T0044141

THE SHAANXI OPERA

OTHER TITLES BY JIA PINGWA

Happy Dreams

THE SHAANXI OPERA

WINNER OF
THE MAO DUN
LITERATURE PRIZE

A NOVEL

JIA PINGWA

TRANSLATED BY NICKY HARMAN
AND DYLAN LEVI KING

AMAZON **CROSSING**

This is a work of fiction. Names, characters, organizations, places, events, and incidents are either products of the author's imagination or are used fictitiously. Any resemblance to actual persons, living or dead, or actual events is purely coincidental.

Text copyright © 2008 by Jia Pingwa

Translation copyright © 2023 by Nicky Harman and Dylan Levi King

All rights reserved.

No part of this book may be reproduced, or stored in a retrieval system, or transmitted in any form or by any means, electronic, mechanical, photocopying, recording, or otherwise, without express written permission of the publisher.

Originally published as *Qin Qiang* 秦腔 by The Writers Publishing House, 2005. Translated from Chinese by Nicky Harman and Dylan Levi King. First published in English by Amazon Crossing in 2023.

Published by Amazon Crossing, Seattle

www.apub.com

Amazon, the Amazon logo, and Amazon Crossing are trademarks of Amazon.com, Inc., or its affiliates.

ISBN-13: 9781542016872

ISBN-10: 1542016878

Cover design by Kimberly Glyder

Cover images: © Romas_Photo / Shutterstock; © Eastimages / Getty

Printed in the United States of America

THE SHAANXI OPERA

TRANSLATOR'S FOREWORD

BY DYLAN LEVI KING

It seems that there will never be a shortage of thick rural novels coming from Chinese writers, but *The Shaanxi Opera* is so much more than simply another dusty countryside story or hinterland family epic.

The Shaanxi Opera reminds me of Zhang Zeduan's famous painting *Along the River during the Qingming Festival*. Look at the painting from a distance, and it's a busy scene of a festival day in Bianjing with more than eight hundred human figures, dozens of buildings, livestock, stray dogs, and Song dynasty urban miscellany. But take a step forward and it reveals carefully sketched scenes of daily life.

Those delicate, quotidian moments are realized with such subtlety in *The Shaanxi Opera* because many are drawn from Jia's own life. This was a deeply personal book for the author and the first novel he set in his hometown (*The Shaanxi Opera*'s village of Freshwind is a stand-in for Jia's own Dihua, a village in Shaanxi recently transformed into a tourist attraction), and he peopled it with characters drawn from his family and neighbors.

The book you are about to read is one of the great epics of modern Chinese literature, written by a man widely considered to be the country's greatest living author. Yet it is very likely that you have never heard of *The Shaanxi Opera*, and even more likely that you are not familiar with the name Jia Pingwa. Despite Jia's stature in the world of Chinese literature—challenged only by Nobel laureate Mo Yan—Jia's works, apart from a single, relatively minor novel translated into English almost three decades ago, were mostly unavailable in English until the 2010s.

Many other Chinese writers have written about rural life, but Jia Pingwa has it in his blood. He was born in 1952 in one of those picturesque, grindingly poor villages that dot the arid landscape of southern Shaanxi. Jia was the eldest of four children. His mother was an uneducated woman with bound feet, and his father was a schoolteacher. With the arrival of the Cultural Revolution in the 1960s, Jia and his mother supported the household, with Jia's father branded a "capitalist roader" and sent for reform through labor.

Jia discontinued his formal studies to support the family and went to work on a production brigade building a dam. He was lucky enough to catch the eye of Party officials working on the production team. These cadres soon noticed his skill at turning out banners and newsletters. He was selected for a spot at Northwest University in Xi'an, capital of Shaanxi Province, and left the village for the first time.

Jia made a name for himself as a writer after leaving college, publishing short stories in the right places and taking advantage of the cultural fever and new openness of the 1980s. After a series of minor novels, he unleashed a thermonuclear device on the world of Chinese letters: *Ruined City*, published in 1993, was something nobody had seen before. It drew from Ming dynasty novels as well as the type of realism considered fashionable at the time, but it went in a completely different direction, abandoning the countryside for literary salons and hotel suites, telling the story of a horny antihero, Zhuang Zhidie, and his innumerable lovers and rivals.

Ruined City fortified Jia Pingwa's reputation as one of the most important writers of the past hundred years. But it is also the reason that most readers of this book will not have heard of him: *Ruined City* was banned, Jia was censured, and it became impossible for foreign publishers and translators to cut a deal with the author for international rights to publish his work.

After a decade in the wilderness, Jia finally returned to center stage with the publication of *The Shaanxi Opera* in 2005. The novel, like *Ruined City*, was monumental. It was a unique and masterful work and a critical and commercial success. It went on to win the 2008 Mao Dun Literature Prize. The follow-up, the slimmer and more accessible *Happy Dreams* (available from Amazon Crossing, translated by Nicky Harman), was another success, and 2009 saw the unbanning of *Ruined City*.

Unlike other rural novels that shoot for national allegory, *The Shaanxi Opera* is concerned with the day-to-day of modern village life. It is set around the time that the novel was written, in the early 2000s, and the concerns of rural life in a rapidly urbanizing China are present. This is a novel about the death of a village; this is the story of the end of a way of life. All able-bodied men and women have left Freshwind to seek their fortunes in Xijing, a name Jia uses in most of his books to stand in for Xi'an. The only ones left behind are the elderly, children, and the disabled. When it comes time to bury the dead, there are scarcely enough men left to carry the coffin to the grave. The local form of opera, which gives the book its title, no longer has enough devotees to sustain touring troupes.

The local opera might be a good comparison for *The Shaanxi Opera itself*, but perhaps a brief explanation is required of what exactly it is. Shaanxi opera, or Qin opera, is an operatic form mostly unknown outside China, although some readers will perhaps have seen performances of Peking opera or Cantonese opera or, more likely, seen Chen Kaige's 1993 film *Farewell My Concubine*. The Qin opera draws from the same folk and literary traditions as other local operatic traditions in China and uses most of the same musical instruments and narrative styles. The performers take to the stage with painted faces, singing to the accompaniment of percussion and flutes, telling highly stylized versions of classical epics of warfare and national turmoil, but also of forbidden romance and domestic strife. Many of the Qin opera tunes are adapted from local folk songs, and the opera tunes are adapted back by village singers and players.

It wouldn't be a stretch to adapt the novel to the operatic form. It reads like just the type of legend that a Qin opera librettist might draw from: two powerful families, the Xias and the Bais, one ascendant and the other fallen into disrepute, united by the marriage of Snow Bai—the prettiest girl in town, pure as her name, filial daughter and keeper of village tradition—and the handsome scholar Rain Xia. It wouldn't make sense to have a love story free of conflict, though, so our narrator, Spark, is madly in love with Snow Bai. And Jia is a student of the Qin opera form, so he knows to throw in some scenes of supernatural spookiness, slapstick comedy, musical interludes, sexual innuendo, and one or two fight scenes.

Like the Qin opera, too, *The Shaanxi Opera* follows a rhythm that might be unfamiliar to most readers. The beats don't seem to fall where you would expect them to. The structure of the novel more closely resembles that of *Journey to the West* or *Heroes of the Marsh* than it does a modern novel. My cotranslator, Nicky Harman, and I came up with Thomas Hardy as possibly the closest comparison, not only in subject matter but also in how Jia puts a story together.

Knowledge of operatic tradition or Ming dynasty adventure novels is not required, of course. *The Shaanxi Opera*'s themes of revenge and betrayal, modernity and tradition, lust and love, decay and growth—these are timeless and universal.

Chapter 1

There's no question: Snow Bai was the girl I loved.

I wasn't the only one. The men of Freshwind followed her like a pack of wolves. I watched her and I watched them watching her. If someone gave her a little gift—a hairpin or a pear—or talked to her too long or said anything bad about her, I'd take a knife and girdle the persimmon tree in their yard, and the tree would wither and die. But she'd never know that I'd done it for her. When she still lived in the village, she used to go down to the cornfield to cut fodder for the pigs, and I'd follow her, stepping barefoot in her footprints. Once I followed her footprints to a puddle of piss. I stood and stared at it for so long that when I looked back, the footprints had dandelions growing in them.

Back behind her family's shithouse, there was a mulberry tree that I used to climb every day around sunset. All I wanted to do was to view the yard, but Snow Bai's mother thought I was stealing fruit and spread shit on the trunk; even that couldn't stop me. One time I fell out and landed on my head, but I didn't give a damn. Nobody in the village understood my love for Snow Bai; they thought I was greedy for the fruit. They had no idea what was going on in my head.

"I'll tell you this—there aren't many girls like Snow Bai around here," Shifty said one day when I went to see him at his brickyard. He was perched on a stone roller, slurping noodles. "In the old days, a woman like that . . . I'd have snatched her up, like a bandit."

I didn't like hearing anyone talking about Snow Bai like that, so I picked up a clod of mud and crumbled it over his noodles. Shifty grabbed me and we clinched up. He gave me a cut on the cheek, ate my noodles, and threatened to smash the bowl.

One of the men watching finally stepped in. "That's enough," he said. "Tell Spark to bring you a flatbread tomorrow. At least this big." He traced a big circle in the air.

Shifty stormed off, cursing me as he went.

I stood up. "I don't owe him a thing," I said. "Why'd you say I'd bring him a flatbread that fucking big? Nobody talks about Snow Bai like that. He can eat his mother's cunt."

"Spark, you're fuckin' crazy," the man said.

I'm not crazy. Never have been.

I picked up a handful of chicken feathers off the street and pressed them to my cheek.

From the doorway of his pharmacy, Big-Noise Zhao called to me, "Where are you going in such a hurry?"

"Nowhere," I said.

"You look like you've got wings with those feathers stuck on you. So I figured you must be in a hurry. Come over here and look in the mirror."

Big-Noise Zhao had a head the size of a persimmon, but he was always one of the sharpest guys in town. He'd invented his own ointment and named it after his shop: Great Qing Ointment. After that nobody cared that he had a head like a persimmon.

The full-length mirror in the pharmacy had been a gift from Snow Bai's mother. She'd had a headache that wouldn't go away, and when Big-Noise Zhao finally cured it, she gave him the mirror to thank him.

I went and stood in front of the mirror, studying my reflection. I blinked, and there was Snow Bai, looking back at me from inside the glass. That was my secret. I had never told anyone that I could see Snow Bai in this mirror. I had another secret: when it was hot, I spat on my finger and rubbed it on my nipples to cool off. I wasn't going to tell my secrets to anyone, especially not Big-Noise Zhao.

Forest Wu was in the shop, too. He had a stutter, but that day he was in the pharmacy for his headache. Big-Noise Zhao had taken off his shirt and was working on Forest Wu, scraping a porcelain chip between his eyebrows. A moment later, a drop of blood appeared. The blood was as dark as soy sauce.

Big-Noise Zhao glanced over in my direction. "Keep your sweaty fingers off my mirror."

A fly walked across the surface of the mirror. Even when I waved my hands, it stayed put. "Big-Noise Zhao," I said, "why'd you bring a fly to work with you?"

"Is it male or female?" he asked.

"Female."

"How can you tell?"

"Only a female would admire herself in the mirror like that."

"They s-say Spark is crazy b-but he can't be . . . ," said Forest Wu.

I didn't say anything; I wasn't interested in talking to someone like him.

I was just about to spit on the floor, but Wisdom Xia came to the door carrying a bundle of red paper, so I went and sat in the corner instead. The elderly school principal had his copper water pipe, too; he sat on a chair beside Forest Wu, and the sound of the bubbling water in the pipe filled the shop as the old man took a long drag.

He exhaled and turned to Big-Noise Zhao. "I'm here to ask a favor. I need you to write some couplets for me."

The pharmacist found his brush and took the strips of red paper. He immediately began writing. "When I heard that Wind Xia finally made his marriage official, I was planning on stopping by to congratulate you. Tomorrow will be a good day to have a celebration here in the village, and it'll be nice to do it at your place. You deserve it, after all these years."

"Well," Wisdom Xia said, "take this as your invitation to my son's wedding."

"What do you think of these?" Big-Noise Zhao said, showing the poetic couplets he had written to Wisdom Xia. They were just right to adorn the new couple's home.

"Beautiful. You should write one for the opera theater, too."

"Is there going to be a performance?"

"The county opera company is coming to perform."

Forest Wu shook with excitement and started gesticulating wildly, as if he were trying to wring a full sentence out of his throat.

"Don't force it," Wisdom Xia said. "Take your time."

Eventually, they figured out what he wanted to say. Forest Wu wanted to offer a toast to Wisdom Xia and congratulate him on his son's marriage. Wisdom Xia took twenty yuan out of his pocket, and Forest Wu ran out of the shop to buy a bottle of liquor.

Big-Noise Zhao finished writing, put down the brush, and took the water pipe from Wisdom Xia. He took a slow drag and held it in his mouth, then started coughing as Wisdom Xia laughed. Big-Noise Zhao said ingratiatingly, "There are two great families in Freshwind: the Xia family and the Bai family. Now, they'll finally be united. It's like the famous chess move: 'The great roc spreads his wings to block the sun.' You're sacrificing your most valuable piece to win the game."

"Come on," Wisdom Xia said. "That's a bit much."

Big-Noise Zhao chuckled. "Fourth Uncle, you're missing the point." Like most people in the village, he always called him "Fourth Uncle" instead of his real name. He was the fourth-born son of the powerful Xia family. "It's much more than simply moving up in the world. Don't be modest. Look at Pavilion Xia. He's the head of the whole village now. The Xia family has prestige and power. How else did Pavilion get that job?"

"There's not much nepotism going on. He's not hiring anybody from his own family."

I coughed a few times, but Wisdom Xia ignored me, so I hocked a loogie and spat toward his back.

Forest Wu came back with the bottle, all smiles. "F-fourth Uncle, the county opera company is putting on a sh-show, right? Is Snow Bai performing with them?"

"No," Wisdom Xia said.

"This'll be the first time anyone in the village has had an opera performance at their wedding party," Big-Noise Zhao said.

"The village government arranged it. The party just happened to fall on the same date as the performance." He got up and stamped the mud off his feet before leaving the shop.

Once he was gone, Forest Wu ripped the lid off the bottle with his teeth. He called me over to have a drink. I waved him away.

"What's gotten into you?" Big-Noise Zhao asked me. "You couldn't even say hello to Fourth Uncle?"

"I bit my tongue."

"Ca-can I go to the banquet, too?" Forest Wu asked.

"Everyone in the village is going."

"I, uh, d-don't have any money to b-buy a gift."

"What's wrong with you? You can't scrounge up some cash?"

The two men drank while I bit my fingernails. "Big-Noise Zhao, who's Wind Xia marrying? Some girl he met in Xijing?"

"Don't play dumb," Big-Noise Zhao said.

"I really don't know," I insisted.

"People come in different classes," Big-Noise Zhao said. "There's only one girl in the village that's a match for him. It had to be Snow Bai."

I felt a buzzing in my head and saw sparks in front of my eyes. "Snow Bai got married? Who'd she marry?" I looked out the doorway of the pharmacy. The street outside tilted up like a wall. I could see the chickens and dogs racing across it, all topsy-turvy.

Big-Noise Zhao picked up his cup of liquor and poured it into his mouth. That mouth had become as big as a washbasin. "What's wrong with you, Spark?"

"But it's impossible!" I howled. "Impossible!" I started sobbing.

Everyone in Freshwind hates it when I cry. Whenever I start crying, my jaws lock shut, and my face turns blue. I can't breathe right, and I usually wind up falling to the ground. Everyone says it looks like I'm dying.

When I fell to the ground this time, Big-Noise Zhao rushed over and pinched me under the nose. "Hey," he said, "don't scare me like that. I can't handle it."

Forest Wu came over, too, and began dragging me toward the door. "W-we d-didn't hit him; he-he ju-just died."

That woke me up. I rolled over and kicked Forest Wu in the balls. As he staggered back, I grabbed the bottle of liquor out of his hand and smashed it on the floor of the shop. Forest Wu loomed over me, his hand raised.

"Come on, motherfucker," I said. "Try and hit me."

Forest Wu thought better of it. He lowered his fist and picked up the bottom of the smashed bottle. There was a bit of liquor left in it. He took a sip, muttering, "N-no one's picking on you. Y-you're crazy!" He took another sip.

I went home and cried until I coughed up blood. I was sitting in front of the clothes-beating stone, and I slammed my fists into the flat stone until it felt as soft as a lump of dough. I cursed heaven. *Why can't you send an earthquake? Tear down the mountains and shake the earth?* If that happened, who would save Snow Bai? Not Wind Xia, that was for sure. Only I could save her.

I would do anything for her. If Snow Bai and I were both beggars, I would still give everything I had to her. I would. If I were starving and found a single crumb, I would offer it to her.

Snow Bai, my sweet Snow Bai. Why did you have to be born so perfect? If only she had a scar across her cheek—or maybe if one of her legs didn't work. Would Wind Xia still love her then? I know I would.

A breeze blew down the alley and smacked a shred of newspaper against the wall. I knew it was my dad's spirit. He always shows up when I'm in trouble. But he was the last person I wanted to hear from. This was all his fault; he'd been a village cadre, but he had to go and die. If he were still alive, our family would still be respected. Village cadres and their families were always respected. They were second only to the Party boss and the village head. The village matchmakers would have been begging him to arrange my engagement to Snow Bai. But my father was dead.

I turned my anger on Wind Xia; I hated him more. He was the real cause of this. He'd gone off to the provincial capital, Xijing; he'd been a success. So why didn't he marry one of the thousands of girls there? Why settle for a crumb when he already had a bowlful of braised pork?

I began to cry again, alone in the yard, sobbing until my guts hurt. I gagged and then vomited, and when I looked down there was a white roundworm wriggling in my puke. I hated Snow Bai, too. *This isn't fair, Snow Bai! It's like Wind Xia was parading around town in a new suit when I was sitting naked and alone—and you went and brought him a new jacket.*

That afternoon I hated everyone I saw. I clenched my jaw and gritted my teeth. Finally, I felt a tooth come loose. I opened my mouth and it fell into the dust. I picked the tooth up from the ground and held it for a moment, then planted it where it had fallen. *This tooth,* I vowed, *this tooth will grow into a seedling, and then it will grow up into a tree, and the tree will have thorns, and these thorns, I promise, will poison the marriage of Wind Xia and Snow Bai. Their life together won't come to a good end.*

Chapter 2

The next day, I went to the theater. The stage was already being set up with lights and a back-drop. The roof was there all the time, covering a stage that looked out onto a wide square, but everything else needed to be set up. Below the stage, the older women of the village had moved in, occupying the space with benches and chairs. Their voices mixed in an unintelligible babble. Children squatted and pissed, their urine running under the benches and snaking across the dusty floor. Clerk's wife had set up an old stove beside the theater. She was taking advantage of her husband's job at the village administration office to set up a stall selling fried rice noodles. She couldn't get the stove lit, and black smoke billowed over the square. Big-Noise Zhao was climbing a ladder to hang the red sheets with calligraphy from one of the pillars near the stage. The dye in the paper was spreading to his hands and his face, leaving them stained a pale crimson. Culture Xia, the son of Treasure Jia, grandson of Justice Jia, was there. He was watching Tongue-Tied, who was holding the ladder up to the couplet:

> Famous and profitable, the theater's the place to show off your
> good fortune,
> Hot or cold, even the best medicine can't cure every
> inflammation.

"Big-Noise Zhao," Culture said, "this sounds more like an advertisement for your shop than a wedding wish."

A bat flew out of the rafters, and Big-Noise Zhao wobbled on the ladder. As he grabbed for a better grip, he dropped his bottle of glue onto Tongue-Tied. Tongue-Tied let go of the ladder and moaned, trying to tell me to help him out. Moaning was all that he could do. He was a mute. I didn't bother. I was in the mood to fight, not help.

On the north side of the theater grounds was a strawstack with a pig rooting around underneath. The pig was staring at me. I walked over and kicked the pig in the teats. The pig thought I was playing, though. She rolled over onto her back. I spat and walked away.

Suddenly, there was a gust of wind, so strong it carried me, spinning, up onto the top of the strawstack. Then the wind picked me up again, and I sank back down to the ground as softly as a leaf falling from a tree.

I should probably tell you a little bit about Freshwind. You know it's the most famous village on the Zhou River, right? Its opera theater, in particular, has a long history. Across the top of the theater are three words, in gold: TRUE MIRROR TOWER. To the east side of the theater, there's the God of Literature Pavilion. The pavilion used to have a gold-plated dome, but it collapsed a long time ago. The roof and the walls are still standing, though.

My dad used to say that the God of Literature was the reason Freshwind produced two scholars. The first was Snow Bai's half brother. He ended up going way out to the frontier—to Xinjiang—to work, and barely ever came back to the village. I remember he told everyone that Xinjiang was so cold that you couldn't even piss outside. As soon as you started pissing, he said, the piss froze solid. There'd be a rod of frozen piss so hard you could lean on it. The other scholar was Wind Xia. He left the village, too, and went to Xijing. He made a name as a writer. They even published some of his stuff in the provincial newspaper. He came back from time to time.

Wisdom Xia had been something of a scholar himself back in the day and served as the principal of the local primary school. He was proud of his son's literary accomplishments and could often be seen rifling through newspapers in the village administration building, pulling on his water pipe and checking for new pieces by his son. When Wisdom Xia found a new piece, he'd carry the paper around for days.

Eventually, some people figured out that if they took a newspaper with his son's writing in it to Wisdom Xia, he might buy a bottle of liquor to celebrate. Wisdom Xia would take out the fifty yuan that he always kept stuffed under the insole of one of his shoes and send for the liquor. When he got home with whoever had found Wind Xia's story in the paper, he'd call for Fourth Aunt to bring out some food. Everyone called his wife "Fourth Aunt" since Wisdom Xia was the youngest of the four brothers. She'd rush to lay out cold tofu, pickled vegetables sprinkled with hot oil, chili peppers, and salt. That meant she'd provided the customary four dishes, as far as he was concerned—chili peppers and salt counted as dishes, too.

Wisdom Xia would always call for the chicken, too. "The chicken," he'd say. "Where's the chicken?" And then Fourth Aunt set the chicken on the table. Wisdom Xia always made sure the chicken was out. It wasn't for eating, since it was carved out of wood. It looked good at the center of the table, though.

The pavilion had plenty of space, so the Middle Street Committee had once commandeered it to put their cows in. The cows were long gone, and the space had been taken over by the local government, who put up a sign that said, CULTURAL CENTER. Apart from a few pamphlets with titles like *How to Raise Mink*, and *Growing Sichuan Peppercorn*, or *Fields to Forest*, there wasn't much in the cultural center, but villagers went there to play chess or mah-jongg.

Big-Noise Zhao climbed down from the ladder and called me over. The wind blew hard again, messing up my hair. "This wind is a bad omen," he muttered. I told him about the wind carrying me to the top of the strawstack. He looked worried and said, "Listen, if you aren't feeling well . . ."

"It really happened," I insisted. I told him that there was a bird's nest on the top of the strawstack and said to check if he didn't believe me.

Culture Xia overheard and carried the ladder over to the strawstack. He climbed the ladder, and everybody was surprised when he tossed a bird's nest down to the ground.

Big-Noise Zhao dragged me over to the cultural center and asked if I wanted one of his medicated patches. "I won't charge you for it," he said.

I said that I'd really been to the top of the strawstack. He ignored me this time and looked back inside.

Someone was saying, "Was it a circle tile? My eyes aren't too good."

"You've been playing mah-jongg all day," Big-Noise Zhao shouted. "No wonder you can't see a thing!"

Wind Xia's brother Rain Xia and the town treasurer, Goodness Li, were both sitting at the table. Rain Xia had drawn a circle tile and was pressing it to his forehead. When he pulled it away, the tile left a mark on his forehead. Goodness muttered that when the game was finished, they'd find an extra circle tile, and Rain started yelling at him.

"What are you doing here, Rain Xia?" Big-Noise Zhao asked. "Your whole family's busy, and you're playing mah-jongg?"

"I came to borrow some tables and chairs and thought I might as well play a few rounds," Rain said and then stood to leave.

"Let me guess," someone at the table said. "Your brother's got a new wife, so you're in a hurry to get in there."

"Sister-in-law's ass, little brother gets half," said another player.

I heard voices from the other side of the pavilion. "I wouldn't go out this shabby normally, but here I feel like I'm overdressed," one of the actors from the opera company said.

A woman's voice answered: "Think you're a prince as soon as you leave the city, huh?"

The man grinned. He looked around. "Doesn't seem very 'cultural' for a cultural center, does it, Mrs. Wang?"

"This is Wind Xia's village," Mrs. Wang said. "Of course they've got culture."

Their conversation caught the attention of Dog-Scraps, who had been watching Rain Xia and the others play mah-jongg. Dog-Scraps looked ghoulish. He was a wretchedly skinny man who looked like he was at death's door, even though he was still shy of sixty. He walked over to the actors and stood with his sun-ravaged face inches away from Mrs. Wang's.

"You're performing *Picking Up the Jade Bracelet*?" he asked.

She nodded.

"I can't believe it," Dog-Scraps said. Mrs. Wang smiled politely. "You're all old and dried out," he said.

The actress's expression changed, but Dog-Scraps's enthusiasm didn't fade. He reached out for a handshake, but she shoved her hands into her pockets.

Later, I heard the full story. This same company had come to Freshwind about thirty years ago, and Mrs. Wang had performed *Picking Up the Jade Bracelet*. Dog-Scraps may have missed some of the details of the love story between the dashing young scholar and the beautiful maiden, but he fell in love with the actress anyway. When he went home that night, he asked his wife to play the part of the maiden. She was so mad they almost got divorced.

Dog-Scraps didn't seem to care that the famous actress was angry with him, so Goodness came over and apologized for him. He said that Dog-Scraps just didn't know how to talk to women, then kicked him and told him to get lost. The incident with Dog-Scraps upset Mrs. Wang for the rest of the day.

That afternoon, the actress said she had a stomachache and was going back to town. Goodness was nervous since the village was paying for the performance and they'd been promised some big names. Wisdom Xia told Big-Noise Zhao to fetch his cups and needles. Mrs. Wang told them not to bother because she was already packing up her things. Wisdom Xia ran and got Snow Bai. Snow Bai begged Mrs. Wang to stay and perform. She took out a few of the Shaanxi opera masks that Wisdom Xia had painted. She showed Mrs. Wang the one he had done for her.

The actress looked at the mask. "Am I really that old?"

"You aren't," Snow Bai said.

"I must be. Everyone gets old."

"Humans age, but art is timeless."

Mrs. Wang looked up from the mask and fixed her gaze on Snow Bai. "Fine. I'll perform," she said. "But I won't be doing *Picking Up the Jade Bracelet*, and I won't wear a costume or act. I'll sing a few arias."

I hadn't planned on going to the Xia family's wedding reception, but Goodness forced me to. I saw Snow Bai in the yard. I couldn't look at her face, so I watched her feet. She was wearing narrow leather shoes. The leather of the shoes was delicate, and the shoes wrapped tightly around her feet, showing off their delicate shape. Her feet were beautiful.

I thought about what Uncle Glory, Mid-Star's dad, had told me about Bodhisattvas—he was a Buddhist and knew about those kinds of things. He said that when Bodhisattvas walked, each footprint sprouted a lotus flower. When I watched Snow Bai walk, I saw rows of flowers trailing behind her, too.

Big-Noise Zhao saw me staring down at the ground. "What are you looking at?" he asked.

That bastard—he knew I couldn't look her in the face. Couldn't he let me stare at her feet? I turned and studied the yard instead. There were flowers there, too: a flower bed planted with Chinese roses blooming bright red.

"Don't drink too much today, Spark," Big-Noise Zhao said.

I walked over to the flower bed and reached out to pull off one of the petals of the rose. I saw the petal shiver and realized I was hurting it, so I let go. Just then, someone set off firecrackers to mark the start of the banquet. Goodness was serving as the host of the reception, and he stood in the yard, greeting the guests.

The Xia family hadn't invited many people, but as Big-Noise Zhao had said, nearly everyone in the village was there. Forest Wu was the last to arrive, calling for his wife, Black-Moth, who had arrived earlier. "Are y-you coming back or not? They're g-going to collect the gifts. Do you h-have any m-money?"

Fourth Auntie saw what was going on and called Forest Wu inside.

"I d-don't have any m-m-m-money for a gift," he protested.

"Who asked you to bring a gift? Come and join us," she said.

After a pause, Forest Wu relented. "Next month, f-f-for my mother, i-it's the third anniversary of her passing, you can come and don't bring, uh, a-anything."

The village head, Pavilion Xia, and Party Secretary Concord Qin arrived together. Concord Qin stopped by the gate of the yard and read the couplet written on red paper:

> Without destruction, there is no progress
> True feeling comes from conflict

"I presume that's Big-Noise Zhao's work," Concord Qin said. "It's very nice."

Goodness pulled Concord Qin and Pavilion Xia inside and got them seated before getting up in front to speak. Goodness was a gifted speaker. He spoke for a long time, but even though he spoke well, most of the guests at the banquet stopped listening after a few minutes.

The speech was about scholars and beauties. Wind Xia was a scholar and Snow Bai was a beauty. The story of Wind Xia and Snow Bai was straight from classical literature. This match, he said, was truly blessed. Although the couple had already had a wedding in Xijing, they'd come back to the village to extend greetings to their relatives and neighbors. Tradition was tradition, after all.

Goodness surveyed the room. He began to list the family members who had arrived: the Xia family, of course, from East Street, and Wind Xia's one aunt who lived on Middle Street, and the bride's family from West Street, and the uncle from South Gully. Finally, he greeted the couple's classmates from their middle school at West Mountain Bend. He invited everyone to raise their glasses to congratulate Mr. Xia, the former school principal, and then raise them again to wish the newlyweds many years of happiness together.

"Are all the glasses raised?" Goodness asked.

"My arm's getting tired. Can you wrap it up?" someone called from across the room.

"Then let's drink," Goodness said. "Bottoms up!"

Everyone lifted their glass and drank.

"Now, don't sit down too fast. Let's refill those glasses. Let's have our Party secretary, Concord Qin, say a few words."

Concord Qin stood, protesting the invitation. He motioned for Pavilion to stand.

"No, no," Pavilion said, "I'm family. You should speak first."

Concord Qin raised his glass and turned to the banquet crowd. "I'm not very good at this," he said, then paused. "Well, let me make it brief. One word: good luck!"

"That's two words," someone from another table said.

Concord was stumped. He stood awkwardly for a moment, then chuckled and sat down. Everyone drained their glasses.

During the banquet, the guests surprised Wisdom Xia by smearing rouge on his face. "The tradition is to prank the bride and the groom," he said.

They told him they thought it'd be more fun to prank the father of the groom instead. They also told Wisdom Xia that he had to perform for them.

"What do you want me to do?" Wisdom Xia asked. He looked around and then called for Fourth Aunt to bring his opera masks.

"They've all seen those."

"Bring them!"

From a big cupboard, Fourth Aunt began pulling ladles that had been painted with masks in the style of the local opera. I knew Wisdom Xia painted opera masks, but I didn't know he also did them on ladles.

Guests began to crowd around the pile of ladles on the table. A few picked them up. Some of them even put them in their pockets and said they wanted to take them home with them. Rain Xia tried to prevent anyone from leaving with the ladles, but his father stopped him. "If they like them," Wisdom Xia said, "let them keep them."

So the guests chose their favorite pieces, and soon enough, the ladles were all gone.

"Now, this is a banquet," Wisdom Xia said, beaming. "I want everyone to enjoy themselves." He went back to his bedroom and returned with a large radio. He put it on a table and fiddled with it for a while before turning up the volume to a broadcast of a local opera performance.

When I heard the music, a strange feeling came over me. It was like the sudden gust of wind earlier that had lifted me off my feet. I began to sing:

> Before my eyes, buildings rise
> Before my eyes, you welcome our guests
> Before my eyes, buildings fall . . .

"This guy is crazy," I heard someone shout.

Goodness put his hand on my shoulder and steered me out to the yard. "Spark," he said, "you've got a voice like a gong, and you can't sing for shit." He put a bowl in my hands, grabbed a pair of chopsticks, and began heaping it with rice. He put a few morsels of meat on top, too. "Sit over there by the flower bed and eat your heart out," he said. "If you feel like singing again, just let me know and I'll fill your bowl again." He left me out in the yard and turned back to the guests. "If you want a song," he called, "I'll sing."

The guests chanted, "Sing! Sing!"

And then Goodness really did sing:

> The king's throne is backward, oh oh no!
> Out sticks his stomach, ho ho ho
> A step forward, a step back, just don't go
> His great-uncle's his uncle, don't you know?

Just then a fly came and landed on the tip of his nose. He batted the fly away and stopped singing. The opera kept playing on the radio. Tongue-Tied led a dog named Lucky into the yard. When the dog heard the music, she stopped suddenly and let out a high, sad whine. Her whine was in perfect harmony with the voice of the singer. All the guests were dumbstruck; they had never seen a dog sing opera before.

"Goodness! That dog sings better than you," one of the villagers said.

The dog howled along with the radio until Tongue-Tied brought her a pork bone from the table.

But Lucky wasn't interested in the bone; she was staring at me. I called her over, and she lay by my feet. I knew that Lucky had been an opera singer in her last life. I didn't want to tell everyone that, though. That was between me and Lucky.

Big-Noise Zhao and Wind Xia were talking over by the crepe myrtle, or "tickle tree" as we called it, next to the flower bed. They'd been classmates in primary school.

"That's the thing with my father," Wind Xia said, pointing at the radio. "Everything has to be about opera."

Big-Noise Zhao smiled. "Your father loves the local opera. I was thinking how perfect is it, Snow Bai marrying into your family. She loves opera as much as your father. Wisdom Xia deserves a daughter-in-law like her."

"Personally," Wind Xia said, "I can't stand it."

"If you don't love opera, then what about Snow Bai—"

"I've got other things in mind for her. She's staying with me in Xijing. She won't be singing opera anymore."

I bit down on a grain of sand and spat a mouthful of rice onto the ground.

Concord Qin joined the two men then, asking Wind Xia if the orchard boss and opera buff New-Life had arrived yet. "I haven't seen him," Wind Xia said. Concord Qin called over Wisdom Xia, who walked over pulling on his water pipe.

I guessed that they were talking about gifts for the performers because I heard Concord Qin say, "Five cartons of cigarettes, ten *jin* of eggs for each person—about eighty eggs each— and a bag of apples; that shouldn't be too hard to take care of, should it?"

Wisdom Xia took a long drag from his pipe. He called Snow Bai over. She walked across the yard, and I could smell her perfume as she passed me. I was close enough to her that I could see a little piece of fluff on her pants leg. If I'd wanted to, I could have reached out to brush it off.

"Just make sure to give Mrs. Wang a red sash," Snow Bai said. "She gets one of those wherever she goes."

"I'm going to need to talk it over with Pavilion," Concord Qin said.

Pavilion was called over, and they repeated everything for him. "We invited the opera company," Pavilion said, "so of course we should take care of them."

Concord Qin looked over at me, and I pretended to be eating. "But the performance," he said to Pavilion in a low voice, "was to celebrate Wind Xia and Snow Bai's marriage."

"So what? Everyone enjoyed the performance. If it wasn't for Wind Xia's marriage, do you think we could have gotten them to come? Farmers can count on a harvest every season, but men like Wind Xia only appear once in a hundred years. He put Freshwind on the map. I'll make an announcement: if anyone of Wind Xia's caliber comes along in the future, the village government will stuff lucky red envelopes with cash and bring them to their wedding and their funeral. We don't have anything to hide, do we?"

Wisdom Xia started to speak, but Concord Qin cut him off. "Pavilion's absolutely right. The thousand yuan to book the theater, plus a red sash, and the eggs and the apples. We'll get New-Life to take care of the apples. Take it out of his fee for the theater." Rain Xia was sent to find New-Life.

Wind Xia whistled and Lucky came to his side. As he walked toward the gate of the yard, he looked back at me. "Hey, Spark," he said, "come on, let's go."

I looked over at Snow Bai. She was going from table to table, offering toasts. "I'm not going," I said.

Wind Xia scowled, grabbed a pack of cigarettes off a table, and left.

Chapter 3

The chickens had gone in to roost, but the sky wasn't quite dark yet. The sun shone red like firelight through curdled clouds. I was out in the yard, using a stick to beat the dust out of my bedsheets, when my neighbor Take-It-Easy looked over the fence. "There's an opera tonight, and that's a lucky sky," Take-It-Easy said. "It's a bit strange, isn't it?"

"What's so strange about it, you bald bastard? It just looks like heaven is running a fever."

"Check your own temperature!"

I did feel like I might have a fever. When I got back from the banquet, I'd fallen asleep. After sleeping awhile, I woke up to find my whole body was burning hot. I beat the bedsheets to see if I'd burned any holes in them—there were no burns, but I did manage to shake out some bedbugs.

I looked out into the yard. A white cat passed from the shade of a tree into the sunlight, its fur stained red by the setting sun, then walked along the side of the house and scraped along the old stove, powdering itself dark gray with soot.

Take-It-Easy cracked his neck and headed out. He was going to the opera theater. But I waited until I heard the cymbals and drums, and until I'd drunk a ladleful of sour broth, before heading over.

When I got to the opera theater, it seemed like everyone in the village was already there. The women and children who had seats were trying to keep sitting, but the late arrivals crowded in all around them. The final stragglers ended up standing on a bench in the back. Their feet were planted firm, but their bodies swayed back and forth. I thought they looked like a field of wheat, swept by the wind in midsummer.

Kids began to climb the walls around the edge of the theater grounds, and then a few boosted each other up to the stage itself. Some of the troupe tried to shoo the kids from the stage, but they climbed back again.

I heard a voice call from the crowd, "Spark! Get Spark over here to get them in line."

I went over to the stage and began yanking the kids down one by one. I heard another voice from the crowd: "This guy's out of his mind. Is he trying to kill them?" But I didn't mind; I knew I was the only one who could restore order.

I left the front of the stage and saw Culture and a few of his friends slip around the back of the theater; when I followed them, I saw them peeking through a crack in the door that led to the dressing room for the performers. I went over to take a look, too, hoping to see Snow Bai, but I only saw the older male actor who had been with Mrs. Wang. He was busy putting on his makeup. That afternoon, Justice Xia's son Treasure Xia sat down with the actor for lunch. Treasure offered him a cigarette. The actor said he couldn't smoke because he needed to protect his voice.

"What are you going to play?" Treasure asked.

"Guess," the actor said.

"The *jing* role," Treasure guessed. That would make sense—a strong male role, like Judge Bao or maybe some warrior.

"Nope."

Treasure asked if he would be playing the *sheng* role. That was the male lead, usually a scholar or an official. Those roles went to experienced male actors, too.

"No," the actor said.

"Then you're playing the *chou* role?" That was the clown. But the actor said no again.

Treasure was sick of guessing. "You're playing with your balls then?" he asked.

"You're getting close."

"Oh!" said Treasure. "It must be the *dan* role." A big guy like that playing the role of the young woman in the play—that was something to see.

He must have heard me make a sound, though, because he got up and stood with his back against the door I was peeking under. I was tired of watching anyway, so I left the back of the theater and walked along the front of the stage, where everything was still reasonably orderly. I went to the strawstack, leaned back, and watched the stars starting to appear. I counted each star I saw, then counted again to be sure, but I got a different number both times. I was about to count again, but I heard a couple talking on the other side of the strawstack.

"Did you see the crowd?" the woman said in a low voice. "Not bad, huh?"

"Farmers are suckers for this kind of stuff," the man's voice answered back.

"Come on, don't talk like that. If anyone overhears, you'll get an earful."

"If you go to see a big concert in Xijing, you'll see how pathetic these opera shows are."

"It wasn't always like that," the woman said. "Riches Wang, back in the day . . . When she performed *Hanging Pictures*, everyone saw it. They even had a saying: 'I'd rather see Riches sing *Hanging Pictures* than be the leader of the whole Republic of China.'"

"But that was back in the twenties," the man said.

"Well, we have our Mrs. Wang now."

"That old bird who does *Picking Up the Jade Bracelet* wherever she goes, right? Supposedly, she gets a red sash . . ."

"You . . . you . . ."

"I'm serious."

"I don't want you talking like that backstage," the woman's voice said.

"I'm not going backstage. There are too many people running around as it is. I'm going to find Big-Noise Zhao."

I realized it was Snow Bai and Wind Xia just on the other side of the strawstack. I shrank back into the shadows; I didn't want them to see me. They seemed to have finished their conversation. Wind Xia was going one way, and Snow Bai was going the other, toward the theater. I watched Snow Bai's legs as she went. Her legs were so straight that it looked like she didn't have knees.

Snow Bai, Snow Bai, if you could ever love me, sneeze to give me a sign!

But she just kept walking.

The sound of drums and cymbals came from below the stage; then the heavy red curtain parted, and the performance began. Members of the company took the stage, singing folk songs and excerpts from operas. They didn't wear makeup or elaborate costumes. The host of the show had introduced the performers as famous actors, but nobody recognized any of them, so nobody clapped. The audience began loudly discussing how fat or skinny the actors were or who had big eyes or who had a long face. The program continued. An actor tried a somersault, and his false beard fell off. The crowd booed him, and someone said, "We want to see the real stars."

Mrs. Wang took the stage next. The crowd expected her in costume and makeup, but she came on dressed just as she had been when she arrived in Freshwind. She was thick around the middle with short legs. As she performed her first aria, the crowd began to buzz like a hornet's nest.

Shifty got up on the stone roller. The heavy cylinder of stone balanced on an equally heavy stone table was usually put to the mundane task of grinding grain, but Shifty was using it as his stage. He jeered. "You gotta be fucking kidding me!"

The crowd cheered for Shifty, and Mrs. Wang stopped singing. She tried to storm off-stage, but the host of the show blocked her way and tried to get the audience to clap for her.

Everyone laughed instead, and someone shouted that she should perform *Picking Up the Jade Bracelet*.

When I heard the show stop and the crowd turning on the performers, I started running toward the stage. The crowd was packed in so tight that some of the kids had started crying. Three different shoes hit me in the head. "Stick that in your mother's cunt!" I shouted, tossing the shoes back into the crowd.

Concord Qin got to me before I climbed onto the stage. "Spark," he said, "we need to get them under control." He jumped up onto the stage and tried shouting for silence. The crowd ignored him, and Concord Qin jumped back down from the stage, defeated. "Where is Pavilion?" he asked me. "He didn't come?"

"Pavilion went up to the reservoir after dinner," I said. "He didn't tell you he was going?"

Concord Qin furrowed his brow. "If this gets out of hand, we could have a real problem," he said. "I think we need to get Uncle Justice."

The opera company's director came around to the front of the stage. "Who's Uncle Justice?" the director asked.

"He's the old village head," I said.

"Spark," Concord Qin said, "you lead the way. Find Uncle Justice. Bring the director with you to make sure he comes."

The director and I jogged over to East Street. There was the sound of a dog barking somewhere. A car passed on Highway 312, and its headlights lit up the wall across the way. "Did you see that?" I asked the director.

"What?"

In the instant the car's headlights had lit up the wall, I had seen Thunder's daughter, Emerald, entwined with Star Chen. "I see how it is!" I shouted into the darkness. "Sucking face is better than watching opera, huh?"

"Mind your own business," the director said. "We're supposed to be getting reinforcements." But I didn't move. I picked up a clod of mud and threw it in the direction of where I thought Emerald and Star Chen were. It was too dark to see anything, but I heard them running away. I led the director on, down a winding alley. The director asked me why the old village head lived in such an out-of-the-way spot.

"Sure, it's nothing special to look at," I said. "But it's got good feng shui."

"You sure about that?" the director asked.

"If you go up Bowed Ox Ridge during the day and look down from the north end of it, you'll see what I mean."

What I meant was, when you look down from Bowed Ox Ridge, you can see that East and West Street are shaped like a ⊔. So with the three neighborhoods, East Street, West Street, and Middle Street, it's kind of shaped like a scorpion. The old village head's home is at the tip of the scorpion's tail.

Before, East Street was where the poor people lived, and West Street was where the rich people lived, and the richest people in the village always came from the Bai family. But the Bai family had two sons who got into an argument about something. The younger of the two moved to East Street but didn't have any kids, so after the younger brother and his wife died, the older brother took over their house on East Street. The older brother was Snow Bai's grandfather. Back in the day, before the days of village heads and committees and the Communist Party, he was Freshwind's headman, responsible for collecting taxes and all that.

When the Communist Party liberated the country in 1949, Justice Xia was given the job of carrying out land reform. He wanted to have Snow Bai's grandfather declared a landlord, but it turned out that the man the Peasants' Association installed above him, at the county level, was a relative of Snow Bai's grandfather. There was a meeting, and he spoke on the Bais' behalf. They had to give up what they had over on West Street and move into the house on East Street, but in doing so got away with being declared middle peasants instead of landlords. That meant that they still had land taken from them, but they weren't tarred with the worst possible label. The Bais' old house on West Street ended up going to Justice Xia's family, of course. The Xia family had four sons, and their father had used the character *tian*, heaven, in all their names. He named the sons Heavenly Benevolence, Heavenly Justice, Heavenly Rites, and Heavenly Wisdom. The four brothers lived together in the West Street house for ten years, and after that they split up and built their own homes. As the eldest, Benevolence Xia was the first to move away, and he went to the north end of the street. Benevolence Xia was Pavilion's father. He was something fierce, but he died young—he wasn't even sixty when he dropped dead. The third oldest, Rites Xia, was the next to move. He went to the bottom of Middle Street and worked as a clerk in Tianzhu Township, which is about fifty *li* away from here. He's been retired for a long time now, though. The second eldest, Justice Xia, went to the tip of the scorpion's tail on East Street to build a house. He had five sons, and for the first four, he used the character *qing*, "celebration," in their names, paired with, successively, Gold, Treasure, Bounty, and Hearth, from the saying "May gold and jade fill your hearth." When Second Aunt was pregnant with their fifth child, Justice Xia decided he wanted a daughter, but when the child was born, it turned out to be another boy. Not only a boy but also an ugly boy. Justice Xia ended up calling the baby Halfwit, and the name stuck. The five sons eventually all moved out and built their own homes, but Justice Xia stayed where he was, at the tip of the scorpion's tail. But I wasn't about to try and explain all that to the director. Even if I did, he'd never understand.

"So," the director said, "the old village head is Wind Xia's uncle?"

"Hey, you catch on quick!"

"But Wind Xia's house is much nicer than the old village head's."

I pulled the director along, ducking under a willow beside the pond. I was about to tell him that Wind Xia's house used to belong to the Bai family, so of course it was nicer, but right then Hearth's wife, Bamboo, appeared, walking toward us. She wobbled on legs as bony as a stork's and pulled hard on a cigarette, squinting at me. "Is Uncle Justice at home?" I asked.

"He was drinking, probably already asleep . . ."

I rapped the iron knocker on the gate. From inside the yard, I heard Lucky barking.

"It's me, Lucky," I said.

Lucky barked.

"I'm looking for Uncle Justice."

Lucky growled.

"Is he sleeping? You gotta get him up. There's gonna be trouble."

"Who's that out there?" said a voice from inside the house.

"Uncle Justice, it's me. It's Spark. Open the door."

The door creaked open. Lucky had slid the bolt open with her teeth. Justice Xia was standing behind her. He was a big man, whose frame filled the doorway. With the lights of the house blazing behind him, he looked even more intimidating than usual. The director bustled forward, fumbling with his pack of cigarettes, and tried to offer one to Justice Xia, who waved him off. "What do you want?"

The director told him about the audience at the theater, how the performance had been disrupted. He was worried there might be a riot.

"That's it?" Justice Xia asked. "And where's Concord Qin?"

"Concord Qin's soft," I said. "He couldn't control them."

"Son of a bitch," he said. He was almost out of the gate when he stopped and turned back to shout, "Hey, you! Bring me my jacket. And my glasses, too."

Justice Xia never called his wife anything other than "Hey, you." Second Aunt was blind, but she knew how to get around. She appeared with the glasses and his jacket. His glasses were big, tinted ovals. Rather than put his arms through the sleeves, he draped the jacket over his shoulders.

I told Justice Xia that he looked like a general.

"Bullshit," he said.

Back at the theater the audience was bubbling like a pot of rice porridge. The crowd had started throwing things onto the stage. Two groups of kids had gotten into a fight. "Fuck your mother!" one of the kids shouted across to the other group.

"Fishy, Fishy, Fishy Zhang!" a kid in the other group shouted back.

That wasn't a curse; it was just the name of the other kid's father, but when the kid heard his father's name, he started to cry.

Concord Qin came over to intervene. "Who cries when they hear their own father's name?" he asked. "Look at Mao Zedong. Everyone says his name."

Everyone laughed except for Concord Qin. The stage lights lit up his sweaty face. Concord Qin tried to bring out the actors to bow to the audience, but below the stage everything was still chaos, and nobody was listening to him. Justice Xia climbed the stairs at the side of the stage, his jacket still draped over his shoulders. He held his hands behind his back.

"The old village head is here!" I shouted.

Justice Xia walked to center stage. "When they told me they wanted to invite an opera troupe, I said no," he said. "The harvest isn't in, and it's not New Year yet, so why hold a performance? But I asked what everyone thought, and you all begged me for a show. And now that you've got what you want, you won't let them perform. What's gotten into you?"

Whap! The stage lights had attracted a cloud of mosquitoes, and Justice Xia slapped one that had been unlucky enough to land on his cheek. "This is an embarrassment. If you don't want to see opera, go home and go to bed. If you want to watch the performance, be respectful." He turned his back to the audience to look at the director, and I could see the skin on his neck, full of creases and folds. "Start the performance," he commanded, then walked back down the stairs.

This time the performance began to a respectful audience. Justice Xia left the theater, looking satisfied.

I followed him. "Uncle Justice, Uncle Justice, Uncle Justice, you looked like you could kill someone." He waved a hand dismissively. "Concord Qin always brags that he went to school longer than anyone else around here. He claims to be an intellectual. Intellectuals can eat shit, though. To be a village cadre, you must be tough, like you." Justice Xia just waved my words off again.

I followed him for a while and then turned back. If he was going to give me the cold shoulder, I figured I should save my breath.

When I got back, I sneaked up behind Forest Wu and slapped him on the neck. He'd been staring slack jawed at the performance, and I scared the hell out of him. He jerked around, and I could tell he wanted to curse me, but he couldn't get a single word out.

The performance continued until near midnight. After everyone left, I helped Tongue-Tied, Halfwit, and Rain Xia carry the opera company's costumes and props to Wisdom Xia's place. I tried to get Clerk to help us, but he was busy with something else. He was walking back and forth, staring at the ground. I knew he was looking for things left behind by the audience.

"You won't find any wallets," I said, "but there's a few bricks over by that wall, if you want them." Without speaking, Clerk went over and began to collect the bricks.

After the show, the performers met at Wisdom Xia's home for noodles with pickled vegetables. Most of them wanted to go back to the city that night, but Wisdom Xia tried to get them to stay. He finally gave up and asked Rain Xia to get Rites Xia's son Thunder to drive them back home. Thunder worked for a state bus company, driving a route between the county seat and Xijing. He drove that route every day and came back every night to the village. Rain Xia went to get Thunder, but he ran into Thunder's wife, Blossom, on the way over to their house in Middle Alley. She didn't want her husband driving anyone that night. "Thunder got back late tonight," she said, "and didn't even get to toast your family at the wedding. And now you want him to take people back to the city in the middle of the night?"

Rain Xia didn't know what to say, so he went back to Wisdom Xia and told him what she had said. "I didn't tell you to talk to his wife," Wisdom Xia said. "Get Thunder over here."

Snow Bai decided to go instead. She knocked on the gate. Rites Xia, Thunder's father, heard the noise from his bedroom and came to the window. "Who's there?"

"It's me, Third Uncle."

Rites Xia yelled for his son to wake up. "Snow Bai's here," he said.

Blossom came to the door. "Oh," she said, "Snow Bai, it's you. I went to the show tonight just to watch you perform. I can't believe you didn't sing."

"Oh, I'm just an amateur," Snow Bai said modestly. "Especially here in the village, it wouldn't be right to get up onstage. Is your husband awake?"

"He's asleep, but I can get him up for you."

"If it's not too much trouble, we wanted to ask him to drive the theater group back."

"Well, trouble or not, if he doesn't do it, who will? In the Xia family, we're always there for each other, whether it's a wedding or a funeral. Thunder is always there to take them there and take them back after."

Three men and two women from the opera company stayed behind. The men went off to play mah-jongg with Rain Xia at a township cadre's house, while the women planned to stay at Snow Bai's mother's house on West Street. Snow Bai told her mother-in-law that she wouldn't be back to their home that night. Fourth Aunt wasn't happy. She kept pestering her daughter-in-law until Snow Bai gave up and told Wind Xia to take the women from the opera company to West Street.

I probably should have gone with Rain Xia and the rest of them to play mah-jongg, but instead, I stayed at Wisdom Xia's house, watching Fourth Aunt, sitting under a lamp, count the money given to the family by guests of the banquet. I got up to leave, but just then Gold's wife, Chastity, showed up. She wanted Snow Bai's opinion on something. Her son, Shiner, had a good voice and was always singing with Star Chen. She was debating buying a tape recorder for him. She wanted Snow Bai to hear her son sing so that Snow Bai could tell her if it was worth the investment.

"Oh, just get one," Fourth Aunt said. "We don't need to hear him sing at this time of night. It's just a radio; how much can it cost?"

"No, this is a tape recorder, not a radio."

"Oh, is that more expensive?" Fourth Aunt asked.

"It's like comparing a wristwatch with a clock," Chastity said, and spat. Fourth Aunt licked her thumb and went back to counting bills. "Did you turn a profit?" Chastity asked.

"What do you mean, turn a profit?" Fourth Aunt asked.

Chastity forced a smile and then looked away. Shiner got distracted and started to wander around the room. Chastity scolded him. She sidled up to Snow Bai and asked in a low voice, "How much did you get?"

"I don't know."

"Why do you think they had a banquet?" Chastity asked. "They're getting back all the money they gave out in gifts over the years at other people's weddings. They probably made a bundle. How much did they give you?"

"Why would they give any to me?" Snow Bai asked.

"Why not? Wind Xia isn't their only son, you know. They have Rain Xia, too. Are they going to give it to Rain Xia? Even if they don't give you anything else, you should at least get to keep the money from your classmates and family."

The two women were whispering, but Fourth Aunt heard enough of the conversation to get the gist. "Snow Bai," she said, "can you go check the chicken coop? Make sure the door is closed. And watch out for weasels."

"What weasels?" Snow Bai asked.

"I don't think she wants me here," Chastity whispered.

"Oh, Chastity, you're leaving already?" Fourth Aunt asked. She took some of the bills and tried to hand them to Snow Bai. Snow Bai wouldn't take them, but her mother-in-law insisted.

Chastity hurried out, scolding Shiner the whole way.

Chapter 4

Years breeze past and the months fly by—it's the days that seem to take forever.

The day after the banquet, Wisdom Xia was the first to awaken. That was normal enough; he'd been sleeping very little for the past year or two. No matter what time he went to bed, he'd get up at five in the morning.

After he woke up, he went to the south side of the village and strolled along the riverbank. He walked back toward East Street with his splayfooted walk, rattling the knockers of gates along the way, shouting, "Wake up! Out of bed!" When he got home, he opened all the doors and windows of the house, then boiled water for tea and lit his pipe. He sipped tea and smoked his pipe while admiring the calligraphy and paintings hanging on the walls of the main room of the house. He stared at them until the figures in the paintings seemed like they were just about ready to climb down off the walls.

The sound of Wisdom Xia puttering around woke Snow Bai up. She'd just married into the family; it wouldn't be right for her to stay in bed. She swept the yard and then went to the well to fetch water. On her way back from the well, she saw Goodness coming down the alley. He was singing "Zhang Lian Sells Cloth":

Why oh why
Did you go and sell our big iron pot?
I put it on to boil, but the water never got hot!

Snow Bai put down her carrying pole, laughing. When Goodness saw Snow Bai, he stopped singing. "What are you doing up so early, Goodness?" she asked.

"I couldn't sleep," Goodness said.

"Why not?"

"I don't have any complaints about Fourth Uncle, but just because he gets up early, why does that mean the rest of us can't sleep in peace?"

Snow Bai laughed.

"You better be careful; the old man is fussy. Did you empty their pisspots yet?"

"Not yet."

"Look at you," Goodness said, "smashing the traditions!"

By the time Snow Bai got back, Wisdom Xia had already finished his first pot of tea. He dumped the tea leaves in the flower bed and asked Snow Bai why Wind Xia wasn't up yet. "Just look at the time!" he said before she could answer. "He should have already gone over to West Street and fetched our guests from the township government offices."

When Snow Bai heard that, she rushed over to their room to wake up her husband. The opera performers who had decided to stay overnight in Freshwind were back and just finishing lunch when New-Life came to the door. Wisdom Xia wanted to know if he'd brought the gifts, but before he could ask, New-Life started making a fuss about not having been invited to the banquet.

"We only had the relatives," Fourth Aunt said. "We didn't invite anyone from West Street or Middle Street."

"I thought you forgot about me," New-Life said.

"How could we forget about you? Didn't we ask you to take care of the gifts for the performers? You never showed up!"

"I was in West Mountain Bend, getting the eggs."

New-Life sent Rain Xia to pick up the apples at the orchard before turning to the bandleader of the opera company to show him a drum score he'd composed. New-Life was a farmer, but his only talent was in the arts. I'd always thought if he'd been given the chance to move to the city, he might've ended up like Wind Xia.

New-Life was like a golden bell that had been buried in the mud, where it would never make a sound. Like his late father, Water-Rise, New-Life could only read a couple of characters. But that didn't stop him from memorizing whole operas word for word, all the roles from *sheng* to *jing* to *chou* to *dan*. He'd performed the *dan* role in some performances by local troupes. Then a few years back, while celebrating the New Year, he'd been too slow to let go of a firecracker. He blew the first two fingers off his right hand. He couldn't do the complicated finger patterns required to perform the female roles, so he turned his attention to the percussion instruments that accompanied the performances. After that, New-Life supplied the drums for all the village festivals. He accompanied the dances for the New Year's festival of lights with his woodblocks.

The bandleader was in the middle of taking a drag from Wisdom Xia's water pipe when New-Life came over. "Master," New-Life said to the bandleader, and he pulled out a rolled-up piece of paper from his pocket. The director saw it was filled with cramped musical notation. "What do you think?"

"Hum it for me," the bandleader said.

New-Life Liu really threw himself into the performance. He hummed until he was blue in the face, then took off his jacket to beat his own belly. Everyone in the yard wanted to laugh but managed to hold back.

"It's amazing, really," the bandleader said when New-Life was finished. "I tell you, if you go to the city, you'll see professors and politicians who are really just farmers, deep down. And now I come to the village and meet a farmer who's a real artist."

Big-Noise Zhao told me later what the bandleader had said. I agreed completely. "Just look at Wind Xia," I said. "He might look sophisticated, but he's really a bum. He's corrupt!"

"You're just jealous because he married Snow Bai," Big-Noise Zhao said.

"I don't care that they got married, but he acts like he owns her."

"You better watch what you say. Go find your own girl, if you're that upset."

"I'd rather go naked than wear rags," I told him. "It's a fur coat or nothing for me."

"Well, I guess that's the end of your family line then."

"Ah, what the hell do I want sons and grandsons for? They'd all be farmers, too. Like our lives aren't hard enough—you want my sons to deal with this shit, too? I'd rather plant a tree. What's a tree got to worry about?"

"Are you losing it again?"

While New-Life Liu was drumming on his belly, I went out for a walk. The men who had been sent to collect the apples and other items for the performers were returning to Wisdom Xia's home with shocking news. It turned out that New-Life had let half the orchard go fallow that year. Freshwind was a town of gossips, and even an egg missing from under a hen started people talking. For a few years, New-Life had made a fortune selling apples, but the year before there'd been an early frost, and then there'd been a drought. New-Life figured he'd cut his losses. It wasn't New-Life's decision to make, though. Even though he ran it, the orchard was still collectively owned. Some of the villagers were hesitant to criticize New-Life, but once they started, they couldn't stop. Finally, someone went ahead and bit into one of the apples. When everyone saw that, they decided they might as well get their fill, too. Pretty soon the apples they'd collected were all gone.

New-Life had already smacked his belly scarlet by the time he noticed a kid walk by snacking on an apple. "Where'd you get that apple from?" he asked.

"Everyone's eating apples out there," the kid said.

New-Life rushed for the door, where he saw that villagers had started raiding the boxes of apples he'd packed himself. Just then, Third-Kid Li's mother was carrying off a half dozen in her apron, and when New-Life grabbed for the apples, she made a dash for it, throwing one of the apples to her grandson. New-Life caught hold of her apron and pulled her to the ground.

"Oh, you're going to beat people up now?" a man in the crowd said.

"The Two Committees ordered them for the performers," New-Life said. "Why the hell is she eating them?"

"That orchard belongs to Freshwind. If you can eat them, why can't we?"

"I'm leasing it," New-Life said. "Those are my apples!"

"Did the village get their cut?" the man said.

"I paid," New-Life said.

"How much?"

"I paid half."

"What about the other half?"

"I'm only using half of the orchard."

The two went back and forth for a while before I butted in. "New-Life," I said, "everyone knows you manage the orchard, so why are you trying to get out of paying half the fees?"

"So what? What are you going to do about it?" He poked me in the chest with the three remaining fingers on his right hand, and I slapped him away.

"When there's a bumper crop, you're there," I said, "but in the lean times, you're nowhere to be found. Are you looking after the orchard for us, or are we looking after you?"

"I'm not talking to you, retard."

I reached into one of the boxes and picked out two apples. I took a bite from one and tossed the other on the ground.

Shifty, who had been pacing at the edge of the crowd, smoking a cigarette, chose that moment to butt into the conversation. "So," he said, "you're saying you changed the contract you had with the village? Let's have a look at that contract."

"You want to see it? I'll show it to you!" New-Life Liu barked back, spittle collecting at the corners of his mouth. He shouted for Rain Xia to take the eggs and what was left of the apples into Wisdom Xia's yard and then stormed off toward the orchard. When Wisdom Xia saw how few apples were left, he was livid. After dividing everything up into smaller boxes, there was hardly anything worth giving.

"Listen," the bandleader said, "all the performers who went home yesterday, don't worry about them. If you only give eggs to those of us who are still in the village, you have just enough to give everyone two boxes."

"No," Wisdom Xia said, "I can't do that. Everyone worked so hard on the performance." Wisdom Xia went into the bedroom to consult with his wife. He decided that the quilts that they had received as gifts would be redistributed to the remaining members of the opera company.

"Why are you getting involved here?" Fourth Aunt asked. "The village was responsible for putting on the performance, so the village should pay. Besides, do you have any idea what these quilts are worth?"

"You know they only put on that performance because of us. And anyway, what do we need so many quilts for? We might as well show a little generosity in this lifetime."

"It's up to you," Fourth Aunt said, but she didn't look happy.

He took a half dozen quilts. "It's better that someone gets some use out of them, rather than letting them sit in the cabinet."

At first the performers wouldn't take the quilts, but in the end, they accepted them and climbed aboard the trailer pulled by Roughshod Ding's small tractor. The tractor left the yard and went down the road, then turned onto Highway 312.

As I watched them go, I started to feel miserable. I knew that with the opera company gone, I had no excuse to go to Wisdom Xia's place. I didn't even want to talk to Shifty and the rest of the crowd that was hanging out waiting for New-Life to get back with the contract.

"New-Life isn't back yet," Shifty said when he saw me leaving. "Where are you going?"

"What the hell do I care what he does with the orchard?"

"Back in the war years, you'd be a fucking deserter."

"Back then, I'd be carrying a rifle, going door to door, looking for my woman."

A man appeared in the alley, dragging a sheep. Rites Xia was behind him, calling for him to stop. "You're being unfair," Rites Xia said.

"We agreed on three hundred yuan, didn't we?" the man leading the sheep said.

"You're right," Rites Xia said, "the sheep is three hundred. But the rope you're leading him with, that's a good hemp rope. And the leather collar, I paid five yuan for it. Let's settle on eight yuan and call it even."

"That's not going to work for me."

"Well, that's just the way it is," Rites Xia said, and he reached for the sheep's lead.

"All right, all right," the man said, "I'll give you five yuan. But I don't have it on me right now. In a few days, when I come through Freshwind again, you'll have it."

Rites Xia looked over and saw that everyone was watching, laughing at him. He waved me over. "This is Spark," Rites Xia said to the man. "You know him?"

"Sure, I know him. Crazy old Spark."

He knew me, but I sure didn't recognize him.

"Spark is going to be our witness, all right?" Rites Xia said. "Our deal is I get my money within three days."

The man left, leading the sheep. Rites Xia asked me what everyone was doing out on the street. I told him about New-Life Liu and the orchard. Rites Xia turned and walked away as if he hadn't heard me.

"What's gotten into you?" I asked.

"I don't have time for this."

"Where you going?"

"The market," Rites Xia said, "over in Teahouse Village."

I noticed he was carrying a black plastic bag. "What's the price of silver these days?" I asked.

He turned and walked back to slap me on the cheek. "What the hell are you talking about?" he said in a low voice.

The fact is, he knew exactly what I was talking about. For a while, Rites Xia had been buying and selling silver coins on the black market. I was the only one who knew about it. I'd been at the Teahouse Village market and seen him leaned up against a wall doing a deal. I even saw him biting one of the coins to test if it was real.

Rites Xia clamped a hand over my mouth. "Who else did you tell?" he said.

"Who did I tell what?"

"Huh? Tell me what you told them!"

"I told them your son Thunder was kind enough to bring his father a sheep. He wanted you to drink milk every morning. And then you went and sold it."

"I don't like fancy things," he said, laughing. "No harm in that, is there?" He saw an apple that had fallen in the gutter. He picked it up, brushed it off, and put it in the plastic bag.

I stood in the road for a while after Rites Xia left. I was deflated. It felt like the air was still hissing out of me. The two idiot girls from the Liu family were over at the Middle Street archway. They looked up at the sky.

"Look at the sun," one of the girls said.

"That's the moon," the other girl said.

They stopped a man walking by to ask him. "I'm not from Freshwind," he said. "I'm not sure."

I tried to laugh but nothing came out. I turned and walked toward Bowed Ox Ridge. That was where the village government was undertaking the Return Grain Plots to Forestry plan. The old field was now full of young trees, arranged in careful rows. Each tree was painted with a white stripe of lime around its trunk.

My dad's grave was in that field. When I didn't feel right, I liked to visit his grave, and today was one of those days. I stood in front of his grave mound and told him, "The woman I love has been married off to the Xia family. Why? Why to the Xia family? I can't figure it out. Her name's Snow Bai. I understand why she didn't marry me. But couldn't she have married someone from another town, far away, so I'd never need see them together? Why did it have to be the Xia family?"

My dad didn't answer.

A wasp busied itself among the brambles on the grave. "Your poor boy . . ." The wasp flew up and stung my forehead. I blocked a nostril, blew snot into my palm, and wiped it over the welt. Then I went around the back of the grave and took a shit.

As I was pulling up my pants, Dog-Scraps appeared in the field. Dog-Scraps had lived a hard life. He made a living collecting shit. He was so hard off that I'd heard he couldn't even afford to buy salt. Just when I was feeling bad for him, though, the first thing he said was, "Spark, your paddy field is full of weeds. Are you ever going to pull them?"

"Why don't you go pull them yourself?" I asked.

"Who are you to order me around?"

"You want some shit to pick up? I'll give you a nice fresh one." When he got closer, I picked up a stone and threw it at mine so that it spattered up at him.

Back at Wisdom Xia's home, the old man had gone back to bed and slept until midday. Fourth Aunt made lunch and then set about preparing thank-you gifts to send to relatives on West Street. She called Snow Bai over and asked her how many relatives she was going to visit. Snow Bai said that there were too many families to visit, but she'd stop by the closest relatives, at least, so there were at least six families that needed gifts. There was plenty of sugar-cane liquor, but there weren't enough noodles left, so Fourth Aunt divided the five remaining bundles of noodles into six and repackaged them in red paper.

Wisdom Xia got up and sat on the edge of his kang. The fire in the furnace below was not lit. The stone bed was cool. He watched Fourth Aunt wrap the noodles. "Wind Xia," he said, "are they still arguing over on East Street?"

"It's still going," Wind Xia said. "New-Life went to get the contract and came back with it. Pavilion and Concord Qin are there now, too. Concord Qin's stamp is on the contract. When Pavilion saw the stamp, he lost it. Concord Qin tried to talk his way out of it, but he broke out in hives. He's not doing too good."

"Give me a light," Wisdom Xia said. Wind Xia lit the pipe for his father. Wisdom Xia took a long drag.

"Pavilion was like a tiger," Wind Xia said. "Who knew he had it in him? But the way I see it, just because Concord Qin's stamp was on the contract doesn't mean Pavilion can put all the blame on him. He raked Concord Qin over the coals, right in front of Shifty and the rest of them."

Wisdom Xia snuffled and exhaled smoke. "You've been in the city too long," he said. "Stuff like this, down in the village, can turn into major problems . . ." He trailed off. "What was that? Did I hear thunder?"

That's exactly what it was. The sound cracked through the big, clear sky, and a single cloud rolled in to cover the whole of Tiger Head Cliff down in South Gully.

Chapter 5

The thunder was like the sound of stone grinding on stone. There had been a few storms like that already, rolling thunder but not a drop of rain, so everyone had stopped paying attention to the clouds. When clouds began to pile up against Tiger Head Cliff, though, the whole town went out to look. Maybe it was because the clouds finally had an audience, but they finally released—though not much, at first. The first raindrop landed in Star Chen's doorway with an audible thud. The raindrop sent a cloud of dust into the air.

Bright Chen was sleeping inside on a bamboo mat. He was still half-asleep when he heard Star Chen shouting that it was raining. By the time Star Chen got to the door, the rain looked like it had stopped, so he spread out his tools in the doorway and got to work repairing a tire, singing to himself as he worked. Star Chen was famous for being the first person in Freshwind to start singing pop songs. He sounded exactly like the singers on TV and the radio. He was singing a song called "The Wanderer":

> There's a wanderer out there
> Missing you, mother dear
> Oh the wanderer, far and wide he roams
> Always missing you, mother dear
> He ain't got no hooooome . . .

When the kids in the alley heard Star Chen start singing, they ran over to listen. Star Chen ignored them. He turned and stared off at some distant place down the street.

When the thunder clapped, I was with Roughshod Ding. None of the Middle Street houses had gateways flanked by pillars. Their gates opened onto long passageways that led to the yards. Roughshod Ding's was no different, and that was where I was sitting, drinking tea with him. When Roughshod Ding came back from the county seat, he scrubbed himself down with cold water. He was even shorter than me, but he had a big, puffed-up belly like a toad's.

"Hey, you're such a midget," I said, "how'd you get such a big name?"

"What's wrong with my name?" Roughshod Ding asked. "My dad came up with it. He wanted me to have a strong name, not some good-for-nothing loser name. He wanted me to be tough enough to look after myself."

He turned and called over to his neighbor, Auntie Wang. "Auntie," he said, "what are you doing still working on a hot day like this? Come and drink some tea with us."

She was working the loom and had sweated through her clothes from front to back. "If I had a son like you," she said, "I could afford to lie around in a chair fanning myself, too. Did you hear the price at the dyehouse went up?"

"Yeah, sounds about right."

The shuttle fell from the loom. Auntie Wang bent to pick it up but couldn't reach it. "The price of everything's shooting up," she said.

"But Roughshod is still as short as ever," I said.

Just then, Forest Wu walked by with a pole across his shoulder, a bucket at each end, one with freshly made tofu, the other with sour broth, the beverage made from fermented greens that everyone drank in the summer. He called out as he went, "Tofu! Sour broth! T-tofu!"

Auntie Wang got up from the loom and reached into her pocket. She fished around for a long while before finally pulling out a tattered bill. By then Forest Wu had already walked down the road. "Hey, dummy," Auntie Wang said. "Are you selling tofu or fleeing the scene of a crime?"

The day was hot, and the heat seemed to be coming right up from Middle Street. Looking east, I could see the archway that marked the beginning of East Street, and then west toward its mirror on West Street, where Forest Wu was selling his tofu. The air shimmered and the street looked like it was melting.

I called for Lucky in a loud voice; I knew she would answer only to her real name. Lucky stopped short when she heard me calling. She was busy chasing Tiger, the black dog that lived down by the village administration offices—apparently, the Xia family had such good relations with the village administration that it extended to their dog as well. Lucky and Tiger were the perfect match for each other. Lucky barked and nipped at any dog that approached Tiger. She escorted Tiger to the door of the dyehouse, yapping alongside him all the way.

The dyehouse had always been run by the West Street Bai family. The Bais were known for being canny businesspeople. The Xia family pretty much kept out of business, though, except for the hair salon that Bamboo had opened. All along Middle Street, the shops belonged to the Bai family. There was the noodle shop, the blacksmith, the tailor, the paper shop . . .

The dyehouse used to be quite small, but the variety of fabrics and patterns and colors on offer increased by the day. The drying racks outside the dyehouse ran all the way south to Freshwind Temple.

It wasn't far from the dyehouse to Freshwind Temple, really—just down a short lane and you were there. The temple was on a field of tamped earth opposite the theater. When was Freshwind Temple built? Nobody knew for sure, but everybody knew that the front hall of the temple was larger than the one behind it. The eaves of the two buildings were off by about a foot, so whenever it rained, the water collected on the steps between them and ran off into the gutters to the east and west. The front hall was divided into four rooms by old wooden folding doors. The doors had gotten so warped that even when they were closed there was enough of a crack left to slide a hand into. The rear hall had two rooms off the main chamber, and in that central room there was a long altar and a bench. If you sat on the bench, you could look out the window of the rear chamber and see the large ginkgo tree in the yard. A family of birds once lived in the ginkgo tree, but three years earlier a hawk had come to the tree and attacked them. It was a fearsome battle, and the ground below the tree was covered in white and gray feathers. People tried to help the birds by throwing rocks up at the hawk, but nobody could hit it. The battle lasted for three days and three nights, and in the end the male bird was pecked blind and fell from the tree, dead. The female bird fell out of the tree shortly after. She could still open her eyes, but she died a short time later. The strange thing was the hawk never even occupied the nest; he flew away after killing the husband and wife. Not long after, the village was hit with a sandstorm that lasted seven days, and the nest was blown from the tree. Two fledglings were found in the nest, dead and dry.

That was around the time that construction on Highway 312 started up. The original plan was for the highway to avoid the village, running from Yijia Ridge and along the river, where the embankment could serve dual purpose as roadway and dike. This plan meant they wouldn't need to occupy farmland in building the road. But eventually this plan was scrapped, and the highway ran across the plateau, ruining the village's feng shui. That turned out to be a serious problem, because once the village's feng shui was ruined, Justice Xia was forced to step down.

Justice Xia had once been the right hand of the Communist Party in the village. During the first round of land reforms, he'd measured out the plots, and when the village was organized into communes a couple of years later, he tore out the boundary stones he'd put in. He had weathered the storm of the Socialist Education Movement of the early 1960s and the purge of reactionaries within the bureaucracy. He had made it through the tempest of the Cultural Revolution without a scratch. When the next wave of reform came with Deng Xiaoping, he was there to divide things again. He set up the brickyard and expanded the apple orchard. Justice Xia was the Mao Zedong of Freshwind—he did what he wanted, and his word was law.

Rumors started going around that they were planning to promote him up the ladder to the next layer of the bureaucracy in the township. Gold Xia went out and bought a bolt of houndstooth fabric and had the tailor on Middle Street make an overcoat for his father to wear when he went to his new position in the township government. But just then, when everything seemed to be going his way, Justice Xia got cocky and decided to help the villagers block the construction of the new highway. They set up a roadblock and turned away the workers arriving to build the new road. When the excavator arrived to start digging, he sent a group of old people to lie down in the path of the machine. The young township head came to oversee negotiations at the roadblock. He gave him the order to disperse, but Justice Xia said, "You owe the farmers an apology."

The township head was furious. "I represent the entire country," he'd said.

The Public Security Bureau sent their men to drag off the old people, and Justice Xia was censured.

After that Highway 312 plowed straight across the northern tip of Freshwind, running along the plateau and cutting Yijia Ridge in half, destroying forty *mu* of farmland and a dozen *mu* of orchard. On top of that, the project to fill Seven Li Gully had to be abandoned. Justice Xia had enough and resigned. I knew that he was trying to send a message to the township government, though. When I went to see him, he asked me, "You've been running all over town, haven't you? So what have you heard?" He was rolling up a cigarette and offered me one, but I said I was fine.

I decided to flatter him. "If you step down," I said, "Freshwind is doomed."

"You really know how to kiss ass," Justice Xia said with a laugh, showing a mouthful of black teeth.

"No, really! It'll be the end of the village."

"Well, if it ends, it ends then."

But instead of asking Justice Xia to come back, the township government gave the village Party secretary job to Concord Qin, who'd originally been on the Public Security Committee. Meanwhile, Justice Xia's oldest nephew, Pavilion, got tapped to serve as village head. His candidacy was announced and there were no objections within the allotted five days, so that was that.

The next day, Justice Xia got up early and prepared to go out. He seemed to have shrunk, and his clothes didn't fit him right anymore. His wife tried to stop him. She was going to fry some eggs for him, but he told her he wouldn't eat. "Get my jacket," he told her. "No, no, not that one, the houndstooth jacket Gold had made for me."

"What do you want to wear that for?" Second Aunt said. "Aren't you worried they'll laugh at you?"

"I haven't done anything wrong," he said. He walked out the door with his houndstooth jacket draped over his shoulders, a cigarette in his mouth, and his dark glasses perched on his nose.

As he passed the public announcement board, people called out to him, "Village head!"

Justice Xia went into a restaurant and ordered his favorite, *liang fen* noodles. That day, he paid with cash instead of putting it on the government tab. After his big bowl of noodles, he ordered a couple of bottles of liquor and ten *jin* of pork ribs.

"I didn't get to finish what I started," he said as he ate, "but now's the time for the younger generation to take up the burden, and for me to go home and take a nap."

"Spark, Spark," Roughshod Ding said, and gave me a shake. "What happened next?"

I guess I'd spaced out for a second. "Where was I? Well, Justice Xia—"

"Call him Second Uncle," Roughshod Ding said.

"I think Second Uncle only wore his houndstooth that one time, right?"

"We were talking about the dyehouse. How'd you suddenly jump to Second Uncle's jacket?"

"Why can't I jump?"

That's how conversations go, from one topic to another, without rhyme or reason. Roughshod Ding ignored me. "We're not going to get anything done," he said, "sitting around here like this. I have to get some money together." I didn't answer. "But how?" he mumbled.

That's Roughshod Ding—even with money in one pocket, he's thinking of how to fill the other pocket. He was getting on my nerves. "You want to make some money? Put some pantyhose over your head, go down to the credit union, and rob them." As soon as I said it, I knew I shouldn't have. The only reason Roughshod Ding had any money now was because he used to work at the credit union. Roughshod Ding was one of the first people they hired. The word around the village was that he'd made himself a bundle through a bunch of loopholes and side-dealing. "I guess I should watch my mouth," I said.

"You can start by getting those chives off your teeth," Roughshod Ding said. I rubbed at my teeth and found a shred of green. "Hey, Pavilion looks like he pissed his pants!"

I looked up and saw Pavilion coming our way with a mean look on his face.

Chapter 6

That afternoon, Pavilion panted with rage the entire way to the Two Committees office. Apart from the scar over his left eyebrow, Pavilion was the spitting image of his late father. Pavilion was much less patient than Benevolence Xia had been, though. He was quicker on his feet, too, and he had a sharper tongue. One time, I was squatting down in the public bathroom when he came in. "Taking a piss?" I asked him.

He grunted.

"I have something to report," I said.

"What is it?"

"It's about my dad."

"You have to go to Concord Qin for that."

"Concord Qin isn't going to be able to figure it out."

"All right," Pavilion said. "When I get the chance, I'll look into it. Right now, there's three more guys waiting outside, asking for favors." He put his dick back in his pants and went out. He was in such a hurry I wondered if he'd even finished pissing before he pulled up his pants.

Pavilion arrived at Freshwind Temple, huffing and puffing. A sign on the temple gate read, Two Committee Meeting Office, meaning the village committee and the local Communist Party branch. Someone had used a charcoal cinder to sketch a phallic-looking tortoise. Pavilion cursed and rubbed the sketch away; then he kicked open the gate.

Goodness was sitting in the courtyard of the temple, drinking tea with Lotus Jin from the Women's Committee. Goodness and Lotus Jin had their shoes off. Their feet were resting on a stone bench. The two sat half in the shade of the ginkgo tree and half in the dappled sunlight coming down through the leaves of the tree. Spots of shade and light spread across them, leaving them looking like a pair of Dalmatians. That year there hadn't been enough rain, and the tree had produced far fewer nuts than usual. The leaves had begun to fall, and Big-Noise Zhao was under the tree, sweeping them into a sack to take back to his shop and turn into medicine. When Lotus Jin saw Pavilion coming, she quickly slipped her shoes back on. Pavilion marched straight into his office without saying anything.

"What's Pavilion upset about?" Big-Noise Zhao asked.

"It's probably because he saw you collecting the ginkgo leaves," Lotus Jin said. "The village cadres depend on that for their spending money, you know."

"Price of ginkgo nuts is only two mao this year," Big-Noise Zhao said, "and these trees aren't producing much."

"They were at five mao before. This is an off year for the nuts, so the leaves are going at a decent price. And you're out here every day collecting them."

"Is Pavilion really that petty?" Big-Noise Zhao said. He continued sweeping up leaves while looking over at the window of Pavilion's office. "I've heard he's always like that—comes in, doesn't say anything until he's at his desk. Even if there's an emergency, you have to be sitting across from him before he'll listen. And he hates it when someone sits in his chair, right?"

"Where'd you hear that?" Lotus Jin said.

"I think it's the right way to go about things. That's preserving the dignity of the office. You don't want to see the manager of the store sweeping up the aisles."

"I see," Lotus Jin said, as if she had suddenly come to some great realization.

Just then Pavilion's office window clattered open. "Big-Noise Zhao," he shouted, "if you haven't got anything nice to say, keep your mouth shut!"

Big-Noise Zhao put his head down, bent to pick up his bag of leaves, and hurried out of the courtyard.

Pavilion called Goodness into his office. Goodness came in and poured a cup of tea for Pavilion, who didn't drink it. Everyone knew Pavilion sweated water out like a sieve. He told Goodness to give him a rundown of the ledgers so he'd have some idea what the village owed and what was owed to them.

"What's this about?" Goodness asked. "Are we being audited?"

"Everyone around here talks too damn much," Pavilion said. "I'm the village head. Why shouldn't I know what our accounts look like?"

"It's simple; thirty thousand yuan left in the budget, with eighty thousand owing on the taxes we have to kick up, a hundred and thirteen thousand owed to the cadres, and twenty-two thousand owed to the restaurant."

Deep furrows appeared on Pavilion's forehead. "Why do we still owe the cadres so much money?" he said.

"It's been building up for a few years now," Goodness said. "Paying our taxes up the ladder is always our priority. There's never enough money left over. The village cadres have had to pay their own expenses, some out of pocket, but most of them have gone to get loans in their own names. There's back pay, too, from six months' to a year's worth. We owed Spark's father a year and three months of back pay when he died. Spark has come by the office to curse me out about it a few times now."

"How much is owed to us altogether?"

"We're still waiting on twenty thousand in agricultural taxes from West Street, plus eight thousand five hundred from Middle Street, and sixteen thousand from East Street. We've collected five thousand of the fees from the orchard, and we're still owed three thousand. As for electricity bills, we've only collected about a third of what's owed. And the trees we were trying to sell along the river—we're still waiting for that to be settled. Spark's father wrote that he had sixty trees. I went and had a look and counted at least eighty-one, and we made the deal at a hundred yuan a tree. Somewhere along the way, he made a deal to sell forty trees to the nephew of the head of the township government. We found out he made that deal for fifty yuan a tree, since they were buying so many. Once he died though, things got complicated."

Pavilion was silent. He reached in his pocket for a cigarette but came up empty. "You got any cigarettes?" he asked.

"Just smoked my last one." Goodness reached back behind the broom in the corner. Before he could scavenge a butt, though, Pavilion had dumped his tea out on top, soaking everything. He sat fuming in his seat. Goodness went to the still-open window. The cicadas hissed their dying song in the ginkgo tree. He watched Lucky squeeze into the courtyard through the open temple gate, followed closely by Tiger. When Lotus Jin saw them, she rose and shooed Tiger out of the courtyard. Tiger, trapped outside, barked for Lucky, and Lucky, stuck inside, barked back. Goodness shrugged, and Lotus Jin opened the gate again and pushed Lucky out.

"There's one more thing," Goodness said, "but I'm not really sure how to bring it up."

"Just say it."

"When Concord Qin went to the county government to ask for the money to cover the reinforcement of the dike, he said he didn't want to bring a knife to a gunfight, so he ended up taking twenty thousand yuan from the village to grease the wheels at county. We got the money to cover the work on the dike, but that twenty thousand never got paid back."

"So ask him what happened to the money," Pavilion said.

"How am I supposed to bring that up?"

"You're the accountant! What do you mean, how are you supposed to bring that up? That money belongs to Freshwind. Are we supposed to just look the other way?"

Goodness didn't say anything. In the distance, he heard the long hee-haw of the donkey pulling the stone roller behind the dyehouse. It had to be the donkey at the dyehouse since it was the only one left in Freshwind.

Now that Pavilion had laid into Goodness, he felt a bit better. "What about this thing with New-Life and the orchard?" he continued in a softer tone. "Everyone's asking questions now. Shifty is saying he wants to file a report. What are we going to do?"

"I was just talking about it with Lotus Jin," Goodness said. "Concord Qin authorized the revision of the contract, but we were wondering if you knew anything about it beforehand."

"I didn't know shit!"

"They really screwed this one up. If you take a shit, you should wipe your own ass, I always say."

Lotus Jin entered with a kettle of tea. Seeing that Pavilion was waiting for her to leave before he kept talking, she set the kettle down quickly and left the office, going back out to the courtyard, where she sat on the bench to paint her nails.

"He took a shit all right," Pavilion said, "but do you think Concord Qin's still going to be able to wipe his ass clean after all this?"

"Shifty is fired up and doesn't care who ends up getting the axe. It's going to be bad for Concord Qin if Shifty really goes after him, but it's not going to be good for us, either. For now, the best option is for you to be seen to be dealing with it. Put some pressure on Shifty and buy us some time."

"I tried to protect Concord, and I've gotten no gratitude. Instead of coming to me, I hear he went to Second Uncle."

"I'm not sure about that," Goodness said, "but the last three times I was at Uncle Justice's place, so was Concord Qin. Maybe he thinks the former village head still has some pull with the higher-ups . . ."

"Sounds like my uncle isn't thinking straight, either," Pavilion said. He got up and left Goodness in the office, going over to the well in the courtyard. He drew up a bucket of water from the shallow well, poured it into a copper basin, and then dunked his head into the basin. Water splashed on the ground.

It really pissed me off when Pavilion and Goodness brought up my dad. Goodness Li was the one who was always causing trouble; he was a wicked little ghoul. But even if he was to blame, whenever anybody brought up a problem in Freshwind, Goodness would start talking shit about my dad. The dead can't argue their case. If the road was full of dog shit or pig shit, he'd try to tell everyone that it must've been my dad's shit. It was different when my dad was still alive. Goodness was over at our place so often he left his footprints in the stone outside our gate. He'd never come empty handed, either. If he didn't bring a chicken for us, he'd at least have an old pumpkin or something. On rainy days, he'd make a mess of the steps, stomping around in his muddy shoes until my dad told him to come inside. Goodness insisted on using a stick to scrape every last bit of mud off his shoes.

The trees were the perfect example of how Goodness always sidelined my dad. My father had been involved in the plan to cut down the trees along the river dike. The trees were being cut down to use in repairs on the school, which was on the verge of collapsing, but some of the lumber was being bought by the nephew of the township head. Of course they had to sell to him; he was connected to the township head, who had authorized funds for the school repair. Who do you think showed up to help haul the trees? It was Goodness, ingratiating himself again. Later, Concord Qin secured funding from the county government to reinforce the dike, but my father was the one who got the ball rolling—nobody likes handing out bribes. My father filled a sack with persimmons and peanuts as a gift, but they wouldn't even let him in the door. Later, twenty thousand did the trick, but you can't expect to get a receipt for that. How stupid do you have to be? What had all my father's hard work amounted to? Busted shoes and nobody willing to give him the time of day. He was so poor he would beg bowls of noodle water from the restaurants to soak his stale bread in, and he wrecked his stomach that way. Nobody cared, and the village still owed him his last paychecks.

While Pavilion washed his face, Goodness rushed over to the walnut tree in the courtyard and picked three leaves. He brought them to Pavilion, telling him to tuck them in the waist of his pants to cool himself off. Pavilion waved him off. "Just scratch my back," he said. When he lifted his shirt, Goodness saw that Pavilion's back was red from heat rash. After scratching for a while, Goodness felt his back starting to itch, too, so he went over to the gingko tree and rubbed his back on the trunk. Lotus Jin followed Goodness and Pavilion back into the office. She plugged in the electric fan and started fiddling with it, but it wouldn't turn on.

"Did you check if the power's out?" Goodness said.

Lotus Jin flicked the switch on the desk lamp. The lamp was dead, too. "The power's out again," she said.

"Go," Pavilion said to Goodness. "I want you to call up everyone from the township government and tell them to meet us at the Liu family restaurant."

"We're bringing the township government down here?"

"I'm sure Shifty's going to report the orchard situation. Let's get to them first. I have another idea, too. I want them to increase capacity at the power station. Forget irrigating the fields; we can't even plug in an electric fan. West Street is riding me so hard I can almost hear them complaining from here. We'll get the township government to cover the expense."

"Should we invite Concord Qin to the meeting?" Goodness said.

"Of course," Pavilion said.

"I'll go let him know," Lotus Jin said and then went out.

Goodness prepared to leave, too, but Pavilion stopped him. "I want you to get Lucky Liu to cook us up some donkey medallions," he said.

Lotus Jin was waiting around the corner for Goodness. She reached up and fixed a hank of hair to cover his bald spot. "What were you talking about when I came in that Pavilion didn't want me to hear?" she asked.

"Pavilion thinks Concord Qin is too close to the old village head," Goodness said.

"Pavilion's worried about his own uncle?" Lotus Jin asked.

"If Concord Qin and Pavilion keep after each other like this, we're the ones who are going to end up suffering."

"It's Concord Qin's own damn fault for being a soft touch," Lotus Jin said. "People are saying that the township government might be pushing for Concord Qin and Pavilion to switch positions. Have you heard anything like that?"

"I asked him about it, and he wouldn't stop asking me who I heard it from. I'm scared to bring it up again."

"Do you think the township head might make the announcement tonight at the dinner?"

Goodness scratched his bald spot. "You know, you could be on to something. I can't believe I overlooked that." He glanced around and then reached down and pinched Lotus Jin's ass. Lotus Jin swatted him away and rushed off to Concord Qin's home.

Busty, with curves in all the right places, Lotus Jin had always been considered almost the equal of Snow Bai among the beautiful women in the village. Her only flaw was the freckles on her cheeks that obliged her to cake on foundation. In the summer, she was always sweating the powder off and had to keep a mirror in her pocket for touch-ups. As she walked, she checked her mirror three times. When she arrived at Concord Qin's house, the door was locked from the outside—nobody was home. On the way back, she happened to run into Concord Qin's wife, who was sitting outside the dyehouse, studying a piece of printed fabric. "Sister," Lotus Jin said, "I'm looking for Secretary Qin." She was sitting next to a couplet that had been pasted on either side of the door of the dyehouse:

> When you arrive
> We'll know your length.
> When you leave
> You'll know our depth.

Another masterpiece from Big-Noise Zhao, Lotus Jin thought to herself. "Sister," Lotus Jin called out again, louder this time, "where's Secretary Qin?"

"'Secretary'?" Concord Qin's wife said. "He's as useless as ears on a deaf guy. They should've cut him loose a long time ago."

"What do you call a man with no ears?" Favor Bai said, coming out of the dyehouse.

"I don't know, what?" Concord Qin's wife said.

"Can't figure it out, huh?"

"Nope."

"Come on! Let me tell you a story. An elephant was strolling down a path, and a snake was coming the other way. The elephant says, 'Get out of my way.' The snake says, 'Who the hell are you? You look awful stupid with a dick growing out of your face.' The elephant says to the snake, 'You look awful funny with your face on the end of a dick.'"

Concord Qin's wife jumped up and pinched Favor Bai's mouth shut. She pulled Lotus Jin aside. "What are you looking for him for?" she asked.

"The Two Committees are inviting the township government to a dinner in the village tonight. I can't find him anywhere, though."

"He's at home."

"I just went there, and the door was locked."

"He doesn't want to see anyone," Concord Qin's wife said. "Told me to lock the door when I went out so that everyone would leave him be. Lotus Jin, you know as well as I do that Concord Qin's a sucker for a sob story. New-Life said he couldn't handle the other half of the orchard after the bad harvests and owing so much money. He told Concord Qin that he was looking after his sick wife. When Concord Qin saw that New-Life was in trouble, he agreed to change the contract. Now, Shifty is getting involved and Pavilion is pissed off. They want him to change the contract back. But what's the point in crying over spilled milk? Not that anyone gives a shit about what my husband has to say about it."

Lotus Jin didn't offer an opinion. She followed Concord Qin's wife back to her house. When the gate swung open, Lotus Jin saw Concord Qin sitting on the stairs up to the house, peeling taro into a basin. When Lotus Jin told him about the dinner, Concord Qin said he wouldn't go.

"You're pathetic," Concord Qin's wife said. "Why not?"

"I don't want to see Pavilion."

"You're a disgrace to your family. What are you scared of Pavilion for? He's not a man-eating tiger, is he? You should let the cadres from the township see how he bullies you."

"Fine. I'll go above his head. I want to tender my resignation directly to the township head."

When Concord Qin and Lotus Jin arrived at the restaurant, the party had already downed three rounds of drinks and Lucky Liu's son had just returned from West Mountain

Bend, where he'd been sent to buy donkey medallions. Lucky Liu was complaining that they could have raised a donkey in the time he was gone. His son grumbled that no one in the market had had fresh ones, so he'd had to convince them to give him a couple of frozen ones. Before they could stop him, Pavilion opened the package himself and saw the two donkey penises. Each penis had a strip of paper attached to it. One strip had the township head's name on it, and the other had the township Party secretary's name on it.

"Looks like we'll be enjoying the organs of our guests from the township government," Pavilion said. Everyone laughed except for Concord Qin, who chose that moment to announce to everyone that he was resigning.

"What's wrong, Concord Qin?" the township head said. "We're having a good time here. What are you talking about, you're resigning?"

"I'm not going to be the Party secretary anymore." The table went quiet, everyone staring at Concord Qin. "I just wanted to tell you in person," he said, and then he got up to leave.

"Have a drink!" the township head said. "Let's drink, eat some donkey medallions, and then talk."

"I'm serious," Concord Qin repeated. Having set himself on resigning, he wasn't going to let anyone distract him. He refused to take his seat at the table.

"You think you can just quit?" the township head said.

"Like they say, it's trying to turn a ball of mud into a Buddha. I'm never going to be cut out for this job."

"Freshwind is right under our nose, so to speak," the township head said. "We see everything that happens here. Concord Qin, we know you get things done. Sure, you can be a soft touch sometimes, but that's why we set you up with Pavilion, the hothead from the farm-machinery depot. When we selected you two to take over, we were thinking of two voices harmonizing. One of you would be the good cop, the other the bad cop. In a big village like Freshwind, we need to make sure things are handled correctly. Situations can't be dealt with the wrong way. I know there have been a few problems here recently. There's no need to panic. Whatever problems come up, we can handle them. For the greater good, we can't allow you to resign. However, we've looked into things and decided that it might be an option for the two of you to switch positions . . ."

Pavilion had been hitting the liquor hard, and his face had gone red. He set down his glass, though, when the donkey medallions arrived at the table. The donkey penises had been roasted, chilled, and then sliced thin. Round with a hole in the middle, the medallions looked just like the copper coins threaded onto a string in times past. "Director," Pavilion said, "give this a try." He looked on eagerly as the township head took a medallion. "Now, as for changing positions, what do you think?"

"I'm open to your suggestions, of course," the township head said.

"I don't think it's appropriate," Pavilion said. "I'm still young. I don't have the experience. I was thinking that it would probably be best if I continue on as Concord Qin's assistant."

"Just forget about me already!" Concord Qin said.

"I think we should do it," the township head said. "Tomorrow, I'll make the move public." After he spoke, there was silence. The township head reached for the donkey medallions again. "They say this stuff is good for you, right?" He smacked his lips.

"Nowadays, they mostly sell them from younger donkeys," Goodness said, "but over in West Mountain Bend, they sometimes get the big ones still. Those have some power!"

"Goodness here married into a West Mountain Bend family," Pavilion said. "His father-in-law used to make donkey medallions at home."

"The secret is," Goodness said, "you need to get a donkey that's at least two years old. You can't make the cut when the penis is soft, either. You must get it hard. The way to do it is to bring over a pretty little jenny. Once the male gets fully aroused, you take the knife and"—he made a chopping motion—"you make the cut."

Blushing, Lotus Jin stood and left the table. "That's enough of that," the township head said. "Lucky Liu, what are we having next?"

"How does noodles in sour broth sound?" Lucky Liu said.

"One bowl of noodles each then," the township head said.

"None for me," Concord Qin said.

Pavilion, Lotus Jin, and a few others refused as well, saying they were full.

Lucky Liu yelled to the kitchen, "Bring out three two bowls!" Shortly after, a group of three entered, also wanting noodles. Lucky Liu called to the kitchen again: "Bring out two three bowls!"

"What does Lucky Liu mean, 'three two bowls,' 'two three bowls'?" Lotus Jin whispered to Goodness.

"'Three two bowls' is three portions of noodles in two bowls. 'Two three bowls' is two portions of noodles in three bowls. Understand?"

"Why, that thieving old—" Lotus Jin started, but Goodness stamped on her foot before she could finish.

Goodness turned back to the table and lifted his glass. "Even if the decision hasn't been officially announced yet," he said, "your word is bond. Let's lift our glasses! First, I'd like to pay my respects to the township government leadership and their benevolent concern for

Freshwind. I'd also like to congratulate Pavilion and Concord Qin. As always, the township government knows best. God's in his heaven; everything is in its right place!"

Concord Qin refused to drink at first, but they finally got him to lift his glass and drink half. His face immediately went red, and spots popped up on his arms.

"Brother, I'll finish your drink for you," Pavilion said. "Since we've sealed the deal, perhaps now is the time to ask for a favor. Freshwind's electrical quota is too low. I know the township is aware of this. We need the quota raised, and we wanted to ask the township to cover the expense."

"Freshwind never asked much of us in the past," the township head said. "They took what they got and didn't complain. But it looks like things are changing now, huh, Pavilion? We'll raise the quota, call it an emergency measure, and the township government will pitch in. But let's be clear, it's not a gift—we're splitting it sixty-forty. Once I get your forty percent, we'll pay our sixty. Sound good?"

"Please, allow me to pledge this half bottle, downed in one gulp!" Pavilion proclaimed.

He lifted the bottle, but Goodness stopped him. "Your ulcer . . . ," he said.

"A bleeding stomach is a small price to pay for their portion of the electricity payment," Pavilion said. He put the bottle to his lips like a trumpet and drained the contents.

The conversation moved to other topics, and the township head began to ask about local affairs—antidrought efforts and the Return Grain Plots to Forestry plan at Bowed Ox Ridge—and then he finally got around to the orchard. "Before I came here," he said, "Shifty came to me."

Concord Qin went pale, and Pavilion hurriedly poured him a cup of water. "Shifty already filed a complaint, huh?" Pavilion said. "It's nothing, really, just some small changes with New-Life Liu's contract. Concord Qin and I discussed it, and the original terms were based on a normal year. But then there was the early frost last year, and the drought this year. I saw it myself; the harvest was really pitiful. We can't blame New-Life for that, can we? But don't worry, now that word's gotten out that we're splitting up the orchard, there are lots of people who'll want to lease it. There's nothing to worry about. We'll have the problem solved before you know it."

"That's good to hear," the township head said. "Shifty made it sound like you two were fighting tooth and nail over this."

"Can you really believe anything he says?" Pavilion said. "If Shifty's not complaining, then he's freeloading or making a mess for other people to clean up. Everyone here in Freshwind knows all that bastard has ever cared about is looking out for number one." Having said his piece, Pavilion slipped off to the bathroom, and Concord Qin followed him.

"You told him lots of people want to take over the other half of the orchard," Concord Qin said, "but how can that be, with the state it's in now? If he finds out we're lying to him, what are we going to do?"

"I've got just the guy," Pavilion said.

"Who?"

"Star Chen."

"You think he'll agree to that?"

"I'll deal with him," Pavilion said. "You just worry about getting the back rent from New-Life Liu."

When they got back to the table, Concord Qin's face had recovered some of its color. He proposed a toast to Pavilion. "Brother," he said, "I'm no match for you. I'll let you take care of things with Star Chen."

"Who's Star Chen?" the township head asked.

"Young guy, not originally from Freshwind," Pavilion said. "Originally, he wanted to set up a shoe store, but our local taxes and fees were too high to make it feasible. We were thinking, if outsiders want to come and do business in our town, we should make it as easy as possible for them. Taxes are taxes, but maybe we can waive some of their other fees. Does that sound reasonable to you?"

"I'll leave it to you two to decide what's best," the township head said. "As far as people moving to Freshwind, the more the merrier, I say! Sesame seeds are easier to overlook than pumpkin seeds, but that doesn't mean they're worth any less. Don't let an opportunity like this slip through your fingers."

Pavilion told Lotus Jin to go fetch Star Chen and have him brought to the restaurant to meet the township head.

Chapter 7

When the sun went down, the crows fluttered down from Yijia Ridge. I never could stand them—crows—I thought they were ugly creatures. Me, I can't stand ugliness. My way of thinking is, if you're going to plant a garden, put the prettiest flowers in it; if you're going to sit down to a meal, get the best cut of meat; if you're going to get married, pick the prettiest girl in the village. As I watched, the crows flew down and perched on the gabled roof of the theater. They called out a chorus of *Hey-wa! Hey-wa!* In the dusk, the crows and the roof were the same color.

That afternoon, Justice Xia had broken an old spade in the dirt and taken it down to the blacksmith to fix. It was getting late by the time the blacksmith had finished up with the spade, and while Justice Xia was on his way back to his yard, he happened to go alongside Thunder's wall and heard the sound of drinking games coming from inside. He went around to the gate and saw Rites Xia feeding his pig with scoops of sweet potato flour noodles. The pig rooted in the dirt, swallowed a few mouthfuls of the noodles, and then looked up at Rites Xia as if to ask for another helping.

Rites Xia swore. "You've got a lot of nerve. You eat better than I do." When he looked up from the pig, he saw that Justice Xia had come into the yard. "Have you eaten yet, brother?"

"Yep."

From one of the rooms in the courtyard came the sound of the TV, and then Blossom grumbling that the reception was no good. She was calling for Culture to climb the tree and put the antenna a bit higher. When she came out into the yard, she saw Justice Xia and said, "Come inside for a drink."

"Again?" said Justice Xia.

"What's the point?" Rites Xia said. "Drinking is just paying good money to ruin your body."

"Who's over?" Justice Xia asked.

"Pavilion, Wealth Zhao, and that other guy, Star Chen. Did you hear? Pavilion is the new Party secretary."

"What about Concord Qin?"

"They switched jobs."

"What are they screwing around again for?"

"Maybe it'll work out for the best. Right after they switched, Pavilion got this guy Star Chen to take over the orchard."

"Really?" Justice Xia went over to the house and pushed open the door. The room was full of smoke and liquor fumes. The men rose and beckoned for him to sit with them and drink a toast. Justice Xia took a seat and lit one of his rollies, packed with dark tobacco. "You young people have your fun. Go on!"

Star Chen poured a glass of liquor and extended it toward Justice Xia.

"That's how you pass a glass of liquor?" Wealth Zhao asked in a stern tone. "With that hand?"

Star Chen paused and looked back at Wealth Zhao, not comprehending the error.

Wealth Zhao took the glass from Star Chen and, holding it with two hands at eye level, passed it to Justice Xia. "Remember, here in Freshwind, if you're passing to your elders, do it like this."

Justice Xia waved off the glass, saying it was too hot to drink, but Wealth Zhao insisted. "Pavilion became the Party secretary today. You're an old cadre yourself, and Pavilion's second uncle; you should drink a toast to him. He brought some honor to the ole Xia family name today."

Justice Xia took the glass but passed it to Star Chen to take the toast for him. He leaned into the younger man and said, "You take care of that orchard, you hear? If you need a hand with any of the technical stuff, you let me know."

"Uncle, you heard the news?" Pavilion asked.

Blossom came in and bent to pick up the empty bottles discarded on the floor. "You drank this much already?"

Thunder called out, "Can I get another plate of this?"

Blossom heard but pretended she hadn't. From where she was leaning in the doorway, she said, "Your uncle knows everything. He knows who every chicken in the village belongs to and whether it lays eggs."

"It looks to me like everything has worked out," Justice Xia said. "Next time we have to deal with a land contract, we need to be more careful. Freshwind Village is certainly a hard place for cadres to work in."

"This time it was Shifty who ended up causing problems," Pavilion said.

Blossom sneezed, splashing droplets of snot on Thunder's neck. "That means someone's thinkin' about me."

"Must be the dog," Thunder said.

She kicked him. "Shifty was just trying to make a preemptive attack."

"Come on, shut up about it."

"I'm not just talking shit here," she insisted. "I've heard him say that the brickyard is going bankrupt. But he's not doing anything to help himself. The thing is, he's not willing to take over the orchard, but he doesn't want anybody else to take it over, either. He must be up to something."

Pavilion said, "Uncle should have decided things, but he didn't. Same with Concord Qin. If nobody can decide, it's going to be a mess."

"What if I didn't retire? What would he do? I'll tell you this: you'll have to check those accounts every month to make sure there's absolutely no corruption. We must guard against graft!"

"Before he took over, it was an issue, too. That's how things are—if there wasn't room for corruption, those people wouldn't have bothered doing the work. But there are degrees. Once things get too corrupt, it's a problem."

"I don't want even the hint of corruption!"

"Like they say, you need muddy water to raise carp," Pavilion said, smiling and pouring liquor into everyone's glass. "Who in Freshwind is going to run a clean operation?"

"You know I can't do it. I didn't win any awards when I tried." Justice waved his hands as he spoke, and his cigarette flew from between his fingers and through the doorway into the yard. At precisely that moment the lights flicked off.

Blossom said, "Power's out. The power's out again." The room fell silent and still, everyone refusing to say a word or budge from their seats. Blossom struck a match and lit the kerosene lamp, calling out, "Emerald! Bring the other lamps." She backed away from the table, and her foot knocked over an empty liquor bottle, smashing it to pieces. The lamp on the table shuddered.

"Again with this; almost every day now with the power cutting out," Justice said.

"Back when you were in charge, nobody even had power," Pavilion said. "Now, everybody's got an electric fan. Anyway, I'll go to town and pick us up a new transformer tomorrow."

"Why do you always have to talk back to me? I was just saying . . . ," said Justice.

Rites Xia was still out in the yard, feeding the pig. He bent down and massaged the pig's back to see how much fat it was putting on. The spine of the hog still stuck out, sharp as a blade. Thunder's daughter Emerald ran over and said, "Second Uncle and Uncle Pavilion are arguing again. Can you go break them up?"

"It's not them arguing; it's their livers fighting. Go get the rhubarb root from the dresser in my room. Let them have some of that."

But Emerald never got the chance to get the rhubarb root. The door to the house crashed open. Justice Xia came out with Wealth and Thunder following him, pleading for him to calm down. Their soothing words fell on deaf ears. Justice Xia's neck stiffened, and the jacket he had draped over his shoulders slipped to the ground. Blossom picked up the jacket and raced after Justice Xia.

Rites Xia barged into the room. "Are you two just about done? Your livers acting up again?"

"It's all my fault," said Pavilion. "To him, every single problem is because we're not running things right. Are we family, or am I just another village cadre? He's trying to pull rank on me."

Rites Xia ignored him and started clearing the empty plates off the table. "I keep telling them, quit drinking so much, quit drinking so much. You get that heat inside of you on a hot day like this. Why would you drink on a day like this?"

"Let's keep drinking!" Thunder said. "You got any left over there? I'll go get a few more bottles." Thunder passed a fresh bottle to Pavilion. He took it and tried to pry the bottle cap off with his teeth. The cap wouldn't budge, so he went over and slotted it into the house's keyhole, slamming the cap off.

Justice Xia grew even angrier when he heard Pavilion calling for more liquor. He went past Wisdom Xia's house without stopping. He kept going, headed toward the tail of the scorpion. From inside the houses on the alleys that branched off the main street, he heard the sound of people cursing the blackout. All those electric fans that Pavilion had mentioned were sitting idle. People came out of their houses with their bamboo sleeping mats to spend the night in the threshing yard.

Justice Xia heard someone call out, "Uncle Liu, are you going to the threshing yard?"

The response came: "I'm staying here."

"You're going to roast in there!"

"Then you can come clean out the ashes tomorrow."

The light from a lantern flickered down the alley, illuminating Justice Xia for a brief moment. He didn't want anyone to catch him out there. He didn't want to have to answer for the power going out again. He stood for a moment beside the wall before the thought came to him, *They're not going to ask me.* He sometimes forgot that he wasn't a village cadre anymore.

He began to stride down the alley. There was nobody around to distract him, and his thoughts turned back to Pavilion. There was going to be trouble, Justice Xia decided. That Pavilion couldn't seem to do anything right, and he wouldn't listen to advice, either. He had sounded so casual when he'd brought up the transformer, but where was the money going to come from to buy it? It was going to be taken out of public funds, of course. The people of Freshwind would have to raise the money. Things never went smoothly when money had to be raised in Freshwind. Justice Xia had been through it before, with the project to fix the roads. Everybody wanted the roads fixed, and they raised the money, but the whole project ended with the villagers calling for his head.

Justice Xia's anger toward Pavilion turned slowly to concern. He looked up and saw that he was back at his own house. He leaned the spade against the gate and went off to find Marvel, the village electrician.

Marvel Zhou had suffered from heart trouble ever since he was a kid. You could tell as soon as you looked at him that he was not a well man—his lips were always tinged blue. When Justice Xia had been running things, he had made Marvel the village electrician because the kid wasn't going to be much help with manual labor. There was some grumbling about favoritism, of course. Dog-Scraps's voice was the loudest among those grumblers. He complained to Justice Xia that he was coddling the kid, and it wasn't fair. Justice Xia didn't bother arguing. He simply said, "If you get heart disease, I'll coddle you, too."

Dog-Scraps had a counter to that. "Too bad my mother wasn't a landlord's wife."

Justice Xia had answered with a stiff right to Dog-Scraps's jaw.

Nobody complained about Marvel after that. But step back for a moment. Can you figure out what Dog-Scraps meant by the line about the landlord's wife? There's a story there. Not many people in Freshwind know that story, except the old folks—and me, of course. The story goes back to when they were doing land reform after Liberation. Marvel's father was labeled as a landlord, and they put him through struggle sessions, of course. That's what they did back then to people with that class label.

But Marvel's father wasn't strong enough to take it, so his wife—Marvel's mother—went to seduce Justice Xia. Marvel's mother waited for him at the mill yard. She slipped off her pants and laid down on the stone roller. When Justice Xia came in and got a look at her body, his blood started pumping. Now, Justice Xia's wife, Bamboo—I call her Second Aunt—wasn't a landlord's wife by any means. For underwear Bamboo wore scraps of an old jacket that she'd sewn together, and when she got her period, she'd line it with cotton wadding from a quilt. Marvel's mother, though, had on red silk panties. Justice Xia thought to himself, *This really is a landlord's wife!* He pounced on her. Even after he finished inside of her, he jabbed his fingers into her. He lifted himself up, giving the landlord's wife's ass a final slap. He looked down, then, and saw that the cow that pulled the stone roller was watching him. Its eyes were as big as bronze bells.

But Justice Xia was still Justice Xia. He couldn't promise to spare the landlord. This is what he told her: "You can't confuse the two things. What we did together has no bearing on his situation."

"So that was for nothing?"

"Were you trying to trap me into something?" asked Justice Xia angrily. He forced himself on her again. She tried to roll away, but he held her firm. Justice Xia clamped a hand over her mouth to stifle her cries, roaring, "Think you can trap me, you goddamn landlord's wife?" She gave up her struggle. She gave in to him. But her muffled cries had been heard outside the mill.

The first to hear the cries of Marvel's mother was Mid-Star's father, who had just come up onto the bank along the edge of the paddy field where he had been pulling weeds. He saw Justice Xia and Marvel's mother in the mill yard, struggling together. He plucked a leaf from a castor plant, wiped his face, and walked away. Mid-Star's father was studying Buddhism back then. He used to tell fortunes. He also liked to run his mouth, and he ended up telling a few people along East Street what he'd seen. Not only did they not care but they also figured Justice Xia was probably doing the right thing, since the woman had tried to trick him.

The second to hear the cries was Marvel's parents' cow. The cow saw the situation differently. Every time the cow saw Justice Xia after that, she took a run at him and butted his ribs with her rock-hard skull. Mid-Star's father told me about reincarnation one time. Like, if you're a human in this life, you could have been a tree in your last life, and you might end up as a pig in your next life. However, how you act in this life decides what you become in your next life. That's why I said Lucky must have been a singer in her last life. Me and Snow Bai must have had some connection in our last life, too. Maybe she was a tree, and maybe I was a stone, sitting in the grass, not too far away from the tree. Whatever the cow had been in her last life and whatever it would be in her next life, she hated Justice Xia in this one. When the village was re-formed as a commune, Justice Xia finally had a chance to get even. He killed the cow, skinned it, and made its hide into a drum. The drum is still around, up at New-Life Liu's place.

Justice Xia despised Marvel's mother for trying to trap him, too, but as the years went by, he softened. After Marvel's father died, he tried his best to look after the family. He also did his best not to let anyone know he was doing it. One time, many years back, after Marvel's mother had finished work, she was cutting through the threshing yard and tried the old trick of stomping across the beaten grain. The trick was, you'd always be able to pick a few kernels of wheat off the soles of your shoes or your pant legs. It was a common way, in those days, to steal a bit of extra grain. Justice Xia happened to be nearby—he didn't let on that he had caught her, but he cleared his throat loud enough for her to hear. It put a scare into her. She was looking around for where the sound had come from and eventually saw Justice Xia. He was suddenly occupied with picking shreds of tobacco off his lap, pretending not to have seen anything. He could have ratted her out but he didn't, and she always felt thankful to him for that simple kindness. Later, she sent her son to call Justice Xia over to their home to eat mugwort steamed rice. Justice Xia never went. But he looked after Marvel when the boy turned out to be too sickly to work with the rest of the villagers.

That night, Justice Xia cut through a few alleys to the persimmon tree at the end of East Street. He could see the gate of the Zhou family courtyard—a big courtyard that had once housed a grand home. After Liberation, the courtyard had been turned over to poor peasant families. A sickly farmer named Tied-Dog Zhang got four rooms, and Marvel's family got two rooms. Justice Xia watched Marvel cross the courtyard, headed to his own door. The electrician had gone out to the generator to change the fuses and had only just returned to East Street.

Before heading into the courtyard, Marvel happened to glance over at the persimmon tree. Below the tree, he saw a glint of light. He thought to himself that it must have been the eye of a wolf and shivered. He saw the light glow a deeper red and realized it must have been someone under the tree smoking a cigarette. "Who's there?" he called out.

Justice Xia came closer, startling Marvel. When he recovered, he invited Justice Xia in to sit for a while. Inside, the smell of pickled cabbage and Marvel's piss bucket filled the room, slowly replaced by the smoke from Justice Xia's cigarette. Marvel always felt personally guilty when the power went out, and when Justice Xia asked about the situation, he immediately launched into a self-criticism.

"I feel so bad about this," he said. "I can't even hold my head up in front of you."

"Save it, I'm not running things anymore. I just want to know why the power went out." Marvel had an excuse, but Justice Xia saw through it. "There's a transformer that has to be changed out, and you've got to raise money for that. Right?"

Marvel was surprised that Justice Xia knew about the transformer and admitted that Pavilion had plans to go to the township government to ask for money to get a new transformer. The problem was, the electrician explained, that the transformer was going to cost forty thousand, and they would have to add another twenty thousand to upgrade the generator. It was either that or get high-voltage wires run out to the village. It was more complicated than just buying a transformer.

"Pavilion wants to get the transformer first and worry about raising the rest of the money later," Marvel said.

"I can see what's happening here," Justice Xia said. "Pavilion doesn't understand the situation. You need to be very careful and make sure the money isn't wasted. Do you understand me?"

"I'll do my best."

After they had talked for a while, the mosquitoes became overwhelming. "Why don't you get some mosquito incense?" Justice Xia asked.

"I usually smoke them out when the sun sets. I don't usually have the lamp on this late. I guess they're coming in through the door somehow, trying to get to the light."

"Well, I better go."

As they walked out together, a lamp lit up Marvel's mother's room. They could see her, silhouetted against the window paper. She called out, "Who's out there with you, in the middle of the night?"

"It's Uncle Justice."

Justice Xia paused as if he were about to speak, but he kept going instead, hurrying out of the courtyard. Once they were out of earshot of Marvel's mother, Justice Xia said, "How is her blood pressure these days?"

"She still gets light-headed sometimes, but it's not that bad."

"Make sure she gets up slowly. She's got to take it slow when she gets out of bed."

"Okay."

"She didn't have an easy time raising you, so now that she's getting older, you have to be there for her."

Marvel felt tears come to his eyes.

Chapter 8

Now, that same afternoon, I was drinking weak tea with Roughshod Ding. The cheap fucker wouldn't put more than the stingiest pinch of leaves into a pot. I decided to go over to the cultural center, where Rain Xia and his gang were playing mah-jongg. It turned out that Bright Chen was over there, too. All that stuff that happened that day, between Justice Xia and Pavilion? It was Bright Chen who told me about it. Bright Chen has a stutter, a bit like Forest Wu, but it's more rapid fire, if you know what I mean. I prefer that, in a way. I told him, "If you can't say it, just sing it."

So he sang:

> More I think about it, it makes me sick.
> I never have, never will belong
> I tell you this now and know it's true
> Not a single good man lives in Hongtong.

"So you can sing local opera!"

He looked pleased with himself and then sang a few more lines.

"Bright Chen, they're going to get your brother to take over the orchard. Why would you say there're no good people in Hongtong County?"

"He started c-c-crying as soon as he s-s-signed the contract."

"What was he crying for?"

"He wants to be a s-s-singer. He was f-f-fixing tires before, but he didn't have to s-s-stay in one place. He could m-m-make a living doing that, wherever he went. Now that he's taking over the orchard, he's tied down to Freshwind."

"He wants to make a living as a singer? I've heard him sing; he'd end up starving to death. If he has to bring you along with him, that'd be even worse. Anyway, where else are you two gonna go?"

"Th-th-that's right."

I asked him about Star Chen and Emerald, and his face darkened. "It's n-n-not like that!"

"You want to stay in Freshwind, you've got to get yourself a piece, right? You know what I mean?"

"I can take c-c-care of myself. We've all g-g-got hands, right?" I felt sorry for Bright Chen and his brother. Happy people are all alike, basically, but every unhappy person is unhappy in their own way.

Bright Chen interrupted my train of thought to say, "You're j-j-jealous of him, aren't you?"

Ha! The idea of me being jealous of Star Chen was a joke. Jealous of him and Emerald? Snow Bai was a ripe, round peach compared with that sour little crabapple. The only guy in Freshwind that I was jealous of was Wind Xia.

I sat watching the mah-jongg game until the sun set and then started walking home. I thought I might bump into Snow Bai on the way back; maybe she'd be on her way from her parents' house on West Street back to East Street. But instead, I ran into Obedient Zhang, who managed the farm-supplies store. I heard him before I saw him.

"Spark! Spark!"

I wasn't in any mood to deal with that pockmarked son of a bitch.

He yelled again, "You think you can pull the same trick as your dad, pretending to be deaf?"

"What the hell did you say?"

"You heard me that time, huh?"

There's a story there, too. My father was Justice Xia's personal assistant. He never left his side. Even when Justice Xia changed positions, my father stayed with him as an assistant. One time, in the middle of whatever the latest political campaign was, Justice Xia had to make a public criticism of my father. My father didn't take it personally. He just shut his mouth and stood there, pretending he didn't hear anything that was being said to him. When Justice Xia was done, he went right back to being his assistant.

I complained to my father about it, and he told me, "That's model behavior. Take it as a lesson."

I asked him why he had to be the lesson. Why couldn't Justice Xia have model behavior? Why did my father have to sit there and take it? He told me I didn't understand. But so what? I still had the right to complain about it, didn't I?

I had picked up a brick and was ready to plant it in Obedient Zhang's temple; then I saw what he'd called me over for. You see, in the shop, they used a straw to siphon the liquor from the big wooden barrels into bottles, but someone had to get down and take a first suck to clear the air from the straw and get things flowing. That someone was going to be me. It took a couple of pulls to get the liquor flowing, and I made sure I got a few good mouthfuls once it was going. The liquor hit my belly, and I felt my head get light and my eyes half close. I wanted to see Snow Bai more than ever. I looked up and there she was! She was going up the street, holding a lantern, her footsteps light, her ass bouncing. Just as I was about to call out to her, I saw Goodness and Lotus coming down another alley.

I overheard part of their conversation. "What's this girl up to?"

"You should be over at Thunder's place, drinking with Wealth."

I looked back where I'd seen Snow Bai and realized that it hadn't been her at all. It was Wealth's wife.

I went over to Goodness and Lotus and said, "All it takes is for a guy to make some money, and his wife suddenly carries herself different."

Wealth's wife turned around and yelled back at me, "What the hell do you know about having a wife?" She turned to Goodness and Lotus. "Wealth can't look after himself when he drinks. Last time he got drunk, he ended up falling in a ditch. Lucky for him it was dry, or he would have drowned."

Goodness said to Lotus, "Thunder never invites us over for a drink. We should just show up there, too."

I decided to tag along since I knew that if I went home, I wouldn't be able to sleep anyway.

At Thunder's place, Goodness, Lotus, and Wealth's wife were steered to their seats by Blossom. But she wouldn't give me a place to sit, let alone a drink. She said, "You're crazy. If I give you a drink, you might end up getting out of control. You can supervise, okay? Make sure everyone takes the drinks they're supposed to."

She might not have meant it, but I took the job seriously. The men drank a few rounds, and when it was time for Wealth to drink, Thunder motioned for me to grab Wealth's arms so that he could pour a shot in his mouth. I grabbed him and, once the shot had passed his lips, I told him to talk so that the liquor would go down his throat.

When it came time for Pavilion to drink, he called me over and told me to drink for him. "One drink won't hurt you. Don't worry about it." I'd already had a few mouthfuls straight from the vat, so a shot or two wouldn't hurt me. I tipped back the shot and saw that Wealth was pissed off. I was supposed to be supervising, after all.

"You aren't playing fair. Why are you sucking up to Pavilion? You think he'll put you in charge of the brickyard? You think you're gonna be the next Star Chen? Now that he's taken over the orchard, you're working an angle on the brickyard? You'll have to deal with Shifty if you want to take over there." Now, at that time, I hadn't heard yet that Star Chen was taking over the orchard. I asked Pavilion if he was serious.

"New-Life didn't cut it, so we needed somebody to take over. I thought about having you manage the orchard, but you're sick. You think you could have handled it?"

"What do you mean, I'm sick? You're the one who's sick, you and the rest of these village cadres. The whole lot of you are corrupt, especially Concord Qin. You know it was my father who nominated him to take that job? What happened after he was gone? Concord Qin didn't do a goddamn thing."

"The man is dead; let him rest in peace," Wealth said.

"The village still owes him five hundred yuan. He paid out the livestock-inoculation tax with his own money and never got paid back."

Pavilion said, "Don't bring that up here."

"Why not?"

"You don't even know what happened. Your dad oversaw getting the money together to fix the street, and you can see for yourself how that worked out. That ended up blowing up in our faces. The dead are blameless, but I'm still here to take the shit. Let it rest, with him. You want to talk about five hundred yuan? Who do you think you are?"

"Is that any way for the village head to talk?"

Star Chen said, "He's not the village head; he's the Party secretary. That's way more important than the village head."

"You're the Party secretary now? If you don't pay back that money, I'm going to file a report."

"Go ahead!"

To be honest, if Pavilion had spoken reasonably with me, I probably would have let it drop. But as soon as he said that, I was mad. I felt like my head was on fire, like there was a cockscomb of flame blazing up from my scalp. I jumped up and stamped on the floor. Dust fell from the roof beams. "You're all corrupt!"

"Who's corrupt?"

"Concord Qin's corrupt, and you are, too."

"You better watch your mouth."

"Corrupt! Corrupt! Corrupt!"

He hit me with a punch that knocked me to the floor.

I reached under the table and found the two false teeth that had been knocked out. I popped them back into my gums and crawled toward the door. "The Party secretary is beating people up!" I stood up and faced him. "You better finish what you started."

Everyone in the room fell back toward Pavilion, as if they would shield him from me.

"Spark, what's gotten into you?" Pavilion demanded. "Are you crazy or something? Are you having an attack?"

I lunged at Pavilion but missed. I smashed my head against the table, knocking off the liquor cups. Wealth grabbed me and led me away.

He scolded Pavilion. "What's wrong with you? What do you hope to accomplish, getting this retard riled up?"

I grabbed at the doorway, but Wealth broke my grip. He dragged me out into the yard and led me home.

When I got into my room, I lay down on the kang. I couldn't sleep, so I stared at the ceiling, watching the mosquitoes. When they landed on me, I didn't bother swatting. I let them prick me and drink their fill. Once each mosquito had drunk its fill, I finally brought my hand down on it. I could smell my own blood, pungent, staining my palms. I started to feel light-headed, and I imagined my skull splitting open like a melon left to crack in the field. From the crack in my skull, I felt a white vapor leaking.

I don't know when or how I had left my kang, but I found myself walking through Freshwind, kicking stones in the street. I waited for someone to come out of their yard to talk to me, but nobody came. I knocked on doors and nobody answered. I knew they hated me. I knew they despised me. Nobody cared whether I lived or died. I went to the front of Big-Noise Zhao's shop and stood in front of the lamp that lit the facade. My shadow rolled out behind me like a cape, stretching on and on, a hundred feet behind me. I stamped on the shadow. My shadow felt nothing, but my foot ached.

When the sun rose, I found myself back on the kang. My body was covered in red welts from the mosquito bites. I looked up and saw that the door to my room and the gate of the courtyard were both open. I thought maybe a thief had come in sometime during the night, but I checked under the kang mat and saw that my money was still there, as were the three steamed buns in the hanging basket.

I went out into the street and watched a pig wander down the lane, its belly scraping the ground. It was one of the pigs that the people on Middle Street put out to scrounge for scraps. Following closely behind the pig was Dog-Scraps, balancing a shoulder pole, one end loaded with a bucket of shit and the other with a bucket of piss. Each time the pig lifted its tail to take a shit, Dog-Scraps stuck out his scooper to catch the droppings.

I'd always looked down on Dog-Scraps. When everyone went out to the city to work and make a good living, Dog-Scraps went along, too, but he came back after a year, got sick, and ended up doing this, wandering around picking up shit. The crotch of his pants had worn out, so the breeze blew down his ass crack and tickled his balls.

I walked down to the village administration office along Highway 312. I saw that Lucky was already stationed in front of the big iron gate, waiting for Tiger. I'd never considered what dogs in love looked like, but I wouldn't have guessed that they'd be this absorbed in it.

I walked back through the village and ended up on West Street. Everyone was out of bed by then, coming out into their yards, rubbing their eyes and scratching themselves. Someone called out, "It's early to be out patrolling the streets."

"Did you hear me knocking at the door last night?"

"Nope."

"I was hitting it so hard I thought I was gonna bust it down."

"You're out of your mind."

Out of my mind? What the hell does that even mean? They're always saying I'm crazy. Is it crazy for me to love Snow Bai? What do I do that's crazy? I went over toward Water-Rise's place. The peonies outside his gate were happy to see me. I smiled back at them and said, "Hello, peonies."

The sun came out right then, and Yijia Ridge glowed white like it was made of cotton stuffing. I was watching the clouds through a break in the wall; they seemed to fill up the gap with white fluff. The break had been repaired with a patch of woven bamboo, and the morning glory vines that threaded through it seemed to be reaching up through the cotton clouds to the blue sky above. I had never seen anything so beautiful in all my life.

I went closer and peeked over the wall; Snow Bai was there, washing clothes. I held my breath and crept back behind the mulberry tree. She had a massive pile of clothes in front of her. On a rack of woven bamboo, there were clothes hung to dry—a shirt, pants, underwear, and a few bras. Snow Bai was bent over a big wooden basin. My whole body tensed each time she twisted the clothes to squeeze out the water. My clenched fists began to sweat. My head swam. I thought, *Snow Bai, Snow Bai, one word is all I need. Turn around. I'm here.* I prayed for her to turn around. I looked up at the sky. Snow Bai stood but did not turn. She let water drip from her hands into the basin and walked back into the main room in the courtyard.

Something came over me, and I darted from behind the tree, leaped over the woven bamboo patch in the wall, and grabbed some of the clothes off the rack. I looked up at the main room's doorway. There was only a cat there, who meowed at me. I ran, dropping some of the clothes but holding on to a pink bra. I ran all the way past West Street to the old dugout without taking a breath.

I took out the bra and held it in front of me, the cups of it balanced in my palms like two ripe peaches. I pressed my nose into the bra. I bit it gently and licked it. I felt a strange feeling bubbling up from somewhere deep inside me. I wanted to throw up. I knew the feeling was love. I knew the feeling couldn't be contained.

A mushroom sprouted from the dirt, and its cap popped open.

I looked down, past the bra, to where that thing was watching me with one cruel eye. It was an ugly thing. I couldn't bear to look at it, poking out of my pants. "Snow Bai, Snow Bai!" I called out to her because I was afraid and thought that calling out would soothe my fears. The eye still stared up at me. It sneered and spat at me.

I won't say anything else about that because, talking about it, I can feel my heart thudding in my chest and goose bumps on my arms. That was when it happened—I was discovered. I heard footsteps, and then some of the Bai family were beating the shit out of me. The worst moment of my life was soon to follow. I ran home, full of remorse, unable to believe what I had done. From my neighbors' yard I could hear a handsaw. Someone was cutting down boards. The sound of the saw was cursing me. *Pervert! Pervert! Pervert!* I said to myself, *I'm not a pervert. I'm a good person!* The room came to life—the furniture, the table, the broom, the hanging basket—all cursing me. *You think you're a good person, huh? As upright as a bamboo pole, huh?* Between my legs, that one eye still stared, but it had nothing to say. It had exposed my deepest thoughts and now had nothing to say. It just dangled there, seemingly unaware that it had destroyed me. I slapped it, hard.

I said to the cat, "Bite it off me!" The cat didn't move. I said, "I'll kill you!" I picked up a straight razor and I killed it. Blood began to flow, staining my pants. I didn't feel any pain. I went out into the yard. Outside the gate, a crowd had formed, and they were pointing at me, jeering and spitting.

I told them, "I killed it."

Favor Bai from the dyehouse said, "What did you kill?"

"My cock." He laughed. Everyone laughed. "I really did it. I cut it off."

Favor Bai ran into my room. He saw that my bloody cock was on the floor, still jerking as if blood still pumped through it. He bent to grab it, but it slipped from his grip, like a frog. He stamped on it with his boot and shouted, "This is the retard's cock! He cut it off!"

The crowd closed in on me, and I expected to feel them kicking and punching me. But they were dragging me toward the pharmacy. I tried to struggle away from them, but they pinned me, pressing me back against the door. The door fell off the hinges, and they carried me away on it like a stretcher.

Later, Big-Noise Zhao told me that when I arrived, he had been singing opera with Xiao Wang from the village government. He had just sung, "Look at your forehead, look at your thighs / Were you really meant to ride a sedan chair?" They carried me into the shop, and as soon as Big-Noise Zhao saw me, he knew the wound was too severe for him to deal with. He told them to go out onto Highway 312 and flag down a car to take me to the county hospital. He sent Favor Bai to run back to my room and retrieve my cock.

While this was all happening, the Bai household was in an uproar. Wind Xia was pacing the room, cursing me. Someone came to tell him the news, and he arrived as I was being carried on the door to Highway 312. He saw the scrap of bloody flesh in Favor Bai's hand and said, "These surgeons can work miracles these days. They'll be able to get it back on."

"It's still warm," Favor Bai said. "There's still life in it."

Wind Xia went back and told Snow Bai what had happened. She started to cry. I was already on the way to the hospital, but I felt like I could hear the cries. I could feel them. I was finally happy; she didn't hate me. The next time I saw her, she wouldn't ignore me.

But when Wind Xia saw her crying, he was angry. He asked, "What the hell are you crying for?"

"It's all my fault," she said.

He went out, slammed the door, and walked back to East Street.

That was the first time they had ever fought.

Chapter 9

The drought continued and the countryside grew parched. Clouds of dust hung in the air above the road. The chickens began to pluck themselves, stripping their bodies feather by feather, until the bare skin on their necks shone red. In the heat of the afternoon, even the stray dogs took shelter, panting under the eaves. Dead fish bobbed to the surface of the pond. Up on Bowed Ox Ridge, the saplings planted as part of the Return Grain Plots to Forestry plan withered and died. Even worse, there was no water to send down from the reservoir into the rice paddies. The raised beds dried out and looked as if straw mats had been flung over them. The lower fields that still managed to get a few drops of water became a refuge for the frogs, and tadpoles swam in the shallow puddles, their tails sticking in the mud. It was the worst drought in a decade. Was it a sign? Was there going to be a death in the village?

I didn't know, but I also really didn't care. I was lying on a gurney in the county hospital. It was too late for my cock. When the doctor received it, it was already dead and black. All his knowledge and skill couldn't have reattached it. I asked them to make a grave for it. They buried it under a peony bush in the hospital garden. Perhaps in its next life, it would bloom as a white peony.

But let me get back to Freshwind. I thought life would go on without me much as it always had, but without me, Freshwind was like a plain bowl of rice with nothing to season it.

Clerk, who cooked in the canteen at the township administration offices, finished washing up one night and carried the dirty water back to his own home. He went down to his plot of land to wait for the water to come. The fields were full of people, waiting for the same thing.

Someone asked, "Are they releasing some water from the reservoir tonight or not?" None of them had any way of knowing, so they simply waited, cursing the weather.

Someone began to sing from an opera:

As the emperor walked from the palace gates,
The carved dragons on the pillar swayed,
Steam billowed from the furnace's golden grate.

A pure blue belt with a Big Dipper inlaid,
Gold buckles on boots of the darkest shade.
The lion guardians dance on rough stone paws.
The palace maidens and the courtesans arrayed
Put their hands together in polite applause.

Someone shouted, "Knock it off! We're about to lose our crops, and you're singing about some old emperor."

The singer called back, "If they're wiped out, we don't have to be farmers. We'll be just like that old emperor."

"Blow it out your ass," Clerk said. He lifted his head and saw Wind Xia coming up from the river embankment. "I'm glad you're here, Wind Xia. If you're here, the water must not be far behind."

Clerk and Wind Xia had been classmates in elementary school. They had shared the same desk. When Wind Xia came into town he avoided his old classmates, but whenever he ran into Clerk, he'd make time to chat with him. One time, after the two had chatted about the old days, Wind Xia gave a cigarette to Clerk before he left. The secretary at the township administration office saw it and asked where it was from. Clerk replied, "I got it from my old deskmate, Wind Xia." The secretary was curious about Wind Xia, so Clerk started telling stories about their school days. He said that when Wind Xia was young, he loved writing—not just writing essays or stories, but simply writing characters. He'd scrawl letters across every available surface. Clerk was never much of a student, though. As soon as he got a pen, he busted it into pieces to make a trap to catch locusts. The secretary laughed. "What a pair the two of you were. Complete opposites!"

Clerk laughed along with the secretary. He said, "I'm just a simple farmer. That's it." He sang a snatch of "One Story of Two Marriages":

Year by year, those days went by,
Turning rows with the plough blade,
Toiling till the sun soars high.
And my wife sewed her brocade,
Should have enough to keep bills paid.
By the light of the lamp, we work to dawn,
Twisting the wick until it's frayed,
Tank up with oil, keep getting on.

Wind Xia moved through the crowd, handing out cigarettes. He was left without one to smoke himself, so he borrowed Clerk's pipe. The two men stood around, smoking. Finally, the topic shifted to me. Clerk cursed me, but he told Wind Xia not to be angry.

"I'm not angry."

"It's not worth being angry at a guy like him."

"'A guy like him'? Is he really crazy?"

"He might not be certifiable . . . He's not wired right, at least."

"It's still a tragedy, though . . . For a man to lose his manhood . . . How can you live after that?"

Clerk put his arm around Wind Xia's neck and said, "Wind Xia, Wind Xia . . . It's like worrying about a bull that's been castrated. You should be worried about bigger things."

Clerk was still holding on to Wind Xia when Shifty ripped into the field on his motorbike, trailing dust and exhaust. He hit the brakes, but he still managed to come dangerously close to the two men, knocking Clerk's shovel out of his hand.

Shifty didn't bother to apologize. "Wind Xia, I just reported your big brother."

"What's wrong with you?" Clerk said. "Go ahead and report him, but don't come over here, shooting your mouth off."

"Why not? You want me to keep it a secret?"

"Why'd you report him?" Wind Xia asked.

"The Xia family thinks Freshwind is their own little fiefdom," Shifty said. "As soon as Justice Xia stepped down, Pavilion Xia stepped up. I've had enough! Now you're covering up for New-Life Liu—can't figure out why you'd bother covering up for someone like that, but you sure as hell are."

"So what?" Clerk demanded. "Go ahead and report him. You don't have bigger things to worry about? You should be worried about your brickyard."

"This is just a preemptive attack. I'm just getting started. Wind Xia might not be safe, either. You watch out, too. These people would steal the lice right out of your hair. Anyway, just look around you at the state this village is in. Once they starve your guard dog, you have to watch your own gate."

"You think you're tough, huh? Tougher than our uncle?"

By "our uncle," Clerk meant Shifty's father. Shifty's father had served as a quartermaster in Chiang Kai-shek's Nationalist army. Back when he was still alive, he'd loved reporting people, too. After Justice Xia had promoted Goodness Li and Concord Qin, Shifty's father had sent off an official complaint to the township administration office. Justice Xia had ended up receiving the complaint and dutifully sent it on to the county government, which had ended up sending it to the township administration, which handed it back to Justice Xia a second time . . . Shifty's father wrote out the complaint again and put it in an envelope and sent it off to the county head. The county head saw the complaint and personally came to Freshwind to mediate. Justice Xia wasn't concerned. He asked the county head, "Do you know what kind of person he is?"

"What kind of person?"

"A KMT quartermaster."

"So, this goes back a long way?"

"Me and him come from different class backgrounds. If things had turned out differently, he'd be where I am—or where you are." The county head didn't investigate further. They went back to Justice Xia's home and ate a meal of corn pudding. After the meal, the county head got in his car and left. When Shifty's father got the news, they say he sucked in one big breath, and his belly swelled up and stayed that way. He was in the ground before the villagers took the first crop of wheat off the land.

"Why do you have to bring him up? I despise the man. It's been three years since I burned joss paper at his grave."

Wind Xia didn't have much love for Shifty, but he couldn't help but laugh. "To be honest, I don't care who you report. There's nothing I can do about it. But your attitude is refreshing."

"Really? I'm glad to hear that. You know where I got it from? Learned it from your father. Everyone in the village administration feared him. He called all the shots. He was a real character."

"Learned it from him?" Clerk said. "You must have missed a few lessons. Unlike you, he wasn't only thinking of himself."

"He used to be in charge of the school," said Shifty. "Some of those students went on to the county government. And look at his son. Hell of a guy. I wish I was half the man he was." A thought came to him then, and he asked Wind Xia, "Did Treasure come back yet?"

"It's Sunday today, isn't it?"

"Huh? Who cares what day of the week it is? He said he was coming today for some bricks. If you see him, tell him to come find me. We just finished baking some bricks, so he better come get them soon." That was when Wind Xia realized Treasure was building a new house.

Chapter 10

When Wind Xia got home, his mother asked him why Snow Bai hadn't come back with him. He said she had to visit her parents' house, then he hesitated for a moment and mentioned Treasure buying bricks for a new house. Wisdom Xia was out in the yard, watering his flowers from a bucket. The roses, white and red, had all blossomed. They were full of life, and there was so much that they wanted to say. Wisdom Xia's was one of the few flower gardens in Freshwind—he'd made a flower bed out of bricks and planted it with roses and peonies. The peony bushes stood higher than the courtyard wall, and when the flowers were all in bloom, you could see them from outside the courtyard. They looked like a clump of rosy clouds spreading across the wall.

Wisdom Xia planted the flowers and watered them, but he probably had no idea that they could talk and listen. The honeybees knew. The butterflies knew. And I knew. Once the roses had drunk their fill, they tried to speak to Wisdom Xia, but he ignored them and turned away.

He looked at Wind Xia. "Bring me my water pipe." Wind Xia passed the pipe to his father and lit a wick so that he could light the bowl. "I wanted to tell you about the house. Past few years, everyone in the family has built their own courtyard. It's just us in the old house now. There's nothing wrong with the place, but you and your brother, you'll need something bigger. You know the production team's old warehouse, over on East Street? We buy it and—"

Fourth Aunt said, "The old warehouse? It's completely wrecked. Who would live in there?"

Wisdom Xia blew out the wick. "What the hell do you know?"

Fourth Aunt went out into the yard and shut the gate to the chickens' enclosure. One of the roosters crowed, and she shouted, "Shut up in there or you'll hear it from me."

"I don't plan for us to live in it. We buy it for the foundation. The new courtyard will go up over the old foundation. When you retire, you'll need a place to stay. What do you think?"

Wind Xia said, "I disagree."

"You disagree? This is an opportunity we can't afford to pass up."

"When do you think I'm going to retire? And when I retire, you want me to come back here and live? By that time, there won't be anyone else my age in Freshwind. I won't know anyone that's stuck around the village, either. Who am I going to talk to? Anyway, think about going to the doctor, getting water, staying warm in winter, and what about kids? Nobody's coming back from the city."

"With kids, it depends on the mother's residency status. The whole family's going to stay in Xijing?"

"I'm trying to get Snow Bai transferred to the city."

"Transferred?"

"I'm going to bring you and Mom, too, when the time comes."

Fourth Aunt said, "That sounds great. A comfortable life in the big city . . ."

Wisdom Xia glared at her. "Go ahead. Why don't you go there right now?" The words seemed to fall from his mouth and clatter to the floor.

"Fine! It seems like nothing I say is right. Just leave me out of it, okay? Are you happy now?"

"We all return home, eventually," Wisdom said. "What is home? Home is the place where you are born, the place where you grow up. Look at all the great men of the past . . . They might leave their hometown, but they don't forget where they came from. When the time comes, they return."

Wind Xia said, "Home is where you two are."

"You're not going to come back to burn incense for our ancestors? You sound so confident now, but can you say, right now, that you will spend the rest of your life in Xijing? What about Defender Lu from West Mountain Bend? He was younger than you when he became a head in the Department of Education. In 1956, he was branded a rightist. Then he was forced to come back."

Fourth Aunt could not contain herself. "What the hell are you talking about? What are you bringing up Defender Lu for? How much is it going to cost to buy that warehouse? How much is it going to cost to build a new courtyard on it?"

"Most of it will get torn down. But we can use the roof beams and the wall posts. We can salvage some of the roof tiles, too. All in, we're talking about twenty-five thousand yuan."

Fourth Aunt sighed with exasperation and looked over at Wind Xia.

"It doesn't matter how much it's going to cost," said Wind Xia. "The problem is that there's no need."

Wisdom Xia walked away without speaking and went into the main room. He sat down on his rattan chair, silently pulling on the pipe.

On the wall in front of the chair hung a scroll painted with a crouching tiger. The great cat's demeanor was sluggish, its eyelids drooping. Wisdom Xia was fond of pointing out to anyone who saw that picture what he particularly liked about it. The tiger wasn't as clever as a fox or as smart as a hare, but when it came time to hunt, no animal was a match for it. When Pavilion had been made the village head, Wisdom Xia had brought him to the scroll for a lecture. It was a colorful speech with plenty of classical allusions and talk about respect for the place you're from, keeping one's own counsel while being decisive, deep stuff . . .

He had pointed at the crouching tiger and said, "Look at this tiger. There's something that sets it apart from the rest of the animal kingdom. You know, we always call them 'old tiger'—is there any other animal that has 'old' in front of its name?"

Pavilion had said, "Really? What about rats? We always say 'old rat,' too." That had shut up Wisdom Xia for good.

Wind Xia still feared his father a little bit, and he felt a shiver run up his spine when he saw the old man retreat to his rattan chair. Whether the old man hoped to work up the energy to talk about the warehouse again or he was trying to summon some of that tiger spirit or he was simply depressed, Wind Xia wasn't quite sure, but within a few minutes Wisdom Xia had closed his eyes and was asleep.

Wind Xia slipped out into the yard and went into the street to look up at the night sky. Just then, Shiner and Tongue-Tied burst noisily out of the shadows. Tongue-Tied was trying to throw something at Shiner but missed, and it came to rest at Wind Xia's feet. After they'd run off, Wind Xia bent to look at what they'd been throwing. It was a dead cat. He thought about kicking it into the road but instead bent to pick it up. *It will make good fertilizer for the flowers,* he thought.

Dinner came late, and when it was ready, Fourth Aunt called Wisdom Xia to the table. He rubbed his eyes and rose from the chair. He said to Wind Xia, "Go to the cabinet and get the old scroll. Get rid of this one here and hang that one up instead. The calligraphy on this isn't what it should be. It's a bit weak."

Wisdom Xia had plenty of scrolls of calligraphy and enjoyed replacing the two strips of couplets that hung beside the crouching tiger. When Fourth Aunt saw him getting a stool to retrieve the couplets, she said, "It's late enough already. You haven't even eaten yet. What are you doing fooling around with those scrolls?"

Wisdom Xia said, "You worry about your own things." He scowled but took a seat at the table and waited for dinner to be served. Fourth Aunt came with his bowl of corn porridge and set it down. She took her own out into the yard to eat. Wind Xia hung the new scroll. It read:

It is with brotherly love that my eyes glow,

When spring winds through these eaves blow.

He chuckled to himself and went into the kitchen. He took the wooden chicken and brought it to the table.

Fourth Aunt called in, "We're eating porridge. What the hell are you doing with that?"

"My father likes it." He set the chicken on the table and took his bowl out into the yard, too.

Out in the courtyard, there was a soft breeze that was enough to keep the mosquitoes away, but mother and son both heard Wisdom Xia inside the kitchen, smacking them off his arms and legs. He wouldn't come out to eat with them, and they weren't about to invite him.

Fourth Aunt said, "If he wants to get eaten alive, let him stay in there."

Wind Xia asked about his brother. He wondered why Rain Xia hadn't come back for dinner.

"He could fall off the face of the earth and I wouldn't hear about it," Fourth Aunt said. "If I had to guess, there's a good chance he went to the Jin courtyard."

"Why?"

"Someone told me he's involved with Lotus Jin's niece."

"Oh."

"That's what your father's so fired up about. He wants to build the new courtyard to make sure everything goes smoothly with those two. He wants him to get married. I'm against it! When you and Lotus Jin had your thing, it was Lotus Jin's mother who stood in the way. She didn't think you were good enough for Lotus Jin. She wanted to know how a farmer could be any match for her daughter, who's already got a job as a teacher. Now, this other Jin girl is mixed up with Rain Xia. I want to know what the hell's wrong with him. He couldn't chase after a girl with a different last name? Why does it have to be Jin? Now, he's always running over there, doesn't have any time to get any work done around here."

"What's Lotus Jin up to these days?"

"She got married to old Zheng's oldest boy. Still working as a teacher. She's on the village women's committee, too. Still a conniving little thing, as always."

"She's doing well then?"

"She broke your heart, and you're still worried about her?" A mosquito landed on Wind Xia's neck, and Fourth Aunt hissed, "Don't move!" She smashed the bug with a slap, then picked a leaf up from the yard to wipe the blood off.

Suddenly they heard dishes being broken. Fourth Aunt called in to Wisdom Xia, "What's going on in there?" No answer but there was another crash.

There were footsteps and a voice calling, "Fourth Aunt, Fourth Aunt!"

"It sounds like someone's calling me," Fourth Aunt said.

"It must be Auntie Chrysanth," Wind Xia said, referring to Treasure's wife.

Fourth Aunt put down her bowl and said, "They're fighting again."

Two bodies tumbled in through the yard's gate, lit up by the moonlight. Treasure tossed Chrysanth up against the wall, and she kept screaming until he clamped his hand over her mouth. She kicked and scratched at him, but he seemed to barely notice her attack. It was Fourth Aunt who pulled him off her. "You're going to suffocate her. What's wrong with a smack on the ass?"

Chrysanth tried to suck air and finally broke into a choking sob. "Help me, Auntie!"

Fourth Aunt turned on Treasure again. "Every day, like this. If you're not beating her, you're cussing her out. What the hell are you thinking?"

Treasure said, "I work my ass off at the school all day, teaching my classes, and drag myself home at the end of that long day. My dinner's not made, there's nothing for me to drink . . . It feels more like raising a pig than having a wife to look after me. You go look for yourself, Auntie. Tell me if it looks like a happy household or a pigsty. Everyone else, their kids go out with their hair brushed and their clothes straight, but mine are going around looking like wild dogs. Get them all cleaned up, fix myself up, and I find two pairs of bloody panties stuffed under the kang."

Chrysanth said, "That's a lie. You hate me now, but when you were single, it was a different story. You say I'm dirty? That wasn't what you said when you were licking me all over."

Treasure slapped her across the face. "Your mouth is as dirty as your mother's."

Chrysanth wailed the name of Treasure's mother.

"Why do you have to bring her up?" Fourth Aunt asked.

"I hate her!"

"What does she have to do with this?"

"Why'd she have to give birth to such a good-for-nothing?"

Treasure punched her twice more. Fourth Aunt moved to shield Chrysanth and pulled her into her own courtyard. "You watch your mouth, too! Stop yelling my mother's name."

"I only said it because he hit me. She gave birth to a cruel monster."

"If you're going to keep saying that, I'm not going to help you. Let him beat you to death."

Wind Xia went to see Treasure after the fight was over. There were two scratches across Treasure's cheek. "Look at what my life has become!" Treasure's home was three rooms, all of them dark, and none of them very big. The rooms were dirty and in disarray.

Treasure had started out on a casual basis at the village primary school, but he'd eventually been promoted to a formal position. It didn't take long before his superiors took notice of his lax attitude to teaching, and he was transferred to a primary school in Baimao Gully. Baimao Gully was about ten *li* from Freshwind. The school was a one-roof affair, with a couple of dozen kids of different ages crammed in together. When he had time off, he'd go and fell a few trees on land owned by one of the parents. He'd carry them on his shoulder all the way home. He planned to use them to build his new courtyard home.

Wind Xia wasn't really too sure what Treasure was up to, and he didn't plan to let him talk much, but he reminded him to go see Shifty about the bricks. Treasure's attitude changed completely. "They're out of the kiln?"

"Shifty said you better come get them soon. If you don't get them, somebody else will."

"I'm not too worried. If I go tomorrow, maybe I can make a deal for them still."

He didn't seem concerned at all about the bricks. Wind Xia left and went home. Chrysanth was still crying in the yard. Fourth Aunt had given up trying to talk to her. Chrysanth's daughter, Bodhi, came over, calling for her. But Chrysanth only shouted back, "Go to bed!" She went back to crying. Then stopped to call after her daughter, "There's some buns in the basket. Cover it up so the rats don't get to it." She went back to crying.

Bamboo came into the yard then and told her, "Stop crying. Your father told me to come over and see what's wrong with you."

Fourth Aunt motioned to Wind Xia. "Give your auntie a cigarette."

Bamboo took the cigarette and said, "Fourth Uncle isn't here?"

"He's inside."

Bamboo stuffed the cigarette in her pocket. "Fourth Uncle's in there, and you're out here crying like this?"

Chrysanth stopped crying. "Fourth Uncle's inside? I want to know what he thinks about all this. That thug Treasure is going to kill me one of these days."

The voice of Wisdom Xia came from inside the house. "Go ahead and cry. Cry some more. There might be a few people in Freshwind who still haven't heard you."

Bamboo pulled Chrysanth out of the yard, hissing at her, "You deserved it! A mouth like that, I'd slap you, too. I know Treasure has a temper, but he must look after the family. You know he's trying to build a new house, too. That's enough pressure on him. He comes home, and there's no food, nothing to drink; of course he's angry."

"He's building a new house for him and Black-Moth."

"That's a goddamn lie, isn't it?"

Chrysanth didn't answer. She tried to pull Bamboo toward the house.

"There's nothing to talk about. You're fine. I have to go find Roughshod Ding anyway."

When Fourth Aunt heard that Bamboo was going to get Roughshod Ding, she told Wind Xia to go along with her to West Street and stop in to see Snow Bai. "And bring her back with you. It's not right. You're married, and she's sleeping on East Street while you're over on West Street."

On the way there, Wind Xia asked, "Who is this Black-Moth?"

"Give me a cigarette and I'll tell you."

"Hearth barely smokes, but you more than make up for it, huh?"

"You're saying he's not a man? Anyway, Black-Moth is Forest Wu's wife. Good man but not much to look at, that Forest Wu. The wife, though, Black-Moth, as pretty as all outdoors, combs her hair out until it shines. I don't know how that Treasure gets along with her so well, but he can't go more than a day without fighting with Chrysanth."

"Treasure and Chrysanth deserve each other."

"Among your generation of Xia boys, Treasure's not as ruthless as Pavilion, not as tricky as Halfwit . . . He's a sack of shit. Chrysanth shouldn't have to deal with him. What can you do? You can't guess how a marriage is going to work out. The wrong people get together sometimes. But you and Snow Bai? That was written in the stars."

On the way to Roughshod Ding's home, they passed the Jin house with its trellis of grape vines. The trellis was buzzing with fireflies, and Wind Xia reached up to catch one. He held it in his hand, staring into space. He had come to the Jin house with Lotus Jin one winter, and she had heated him up some liquor in a clay kettle set in the coals of the firebox. Right after she'd nestled the kettle in the coals, she'd stepped away and it tipped over. The liquor spilled over the coals, extinguishing them and sending up a cloud of ash. He'd had a premonition then that things wouldn't work out, and he'd been right.

"What's wrong? You thinking about Lotus Jin?"

Wind Xia laughed, and Bamboo grabbed his arm and pulled him toward the gate to their courtyard. He pulled away. He reached up and plucked from the trellis above the gate a single unripe grape. The firefly flew away, headed into the courtyard. He chewed the grape.

The night seemed normal enough. Water-Rise's kid came home with bad grades and got slapped. Third-Kid Li's mother's asthma started acting up again. At New-Life's place, the chicken fell in the latrine pit and had to be fished out again.

But something out of the ordinary did happen. Something I can't skip over. I was the cause of it, after all. This is the story of how I ruined Wind Xia's leg. It might sound a bit strange, but think about it for a second, and it doesn't seem that odd, given the way this world works. Like I was thinking, a dog has a tail, and a rat has a tail, but why don't humans have tails?

Turns out, when I was in the hospital, there was a little girl in there having surgery to get a tail sliced off. So that night, while I was lying in the hospital, I was looking at the mold on the wall and I thought to myself, *That looks like Wind Xia; how he'd look if I saw him from the side? Wind Xia has had such a lucky life. Why does he seem to pick up good luck like Dog-Scraps picks up shit? If he was a cripple, things would be much fairer.*

I had that thought, and I thought it real hard. It was right when he was standing in front of Lotus Jin's place, chewing the grape. The grape was hard and unripe. He shivered because it was so sour. He told Bamboo he wasn't going to go with her to Roughshod Ding's house. He told her he had to go to West Street, and he walked away. But right as he walked away, his knee popped, and he fell to the ground.

"What's wrong?" Bamboo asked.

Wind Xia staggered to his feet. "I'm fine." And he was right: he was fine. But three days later, climbing a flight of stairs, he felt a faint, dull pain. He went back to Xijing to shoot a film, and that was when the knee finally gave out. He ended up having to go for surgery.

Let me get back to Bamboo's visit to Roughshod Ding. When she showed up at his place, the lights were out, but he was watching TV and the electric fan was blowing. Rain Xia was over, and the two of them were talking. When Bamboo went in, Rain Xia got up and left.

Bamboo said, "Roughshod, you've always been a clever son of a bitch, so I guess you already know why I'm here."

"At least I'm not wasting any electricity."

"That's the spirit," she said sarcastically. "But there's more to it than that, I'm afraid. Everyone on East Street knows you're stealing power. You know I head up the residents' committee. How are we going to deal with this?"

"I heard there are some people on Middle Street who didn't pay their fee. I might as well use the electricity they're not using."

"Here's what I heard: they can't pay their electricity fee because you screwed around with the meter."

"That's a lie!"

"I don't care one way or the other. That's a problem for the residents' committee over there to figure out. I'm here to deal with you stealing electricity from East Street."

"I just used a bit. I put the fan on at night, watch a bit of TV, put a light on. Not even every night. Twenty times at the most. It's like twenty or thirty yuan worth of electricity. I'll pay for it, eventually."

"I want it in writing."

"You don't believe me?"

"No way!"

Roughshod Ding wrote up a contract. Bamboo wasn't satisfied. She wanted him to bite his middle finger and leave a bloody fingerprint at the bottom of the paper. He smacked a mosquito and stuck his finger into the blood in his palm. He put his fingerprint at the bottom of the contract. "I feel sorry for your husband."

"What the hell did you just say?"

"I realize now what Hearth has to live with."

When Bamboo got home, she told Justice Xia what had happened. He told her, "You should have made him pay the fee right there and then."

"I've got the contract."

"You know how long you're going to wait to get the money? The way things are at the brickyard, the money's never going to come. Everyone is too damn soft. Things are never going to get set right in Freshwind."

"You shouldn't say things like that. Pavilion is in charge now. He'll deal with any problems."

"The problems are going to deal with him."

Second Aunt looked over from the kang and rolled her eyes. She went back to cracking roast peas. She bit at the shell of one stubborn pea and then put it on the edge of the kang to crush with her palm.

Justice Xia looked over at his wife and yelled, "What are you doing over there? You people will be the death of me."

Bamboo cut in, "Ma, what did you eat for dinner tonight?"

"Porridge with daikon. Barely enough to fill my stomach."

Justice Xia scowled. Whenever he got into one of his moods, his face got long, like a winter melon. Bamboo got up to go, and he asked her, "Did Pavilion and Marvel get back yet?"

"They should be back tomorrow."

"Tell Pavilion that I don't care how he does it, but he needs to make sure West Street and Middle Street have power. When it's this hot, how can people live without power?"

"A little heat never killed anybody. The real problem is this drought."

"I'm worried about that, too. I can't figure out what's going on with the reservoir. They must send some water down to us, soon. But is anybody else worried about it? No. Everyone's going around without a care in the world, right when the village is about to dry up and blow away."

Bamboo didn't know what to say, so she took the cigarette out of her pocket. She lit it and blew smoke out her nose.

"You need a cigarette that bad?"

She pinched it out with her nails.

As Bamboo was leaving, she heard the rooster crowing. Justice Xia sat in angry silence on the edge of the kang.

Second Aunt said, "Us Xia women always smoke. We've been smoking for generations. She's part of a long line of Xia women. Don't worry about it so much."

The sound of scratching came from out in the street. Lucky, who had been lying beside the kang, suddenly got up. Lucky wagged her tail and then walked out. Justice Xia barked at the dog, "Where the hell are you going?" The dog turned back, looked at Justice Xia, and then hung her head. The dog went back to lying beside the kang. When the lights went out, the sound of scratching came again.

"Tiger came early?"

Justice Xia didn't say anything. He stretched out his legs, pushing his feet into Second Aunt's face. She covered them with a pillow.

Chapter 11

When Treasure arrived at the brickyard, he found that not only had Shifty not raised the price, but he'd also added a thousand extra bricks to Treasure's load. You should always be careful of people like that. They make a show of how loyal they are—they'd even slice meat off their calf to feed you—but if you cross them, they'll be on you like a snapping turtle. You know how they are: you can smash them to pieces, and their beak will still be locked onto you.

Treasure slipped a hundred-yuan note into Shifty's hand. "I'm not going to buy you dinner, but go ahead and use that to get a bottle of something nice."

"Hey, what are you doing?" Shifty said. "I'm a man of culture. But if you really want to show your appreciation, there is something you could give me."

"What?"

"Last year, when your father-in-law passed away, I went up with the family to his grave. He had an old porcelain flagon . . . He's not going to be warming his liquor anymore, but I sure could use it."

"I'd love to give it to you, but it's not that easy. Actually, I took it from the house for myself, but Chrysanth doesn't like me drinking, so she ended up giving it to Fourth Uncle. I can't just go and ask for it back now."

"A cheap bastard like you, give away something like that? If you don't want to give it to me, that's fine. But maybe there's something else you can do for me. I need something arranged."

"What?"

"I want to learn from you how to handle money. And I'd love to know how you manage women."

"What the hell are you talking about?"

"Big-Noise Zhao fixed you up when you had a dose of the clap, right?"

"That fuckin' Big-Noise Zhao was fucking with me. It was just an infection or something. Whoever told you that must be—"

"Treasure, come on. You think you've got exclusive rights to the clap? Give the rest of us a chance. I've seen Black-Moth's sister around. I thought you might be able to set us up."

"That's not gonna happen."

"Fine. You can take these bricks and pretend you don't know me, but I know you're fixing up a new house for yourself. One day, you're going to come back here for a load of tiles."

Once he'd gotten the bricks, Treasure could start laying the foundation and putting up the base for the walls. In Freshwind there was a rule that everyone pitched in to help, whether it was a happy event or a sad event, a wedding or a funeral. If somebody got help with something, they'd return the favor by helping whoever had pitched in. The only payment was a meal—money never changed hands. Treasure called over the best bricklayers from West, East, and Middle Streets, and a few strong young men from East Street. He called on the four Xia households and got Mid-Star's father to bring over his compass and figure out the right direction to get the best feng shui. When the day came, Treasure set off a string of firecrackers, and everyone got to work.

After Pavilion and Marvel got back from the city, they'd gone to the township administration a few times to sort out financing and then headed back to the city again to buy the transformer. When Pavilion heard that construction on Treasure's house had started, he sent his wife to help. When she got there, she apologized, saying that Pavilion had been out of town for a few days.

Chrysanth said, "That's fine. At least you're here."

But Pavilion's wife, Cutie, had three pigs to look after, so she had to go back to her house three times a day to feed them. She brought a bucket over to Chrysanth's kitchen and, whenever no one was looking, slipped in some scraps to bring home for the pigs. Finally, Chrysanth got Bodhi to stand guard in the kitchen and make sure she wasn't filling the bucket.

Treasure had put Rites Xia in charge of the construction, but nobody listened to him. He finally gave up and took to going around the jobsite, picking up nails, screws, and pieces of brick. He'd sometimes flex his muscle by scolding people over minor things. He laid into Tongue-Tied for screwing around with a bag of cement, and went after Culture for being too generous with the pinches of tea leaves he was putting in a kettle.

Around noon, when the sun was high overhead, one of the workers called out, "That's enough for now. Let's wash up and get something to eat."

"When the food is ready, they'll call you," Rites Xia said. "Keep going a bit longer."

The sun kept going across the sky, but Chrysanth still hadn't called them for lunch, and the men eventually put down their tools. They stood around, listening to Mid-Star's father talk about reincarnation.

Mid-Star's father had a goatee that he stroked while talking, and an impressively long pinkie nail that he used to dig wax out of his ears. He was telling them how to learn the fate of the deceased's soul: If the person's forehead was still warm twenty-four hours after they died, they'd gone to heaven; if their chest was warm, they'd been reborn as a human; if their belly was warm, they'd been reborn as a pig or a cow; if their legs were warm, they'd been reborn as a wild animal; if their feet were warm, they were in hell.

Someone asked, "If everyone gets reborn, why are there ghosts?"

"Ghosts have slipped out of the cycle of rebirth. They're wandering spirits. If someone dies violently or they're in a bad state of mind when they pass, they can become ghosts."

One of the workers said, "Builder Li, over on West Street, he was working in the city and fell off a scaffold . . . Did he become a ghost?"

"Definitely."

"That's what I thought. Builder Li's wife told me that she always hears a sound in the kitchen, like someone's rattling chopsticks in a bowl. She's even called out to him. She said to him, 'Builder, my dear, don't worry. I'll go to your grave and burn ghost money; then you won't be so hungry.'"

Mid-Star's father said, "Think about it. Around here, the police can't even solve robberies, right? Now, you heard about that murder in Teahouse Village, right? The cops never caught up with the murderer. It was the ghost of the victim that got to him first. That's how things usually go. Ghosts are more reliable than the police."

"So, you're saying Builder Li's ghost is still hanging around?"

"Of course."

"Really? Can you really tell? Do you know where he is?"

Mid-Star's father looked at the man. "You borrowed money from Builder Li, didn't you?"

The man turned pale and started to sweat. "That's a load of bullshit," Rites Xia said.

"No, it's not."

"Enough with this ghost stuff; how about you predict when lunch is coming?"

Mid-Star's father looked down at his fingers and seemed to be counting. He mumbled something. There was a gurgling sound from the back of his throat, like rice porridge glugging out of a kettle. "Give it an hour," he said.

"The hell with that. We're stopping now. Let's go eat!" The workers all stood up. They might have been in awe of Mid-Star's father's powers of prediction, but their stomachs were growling. They put away their tools and started jogging toward Treasure's house.

Rites Xia reported to Treasure what was going on at the new house, and Treasure made sure Mid-Star's father wasn't there in the afternoon. Things were quieter when everyone got to work again. But then Wisdom Xia showed up. Tongue-Tied brought over a bench for him to sit on. Wisdom Xia watched the workers, pulling the whole time on his water pipe. Wisdom

Xia hadn't issued a command, but the workers sprang into action. Before long everyone was dripping with sweat. They looked like they'd just crawled out of the river after a swim. They didn't take a moment's break.

Around then, the oldest son of the Lu family came over from West Street with an envelope of cash for Wisdom Xia. It was his pension from the Bureau of Education. As everyone watched, Wisdom Xia wet a finger and counted the money.

Someone exclaimed, "You get that much a month, Fourth Uncle?"

"It's not much."

"That's not much? When are you taking us drinking?"

"You want to drink? How about tonight? Come over to my house."

"I don't want to wait until tonight."

"Do you see any liquor here?" Rites Xia asked. "Let's keep working. We're supposed to be helping Treasure. If you want to drink, let's do it after we're done here. End of the day, you can go get Treasure to buy some liquor."

"You're not in charge anymore," one of the workers pointed out. "Fourth Uncle is here."

Wisdom Xia said, "Let's listen to some opera. That's better than drinking. Tongue-Tied! Where are you?"

The mute was mixing cement. He looked up and exclaimed, "Wa!"

"Go into my bedroom and get the radio." Tongue-Tied brought the radio out, but there seemed to be something wrong with it. The mute smacked the radio a few times, trying to tune in a station with opera.

Rites Xia grumbled, but he knew he wasn't in charge anymore. "These guys are just like that machine. Gotta slap 'em around to get them to work."

Wisdom Xia said, "When soldiers go into war, they need the propaganda team!" With a final hard slap, the radio crackled to life with the sound of local opera. The workers' mood improved instantly. The bricklayers sang along, letting their trowels clank to the rhythm of the drums. The workers carrying bricks picked up their pace, and so did the boys who were carrying bags of cement. A blob of wet cement landed on the tip of Rites Xia's nose.

Eventually, the opera was drowned out by static, and no amount of slapping could bring it back. Wisdom Xia hummed a tune and said, "It's hot out today. Let me sing 'Rocking Lake Boat.'" He sang.

The workers applauded and shouted, "That was great!"

Wisdom Xia grinned.

"Fourth Uncle, when did you learn that song?" someone asked.

"I learned that one during the Cultural Revolution. They locked me in a barn and brought me out three times a day for struggle sessions. I didn't have the strength to go on. One night, I got a rope, tied it up in a window frame, and planned to hang myself. Right then, I heard someone outside the barn, singing local opera. They had a great voice. I was just about to put the noose around my neck, but when I heard that voice, I thought, 'How can I kill myself when I haven't learned that song yet?' I untied the rope. That opera saved my life. But I don't really do it justice. You have to hear Snow Bai sing it."

One of the workers said, "It shows how close you two are when you say her name. You should bring her over here, get her to sing it for us. What do you think?"

"Sure, sure . . ." Wisdom Xia looked up and saw Take-It-Easy coming toward the work site, leading a child with a round head and a cowlick that stood up like a garlic sprout. The child stopped in front of Wisdom Xia and kowtowed. "Who are you?" Wisdom Xia asked.

"I'm Badge Zhang."

"That's a rather awkward name."

Take-It-Easy said, "Maybe you could give him a name, Fourth Uncle."

Wisdom Xia asked the child, "Do you know your uncle Wind Xia?"

"Yes."

"You should follow in his footsteps. Let's call you Like-Wind Zhang. You'll stand out in the crowd, just like he has."

"This is a special child," Take-It-Easy said. "You should hear him sing Shaanxi opera!"

The child sang. He had a good voice.

"Not bad, not bad," Wisdom Xia said. "But remember, if you want to sing, you must study."

Take-It-Easy said, "He's already started school. But his father wants him to quit."

"Who's the father?"

"Zhang Ba is his father. He's so hunchbacked he can barely lift his head. He's got no way to make money now. He can't even help out in the fields. There's no money to pay the boy's tuition. That's why he wants him to quit."

"This is Zhang Ba's kid? He can't afford to ruin the kid's education. From now on, Like-Wind Zhang, your grandpa's paying for your tuition." Take-It-Easy pressed Like-Wind to the ground again, and he kowtowed to the old man. The sound of the boy's forehead hitting the dust echoed across the yard. Wisdom Xia rose from his bench and walked away.

After the old man had left, one of the workers said, "They must have planned that, bringing the boy to sing opera when they knew Wisdom Xia would be here."

Take-It-Easy didn't argue. "Who else could have helped this boy? You think Third Uncle would have done the same?"

Rites Xia overheard the discussion. "I don't have any money to help. And even if I did, I don't want to wear that hat."

Actually, I have to explain this a bit. Almost everyone in Freshwind is tight with their money, and Rites Xia is the tightest. Most people are cheap because they haven't got any money, but Rites Xia isn't exactly poor. I could never figure out why he was so cheap. One time, after he got in a fight with his wife, he showed up at Clerk's wife's restaurant. I said to him, "You're here to eat, too?"

He brushed me off and ordered a *shaobing*. He took a big bite of the flatbread, and a sesame seed fell into a crack in the table. He tried to dig it out, but he couldn't. I told him, "Third Uncle, I'll hit the table and you grab it." I pounded the table, the sesame seed flew out, and he grabbed it. Of the four Xia brothers, Benevolence Xia was already dead, so I don't know much about him, but Justice Xia worked as a farmer and was always healthy; Wisdom Xia and Rites Xia were completely different.

I asked Justice Xia once how Wisdom Xia stayed healthy. "I heard Rain Xia say that his dad never gets sick. How does he do it?"

"It's a secret," Justice Xia said. "You really want to know?"

"What's the secret?"

"Do good deeds."

He might have been right, but if you applied that advice to their other brother—Rites Xia—it didn't seem to hold true. Rites Xia was the last person you'd count on to do a good deed. So what was *his* secret? I already told you about his selling silver coins on the black market, but that wasn't even the half of it. I caught him another time, early in the morning, dumping something out of an old pot at the crossroads. I figured that he must have been getting up early in the morning and boiling himself some kind of herbal medicine, but when I went to check what he'd dumped, it turned out to be soggy banknotes. That's what he was drinking! He got up every morning, used a pair of scissors to shred some cash, then made a tea from it.

Everyone at the new house, from the most junior laborer to the bricklayers and carpenters, including Treasure, was hoping that Justice Xia would not pay a visit. But he came anyway. He studied the foundation for a moment and then paced it off, muttering to himself, "This isn't right at all."

"Dad, Goodness measured it out himself," Bounty said.

"You trust him more than your own father?" Justice Xia paced off the foundation again. "We've got to bring these walls in. They're outside the boundary."

"Treasure's going to be pissed off if he comes back and sees this," Bounty said.

"Enough. You're so worried about pissing him off, what about me?" Bricks had already been laid on the base of the walls, and Bounty didn't want to give the order to tear them down. He said he'd wait for Treasure to make the decision.

Justice Xia went over and kicked down one of the low walls. "If you steal an inch of the collective's land, someone else will take a mile." He crouched beside the broken wall and lit one of his rollies. He watched Bounty and the workers tear down the rest of the wall and start rebuilding it farther in. Culture had already run off to get Treasure.

When Treasure and Culture got back, Treasure stood a short distance away from his new house, watching the workers. Everyone's head was capped with a straw hat except for Justice Xia's, whose head was bare. Justice Xia's fat neck glowed red in the sun.

"Get him a hat, Culture," Treasure said. They walked over to where Justice Xia was crouched.

"I told them to move the walls in," Justice Xia said.

"That's fine. Whatever you say."

Justice Xia brightened. "You've got enough bricks, right?"

"Should be fine."

"What about lumber?"

"We're missing three posts for the pillars. They're ready to go; I just have to bring them over here."

Justice Xia rose and clasped his hands behind his back. He looked as if he were about to leave, but he paused and asked, "Who's teaching your classes while you're working over here?"

"I gave the kids some homework."

"What? You should be teaching your classes."

"Listen to me . . ."

"Listen to what? Get over there right now. If you can't find anybody to fill in for you, you should stay there."

"Fine, fine." Treasure watched Justice Xia go.

After the old man had left, Take-It-Easy asked Treasure, "Are you scared of your dad?"

"The guy could rip my head off; of course I'm scared of him. Everyone does this when they build a new house; nobody worries about taking a bit of extra land. But me? I have to follow the rules. I have to follow the Great Helmsman's orders."

"Don't talk like that. Anyway, nobody's going to build next to here. Not much chance someone'll come along and try to plant something, either. There's a gully over there. Once you build your three rooms here, you'll have an empty space there anyway."

Treasure laughed. "I owe you a drink one of these days. But don't go around telling anyone what you just told me."

"You're a teacher and I respect you," Take-It-Easy said. "My lips are sealed. I'll open them up for that drink, though. Let's go!"

"Thirsty, huh? It'll have to wait. I'm going to the school right now."

But Treasure didn't go to Baimao Gully. He went to Zhang Ba's place. The house that Zhang Ba had been granted during the land reform had collapsed a couple of years before, and Zhang Ba had moved into the shed that the family had once kept cattle in. The old house was mostly ruined, but a few of the pillars and four of the lattice windows were salvageable. Treasure had already cut a deal for the pillars, and now he cut a deal for the windows. He carried them back toward the new house. He dropped them off and went over to his old house. He saw Snow Bai in the kitchen, helping wash vegetables. He saw his mother hobbling toward the house on her walking stick. He called out, "Chrysanth, Mom's coming over."

"What the hell is she coming for?" Chrysanth asked. "She's just going to get in the way."

Second Aunt heard her but didn't say anything. She rolled her eyes and sat down outside the kitchen. Being nearly blind, she couldn't do much to help, but there was nothing wrong with her ears. She heard everything that was going on around her. She heard Snow Bai washing vegetables and called her over. "Take a rest. Let them work for a while."

Snow Bai saw that the old woman's clothes were dusty and patted her down. Second Aunt caught Snow Bai's hand and held it while she brushed her fingers over the girl's face. "Your skin is so soft. I hope I didn't get it dirty." She went on, as if talking to herself, "Wind Xia is so lucky. For such an ugly man, to snag a wife like this . . ."

Bamboo appeared in the doorway. "All the Xia women are the same. We're flowers growing from a mound of shit."

Second Aunt said, "You think you're a flower, do you? A cattail at best. It's true, though. Wind Xia is ugly, but he's special. He went to college. He's read books. Books as thick as bricks! Did you graduate from high school, Snow Bai?"

"No . . . I don't deserve your Wind Xia."

"It doesn't matter. You're a girl. You're supposed to get married off. Your job is to work in the house and look after the kids."

Snow Bai laughed. "Second Aunt, how long have your eyes been bad?"

"Seven years now. I can't see a thing. Just darkness."

Snow Bai leaned forward and lifted one of Second Aunt's eyelids. "It looks like cataracts. You could fix it. You'd have to get surgery."

Second Aunt shouted, "Hearth, Hearth!"

Hearth was scorching the hair off a pig's head. He looked over. "What is it?"

"Snow Bai says I could fix my eyes."

Hearth didn't say anything. The pig's eyes were shut, and there were wrinkles on its forehead. Bounty's wife, who was helping hold the pig's head while Hearth worked, looked up. "You can't fix it now. It's been too long."

"She could fix it," Snow Bai said.

"When are you moving to the city, Snow Bai?" Bounty's wife asked. "You can bring her to the city for the surgery."

"Fine."

Bounty's wife shot a glance at Halfwit's wife, who said, "Old people get sick. If they're not sick, they're dead."

Chapter 12

From every doorway in the village came puffs of white smoke. It was dusk: time to smoke out the mosquitoes. Fires were lit under damp firewood. Smoke gathered in yards and drifted out into the street. I was on my way home, and I wandered through the smoke, floating as if borne on a sedan chair held on the shoulders of sprites. The houses along the street seemed to have shrunk, so I could look down into them. I could see everything taking place within the walls—men and women, children and old people, chickens and pigs, cats and dogs. The smoke grew thicker, and it stung my throat every time I breathed in. It tasted like pickled vegetables and then it tasted like piss and then it tasted like sweat and then it tasted like rotten fish.

The gold letters above the God of Literature Pavilion glowed green. The red lamp hanging at the door of the pharmacy lit the smoke crimson. At the blacksmith's house, the family sat around the table, slurping from bowls as big as their heads. An old woman shuffled across her yard, carrying her grandson. She was too old to care about modesty. Her tits drooped out of her robe like two empty sacks, and her grandson hungrily sought for her nipples. Favor Bai sat on his straw mat and suddenly called to his wife. She came into the room, and he told her, "I'm ready now." With two rough hands accustomed to kneading dough, she slipped off her pants. But when he saw her naked before him and her pussy fat as a slab of pork belly, Favor Bai lost his nerve.

The gate to the yard was closed, and two sparrows perched on the wall. The sparrows chirruped sadly, as if they knew Favor Bai's whole miserable story. But they ignored me. Only the trees waved a greeting. To each one in turn I said, "I'm back! I'm back!" The smoke grew thin, and I could see a sheet of dark tiles slide suddenly from the roof in front of me—it was just crows again. I stood in front of my own door. The electrical pole was still there, and under it, half a stone roller. Mid-Star's father used to say that I would always be a bachelor because of that electrical pole. He said it was bad feng shui. I asked Pavilion to move the pole, but he turned me down. The plaster on the wall around the yard had started to peel and fall away, but nobody had offered to help. I thought about the plot of land I'd been granted, that I still had to get out and plow—nobody was going to help me with that, either.

From out of the sewer pipe climbed a rat. The rat looked up at me. I recognized the rat: my house rat. I said, "You haven't been eating well?" Beside the gate a few cloth sacks of chaff had been stacked, and I thought the rat might get into them, but it shrunk back into the sewer pipe. I called out loudly, "Whose pig is eating this chaff?"

From next door, Take-It-Easy emerged. I saw that the sores across his bald head were worse than ever—his scalp looked like the skin of a roasted persimmon. "It's mine. Your gate was clear, so I was using it to crush some chaff for the pig."

"Could I get a bowl of rice from your pot?"

Take-It-Easy began to carry the bags of chaff away. "So . . . even with the . . . it was just a couple of days?"

"How long did you want me to stay in there?"

"Everything's fine?"

Take-It-Easy wasn't angry, and I wasn't, either. I told him, "I'm fine."

But he asked me, "Are the balls still there?"

I hissed at him and went into my house. I pulled the cord, and the light unexpectedly came on. The bulb had burned out a while ago, so I hadn't expected that. I didn't bother investigating why the light was suddenly working and instead lay down on the kang and thought about what Take-It-Easy had asked. I had sacrificed my future. I only had half my equipment left. I had crippled myself. What would everyone say about me? I began to feel between my legs. But I stopped—who was watching? The rat, of course, and the spiders, and the snails that climbed the walls each night. I switched the light off, but my brain was still lit up. From somewhere in the light came the sound of clucking, and then a chicken and a cat and a pig and a sheep and a cow.

The chicken said to the cow, "They have family planning, but I have to lay eggs every day. It's not fair."

The cow said to the chicken, "What's the big deal? Everyone drinks my milk. What about my own children?"

How come all that's going on in my head? I put the light on again and thought about Snow Bai. When I thought about her, I was like an ant burrowing into a sesame dumpling. I pulled the sheet over my head and burrowed into that, too. I said this to myself: *If I can talk to her tonight in a dream, it means I will be able to talk to her for real.* And I did. I dreamed about her.

When I awoke, sun had filled the room and there was a single flower on my table. How did it come to be there? I wasn't sure. But it was definitely there, definitely a real live flower.

If Snow Bai would talk to me, I knew I wouldn't be afraid to face anyone. And nobody would be afraid to face me. When I went outside, Forest Wu bumped into me and spat on the ground. I spat in his face. A group of boys saw me and took out their dicks and started competing to see who could piss the highest in the air. "Fuck off!" I told them. I sent a kick toward them and they scattered. I cranked my belt tighter. The belt felt as if it was wrapped around me three times, but the end of it still whipped around in the dust behind me, scaring off the crows.

I ran into Marvel next. He didn't say anything but pressed a steamed bun into my hands. I was grateful for that act of kindness. I told him I would go with him on his rounds, checking each home for signs that they were stealing electricity.

The transformer had been replaced, so the power was back to normal, but Freshwind was still experiencing a drought. The reservoir still hadn't released enough water down to the fields. The rice crop had hung on, though, and was starting to flower. Treasure had gotten electricity run out to his new house and had just rigged up a few light bulbs so that the bricklayers could still work. But soon enough the bricklayers were called off to head down to the rice paddies. Everyone was waiting for the reservoir to send water down. There was only Bounty left to work on the walls, and eventually his wife came for him, too.

"Everyone else is gone," he said. "I have to stay."

"Says who?" his wife asked. "If the harvest fails, do you think your brother is going to help you? He won't give you a single grain of rice."

"What the hell are you whining about?" He didn't come down from the scaffold. She went over to where his jacket was hanging from a tree, rifled through the pockets, and came up with the three yuan he'd stashed. "That's for Roughshod Ding! I was going to give it to him tomorrow. It's been three years since his mother died." He jumped down from the scaffold and tried to take the bills out of her hand. They both tugged at them until finally the bills were torn into pieces.

Treasure came over and saw the aftermath. "That's enough. We're done for today."

Bounty hung his head, unable to meet his brother's gaze.

Now, where did everyone get the idea that water was going to be released from the reservoir that night? Nobody was quite sure, but the situation had become so desperate that people were grasping at any scrap of hope. They were like children who wake in the night, calling for their mothers. In the end, the reservoir did not answer their call. They cursed heaven. They cursed the village cadres. Someone brought up Justice Xia, and they thought back to what things had been like when he was in charge.

Someone asked Culture, "Where's your grandpa? How come he hasn't been around?"

As Justice Xia had grown older, he'd been afflicted with a peculiar ailment—an itchy back. That night when Culture arrived, Justice Xia was sitting on the edge of the kang, letting

Second Aunt run her nails up and down his spine. Culture tried to tell him how the reservoir had let them down again. But Justice Xia only said, "Higher, yeah . . . Just a bit higher. To the left." Second Aunt couldn't quite find the spot. Tired of taking orders, she turned and went out of the room.

Justice Xia got up and went out, too, headed straight for Pavilion's house. Pavilion was asleep on his kang when Justice Xia arrived, and even Justice Xia's shouting couldn't wake him up.

"It's been days since he had a good night's sleep," Cutie said. "This morning, he fell asleep the moment he lay down. He's been like this all day, sound asleep, hasn't even eaten."

Justice Xia left and went to Concord Qin's house.

Concord Qin said that he'd already been up to the reservoir. The situation was this: there wasn't much water to go around, Freshwind was already better off than most of the villages in the area, and what little water was left had been sent to West Mountain Bend and Leijiazhuang. There was a good chance no water was going to come.

Justice Xia swore. "That's bullshit! We grow rice over here. If there's no water, we'll be in big trouble. You heard that they weren't going to send water, and you just came back?"

"That's right."

"You should have sat right there until they agreed to send water."

Concord Qin's wife brought a bowl of green bean porridge for Justice Xia, saying, "This will cool you off. Green beans are good for getting the heat out of you."

"I'm ice cold already."

"You've got blisters on your lips. You must have some heat inside you."

"I don't!"

"You're a stubborn man, Second Uncle."

Justice Xia scowled. "Tomorrow, you're going up there again. And I'm coming with you."

Pavilion slept for two days straight. When he got up, his head was throbbing. Cutie had just come back from Treasure's place. "Have they got the walls roughed in yet?" he asked.

"The walls are already as tall as me. I was thinking, Treasure's got a new house . . . You're a village cadre, and we're still living in this old place."

"This place is plenty big for us. What do we need a new house for? What's been going on around here while I've been gone?" Cutie told him how Snow Bai was talking about surgery for Second Aunt and offending the in-laws. "Second Uncle keeps a firm grip on everything except his own family," Pavilion said. "Look at all his daughters-in-law. The only one worth a damn is Bamboo. That woman Halfwit married has already started planning how to divide up the old man's estate. It's going to be a mess when he dies. I don't even know what to say when people ask me what's going on there. Big-Noise Zhao had it exactly right when he said Justice Xia is a dragon and all his family are fleas. What else did I miss while I was gone?"

"They sorted out the power. But everyone's still angry about the water issue . . . ," Cutie said.

"Didn't Concord Qin go up to the reservoir like I asked him to?"

"Yeah, he went up there. I don't think it did much good. Second Uncle started lecturing him about it, saying when he was in charge, there was never any problem with irrigation."

"He never had to deal with a drought." Right as he spoke, Justice Xia and Concord Qin came into the room.

"Speak of the devil," said Cutie. "We were just talking about you, Second Uncle. And here you are."

"What the hell were you saying about me? And you, you're finally awake?"

"I'm up, but I've got a headache."

"You've got to get out and get moving. Let's go up to the reservoir."

Pavilion got Cutie to massage his forehead. He finally said, "All right, let's go." From the cupboard, he took a bottle of liquor and tucked it under his arm.

After Marvel and I were finished checking the houses, we went and sat on the stone roller under the arch at the entrance to East Street, watching people go by. There weren't very many people out and about. We saw Roughshod Ding whiz by on his motorcycle. Favor Bai came by leading his donkey. A little way up the road, the donkey broke free from his master and rolled in the dirt, kicking up a cloud of dust that blew down the road toward us. Another donkey came down a side road leading to Highway 312, this one smaller and pulling a cart. A man was asleep on the cart, his head rolled back against the headboard. The donkey was going where it pleased. Shifty appeared by the side of the road and reached up to grab the donkey's reins. He managed to send the donkey and cart and sleeping driver off in another direction, but it wasn't long before they turned back toward him again.

Marvel laughed. "That fucking Shifty just has to stir up trouble."

"Marvel, are we all made of dirt?" I asked. "And if we're made of dirt, are animals all made of grass?" I looked up the road and saw the people coming and going, seemingly replaced with clumps of mud and dust. The donkey that had shaken off Favor Bai, and the smaller donkey pulling the cart, were woven from grass and brush.

Marvel slapped me on the back of the head. "What the hell are you talking about now?"

As soon as he hit me, the people on the road turned from dust back to flesh and blood. It was kind of like Wisdom Xia's radio—one firm smack could fix my short-circuiting brain. Were there wires and circuits in my head, too?

I gave my head a shake and looked up to see Snow Bai and her mother coming toward us. To be sure I wasn't seeing things, I gave my own head a smack. It really was her. She was wearing a yellow dress that seemed to light up the street. I must have been staring because Marvel called me twice and I didn't even hear him. But Snow Bai's mother heard my name being called, looked up, and dragged her daughter down an alley.

Marvel waved a hand in front of my eyes and called me again. "What's wrong with you?" He added, "They're gone. They went down that alley."

"That witch . . ." I was talking about Snow Bai's mother.

Marvel said, "You really love Snow Bai?"

I ignored him. What use was it to tell him that I loved her?

"Listen to me, brother," he said. "It doesn't matter whether you love her or not."

I wasn't expecting that. "Why not?"

"That's just the way it is. Everyone has their place. Rich men eat delicacies, and poor men get the scraps."

I didn't want to hear it. "Get out of here," I said, and waved him off. He stayed where he was, but a fat bluebottle that had been drinking from a puddle of spit beside my shoe flew into the air.

"You should listen to me, Spark. I'm trying to look out for you. She's not for you. You'll be lucky to get the scraps."

I stood up. I was never going to work with them again. Things were never the same between Marvel and me after that. I walked away, drifting down the road, wanting to cry, and just as the tears came to my eyes, I saw Pavilion, Concord Qin, and Justice Xia coming toward me.

Justice Xia called out to me. "Spark, what's wrong?"

"Nothing."

"Then lift your head up."

"Are you really okay?" Pavilion asked.

"I'm fine."

"Then come up to the reservoir with us."

"What do we need him for?" Concord Qin asked.

Pavilion said, "Everyone and everything has their use. Even an old rag can still be stuffed into a crack in the wall." To me, he said, "You coming or not?"

"Okay."

"All right, if you're coming, go grab that rooster over there."

We were outside Concord Qin's place, where a rooster was prancing around two hens. The rooster dipped his comb and strutted arrogantly to the left, circled back around to the right, stretched out his neck, and crowed. I slipped off a shoe and came up behind the rooster and knocked it down with a slap of the sole. As I grabbed the bird around the neck, I heard Chastity shouting inside the yard: "Thief! Thief!"

"Pipe down," Pavilion said. "I'll give you the money for it later."

The four of us headed out to the reservoir, ten *li* north of Freshwind. In 1976, when the dam was being built to create the reservoir, Concord Qin, Pavilion, and Justice Xia had all worked up there. Pavilion's father, Benevolence Xia, had died on the site, blown up when a stick of dynamite that was supposed to have been a dud went off in his hands. It was only when we got up to the administration office that I realized we were there to ask them to release water down to Freshwind's fields.

Pavilion told Justice Xia and me to wait outside. He said things would go better if he and Concord Qin dealt with things.

I told him, "I thought you wanted me to come along in case things got rough."

"You stay with Second Uncle," Pavilion said. "Wait for us to come get you." He tossed me a pack of cigarettes and took the rooster, along with the bottle of liquor, and went inside.

I understood what was going on. This was like two generals of opposing armies negotiating a ceasefire. Wisdom Xia had told me before that the smartest general is the one whose army wins without firing a shot. When Chairman Mao was alive, would you say he was a rich man? Of course, he wasn't broke. But he could get through life without a single yuan in his pocket. Wisdom Xia told me that last year, too.

I sat with Justice Xia on a slope outside the administration building; he was smoking his rollies with their fragrant black tobacco. After smoking a few in a row, he must have wanted to cool down his mouth, so he stood and ripped a few leaves down from a walnut tree and chewed them.

He suddenly asked me, "When we saw you this morning, why were you crying?" Justice Xia was Wind Xia's uncle, and Snow Bai had married into their family, so I was sure he knew what had happened between me and Snow Bai. I thought he must have been waiting for the chance to cuss me out. But he didn't mention that. He didn't mention what I'd done to myself or how I'd been in the hospital. He asked, "The third anniversary of your father's passing is coming soon, isn't it?"

"You remember?"

"I can't believe it's been three years already. I'll tell you this, if your father was still around, we wouldn't have had to come up here." I started to cry, the tears dripping off my cheeks. "Hey, we're in a drought. Don't waste those tears. When Pavilion asked you to come up, I didn't think you'd come. I thought you still bore a grudge against him."

"You've argued with him before, too, but you still came."

"Ha, that's right. You know, you're a lot like your father. I can't believe the village is in such a mess. The growing season is already short enough without a drought. I'm worried that if we don't get any water, harvest season will be a disaster."

"Everyone talks about when you were in charge of things."

"Really? What do they say?"

"They said we never had a bad harvest when you were running things."

"We never went through a drought like this."

"Why not? You were lucky. That was your fate, I guess, to never have to face a drought."

"Don't go around talking like that."

But I had more to say. "The cadres now aren't half as good as you were, and the weather's turned bad, too. There's the saying, 'Lament in the heavens and anger from below.'"

Justice Xia lit another one of his rollies. The smoke was bad enough to choke you, but even worse, he stashed all the old butts in his shoe. The stench of feet and tobacco filled the air around him.

"I don't know about the heavens . . . ," he said. "The people are angry, that's for sure. Freshwind is a good place, but the state that it's in, so poor . . ." He trailed off and began mumbling. I wasn't sure if he was talking to me or to himself. It sounded like he was doing some calculations. "One *mu* of paddy field produces 600 kilos, a kilo sells for eight jiao and six fen, take 150 kilos off the wheat fields, one yuan and six jiao for every kilogram, a family of four, three *mu* for each person, income for the whole year is 7,000 yuan, all the taxes put together, subtract 2,500 yuan from that, and 1,500 kilograms of grain get held back to use at home, adding up to about 1,260 yuan, 250 kilograms of cooking oil at one yuan and six jiao per kilogram, which adds up to another 400 yuan, and altogether that adds up to 2,500 yuan. Subtract 2,500 yuan from 7,000 yuan, you've got 2,000 yuan left. With that 2,000, you have to cover electricity, daily necessities, sending kids to school, money for weddings and funerals, and there must be some for illnesses and emergencies. And those numbers are for a year with a good harvest. A year like this, there's no way anyone will be making that much. You have to save a bit of that money for other things, too, like subsidies to the village cadres, paying the salary of the community teachers, fertilizer, pesticide, plastic for covering seedlings, seeds, and the prices for those are always going up. It's tough to be a farmer."

I could see the worry on his face and the deep lines in his forehead. "You're giving me a headache. Why bother with the numbers? Everyone just muddles through. If they don't starve to death, they make their harvest and live another year."

"That's exactly what your dad would have said."

We sat on the slope together until the sun began to dip toward the western horizon and our stomachs were growling. "Did they forget about us out here? They're in there, drinking."

Justice Xia pointed to the garden farther along the slope and said, "Do you want a radish? Get one for me, too." I was walking over to the garden just as Concord Qin came out of the door with the chicken's steamed head and claws. He gave the head to Justice Xia and the claws to me.

"You cooked the chicken?"

"We already ate the chicken. The liquor's all gone, too. But still no progress."

Justice Xia tossed the chicken head to the ground and walked toward the office.

The office was made up of three rooms in a timber shack. Behind the office was a row of smaller shacks where the workers lived. Some of the workers were out in the yard, sitting under a walnut tree, playing chess. There was the faint sound of Pavilion shouting. Justice Xia strode up to the door of the office and kicked hard at the door.

The reservoir manager came to the door. "Hey! When did you get here?"

"I've been waiting out here all afternoon, while you were in their drinking."

The reservoir manager said to Pavilion, "This ain't right, bringing Second Uncle up here to put the screws to me. You didn't even tell me he was out there waiting."

"We brought some muscle, too," Justice Xia said.

I balled up a fist and walked toward the manager, trying to look as menacing as I could. I stubbed my toe trying to kick a rock and pretended that it hadn't hurt.

"Listen, my hands are tied," the manager said. "I follow the plans that were given to me. If it was my call, I'd be more than happy to send some water to Freshwind, even if there was only a spoonful left in there."

"I managed the workers from Freshwind that came up to work on the reservoir," Justice Xia said. "Pavilion's father died up here. How can you say we can't have our share of the water? That's unacceptable. If you won't open those gates, I'll open them myself."

The manager was startled and could only stammer, "Director, p-please, c-calm down."

"'Director'? There's no need for that. I retired a long time ago. Even the mice aren't scared of this old cat anymore." He strode off toward the dam. Concord Qin and Pavilion grabbed the manager's arms. He was a thin man, and though he struggled with all his might, he couldn't break free.

The workers who had been playing chess jogged over, but I grabbed a sickle down from the office's windowsill and waved it menacingly.

"Calm down, Spark," Concord Qin said. "Don't get crazy."

I didn't want to hurt anyone. I swung the sickle, letting the blade whistle in the air. I stuck out my left arm and pressed the sickle's blade down into my flesh until it drew blood. A droplet of blood fell from my arm like a ripe peach falling from a tree. The workers didn't dare take another step forward.

Justice Xia turned back and said, "That's enough. Let the manager come up with me."

"Irrigation is the lifeblood of these farms," the manager said. "If you damage anything, you'll pay for it. I won't have any part of it."

"Lifeblood, huh?" I said to him. "Freshwind is about to die. I've got nothing left to live for, without that water. Bring him up here. Let him open the gates himself!"

Concord Qin and Pavilion dragged the manager up toward the dam.

While they watched, the manager cranked open the gates that fed Freshwind's irrigation canals. Pavilion sighed, looked at the water flowing down from the gates, and said, "I gotta take a piss after that." He took his dick out and pissed in the dust. His face loosened, and his eyes closed in silent ecstasy.

I shut my eyes, too, and listened to the voices that came indistinctly to my ears. To the sound of fish splashing in the reservoir, breaking the surface of the still water. I heard a locust jump from the tall grass, then land near my feet.

When I opened my eyes, Pavilion still had both his hands on his dick. "Are you taking a piss or playing with it?" I asked.

"You fuckin' piece of shit! I didn't say a goddamn thing about you, so why do you have to talk shit about me? Why don't you go play with your own!"

I knew what he meant, that I didn't have my own to play with. But the insult satisfied him, and his satisfaction somehow soothed me.

Right as Pavilion prepared to turn on me again, we were both distracted by the sound of a loud splash. Justice Xia had jumped into the irrigation canal. The gates of the dam were wide open, and Justice Xia could not stand in the rushing water. His head stayed under the water for a long time, with only his hair floating above the flood like long grass. I saw his handkerchief and his pouch of tobacco swept downstream.

I suddenly realized that nobody else was reacting, either. Even the reservoir manager seemed to be in shock. I shouted, "Second Uncle!" But he did not lift himself out of the water. He was like a fish. A fat gray catfish, stuck to the bottom of the canal. Concord Qin jumped in after him. Just as he reached the old man, Justice Xia rose from the water, spraying water from his mouth.

"Fuck, you scared me," the manager said.

Justice Xia stood. "I drank eight mouthfuls. Eight! Tastes so sweet I know you cocksuckers are putting sugar in that reservoir."

"I'm telling you, old man. My job is to follow the plans. When the other villages come up here to ask me what the hell is going on, I'm sending them to you to deal with."

"You want to blame it on me? You opened those gates yourself, you little bastard. I'm not a cadre anymore. If you want to keep sucking off that government teat, you better figure out an excuse or retire like me." Justice Xia went up to the dam, blew his nose on his fingers, and wiped it on the manager's back. He leaned in and whispered something in the man's ear. I couldn't hear what he said, but whatever it was, the manager first looked shocked and then chuckled.

I asked Justice Xia later, "What did you say to him?"

"I told him we'd send him a banner to hang up on the dam."

I don't know whether they ever sent a banner. Pavilion stayed up at the reservoir to make sure the water kept flowing. The gates had to stay open for at least twelve hours. Justice Xia and Concord Qin rushed back to Freshwind to get everyone ready to irrigate their fields. I was sent to walk down the canal to make sure that nobody dammed up or diverted the stream.

It was after midnight when I saw the fish in the canal. It had a big head, sharp teeth, and long black fins. I'd never seen a fish like that before. I walked along the canal, and the fish swam alongside me. The moon was high overhead. Halfway down the hill, the canal made a turn. I felt a bit scared, suddenly, and I asked the fish, "Who are you?"

"Ya! Ya! Ya!" the fish said.

"Are you Second Uncle?"

"Ya! Ya! Ya!"

Mid-Star's father had told me that whenever you meet a person or an animal you've never met before and you feel a connection, you must have had some connection in a previous life; they were your relative or your close friend. I wondered whether the fish was Justice Xia or if maybe Justice Xia had been a fish in his last life.

We followed each other down the hill, side by side, between the steep-sided dirt cliffs and following the curves in the canal. When we got to Freshwind, I stood on the ridge between the first fields at the edge of the village and shouted, "Water's here!"

The villagers waiting at the edge of the fields had mostly fallen asleep, and they staggered to their feet, rubbing their eyes and saying, "Water?" They spun around, trying to find where the shouts had come from. Forest Wu started shouting, too, suddenly losing his stammer. When they heard him shouting, the rest of the villagers began to shout, too, until they were all howling together like a pack of dogs.

The news spread through the village, and everyone rushed to the fields. I sat down on the edge of the canal and looked down at the water. The fish was gone.

Chapter 13

There's nothing more I can say about the fish because no one else in Freshwind Village saw it. I asked the first man who went out to water his crops, Dog-Scraps, but he said he hadn't seen it.

"How could I have missed a fish as big as that?" he said, then made me sniff his fingers and look in his mouth. Neither smelled fishy.

The last ones to get a turn at the water were Bounty and Forest Wu. Bounty told me that while they were waiting, Roughshod Ding had brought him some bad news, saying they were going to run the water through a culvert on Highway 312, five *li* west of here, and the Highways Department had decided that the villagers would do the work. Goodness set it up with Excellence, who had started lining up the workers. As soon as Bounty heard that, he went looking for Goodness; he didn't even stop to water his crops, so how could he possibly have seen a fish?

So as I was saying, Bounty went looking for Goodness. Only Goodness wasn't well; he hadn't taken a shit in days, and he was in a very bad mood.

"The Highways Department put Excellence in charge; it's nothing to do with me. Besides, when good things happen, don't they always happen to you Xias?"

"You're the bookkeeper and a village cadre; how can you talk like that?" protested Bounty. "East Street is full of Xias, but that doesn't mean the good things happen to us."

"You just count 'em up. Start with the new houses on East Street—who built them? The Xias, wasn't it?"

"Anyone can build a house, so long as they can do the work. It's not as if we're stopping anyone else."

"And where do you Xias get the money from?" Goodness pursued. "Ever since the 1970s, if anyone gets a job in the army or in recruitment or leaves the village, you can bet they're a Xia. Most of the Xias get government jobs; they keep getting richer, and the poor get poorer."

"You've got to come from a good family for an army or recruitment job—you know the policy as well as anyone. You're surely not blaming the Communist Party, are you? I mean, how did you get to be bookkeeper when you're not from a big clan?"

Red faced with fury, they carried on shouting at each other until bystanders finally succeeded in pulling them apart.

Treasure had brought the timber back from Zhang Ba's and was sitting over his tea, feeling pleased with himself, when Halfwit came hurrying along. "Second Brother, you're needed!"

"What's up?"

"Third Brother's having a fight with Goodness. You better go. Blood's thicker than water, isn't it?"

"Let them fight! There are fights every day in the village; they're not going to kill each other. Even if they look like they're going to, his wife's a terror. She can go and sort it out."

And without even offering Halfwit any tea, Treasure slung his jacket over his shoulders and set off for the brickyard.

Shifty was asleep in the brickyard shed. Winter or summer, Shifty never wore any underpants when he slept. He didn't get up when Treasure turned up; he just lay there with his dick resting on his thigh like a bit of dead snake.

"Aren't you afraid the cat'll pounce on it?" asked Treasure.

"I didn't think you'd be long," said Shifty.

"I haven't come to buy tiles. I want to know if you've met White-Moth."

"Who's White-Moth?"

"Black-Moth's kid sister."

Shifty sat up with a jerk, his eyes glittering.

"And you can get one thing clear: it's okay to know her, but just you keep your hands off her!"

"So where is she?" asked Shifty.

"Gone to her sister's."

Forest Wu's home only housed the one family. Inside was a yard with a main house with three rooms, and a smaller building down each side. The eaves of the main house had come down at one corner and were covered with a sheet of plastic. When the wind caught the plastic, the flapping sounded like a ghost clapping its hands. The gate was not locked, and the two sisters, White-Moth and Black-Moth, were indoors sluicing themselves down with a basin of cold water. When they heard the shout, "Is anyone at home?" they hurriedly blew out the lamp.

"Who is it?" Black-Moth asked. But instead of answering, Treasure rapped the gate ring three times and went in. Black-Moth came out, wrapped in a sheet, but hurriedly dodged back inside as soon as she saw that Shifty was there, too. Treasure and Shifty sat on some steps under the eaves where the cloth bag and wooden box for making tofu were drying.

"Where's Forest Wu?" asked Treasure.

Black-Moth came out, properly dressed now, and carrying two bowls of mung bean broth. "He's gone to the field to wait for the water. Did neither of you go?"

"You asked me to find a job for White-Moth to do. I told Shifty, and he wants to see if she's up to doing some work in the brickyard," said Treasure.

"White-Moth! White-Moth! Come out here, quick!" shouted Black-Moth.

White-Moth came out, carrying a kerosene lamp, which shone on her face, lighting up her pink cheeks and bright eyes.

Shifty got to his feet and approached her. Treasure gave a cough.

Shifty reached out his hand and took hold of the lamp. "Haven't you got electricity?" He sounded flustered.

"My sister's family doesn't have the money. They're dirt poor; my brother-in-law thinks I'm mooching off them—I've got to get a job."

"Come to my brickyard. I'm just worried that it's so dusty your fair skin will end up black."

"Well, there's such a thing as black peonies," said White-Moth.

"You're shameless!" retorted her sister.

"It's the truth, isn't it?" said White-Moth.

"It certainly is," said Shifty.

Treasure could see the sparks beginning to fly and shot a look at Black-Moth.

She took the hint. "Let's talk indoors."

"Fry some eggs. Boil some water. Why's there no water in the bucket?" asked Treasure.

"Sit down; I'll go to the spring for some water," said Black-Moth.

"I'll go with you," said Treasure. And they went out and shut the door behind them.

But they didn't go to the spring; they nipped into the side building instead, and Treasure pressed Black-Moth up against the stove. The moon shone in through the window. A large boiler for making tofu sat on the stove, with a bowl of cold tofu in it.

"You want some?" asked Black-Moth, but Treasure was busy tugging at her pants. Black-Moth grabbed a bit of tofu and shoved it into her mouth as he pulled her pants down. "Shifty's in the house; there isn't time for anything."

"Hold on to the top of the stove; I'll put it in from behind."

"I'm on the rag," said Black-Moth, still stuffing tofu in. She pulled a wad of paper from between her thighs.

Treasure grunted in annoyance. "Then you can bring me off."

They stood with their arms around each other, and Black-Moth brought Treasure off with her hand. He spurted onto her shoe.

Black-Moth wiped them clean. "You owe me for these shoes."

"I'll buy you some tomorrow at the market."

"I want some clothes, too."

"You want shoes and clothes? I'm building a house; where am I supposed to get the money?"

"You're so tightfisted!"

They straightened their clothes, and Black-Moth was heading back to the house when Treasure stopped her.

"Better tell him all about it."

But Black-Moth objected, "Shifty's a monster. White-Moth can go; he won't give her a bad time."

"Who will give whom a bad time?"

"Well, just you tell Shifty that he's got to take White-Moth on at the brickyard, provide all her meals, and decent pay, too!"

They could hear giggling coming from the house, and then there was a gasp from White-Moth. In the quietness of the night, it was a very loud gasp, and Black-Moth called, "What's up, White-Moth?"

Silence.

Then White-Moth said, "Sis, there's a rat in the room! Ai! Ai!"

Treasure hastily pulled Black-Moth back inside.

"Let's have some light. If we're not getting fried eggs, you do some tofu with chili and vinegar, and we'll eat that."

They lit the lamp, prepared the tofu, and carried the bowls out.

Treasure called, "Come and have some tofu out here; it's cooler in the courtyard."

White-Moth came out first and shot around to the shithouse at the back. Then Shifty emerged, his legs wobbling so much that he nearly tripped over the threshold.

"It's hot as hell in here; don't you have a fan?" he said.

"There's wishful thinking," said Black-Moth.

"White-Moth can come and get a fan from me tomorrow," said Shifty.

"Even if we had electricity, which we don't, White-Moth can't go taking stuff off you like that," said Black-Moth. "And I haven't asked her if she wants to work in the brickyard yet."

From inside the shithouse, White-Moth called, "I do!"

Treasure and Shifty ate their tofu and left. Forest Wu, meanwhile, was still out in the fields, waiting his turn to irrigate his crops.

"Did you get any?" asked Treasure.

"That's a lot of water," said Shifty, evading the question.

Treasure was quiet for a moment, then said, "Give me a smoke."

Shifty passed him a pack, and Treasure took one out and lit it, then put the whole pack into his own pocket.

"You only met her today, and you . . . ," Treasure said.

"If a cat sees a fish and doesn't eat it, what kind of cat is that?"

"It took me years to get into Black-Moth's panties, and you're in there with White-Moth the minute you meet her."

"You're too educated, that's your trouble!"

Treasure ground his teeth in rage.

Chapter 14

Pavilion had spent three days and four nights at the reservoir. After a few arguments with the reservoir manager, they made their peace, and Pavilion came home with some soft-shelled turtles he'd caught in the reservoir. It was noon by the time he arrived, and he told Cutie to invite Wind Xia and Big-Noise Zhao to come and eat with them. Big-Noise Zhao arrived early and soon had Pavilion cracking up at his jokes.

Then Wind Xia came in. The others fell silent. "What were you saying that you don't want me to hear?" he demanded.

"Why would you want to listen to stuff like this?" asked Big-Noise Zhao. And he recited, "'Fooling around, if you do it properly, it's called romance; taking by force, if you do it properly, it's called marriage; frigidity, if you do it properly, it's called virginity; impotence, if you do it properly, it's called integrity.'"

"Who the hell said that, and what's it about?" said Wind Xia.

"Spark . . . the useless ignoramus. He's always thinking up stuff that would never occur to anyone else."

Big-Noise Zhao must have felt awkward talking about me like that because he fell silent. He glanced at Wind Xia, but Wind Xia changed the subject. Looking at the turtles on the chopping block, he said, "Hey, turtles for dinner, delicious! You're really spoiling us."

I'll tell you this for free: The reason why Big-Noise Zhao shut his mouth in a hurry was that he realized that Wind Xia didn't like people mentioning my name. But when Wind Xia changed the subject to turtles, it showed that my little saying had hit home all the same. He'd taken someone by force, all right, and that someone was Snow Bai!

While they were on the subject of turtles, Big-Noise Zhao said to Pavilion, "I know you got me here to see how they're cooked. But your sister-in-law thinks you need feeding up after all that work you've done."

"Big-Noise, if your lips were tiles, you'd have broken them with all that flapping," said Cutie.

"What's the matter? A sister-in-law should look after her husband's brother, shouldn't she? You know what they say, 'sister-in-law's ass, little brother gets half!'"

Cutie was just slicing open a turtle and stopped Big-Noise's mouth with one of its eggs.

"Your trip to the reservoir was a lot of work, Pavilion," said Wind Xia.

"It's a pity you didn't go; you could have written a good article about it. I had to play good cop *and* bad cop, but I forced him to back down in the end. While I was still there, he stopped the flow after half the water had run out. I could have wrung his neck, but I didn't; I tried a bit of gentle persuasion. I told him, 'If I were a woman, you could screw me, but I'm not, so I'll have to take a knife and make a hole in my thigh instead.'"

Cutie was just chopping up the turtle claws. She threw one at Pavilion's head. "Pavilion, don't be so damned crude!"

Pavilion wiped the turtle blood from his forehead. "You've got to go low to come out on top. The reservoir manager's not a pervert, but he is a drunk, so I took some bottles to share with him. Then he tried to give me a hard time; he said, 'If you can down a bottle in one, I'll turn on the water for you.' I said, 'You better be as good as your word!' and I picked up the bottle and drank. It made me so drunk I fell off my chair. Wind Xia, you write that up, and I guarantee that'll be a good article."

But Big-Noise Zhao said, "That's not what good writing is. Pavilion, you don't know a thing, do you?"

Wind Xia just laughed.

"Maybe I don't, but I've read Wind Xia's book," said Pavilion. "And I can tell you this, Wind Xia, your book's boring; the only thing I like is the poem inside the front cover."

"What poem?" asked Big-Noise Zhao.

"It's dedicated to Isaac Newton," said Pavilion. "It goes like this: 'Nature and the laws of nature / Are concealed in the darkness. / The Lord said, Let Newton do his thing, / And then there was light!'"

"You're a clever man, Pavilion, to know all about Newton," said Big-Noise Zhao.

Pavilion said, "You think you're the only one who can compose couplets, and everyone else is a hillbilly? I always liked poetry at school, and when we went back to the village after graduation, Wind Xia and I both used to write; you ask him."

"It's true, I know Pavilion here likes Pushkin's poems; he's always reciting them to me in his best Mandarin. He didn't just crawl out of a hole in the earth, you know," said Wind Xia.

"I'm convinced that if Pavilion gets to be section chief, he'll be doing the county head's job, and if he gets to be county head, he'll be doing the provincial head's job. He'll be a Lin Biao, out to get Chairman Mao," said Big-Noise Zhao.

"Is that a compliment or an insult?" asked Pavilion.

"Would I dare insult you? Do I want to end up like Concord Qin?"

"Big-Noise, you're always shooting your mouth off, but it's true that a lot of the villagers feel sorry for Concord Qin. I'll tell you something; no matter whether you're Party secretary or village head, it's shitty being a cadre. You're being tripped up all day long, your bosses are always on your case, and the people under you are always trying to get the better of you. You're like a bean being ground to flour between two stone rollers. If you're a township head or a county head, you can line your own pockets, but in the village there's nothing to line your pockets with. I went to a meeting in the township a few days ago, and I told them they should feel sorry for people like us. We go for a meal and a drink at someone's house and get cursed to hell and back."

"It's not as bad as that. Isn't there a folk song about local cadres all having 'mothers-in-law in every village'?" Big-Noise Zhao asked.

"I'd almost forgotten that. But I'll tell you something; a couple of months ago, your sister-in-law here threw a screaming fit at me, and I thought, 'Uh-oh, she's fallen behind with her grain tax for sure!'"

Cutie flushed and yelled at Pavilion, "How dare you say stuff like that! Big-Noise, I've split open the turtle; come and see how it's cooked." And she went off to the kitchen.

"She's crazy," said Pavilion. "You'll see; she'll bring the food and ask if it's good. And the more you say it is, the more dishes she cooks for you."

Sure enough, when Cutie brought the first dish in, she asked, "Is it good?"

"Very," said Big-Noise.

"You've had dinners all over China; I'm sure you're poking fun at my cooking."

"No, it's really delicious."

"Good, I'll go and knock up a few more dishes then."

While they were waiting for the turtles, the three men drank a beer each, and the scar on Pavilion's face turned a vivid red. "Wind Xia's a big shot now; he's been doing big things," he said. "It's made me think I should do big things in Freshwind. Chairman Mao ruled the country; can't we rule one small village?"

"Let me read a poem first," said Big-Noise Zhao. And he recited:

> Ah ocean, you're full of water
> Ah stallion, you have legs that canter
> Ah love, you are lips to lips
> If you walk the streets at night, you'll bump into a specter.

Wind Xia banged the table and roared with laughter.

"What are you on about?" asked Pavilion.

"I figure Freshwind Village is a lost cause—no industry, no investment, too many people living on too little land, the only way out is education—but even for people with education, how many of them have done as well as Wind Xia?"

"It's exactly because there's a shortage of land and no resources that I want to do something different. Every village cadre should leave their mark," said Pavilion.

"Old Mr. Wang built a bridge, Mr. Xi built an extension to the school, Spark's dad built roads, and your second uncle did the most of all. He built the river dike, he transformed the beach at the bend in the river, built field terraces at Beiyuan, dug canals, and made an orchard, too. If any new temples are ever built, we'd have to dedicate one to your second uncle," said Big-Noise Zhao.

"You make it all sound hunky-dory, but you haven't mentioned any of the downsides," said Pavilion. "Three people died building the bridge, and the new roads are causing a lot of trouble. Maybe he did leave an orchard, but only half of Seven Li Gully has been filled, everyone's exhausted, it's all cost heaps of money, and now he's stepped down without even finishing the gully-filling. When I took over, it was going around the township that your ancestors must have been smoothing the way for you—they said Freshwind Village had started poor, then struck it rich, and we were living in a golden age. No one knew that the village coffers were empty and the accounts were in a mess. Second Uncle got the 'poor village' label taken off, but all that meant was that we got no more emergency aid, and they slapped taxes on us. Then the drought came. Times are really hard now.

"But I've achieved two things since I've been in office: One is making sure there are no disturbances. Freshwind folk have always been a mulish lot—even the township government says as much—and cadres here have a helluva job managing them. But I've settled them down. There's been no trouble over the reforestation project, even though reforestation is hell to manage—in fact, Bowed Ox Ridge is a model of its kind. The second thing I did was to get that 'poor village' label restored. I know it doesn't sound good, but there are real benefits. The county and township governments can't slap more projects on us, and we can ask them for funds—the money for our transformer came from the township. Next, I've got my eye on building a farmers market. That'll be something to boast about: an agricultural-products center to be built on some land in the east of the county." And Pavilion jumped to his feet, his eyes rimmed with red.

"Are you crying?" Wind Xia asked.

"I'm so excited about the farmers market that every time I think about it, tears come to my eyes!"

Big-Noise Zhao bent his head to hide a smile.

"You don't think it's feasible?" said Pavilion, and he got out a sheet of paper. On it was a sketch of a large market built on the triangle of land formed by the two streets that led out to Highway 312. There was a guesthouse—a three-story building with six rooms—an area of thirty thousand square yards laid out for vendors' booths, a grand decorative archway, and three rows of small shops.

"It's a great design," said Big-Noise Zhao. "But it's a huge project. Will there be the political will to drive it through to completion? Concord Qin said the Seven Li Gully–filling project was going to be stopped, so . . ."

Pavilion interrupted him. "To hell with Seven Li Gully. They've been at it three years, and what's been achieved? Even if the job gets finished, how many new crops will it grow? The main problem right now isn't grain; even if we don't harvest a single grain for two years running, the people won't starve. The problem is there's no money; we must solve the problem of the villagers having no money. I'm Party secretary, and I have to be the flag-bearer."

"Hang on a moment," said Big-Noise Zhao. "When Concord Qin was Party secretary, you said he only represented the Party; he couldn't represent the village committee. Now you're Party secretary, you're saying the Party's the flag bearer. You can't have it both ways."

"You tell me, was Concord Qin capable of driving through a project that big?" said Pavilion.

Big-Noise Zhao was silent.

They heard shouting outside the yard gate. "Cutie! Cutie!"

"That's Fourth Auntie," said Cutie, and went out. Then she came back and said, "She's looking for Wind Xia."

"Ask her in to eat," said Pavilion.

"They've got guests, and Fourth Uncle is pissed off because Wind Xia hasn't come home." She turned to Wind Xia. "Have you fallen out with him?"

"The guests are from the county opera troupe. He's annoyed because he thinks I'm snubbing them."

"Is Snow Bai there?" asked Pavilion.

"Yes, she is. So why on earth does he want me there as well?"

"Does Snow Bai know the people in the County Department of Commerce?" Pavilion asked. "I've got a bit of business . . ."

"What business?" asked Wind Xia.

But Cutie broke in. "Fourth Uncle's at home and he's angry; forget your other business."

As Wind Xia left, he patted his pocket and realized he was out of smokes, so instead of hurrying straight home, he headed to Middle Street.

On Middle Street, Forest Wu and Bright Chen were having a fight. It was the most interesting fight Freshwind had ever seen. I was there, too, egging them on.

Forest Wu had been up at first light to collect the manure. Then he wanted to mill the soybeans to make tofu and shouted to Black-Moth to come and help. Black-Moth was sitting listlessly on the doorstep. She hadn't washed her face or combed her hair.

"What's up with you?" said Forest Wu.

"I'm not feeling well," said Black-Moth. She spat again and again until the cloth-beating stone at her feet was covered in spittle.

"All that sp-spitting, a-are . . . y-you pr-pregnant?"

Black-Moth said nothing.

Forest Wu was suddenly excited. "You m-m-might b-be having a-a . . . !" Forest Wu had always wanted a child, but the years had gone by without Black-Moth getting pregnant. "G-go back to bed; I'll m-make the tofu on my own. I know how to do it."

But Black-Moth said she didn't feel like eating, so Forest Wu gave up on the tofu and chased the brown hen around the yard instead. He was going to kill it and make chicken stew for Black-Moth until she shouted at him, "You idiot! The hen's still laying. Are you going to sell her bones to buy fertilizer and pesticide?"

"Would you like *liang fen* noodles to eat then?"

"No, I want an apple."

"Give me some money, and I'll buy you an apple."

"When have you ever given me any money?" Black-Moth retorted.

Forest Wu went to the corner of the room and extracted an old sock from a crack in the wall. He took out the two yuan he had squirrelled away in it and went to New-Life Liu's orchard. As it happened, New-Life Liu wasn't there, but Star Chen's orchard was next door. Star Chen and Emerald were making out in the straw hut. They were not in the slightest bit embarrassed when they realized he'd caught them at it, but *he* was, and hurried back into the village. On the way, he happened to pass Bright Chen, sitting in his shop doorway, mending a shoe.

Forest Wu spat contemptuously, and Bright Chen asked, "Wh-what are you sp-spitting for? Wh-what have I d-done to off-offend you?" and spat back at Forest Wu.

Forest Wu was a man who could keep secrets. He just said, "N-now we're o-on a level." And he sat down to rest his feet. Some folks with nothing better to do were sitting inside Bright Chen's shop—me, Favor Bai, Pillar Zhu, and Obedient Zhang from the farm store.

I said in a low voice, "Forest Wu is a slow stutterer, and Bright Chen is a fast stutterer. What on earth could have made them fight?" Then I offered Forest Wu a smoke. Forest Wu had a drag, then hung his hat on the door bolt and went off to the shithouse, not for a piss or a shit but because he wanted to hide his two yuan. He couldn't tie them into his pants belt or put them in a pocket, so he hid them inside his shoe. When he came out, he saw his hat had been daubed in black shoe polish.

"Who did that?" he demanded. I pointed to Bright Chen. Forest Wu flung at Bright Chen, "Y-you m-made my straw hat d-dirty!"

"N-no, I d-did not. Wh-why would I w-waste good shoe polish on a sc-scruffy old h-hat like that?"

"Y-you d-did!"

"I d-did not!"

"You're so p-pigheaded, why c-can't you admit it? Y-you, an outsider, you c-come and tr-treat a local man like th-this."

"What d-do you mean, out-outsider? I've got a t-temporary-residence p-per-permit. And we've got a l-lease on an or-orchard, too. Have we ever taken any f-food or d-drink from you?"

"You're d-drunk! Does the chick tr-tread on the old h-hen's e-egg?"

Bright Chen had no idea what that meant.

"F-fuck y-your mother!" finished Forest Wu.

"F-fuck your grand-grandmother, y-your mo-mo-mother, and your wom-woman!"

Forest Wu glared furiously at Bright Chen, poked his finger in his face, and yelled, "And th-the s-same to y-you!"

We all stood around watching and listening. Every time one of them opened his mouth, we did the same, trying to follow his rhythm and swear along with him, but it was hard to do the stutter; we couldn't get it right.

"Lay into each other, why don't you?" I said.

And that's just what they did. Bright Chen was quicker on his feet and got in the first punch. Forest Wu kicked out at him but kicked his shoe off, and Bright Chen grabbed it and flung it three yards away.

At that point, we tried to stop the fight, but Forest Wu wasn't giving in. "I-I'm n-not as strong as him; h-he can get his br-breath back quicker." Then he suddenly remembered the money in his shoe and went to pick it up. But the money was nowhere to be seen, and he burst into tears.

At that very moment, Wind Xia arrived on Middle Street to buy his cigarettes. As soon as I saw him, I slipped away. I didn't want to meet him. The truth was, I feared him more than disliked him, maybe due to a guilty conscience.

I walked over to the barbershop that Zhu Qing had opened and told his assistant to cut my hair. The back door was open, and I could see a peony bush growing in the yard. The kid had been tying a bamboo stick to it for support. As he was cutting my hair, he kept looking back at the peony.

"Colorful, isn't it?" he said.

"Very," I agreed.

"How come the flowers are so colorful?"

"Just do a good job on my hair; stop looking at the flowers," I said.

He couldn't look, but I could. The peony flowers really were colorful. Bright flowers attracted the butterflies and the bees to pollinate them. So the flowers were like the peony's genitals. Why did it wear them on its head?

"Did Forest Wu and Bright Chen have a fight?" the kid asked.

"Yup."

"They stopped as soon as Wind Xia turned up. Are they scared of him?"

"Why'd they be scared of him?"

He started to cut my hair ends. It hurt, and I told him so.

"That's weird. No one's hair hurts when you cut the tips. I'll give you a part like Wind Xia."

"I want it on one side," I said.

"All the guys want to be like Wind Xia, 'cause he's married to that beautiful girl, Snow Bai. She's like a flower."

I got angry at that. "Cut the crap! So what if he married Snow Bai?"

That annoyed him, and he cut my hair so short I told him just to go ahead and shave it, then I didn't give him any money.

Wind Xia saw Forest Wu crying his eyes out. "What's the matter?" he asked.

"I lost my money."

Wind Xia took out five yuan, but Forest Wu refused to take it; he said he wanted his own money back. Things were getting serious. In a big place like that with just a few people in it, the two yuan couldn't have just disappeared, and everyone suspected someone else of being the thief. They hunted around, but nothing was found.

Finally, Favor Bai asked, "Was it one two-yuan bill or two one-yuan bills?"

"O-o-one bill," said Forest Wu.

Favor Bai emptied all the money out of his pocket. He had twenty yuan but no two-yuan bill. "I didn't pick it up; you can take a look and see."

Pillar Zhu and Obedient Zhang did the same, and they didn't have a two-yuan bill, either.

"You can s-search me," said Bright Chen, "and i-if you find a single c-cent on me, then I t-took the m-money! Why don't you sh-shout for Sp-Spark; he's g-gone; maybe he went off with it."

Just as Pillar Zhu came running over to the barber's for me, Wind Xia said he'd found the money. What he'd done was throw a bill of his own on the ground; then he picked it up, said he'd found it, and gave it to Forest Wu. Forest Wu sniffed the bill, held it up against the sunlight, then gripped it in his hand. He bared his teeth in a grin.

When Wind Xia got home with his cigarettes, Snow Bai was waiting for him at the door.

"Where did you go?" she asked. "You're such an asshole; what made you stay out so late? Dinner's ready and you've kept us all waiting."

"You all eat your dinner," said Wind Xia.

"You need to stay here and talk to Master Qiu," said Snow Bai.

"Hasn't he gone yet?"

"What are you talking about? He's come specially to meet you. How do you think he's going to feel if you snub him like this? How am I going to feel?"

"So he wants to meet me, but I don't want to meet him. I don't like the look of him at all."

"But if you admire someone's art, what does it matter what he looks like?"

"I don't admire his art."

"Well, you may not like Master Qiu, but he's a big shot in the troupe, as big as Master Wang—you've met him. He's not just a good actor; he knows all about the theory of Shaanxi opera, and he wrote the chapter on opera in the county annals," Snow Bai said.

"Did he indeed?" said Wind Xia. "A big shot in community theater, eh?"

"No need to be so pissy," said Snow Bai. "The troupe was about to split into two, but his prestige brought it back together, and now he's come to recruit me."

"I don't care if his crappy outfit splits into four or five; you're coming to the provincial city with me."

"And what will I do there?" Snow Bai protested. "I've spent a dozen years practicing my opera skills. I'm not going unless I can keep going with it."

"You're so pigheaded! Shaanxi opera's nothing nowadays; what's the point of being known for your opera skills? What are you, a lemming? You get yourself a job transfer and come with me, and I'll speak to your Master Qiu and tell him you're not joining his troupe."

Snow Bai was furious. "Don't you dare!"

When Snow Bai was angry, a red mark appeared above her eyebrows. Wind Xia looked at her. He suddenly burst out laughing.

"What are you laughing at?" demanded Snow Bai.

"I thought of a story I once read. It was about two women who both claimed to be princesses, but only one of them could be, and no one knew who the real princess was and who was the fake. So they put a pea under twenty mattresses and made the princesses both sleep on top. The one who slept through the night was the fake; the one who was kept awake because the pea was digging into her was the real princess."

"I know I'm worthless," said Snow Bai. "A dog eats meat but doesn't lay eggs. A hen eats grass and grit and wants to lay eggs; in fact, she gets all backed up if you don't let her drop that egg out."

They carried on arguing until Fourth Auntie came outside. Wind Xia instantly buttoned his lips, went into the yard, and headed for the main house. Snow Bai ran after him and batted the dust off the back of his jacket.

Inside, Wisdom Xia and Master Qiu were talking over their dinner. Qiu was an old man by now. He was completely bald, and his nose was so big it took up half his face. He raised the cup to his lips and drank.

"Are you saying you need to spin three hundred and sixty degrees to do your somersault?" Wisdom Xia was asking.

"Sure. It's the only way I can land on my back facing up," said Master Qiu. "Landing on your butt and shoulder, that's for limber young actors."

Wisdom Xia asked another question: "And balancing things on your forehead—does that require drawing your brows together in a frown?"

"You've got to be able to move the skin on your whole skull," said Qiu, and he demonstrated by wriggling the skin on the top of his head. Then he put a dish on his forehead and moved it backward so steadily that the food in the dish didn't move.

Wisdom Xia applauded, and Fourth Auntie and Snow Bai followed suit. Wind Xia looked at the row of wooden ladles painted with opera masks newly hung on the reception room walls. "That's Zhang Fei's face," he said.

Snow Bai trod on his foot under the table. Wind Xia looked at Zhang Fei, and Zhang Fei looked back at Wind Xia.

Wisdom Xia turned to Master Qiu. "I saw you spitting fire last year in the county seat. The others only managed it once, but you spat fire sixteen times in a row. You must have had a helluva lot of pine resin in your mouth. How did you manage it?"

Master Qiu took a gulp of his wine. Wind Xia looked at his mouth. Master Qiu's upper and lower lips were a mass of wrinkles. Behind him, a fly landed on the wall and stuck there like a nail. "By reverencing the gods," pronounced Master Qiu.

"Reverencing the gods?" asked Wisdom Xia.

"Young Six in our troupe didn't pay his respects properly, and when he spat fire, his whole mouth went up in flames. If you reverence the gods, then they're with you, they possess you. That's the only way to do anything well. Think of the yin-yang masters. Do any of them have any education? No, they don't. But when they practice their art, the gods possess them. You do what they say, and you're safe; you ignore them, and you can expect trouble. Wind Xia, does it work like that when you write your articles? I once met a writer at the County Cultural Institute, and every evening he invoked the spirit of Cao Xueqin, the writer of the great classic *The Dream of the Red Chamber*, to write his novels for him."

"Not likely," said Wind Xia. He reached out with his chopsticks and picked up a peanut, but it bounced away and spun in a circle on the tabletop.

Master Qiu pounced on it and stuffed it in his mouth. "Have you met the writer I was talking about?" he asked Wind Xia. "Chen, his name is. All his teeth are stained black."

"I've read his articles; they're dog shit."

His father glared at him, and Wind Xia got to his feet and clinked his cup respectfully with Master Qiu's.

"Your father loves his opera; I'm sure you must have that love in your genes, too," Qiu said.

"You know about genes?" asked Wind Xia. Behind Master Qiu, he glimpsed Lucky's head. *When did the dog get in?* he wondered.

"*Genes* is a modern word, but our forebears knew all about them all the same. Fan Zidong's opera *The Three Drops of Blood* is all about proving or disproving paternity with drops of blood, and now genes make a cat say *meow*. You write an opera for us, and Snow Bai and I will sing it, and I guarantee it'll be a sensation. It might even win a prize!"

Wind Xia beckoned to Lucky, and the dog squeezed under the table. Wind Xia puffed cigarette smoke in the dog's face. "I don't know anything about opera," he said.

"Wind Xia, can you go and fetch the rice?" asked Snow Bai.

Wind Xia went into the kitchen, and Snow Bai followed him.

"Why are you talking to Master Qiu like that?" she demanded.

"How should I talk to him? If he says the light bulb's black, am I supposed to agree it's black?"

When they went back, Master Qiu was pouring himself more wine. He splashed some of it on the table and bent his head to slurp it up. "Anything in this world can be wasted, but not wine."

"You're a real Wine Immortal; aren't you afraid it'll damage your voice?" said Wind Xia.

"That's the Qinqiang singing style. We Qinqiang folk can only sing if we eat chilies and drink strong liquor. Not like southern opera. Wild horses couldn't drag me to watch that stuff; it's just flimflammery! How do you think the Qin empire vanquished the Six Dynasties? Do you know?"

"No."

"The Qin drank strong liquor and ate all the chilies in their hotpots. That protected them against cold and hunger. When they got their marching orders, they were off at lightning speed. The southerners pitched camp, and then they had to wash their greens and rinse the rice. Before they had dinner ready, the Qin had swooped down and slaughtered them all. You should write an opera piece for us about how the Qin soldiers did things, right?"

"Let me pour you some tea," said Wind Xia. The teapot was empty, and he went to the kitchen and put the water on to boil but then didn't come back with the tea.

Snow Bai left the room and saw Wind Xia and Tongue-Tied playing with Lucky in the yard. She went pale with anger. But Wind Xia smiled mischievously. "Hey, Snow Bai, I've got something to ask you."

"And what would that be?"

"Do you know anyone who works in the County Commerce Department?"

"Why?"

"Pavilion's setting up this farmers market, and he wanted me to ask you if you've got any friends there, because he wants some support."

Snow Bai grunted.

"What's up?"

"You go and ask Master Qiu. His son's head of the department."

"Hah!"

Master Qiu had had too much to drink and was sleeping it off on the kang. Wind Xia went to get Pavilion, and Pavilion sat down by the kang. When Master Qiu woke up, he invited him to his house for more drinks. Wisdom Xia and Snow Bai were invited, too. Obviously, the talk was all about how wonderful Shaanxi opera was. Then they got on to the farmers market.

Master Qiu thumped his chest. "No problem! My son may be a minister of state, but he still calls me Dad when he's back home. I'll tell him."

Pavilion was delighted. "Master Qiu, you're such a hero that I have to serenade you. I'm not good at arias, but I'm going to sing one anyway." And he began singing an aria from *The Pomegranate Doll Lights the Stove*:

I pump the bellows and think of my mother,
I think of my mother at home
Oh mother, mother tell me true:
Why do you leave me alone?

He sang horribly out of tune, and it was not long before his listeners protested. "Your mother never did anything to hurt you; why are you punishing us like this?"

"You sing then, Snow Bai," said Pavilion.

Snow Bai took up the song:

> Life is hard for a girl like me
> I got myself a man, he was a beam supporting little
> Oh, life is hard for a girl like me
> The next man I found, he was just a pimple
> Oh, my man, what a pimple was he!

The next morning, Pavilion was to accompany Master Qiu to the county seat. Snow Bai wanted to go, too, to see the opera troupe. She was hoping Wind Xia would go with her, but a grim-faced Wind Xia said he had to go back to the city.

Chapter 15

I still remember the rat that used to squeeze in through the drainpipe. It was my pet; it would dance around on the rafters for me, and when it got tired, it would stop and eyeball me. Its eyes had no whites; they were just two black beads with a faint, sinister gleam. No cats dared come by our house. Nor did any of the villagers after Dad died, and no one had any idea what I got up to on my own, except that rat. I used to get up early, burn three sticks of incense in front of Dad's memorial portrait, and sit down to write my diary. (I'm the only person in Freshwind who can write enough to keep a diary, you know.) Blue-gray smoke coiled upward from the incense burner; the rat thought it was a rope and tried to climb down it from the rafter. It fell and landed with a thud in the incense burner. Rats are supposed to be clever, but this one was clumsy. All the same, it stuck around in my house and kept me company for ages. That's how you could tell I still had food to eat. Apparently, a boy on East Street fell ill last year, and the family had to sell all their grain to pay a doctor to treat him, whereupon all the rats deserted his house. There's something else: my house rat was educated. When I wrote in my diary about Snow Bai, the rat chewed those pages up. I was amazed.

"Rat," I said, "you know how I feel about Snow Bai now. Well, you go and tell her, if you can." And sure enough, my rat went over to Wisdom Xia's house, and ran back and forth all night over Snow Bai's mosquito net.

"You're evil!" she shouted, and threw an empty powder compact at it. There was still a little face powder in it that got on its ear—a rat with Snow Bai's face powder on it. The pity was that when it squeaked at her "Spark loves you! Spark loves you!" Snow Bai didn't understand. So then my house rat had a good chew on Wisdom Xia's calligraphy and painting scrolls.

Wisdom Xia used to change the scrolls when the fancy took him, hanging them up by turns, and the ones in the main room of the house had to be done by painters with a good reputation in the community. Soon after, Wisdom Xia went looking for the calligraphy scroll by the deputy head of the County Literary Institute, only to discover that the rat had chewed it to tatters. He shut all the doors and windows and hunted the beast down, then told Tongue-Tied to kill it. Tongue-Tied poured kerosene all over it and set it alight in the square in front of the opera theater. The rat screamed and dove into a barley strawstack, setting that on fire, too.

A meeting of the Two Committees had just begun in the temple building. Pavilion, new in the post as Party secretary, was at loggerheads with Concord Qin over the new plans. In Pavilion's mind, the farmers market would be built on the corner of Middle Street and East Street—that is, the triangular patch of ground on the way to the township government offices—and would bring together the farm produce of six local townships.

Pavilion was getting so worked up he'd taken off his jacket. This project, he proclaimed, would revive both the township and the County Department of Commerce, and would be the means of rescuing Freshwind Village from its decline. In fact, it could stimulate the economy of the entire township. He told the meeting that he'd been in touch with the township government and the Department of Commerce, who supported the project, and he'd had drawings done. Then he rolled out the plans—the decorative archway that would be visible from Highway 312; the three-story guesthouse, to be built in the style of the county seat's Fu Lin Restaurant; and the vendors' booths, blue, rainproof shelters, standing on concrete bases. Pavilion talked till he was parched.

"Bring some tea," he demanded. "There's some good stuff on my office desk."

Lotus made the tea, and Pavilion poured cups for everyone.

"We need a market management committee," he went on. "I've given it my consideration, and I think Concord Qin should chair it, and Goodness and Lotus should be vice chairs." Without waiting for anyone to respond, he got a stick and sketched some calculations on the wall. "Freshwind used to have a weekly market. From now on, the new businesses will be open every day, we'll charge the vendors so much in fees, and they'll have a daily turnover of such and such, and they'll pay so much in taxes and management fees . . . times two hundred vendors . . . how much is that a year . . . ?"

He sat back down in his chair and looked around at everyone, fully expecting a round of applause so that he could say, "Excellent! I'm glad to see there's a smile on every face." But there was dead silence in the room.

Concord Qin sat with his head bowed, puffing hard on his cigarette and inhaling the smoke deep into his belly, then exhaling a plume that hit the tabletop and coiled upward, hiding his face from view. Lotus stared fixedly at a mosquito flying around in the smoke as if it were a crane in a cloud. Goodness's eyes were red and inflamed. He dabbed at them with his sleeve, once, twice, but his eyes continued to leak as if they had diarrhea. At least Goodness sat still, unlike the others, who fidgeted, blew their noses noisily, or got up to go to the bathroom or pour more tea or spit gobs of phlegm out the window.

Pavilion tapped his fingers on the table. "Speak up!" he said. "Everyone should be part of deciding a major policy like this."

Still, no one said anything. They didn't even whisper among themselves, so it was impossible to guess what they were thinking.

Finally, Concord Qin spoke. As was his wont, he stumbled over his words and spoke so quietly that he was barely intelligible.

"What was all that about? I couldn't make out a word you were saying," said Goodness.

"Really? Then I'd better say it a bit louder."

Just then, they heard a shrill yell coming from outside the temple compound. "Fire! A strawstack's on fire!"

Lotus went to look out the window. A trail of black smoke roiled in the air like a dragon, and flames shot up above the compound wall, sparking and licking.

"It's a real fire!" she exclaimed, and everyone rushed outside.

One corner of the barley strawstack glowed red hot, and a crowd of children were shrieking in wild excitement. Tongue-Tied had taken off his jacket and was desperately trying to swat the flames with it, but the flames had caught his jacket and even his hair.

Pavilion rushed over and pushed him out of the way, took off his own jacket, and carried on, swatting and shouting, "Bring water! Bring water!"

One bucket of water had no effect, and they brought shovels and spades and earth, but the fire crackled merrily away. Concord Qin could see that the fire was out of control and shouted that they should pull away the half of the stack that had not yet caught. After an hour of frantic effort, half the stack had been pushed aside, though the rest was beyond saving. The villagers' faces were blackened with soot, only their eyes showing white.

"How did the fire start?" asked Pavilion.

He was answered by a chorus of children. "Tongue-Tied set a rat on fire, and it got inside the stack!"

Pavilion gave the boy a kick up the butt. "You're lucky you didn't get burned alive!" he yelled.

Tongue-Tied looked like he'd just come out of a coal mine. He had no hair left, and his jacket was half burned away. He let out a wail and then burst into tears. When Tongue-Tied was angry, no one in Freshwind could get near him, but when he was in the wrong, he just cried.

And where was I, Spark, all this time? When the stack caught alight, I had just come out of the alley and was walking past the theater. My first thought was that I was sorry the bird's nest at the top had gone up, but when I heard that Tongue-Tied had chased a rat out into the square and sprinkled kerosene over it, I realized that my house rat had paid with its life.

I was livid with Tongue-Tied. But after the boy got a kicking from Pavilion, I stopped bothering about his assassination of my house rat and went and told him, "You better go and see Big-Noise Zhao. Get some gentian violet to soothe those burns on your head."

"To hell with the gentian violet!" Pavilion raged. "You go and tell your dad to pay back the owners of the strawstack this minute!"

The Two Committees went back inside Daqing Temple to resume their meeting, but after all the excitement, it took them a while to settle down. The strawstack had apparently belonged to Old Wang's family, who had a rice wine business. Old Wang's wife was always shooting her gob off; she'd give Bounty a hard time, for sure.

Pavilion called them to order. "That's enough of the fire. We have things to discuss."

"You know what they say, 'A fire burns the barriers down and luck comes in its wake,'" Goodness said. "This fire was outside the government offices, so we'll soon be rolling in it, won't we?"

"That's enough of that; tell us what you think of the plan," Pavilion urged him.

"But Concord Qin was talking, wasn't he? Concord Qin, you finish what you were saying."

"Where did I get to?" asked Concord Qin.

"You were talking like you had a walnut in your yap. None of us could understand a word—start over," said Goodness.

"Start over? What can I say? Pavilion's done a helluva lot of work on this, right? He's thought of everything; he's been everywhere. It's no kind of a life being a village cadre. It's not just all this running around; it's having to beg favors and being at other people's beck and call. Pavilion is a really good Party secretary. He's really put himself out for our village; he's worked himself to the bone. He's a better man than I am. I'm older than Pavilion, but I haven't achieved half as much as he has. No one here present today is as good a man as Pavilion is."

"Please don't say things like that," said Pavilion.

"I speak what I feel," said Concord Qin. "Pavilion is a brave man. But rightly or wrongly—and please correct me if I'm wrong—I have the feeling that though the market plan is good, and of course it is, perhaps Freshwind Village isn't ready for it quite yet? Number one, even though Freshwind only has a weekly market, the township to the east of us, Heilongtan, has five markets a week, and Xishantan, to the north of us, has three markets a week, and Teahouse Village to the west has a market every day of the week. And that's the way it's evolved over a hundred years or more. We're a mountain village. Do we really have enough produce to sustain a farmers market? Say we set up this distribution center. What gives us the edge over anywhere else, apart from our proximity to Highway 312? I'm just not sure."

"Number two, business doesn't have a firm footing in the village; we don't do enough trade. Look at the orchard. New-Life Liu has only been able to lease half of it, and the brick-yard hasn't been profitable for years. As for the township fishpond, from what I hear, it's like a pissing widow—all outgoing, nothing coming in. And then there's the river dike and the water mill . . . None of the village projects have made us any money. The dyehouse is not doing badly, for a hole-in-the-wall business, and our building team has a good reputation hereabouts, but that's privately run. The farmers only have their land and what they can grow on it to keep them alive, and there isn't enough land to go around in Freshwind. That's the problem we need to resolve; otherwise we're screwed. In the last few years, a lot of land has gone to building houses, and Highway 312 has taken even more land. The farmers market will not only not solve the land problem but will also take up a substantial area, all of it good farming land. That soil's so fertile that Justice and his team are getting yields of a thousand *jin* per *mu*, and the county awarded them a Red Flag commendation."

Pavilion snorted at that point, and Concord Qin fell silent. Pavilion did not say anything, either. He stubbed a cigarette down hard on the tabletop several times over; then he dipped the butt into his tea and blew hard on the cigarette so the tea squirted out through the filter.

"Go on," said Goodness.

"I've finished," said Concord Qin.

Pavilion's eyelids fluttered and he said, "We on the Two Committees really have to make things happen. If we stick to how cadres used to work, just collecting grain taxes and dragging women off for abortions, I don't want any part in it." He reached out and snatched the mos-quito, pulled one wing off, then the other one, then splatted its body. He sniffed his hand; it smelled bad, and he wiped it on the table leg.

Concord Qin spoke again. "What I mean is, yes, we should make things happen, but the best things are the ones we've inherited from our predecessors; they had big projects, too. Justice and his team never finished the gully-filling at Seven Li Gully, mainly because of the drought. But I don't think the drought will last forever, do you?"

"I knew you'd bring up the gully-filling project. A few days ago, when I was at the res-ervoir, I made a point of coming back via Seven Li Gully to have a look. It's true you could create several hundred *mu* of arable land there. But how long would it be before the project begins to show results? Have you thought about that? And let's suppose the gully is filled and we have that extra land. If the farmers only have the land to rely on, what will the yield be, and how much money can they sell the grain for? The world today isn't like it was ten or twenty years ago; you can't live well just by growing grain. Freshwind used to be one of the county's better-off villages, but not anymore. Grain prices have plummeted, and the cost of stuff like fertilizers, pesticides, and seeds has soared. No matter how much extra land you create, it isn't going to bring the farmers any real benefit. Four people have gone to work in the city from East Street, seven from Middle Street, and five from West Street, and their land's all gone to waste. Getting jobs in the city, I support that, but we can't have all the Freshwind farmers waltzing off there. Life's not a bed of roses for farmers in the city. You're at everyone else's beck and call, you do the work the townsfolk don't want to do, sometimes they don't pay you, industrial accidents are common—I've even heard of villagers being reduced to begging and prostitution. Would you want to beg on the streets? Would you want your wife or daughter to be a prostitute? But they all need the money!" Pavilion was so worked up he waved his arm and knocked his teacup over. The tea snaked across the table, and the cup crashed to the floor and shattered, making everyone jump at the noise. Lotus bent down to clear up the pieces.

"Never mind that, Lotus," said Pavilion, and he kicked the fragments under the table. "Go on, Concord Qin."

"That's what I think," said Concord Qin.

"Nothing more?" asked Pavilion.

"Nope."

"Then let's hear what everyone else thinks," said Pavilion.

No one spoke.

It was quite normal for people not to open their mouths during the Freshwind Two Committees meetings; they left the talking to the people running the meeting. In general, Justice Xia was the most voluble. He was not as educated as Pavilion. But he had a good memory, and he had the gift of delivering fine-sounding paired phrases, so he could fire up his audience. He was always swearing and using bad language, too, which had the curious effect of making him sound furious and heartfelt at the same time.

Justice Xia and my dad, when he was alive, were polar opposites, and one time when Justice Xia had a birthday dinner, my dad had fallen out with him and refused to go. Justice Xia stood on top of the dike looking down on my dad on the river beach below and yelled, "Why the fuck won't you come to my birthday? Do you hate me that much? Tonight, you've got to come and drink with me, and you've got to bring me some booze. I'm telling you I'll drink you under the table, you fucker!"

My dad didn't mind being sworn at, and that evening, he set off cheerfully to Justice Xia's house, carrying the liquor.

Pavilion Xia just didn't have the same popular touch. Instead, he worked himself up, talking until the scars on his face glowed bright red and the spittle gathered at the corner of his lips. He also used to tug so hard at his forelock when he was talking that he gave himself a bald patch.

Still, no one in the meeting spoke up, and Pavilion got worked up again and started tugging at a tuft of hair.

"You say something," one of the Public Order Committee members urged Goodness. "If you don't speak up, Pavilion will pull all his hair out."

Lotus burst out laughing, then hurriedly suppressed it when she saw the others staring fixedly at a long crack in the wall opposite with poker faces. It looked like a tree was growing through.

Goodness rubbed his eyes, then lowered his lids. "Listening to Pavilion, I felt what he said made sense. But then Concord Qin spoke, and I felt he made sense, too. If Pavilion says anything more, I expect that'll make sense, too. It's all very difficult; we're only trying to do the best for the community. We have to consider all the options carefully, very carefully indeed."

"That's as bad as saying nothing at all," said Pavilion.

"I'm not trying to paper over the cracks," Goodness protested. "But whatever we do, whether it's build a farmers market or fill in the gully, we have to shell out money. I'm the bookkeeper; I know how little money there is in the village coffers. Where are we going to get the starter funds? Justice Xia never managed to turn his good intentions into real achievements before he stepped down; that's something we should draw lessons from."

Pavilion got to his feet and stood there for a few moments, then went out of the room.

"He gets so fired up, and he feels like we've poured cold water on his big project," said Lotus.

"He's gone to the bathroom," said Goodness.

"He's so upset, his piss'll come out black," said Lotus.

"The rest of you, speak up," said Concord Qin. "I know you've got firm opinions about it. Why can't you open your mouths in these meetings?"

Pavilion came back in, his head dripping from the dousing he'd given it under the courtyard faucet. "It's time for lunch," he said, "but not until the meeting's worked out some ideas."

After some grumbling ("An army can't march on an empty stomach . . . Feed us properly, and then we'll tell you what we think . . ."), they began to speak. But still, opinions were divided—some for the farmers market, others for the gully-filling project.

"You're hopelessly at odds with each other," said Pavilion. "I've heard that in Shanmen County, their cadres are directly elected by the villagers. I can't imagine how that system works."

"If you get ten people in a room, you'll get ten different opinions," said Lotus. "We wouldn't reach agreement if we talked until tomorrow. Democratic centralism means democracy *and* centralism, so the leaders have to decide."

Pavilion spat on the floor. "Okay, meeting's over."

While this raucous discussion was going on in the temple building, Old Wang's wife had wasted no time in running to Bounty's home to demand compensation for the loss of their strawstack.

Bounty had no idea what she was talking about. "I need to ask Tongue-Tied what happened," he said.

"He's mute; how's he going to tell you?"

"He knows how to nod and shake his head, doesn't he?" But Bounty couldn't find the boy anywhere. That was because he was hiding at mine.

When Bounty couldn't find him outside, he turned round and went back home, where Old Wang's wife was still kicking up a fuss. "Tongue-Tied's a counterrevolutionary!" she wailed. "He deliberately set that fire. And you're deliberately shielding him, and that's counterrevolutionary, too. And counterrevolutionary fires kill people!"

Bounty tried arguing with her until he had nothing left to say except, "A man shouldn't fight with a woman."

Old Wang's wife was so enraged she grabbed a bit of rope and slung it over the doorframe. "I'll string myself up right here and give you a human door curtain!"

At that, Bounty gave her his own family's barley strawstack in compensation.

Later that afternoon, Tongue-Tied crept home. Bounty tied him up with a rope and gave him a beating. Culture went straight and told Justice Xia.

Justice had come back from the rice paddy, his legs coated with gray-black mud, which he was scraping off with a strip of bamboo. "It's what he deserves," was his response.

Culture left again, then came back to report that Tongue-Tied had been strung up from the doorframe and his dad had beaten him so hard he'd broken the stick he used to wedge the gate shut.

Justice Xia was stewing up some tea leaves for himself. When it was good and strong, he repeated, "It's what he deserves!"

Culture left again, then came back to report back that Tongue-Tied had been beaten so badly he'd pissed his pants.

Justice Xia was smoking one of his rollies, packed with dark tobacco. "It's what he deserves!"

When Culture left once more, Justice Xia shut the yard gate behind him. After a little while, he heard the gate ring twisting back and forth, creaking and groaning. "I don't want to know!" he yelled.

But it was his wife, Bamboo. She told him what had happened in the Two Committees meeting, and Justice Xia laughed.

"Why are you laughing, husband?" she asked.

"Concord Qin's making progress."

"Right, Concord Qin's not afraid to speak out, but there's no way Pavilion is going to listen to him," she said.

"You better go," he said.

As soon as she'd gone, Justice, his cigarette dangling from his lips, draped his jacket over his shoulders and let himself out. He passed Bounty's place and heard Tongue-Tied's hoarse cries inside the yard. Justice Xia coughed once, and Bounty stopped his beating. Tongue-Tied yelled louder than ever, but, disappointingly, his granddad didn't come into the yard, and they heard his footsteps fading into the distance.

As Justice Xia strolled along East Street, Middle Street, and West Street, a lot of people were learning that members of the Two Committees disagreed and that the old village head was against Pavilion's proposals. There had been an outcry when Justice Xia hadn't succeeded in filling the gully, but when he stepped down, the villagers felt they had been unfair to him. Justice Xia was always the last person to line his own pockets, after all. He had far more experience than Pavilion, and if he was against Pavilion's plans, then maybe Pavilion was being rash. And there was something more: Pavilion had put Marvel in charge of the newly installed electricity transformer and paid him an increased fee. In other words, Pavilion gave nice jobs to people who were nice to him. The farmers market, the archway, the hotel building, and the market area would all need to be built, and who knew who would get those nice jobs?

"We're against the market, too. Better for us all to be poor than for a few to get rich," was the general opinion.

I was against a local specialty products market, too. I tagged along behind Justice Xia. He went to the dyehouse, I went to the dyehouse; he went to the Great Qing Hall to talk to Big-Noise Zhao, I went to the Great Qing Hall to talk to Big-Noise Zhao.

I talked to people. "Don't you think it's a crazy idea to build a farmers market there? That land is so fertile you can stick a chopstick in the earth, and it'll burst into bloom. It's a waste of good land."

The villagers turned to Justice Xia. "You used to be the village head; what do you think?"

"You're not a farmer unless you have land."

"Then we're with you!"

Justice Xia did not respond. He clasped his hands behind his back and walked on. Folds of flesh rippled down the back of his neck and jiggled with every step he took.

I jogged up behind him. "Uncle Justice, Uncle Justice, the back of your neck's all greasy."

Justice Xia ignored me.

"Your collar has grease on it!"

He still took no notice.

"Won't it ruin your jacket?"

Beside me, Roughshod Ding said, "You're just the same as Lucky, Spark."

I didn't like that comment at all. When Lucky was out with Justice Xia, anytime Tiger appeared, she chased after him instead. I didn't switch allegiances like that.

We finally got to the restaurant run by Clerk's wife on Middle Street, and Justice Xia looked around at me. "You want some *liang fen* noodles? It's on me."

"You hit Clerk last year; will his wife sell them to us?" said I.

"I hit Clerk?"

"During the reforestation project at Bowed Ox Ridge, Clerk was going on about exchanging his land, and you hit him across the face."

"I'd forgotten, and you still fucking remember." He stood at the restaurant door and sucked hard on his rollie.

Clerk's wife hailed him. "It's Mr. Xia!"

"Call me Second Uncle, please," said Justice Xia.

"Have you eaten, Second Uncle?" the woman asked. Then, without waiting for an answer, she said, "Please, take a seat." And she wiped a stool clean with her sleeve.

"Spark here tells me I hit Clerk last year, so he thinks you'll refuse to sell us *liang fen* noodles," Justice Xia said.

"He's crazy, so he talks crazy talk. You've known Clerk since he was a little boy; why shouldn't you hit him? 'Spare the rod and spoil the child'! It's all part of tough love."

"Fine, then wash a couple of bowls and give us two portions of *liang fen* noodles."

And Justice Xia and me, we hunkered down in the restaurant doorway and ate our *liang fen*.

Justice Xia couldn't take strong drink. What he loved was a rollie, packed with dark tobacco, plus a bowl of *liang fen*. During the "struggles" of the Cultural Revolution, once the parades of struggled-against people in their clownish tall hats were over, he used to treat himself to a bowl of *liang fen* at a street stall. The day he was forced to step down as village head, there he was, sitting on the sidewalk, eating his bowl of *liang fen*. Whenever he had something important going on, he had to have a bowl of *liang fen* with plenty of vinegar and chilies. The most important organ in his body, I reckon, was not his brain; it was his stomach. Now he sat there, taking a puff on his rollie and then a mouthful of noodles, his mouth stained red with the chilies, the sweat pouring off him.

Pavilion rode along West Street on his motorbike and got off at the archway. He hadn't seen Justice, whose head was bowed over his noodles.

"Pavilion was driving fast," I said.

"He's upset," said Justice Xia.

Chapter 16

By now Pavilion was getting anxious. He'd sounded out the villagers and discovered that not nearly as many of them supported the farmers market project as he'd thought. So he got on his motorbike and went to the brickyard to talk to Shifty. He normally didn't waste much time on Shifty, but the other villagers feared him and would do a lot to avoid getting on the wrong side of him. Given the influence that Shifty seemed to wield over them, Pavilion felt he could use him to drum up support. He found the man sprawled on the kang in the brickyard office, his shirt pulled up to show his great belly, while by the window a girl was chopping up the filling for dumplings with rapid smack-smack-smacks of her cleaver.

"You live a good life, Shifty; no wonder people are jealous of you."

Shifty sat up. The crisscross pattern of the kang matting had made marks all over his back.

"Your tree roots don't shift in a gale, Pavilion, and even the treetop doesn't sway much."

"How do you know my roots don't shift, Shifty?"

"I may be a peasant," said Shifty, "but I can't stand the dumb way peasants make fun of you if you're poor but resent it if you do well. I've been running this brickyard for years. I've never earned that much for the village, but I haven't messed it up, either. Now there's all this talk about someone else taking over the lease, but I'm telling you, there's not one person anywhere in the village, from East Street to West Street to Middle Street, who's capable of doing any better with this brickyard—you'll understand that, even if no one else does."

"You know Freshwind inside out, Shifty."

"Well, there aren't many souls to know, even in the graveyard," said Shifty, then continued, "Pavilion, you spend your time making plans for Freshwind Village, and it all comes to nothing. They've even poured cold water on the market plan."

"Is there anything you don't know? Tell me what you've heard."

Shifty suddenly became friendlier. He gave Pavilion a smoke and a cup of herbal tea, then said to the girl, "You've minced it enough. Take it outside and make the *jiaozi*, and make plenty; the Party secretary is staying for a meal."

When she'd gone, Pavilion asked, "Who's that? How come I haven't seen her before?"

"Lovely fair skin, eh?" said Shifty. "It's like that all the way down her body, too."

"Now then, just behave yourself."

"Would I dare? That's White-Moth, Forest Wu's sister-in-law; she's doing a bit of work for me in the brickyard." Then he went on: "The villagers are all saying something different about the farmers market; they're getting it all out of proportion."

Pavilion looked thoroughly disheartened.

"I've shot my big mouth off again, haven't I?" said Shifty.

"No, carry on."

"Are you really up for all that work?"

"I'm a big boy; I'm not worried."

Outside, White-Moth was busy making *jiaozi* dumplings. All they could see of her through the door was one long leg stretched out and a sandal-clad foot with a big toe markedly longer than the others.

Pavilion shifted his stool till he couldn't see that foot any longer and said, "I know what I'm doing; that's why I'm Party secretary."

"Right," said Shifty. "So this is how I see it: the villagers are scared shitless because they're poor and don't want to fund projects. The reason they don't want the farmers market is they figure outsiders will get the contracts and get rich from it. Plus, who's going to get the sellers' stalls?"

"You've always got to have some people getting rich first, and they pull the others along behind them. I'm not my second uncle, or Concord Qin."

"Yes, anyone who puts in money should get a stall—that should be the rule, no exceptions. That way, you'll get a lot of support."

"How much support, do you think?" asked Pavilion.

Shifty went through all the households from East Street through to West Street, one by one. He figured there'd be more support from West Street because fewer cadres lived there; it was mostly small traders. A fair number of the folk on Middle Street should be in favor, too. But he didn't think there'd be much support from East Street, "apart from your second uncle, maybe."

"Well, the only thing I care about is that you don't screw things up for me," declared Pavilion.

"I know which side my bread is buttered on," said Shifty. "You could ruin my business just like that, if you had a mind to."

"And I want you to speak out in favor of it, too."

"No problem, just so long as you treat me well in return."

But Pavilion told him, "You've got a few days, and then you've got to pay over what the brickyard owes. The village needs the money. And get the bricks ready for the archway and the hotel. You'll get paid for those after the market starts to make money."

Shifty stared at him. "Pavilion, did you come to ask my advice or to put me in my place?"

"Both."

"If I'd known, I'd have made myself scarce."

"Too late for that; I haven't had those *jiaozi* yet."

They finished their dumplings, and Shifty saw Pavilion to the gate.

Pavilion whispered to him, "If you keep that sister-in-law of Forest Wu's here, your wife will come and kick up a fuss with me, and I won't be able to defend you."

"All right, I give in. After all, you surely won't stop at village Party secretary. You'll be promoted one day, maybe as high as county head."

"Well, if I get to be county head, I'll give you a department to run, and that's a promise." And Pavilion put his arm around Shifty's shoulders. "Shifty, you're a scoundrel, but I can't help liking you."

Pavilion set off on his motorbike, feeling much more cheerful. He rode right around the triangular site of the proposed market, then stopped and got off. Hands clasped behind his back, he paced it out, width and length. Then he reached into his pants and began to piss, tracing the characters of his name as he did so. By this time, night had fallen, and Pavilion pushed his motorbike into the alley off East Street, passing by Wisdom Xia's home. The gate was open, and he could see Rain Xia in the yard, scratching the trunk of the tickle tree. The whole tree shook with his movements, and the leaves rustled as if they were laughing.

"You're back late. Come in," said Rain Xia.

"Has your brother left?" asked Pavilion.

"Long time ago."

"And Fourth Uncle?"

"Dad's indoors with Second and Third Uncles. Come on in."

"No, I don't want to butt in on the old boys' conversation."

Snow Bai was back from the county seat with a bottle of good liquor, and Wisdom Xia had invited his older brothers over. They filled their cups and toasted each other, and it all went down very nicely. The four Xia brothers were well known in Freshwind Village for their closeness; if any of them had anything good to eat or drink, like red-cooked pork, a jar of tea, or a bunch of Chinese toon sprouts in springtime, they'd be sure to invite the other three along to share it.

"Good wine," said Wisdom Xia appreciatively. There was a noise in the yard outside. "Who is it, Rain Xia?" he asked.

"Pavilion, but he's gone already."

"Why did he go, if he knew we were having a drink?" said Wisdom Xia.

"He's avoiding me," said Justice Xia.

"Why?"

"I don't want to talk about it. Have another drink."

Suddenly they heard the sounds of an argument next door.

"Treasure and his wife are a match made in hell," said Wisdom Xia. "They're always fighting. The sooner the new house is built and we can move out of here, the better; that way I can get some peace and quiet." He turned to his wife. "Go and see what it's about, will you?"

Fourth Auntie went, but she didn't come back, and the shouting got louder. It didn't sound like Treasure and his wife now; it was Gold's wife bawling out Halfwit, and the yells were earsplitting. Rites Xia went out but came back to say, "Wisdom, you go."

Justice Xia was furious. "They're like a fucking flock of cocks and hens pecking each other in the henhouse. The poorer they are, the more they fight, and the more they fight, the poorer they get!" He was about to rush next door when Wisdom and Rites got hold of him.

"I'll go," said Wisdom Xia. And he went, carrying his water pipe. Justice Xia was still pale with anger. "How on earth did I give birth to trash like this, brother? They're an embarrassment," he said to Rites.

"All families argue. Don't take it to heart. Wisdom's gone to sort them out; no one's going to argue with him."

And the shouts had indeed died away.

The old way in Freshwind was not to grow eggplant in one row and cowpeas in the next, but to sow everything all mixed together. When you harvested the ripe walnuts from the trees, you whacked the branches with a long bamboo cane. The odd thing was that once you thought you'd gotten every walnut off, if you moved around and took another look, suddenly you'd see one that you'd missed. You could never completely clear a tree of walnuts.

Village issues were always messy like that, too. Pavilion and Concord Qin had swapped their jobs in Freshwind; one wanted to build a market, and the other wanted to finish the gully-filling. A lot of people had strong feelings about all this; everyone was convinced their views were vitally important, and everyone felt they had a responsibility to make those views known.

Arguments raged throughout the village. Passions ran so high—tables were thumped, benches were kicked over—that the more timid villagers slunk off home and refused to go out anymore, or to express an opinion. Pavilion asked Bounty Xia to pull together a work team to build the archway and the hotel, his condition being that Bounty get the folk from East

Street on board—in particular, his Xia clan. Of course, Bounty was delighted to oblige until he discovered that his dad was for the gully-filling.

Next, Concord Qin tried to enlist his support for the gully-filling on the grounds that it would bring long-term benefits and be good for their dad's track record and reputation, too. The five Xia brothers couldn't make up their minds. After dinner that day, Treasure got them over to his house for a family discussion. Gold wasn't there, having gone to his work to try to transfer his job to his son so he could retire, but Chastity came in his place. She sat on the edge of the kang, stitching shoe soles as she listened, the linen thread hissing as she pulled it through her fabric.

They managed to come to an agreement. They would not take one side or the other; they'd wait it out and see how things developed. If the village decided to build the farmers market, then Bounty would definitely get the commission and would get a few stalls, too. If the gully-filling project won out, then there was the matter of moving the family graves to consider.

Three years previously, when the Seven-Li Gully project had been put on hold and their dad, Justice Xia, stepped down, he didn't seem to mind and simply went out to get himself a bowl of *liang fen* noodles in the village, while their mom was so furious she made herself ill. Afraid she was going to die, the brothers divided up their duties. Gold, as the oldest, would arrange the funerals of both their parents when the time came; Treasure and Hearth were responsible for the funeral shroud and the coffin for one parent each; and Bounty and Halfwit were responsible for the graves. They settled on a twin tomb to accommodate both parents but couldn't decide where the plot should be sited. Finally, their father chose the foot of the slope in Seven-Li Gully.

"That's where I want to be buried," he said. "I've battled through all the odds in my life, but Seven Li Gully has been my downfall. So I'll stand guard over the place when I'm dead."

They dug out the graves, but then their mother recovered, although she did lose her sight. Now, if the gully was really going to be filled, the graves would have to be moved.

"Bounty and I spent twelve hundred yuan getting those tombs built," Halfwit said. "When we move them, we'll be able to reuse some of the old bricks, sure, but a lot will be wasted. And we'll need to pay a bricklayer, too, and buy more cement and lime. I've done a rough estimate—I figure it'll cost us six hundred to seven hundred yuan. We'll do the moving, we'll put ourselves out, but it's not fair that we should have to fork over that much. I suggest we share the expense between the five households."

Chastity protested. She jabbed the needle into the sole of the shoe she was stitching. "We agreed all this a long time ago. Why change it now? Take the funerals. We took that on and agreed to a feast for fifty guests. What happens if eighty people turn up? I can't turn them away, can I? What happens if they croak, and we can't bury them within the three days because the yin-yang master says it's not propitious? Suppose we have to wait six or seven days for the funeral; are you all going to split the costs of meals for the extra four days?"

Treasure and Hearth agreed. "Sister-in-law's got a point. We're not forking out for moving the graves."

"Well then, let's change who's doing what. I'll hold the funerals; you can dig the graves," said Halfwit.

"And we all eat shit?" said Chastity. "You're the youngest, and the parents have always protected you. You've got nothing to complain about."

"Yeah, I'm the youngest, and I've never had a share in the benefits my older brothers get."

"No? And what about when you wanted a wife? The good ones wouldn't look at you, and the others all wanted expensive gifts. Our dad said we should all chip in, and we did, even though we'd all set up separate households by then. How can you treat the old folks with such lack of respect now?"

"Me? Lack of respect? What about you? Our dad looks after your family's land for you, but have you even bought him a scrap of cloth for new clothes? Big brother has a government job and earns a good salary every month, and what kind of clothes do our mom and dad have to go around in? You know why our mom got sick? It's because she couldn't stand to see you two eating meat and our dad standing at your gate asking if you'd brought the harvest in yet, and you were too scared to open the gate to him. That's what made our mom ill with anger."

"So you're putting the blame on me for that?" Chastity exclaimed. And she whacked Halfwit over the head with the shoe sole.

Halfwit had a big mouth, but at heart he was a coward. He grabbed the broom and hit Chastity with it, then fled out the door.

Treasure, Bounty, and Hearth stopped Chastity from going after him. She slumped to the floor and burst into floods of tears. Fourth Auntie tried to calm her down, without success, and Rites Xia had even less success, but when Wisdom Xia turned up, Chastity hurriedly stopped wailing, and Halfwit, who was standing outside the door, stopped his swearing, too.

"Bring a chair out," Wisdom Xia commanded. Hearth hurriedly obeyed. Wisdom Xia sat down. "Now then," he said. "Why have you suddenly stopped all this crying and swearing? It must have been something good; I want to hear it. Come on, spit it out!" Treasure, Bounty, and Hearth almost fell over themselves to apologize.

Then Bounty said, "Halfwit, say sorry to Fourth Auntie."

"Only if we settle who's going to fork over the seven hundred yuan," said Halfwit.

At that, Wisdom Xia's hands shook, and he almost choked with fury. Chastity shot him an urgent glance, and he said with a grim smile, "If you don't want to fork over the money, then why don't you let your mom's and dad's corpses rot in a ditch and be done with it!"

Treasure kicked Halfwit. "Let's stop the meeting. In the future, if we need to discuss family business, we'll make it just the brothers and keep the womenfolk out of it. Off you go, everyone! I'll stay and calm Fourth Uncle down."

He lit Wisdom Xia's pipe, but the old man sat motionless and wouldn't take it. Bounty set a cup of tea beside him, but he ignored that, too.

"Take him home," said Fourth Auntie.

So Treasure and Bounty picked up the chair with their uncle in it between them and carried him back to his gate.

Having quelled his nephews and niece and arrived home, Wisdom began to drink with Justice. But his brother was not in a good mood, and before he'd finished one bottle, he was drunk. Rain Xia helped his second uncle along the road toward his home in the scorpion's tail of the village. Justice clung to his arm and shambled along, muttering, "Your third uncle's not well; I gotta go and help him home." But once at his own gate, he yelled, "Open up! Open up!" There was no response from Second Auntie, and he gave it a hefty thump with his foot. The bolt had been shot across inside, but now it burst open, and Justice fell backward into Rain Xia's arms. Inside the yard, the house's front door was bolted, too.

Rain Xia whispered, "Second Uncle, wait! This door's got panes of glass in it."

"Okay," Justice Xia muttered. "Panes of glass; I'd better not kick it then."

Not many of the village folk ever got to hear about this incident.

For the next three days, a great red sun hung in the sky by day, no stars were visible after it got dark, and the wind blew hard. Mid-Star's dad had had the runs for a long time—and that evening he went out to buy an herbal remedy. On his way back, he bumped into Treasure pushing a handcart to the brickyard for some bricks.

"What's up with you?" asked Treasure. "You spend all day reading the signs for other people; how come you've fallen sick yourself?"

"Physicians can't heal themselves," said Mid-Star's dad. Then he asked, "Is the market going ahead?"

"Why would you care?"

"It's just that if it is, Pavilion should go and talk to Mid-Star, because he works in the county government." His stomach was giving him trouble again, and he hurried off, holding up his pants with one hand, to find an out-of-the-way spot.

Talk to Mid-Star? Fat lot of good that'll do, thought Treasure. Mid-Star had transferred to the county offices after leaving the army, but he had no particular responsibilities there. Treasure laughed in the darkness and went on his way to the brickyard.

In the brickyard, Treasure told Shifty about the family argument; once he'd left, Shifty went to pass on this tidbit to Pavilion. His analysis of the situation was that if Justice Xia's family were having all these fights, then opposition to the gully-filling might build up and East Street would not present them with much of a problem. However, he added the further news that Concord Qin's supporters were doing a lot of lobbying on Middle Street and West Street. He'd just passed a bunch of them—Righteous Lian, Soldier, New-Life Liu, and Goodness Li—on their way to the cultural center with Concord Qin. Ten to one, they'd be urging him on over a game of mah-jongg.

Pavilion heard him out, then said, "You like a drink?"

"No, thanks," said Shifty.

But Pavilion got out a bottle and made him take it anyway.

As he escorted Shifty out, Pavilion saw White-Moth sitting at the end of the alley on the stone roller, cracking melon seeds between her teeth, but he pretended he hadn't seen her.

Back home, Ma Qiao said to him, "What's Shifty doing, taking Forest Wu's sister-in-law around with him everywhere?"

"I don't know," said Pavilion. And he picked up the phone on top of the counter.

That phone call changed everything in Freshwind Village—and that's no lie. Pavilion was calling the township local police. He never told them that he was Pavilion Xia; as the village Party secretary, he simply said he had something to report: there were a bunch of people gambling in the cultural center. He made his call, then went to bed.

He slept like a log. He slept right through Old Wang felling his toon tree nearby; not even the heavy thuds of the ax, the tremendous crash the tree made when it fell, the squawking of the hens, or the barks of the dogs woke him. Old Wang picked up his flashlight and shone it on the stump of the toon—and got the fright of his life. The whole stump was covered in blood. He looked at the end of the tree trunk, and that was pouring blood, too. In a panic, Old Wang grabbed his ax and rushed off home. No one believed it when the story came out, but you can take my word for it—it was absolutely true.

At that moment, I was hiding behind a low wall with Tongue-Tied, and we were cooking up a practical joke. Tongue-Tied had come to my house before nightfall and waved his hands and signed until finally I understood that Old Wang's wife was bending his dad's ear about the strawstack fire. He was terrified of getting a hiding from his dad and wanted to get revenge on the woman. Tongue-Tied didn't know his own strength, and I was worried he might take it out on the Wang boy and do him an injury or destroy their crops, so I suggested something different: Why not put a turd in a snack box and leave it outside their gate for Wang or his wife to pick up, ideally when they were carrying their *laozao* rice drink, balanced on a shoulder pole?

So Tongue-Tied and I were hiding behind a low wall, waiting to see what would happen. Neither of them came out; instead, Goodness came hurrying by. He spotted the box, looked around to make sure there was no one in sight, grabbed it, and scurried away, then opened it and threw it back down again. It was a pity but still funny, though Tongue-Tied and I didn't dare laugh. We waited until Goodness had gone some distance before we emerged, and just at that moment Old Wang came home, carrying his ax.

He caught up with Goodness. "The toon tree bled when I felled it. Why do you think that is?"

"Don't talk nonsense; you're not Spark!"

"It really did bleed." And Old Wang took Goodness and Tongue-Tied and me to have a look. The blood had formed a big puddle.

"It's a woman tree; it's got its period," I said.

Goodness dipped his finger in the blood and tasted it. "Nonsense," he said. "Toon tree sap's red; this is just a bit redder than usual, that's all." And he laughed at us for being so easily taken in.

I didn't agree with Goodness, and I was getting ready to tackle him when Concord Qin, New-Life Liu, Righteous Lian, and Soldier came by and shouted that they were off to the cultural center to play a few rounds of mah-jongg. Tongue-Tied and I wanted to tag along. If they were going to play, then so were we.

"Who asked you two to come? We have stuff to talk about," Goodness said.

"What are you talking about that you're worried we'll tell?" I protested. "I'm hard of hearing, and Tongue-Tied can hear but can't speak."

"Come on then," said Concord Qin. "You're not outsiders."

"Oh, okay," said Goodness. "But if I lose, you can cough up the money, Spark."

"You're bound to lose," I muttered. "You've got rotten luck."

So there they were in the cultural center, playing mah-jongg and chewing over the gully-filling project. They got me and Tongue-Tied to serve them; we could watch, but we had to keep quiet. They had just played one round when three of the local police crept into the courtyard. The first to see them was Tongue-Tied, who was standing in the doorway taking a sneaky drag on Goodness's cigarette. He watched as they crept past the tower looking just like Japs in a war film, then suddenly split up, one racing round to the back window and the other two rushing the front door.

Tongue-Tied threw down his cigarette and gave a howl. He couldn't talk, but he tried frantically to block the doorway. The police tried to pull him out of the way, and when he wouldn't move, they gave him a shove and the door banged open and Tongue-Tied tumbled backward into the room. Goodness was the lucky one; he had gone out to the bathroom just three minutes before. The others—Concord Qin, New-Life, Righteous Lian, and Soldier— were caught red-handed. They stood rooted to the spot, stupefied.

I made a dive for the back window, fell out, and felt the third policeman gripping my hair. "Think you'll escape this way, do you?" And he dragged me back into the room. New-Life Liu had gone green around the gills. He quickly swept the bills off the table, but one of the policemen spotted him. "Put that money in here!" he shouted and flung a cloth bag onto the table.

"But everyone plays mah-jongg. You do, too!" Righteous Lian protested.

"Of course we do," said the policeman. "Difference is, you're going to be arrested for it."

"Where are you from; how come I don't recognize you?" New-Life asked them.

"You'd know our sergeant, for sure, but our sergeant's not going to come in person, is he? You'll know Constables Wang and Wu, too; they were here a week ago, checking up on the teahouse. We're new; this is our first visit, but you know us now."

Concord Qin spoke up at this point. "Comrades, see, the thing is, we came here to talk something over. The mah-jongg was just a bit of fun so we didn't get bored . . . And, hey, don't the local police usually turn a blind eye to betting a couple of yuan here or there?"

"We used to turn a blind eye, but now we've got quotas. Every year, each one of us has to collect and pay over five yuan in police fines, so if we didn't come today, how would we reach our targets?"

I couldn't stand the way the policeman was obviously winding us up, like a cat torments a mouse. Tongue-Tied was glaring at the police officers. He suddenly jumped on the one guarding the doorway and shouted, "Run! Run!"

Two of them pinioned his arms and twisted them behind his back. "Don't you dare move. We'll cuff you!"

The rest of us didn't dare move, either. "Tongue-Tied, you can speak!" I exclaimed. But those were the only two words that Tongue-Tied ever spoke in his whole life.

Meanwhile, New-Life Liu picked the bills up off the floor and put them in the bag. Then he reached into his pockets, pulled out some more, and added them. "That's all there is."

Soldier got some bills out of his breast pocket. He went to put them in the bag, but his hand wouldn't lose its grip, and one of the officers struck him on the arm. His fingers opened, and the bills fell out.

Concord Qin had no money on him. He said he hadn't brought any; he'd borrowed from the others and lost it all.

Righteous Lian smiled unctuously. "Please feel free to fine us all you like. But Mr. Concord Qin here is the head of Freshwind Village, so you'd better let him go."

"You mean the village head is a gambler? In that case, we certainly can't let him go; our chief'll have to deal with this." The officers swept up the whole tablecloth, complete with the mah-jongg set, and got ready to haul us all off to the local police station.

There was a sudden thud from behind the tower and the sound of running feet. I knew it was Goodness—he was the one who'd picked up the snack box with the turd inside it, and now he'd had the luck of the devil. I couldn't get my head around it.

"The boys weren't playing; can't you let them go?" said Concord Qin. The police officers looked at Tongue-Tied but ignored him because he couldn't talk. Then they searched me. There was nothing in my jacket pocket or in my cuffs. They looked at my pants.

"Anything down there?"

"Nope." I meant I'd cut off my thing, but they thought I meant I had nothing in my pants pocket, and they pushed me out of the way. Huh! I was cleverer than they thought. I had 122 yuan in my pants pocket. Concord Qin, Righteous Lian, and New-Life went out of the room, but Soldier stood right where he was.

"Out with you!" shouted one of the officers.

"Coming," said Soldier. He put his foot under the table and kicked something toward me, then followed them out of the room. I looked down at my feet, saw a roll of hundred-yuan bills, and quickly picked it up and palmed it.

In the station, the sergeant recognized them, of course. He didn't take them into custody or fine them or take written statements, but he hung on to the money in the bag, on the grounds that it had already been confiscated, so they couldn't give it back. Concord Qin felt he'd been particularly treated unjustly because he wasn't a habitual gambler, not compared with the many Freshwind villagers who played mah-jongg a lot and never got arrested. There was something odd about the whole business. When the sergeant went to the bathroom, he inspected the phone on the table and noticed that Pavilion's number was displaying as the last call. Everything went black before his eyes, and he collapsed and hit his head on the corner of the table.

By the next day, the news was all over the village. The only thing anyone was interested in was that Concord Qin had been arrested for gambling; no one cared who the others were. Some of them had a good laugh about it; others were angry with Pavilion.

Goodness, who loved his mah-jongg, was the angriest. In the village government offices, he said to Lotus, "You do what you can, and you don't do what you can't, but you can't use underhanded methods like that."

Pavilion happened to overhear his comment and was mortified. He shouted furiously, "Yes, it was me who reported them. And from now on, I'll report anyone in Freshwind who gambles!"

Goodness muttered angrily, but he was a mild-mannered man and not given to arguing, so he let it drop.

Concord Qin, however, actually fell ill and stayed home for a few days. When Pavilion came by the office, Goodness wouldn't speak to him. Pavilion was definitely out on a limb. But he needed to call a meeting to discuss the market project, and so one day he brought some wine with him so he and Goodness could share a few drinks. When he got there, there was no one to be seen. The bookkeeper's office door was shut, too. Pavilion called a few times, but no one answered, and he sat gloomily on the steps of the main hall and waited. He needed to bring everyone together again, and he'd wait for Goodness for as long as it took. After about half an hour, the bookkeeper's office door opened, and Lotus came out. As she tiptoed away, she spotted Pavilion and gaped at him in shock. Pavilion felt a throbbing in his temples. He got to his feet, then sat down again.

"Mr. Secretary, haven't you gone yet?"

"Have you finished what you were doing?"

"I was helping Goodness reconcile some accounts."

Goodness heard their voices and came out himself. "Were you looking for me?"

"You look hot; better go and wash your face," said Pavilion. Goodness washed his face in the washbowl, and his hair, and he made sure to spend a long time over it. Then he slowly came back to Pavilion, who said, "And hadn't you better clean up down there, too?"

Goodness looked down to see some white crud on the zipper of his pants. He slumped down on the steps.

"Pavilion, we only did it once; please don't tell anyone."

Pavilion heaved a sigh, then smiled. "What is there to tell? You haven't done anything that I can see. Lotus, go and buy us some snacks; Goodness and I are going to have a few drinks."

Lotus hurried out into the street, examining her hair in a hand mirror as she went.

Chapter 17

One day passed, then two, and Concord Qin didn't get better—in fact, he got worse. He gave notice that he was quitting his job and stopped going to the village offices. The township government refused to accept his resignation, however. On top of that, they enthusiastically endorsed Pavilion's market plan. In fact, the township head took up his brush and personally did the calligraphy for the characters to be engraved on the decorative arch. FRESHWIND VILLAGE MARKET, it read.

For a few days after that, Justice Xia went around with a face as black as thunder. He refused to go out of the house or let Lucky the dog out, either. He said he was going to plait some straw shoes. This was something he hadn't done for ten years, but he got out the shoe frame and some dried pondweed, hung the frame from the lintel, and tied the rope end around his waist. Then he rubbed the strands of straw between his fingers until they rustled. He worked in silence, not even answering when Second Auntie spoke to him. It took him a while to get into his stride, and his first efforts were either too big or too small, so he unplaited the straw and tried again. He worked for the best part of a morning but still had not made a decent pair. Come midday, Wisdom Xia dropped by to invite his second elder brother over— Fourth Auntie had picked some pumpkin flowers and was making pancakes. Justice ate two, then stopped and sat staring fixedly into the distance.

"Would you like to listen to some opera, brother?" said Wisdom, but after twisting the radio dial back and forth, he still couldn't find the right station.

"Forget it. I don't like listening to opera," said Justice.

The two of them fell silent, gazing outside at the roses and peonies in the flower bed. The flower stems and leaves looked as if they were crawling with black insects. There were ants, too.

"What's up with the flowers?" Wisdom wondered aloud.

"I'll go and have a look," said Justice.

Wisdom let him get on with it and sat at the table, sketching opera masks. Justice scraped the earth away from the roots with a trowel and uncovered a dead cat, one that Wisdom had buried there to serve as fertilizer. It was the maggots in the rotting corpse that had attracted the midges and the ants.

"Who buried this cat?" called Justice, but Wisdom was deaf to everything when he was painting opera masks. Justice threw the cat's corpse into the latrine pit and, seeing that Wisdom was absorbed, quietly made his way back to his home in the scorpion's tail of Freshwind.

Fourth Auntie had gone to Bounty's house for a chat, so she missed seeing Justice; she got home to find Wisdom with his mouth daubed with blobs of color—as he painted, he was constantly wetting his brush on his tongue. He looked as grubby as a baby's butt.

"Where's Second Brother?" she asked.

"Tending to the flowers," said Wisdom. But Justice wasn't there anymore.

"That brother of mine!" exclaimed Wisdom. He felt sorry for Justice, not having any education or a hobby to take him out of himself. He went to find Goodness.

As a result of that, Goodness set off for the scorpion's tail without delay. When he got to Justice Xia's gate, there was Tiger, prowling around. Tiger hadn't seen Lucky for many days, and his tail drooped in the dust. He cocked his leg against the wall and pissed, and Goodness saw the dog had a stiff dick.

Goodness had to knock for a long time before finally the gate was opened. Justice stood there and spluttered angrily at Goodness for not sticking to his principles, showering Goodness in the face with spittle.

Goodness, good-natured as always, wiped his face and merely said, "I haven't got an ounce of influence now that Concord Qin isn't there anymore."

"I don't want to hear any more about it!" exclaimed Justice, but he couldn't resist asking whether Concord Qin was better or not.

"I've been too busy to go and see him these last few days," said Goodness. "But Lotus tells me that his daughter has been to pick up medicine from Big-Noise Zhao a few times."

"Have you not been because you want to steer clear of trouble?" Justice pursued.

"I don't have anything to be scared of. I'm only the bookkeeper; I have a skill that puts food on the table. If anyone with more ability wants to swap places with me, I'm easy about it."

"If only Concord Qin was a steady hand at the tiller like you are, Goodness. He's useless; he chose the wrong time to be playing mah-jongg, and to get sick."

"Second Uncle," said Goodness, "a new ruler means new ministers. With Pavilion busy with his job, for better or worse, it's all up to him. He has his reasons, and maybe they seem unfair, but time will be his judge. When you started the gully-filling project, there were a lot of protests, but now, just a few years later, everyone's talking about all the good you've done for the village. You can rest on your laurels now you've retired. Don't upset yourself; it's not worth it. You have an unblemished reputation already. Take a step back, like you're standing on the riverbank watching the waves, and you'll rise even higher in their estimation."

"It really doesn't matter; I'm not bothered," said Justice Xia.

Goodness took him off to New-Life Liu's orchard and got New-Life to play drums for them. Justice Xia had forgotten how mercurial Goodness was. He inflated himself like a ball bouncing all over the place one minute, and the next minute, he shriveled like a pricked balloon.

Justice Xia looked up at the sky, his mouth agape and all his black teeth on show. Just then a solitary bird flew by and from its rear end released a drop of shit that landed right in Justice Xia's mouth. That was really bad luck, but he didn't make a sound or even clean his mouth out. Instead, he just stared silently up at the bird and said to himself, *I'll remember you!*

They arrived at the orchard. The original shack Justice Xia had built was no longer there, and New-Life Liu, after leasing the orchard for some years, had replaced it with a brick house to which he had now added two additional floors. On the first floor was the room where he received guests; on the second floor he'd built a kang, and on the third floor, the roof level, stood a small pavilion. It made the house look a bit like a fort. Because it was so hot, his wife had gone to the embankment at the southern end of the orchard to pick Sichuan pepper leaves, while New-Life and his son dozed on straw mats in front of their door, dressed only in patterned boxer shorts.

New-Life had been trying to teach the son a drum rhythm, but the son kept forgetting what he had learned. "You're as stupid as a pig!" New-Life shouted and tapped out the rhythm on his belly. As soon as Justice Xia and Goodness appeared from behind the wall, New-Life's wolf dog reared up on its hind legs.

New-Life looked around, then sat up. "Grandad! And what are you doing here, Second Uncle? Hurry up and make us some tea, son." And then, in a louder voice, "Wife, come back to the house. Come and see who's here!"

"Your reputation has preceded you, Second Uncle. Look what a fuss your arrival has caused," Goodness said to the old man.

But Justice only said, "If I ever live to see New-Life snub me, I'll bash my brains out against the shithouse wall."

"I may not be up to much, but I do know right from wrong," said New-Life. "The country is a big village, the village is a small country, and Second Uncle is Freshwind's very own Chairman Mao."

"What are you talking about?" said Justice Xia.

"When you were village head, didn't I say that to you? A few days ago, Iron-Man's mom said we ought to fix up a room on the third floor and we'd be very pleased if you, Second Uncle, wanted to move in. We'd see you have everything you need. It's quiet here, and it's a nice view. That's what Iron-Man's mom said."

Then he yelled again, "Hey, wife! Have you gone and died somewhere?"

New-Life's wife was a hunchback, so bent over that she couldn't even raise her head. She looked like she'd been flattened between stone rollers.

"Coming, coming!" she shouted back.

Meantime, Justice Xia's spirits had revived. He stood up a bit straighter, lit one of his rollies, and said, "Goodness, there are two kinds of people I can't abide: one is drunkards, the other is flatterers. When they pay you compliments, you can't accept them or reject them; all you can do is listen earnestly and smile."

Obviously Justice Xia was in a much better mood.

"Second Uncle, you know it was me who told New-Life," Goodness made a point of telling him.

"And you did well. I'm not worried about you telling; I'm worried about you not telling!"

They heard the cracking of branches, and New-Life's wife pushed through the fruit trees, bent almost double. In one hand, she clutched a bunch of Sichuan pepper leaves.

"Second Uncle's here!" she exclaimed. "You're all staying for lunch then. I'll fry these."

"Never mind the pepper leaves; Uncle likes *liang fen* noodles," said her husband. "You get some pea flour and make us *liang fen*."

"Liang fen, liang fen!" Justice Xia echoed him and then sat down to sip his tea.

As they drank, Goodness said to New-Life, "Haven't you taken your wife back to the doctor?"

"Nah, what's the point? Spark had a bright idea. He said to press her between two doors; that'd straighten her back. But I said it'd kill the woman. Spark is a scoundrel."

"What made him say something like that?" exclaimed Goodness.

"It was just a joke."

"It's not a laughing matter!"

"Some things you just have to laugh at. I told Iron-Man's mom, you just have to grin and bear it; if you fret about it, it'll kill you. Don't you think?" He turned to Justice Xia.

Justice Xia gripped his shoulders wordlessly, then lifted his teacup to his lips and sipped. That made his glasses steam up, and he took them off.

"New-Life's a happy guy," said Goodness. "Play your drum, New-Life, for Second Uncle to listen to."

"Very good!" said New-Life.

The three of them went up to the third floor. Half of it was taken up by the extra room, and the other was a flat roof with a pavilion from which you had a good view of the orchard. Inside the pavilion hung a large oxhide drum. Just looking at it gave Justice Xia goose bumps. It reminded him of the crazy things he'd done as a youth. He picked up the drumstick, struck the drum three times, spat, then said, "It was me who flayed you, ox!"

New-Life began to wax lyrical about the quality of the oxhide, which had been in use for years and years without ever splitting or cracking. "What would you like to hear?" he asked.

"Something from a festival, of course," said Goodness.

"That's all so old. How about something new? There's a traditional Freshwind piece called 'King Qin's Eighteen Drums.' I've rewritten it. Have a listen."

And he told his son to play.

I heard the drumming. I was chatting with Tongue-Tied, Rain Xia, and Roughshod Ding in the shade of a pagoda tree by the West Street archway. We'd watered the rice fields and spread the fertilizer, so there was no work for us to do, and we mooched around the village, sitting down wherever we could find a scrap of shade. Roughshod Ding and I had been playing "the wolf eats the baby" with squares scratched in the dust, but he could work out the game three moves ahead and I was never going to beat him, so I stopped and studied the tree instead. I could see it wasn't random, the way the branches grew thick or thin and bent this way and that. Those branches had feelings. This one leaned toward that one affectionately but couldn't stand another one. Some pairs were husband and wife; others were talking to each other. I could see it all happening, and I was really enjoying it. Then suddenly the drumming broke in.

"Where's that coming from?" I wondered. Tongue-Tied listened and flapped his hands. I said to him, "If you're dumb, your ears should be sharper. Can't you hear it?" He just flapped his hands again. I could tell it really was a drum, and I looked up, thinking it must be the wind drumming on the sun. But the sky was dense with thick clouds.

"It's so loud," I said.

"Don't talk crazy," said Roughshod Ding. "Come and play another round with me." So we did. As we played, the drumming got more melodious, and I knew that my soul had found its way out of my body. Now there was one "me" playing "the wolf eats the baby," while the other "me" had run off in pursuit of the drum. That me got to the orchard and sat down on New-Life's third-floor roof. Justice Xia, Goodness, and New-Life couldn't see me, but I could see them. They were acting like a bunch of crazies; they had forgotten their sorrows, they'd forgotten how old they were, the drumbeats were booming out, and Justice Xia was shouting, "Beautiful, beautiful!" I could see the drum was turning into the head of an ox, and Justice

Xia was shouting that his rib cage was missing a rib. A plane passed overhead, looking like a laundry club. A sheep was tied up next to the orchard, pawing the ground with its hoof, and in the belly of the sheep there was a lamb.

The thing is, Justice Xia used to be in the Freshwind drum band in his youth. Old Zhao from Middle Street (Big-Noise Zhao's third uncle) was the lead drummer, and Justice Xia played a small gong. After the old man died, his pupil, New-Life Liu, took over as the lead drummer, and under his management the band provided entertainment at all the village festivities, New Year, and so on.

New-Life always said the two things he most loved were mah-jongg and drumming. If he was playing mah-jongg, it made him forget the drumming, and vice versa. The other villagers said that it was his love of mah-jongg and drumming that had turned his wife into a creature who looked like a river shrimp, and he could only live with a river shrimp for a wife if he lost himself in those two loves. His son had just played the first and second part of the piece and was starting on part three. New-Life looked on, occasionally shouting, "Rapid fire, three!" The boy struck the drum simultaneously with both sticks twice, then struck the very center of the drum once.

New-Life shouted the names of five different beats, and the boy followed his instructions. He struck the right-hand side of the drum lightly with the right stick, and did the same on the left, then the right stick beat a rapid fire on the right, followed by the same on the left side, finishing with a right-stick strike in the very center of the drum. New-Life shouted, "Eight taps and thirteen dongs!" His son pressed down on one side of the drum, then, working both sticks together, struck the different beats until he'd played thirteen "dongs." By this time New-Life and his son were both running with sweat, their hair stuck to their foreheads, and there were damp patches on the crotches of their pants. The sweat ran into their eyes so they couldn't open them, and then down from their faces to splatter on the ground. The drumbeats had no sooner faded away than Justice Xia burst into applause, and they heard a shrill cry in the distance: "Bravo!"

Justice Xia looked up. A man and a woman were standing in a shack on the east side of the orchard, and that was where the cries had come from.

"Is that Star Chen's shack?" asked Justice.

"That's right," said New-Life, and he beckoned them over. But Star Chen didn't move, nor did the woman.

"Is that Emerald?" asked Justice Xia.

"Of course it is," said Iron-Man. "She's always there."

New-Life glared at his son. Justice looked bemused.

Goodness changed the subject in a hurry. "New-Life, you're talented. You should be more than a peasant."

At that moment, the hunchback woman climbed up to the third floor (yes, she could climb stairs) and shouted that the *liang fen* noodles were ready. She'd overheard Goodness's comment and said, "Once a peasant, always a peasant. Drumming doesn't fill your belly. If he spends his time drumming and lets the orchard go to rack and ruin, he'll just bring a heap of trouble on us."

"The hell you know!" said New-Life. "If I play well, I might get a job in the provincial city."

"The provincial city?" said his wife. "Fancy yourself as Wind Xia, do you?"

I was annoyed at that. Wind Xia was nothing but a hack journalist. Fair skin covers a multitude of shortcomings. Could Wind Xia winnow or make mud bricks? No, he could not. If he was still in the village, he wouldn't even have found a woman to marry, or if he had, she'd have been quickly snatched away by another man.

"Drums have got to be beaten, and orchards have got to be managed," said Justice Xia. "You and Star Chen are in competition now, and you better measure up to him, or else!"

New-Life bowed to Justice Xia by way of a solemn promise, and they went downstairs to eat their *liang fen*.

At that point, I left. I'd already lost four times to Roughshod Ding, who was very pleased with himself and demanding sour-broth noodles from me as his winnings. We went to Clerk's wife's restaurant and were eating our noodles when a bunch of kids armed with sticks came along, chasing after Lucky and Tiger. The dogs were stuck together, Lucky running forward and Tiger, who'd mounted her, scrabbling along backward. Tongue-Tied chased the kids off, and the dogs stopped and separated. I kicked Tiger away.

While we were eating, Justice Xia was getting drunk on noodles at New-Life's house. Yes, that's what I said. Surely it was alcohol that made you drunk, not noodles? But Justice Xia really was drunk as a skunk. He'd slurped one bowl of noodles and exclaimed, "Delicious!" Then he'd slurped down another bowl. Then another, but by this time, he didn't look right. His legs trembled and his forehead was covered in sweat. "Did you put poppy-shell oil in these noodles?" he asked.

New-Life answered, "There's a bit too much mustard in it."

Justice Xia was up for more, and New-Life prepared him another bowlful. But before he'd had time to add the chili, vinegar, and mustard, Justice Xia had dug his chopsticks in. A strand of noodle fell on the cooker top, and he retrieved it and shoved it into his mouth. New-Life had never seen him eat like this before, and he was delighted.

"If you're enjoying the *liang fen*, that must mean they're well made."

Goodness came over and removed the bowl. "No more, Uncle," he said. "You're drunk on noodles."

"How can *liang fen* get you drunk?" asked New-Life in disbelief.

"It happens all the time. First the drumming, then all the noodles he's eaten; obviously, he's drunk."

"Uncle can eat any amount of *liang fen*," said New-Life.

"Maybe so, but it's not normal to have three helpings and then ask for more. And when he's drunk, he looks happy, like now. If he wasn't drunk, he'd be crying."

"Nonsense," said Justice Xia. "When have I ever cried?" And right then and there, he began to do just that. Mud-colored tears coursed down both cheeks, along the furrows of his wrinkles.

"You must not be drunk, the way you're crying," said Goodness.

"I'm crying from happiness. I haven't been so happy in ages! Didn't you know that people cry from happiness? Back in 1935, under the Nationalists, there were bandits in Freshwind, and they were always dropping dockets."

"What've bandits got to do with anything? And what dockets?" said New-Life.

"The dockets had the name of the head of household, how much they were worth, and a deadline. Every household had to hand over their money to the local boss, Ma, from Liujiapo Village. If they couldn't pay up, the 'slash-and-burn brigade' would be onto them."

"You're drunk. That was years and years ago."

But Justice Xia went on anyway. "Big-Noise Zhao's family were well off, and they got the docket. His granddad sold what they owned and bought the bandits off with two baskets of silver dollars and a bag of opium. After that the family was broke and started working as herbalists." And he helped himself to another bowl of noodles.

"That's ancient history," said Goodness, and tried to take Justice Xia's bowl away from him, but the old man got another mouthful in anyway.

"You're so fucking like your uncle!" he said. "I'm telling you, my family got the docket, too, only the sum the bandits demanded was too high and when the seven days were up, we didn't have the money, so the whole family took off to hide in the mountains. Except me; I hid in a big tree behind the house. When darkness fell, the bandits came with torches and searched the house from top to bottom. They took away anything of value; then they set fire to it and burned it. There were twenty or thirty gun-toting bandits, but none were from around here except your uncle; he was the only one I recognized. As soon as the bandits had gone, my granddad got all the Xias together to go and hunt for your uncle. They tracked him down to the opium den in Chafang Village and went and tied him up with ropes. At first, they were going to bash a hole in his skull, fill it with kerosene, and make him into a human candle, but then your Li clan begged them to be merciful, so they strangled him instead. You know how much corn spirits the Xia clan got through that year? Eighteen jars full. I was a kid back then, and I managed three bowls of spirits without getting drunk. So you think three bowls of noodles is going to make me drunk? I love *liang fen* noodles! In all my years serving as a cadre, I've eaten more *liang fen* than you've eaten grain."

"All right, all right, so my uncle deserved to die, but you've got to stop eating now; you really are drunk," said Goodness.

New-Life put in, "Was your uncle really an informer for the bandits?"

"Damn all to do with me," said Goodness.

"That's right," said Justice Xia. "He doesn't have anything to do with Goodness; he was Excellent's grandad."

"But Excellent's such an honest guy; how could his granddad have been an informer?" asked New-Life.

"People are weird and unpredictable," said Justice Xia. "If we didn't have the Communist Party, what kind of a world do you think we'd be living in nowadays? I've been a Party member all my life. If the Party tells me to stand, I stand; if it tells me to squat, then that's what I do. But cadres nowadays think they know everything; they think they can do exactly what they want."

Goodness and New-Life could think of nothing to say at this outburst. The tears ran down Justice Xia's face, and he began to sob in earnest. New-Life did his best to comfort him, but that only made Justice cry harder. He went on telling them stories about when he had been village head, about the half a lifetime he'd spent working for the village, and about the two things he most bitterly regretted: he'd spent everyone's money on the gully-filling project, but it was still unfinished, and the fact that when he was young, he shouldn't have . . . But then he stopped.

New-Life had never seen Justice Xia cry like this. It scared him, and he hastily cleared the *liang fen* bowl away.

"Let him eat," said Goodness. "He'll only stop crying if he eats himself thoroughly drunk." And he gave the bowl back to Justice Xia. But the old man only had one more mouthful, then slumped over the table and fell fast asleep.

"Well, at least he's calmed down. But how are we going to get him home?" said Goodness.

"You give him a piggyback ride," said New-Life.

"I'll get an earful from Second Auntie if I do that, for sure," said Goodness.

"Then he can stay the night with me," said New-Life. But Goodness carried him home anyway.

Tongue-Tied and I dangled a bit of pork rib in front of Lucky to lure the dog back to the pond outside Justice Xia's gate. When we got there, there was Goodness. He had set his burden down for a rest on the stone roller and shouted for Tongue-Tied, but when the boy saw his granddad sprawled on the roller like a lump of clay, he wailed fearfully at Goodness.

"Don't blame me," said Goodness. "He got drunk all on his own."

Tongue-Tied picked the old man up and carried him into the yard.

I didn't go into Justice Xia's yard because just at that moment, I saw Snow Bai in the gardens at the south end of the pond. The celery was green, her jacket was red, and when she stood up, she was dazzling, a sight for sore eyes. I stood rooted to the spot. Mid-Star's dad had said there were such things as goddesses in this world, as well as demons and fox spirits, and they often assumed human shape and moved among us. So when Snow Bai stood up in the vegetable patch, I couldn't believe it was really her. But it was, of course. She was holding three pumpkins she had just cut and crooning some lines from "The Peach Blossom Hut":

A year ago in this house, your cheeks had a peach-blossom glow
Now you are gone, but the peach blossom still smiles when the zephyrs blow.

The last time I'd seen Snow Bai, she was with her mom, and they'd scampered away from me into an alley. This time she'd have to stick to the little path that led from the vegetable patch to the pond. I wished the path was even narrower, as narrow as a log; that way Snow Bai couldn't avoid me. I gazed at her as she approached. Finally, she looked up and I hurriedly pinned a smile on my face. She startled, and then her face fell.

"What are you smiling about?" she demanded.

I suddenly felt flames envelop me from head to foot. I burned like an ingot in the forge. Then I was plunged into cold water and turned into a lump of iron. I could not think what to say. My lips trembled, but no sounds came out. I didn't dare block the path, so I shifted to one side and stood sideways so she could pass. And pass she did, trailing a whiff of something fragrant and warm in her wake. I saw three yellow moths and a ladybug on her pants leg. Then a dragonfly flew toward her, and I reached up to catch it—and tumbled into the water. The pond wasn't deep, and I stood up right away, but Snow Bai had come to a halt and looked terrified.

"I'm fine, I'm fine," I told her.

"Quick, get out of there!"

Her concern for me made me glad that I'd fallen in the pond, and I made sure to fall back in again, just so that she'd feel even sorrier for me. I let my head go under and swallowed a mouthful of filthy water, too. But she must have seen through me, because when I came up again, she was gone. There was a pumpkin lying by the path; she must have left it for me.

"Snow Bai! Snow Bai!" I called. She was scampering up the slope past Justice Xia's house. Why had she given me a pumpkin? I mean, she hated me enough to scratch my eyes out and spit at me, didn't she? So why had she given me a pumpkin? I stood in the pond, and suddenly I had so much to say. Why hadn't I talked to her when I'd had the chance, even if she was glaring at me? I whacked myself across the face so hard that I made myself cry.

My wails scared Tongue-Tied, who had come out of Justice Xia's house. He stood at the gate and went, "Wah? Wah, wah?" I stopped crying. Looking at him, I thought how lucky I was. So I got out of the pond, clutched the pumpkin to my chest, and ran off home. As I ran, my legs got lengthened until they were two or three yards long, and my feet were as big as winnowing baskets as I leaped through the Freshwind alleys.

"That Spark, he's really off the wall!" I heard someone say.

I paid no attention and ran on. When I got home, I put the pumpkin on top of the cabinet in our big room and told my dad's picture, "I've brought a pumpkin home, Dad!" I was sure that he'd understand this as, "I've brought a wife home!" I left the pumpkin sitting there and sat in front of the cabinet and sang the first thing that came into my head—opera. Snow Bai sang opera, and now I did, too. It was a line that went, "Ai-ya! You've come to me!" But I couldn't remember the next line.

Chapter 18

I was deliriously happy for three whole days. Favor Bai from the dyehouse had hung out some patterned cloth to dry and was singing some lines from "The Vermilion Brocade Mountain":

> I open my door and stand leaning on my cane,
> I'm a wealthy gent, a very fine swain!

A very fine swain, my ass. What a laugh! I hurried past the dyehouse door to wait for Snow Bai on the pond path. The sun overhead burned bright as a ball of fire, so hot it felt like bunches of needles thrown at my scalp. I held a castor oil leaf over my head so that Justice Xia wouldn't see me when he came out of his house, and Snow Bai wouldn't spot me from the vegetable patch, either. But Snow Bai stayed away. I walked along the path until I got to the vegetables and wondered whether I could just capture Snow Bai's shadow. I couldn't; the only thing I captured was a sloughed snakeskin.

I took it to the Great Qing Hall to sell to Big-Noise Zhao, because he used pounded snakeskin and camphor tree sap to make a cure for inflammation of the middle ear. But Big-Noise Zhao didn't offer me any money for it. In fact, he more or less ignored me. He was flicking through a magazine, and when he came across the head shot of a film star, he exclaimed, "What could she be eating to get this beautiful?"

I took a look, but she wasn't anything like as beautiful as Snow Bai.

He cut the photo out and stuck it at the head of his bed, then said to me with a smile, "I love writing couplets; does that make me an artist?"

"I don't know."

"A love of beauty is the sign of an artistic soul."

Big-Noise Zhao was a good man, but he could be a bit sharp tongued and grumpy. He was convinced that he was on a level with Wind Xia, and he looked down on me. I didn't say any more, just set off for home, singing a song to myself.

I didn't see her at all that day, so at home in the evening I began to call her name very softly. I was sure that if I called to her, her ears would burn. I called and called until my voice began to shake, and then I raised my voice a bit. The neighbor must have heard because he chucked a piece of broken tile into my yard. I ignored it. I said to a cricket on the tree in the middle of the yard, "You call for me! Go and call in his yard." And the cricket did just that. It landed on my neighbor's tree and called, "Snow Bai! Snow Bai! Snow Bai!"

There was no entertainment in the village at night except drinking or playing mah-jongg or turning the lights out and getting down to it on the kang with the wife. I roamed around the alleys, looking for someone to talk to, but the doors were shut and all I could hear were squelchy sucking noises through the windows. I went home and lay on the kang, thinking about how Big-Noise Zhao had pasted up the picture of the movie star. It was a shame that I had no photo of Snow Bai. In the dark I stared at the wall above the kang and imagined I could see her face there, and somehow my hand crept between my legs.

I'd had a miserable life as a kid, no toys to play with, not even a ball, but at least I'd had my dick. But now when I reached down there, there was nothing; all that was left was a little stub. Then something leaked out. I've never told anyone that. After that stuff leaked out, I was sorry I'd let it happen. I was such a jerk. But Big-Noise Zhao had said that artists could be inspired by beautiful women. I wondered if jerks like me could sleep with a woman. And do artists suffer if they don't? I couldn't write couplets, so I wasn't an artist, but maybe I wasn't a jerk, either. After all, I was home by myself with the windows and doors closed and only the mosquitoes and ants to see me.

But the truth is, that wasn't the only time I'd played with my dick. I did it often, and this time it got inflamed and hurt like hell, worse than hemorrhoids. I couldn't even walk. So I went to the county hospital for treatment. While I was there, when no one was looking, I went and found where they'd buried the bit I'd cut off. There was a tree seedling growing from the spot, with three leaves on it. I knew it would shoot up really fast.

While the sapling was shooting up, work started on the Freshwind market project. Pavilion consulted his predecessors in the job and decided it would be rash to impose levies, so he borrowed money from the credit union instead. He handed the whole project over to Bounty. Bounty wasn't as powerful as Excellent Li, but he still managed to tempt Excellent Li's construction team to join him—in particular, some of the key craftsmen. Excellent Li was very upset because it left him shorthanded when he and his team went to build the culvert for Highway 312. His young brother, Citizen Li, worked himself up into a drunken rage because of that and knocked the head off the lion on the East Street archway. Before he could start the project, Pavilion had to kill the chickens to frighten the monkeys, as they say. He got the local police to arrest Citizen Li and keep him locked up for the night and make him pay for the lion to be repaired, too. Citizen Li came out of the police station the next day and punched the earth with his clenched fists.

"I'm leaving and I'm never coming home again, even after I'm dead," he declared. And he went off to the provincial city and was never heard from again.

I didn't see Snow Bai when I came back from the county hospital. According to Rain Xia, the original plan to divide the opera troupe into two had gone wrong. When it came to split up the props and the costumes, there were arguments, and even fights. So the prop boxes were sealed, and for the time being no one could get access to the contents. Wind Xia, meanwhile, was constantly on the phone, trying to persuade Snow Bai to join him in the city. The breakup of the opera troupe plunged Snow Bai into gloom, and Rain Xia's bet was that she might not stick around for much longer; she might try and get as far away as possible. I nearly fainted when I heard that. As if I hadn't already had a really shitty life, what with Snow Bai marrying Wind Xia . . . But at least up till now she'd still been in the county seat, and every couple of weeks, she'd pop back to Freshwind and I could see her. But if she went to the big city, there wouldn't be any more moonlight on water for me, or flowers in the mirror.

For a few days, I was so anxious I could hardly breathe. In the road, I walked on ants, and if I went to the spring to draw water, I had to take a breather halfway back when I reached the gables of Citizen Li's house. I could hear his wife sobbing in there. Her husband had gone, and their place was deserted, no sign of man or beast. The wife sat, doing nothing, day in, day out. Some of the older women tried to cheer her up, told her to hang a pair of Citizen Li's old shoes in the hole where they stored sweet potatoes, and that would bring him back. That gave me an idea: I could do the same with a pair of Snow Bai's old shoes, so she'd have to stick around. But where could I get a pair? I was too scared to tell Rain Xia, let alone go to the Xia house. Just as I was feeling really miserable, Mid-Star Xia came back to Freshwind for a visit, and everything changed again.

Mid-Star was a Xia but only distantly related to Gold, Pavilion, and Wind Xia. He'd lost his mom when he was little and had been brought up by his dad, a God-fearing man who didn't eat meat, or drink, or eat spicy food, and was up at the crack of dawn every day to collect manure for the fields. Every couple of weeks he'd go and burn incense at the Tiger Head Cliff shrine. But he'd been poor as a young man, and he was still poor when he was old. Every village needed someone who knew about feng shui, and yin and yang, and Mid-Star's dad ended up playing that role for Freshwind. It was he who chose the day for every family celebration, and the location for every house to be built, grave to be dug, cooker to be built, or kang to be positioned. Payment was usually in kind, not cash, and although Mid-Star's dad did his best to change that (his house was covered in little notices: "Choosing a day = 5 yuan" and "Choosing a site = 7 yuan"), people still used to bring oil, fuel, salt, or grain and deposit it on the cooker top—their hands never dipped into their purses. He used to say angrily, "I'm not well today!" but in the end he'd pick up his cloth bag and go with them anyway. The gifts in kind were usually a bag of sugar, a *jin* of dried noodles, a bottle of wine, or a carton of cigarettes. He could never get through all that, and he didn't want to, either, so he took the gifts to Clerk's wife to sell in her restaurant. Of course, she wouldn't give him the original price; she'd slash it by as much as a half or two-thirds, so they were always arguing about that.

Goodness warned her about getting on the wrong side of the old man. "He's a yin-yang master," he said. "He could jinx you."

But Clerk's wife was dismissive. "Just let him try; when have any of his predictions been right? I wouldn't like to say whether his prayers for the sick work or not, but his fortune-telling's lousy. When my dad got sick and his legs swelled up so bad that when you pressed a toe it made a dent, I asked him to predict if Dad's illness was dangerous. 'I charge for making predictions,' he said. I gave him ten yuan, and he spent a long time examining Dad's fortune and finally said, 'He'll be fine.' I told him, 'You know what they say—swollen legs in a man and swollen head in a woman, they're both fatal. And his legs are terribly swollen.' But he said he had divine inspiration and my dad would be fine. 'But you're not divine,' I said. He said, 'I've been doing this work for a long time, and I'm possessed by the spirits.' 'Possessed? How does that happen?' I asked. He said, 'It's like when someone becomes a cadre, they take on the spirit of officialdom, don't they? Same with a police officer.' Well, I'd seen that, so I believed him. But my dad was dead before ten days were up."

When Mid-Star was a bit older, Justice Xia tried to get him into the army, but he failed the medical—high blood pressure. Never mind Mid-Star's dad; it was Mid-Star the clan felt sorry for. He was a motherless boy, and as a young man he already had high blood pressure. Justice Xia was furious that he hadn't made the grade and twisted the arm of the recruitment officers, getting them to agree that he could take the medical again. Big-Noise Zhao then cooked up a plan: Mid-Star should drink vinegar before the blood pressure test. So Mid-Star drank a whole calabash full of vinegar, and his blood pressure came right down.

After he'd done his military service and was discharged, the rules said he had to come back to the village, but his dad went crying to Wisdom Xia to get him a job in town. Wisdom went off to the county seat and pulled strings and got Mid-Star placed in a county government department. And after that Mid-Star's dad got himself a gold tooth, which he bared in a smile whenever he met someone. And when he went out early to collect manure, he hopped and skipped along like a sparrow.

The only trouble was that Mid-Star didn't get a proper job in the county government; he was just supposed to help out whenever there was a need. He spent a bit of time in the county head's "deprived villages"; he toured the county, checking on the reforestation plan, and he spent six months reorganizing the county's winery. Then with the breakup of the opera troupe, the troupe head got transferred to the cultural center, and first there were rumors that someone would be sent to replace him, then rumors that the person had turned the post down and someone else would come instead. But in the end no one came—until Mid-Star turned up.

"Aren't you pissed that you've ended up in the opera troupe?" the villagers asked.

"Not me. I'm not worried," said Mid-Star. Of course he wasn't worried. Heading up the opera troupe meant being promoted to a senior admin grade. On his first day he carefully combed his hair, although in fact he was completely bald on top and had to comb over a long tuft that started behind his right ear and glue it down with hair gel. The troupe members all laughed at him, and the fat singer who sang the *jing* painted-face role said that he could hardly resist the urge to get hold of that tuft and give it a sharp tug. Undeterred, Mid-Star began by improving morale; he reunited the two troupes into one and had them rehearse a new opera. Once it was ready, he had grandiose plans to tour every village and township in the county. Mid-Star was filled with boundless ambition. Under his leadership, Shaanxi opera was going to be revitalized. When this news reached Snow Bai's ears, she swayed irresolutely, like a reed in the wind, but finally made the decision not to join Wind Xia in the provincial city.

Mid-Star Xia was now my favorite person. And revitalizing Shaanxi opera was the best idea in the world. Though to be truthful, I'd never been that fond of opera before. Star Chen was always laughing at the villagers who went around singing arias. According to him, they all had bull necks and big mouths, and what they did wasn't singing so much as engaging in shouting matches. It made him want to stuff cotton wool in his ears.

"You're going to the county agricultural college to learn fruit-tree grafting," he told Bright Chen. "You don't want to? Then I'll make you listen to opera."

I'd never minded Star Chen bringing opera down like that. But now that Mid-Star was going to revitalize it, that meant Snow Bai would stay around, so I changed my mind. Opera was the best thing ever! I didn't know how many operas there were, and I couldn't remember any of the words, but all the same, if I had a free moment, I'd hold a steamed bun in one hand and a fresh chili in the other and take a bite of each and belt out a few lines.

It was Obedient Zhang of the farm store who brought us the news that Mid-Star was going to be heading up the opera troupe. No one believed it at first, and they paid him no attention. But for some reason I did believe it was true, and it cheered me up. I bumped into Mid-Star's dad at the river bridge at the east end of the village. He sat on the stone pier, working out his predictions. He had been collecting manure, but he also had a small cloth bag slung across his shoulder, holding a box of Number Nine Lotus incense sticks and a bundle of yellow temple-offerings paper, a stamp carved from a piece of lightning-blasted jujube wood, a pen, and a small notebook. The manure basket sat right in front of his nose, but despite the stink, he was completely absorbed in working out the trigrams.

"Uncle Glory!" I shouted. He had the character 荣, meaning "glory," as one of his given names, so we always called him Uncle Glory.

He looked at me. "Are you bringing me someone to take me out on a job?" By "going out on a job," he meant choosing a propitious day for an event or a site for a grave or something. "I'm telling you straight up, that'll cost you. Gifts in kind and cash payment: six yuan for choosing a day, eight yuan for choose a site. It's gone up one yuan since last time."

"No, nothing to do with a job," I said. "I've got a question to ask you."

"No questions; I'm busy working out predictions."

"Who for?"

"For myself, to see if tomorrow's a good day for making money."

"You'll surely get some gifts tomorrow, now that Mid-Star is taking over the opera troupe—"

But he interrupted. "Spark, let me correct you. Mid-Star's a cadre in the county seat government; he's not in the opera."

It occurred to me that Mid-Star's dad didn't know about his son's new job. Obedient Zhang must just have been spreading rumors. Suddenly, my excitement evaporated, and I got up and left.

But that very afternoon, Mid-Star's dad came to my house to tell me that just an hour earlier, his son had called with the news that he was going to head up the opera troupe. "There's only one troupe in a county as big as this, and he's going to be the head. You must have come to ask me that this morning, right? And I wouldn't let you talk. I'm sorry."

"You're just sorry because you missed out on my congratulatory gift."

He smiled at me, but I didn't smile back. I ran off to tell Roughshod Ding the good news, as well as Marvel and Hearth. Then I went to tell Big-Noise Zhao. He was sitting in the Great Qing Hall talking to a bunch of people. I didn't go in; what I did was, I walked slowly past the front gate singing a snatch of an aria from *Zhou Ren Returns to His Residence*. The lines go:

> If Prince Du had not been jinxed
> How could I, Zhou Ren, rise to such an exalted position now?

There was a shout from Zhou Big-Noise. "Hey, Spark, can you sing opera, too?"

I didn't answer immediately. I wanted to go on singing, but I only knew those two lines, so I hummed a bit more of the tune. Then I asked him, "What's up?"

"What's this nonsense about 'rising to an exalted position'?"

"Didn't you know that Mid-Star has become the new head of the county opera troupe?"

"Why are you so happy about that?"

"Think!"

"I'm thinking."

"Have you thought?"

"Nope."

"Dumbass!" And I carried on humming the last, long-drawn-out note.

Five days later, Mid-Star arrived. It was dusk by the time he got off the bus at the entrance to the township government offices and headed home to the village, his head down and his army pack on his back. Rites Xia had just come out of the store with a bag of fertilizer, and he put it down on the dike while he took a breather.

"Is that Mid-Star?" he shouted.

Mid-Star looked up. "Oh, Third Uncle. You've been buying fertilizer?"

"I was just saying, 'A man with his eyes on the ground has his head in the clouds,' and there you are, Mid-Star. It's the talk of Freshwind, your becoming the head of the opera troupe. Everyone's been telling your dad he's got to buy them a round."

"What's the big deal? It's only an opera troupe."

"Don't talk like that. This is your big break. Nowadays in government jobs, the really hard thing is to get from an admin job to head of an admin department, but once you're a department head, you're on your way. The sky's the limit!"

Mid-Star smiled. "Third Uncle, you haven't got any land; why are you buying fertilizer?"

"Thunder's worried about his land. I'm helping him out."

"Is he still farming? He wouldn't starve even if he didn't harvest a single grain."

"Everyone says Thunder is well off, but it's not true. How well off can you be when you've got a government job? In state-run businesses nowadays, you're fine if they're going well, but if they're not, you can end up in the shit in just a couple of years. I'm worried for Thunder. He's not like you. You may not be married, but you'll be able to find yourself a wife in the county seat, and you can move your dad into town with you, too. Me, I've been a township cadre all my life, and now that I'm old, all I've got to keep me going is a bit of farming."

Mid-Star passed Rites Xia a cigarette.

"What a fine cigarette!" the old man exclaimed. And he put it in his pocket instead of smoking it.

With Mid-Star carrying the fertilizer for him, they walked along together until they reached Freshwind's East Street. As they passed the alleys, everyone came out to congratulate Mid-Star, and he handed out cigarettes, one after another.

"Come to my house; the drinks are on me!"

They all tagged along behind him except Rites Xia, who had stopped and was staring into the distance until Bamboo, dangling a cigarette between his fingers, approached him. "Third Uncle!"

Rites Xia pulled himself together. "Did you know Mid-Star's back?"

"Right." Bamboo was noncommittal.

"He fucking got his break, but I never got mine. I was on an admin grade till I retired, but he's already on the senior grade at his age." He got Mid-Star's cigarette out of his pocket and offered it to Bamboo.

"Is he really heading up the opera troupe? And does Fourth Uncle know?" asked Bamboo.

Wisdom Xia was sitting at his eight-seater dining table, his "Eight Immortals" table as they were called, painting opera masks on the back of gourd ladles. First, he painted Lord Guan, then General Cao Cao. Rain Xia burst in and started rifling through the cabinet.

Wisdom Xia looked at him for a minute, then took off his reading glasses and said irritably, "Bandits after you, are they?"

"Where're the pliers?"

"Why do you get into such a bother about finding a pair of pliers? If I put you in charge of something big, you wouldn't know where to put yourself."

Rain Xia finally found what he was looking for in a box at the bottom of the cupboard and was about to rush off again when Wisdom Xia said, "Come and give my back a scratch."

"You've got a back-scratcher on the table."

"I want you to do it."

As Rain Xia obediently scratched his back, Wisdom said, "Up a bit, up a bit more, left—left, I said. Can't you tell your left from your right?"

"You're not easy to please, Dad."

Wisdom Xia laughed. "And how many times have I told you, tread heavily when you walk. That's the only way to get things done in this life. Don't be like your uncle Glory, hopping along like a sparrow."

"Like a sparrow?"

"He's a lowlife."

"Uncle Glory's a low-life? Well, at least Mid-Star's done well for himself, heading up the opera troupe now."

"Really? Who told you that?" Wisdom Xia exclaimed in astonishment.

Rain Xia took that as his cue to stop the scratching and hurried off with the pliers.

As he went out, Wisdom Xia said, "Head of the opera troupe? Well, he's treading heavily!"

Out in the yard, Rain Xia walked at a measured pace. But he couldn't keep it up, and when he got out onto the street, he broke into a run.

Fourth Auntie went in and said to her husband, "You're always going at him. Why don't you just make him drag a stone roller behind him? That'll weigh his footsteps down."

"I've watched him grow up, and I know him inside out. He'll never come to any good. What did he want the pliers for, anyway?"

"He's working on the market project. He came home for lunch, but all he did was gulp down a bowl of corn porridge. I asked him what was up, but he wouldn't say. You know, you two are peas in a pod, both of you. If you don't eat properly, your brains go out the window."

"You know those noodles you made today? Noodles should be thick, a finger's width and four fingers long, and you're supposed to sprinkle them with oil and chopped green onions."

"All right, all right, we're having rice tonight—I told Rain Xia that, too—you go and buy some tofu."

"Where am I going to get tofu at this time of day? Anyway, your son should be buying it if he wants it, instead of his old dad having to go and do the shopping."

They heard footsteps at the entrance, and Fourth Aunt shushed him. She went out to see who it was. "It's Mid-Star!" she cried and then ushered him indoors.

Mid-Star was dressed in a pair of sharply pressed pants, and a bunch of keys hung from his belt. Fourth Auntie called to Wisdom Xia that they had a visitor, but Mid-Star said, "I don't want to bother Fourth Uncle; I'll say what I have to say to you," and he followed her into the kitchen instead, pulling up a low stool and then sitting down as she put the water on to boil.

Mid-Star apologized fulsomely for not coming to offer his congratulations on Wind Xia's marriage. He hadn't known about it; otherwise he would have come back no matter how busy he was. It was only after he'd gotten his job with the county opera troupe that he'd found out that Wind Xia had married Snow Bai. Snow Bai was one woman in a million, a good person and a superb performer.

Fourth Aunt had the fire blazing merrily, and her cheeks turned rosy with the heat. "You've really made good. Made your dad proud!" she exclaimed. "What's the weather like in the county seat? Is it hot? Snow Bai's developed a heat rash on her neck. Will the spots fade, do you think?"

Mid-Star sighed admiringly. "What a good mother-in-law you are, so fond of your daughter-in-law. A good mother-in-law gets the good daughter-in-law she deserves. Now then, I've come back for two things: one, to visit my sick dad; and two, Snow Bai asked me to collect a bed coverlet for her because she's busy rehearsing the opera before they take it around the county."

"What's she doing touring around the villages when she's supposed to be in the provincial city?" said Fourth Aunt.

"The opera troupe's just been reorganized, so none of them are going anywhere."

"But Wind Xia wants her to transfer her residency to the city and give up her singing. Why can't she leave?"

"I'm head of the troupe now; I'm not letting her go."

"You're head of the opera troupe?"

"That's right."

"That's a good thing. Means you can take good care of Snow Bai. But touring around the countryside, that's no way to live."

"Fourth Aunt, the troupe has its rules."

"Well, why can't you pull strings for her and put in a quiet word? Like Fourth Uncle put in a quiet word for you when he got you your job in the county government."

"I've only just arrived. I can't go doing things like that. Besides, if one person leaves, then they'll all disappear."

Fourth Auntie looked unhappy. She prodded the poker through the stove opening, twice, three times, and the flames went out. She bent down and blew through the hole. A cloud of black smoke belched out, and she and Mid-Star both began to cough.

When Mid-Star first arrived, Justice Xia had put down his paintbrush, but at the words "I don't want to bother Fourth Uncle," he stayed sitting where he was, looking pensive and puffing on his water pipe.

Then Bamboo slipped silently in, startling him, and announced, "I just came to tell you Mid-Star's news, and he's gotten here before me."

"What's his news?" asked Wisdom Xia.

"He's been promoted to head of the county opera troupe."

Wisdom Xia appeared unmoved. "Is that all you came to tell me?" he said, blowing on the wick and inhaling.

"That's right."

"Well, I already know, so you can be off."

Justice Xia was the epitome of the kindly old man to anyone who didn't know him well, but he kept the younger family members strictly in line. Bamboo turned to go.

"Take this with you," Wisdom said, pointing to a pack of cigarettes on the table but obliging Bamboo to go and pick them up himself.

"Thanks, Uncle."

A little time after he had gone, Wisdom Xia got up, too, and went and stood on the steps outside. He stretched, then gave a cough.

Mid-Star heard and hurried out of the kitchen to greet him.

"Ah, Mid-Star! Hasn't she brewed you some tea yet?"

"I asked him if he'd like some sour broth, but he said no," said Fourth Aunt.

"He's head of the troupe now; what would he want with sour broth? Do him some proper tea."

"You heard the news, Uncle?"

"Good news like that? Of course I did. You're in the troupe, and our Snow Bai's there, too. That makes two Xias in the troupe."

"There's nothing good about it," said Fourth Aunt. "Snow Bai was going to leave the troupe, and now she can't!"

"Now Mid-Star's taken over as head, Snow Bai should stay and support his work," said Fourth Uncle. "Why would she give up all that? And why would she want to stymie his great plans? Besides, what would she do in the big city, anyway? She's too young to give up her career. Not after all the effort she's put into learning to sing opera."

"You haven't changed, Fourth Uncle," said Mid-Star. "Anyway, Snow Bai wouldn't dare leave. My plan to revitalize the local opera would crumble if she goes."

"You've got a plan to revitalize Shaanxi opera?" exclaimed Wisdom Xia. "Come and sit down with me, Mid-Star. Your auntie will make you some dinner, and you and I can have a chat." The old man was fizzing with excitement.

Mid-Star spoke eloquently about his big plans. The trouble was, it was all empty talk because Mid-Star knew nothing about opera. Wisdom Xia recommended starting with the opera *The Orphan of Zhao*, but Mid-Star had never heard of it. So Wisdom Xia recommended *Seizing the Brocade Pavilion*, but Mid-Star had never heard of that one, either. Wisdom Xia reeled off the names of several other operas.

"Have you heard of those?"

"Nope."

"Well, if you're going to head up the troupe, you'd better get a few operas under your belt." Then he went through his cupboards and pulled out the ladles painted with opera masks.

One by one, he went through them, explaining to Mid-Star which opera they came from, which role they belonged to, and why some had white faces and some red.

Mid-Star gaped in astonishment. "How do you know all this, Uncle?"

Wisdom Xia leaned back in his chair. "Isn't the dinner ready yet? Bring it in!" he bawled.

There was no response from Fourth Aunt outside in the kitchen. Only the rice was done, but there was no tofu. She had been going to fry eggs and a dish of potato slices, then decided she'd do a dish of greens cooked in sour broth instead. Wisdom Xia yelled again, and she shouted back, "Rain Xia's not home yet!"

"So we're not allowed to eat if he's not here? Mid-Star, you must try some of your aunt's cooking."

"What cooking? There's nothing cooked!" shouted Fourth Aunt.

Mid-Star got up. He had to go; he couldn't stay for a meal, he said, but if Fourth Uncle could give him one of the masks, he'd like to hang it in his office. That would make him very happy.

Wisdom Xia handed over one, then one more, and ended up giving him five. "If you like them, I can give you more," he said.

Wisdom Xia saw Mid-Star out, then shut the gate and turned on his wife angrily. "What's up with you today?"

Fourth Aunt was tipping a bowl of slops over the flower bed, and a vegetable leaf stuck to the clump of peonies. "What do you mean?"

"I mean the way you behaved with Mid-Star."

"What's up with *you* today?" his wife retorted. "He's only just become head of the troupe, and you're offering him dinner and giving away your ladles."

Wisdom Xia was nearly apoplectic. "Woman, you've dragged your feet over every single thing I've done, ever."

I won't say any more about the quarrel between Fourth Uncle and Fourth Aunt. What family doesn't squabble sometimes? At any rate, they never raised their voices when they had a disagreement. So let them get on with it.

I'm going to talk about me instead. Just about when Fourth Uncle was showing Mid-Star the opera masks, I was at Mid-Star's, looking for him. Only his dad was there, bent over the stone table in the yard, writing something in his notebook. There were three copper coins on the table, too.

"Uncle Glory, who are you doing predictions for?" I asked, but he snapped the notebook shut.

"Were you looking for Mid-Star? I'm afraid he's very busy. He's only just come back, and people keep calling and he's gone out." Then, after a pause, "Spark, do you know how to kill a chicken?"

"Are you inviting me to dinner now that Mid-Star's become head of the troupe?"

"It's a shame; Obedient Zhang's just brought me a chicken as a present, but he's given it to me alive. Trying to show how well off he is!"

"No, I don't know how to kill a chicken," I said.

He smiled at me, and smiled again, and it turned into a grimace, and he set off at a run for the shithouse, holding up his pants. I took my chance to flick through his notebook. (Normally he wouldn't let anyone look at it.) It was full of scribbled notes on the jobs he'd done mapping feng shui, choosing propitious days, and the divinations he'd worked out. The most recent entry was this: "Divination of my own illness." I couldn't make heads or tails of the hexagrams, but underneath, he'd written his interpretation: "Health generally good, but the trigram lines show my yin and yang are out of kilter. The last ten days I've had diarrhea three times a day, and in the last couple of days, it's been twice on the trot. Does that mean I'm taking a turn for the worse? The twelve increase-decrease hexagrams look good for the ninth month. Good for noblemen; not good for common folk. I'm taking it that I'm a nobleman."

I was startled. This man spoke for the gods and the spirits; that was his job. Nothing in this world or the next could faze him, and yet he was scared when he got a bit of diarrhea? I flicked back a few pages. On one, the heading was, "Expect large takings within three days." Below that, he had interpreted the trigram lines in different ways, but beside each, there was the note, "No large takings." It seemed like he was no different from anyone else; if push came to shove, he'd use charms. In the margin he had written vertically, "In three days, only two gifts of food and three yuan in cash."

I laughed out loud. Then the gate banged open and Mid-Star burst in, carrying the five ladle masks.

Mid-Star's dad was not at all happy when his son turned up with the ladle masks. "Wisdom Xia and his family have loads of good stuff. What do you want with these? They're no use to anyone, and he acts like he's doing you a favor."

But Mid-Star kept telling him how wonderful these masks were, and besides, he was head of the troupe now, and he was smitten with anything to do with opera. He was personally going to revitalize the art, and Fourth Uncle was a model in that regard. They were going touring, and the ladle masks were going with them. They were good publicity.

Suddenly, I had a brilliant idea, "You could take all his ladle masks and make an exhibition of them."

Mid-Star looked at me approvingly. "You do have some brains in your head, after all."

"My mom and dad gave them to me."

"Brains, my ass," his dad grumbled. "Brainy people don't have thick hair, and look at him—his hair's so thick it looks like pig's bristles."

Mid-Star neatened his comb-over and turned to me. "Here's a good-quality cigarette for you. And when we go touring, we'll set up an exhibition and we'll get Fourth Uncle along and he can give talks."

"He won't go," said Mid-Star's dad.

"He might; he loves our local opera."

"Well, even if he does, will you have time to give him the kind of care and attention he needs? He's fussy, I know that. He likes a high pillow winter and summer, he wants a summer sleeping mat and a pillowcase, and he can't sleep if there's too much noise around him. He has to sit down at the table to eat, and he has to have at least four different dishes. If it's *laomian* noodles, they have to be the right width, and he likes persimmon vinegar and plenty of chili on them. He has to wash it all down with the broth from the second boiling of noodles. Fourth Aunt's been looking after him all her life, and he still says she doesn't get it right, so how do you think you'll handle him?"

"It would be best if he didn't come along," I said. "Then I can come with you instead."

"Could you?" said Mid-Star.

"I have strong arms; I can do the heavy work, and I'm really careful, too. I eat anything, I'm not picky. You can give me a straw mattress to sleep on. And I don't want wages, either."

Mid-Star was so excited he wanted to go straight around to Wisdom Xia's house to talk to him about it.

"What are you in such a hurry for?" demanded his dad. "Wait till you've had your dinner."

But Mid-Star went anyway. I ran after him. "Whatever you do, don't say you're going to have me oversee the exhibition."

"Why not?"

"Just don't mention me at all. Not if you want this plan to work."

When I got back, Mid-Star's dad said, "It's hard work, being head of the troupe. It's a big headache for him. And Mid-Star, when he takes something on, he puts his mind to it."

"Who doesn't put their mind to it?" I asked.

He smiled at me. "Want some snacks?"

"Sure. I know you've been getting plenty of food gifts!"

He took me into the big room and opened the cabinet. Inside was bag after bag of presents. There was a piece of cake in a bowl with one bite taken out of it, and he gave that to me, but first he pinched off some crumbs and put them in his mouth. "Nice!"

I was pretty pleased with myself, and so was Wisdom Xia, so neither of us got much sleep that night. At dawn, I got up to see Mid-Star off on the bus. He was taking two sacks full of ladle masks to the county seat and promised that as soon as they were ready to start touring, he'd let me know.

Once he'd left, I got a sudden craving for some fish. When you're happy, it gives you an appetite. But I didn't go and buy one at the pond, which Shifty managed. I figured that with my run of good luck, I'd be able to snatch one from the river. There was a deep pool at the head of the dam, and there were usually catfish between the cracks in the rocks. That kind of catfish had long whiskers and smooth skin. Most people found them hard to catch, but I could manage it, I was sure. I put my arm in the water and got hold of one. I walked back through the village. Coming toward me was Star Chen, singing,

This is love, Can't be put into words,
This is love, And it's got me all confused.

I can put it into words, I said to myself, *but I'm not going to do it for a numbskull like you.* I swung the fish in his face as he passed. He stopped singing.

"You got fish?"

"I'm starving," I told him. "Let's go to Clerk's wife's shop and get her to steam it for us."

Wisdom Xia, on the other hand, woke up sick. His head felt like it was going to explode.

"You should be happy, now you've given all your ladles to Mid-Star, but instead you tossed and turned all night," Fourth Aunt told him. All the same, she told Rain Xia to go and get some scallions from their vegetable patch. She'd make Wisdom Xia some soup so he could sweat it out.

Wisdom Xia felt that was all too much trouble and took himself off to Big-Noise Zhao's pharmacy for some painkillers. Coming out of the alley, he bumped into Rites Xia talking to Citizen Li's wife. As soon as she caught sight of him, the woman hurried away.

"Have you eaten?" Wisdom Xia asked his brother.

"I have. And by the way, the restaurant is now selling fried breadsticks and soy milk. Why don't you tell Rain Xia to get you some?"

"I wouldn't go in there. Have you seen that they keep their piss bucket indoors all day? The food Clerk's wife sells will be just as dirty."

"Are you going to the West Mountain Bend market then?"

"No, there's nothing I want, and it's too far."

"When our new market's built, there'll be a market every day to go to."

"I haven't been to the site for a few days. Have they finished the main building yet?"

"No. Bounty's got a lot going on. He's building a house for Treasure and building the market, too."

Wisdom Xia grunted, then looked up at the sky, where little fluffy clouds danced. It would be another sunny day.

The brothers walked out of the alley together, and then each went their separate ways: Rites went northward, walking splayfooted, and Wisdom headed to Middle Street, where he bumped into Blossom. "Have you got no money, or are you deliberately mistreating your dad?" he asked her.

"What are you talking about, Uncle?" asked Blossom.

"I'm saying, he's off to market in a pair of shoes that must be really uncomfortable, because the heels are worn right down on one side."

"That's just the way he walks. He wears out all his shoes on one side."

"Why don't you buy him a few pairs at a time, see if that helps?"

Meantime, I went to the restaurant and asked Clerk's wife to gut and steam the catfish, and Star and I hunkered down in the doorway, drinking our soy milk. We watched as Wisdom walked down the street, with everyone greeting him and him nodding away.

I said to Dog-Scraps's son, Leg Sores, "Want some soy milk?"

He stared at me, his Adam's apple jerking up and down, and finally said, "Yes."

I slapped him across the face, and he looked like he wanted to hit me, but I said, "Go on, cry!" and he broke out into a wail.

That brought Wisdom over. "What are you crying about?" he asked.

I answered for Leg Sores. "He wanted some soy milk, but he didn't have any money, so he asked for it on credit, but Mrs. Clerk told him, 'Who d'you think you are, a township cadre or something?' And that made the kid cry."

Clerk's wife was still looking dazed at my story when Wisdom said to her, "Why are you cussing the kid for wanting a bowl of soy milk? Give him a bowlful, and two fried breadsticks, too." And he threw a one-yuan coin down on the counter.

"Fourth Uncle, let me serve you a bowl, too," said the woman.

"I don't want any. And put a bamboo basket over the breadsticks—look at all those flies buzzing around."

"But Uncle, they're only food flies," protested Clerk's wife.

By that time, a bunch of people had gathered a little bit down the alley on the other side, and we heard the spluttering of firecrackers. So I'd better explain what the firecrackers were all about. On the triangle of land where the market was being built, at the north end, there was a chinaberry tree. Obviously, the tree had to be cut down, but Pavilion thought it was a pity, so he had it dug up by the roots and transplanted to his backyard. Along with the tree, they dug up two large stone statues of a man and a woman. They looked a bit strange, but no one thought they were very valuable. Bounty struck one of them and knocked a bit off its shoulder, and just at that moment, along came Third-Kid Li's mom to see what was going on.

"Aren't they the Earth God and the Earth Goddess?" she said.

And when everyone looked closer, they could see the statues were wearing head towels and long gowns, had long faces and flat noses, prominent eyes with no dents for the pupils, and deep wrinkles all over their faces. The older villagers all agreed with Third-Kid Li's mom: these must be the Earth God and the Earth Goddess. If that was the case, then they were divinities. All right, they were only minor figures, but they were still divine. So they were moved to the Earth Shrine.

There was one Buddhist temple and one shrine in Freshwind Village, both built by my grandad's grandad. The temple was Freshwind Temple, and the shrine was the Earth Shrine. It was in North Alley off Middle Street, and, as I remember, it was about the size of a big stone roller. Inside it was empty, but there were two pine trees outside, and we often sat under them, picking up pine nuts and cracking them between our teeth. Sometime later, shops were built on either side, and the Earth Shrine was squeezed between them. In fact, the builders used it as a dump for their rubble, broken bricks and tiles. The pines were felled and used to make the table in the village office's meeting room. The shrine door vanished, too, and all that covered the doorframe was a spider's web with a big fat spider in the middle.

As we sat drinking our soy milk, a bunch of people were sweeping out the Earth Shrine and moving the statues inside. I hadn't known anything about this business beforehand; nor had Wisdom Xia. It struck me as very strange that anything—big or small—could happen in Freshwind Village without Wisdom Xia and me knowing about it. So I carried my bowl over there and sat on the shrine steps and watched the firecrackers being let off. I had no interest in the statues, and as for the man letting off the firecrackers, he was useless. He twirled a firecracker in the air, then dropped it in a hurry when there was still a long section unburned, and the unburned bit flew into my face. I stayed quite calm, didn't even get up, just caught the firecracker between my chopsticks, easy as anything, and held it up so it sparkled and spat.

Wisdom Xia arrived, and the crowd fell back to make way for him. He took a long look at the statues and finally said, "The gods have come home!"

Everyone pressed around him and bombarded him with questions. How come they'd ended up under the chinaberry tree at the north end of the triangular building site? Why had they been buried there? Was it done when the main street was widened, or had they been thrown out during the Cultural Revolution? And how had the chinaberry tree grown on top of them, anyway? No one had any idea. It was a mystery even to Wisdom Xia. But everyone agreed that it was a good omen that they had been unearthed; the new market was bound to be a success. What a good thing it was that they hadn't backed Concord Qin's gully-filling project. After all, the gods were never going to smile on Concord Qin the way they did on Pavilion. Concord Qin didn't even look the part, with his small nose and mouth.

"Huh!" I said scornfully when I heard that.

"What do you mean?" said Big-Eighth Zhang, the one who always had a stuffed-up nose.

"I mean, maybe Pavilion buried the statues himself."

You could have heard a pin drop.

"Who said that?" Wisdom Xia demanded.

The crowd fell back, and there he was, standing five yards away, glaring at me. I didn't dare look him in the eyes. He had a long face and deep creases on either side of his lips. A cloud of dust eddied up in front of me—his words had raised the dust, falling from his lips and striking the ground. Clerk's wife was standing behind me, and she grabbed the soy milk bowl out of my hand and swiped me over the head with a dish cloth.

"You're crazy!" she hissed.

"Did I say something crazy?" I asked Fourth Uncle.

Wisdom Xia raised his voice. "You're not crazy; your words aren't crazy. You're just devious. I'm telling you: these statues disappeared when Pavilion was just a kid."

I sat down on the steps, mortified. Everyone was laughing at me. I turned on Clerk's wife. "You don't touch a man's head or a woman's foot. Why did you hit my head? Bring me another bowl of soy milk, you hear that? Another soy milk!"

When Wisdom Xia arrived at the Great Qing Hall, Big-Noise Zhao was inside, writing couplets. He looked up to see the old man looking grim. Before he could ask anything, Wisdom Xia said, "I need to wash my face."

Big-Noise Zhao hurriedly poured water into a washbowl for him.

Looking much brighter, Wisdom Xia said, "That fucking Spark. Why's he always trying to stir up mud when the water's clear?"

"Has he made you mad?"

"Yes, but it's made my headache better. What are you doing? You're an herbalist, but I never see you reading medical books. All you do all day is write couplets."

"Well, that's what I'm good at," Zhao said. "I don't want to blow my own trumpet, but I could have been a university professor. I just wasn't destined to turn out like Wind Xia, so all

167

I could do was make my living as an herbalist. Trouble is, the only worthwhile thing in this world is education. Who wants to live just to fill their belly?"

"Well, you're such a blabbermouth, you would probably have been demoted from prof to herbalist anyway. And who's getting married?" he added, eyeing the couplets.

"No one's going to get married without inviting you, right? These are for the Earth Shrine."

Justice Xia took a closer look.

The first line read, "This village is full of jokers." The next one, "We two say not a word."

"It's nicely written," he said. "But if the Earth God and the Earth Goddess don't speak, then someone has to speak for them."

Big-Noise Zhao applauded. "There's to be a horizontal tablet, too." And he set brush to paper and wrote, "Everything stands and falls with the Xia clan."

"Have you had any complaints about the Xias?" said Wisdom Xia.

"Never about the Xias, and even if I did, it wouldn't be about you, Fourth Uncle."

"Things are complicated in this life," said the old man with a smile. "Some people are good but dull, so you don't want to hang around with them. Others, you know they'll do you harm, but they're fun, so they stick in your mind."

"Who are you talking about?" said Big-Noise Zhao cheerfully. He then brewed some tea for Wisdom Xia.

Wisdom Xia opened the sachet, dissolved his painkillers in water, and drank it. A sheen of sweat appeared on his forehead. He slowly sipped his tea.

"How many couplets have you written?" he asked.

Big-Noise Zhao added them up on his fingers. "Two hundred. There may be more; I can't remember."

"Well, if you've written so many, you should get Wind Xia to put you in touch with a publisher in the provincial city, see if they can publish a volume of your work."

"Is it Wind Xia getting his work published that made you think of that? But who's going to want to publish mine? I'm just a peasant."

"Wind Xia says that if a book is going to sell, the publisher will pay you, and a volume of yours would sell well, unlike mine," said Wisdom Xia.

"Have you had a book out, too?"

"My opera masks. The troupe have been at me for a long time to get them published, but the only buyers will be researchers of Shaanxi opera. So I'd have to pay for the publication."

"You could afford that, couldn't you?"

"From ancient times to the present, when have scholars ever been rich?" said Wisdom Xia. "The noble have always been poor, and the rich have never been noble. Except for the emperor, of course, who has wealth and nobility all rolled into one. Still, if I ever get to publish, I'll be sure to come and borrow some money off you."

"I can lend you a bit, not a lot. There's someone else you should ask, too," said Big-Noise Zhao.

"Who?"

"Your brother, Third Uncle."

"He doesn't have money; Thunder does."

"You've got it wrong; he's got the most money."

Big-Noise Zhao was a real blabbermouth. As soon as you told him anything, even the local pigs and dogs knew about it. Now he told Wisdom Xia that last August, on the eighth, someone had turned up asking if he had silver dollars. He could tell he was a smuggler, so he refused to talk to him. But the man then asked if there was someone in the village called Rites Xia and, if so, where he lived. Big-Noise Zhao had pointed him in the right direction, and the man went off. Then this spring, he'd seen Rites Xia carrying ten silver dollars in a cloth bag. Each silver dollar went for seventy or eighty yuan, so if Rites Xia had been dealing in them for some years, he must have been rolling in it.

Big-Noise Zhao's eyelids blinked rapidly as he talked. Justice Xia thought back. It was true that Rites was always running off to regional markets, but he never seemed to take anything to sell, or to buy anything. And he had just seen Rites talking to Citizen Li's wife, and the pair of them stopped talking the moment they caught sight of him. Citizen Li's family had been wealthy before the revolution. His dad had been a bandit, so it was perfectly possible that his wife had been selling silver dollars to Rites Xia.

With a heavy heart, grim faced once more, Wisdom Xia said, "Can you vouch for everything you've just said?"

Big-Noise Zhao looked at the old man, and, startled by his sudden seriousness, said, "It . . . it . . ."

"You're talking serious lawbreaking. If you haven't got proof, then don't go spreading rumors."

"I know that. I wouldn't have said anything if you weren't his younger brother. If you weren't Wisdom Xia, Fourth Uncle, the words would have stayed rotting in my belly."

Wisdom Xia suddenly gave two sneezes.

"You're better!" exclaimed Big-Noise Zhao.

"One sneeze is because someone's talking about you. Two sneezes, and someone's bad-mouthing you. Fuck it, who's bad-mouthing me?" asked Wisdom Xia.

I was the one bad-mouthing Wisdom Xia, because he'd bad-mouthed me in front of so many people. That was many times worse than Pavilion beating me, so obviously I was bad-mouthing him. But deep inside, I was grateful to him. Other people said I was crazy; Wisdom Xia said I wasn't, and I didn't talk crazy, either. Thing is, even if you hated Wisdom Xia, you couldn't help respecting him.

After I'd eaten my steamed catfish and gone back to the Earth Shrine again, I heard comments like, "The crazy's done well for himself; he's bought a fish to eat."

"The next person who says I'm crazy had better watch out," I said. "I'll fuck their mother!"

There was loud laughter. "And what are you going to fuck their mother with, your head? You don't have anything down there."

"Don't tease Spark," said Mid-Star's dad. "You should feel sorry for him."

Suddenly I was furious. "I don't want your pity!" I shouted.

"All right, all right, no one's allowed to say that Spark's given himself the chop. He's still one of the funniest people in Freshwind Village. Let's get him to make us a speech." There was loud applause.

I was still angry, and I really wanted to sling a bit of mud at Pavilion, so I spoke loud and clear. "Fellow villagers! Life is not easy for us, and our work is hard, but we have big dreams. One day, we'll have money, and we'll all be able to afford fried breadsticks. There'll be white sugar and brown sugar, and we'll be able choose which one to dip them in. When we want soy milk, we'll be able to buy two bowls, drink one, and pour the other away!"

There was another burst of applause.

I went on. "This is Party Secretary Pavilion Xia's dream for us, that we should all get rich with him."

Shifty stood up. "Spark, that's crap! What kind of a 'dream' is that? What would two muck-raking oxen say about it?"

I was furious at Shifty for butting in. "If you understand what muck-raking oxen say, then you tell us."

And he did. "If two muck-raking oxen are talking about dreams, one says, 'Just you wait till I have a bit of money. I'll contract for all the muck for ten *li* hereabouts. No one else will get their hands on it.' And the other says, 'That's in poor taste. When I have money, I'll hire two girls to come and crap for me, and I'll eat it while it's fresh and tasty!'"

But it was Shifty who was in poor taste. His joke was disgusting, and it diluted the significance of what I'd said. I wasn't going to take any more of this and was turning to go when Big-Noise Zhao came over with the couplets he'd been writing.

"Spark, Spark, don't go."

"Who are you giving those to?" I asked.

"To the Earth God and Goddess." And he stuck them up on either side of the shrine entrance.

I looked at them. "Big-Noise, you're an educated man. Tell me, are these gods important?"

"No, they're minor deities, the smallest."

"But they look after the earth; how can they be the smallest? They should be up there with our top-grade cadres."

"Like Pavilion, you mean?"

"But if Pavilion was an Earth God, surely he'd have finished the gully-filling?" I said.

"Why's your head so full of crap nowadays?"

It was true: my head was full of crap. I pulled off the couplets and ran away with them. Big-Noise Zhao set off after me, but I shouted back, "If you chase me, I'll tear them up!"

He stopped then and cursed a blue streak.

Let him curse and swear; words couldn't hurt me. I went and pasted the couplets up on Justice Xia's gate. To this day, I don't know what made me do that. To be truthful, I wasn't thinking; it was as if I was acting under orders. I rubbed my fingers along my teeth and used the gunk to stick the couplets up. They wouldn't have stayed there, except that just when I'd gotten the top edges stuck down, a ripple of a breeze flattened them against the gate frame. Then a myriad dragonflies turned up from the village pond. They had red wings, and there were so many of them that they formed a red cloud in front of the gate.

What on earth was going on? I was so astonished that I went down to the pond to see. Looking back, I could see the air above the gate was red with dragonflies; it looked like it was on fire. Later, I described this phenomenon to Big-Noise Zhao, but he didn't believe me. He said I was just pretending to be fey.

"If I'm not telling the truth, may I turn into a pig!" I swore.

"Maybe it means that Justice Xia will succeed!" exclaimed Big-Noise Zhao.

I'd never set much store by what that man said, but in this case, his words came true.

Chapter 19

A day had already passed before Justice Xia noticed the couplets above his gate.

The night before, Gold had come back from his work unit with a spring in his step and a bottle of liquor under his arm, having secured his son a position. To accompany the liquor, he picked up three *jin* of lamb and a pack of salted, dried tofu. When he got in the door, Chastity told him her side of the argument with Halfwit. As the oldest son, he should have taken some responsibility, but he'd ended up annoying his father instead. There wasn't much he could do at the moment but scold Chastity.

Chastity very quickly turned the tables on him. Gold had yanked a tiger by the tail. When he'd come home, Chastity had been rolling out dough to make noodles, but now the dough was left untouched on the table.

She let him have it. "You're a coward! A soft-shelled egg! Soft all over! A man is supposed to look after a woman. I'm still waiting for you to look after me! A man should be a big tree for a woman to take shelter under. Where's my shelter? You're about as good as an umbrella in a gale."

When Gold saw that the noodles were not going to be coming, he tucked the bottle of liquor back under his arm and went out the door. He stopped beside the stone roller. "This is how you treat my parents?" he shouted at the stone. "You'll be old, too, someday. You're going to be the death of me, woman. I can't take it."

As Gold shouted, Marvel walked by and paused to watch. He asked, "Who are you talking to?"

"I'm not talking to you. I'm talking to that wife of mine."

"Well, where is she? Is she in that stone?"

Gold gave the stone roller a kick that failed to budge it. He looked down and saw he'd ripped his shoe.

Justice Xia was in Treasure's paddy field, spreading fertilizer, while his wife worked in the kitchen. She peeled a half basinful of potatoes and set about boiling them to add to a pot of dough-drop soup. Tongue-Tied was in the yard, splitting firewood. He was working with his ax on two thick logs. It was slow going. When he finally split one of the logs, Second Aunt called over, "Take it easy over there. You're going to end up hitting me." Tongue-Tied kept swinging.

After Halfwit got married, he was the final son to move out, and Justice Xia and his wife lived alone. Their five sons had proposed that the parents eat at a different one of their houses each night of the week, but Justice Xia hadn't agreed. He thought about how busy his daughters-in-law were, especially when it was harvest time. When they were pressed for time, they could throw together something quick, but if Justice Xia and his wife were there, they'd end up being distracted from the work at hand.

Justice Xia was set in his ways. He didn't want to drag his blind wife from door to door, as if he were begging for food. Justice Xia told them, "I'm giving up our plots of land to divide among the five of you. All I ask is that a couple of times a year, you give us fifty *jin* of wheat, a hundred *jin* of rice, five *jin* of beans, and whatever else you've got, and let us use what we need from your gardens. That way, we can make what we want to eat, when we want to eat."

There was something else that Justice Xia didn't want to bring up: the wives of his five sons were not easy to get along with. He knew that if he was going to go from house to house every week, there would be problems. He thought it better not to put pressure on his sons or their wives. As the old saying goes, "Even the filial son leaves his father's deathbed if he lingers too long."

That system held up for a few years. Justice Xia kept working, helping his sons in the fields. But the old man wasn't the worker he'd been in his younger years, and even his small contribution started causing problems. The daughters-in-law started to complain about the division of labor, that he'd done more work here and less work there. Justice Xia didn't think too much of it. He worked in the fields because he wanted to work. Getting his hands dirty was what kept the old man going. If he didn't work, he started to get restless.

Eventually, it got to be too much, and Justice Xia withdrew from the family. Justice Xia's affection was soaked up by Tongue-Tied. The boy spent most days in his grandfather's home. Tongue-Tied was a faithful companion to his grandfather, and he could pull his weight, too.

He was just getting through the second log when Clerk's wife arrived to call him home. She told him she wanted him to look after Lucky. The dog was going down to the township administration every day to chase after Tiger. Secretary Liu was nervous about Tiger's virtue. Tiger had been crossbred from a foreign breed, and Lucky was a common village dog. And he wasn't fond of the way Lucky showed up at the township administration and started barking like crazy. It was starting to interfere with the regular operation of the township government, he said.

Tongue-Tied couldn't speak but he could understand. He moaned a response.

Clerk warned him, "Don't talk to me that way. I'm just passing on Secretary Liu's message."

Tongue-Tied moaned again.

"Freshwind has plenty of dogs. Why does Lucky have to chase after that one?"

Second Aunt looked up from the potatoes she was peeling. "Watch the way you talk about our Lucky. Lucky didn't go chasing after Tiger. It was Tiger that came over here first."

She put down the peeler, grabbed her walking stick, and headed toward the bathroom. Tongue-Tied rushed to get the piss bucket for her, but she brushed him off.

Clerk said, "Don't worry. You don't have to go all the way there . . ."

"I might be old, but I'm still a woman."

"Well, okay. I should be going. I just came to pass along the message from Secretary Liu. Use your bucket."

She went out of the yard and ran right into Tiger, who barked at her. "You picked the perfect time to leave, huh?"

When Justice Xia came into the yard, his legs were bare, and he was carrying his shoes. He bent at the waist, completely exhausted. He didn't notice the fat red tick crawling up his calf. Tongue-Tied rushed over and slapped Justice Xia's leg. He shouted, "What's wrong with you?" He looked down and saw the tick fall into the dirt. Justice Xia hadn't even felt the tick sucking blood from his leg. A trail of blood ran down his leg like a worm.

Tongue-Tied picked the tick out of the dirt and cut it into four pieces with his thumbnail.

Justice Xia swore. "The hell are you doing? Go ahead and kill it, but why do you have to be so cruel? It's disgusting."

Tongue-Tied ran off.

Second Aunt said, "We're about to eat. What did you do that for?"

"He can go home and eat. We can't be feeding him every day. What are we eating, anyway?"

"Dough-drop soup with potatoes."

He went into the kitchen, came back with a bowl for her, and then filled his own bowl. He was about to take a sip when he looked down and saw that the bowl was full of maggots. He pulled the bowl out of her hands. "It's got worms in it. Why didn't you put a net over it? I'll make you something else to eat."

"Worms? Just pick them out. Fish them out like they're bones without meat on them. It'd be a shame to waste it."

Justice Xia agreed that it was a shame to waste the food. He picked out the worms one by one. He was ready to eat when Gold came into the yard with a bottle of liquor. When Justice Xia saw his son coming, he felt a pain in his gut. It hurt so bad that he had to put down the bowl and chopsticks.

It was Second Aunt who spoke first, calling out her son's name—she could tell from his footsteps who it was. Gold put the liquor on the shelf. She said, "What are you angry about? It was Chastity and Halfwit fighting. What are you blaming Gold for?"

Gold sat down beside his mother. "What are you eating? I'll have a bowl, too."

He was trying to be cheerful. He got up and went to the kitchen, but when he saw the mass of maggots, he felt sick. He tipped out the rice and started over, making his parents a fresh pot.

Justice Xia's anger dissipated as he watched Gold wash the rice in the bucket. "Everything's set with Shiner?"

"Everything's set."

Justice Xia said, "When does he start?"

"Probably another couple of weeks."

"Tell him that when he works for the public, he can't act like he's working at home. He has to take it seriously. I saw the way you raised him. The fields could be full of weeds, and he wouldn't lift a finger."

Gold grunted. He went back to washing the rice and put it on to cook. He took down the bottle of liquor and passed it to Justice Xia. The old man tried to open it with his teeth and then gave up and pried it open on the doorframe. He took a sip and said, "This is the real deal."

"You're in a good mood now, huh?"

Justice Xia called to Gold, "I'm going to make a fire. Go get Third Uncle and Fourth Uncle. Tell them to come and drink."

In Freshwind, arguments aren't uncommon. You have fathers feuding with their sons and sworn brothers becoming foes. But Justice Xia, Rites Xia, and Wisdom Xia had never argued before. Good fortune for one was good fortune for the rest of them. Gold went to Fourth Uncle's place first. Wisdom Xia, trailing smoke from his water pipe, rose to follow him.

Fourth Aunt called after him, "You've got a cold. What are you going out drinking for?"

"My brother called me over. I have to go. Put some green onion in a steamed bun for me. I need some food in my stomach."

Gold went to Third Uncle's place next. Rites Xia was working at patching a hole in the kang. His face was drenched with sweat. He looked up. "You want to drink on a hot day like this? I'm staying here."

Gold dragged him out the door. Rites Xia pulled away and went around to shut the windows and lock the door. He put the key above the doorframe and went out of the yard. Before he'd gone a hundred steps, he turned back and got the key down from the doorframe and put it in his pocket.

Emerald, who was lying out in the yard, cooling off, called over to him, "Nobody's going to open your door, Grandpa."

"You sure about that? Well then, tell me what happened to my glasses. I put them in my hanging basket, and now they're gone."

"Who would take your glasses?"

"I saw Bright Chen wearing them yesterday. How do you think he got his hands on them?"

"Don't be like that. He's probably just borrowing them for a few days. He'll give them back. You know he has pink eye. Go and get your shoes fixed and see if he charges you."

Rites Xia stamped away.

The three brothers and Gold shared a bottle of liquor and bowls of rice porridge. Justice Xia knew one bottle wouldn't be enough, so he pulled another one out of the cabinet. Gold retreated from the table to sit on the kang with his mother. Bamboo had showed up, too, and she took a seat at the edge of the kang and lit her second cigarette.

Gold said, "You're hooked on those things worse than I am."

"It soothes my nerves."

"What about my nerves?"

"What do you have to worry about? You've got Shiner all set up now. What about my son? Who is going to set him up? His destiny is running a plow and staring at a cow's backside."

"Shiner's not going to be making much more money down there than a farmer would. If he was made of stronger stuff, I would have told him to go to the city to work. You can make a name for yourself that way."

Second Aunt sneezed, and Gold and Bamboo stopped talking. She said, "Who's at the gate?"

Gold couldn't hear any sound from the yard. "Sharp ears. What do you hear out there?"

"Someone's at the gate."

Bamboo stood and went to look, but nobody was there. She came back and told Second Aunt. She turned back to Gold. "Out of our four families, they're the luckiest. But our five sons can't measure up to Thunder, let alone Wind Xia."

"Goodness said it the best. Wind Xia took all the talent for himself, a century's worth of Freshwind's talent . . . The rest of the Xia boys have barely got a pulse."

"It's like making money. If you have money, it's easy to make more. If you've got none to start with, you're shit out of luck. Wind Xia's heir has to be a dragon or a phoenix. Fourth Uncle, is Snow Bai pregnant yet?"

"You can't ask him that," Gold said. "If she was pregnant, you'd know already because Fourth Aunt would quit grumbling about it."

Second Aunt sneezed again and said, "Who's out there?"

"It must be the wind," Bamboo said. She went on talking about Shiner and the Xia boys. Lucky ran into the room with Tongue-Tied following, moaning something.

Bamboo and Gold couldn't understand, but Second Aunt said, "Your uncle's kid got burned?"

Tongue-Tied moaned.

"What about your uncle?"

Tongue-Tied gesticulated wildly.

"Go over to Halfwit, Bamboo. That wicked daughter-in-law of mine burned the kid."

"How? And where is Halfwit?"

"He went to play mah-jongg."

As Bamboo went out, Second Aunt was already crying. She called out, "Bring vinegar with you. Rub it on the child's burns."

Justice Xia, Rites Xia, and Wisdom Xia had kept drinking through all of this. They heard bits and pieces of the conversation, floating over to their table, but it was only when they heard Second Aunt sobbing that they knew something was really wrong.

Justice Xia scolded her. "What are you crying about over there? What's wrong with you?" He went on to curse Halfwit for his mah-jongg habit. Even when Halfwit had no money, he'd still hang out over there. What was there to see around a mah-jongg table?

Rites Xia tried to come to Halfwit's defense, saying that out of the nine children of Gold's generation, Halfwit had it the worst, so it was no wonder he'd end up doing something like sitting around a mah-jongg table all day, watching the tiles. Rites Xia told Bamboo to go over to see how badly the child was burned.

"And that wife of his, can't even look after a child," Justice Xia said. "If the kid doesn't have a cough, it's the runs . . . The kid is like a sick rat!"

"What's the point in complaining now? He already married her. Have a drink instead. Have a drink!" said Rites Xia.

"You're right about that, brother. But I'm telling you, if you have a useless son, don't let him marry an even more useless woman."

"You'd be happier if he didn't get married?" Second Aunt asked. "You want him to be alone his whole life?"

"What the hell are you talking about? What did I do to be cursed with a woman like you? You gave me a litter of pigs and dogs."

Second Aunt started to cry again, even louder this time.

Bamboo took the bottle of vinegar from the kitchen and tried to comfort Second Aunt. She said to Justice Xia, "Don't talk to her like that."

Gold told her to hurry up and bring the vinegar over to Halfwit's house. He led Second Aunt into the kitchen to sit down and then went back to the table to refill his glass. He looked across the table at Wisdom Xia.

Wisdom Xia drained his own glass and set it back down on the table. "You should go, too, Gold. If Chastity and Halfwit get into it, it'll be better if you're there. If the burns aren't too serious, go over to my house and get some badger-fat balm for the child. If it turns out to be serious, you'll have to bring the child over to Big-Noise. Tell him that I'll cover the expenses."

Gold and Bamboo rose and left together. After a couple of hours, Gold came back alone, saying that Halfwit's wife had burned the child while making dinner. One of the child's arms was burned, so he put some of the badger-fat balm on it. He told them that Bamboo had already gone home. Everyone breathed a sigh of relief.

Someone said, "That's enough drinking for today." Everyone went home to sleep.

Wisdom Xia was tipsy. He hung his head and walked down the alley, heading home. He fell into a dark mood, thinking over what had been said at the table. He also felt ill, and when a cold wind blew down the alley, he bent over and spilled the contents of his stomach on the ground. He stumbled over to a tree and leaned against its trunk. He looked up and saw that across the alley, in the courtyard of Mid-Star's place, all the trees were lit by candles. An altar had been brought out into the yard, and Mid-Star's father knelt silently beside it.

Marvel was going around to each tree and pulling down branches. He wove them into a leafy crown that he put on his head. Marvel went to the altar and placed some offerings, lit sticks of incense, and poured out some liquor. From a sheet of paper he read, "I invite the Lord of the Big Dipper to take a seat in this humble setting. All twelve trees of this yard, lit with candles and incense, welcome you. The master of these trees, Xia Shengrong, born on the eleventh day of the month of Wuyin and now sixty-six years of age, has for his entire life been industrious, frugal, and charitable. He cares deeply about the people of the village. He has raised a son who has shown great promise. But he has also looked after the other sons of the village, including me.

"Now, he is sick and suffering. My twelve brothers—the eldest, elm; the second brother, peach; the poplar, the plum tree, the persimmon, date, lilac, cherry, toon, pear, and willow trees, and the *huajiao*—pledge a year of their lives to him. When the trees flower and fruit, all will be offered to the Lord. We will light firecrackers and show a movie and burn incense. This is the pledge of the people and the trees. Please hear our prayers. Let this document serve as proof."

After the prayer was read, Wisdom Xia felt a cool breeze pass over him, and he shivered from head to toe. He had never cared for Mid-Star's father, but it was sad to see Mid-Star fall ill just after he'd been appointed head of the opera troupe. He knew the father's pain. He thought back to his own mother, who had always been sick in her later years. Benevolence Xia had always been the one to go to the hospital and then come back to the altar to pray for her life. "Take ten years from my life and give them to my mother."

Her health improved, but Benevolence Xia had died at fifty-five. Their mother had said, "He should have lived until sixty-six. He died ten years early. Those ten years, he gave to me." Maybe there was something to the prayers, after all. But Wisdom Xia didn't understand why they were praying for Mid-Star's dad instead of Mid-Star—and why was Marvel acting as the representative for the twelve trees of the courtyard?

He stood for a while there, until Marvel came out of the courtyard. Wisdom Xia called out quietly and Marvel jumped. "Fourth Uncle! Why are you still out and about?"

"Why are you praying for Mid-Star's father's life?"

"How did you know? He's sick, too. I wanted Mid-Star to pledge some years of his life in the prayer, but he wasn't willing. So, it was the trees. They can't speak, so I was there as a representative, to read that prayer for them. Do you think this kind of thing really works, Fourth Uncle?"

He grunted, then turned and left. As he went, he said, as if to himself, "Maybe, maybe . . ."

By the time Wisdom Xia got home, Fourth Aunt was already asleep. He sat in the rattan chair in the main room and lit his water pipe. The room was completely dark except for a small triangle of light that fell on the floor. When Rain Xia finally got home, he pulled the courtyard gate, which opened with a creak. He pulled out his dick and pissed on the hinges. The gate swung open and closed behind him without a sound. He crept into the house. He was sneaking through the main room when he heard Wisdom Xia. "You're back, huh?"

Rain Xia jumped with fright. "I was going to come back earlier, but Roughshod Ding wanted to play for a while longer. He lost again . . ."

"So, you won?"

"Well, um . . . I'm never playing mah-jongg again. I promise."

"If you win, there's no problem."

"Father . . ."

"If you're not going to bed, take out the money. Go over to Big-Noise's and get me some qi supplements. I need twelve packs."

"What do you need that for? At this time of night? Who's sick?"

"I told you to go, so go. Big-Noise will be sleeping, so you'll have to get him up."

Rain Xia was confused, but he went out, happy that his father hadn't cussed him out again. He jogged down the street. When Rain Xia came home with the pills, Wisdom Xia tossed them in a basket and told Rain Xia to grab a spade and follow him. "When I tell you to do something, you do it. Keep your mouth shut." The two went out to the northeast corner of the courtyard, and Wisdom Xia told his son to dig a hole. He tossed one pack of pills into the hole. They moved to the northwest corner and repeated the process. They did the same in the southeast corner and the southwest corner. Rain Xia glanced at his father, but Wisdom Xia didn't speak. Rain Xia didn't dare question him.

Wisdom Xia and his son walked over to Rites Xia's home. They went around to the four corners of his courtyard and buried packs of medicine. After that, they went to Justice Xia's courtyard and did the same thing. When they were at the northeast corner of Justice Xia's courtyard, Second Aunt was alerted by the sound of their spades and pounded at the window, shouting, "Who's out there? What are you doing?" Wisdom Xia motioned for Rain Xia to stay silent, and they finished burying the medicine. Second Aunt kicked her husband awake and said, "Did you hear that? What was that sound?"

Justice Xia listened for a moment. "What? I don't hear anything. Just because you can't sleep doesn't mean I have to suffer, too." He went back to sleep, and the room was once again filled with the sound of his snoring.

Rain Xia had no idea what his father was doing, burying qi supplements in the middle of the night. It came up again a few days later, when he and Roughshod Ding were sitting around, drinking tea. I was over there, too, actually. Roughshod Ding had no idea, either. I just laughed.

He said, "What are you laughing about? Do you know why he buried them?"

Of course I knew. Whatever you eat, it cures that thing—like, Big-Noise Zhao had told me to get my father to eat pork stomach when he had a stomach problem, and they say you should eat walnuts if you've got bad lungs. So even though the Xia family's men had never amounted to much, apart from Wind Xia and Thunder, Wisdom Xia thought the supplements might help bolster the masculine qi of the clan's men.

I didn't bother telling this to Rain Xia. There are some things you just can't say. If I'd let slip what Wisdom Xia was doing, it would have meant revealing a secret that shouldn't have been revealed. Rain Xia went back to ignoring me. I saw him glance out the doorway at White-Moth, who was sitting on the grindstone.

White-Moth was wearing a short skirt that showed her plump white legs. They looked like a pair of daikon. From her perch on the grindstone, she cast glances toward the west end of the street.

Roughshod Ding said, "Shifty's going to get here any minute now."

"You think she's wearing any panties under that skirt?"

"Who'd wear a skirt without panties?"

"I bet she's not!"

They both snickered.

White-Moth hopped down from the grindstone and said, "What are you laughing at?"

"It was just Spark . . ."

White-Moth looked at me and said, "You're Spark? I've heard Shifty mention you."

I knew he couldn't have sung my praises, whatever he'd said to her about me. I said, "What did he say about me? You know what I do to people who talk about me behind my back? I cut their tongues off."

"Really? I heard you cut other things off, too." She laughed. I knew exactly what she was laughing about. I stood and was about to go, but she stepped closer and pinched my cheek. "I didn't expect you to be a pretty boy."

Just then, Shifty roared up on his motorcycle, and White-Moth ran to take a seat behind him. The pair ripped off down the street, but right before they were out of view, a blast of wind lifted White-Moth's skirt, and I saw that she really wasn't wearing panties. Rain Xia and Roughshod Ding laughed as she pushed her skirt back down to cover her ass.

Rain Xia turned to me. "The way she pinched your cheek like that, she was into you."

I spat on the ground at Rain Xia's feet.

It wasn't unusual for people in Freshwind to make fun of me, but it still upset me. I had never had an issue with Rain Xia, but after that day when I spat at his feet, I always steered clear of him. If I needed something, I'd go to Tongue-Tied. He was a good man. But where was I? I've gotten off track. Let me get back to Justice Xia.

A couple of days later, when Justice Xia went out carrying the piss bucket to dump on Halfwit's green onions, he noticed the couplet pasted to his doorframe. He was momentarily shaken from his ruminations on the properties in fresh urine that made green onions grow so fast. He said, "Who put this here?"

Second Aunt, who was sitting combing her hair on the stairs in the main room, said, "I heard someone moving around out there. That must have been right when they were putting up a big-character poster."

Justice Xia read the couplet aloud and paused. "I'm the Earth God now?"

"Read it one more time."

"You talk too much to be an Earth God."

Justice Xia was silent for a while; then he scoffed, picked up the bucket of urine, and went out of the yard.

Past East Street, the land was divided like this: A third was paddy fields and wetlands, another third consisted of the strips of land on both sides of a stream that ran through the eastern end of the village, and the final third was along the base of Bowed Ox Ridge, out at the northern edge of Highway 312. Bowed Ox Ridge had been chosen for the model plots of the reforestation plan.

Along the base of the ridge, Halfwit grew eggplant, string beans, and green onions. Justice Xia dumped the piss bucket on the onions, cursing Halfwit the whole time. Halfwit had been a troublemaker ever since he was young. There were very few people he hadn't tangled with in the past. If he hadn't cursed them out, he'd swung on them. It was perfectly normal for him to return home with a bump on his head. The boy still wasn't safe once he got home, either. Justice Xia wasn't shy about pulling out his leather strap and giving Halfwit a few strokes. But as much as Halfwit made life for Justice Xia difficult, Justice Xia never gave up on his son.

After the household was divided, Halfwit had a particularly tough time of it. Even though Justice Xia tried to be impartial, he often stepped in to help Halfwit. When the bucket was empty, Justice Xia looked over at the field closest to Halfwit's garden. The field was only about two *mu* and was almost completely overgrown with aster, juniper, and ephedra grass. He knew the plot belonged to Virtue, Marvel's older cousin.

Justice Xia's brow furrowed as he thought about Virtue. He was a hell-raiser who had knocked up his wife three times and had welcomed three daughters into the world but still hoped for a son. Virtue was broke, even before he'd been fined three thousand yuan for breaking family planning rules. When things became truly desperate, he'd run off to Xijing to work as a trash picker. When Virtue was getting ready to go, everyone laughed at him, but never to his face. He showed up back in Freshwind after a few months, dressed to the nines with a watch on his wrist. Roughshod Ding claimed that the watch was bunk. He said neither hand ticked. But Virtue headed off to the capital again, bringing his wife and daughters. Everyone in the village assumed he'd struck it rich in the big city, and some regretted not going with him.

Looking out at the plot, overgrown by weeds, was enough to make Justice Xia forget all about his worthless son. He bent down and pulled out a handful of asters. As he went through the field, pulling up weeds, he cursed Virtue. Then he saw Marvel coming down Highway 312 with his electrician's pouch. He called, "You're going to burn that aster? You need some firewood, Second Uncle? I can bring some over for you."

"You think this is for burning? I just got sick of looking at it. Nice piece of land like this, all full of weeds. Why don't you clear it and plant it? Has Virtue been around lately?"

Marvel's face fell. "He came back over the New Year, but he hasn't been back since then."

"What about Tomb-Sweeping Day? He didn't come to burn incense?"

"Nope."

"Does that mean he doesn't plan on coming back here?"

"He has to come back someday, right? If he stays in the city, where are they going to bury him?"

Justice Xia cursed. "He can bury his mother's foot! Look at what he's doing to the land. Why don't you plant it instead?"

"He told me to plant something here, actually, but he wanted me to send him two hundred *jin* of grain a year in exchange. I'd have to pay the land tax, too. It wouldn't be worth it for me. I'm never home these days anyway. You should see the garden over there."

"Get him on the phone and tell him I'm planting here now."

This is the beginning of another story. That day, Marvel went home and told his mother about Justice Xia's plan. The old woman laid her head on the edge of the kang. She was silent for a moment and then said, "There's no way." Marvel found this a bit unusual. He asked her what the problem was. She told him to bring her a bowl of water so that she could take her medicine. Before he could fill the bowl, they both heard Justice Xia outside the gate, calling for Marvel.

Justice Xia was not a patient man, and after not hearing from Marvel for a few hours, he had gone straight to his house to ask if they'd decided. Marvel rushed out, told Justice Xia that he hadn't made the call yet, and motioned him inside. Justice Xia hesitated for a moment and then followed Marvel into the house. As he went, he gave a few theatrical coughs. Marvel's mother didn't have time to hide, or maybe she didn't want to hide. She spat in her palm, slicked down her hair, and stood up to meet them.

Marvel saw that she had brightened up. He was going to ask her if she was still feeling light-headed, but she busied herself boiling water.

Justice Xia said, "How about some sour broth? That'd be nice."

The old lady ladled out a bowl for him and dumped in a spoonful of sugar. She passed him the bowl and sat on the edge of the kang.

Marvel called Virtue on the phone. Virtue was not interested in planting the plot himself and agreed to lease it to Justice Xia on these conditions: Justice Xia would pay the land tax and provide to Virtue a hundred *jin* of wheat and a hundred *jin* of rice each year.

As they wrote up the contract, Justice Xia blurted out, "Hey! You know what? Before Liberation, I used to farm for your family, too. That's going back sixty years now. And now I'm doing it again."

Marvel's mother shifted as if she were about to stand, but she stayed on the edge of the kang. "Why do you have to bring that up? I wouldn't have said anything. Look at you—at your age, you're still worrying about a couple of *mu* of land. Are you starving or something?"

"I can't let the land go to waste. It's like wasting food. Doesn't that bother you? And I'm not that old yet, am I?"

"As long as you stay strong." The old lady laughed. Justice Xia went silent, feeling for his tobacco pouch in his pocket.

Marvel said, "Please! Mother!"

"I better get to bed. You two have your little talk." She tottered out of the room.

Once the old lady had left, Justice Xia said it was time for him to go, too. Marvel walked him to the courtyard. The night sky was full of bright, blinking stars. Justice Xia was in a good mood. He sang to himself:

Old, old, truly old

Wang Baochuan grew old, waiting eighteen years.

Marvel said, "You can sing *Wudianpo*?"

Justice Xia stopped singing. His face flushed. He said, "How many buns do you eat with your dinner?"

"Buns? I usually eat two."

"I eat three."

"You can still eat three?"

"When I was your age . . ." He trailed off. He went down the alley, lengthening his stride as he approached a set of stone steps at the bottom of a short slope. He tried to jump them, but

184

his foot caught on the step, and he was sent crashing to the ground. Marvel rushed to his side, but Justice Xia waved him off and pulled himself to his feet. He went down the alley with his shoulders rolled back and his chest puffed out. Marvel turned back and went into the yard. His mother was sitting on the stone slab that she beat clothes on. Two bats hung from the eaves.

Other than Justice Xia's five sons, nobody else knew about the plan to plant Marvel's plot. When Marvel went to collect the electricity fee at Wisdom Xia's home, he told the news to Fourth Aunt, and she told Wisdom Xia. He put down the opera mask he was painting and rushed to find Gold. Gold was sitting around with his four brothers, discussing the issue of Virtue's plot of land. He heard Wisdom Xia call him, and he went out.

Wisdom Xia stared down his nephew. "Are you looking after your father or what?"

Gold took a step back, bewildered. "What are you talking about?"

"I'm telling you, if you don't look after him, I'll bring him to live with me."

Gold brought a stool over for Wisdom Xia to sit on. He was ready to light Wisdom Xia's pipe, too, but the old man hadn't brought it with him. "Shiner, go get your grandfather's pipe." Shiner ran to get the pipe. "I'm listening, Fourth Uncle. What are you trying to say?"

"A son should look after his father in old age. What the hell are you doing? I know he's out there all the time, helping you and your brothers in the fields. I can barely stand it. And now you're sending him to go plant another plot of land?"

Gold tried to explain. They hadn't known about the plan, and they were trying to figure out what to do about it.

Wisdom Xia stood and said, "All right, you go ahead and discuss it. Once you come up with your solution, I want a full report."

Gold tried to grab at Wisdom Xia's sleeve, but the old man shook him off and left. Gold went back into the room, suddenly pale.

Treasure said, "Fourth Uncle is trying to pull rank, huh?"

"Don't talk like that," Bamboo said. "He's got his brother's best interests in mind."

"He's from an older generation, and I respect his right to speak, but I don't have to listen to him," Treasure said. "Our father's the oldest of the three living brothers. He should be allowed to run his own affairs without his youngest brother poking his nose in."

"I told you not to talk like that. We have to think this through. Why would he want to plant somebody else's land?" asked Bamboo.

"Maybe we didn't give him enough to eat," said Hearth.

Halfwit's wife, cradling their son, whose arm was still wrapped in a bandage, said, "That's impossible. Those two eat better than we do. Our son goes there every day, begging them to put something in his bowl."

"You're the one who told him to go over there looking for food. You want the older generation to feed and look after your kid," said Bounty.

"Is my son going to eat them out of house and home?" asked Halfwit. "One little wooden bowl, that's all he'll eat. You send Tongue-Tied over there all the time, too. He eats his fill over there every day. We give the old folks their share, but he eats it all up."

"You're worried about what he's eating, but did you notice all the work he does for them? Who do you think hauls water for them? Who do you think chops firewood for them? Who goes out to the doctor for them in the middle of the night?" said Bounty.

His voice rising, Gold said, "Cut it out! The point of dividing the land was to give our father a break, but you've seen what he's like . . . He's still got plenty of life in him. He'll pitch in anywhere someone needs a hand. So he must have figured that instead of helping out everyone else, why not get a piece of land for himself?"

Treasure said, "You think that's what's going on? He was a village cadre, and now he's got nothing to do. He'd love to stay involved, but Pavilion wouldn't listen when he went to try to talk to him. He needs something else to fill his time. If he wants to farm someone else's land, just let him do it."

"But it won't look good for the family," said Bamboo.

Treasure said, "Father was a village cadre, but at the end of the day, he's still a farmer. It's only natural that he wants to plant that plot. Wisdom Xia has been eating off public funds his whole life, so if his own brother is still farming, it could look bad for Wind and Rain Xia."

Around then, Shiner arrived back at the house.

"Where's the pipe?" Gold asked. Shiner said that he'd run into Fourth Uncle on the way, and he'd taken the pipe from him. "How did he seem?"

Treasure said, "Why are you worried about that? We have to deal with our own family's issues."

Wisdom Xia waited for Gold's report, but it never came.

In the days after Wisdom Xia showed up to interrogate him, Gold kept a low profile. From what Wisdom Xia had heard from Rain Xia, it sounded like Gold and his brothers agreed with their father. That put Wisdom Xia in an awkward position. Wisdom Xia walked around his courtyard, cursing Gold for making his brother work himself to death. Justice Xia was fine, for now, but someday all that work would catch up with him. Rain Xia didn't want to intervene, but he knew he had to distract his father. He went out and came back home with two *jin* of pork. He was going to make red-cooked pork for the old man.

"Let's eat meat," Wisdom Xia said. "We can still feed ourselves here." The pork was braising in the pot when Pavilion arrived. Fourth Aunt told him to stay and eat with them.

"Red-cooked pork?" Pavilion asked. "I can do better than that. I'll treat Fourth Uncle to bear's paw."

"Where would you get bear's paw?" Fourth Aunt asked.

"I've got the real deal." Pavilion told Wisdom Xia that a few days before, someone had stopped by Lucky Liu's restaurant with a bear's paw. The wily restaurateur Lucky Liu had offered it to Pavilion, who had turned it down because he thought it was a bit expensive. That day, the county's director of commerce was stopping by to inspect the market. Pavilion decided to offer it to the director. He knew it was a good chance to grease the gears.

"You said you were going to treat me, but it sounds like you just want me to accompany you."

"It would be good for you to come."

"I don't even have local residency papers. You should bring Justice Xia instead."

"You're the one that I want with me."

Wisdom Xia was flattered. The issues with his brother and his sons were momentarily forgotten. "I thought there might be an issue with you and Second Uncle, but if you want him to come, too, I can invite him."

"That's fine."

Wisdom Xia slipped on a new pair of pants and looked around for his suit jacket. The jacket had been bought for Wind, but he rarely wore it. When Wisdom Xia got the jacket out of the closet, Fourth Aunt said, "It's so hot outside I want to peel my skin off. What are you thinking, putting on that thick jacket?"

"You don't understand." He slipped on his leather shoes. "I'm the face of Freshwind. I have to make a good impression."

When Pavilion and Wisdom Xia got to the temple, the director of commerce hadn't arrived yet. Lotus was out in the courtyard, drilling a couple of dozen elementary school students. She said, "Now listen. When I say, 'We extend a warm welcome,' I want all of you to wave and shout, 'Warm welcome!' Everything I say, you shout the final part. You just need to finish the sentence and wave. Okay? Got it?"

The kids called back, "Got it!"

"Okay, let's practice. Uggo, quit fidgeting." Uggo was the blacksmith's grandson. He stood up straight. "We extend a warm welcome!"

The kids waved and called out the final half along with Lotus: ". . . warm welcome!"

"The director works so hard!"

". . . works so hard!"

Lotus saw Wisdom Xia coming into the courtyard. She said, "Fourth Uncle, you came."

The kids chorused: ". . . you came! You came!"

Lotus turned back to the kids. "Who told you to repeat that?"

Wisdom Xia sat down in the conference room, beads of sweat already forming on his forehead. "Is the director here yet?"

"He should be here around twelve or so," Pavilion said.

Goodness came over with a document for Pavilion to sign. He read aloud from it. "'One bear's paw, two *jin* of salt, one *jin* of vinegar, fifty *jin* of flour, five *jin* of vegetable oil, ten *jin* of chicken, ten *jin* of pork, ten *jin* of eggs, fifty *jin* of potato, thirty *jin* of radish, ten *jin* of fish, ten *jin* of ribs, one *jin* of wood ear, three *jin* of fiddleheads, ten *jin* of tofu, one *jin* of MSG, one *jin* of spices, one *jin* of Sichuan peppercorns, fifty *jin* of cabbage, fifty *jin* of rice.' All of that for one meal?"

"This is supposed to be enough for the director and his staff."

"I don't care how many people are on his staff. They're not going to eat all this. Two *jin* of salt? Are they camels?"

"The Two Committees owe the Liu family's restaurant tens of thousands of yuan. If we pad the budget a bit, we'll be able to use some of that to pay off that debt."

Pavilion tugged at the hair at his temples and stared down at the paper for a while without speaking. He finally said, "What the hell is going on here?" He picked up the pen and signed his name.

In the countryside, most people eat lunch later in the day, usually two or three in the afternoon. At around twelve o'clock, Lotus led the kids down to the intersection of Highway 312 that turned into the village. Pavilion and Wisdom Xia followed the kids, and the other village cadres followed them. The sun was directly overhead, scorching down on them. It hit them so hard that it felt like they were being pelted with handfuls of grain. Wisdom Xia, wearing his heavy jacket, had already sweated through his undershirt, and his head swam in the heat. But he turned down an offer to sit under the shade of a nearby tree or put on a straw hat to shield his bare head. He wanted to be a model for the children.

Pavilion said, "I'm sorry for dragging you out into this heat."

"Heat? What heat? A little bit of sun can't stop me from serving the people."

Some of the villagers who passed by stopped to watch. They knew that the village cadres must have been waiting to receive a superior, but they weren't sure who exactly they were waiting for. Only Shifty was shameless enough to stroll up to the waiting cadres, slurping noodles from a bowl. He had a ring of chili oil around his mouth. Lotus told him to leave. She told him that it didn't look good for him to be hanging out eating noodles while the village cadres were earnestly doing their job.

Shifty didn't take it well. He dropped the bowl on the ground in front of Lotus. Pavilion watched but said nothing. Shifty crossed his arms over his chest and said, "My old lady told me to wash her panties. I told her I wouldn't. She said that it was an honor. Even if another man offered, she wouldn't let him."

Wisdom Xia wasn't interested in getting into it with Shifty, but Pavilion took the bait. "What's wrong with you, Shifty? Why the long face?"

"I'm going to report someone."

"Who are you reporting this time?"

"Guess."

In a low voice to Pavilion, Wisdom Xia said, "The director and his staff are going to be here any minute now. Just get rid of him. If he's here when they arrive and starts making trouble, it's going to get ugly."

Pavilion went over to Shifty and whispered something in his ear.

Shifty turned and left.

Lotus asked Pavilion, "What did you say to him to make him leave?"

"I asked about White-Moth. I knew he'd leave."

Wisdom Xia didn't understand. He was about to ask if she was Forest Wu's sister-in-law, but before he could open his mouth, he felt suddenly faint, his arms and legs started to shake, and fat beads of sweat broke out on his forehead.

Pavilion said, "Are you okay?"

"I'm fine." But he started to shake even harder, and his face went beet red.

Lotus said, "Is it heatstroke? I have some tiger balm here."

"Just low blood sugar." Wisdom Xia steadied himself against Pavilion, who called for someone to take him to the Liu family restaurant. Even after being assured that he didn't have to be there to greet the director, Wisdom Xia still protested as he was walked over to the restaurant.

If you have low blood sugar, it usually means you haven't eaten. When Wisdom Xia got to the restaurant, they were selling pulled noodles. He called out for a bowl. But business was good that day, and the bowls of noodles were going out to the already-waiting customers. He watched helplessly as customers slurped and Lucky Liu's wife worked, dunking new batches of noodles. He collapsed on the table, completely drained.

A bowl of *chemian* was finally brought over to his table. He felt like there was a worm in his belly. Even after half a bowl was down, he was still hungry. But once he'd finished it, the color returned to his cheeks. He'd sucked down the bowl so fast that he felt embarrassed to call for another. He said, "I guess low blood sugar is good for the appetite."

Lucky Liu's wife called over, "I'll bring you another bowl."

"Can I get a napkin, too?" He wiped his mouth. "Don't let me get too full, though. I need to save room for that bear's paw. Is the food for the banquet ready yet?"

"It's all on the back burner now."

"Excellent. I want everything to be perfect."

But by three o'clock, the director still hadn't arrived. Pavilion decided to call his office to see when he might arrive. The secretary answered that the director was in an emergency meeting and wouldn't be able to go.

Pavilion was furious. "Bureaucrats!" He sent Lotus off to buy the kids Popsicles. He rounded up the village cadres and led them toward the restaurant. He said, "The way these bureaucrats operate, we need another Cultural Revolution to thin the herd. If they aren't going to come, the hell with it—we might as well go eat."

The meal was quite impressive, but unfortunately the bear's paw came out of the steamer still tough as old leather. Lotus chewed at her helping for a long time before finally giving up and spitting it out.

Pavilion said, "Just eat it. One mouthful of bear's paw is better than three steamed buns."

Wisdom Xia managed to choke down four pieces, a decision that came back to haunt him when he got home that night and his stomach swelled up like a balloon. Fourth Aunt was at his side, rubbing his belly, but even that didn't offer any relief. Finally, he stuck a finger down his throat and emptied the contents of his stomach.

The next day, Wisdom Xia got out of bed very late. He went to his flower beds and saw that there were three blossoms on his China rosebush. In the distance, he heard the sound of firecrackers, and he asked his wife, "Nobody came to get me?"

"What do you mean?"

"Who's setting off firecrackers?"

"Rain Xia set them off. Treasure is raising the roof today."

Wisdom Xia said nothing and busied himself watering the flowers.

He splashed a bit on his shoes. He set down the ladle and went back toward his bedroom, saying to his wife, "If anyone comes for me, tell them I wasn't feeling well and I went back to bed."

"Who the hell is coming to see you?" She bent down to catch one of the hens. Just as she was feeling around up its ass to see if there was an egg, Treasure arrived.

He asked, "Where's Fourth Uncle?"

"Speak of the devil! He said you'd be around. You're raising the roof today, right?"

"That's right. So I thought I'd come and ask Fourth Uncle to come over."

Fourth Aunt jerked her chin in the direction of the bedroom window.

Treasure went closer to the window and called out, "Fourth Uncle, it's Treasure. We're raising the roof of my new house today. I'm here to invite you over."

From his kang, Wisdom Xia called back, "What the hell do you need me over there for? I'm not fit to do any kind of work."

"Who said anything about putting you to work? Come over and smoke your pipe, watch for a while. When it's time for lunch, you can sit at the head of the table."

"I can't go. I'm not feeling well."

Gold said, "It was hot as hell yesterday, and you still went out with the village cadres. How many times is your nephew going to build a house? You can't miss this. It'll get them working even faster, anyway."

"You think I could make them work faster?"

"It wouldn't look good for me if you didn't come."

"I might as well go over and rip a fart, for all the good me showing up there would do you."

Wisdom Xia reached over to the radio on the kang and fiddled with the knob, trying to tune in a local opera station out of the static. Gold scowled and turned to leave.

From the new house he heard the sound of firecrackers and from the radio the sound of "The Smoking Cave."

The firecrackers that Treasure was hearing had been set by me and Tongue-Tied. We set off three strips of them at the doorway and then got up on the roof beam and set off another five strips. Tongue-Tied was being stupid, setting off a strip and dangling it from the same hand he held the matches in. I told him, "Let it go! Let it go!" He ended up tossing the matches, but when the firecrackers got close to his hand, he almost fell off the beam. After we were done, I asked him, "Why didn't your grandpa come over?"

Tongue-Tied mimed Justice Xia digging.

I said, "This is a big deal, though. What was he digging that was so important?"

He just glared at me. When it was time to eat, he sucked down two big bowls of rice. When he saw that I had eaten my fill, he filled up another bowl, passed it to me, and motioned for me to go to the back of the house. He followed soon after with a bowl of morsels plucked from the lunch table. I wasn't sure what he had in mind. He looked back a few times, but only Lucky had followed. I realized he was taking this food for Justice Xia.

Justice Xia was just where Tongue-Tied had mimed he would be. He was resting after digging up the soil, his jacket off, one elbow up on the path between the plots, smoking one of his black cigarettes. Between the plots of land there grew wild jujube vines, leafless and twisted up like a mass of snakes. Wisdom Xia had dug up most of the plants so that their roots lay exposed. But a few of the plants still bore fruit, and Wisdom Xia reached out and plucked a jujube and put it in his cheek.

He sucked on the fruit and looked over at the village. He was so absorbed in the scene that he didn't notice us coming. Tongue-Tied wanted to call to him, but I gave him a kick to shut him up. I looked out over the village. The sky over Freshwind was red, and the land around it was yellow. The streets were white. The houses were black.

I said, "What the hell is he looking at?"

Justice Xia looked back, surprised. "Ha! You brought out some food for me, huh? Something good, I bet."

He stuck his cigarette in my mouth and started eating.

I spat the cigarette out and watched him wolf down his meal. Justice Xia wasn't a young man, but he sure could put food away. It wasn't long before he'd polished off both bowls. Sweat dripped down his back.

There was still a bit of rice left in one bowl, and he rose and went to the low dirt ridge between the plots, blew a spot clean, and set the rice there. He came back and said, "You both had something to eat?"

A flock of sparrows and a pigeon landed, as if they had been waiting for a signal.

"Second Uncle, are these your birds?"

But Justice Xia lay down and went to sleep, snoring like a mighty bellows.

Tongue-Tied and I decided it was time to leave. But Dog-Scraps was approaching, shouting for Justice Xia. Not only Justice Xia, deep in slumber, heard him but so did the ghosts gathered around the nearby tombs.

Poor old Dog-Scraps only had a few days left on this earth, but he didn't know it yet, and he was still worried about his twelve walnut trees. His plot of land was a little way off from the model reforestation field on Bowed Ox Ridge. When he got the money as part of the project, Goodness had ordered him to replace the dead trees, and he had done just that. Three years before, he had gone to work in a gold mine in the Tong Pass and had come back that spring without much money and a bad case of silicosis. He had trouble getting around after that. Dragging the water up to his replanted stand of walnut trees was incredibly difficult for him. He had to rest every few steps.

It was while he was resting that he saw Justice Xia and started yelling, "Mr. Xia! Mr. Xia! You're farming Virtue's land now?"

Justice Xia shook himself awake and said, "What are you doing? Your face looks like a busted burlap sack."

"I'm replanting those saplings."

"You're in the wrong season. You think they'll make it?"

"I was twelve trees short, but I still wanted the subsidy. I was going to wait until the winter, but Goodness told me to replant them right away."

"You're still going to be twelve trees short when those die."

"If they die, they die. If you see my land from far enough away, it'll look fine. How come you're planting on Virtue's land?"

"I'm going to pay the tax on it and give him two hundred *jin* of grain."

"Sounds like a waste of time."

"I can't let the land go to waste."

"It does hurt me to see good land going unplanted. Like this Return Grain Plots to Forestry campaign they've got going on—they've got people planting trees in the fields. But they're so tiny and spread out, it feels like a waste of good soil."

"It is."

"We should be able to grow something in the space between the trees."

"I don't think it'd harm them."

Dog-Scraps smiled. "How would it harm them? It wouldn't. And even if you can't grow wheat, it wouldn't hurt to plant some vegetables."

And Dog-Scraps did just that. He went to his plot of land and started to till the soil between the trees. In Freshwind, it's monkey see, monkey do, so it wasn't long before half a dozen or so other families started tilling the soil in the plots they'd turned over to trees. After that, everyone waited for a nice wet day.

No matter how long a drought goes on, it has to rain eventually, and everyone expected that day to come soon. It wasn't long after the villagers dug up the land on Bowed Ox Ridge that the sky turned dark. The sky was unusually dark, in fact. A mushroom cloud sprouted over the ridge and kept growing taller and wider until it darkened half the sky. Black clouds gathered above the bank of earth south of the theater. But they weren't black clouds at all; they were flocks of crows. Where were all the crows coming from?

The gingko tree outside Freshwind Temple turned black, and an owl hooted from within it. Do you know what that meant? The owl hooted because it knew that somebody was going to die. Dog-Scraps's wife heard it, and she shuddered as she thought to herself, *Will it be Dog-Scraps?* As soon as she thought it, she cursed herself and slapped herself hard across the face. She was on her way up to Bowed Ox Ridge to find Dog-Scraps when she saw him coming toward her. He was running, she saw. His shoes had fallen off, and he held them in his hands. He stopped beside the road and tried to catch his breath.

Wisdom Xia happened to be coming up the road. "How is the child doing at school, Dog-Scraps?"

Dog-Scraps fell to the ground, kowtowing to Wisdom Xia. "It's only thanks to you that the child could get back to school and study. I still haven't had a chance to thank you."

"Get up, get up. I wasn't waiting for you to thank me. What are you doing? You can barely breathe!"

Dog-Scraps tried to answer, but he could not speak. He lifted his hand toward the sky.

"It's raining," Wisdom Xia observed.

"It's heaven's will!"

"It was bound to rain someday." Wisdom Xia turned and walked away.

When he got back home, the courtyard was hung with his ladles painted with opera masks. Fourth Aunt was putting up a straw mat around a sapling, but Wisdom Xia told her not to bother. "It's not going to burn up. Should be some rain coming in today."

"That's why I'm putting it up. I don't want the rain to flood the sapling."

Wisdom Xia grabbed a basket to put over the sapling instead of the mat, and when he bent to examine it, he saw how delicate the tiny plant was, only four fingers tall with leaves as delicate as dewdrops. He covered the elm sapling and began to collect the opera-mask ladles. Right then, Dog-Scraps arrived, carrying a chicken. Wisdom Xia said, "I told you, I don't need your thanks. What did you bring that chicken here for?"

"It's a hen. It stopped laying eggs this summer."

"I don't need your chicken. I'm not taking it." He pushed Dog-Scraps toward the courtyard gate, but Dog-Scraps grabbed ahold of the gate frame and held on tight.

"Fourth Uncle, there's something I need to tell you. You know I'm not good with words, but please . . . I just need you to listen. If you disagree with me, that's fine."

"Quit babbling. What do you have to say?"

"If you don't take the chicken as a gift, can you at least loan me some money in return for it?"

"What are you talking about? What do you want me to do with the chicken?"

"I don't know how to explain."

Wisdom Xia barked at Dog-Scraps, "Speak!"

"It's going to rain today, and I was thinking about planting some vegetables, but I don't have any money to buy seeds. I tried to sell this hen to Clerk's wife, but she said she wanted a hen that was laying. But if it was still laying, why would I sell it? I didn't know what else to do, so I came to you. I'll give you the chicken, and you could lend me some money. Once I sell the vegetables, I can pay you back."

Wisdom Xia listened and his anger faded. He said, "Have a seat." He told Fourth Aunt to pour a bowl of water for Dog-Scraps. He asked, "You said you're growing vegetables, right? On what land?"

"On my land over by Bowed Ox Ridge. It got turned over to trees, but the trees are still small enough that I can grow some vegetables between them. I tilled all the soil already."

"You can grow vegetables there?"

"I think so. Everyone else is tilling the ground between the trees. It's heaven's will—when we started digging up the plots, the rain came."

Wisdom Xia looked up at the sky. The massive black cloud had broken into two long strips that formed a black X. A stone dropped into the yard. Fourth Aunt shrieked. She went over to where the stone had fallen and saw that it was a sparrow, its tiny skull smashed. She was hysterical. "How could a sparrow just fall like that?"

Wisdom Xia said, "Take your chicken with you. I'm not going to lend you any money. You can have some seeds. We have a few *jin* of cabbage seeds, and you can take some."

Dog-Scraps rubbed his hands together. "I don't need much. Just a bit."

"Take it all. Give it to anyone who needs it. Bring me a basket of cabbages at harvest time, and we'll call it even."

Dog-Scraps dropped the hen, took the sack of seed, and left. Wisdom Xia called him back and told him to take the chicken with him. Dog-Scraps grabbed the chicken around the neck, and the hen's comb went from red to purple. The chicken stared at Dog-Scraps with her quartz-black eyes, and Dog-Scraps stared back at the chicken. The man and the chicken stared at each other for several minutes before Dog-Scraps brought his hand back and slapped the hen hard. The chicken's head drooped, and it shut its eyes. "If you don't want a live chicken, Fourth Uncle, maybe you can do something with this."

He tossed down the chicken and left. Fourth Aunt stared down at the dead bird without speaking. Dog-Scraps was already out of the courtyard. As she watched him go, she said, "Poor old Dog-Scraps . . . Too stubborn for his own good."

Just because you feel sorry for someone doesn't mean you have to like them. That was the case with Dog-Scraps, and Forest Wu, and Halfwit, too, and even Concord Qin.

Concord Qin's illness was not particularly serious, but he still refused to leave the house. He got flustered whenever he saw a crowd. But his situation only seemed to worsen as the days went by. Concord Qin's wife couldn't figure it out. Back when Concord Qin was running things, there was no shortage of people stopping by the house to see him, but the visits had ceased. She wanted to find someone to talk to him about whatever he was going through, but she felt uncomfortable bringing it up with people in the village. Concord Qin's wife wept in secret. Pavilion did keep coming, though, and when Concord Qin's wife saw him pull up to the front gate on his motorcycle, she was happy to see him. She rushed back inside to tell Concord Qin, who asked, "What does he want? Is he here to laugh at me?"

"It's good that he's here to visit."

"Who else is with him?"

"It's just him."

Concord Qin burrowed under his blanket and said, "I'm going to take my medicine and have a nap."

Pavilion came into the courtyard with a basket of eggs and asked Concord Qin's wife how her husband was.

"You know how it is . . . I'm worried he's never getting out of that bed. He already resigned. Did you see the letter?"

Pavilion said, "How would Freshwind get by without him? He just needs a chance to rest and recuperate. There's plenty of work left for him to do."

Concord Qin was listening from the kang and trying his best not to make a sound. His throat itched and he swallowed hard.

Concord Qin's wife said, "He was so happy when you two switched positions. He told me, 'Pavilion is capable. Pavilion will get things done.' I didn't think anyone had it in for him. I can't believe they'd arrest him when everyone plays mah-jongg in Freshwind. You know how he is; he keeps everything bottled up. I told him, 'What's the point of burying your head in the sand? You need to get out there and deal with whoever reported you.'"

Pavilion waited for Concord Qin's wife to finish, and then he looked at her and said, "I know you're angry at the person who reported the game. I have something to tell you; it was me."

Concord Qin's wife was about to launch into a tirade, but the words caught in her throat. Behind her on the counter, rats were stealing one of the eggs from the basket. One of the rats rolled onto its back with the egg wrapped in its paws, and the other rat bit its tail. They scurried away, rolling the egg. Concord Qin's wife saw the rats, but she ignored them. She said, "It was you?"

"It was me. How could I have known he'd be in there, playing mah-jongg? I don't know why, but they had a staff change at the station, too. I heard some rumors of what went down, and I told the sergeant not to investigate any further. Concord Qin got the wrong idea and wound himself up."

Concord Qin's wife finally shooed away the rats, and they scurried away, leaving the egg leaking its yolk out onto the counter. She said, "Well, if you put it that way, there's no way I could possibly be angry at you. The way I see it, the two of you are like your second uncle and Spark's father; you can't live without each other."

"That's right. But I can't do anything for him now."

Pavilion walked into the house, and Concord Qin's wife called after him, "He just had his medicine, and he's taking a nap."

When Pavilion entered the room, Concord Qin turned to face the wall.

Concord Qin's wife said, "Concord Qin, Concord Qin, Pavilion came to see you. He brought a basket of eggs." Concord Qin didn't move. She said to Pavilion, "He's fast asleep. He had his medicine."

"Then I'll get going," Pavilion said. "Look after him. Let me know if there's anything I can do." He swatted at a fly that was crawling across the blanket and caught it in his hand. He gave it a squeeze and let it fall to the floor. Concord Qin's wife saw him out.

When Concord Qin's wife came back into the room, Concord Qin immediately started to reprimand her. It seemed to him as if his wife was begging Pavilion for forgiveness. She told her husband that she wanted Pavilion to understand what he had done, that Concord Qin's illness was the result of his carelessness. She said that Concord Qin was being too petty, and that a visit from Pavilion might have made him feel better. Concord Qin said that it was wrong to compare him and Pavilion with Justice Xia and my father. Justice Xia and my father were two sides of the same coin, and they had known each other like brothers. Pavilion had learned a few things from Justice Xia—mostly how to cause a stir—but was nowhere near as honest.

Concord Qin said, "You sold me out! You think Pavilion wants me to get better? You think Pavilion is going to be waiting by my bedside?"

Just as Concord Qin said, Pavilion never came back. Concord Qin's wife saw him once, near the construction site of the new market. Pavilion was shouting out orders, making a show of running things. He saw Concord Qin's wife but ignored her. She sobbed as she realized that her husband had been right.

The basket of eggs that Pavilion had brought that day went uneaten. Concord Qin refused to eat them, and his wife left them on the counter, wrapped in the wheat straw Pavilion had packed around them. The eggs rotted and stank in the hot kitchen.

When the Earth God and Earth Goddess were pulled out of the ground below the construction site for the market, Concord Qin's wife came home to tell her husband. She said, "Everyone says it's a good sign. Maybe you were wrong."

"Wrong about what? I'm not even in the ground yet, and you're looking for someone else to take care of you?"

She crouched in the kitchen and thought bitterly to herself, *Everyone else has brought in two crops already. I don't even have time to work the fields now. Everyone else is down at the construction site, having a good time, and I'm cooped up with Concord Qin.* She felt sorry for her husband and hated him at the same time.

A turtledove flew over from a locust tree on the edge of the village and perched on top of the house. The turtledove cooed, but she could hear only an echo of her own unhappiness in its call. She picked up a broom and tried to knock the bird off its perch. She only managed to knock some clothes off the bamboo rod they were drying on. The bird skipped along the roof, leaving a splatter of pure white shit on the tile. She took it as a sign and spat twice in the dirt.

Concord Qin heard his wife spitting and barked from inside the house, "You got a mouth on you like a dog that just ate a dead baby. What are you spitting for?"

"Oh, Concord Qin, it's a sign. You're going to outlive me."

Concord Qin didn't speak but got up and went out into the courtyard. He picked up the fallen clothes from the ground and hung them back on the rod. His body had weakened, and even the effort of bending to retrieve the clothes had him sweating. He said to his wife, "Where are the Earth God statues now?"

She ignored him.

He said, "Does Uncle Justice know anything about this?" She continued ignoring him, and he spoke as if to himself. "It's been a long time since I saw Uncle Justice around here. Go get the notebook from under my pillow."

She came back with the notebook, and Concord Qin reviewed it. He had recorded who had visited him since he'd gotten sick—there were a total of eight names recorded.

His wife couldn't take it. "What the hell did you write all that for? It's only going to upset you." She tore the notebook out of his hands and ripped out the page.

"I can understand some people not coming—but Goodness?" He aimed a kick at the washing stone and missed, sending his shoe flying across the courtyard. The shoe landed with a thud at the gate, where Wisdom Xia happened to be passing by, carrying a dead chicken.

That afternoon, as Wisdom Xia and Concord Qin ate the chicken, it started to rain. The rain smacked down into the thick dust that coated everything in the drought-stricken village and kicked up a gritty fog that enveloped Freshwind. The fog of dust hung in the air for half an hour, making everyone—even the chickens and dogs—scatter, sneezing and coughing as they ran. As the air cleared, the rain became visible, coming down in streaks, piercing the parched earth. The sound of drumming rain filled the village. Most people didn't bother taking shelter. They stood in the rain and let it wash over them. The old donkey out back of the dyehouse brayed; the villagers shouted with joy; everyone and everything called out in unison.

The afternoon the rain came, Halfwit had been up on Yijia Ridge, cutting weeds. He'd cut down a lacquer tree, and his skin had broken out in a rash and his eyes were swollen shut. As the rain came down, he ran down into the village, hugging everyone he came across, rubbing his face on their faces, trying to rub the poison from the lacquer tree onto them. The villagers swore at him and pulled away, but he didn't mind. He ran, jumping and shouting, and then fell down and rolled in the mud.

Some of the villagers worried that the rain wouldn't last. They put out buckets, basins, and jugs to catch what they could. They opened up the embankments around their cesspits to let the water flow in from the streets. But the rain kept coming until after dark. Every courtyard in the village flooded, and the streets turned from rivers to lakes. The cesspits overflowed, and logs of shit floated across courtyards.

I had the only pair of rubber boots in Freshwind. My dad used to wear them in the winter when he'd go out into the pond to dig up lotus roots. The day of the big rain, I wore them all over the village. I watched a chicken gasping for air, trying to keep its beak above the water. It swallowed one beakful of water and then another, and then it drowned and lay motionless in the muddy water. The wall around back of the tinker's place collapsed. The wall fell on a sow, which immediately miscarried her piglets. A swarm of rats climbed up the opera theater, and seven snakes wound their way up the willow tree in front of it.

A crowd came running down from where they had been planting up on Bowed Ox Ridge, with Dog-Scraps, panting hard, taking the lead. When he saw me, he said, "Anytime you want some vegetables, come and see me, brother!" I followed along with the crowd, who were all barefoot. I took pleasure in splashing in the puddles with my boots, soaking everyone, letting them grumble and curse at me.

But then suddenly, there was a flash of lightning. I saw in the flash a tree coming down, a big red tree, falling toward the field. It looked like a ball of fire, as big as a night soil collector's tub. It flew over a wheat field, crashed against a grindstone, and ripped into a heap of straw that immediately caught flame. The rain put the fire out soon enough, but I wanted to get a better look. As I turned to head toward the strawstack, I heard a buzzing in my ears, and something hit me. I fell to the ground.

When I came to, I knew I wasn't dead, at least. I struggled to open my eyes and heard someone calling in the distance, "The dragon caught Spark!"

That's what we say in Freshwind—caught by the dragon—when someone gets hit by lightning. Seven years earlier, Vigor Bai over on East Street had been caught by the dragon. He was six feet tall but ended up a chunk of charcoal. I looked down and saw that my body was still in one piece. I saw that a coin had fallen out of my pocket and reached down to stick it back in. I couldn't do much more than that—my body felt as if it was locked in place. I saw people running over to me. They thought I was dead, but they didn't look upset. They were saying I must have done something bad to get snatched up by the dragon. I was angry enough to overcome whatever had held me in place, and I sprang to my feet. My ears were filled with a loud rustling sound, like someone was crunching wheat straw beside my head. The rustling became voices, even though nobody's mouth was moving and I heard what they would have said—what they were thinking deep down was, "He's still alive? This son of a bitch has got nine lives. He's got those rubber boots on. You know how his dad got them? He bought them with the village's money."

"Fuck your mother's ass!" I howled back at them, and then I went home and went to bed.

A rainy day is the only time farmers sleep soundly. When the rain comes down, they crash on their kangs, head down, balls up. On those days, farmers sleep until their heads ache. But that night, I couldn't get to sleep. I couldn't shut out the voices. I could hear everything that was happening in the village. When it rained, the work in the fields stopped and another kind of labor began. I heard it all, the sounds of the men pounding and grunting, the women squealing like stuck pigs . . .

I heard Dog-Scraps, too, whimpering, "I'm gonna die! I'm gonna die!"

There was silence then, and I heard his wife say, "Go ahead, die!" I heard them cursing each other.

That was not the right time to think about Snow Bai, but I did anyway. I thought it was disrespectful to place her on par with all the other women of Freshwind. I asked myself, *How are you missing her?* I answered myself, *With my whole body.* I asked, *Tell me the truth—where is that feeling coming from?* I said, *I feel it down here first, but then I feel it in my heart.* I slapped myself across the face. I thought, *What is Snow Bai doing right now? Is she rehearsing an opera, or is the troupe already out on tour? If they were on tour already, Mid-Star Xia would have told me,* I thought. I would regret it forever, letting Snow Bai come to mind at that moment, because the moment she did, the voices stopped. I could no longer hear what people were thinking, but I had no idea what Snow Bai was doing, either. It was after midnight. The rain slowed. The sound of rain drumming on the roof was replaced by the sound of rain dripping from the eaves, and then by silence.

I woke up at noon the next day with the sun beating down pure white rays on the courtyard. The cracks between the mud bricks of the house's walls were already sprouting weeds watered by the previous day's rain. The courtyard wall was still drying out, and it looked as worn as a thirty- or forty-year-old wall could look, with the plaster peeling off it here and there and the cracks across the top covered up with scraps of broken porcelain tile. But it hadn't collapsed, at least. The moss that grew across the wall's crown had turned from black to green since the shower, and from the carpet of moss had blossomed a single flower, which had grown to about the length of a cigarette butt just since that morning. I knew the flower had to signify something. It had to be a sign, I was sure—but of what? There are some things you just can't say. It would be revealing a secret that shouldn't be revealed.

I was suddenly happy and ran to get some money from under the kang mat to gamble on one of Roughshod Ding's games. When I got to his place, there were already two tables set up with people playing mah-jongg. As the players entered, they'd scraped their shoes on the gate's threshold, and a giant ball of mud had collected out front.

I said, "You should take a shovel to that before someone trips and twists their ankle."

"It's good luck! I like to say, if your walkway is smooth, it means nobody ever comes to visit you."

I tried to sit down at Roughshod Ding's table, but he told me to join the other table where four women were playing.

I said, "It's just a bunch of women over there."

"A woman over forty doesn't count as a woman."

I sat down with them and started to play. In Roughshod Ding's courtyard, there was a walnut tree that used to bloom with catkins that looked like caterpillars. The whole tree used to be full of them, but later it withered and stopped flowering. The bare branches looked like hands grasping at something in the air. Grasping at what? What was there to grasp? I was too busy trying to figure that out to focus on the game.

By the afternoon, I was already a hundred yuan in debt, and I'd scratched a dozen marks on the wall behind me. Roughshod Ding was right; these weren't women at all. They were worse than Shifty. I had to run home to get more cash to pay them off. I told Roughshod Ding as I was leaving, "You should cut down this tree."

He laughed and called back, "Everything looks like shit when you're losing, huh?"

What did losing a hundred yuan or so really matter? I felt worse for Dog-Scraps. That was the day he died.

After it happened, I heard Obedient Zhang from the farm store say that Dog-Scraps had come around late that afternoon to buy a bottle of pesticide. Dog-Scraps didn't have the cash to buy it, so he'd asked Obedient Zhang to give it to him on credit. Obedient Zhang had written out the contract and gotten Dog-Scraps to put his fingerprint on it. Dog-Scraps put his thumbprint three times at the bottom of the contract and walked out with the pesticide.

The day before, as the rain was rolling in, the township head was on his way back from the county in the township government's jeep. Soft rain started to bead up on the windshield and then turned to sheets of water across the glass. The township head crowed happily, "It's coming down now! Beautiful!" He stuck his hand out the jeep's window to feel the rain on his skin. It was precisely then that his day was ruined. The jeep was approaching Bowed Ox Ridge and the model forestry plots that the county head himself had ordered. It was the township head's efforts to promote the Return Grain Plots to Forestry campaign that had gotten him on the short list for a promotion. He didn't expect to see farmers out on the plots planting. The township head had spent the night tossing and turning and had gone out early the next day to investigate the situation at Bowed Ox Ridge. It was easy enough to see that the plots had been tilled and planted.

In a fit of rage, he summoned Pavilion and lectured him on the severe consequences that would be faced by anyone found to be subverting state policy. Pavilion immediately set about investigating the situation, and it quickly came to light that Dog-Scraps had been the first to violate the policy. While the seven other households had held back a bit and only planted two rows each of vegetables, Dog-Scraps had dug up and planted every available inch of land between the saplings. Pavilion called a meeting of Dog-Scraps and the other seven households at the township government offices. When the township head arrived, he tore into them. The final ruling was that the township government would revoke the fifty-yuan cash subsidy that each family received per *mu* of land planted with saplings, as well as the yearly payment of two hundred *jin* of grain and twenty yuan. Each of the seven families was fined fifty yuan, while Dog-Scraps was levied a two-hundred-yuan fine. Dog-Scraps returned home, only to break down in the courtyard, sobbing in the mud.

Dog-Scraps's wife helped him into the house and listened as he told her what had happened at the meeting. She was shaking as she said, "They won't be happy till we're dead! How are we going to pay that fine? It's more than the subsidy. Even if we sold our roof tiles, it'd be barely two hundred yuan. You must go see the old principal. He's generous, and he might have some power with them. He was the one that gave you those seeds, wasn't he? He will be able to help you talk to them."

Dog-Scraps put a hand over his wife's mouth and said, "Just shut up. Wisdom Xia gave me the seeds, but if I go to him now, someone'll get wind of it, and he'll end up in trouble, too."

Dog-Scraps's wife seethed, "Why did you have to go plant up there? You've got the brain of a pig. Your name suits you perfectly, so worthless a dog wouldn't even touch it."

Dog-Scraps knew he was in the wrong. He had nothing left to say. Even when his wife clawed at his face, he didn't bother hitting her. He went out of the house. He went to the farm store and got a bottle of pesticide. Under the archway at the head of West Street, he paused and looked up and down the road. Seeing nobody around, he drank the entire bottle. The poison began to take effect as he walked home. His vision went hazy, and he began to stagger down the street. He stumbled into Mid-Star's father and asked, "Where is my father? Where is Boss-Man?"

"You aren't going to find them around here. They're all dead."

After Dog-Scraps's father died young, Boss-Man had taken Dog-Scraps to work in the mines. Three years earlier, the years underground had caught up with Boss-Man, and he'd died of silicosis.

"But I never saw their ghosts . . ."

"Have you been drinking?"

"Yes. I drank a whole bottle!"

Dog-Scraps wanted to die at home. He wanted to eat one last bowl of noodles, stir in chilis until the whole bowl was red, and then smear in a bit of lard. He wanted to change into clean clothes and lie down on his own kang. But he was still thirty paces from his gate when he collapsed in the mud, unable to go on.

Mid-Star's father did not come to help him. He yelled down the road, "Hey, who's looking after Dog-Scraps?"

From inside the yard, Dog-Scraps's wife yelled, "Is he drinking again? Let him die out there."

Mid-Star's father didn't care, one way or the other. He turned and left. Dog-Scraps's wife didn't care, either. Much later, when the hens had gone back inside the coop to roost, she went out to look for him. Dog-Scraps's face was green, and his chin was covered in frothy spittle.

Dog-Scraps's wife dragged him to Big-Noise Zhao's pharmacy at the Great Qing Hall. Big-Noise Zhao told her that Dog-Scraps was barely clinging to life. He poured green bean soup down his throat and stuck acupuncture needles in the pressure points that could make him vomit. But Dog-Scraps refused to give up the poison in his belly.

In a panic, Big-Noise Zhao called out, "Bring me an ox!" Since the household-responsibility system had been introduced in Freshwind, nobody had their own oxen—they pulled their own plows—but the dyehouse had a donkey. The donkey was led over, and Dog-Scraps was thrown over its back. Dog-Scraps's wife sobbed as she led the donkey in a circle, hoping that the poison could be shaken out of her husband's stomach. But still Dog-Scraps would not give up the poison.

Wisdom Xia had gone to bed early and hadn't heard about Dog-Scraps. The next day, he awoke early and went for a walk along the dike, then stopped to drink tea. It was Rain Xia who told him about Dog-Scraps drinking pesticide. Wisdom Xia said, "You mean they drove him to drink pesticide. Will he pull through?"

"He was still breathing last night when he got to Big-Noise Zhao. I don't know how he's doing now."

"Why didn't you come to tell me as soon as you found out? And why haven't you gone to check on him? Huh?"

Rain Xia went to Dog-Scraps's home. Wisdom Xia poured himself another cup of tea. He tried to take a sip but found he couldn't swallow it. He rose and went as quickly as he could to the township government offices.

The township head was in the middle of leading a meeting. He was indulging in his usual habit of opening the meeting by reading newspaper editorials and official edicts. As he was reading, Wisdom Xia came up to the office window and rapped on the glass. Everyone turned to see Wisdom Xia at the window except for the township head, who only looked up to offer stock encouragement to the assembled cadres, "We must be diligent! The work becomes easier once we have a thorough grasp of policy!" The township head went back to reading as Wisdom Xia pushed open the door. He didn't notice the intruder until Wisdom Xia brushed the sheaf of documents out of his hand. He looked up and, seeing it was Wisdom Xia, softened his tone slightly. "Can this wait until the meeting is over?"

"Did you know that Dog-Scraps drank a bottle of pesticide?"

"How would I know? There's a real problem in the rural areas of villagers threatening suicide. I oversee a township of more than ten thousand households. You think I keep track of every single death and birth?"

"Then let me be the first to inform you. Dog-Scraps drank pesticide! I'm sure you can figure out what pushed him over the edge, can't you?"

"I don't understand."

Wisdom Xia lost his temper. "You don't understand?"

"We're in the middle of a meeting."

"Fine. Have your meeting. I'll be waiting for you outside."

The township head went back to reading, but a short time later, he stopped and said, "This meeting is adjourned." He went out to see Wisdom Xia, who was crouched in the courtyard of the offices. He called Wisdom Xia to come to his office and sent out all his staff. He said, "What were you trying to say? How would I know why Dog-Scraps drank pesticide?"

"He was farming land he'd already signed over to plant trees on as part of the reforestation campaign. You planned to revoke his subsidy and fine him two hundred yuan. Am I correct?"

"So, that's what you're trying to say . . . I have the utmost respect for you, Principal Xia, and you know I'm always prepared to assist you however I can, but if you think I can stand by while state policy is subverted, then you are gravely mistaken. You know as well as I do that Bowed Ox Ridge was selected by the county head himself as the site of the model forestry plots of the Return Grain Plots to Forestry campaign. You are also aware that their location along Highway 312 means that everyone can see what's going on over there. Leaving aside the question of what digging up those plots will mean for our plans to combat erosion, how do you expect me to report to my superiors that their model plots have been turned over to vegetable gardens?"

"The only thing you're worried about is your own promotion."

"Principal Xia, please, how can you talk like that? I will not let personal considerations cloud my judgment. Whoever violates their agreements as part of the Return Grain Plots to Forestry campaign will be severely punished."

"Then you can severely punish me, too. He was planting the seeds I gave him. If Dog-Scraps violated the policy, then I'm just as guilty. I'm here to put my neck on the block."

The township head's eyes widened. "You are making things impossible for me, Principal Xia. Where's the tea? Why didn't Principal Xia get a cup of tea? Hurry up!"

Clerk, who worked in the canteen of the office, scurried to bring a cup of tea to Wisdom Xia and then waited outside the door.

Wisdom Xia ignored the tea and raised his voice so that Clerk could hear. "Clerk! Go to my house. Bring my rattan chair and my pipe."

Clerk poked his head in the door. "Okay, okay! Fourth Uncle wants to sit in his chair and smoke his pipe."

Wisdom Xia called after him, "And tell Rain Xia what's going on. Let him know that I might be held up here a day or two. Tell him to bring over some of my calligraphy. I want to hang it up in here."

The argument between the two men continued, and the township head put up a good front, forcing the occasional chuckle while he pulled on his cigarette, but he was beginning to grow worried. As he headed out to the bathroom, he quietly sent someone over to check on Dog-Scraps. He stayed for a long time in the bathroom, letting his piss wash over the pearly white maggots that filled the trough, and then standing there for a long time without doing up his pants. Finally, the man he had sent to check on the situation returned and reported to the township head that Dog-Scraps had died. The township head lost his balance and stepped into the trough as he tried to right himself. Beads of sweat formed on his forehead as he scraped shit off his shoe.

By the time he returned to his office, the township head's tone had softened. He said, "How can we deal with this situation?"

"Now, that's the way I expect you to talk. You're the township head, and I don't want to undermine your authority. When you work for the Communist Party and eat off a state salary, mistakes can be tolerated. But you must know, when it comes to human life, there is no room for carelessness."

"I'm young. I don't have much experience. I want to hear your suggestions."

"Well, here they are: Put a stop to all cultivation of the land that's been entered into the reforestation plan, but there's no need to revoke subsidies or levy fines. Make it clear to everyone in the township that growing vegetables on those plots is completely forbidden."

"Agreed."

"I bear some responsibility for this, too. I will help paint some slogans along Highway 312 to spread the message."

"I don't want to embarrass you."

"I volunteered to do the slogans. But I want you to go to Dog-Scraps's home. Dog-Scraps is truly in a rough situation. If you can do anything to help him out, it would be appreciated."

"All right, all right, all right. I will take care of the revoking of the subsidies. That's not a problem. As for helping Dog-Scraps, let me see what I can do. There's nothing for you to worry about. But as for him drinking pesticide, Freshwind is going to talk about it. I need some help there. We need to put out the fire before it starts. We don't want rumors circulating."

Halfway back from the township government, Wisdom Xia met Clerk and Rain Xia. They were carrying the rattan chair, a water pipe, and a bundle of scrolls.

Wisdom Xia smiled and said, "If the township head didn't cooperate, I really was going to occupy the place." It was then that Rain Xia broke the news that Dog-Scraps had passed away.

Wisdom Xia turned and began walking toward Dog-Scraps's home. Dog-Scraps was laid out on a plank bed set up behind a mourning pavilion erected in the courtyard. A sheet of rough hempen paper was laid over his face. Wisdom Xia lifted the paper and looked down at Dog-Scraps's greenish-black face. He reached down and patted the dead man's cheek. "What did you do it for? Did you have to fucking use pesticide?"

He went out of the courtyard toward the village offices at Freshwind Temple. He asked Lotus to play over the public address some of Dog-Scraps's favorite opera. Dog-Scraps used to love when they played local opera over the village loudspeakers. They played "Spinning Thread Tune" that day. They played it five times.

Chapter 20

Dog-Scraps was buried in the wardrobe that had stood in his bedroom. The four legs on the bottom were sawed off, and the inside of it was packed with ash and juniper fronds. Dog-Scraps was laid to rest in the coffin, and it was buried in the ground. For the next three days, a north wind blew through Freshwind. The wind was not strong, but it had enough force to stir up the leaves. Everyone who got caught out in it came down with a headache shortly after. Mid-Star's father said that because Dog-Scraps had died a violent death, his spirit would haunt the village. The streets were deserted once the sun went down.

I wasn't scared. When I ran into Obedient Zhang in the street, he wouldn't talk to me. I asked him if he needed any help siphoning the liquor out of the barrels. The north wind kept blowing, and the dust flew up into a whirlwind beside him. I saw his expression change. I asked him, "Are you going to ask Dog-Scraps's wife for the money for that pesticide?"

"It's a state store, so that's state money. I have to get it from her."

"That's fine, but do you really want to stir up a ghost? He's dead. You still want to get that money?"

"When a criminal gets executed, they send a bill for the bullet to his family." The whirlwind swept around Obedient Zhang again, blowing harder and harder until his jacket billowed and the buttons popped one by one. The jacket was blown down the street.

"If you want Dog-Scraps to leave you alone, you better rip up that debt," I said.

Obedient Zhang unbuttoned his rear pocket, took out a sheet of paper, and tore it up. The whirlwind blew itself out with a sigh, stirring up the leaves on the trees with its final gust. Obedient Zhang told the township head what had happened.

Seven days after Dog-Scraps had died, the township head paid a visit to the dead man's home. In the name of poverty relief, he had officially withdrawn three hundred yuan out of a township government account and given it to Dog-Scraps's family. The whirlwind wasn't seen again after that.

Wisdom Xia was as good as his word and went out with Big-Noise Zhao and a bucket of lime wash to paint slogans promoting the reforestation campaign. He had Dog-Scraps's wife sit down with Big-Noise Zhao to write a letter of thanks to the township government, and they stuck it to the gate of the offices. And with that, the Dog-Scraps affair was quietly put to bed.

Shortly after that, the township head received his expected promotion to the county government, and an even younger and less experienced township head was appointed to take his place. The new township head paid a visit to Wisdom Xia, who didn't mention the Dog-Scraps affair specifically but cautioned the new township head to pay attention to the disparity between rich and poor villagers in Freshwind. Wisdom Xia counted on his fingers twenty-three households that the township head should pay attention to. They included the mentally disabled, men crippled while working in the city, shut-ins, and families whose homes had burned down or who had too many children . . .

He told the township head that the relationship between the people and the village cadres was uncomfortable. That wasn't to say, Wisdom Xia explained, that the village cadres were corrupt or working in their own self-interest, but they were forced to push the villagers to give up their grain and taxes. The village cadres worked hard, but they had their own challenges: first, the demands placed on them by policy decisions from higher levels of government, and second, the lack of sufficient funding for the village-level government, which made it difficult to pay the salaries of the cadres and also cover the cost of employing the community teachers not on the county government payroll.

Wisdom Xia told the new township head that if he could let the higher levels of government know the situation and push them to take on at least those two expenses—the wages of community teachers and stipends for local cadres—the village government could increase the amount of tax revenue passed upward. With more taxes being passed on, rather than kept in the village, there would be less pressure on the village cadres to cater to the whims of the villagers, and there would be an improvement in the cadres' performance. There was too much poverty in the village, and poverty made people desperate. With a few improvements, it would be possible to improve cooperation between cadres and villagers.

Wisdom Xia spoke slowly, using the tone he had used to lecture students when he was a principal. The township head sat obediently and listened closely, jotting down notes. When Rain Xia came in to pour tea for his father and the township head, he stole a glance at the township head's notebook. He noticed first the township head's excellent penmanship—but then he looked closer and saw that the township head seemed not to have heard a word that Wisdom Xia had said. The township head was nodding along with the lecture, but it was all a show. He was simply copying down sentences from the calligraphy Wisdom Xia had put up on the walls of the main room.

Rain Xia stepped out into the yard and called his father over. "He's not even listening to you. What are you lecturing him for?"

"I don't want him to make the same mistakes his predecessor did."

"Mother wanted to know if he's going to stay here for dinner. She'll have to start cooking if he is."

Wisdom Xia grunted and went back into the room where the township head was admiring the calligraphy on the walls. "How old are you, Township Head?" Wisdom Xia asked.

"Thirty."

"The same age as Wind Xia."

"He's accomplished much more than me in the same number of years."

"Well, being appointed township head is quite an accomplishment. If you're successful here, you'll have a bright future ahead of you. What do you think of the calligraphy?"

"Very nice! I've heard that you also paint opera masks . . ."

"Where did you hear that?"

"Mid-Star Xia mentioned it."

"He's my nephew. He told me when he goes on tour with the opera troupe, he's going to display my work. The truth is, it's just a hobby. None of them are masterpieces." He went into his bedroom and came back with a wooden trunk. From the trunk, he produced eight of his painted ladles. He took out each ladle in turn and explained which opera the mask painted on it was from. He suddenly remembered Rain Xia's question. "You have to stay with us for lunch, Township Head. My wife isn't much of a chef, but she can put together something simple for us."

"Oh no, I'm afraid we're having a lunch meeting today."

Wisdom Xia hollered for his wife: "The township head isn't staying for lunch. Boil him some water!"

In Freshwind, when we say "boil some water," it means to poach eggs. When Fourth Aunt put water in the pan and stoked the fire, she saw that the sugar jar was empty. She sent Rain Xia over to Thunder's house to borrow some. That was when she realized it was Thunder's forty-ninth birthday.

Let me get off track here and talk about Thunder for a while. Rain Xia was close to his younger cousin Thunder, but Blossom invited me instead of him to celebrate Thunder's birthday. Ever since his thirty-sixth birthday, Thunder had celebrated at home with his friends and relatives. He set up a few banquet tables, and he and his guests ate and drank late into the night. A forty-ninth birthday is important, since it's the threshold of middle age. In the days before his birthday, Thunder's wife had gone around the village to let everyone know the date was coming.

Blossom went and bought silk and then went to the dyehouse to have it tinted bright red. She cut the silk into a pair of panties and a backless bodice. At Forest Wu's place, she got a basket of tofu and then went to the oil mill for a bucket of vegetable oil. She hired the butcher to come over the day of her husband's birthday and slaughter their family pig. I was over at Mid-Star's father's home asking about the opera troupe when Blossom came around to borrow their iron tub. She invited me to Thunder's birthday, and I helped her carry home the tub. When we got to her yard, Star Chen was swinging an ax, chopping firewood.

I watched his steady pace and shouted to him, "Keep it up!"

That was around the time Rain Xia came over to borrow the sugar. He asked about the birthday banquet. "How many tables will there be?"

"Probably ten or so," Blossom said.

"I don't have any money right now, but I'll pitch in however I can. Just let me know."

"You might be broke, but I know Wind Xia's got money. He didn't come back to the village, even when he knows Thunder's birthday is coming up."

"You can't blame him. He's a busy man these days. You know he's a pretty big wheel. Even before his marriage leave was up, his company was calling him back to work."

"He might be a big deal, but how does that help out the Xia family? From what I've seen, it hasn't benefited the rest of you. Every time he goes back and forth between here and Xijing, Thunder takes him on his bus. If you add up all the trips since Wind Xia went to college . . . How much would it have cost him to buy the tickets himself? Ten thousand? Eight thousand? Either way, he's never even bought Thunder dinner."

"I'm sure he hasn't forgotten about Thunder. Snow Bai always asks how he's doing, too. Since my brother and his wife are out of the village right now, how about I take care of buying firecrackers for the birthday?"

"Are you serious? Don't let Fourth Aunt know you're buying them. She doesn't want you wasting your money."

I felt bad for Rain Xia. Blossom took his offer at face value. I quietly asked him, "Where are you going to get the money? You know how seriously she takes his birthday. She's going to want a bundle of firecrackers."

"You heard how she was talking! I had to offer, and I can't go back on it now. Could you lend me two hundred yuan?"

I didn't have the money to lend, but I did have a plan. I called over Star Chen and brought him and Rain Xia to the locust tree over the road. I asked Star Chen, "You and Emerald have something going on, don't you?"

"Yes."

"We don't have a problem with that, ourselves, but what you're doing is considered corrupting public morals."

"'Corrupting public morals'?"

Rain Xia kicked him in the shin and said, "You know what we mean. You think we don't know what you're doing with Emerald? You're pretty fucking bold. You're over here splitting firewood like you're already the son-in-law. I'm telling you, if everybody finds out what you're up to, these villagers will beat the shit out of you and dump you on the road out of town."

Star Chen's face went pale. "Are you threatening me?"

I said, "That's right. What are you going to do about it?"

The truth is that there wasn't much Rain Xia and I could do, but Star Chen was spineless. He said, "What do you want from me?"

"Three hundred yuan—or everyone will know about you and Emerald."

Star Chen went to get the money. That was the first time I'd done anything like that. Rain Xia asked, "Do you think we went too far?"

"Everything in this world comes at a price."

That night, when Thunder parked his bus and walked home, Blossom told him that Rain Xia had offered to buy firecrackers for his birthday. "Why do other people have to buy things for my party?"

"He offered to buy them, since Wind Xia won't be around to pay for anything. You're the one who runs Wind Xia back and forth—he owes you. These birthday banquets aren't cheap. Even with Rain Xia helping out on the firecrackers, it's still going to cost us a few thousand yuan."

"Are you serious?"

"You've never run a household. You have no idea how much anything costs." She counted on her fingers. "We're slaughtering a pig, so we've got meat and lard, but we need vegetable oil, too, at least ten *jin*, then a basket of tofu, five *jin* of wood ear, ten *jin* of vegetables, five *jin* of fiddleheads to go with the braised pork and some to make soup, ten chickens, ten ducks, at least thirty *jin* of fish . . .

"Nowadays, everyone wants seafood, so I got Wealth to pick up ten *jin* of shrimp and six *jin* of squid. If we have ten tables, that means we need at least ten turtles, too. At least fifty *jin* of fruit. And then you gotta have cigarettes. Cigarettes are a money pit. Even if we skimp, we'll need at least ten cartons. A basket each of radish, cabbage, leeks, celery, lotus root, eggplant, pumpkin, onions, potatoes . . . I won't even bother telling you about the noodles and rice. Thirty yuan, at least, for the *laozao*, jujubes, gingko nuts, raisins, chilies, Sichuan peppercorns, mustard . . . And liquor? Liquor, we'll need at least three cases."

Thunder waved her off, saying, "You're giving me a headache. I don't want to hear all this."

"You think you're a prince!" She grabbed her husband by the collar and jammed her hand into his pocket, hunting for any cash he might have hidden. Thunder jerked away, but she had already run into the courtyard with a handful of money. "What are you doing with all this money in your pocket? It's not good for your health. Here, I'll give you back two fifty."

"That's all I'm worth?"

"You want what you're worth? Here's ten yuan."

Rites Xia, who was watching the scene unfold, couldn't take it any longer. "If you take all he has, he'll have to go beg in the street for more."

Blossom said, "This is for his birthday! Anyway, if I wasn't looking after the money, a banquet would bankrupt him."

"You should be making money with a banquet. Everyone that comes should slip him some cash."

"Of course! But that's why we need at least ten tables. Anyway, what does he need to carry around all that money for? He'll end up getting himself into trouble. What kind of man goes around with three hundred yuan in his pocket?"

Thunder said, "She's just saying that because she heard Goodness say a prostitute costs three hundred yuan. She doesn't realize that a man like me doesn't have to pay to fool around with girls—they'd be paying me."

Rites Xia grunted and shut the door.

"Fine," Blossom said. "If you've got girls paying you, then I can keep this money."

"How can a woman talk like that? You're only in love with money."

"You think I'm in love with money? You think everything pays for itself? You have no idea what it costs to support this family. And I give whatever I can save back to my parents. Chastity told me the other day that without me the family would fall apart."

"Why do you listen to her? Look at how she's dressed, then go look in the mirror."

"I dress up for you! You said you liked it." Blossom gave her husband the clothes she'd made. "I have to do something to get you into bed."

Thunder jerked his chin in the direction of the house, nervous that his parents or the kids would hear.

"What are your plans?"

"I'm taking some time off. Wealth Zhao can work my shifts."

"After all this money we're spending on your birthday, you're letting Wealth take your shifts? Are you retarded? Tell him you can work the shifts yourself. Remember the last time I

212

helped you, selling tickets? We can do that again, for the next couple of days. A few days of hard work, then take some time off for your birthday."

"You want to work me to death, don't you?"

"I've got something else you can work on, too . . ." She pulled him into the house.

Rites Xia chose that moment to head out to the bathroom. He saw Thunder and Blossom before they saw him, and he turned back to his own room, giving a few theatrical coughs.

The next day, Thunder called Wealth Zhao and told him to park the bus at the township government offices when he arrived back in Freshwind from Xijing. He let Wealth know that he wouldn't have to pick up his shifts. At dusk, when the bus rolled back into the township, several villagers stopped by to ask about getting a ride into Xijing. Blossom met them at the door and said, "You'll have to buy tickets. The company is cracking down on free rides."

Everyone nodded. Someone said, "We just want to reserve our seats."

"You have to get to the township government office by six."

After they left, Thunder said, "Those are our neighbors! Why did you tell them they have to buy tickets?"

"Why shouldn't they? You've let them ride for free for too long. What do you get out of it? All of them are running stores on Middle Street and going into the city to buy merchandise. If we go into one of their stores, are they going to let us take things off the shelf without paying? Why should they get a hundred-mile ride for free?"

"I don't feel right about it."

"You just don't have the balls to tell them. Do you think Wealth has seven or eight people riding for free when he drives in?"

That night, Thunder and Wealth Zhao sat down to a bottle of liquor, and Thunder got up early the next morning to start his route. Blossom went along with him. The five passengers waiting for the bus paid Blossom for their ride, but she waved them on board without giving them a ticket. When the bus got to the county bus station, the station agent asked about the tickets, but Thunder said, "I'm just giving my relatives a ride into the city."

"Don't make a habit of it. I can't take responsibility for whatever happens."

The bus continued to Xijing, picking up passengers along the way. Blossom took cash but kept the tickets. She repeated the procedure on the way back. She took in four hundred yuan on the first circuit. They repeated the route over the next four days, working until they were on the verge of collapse. A day before the birthday party, with one last run to make, Thunder told Blossom to stay home. As he was sending her off, Concord Qin's wife arrived. Concord Qin's wife was bad luck—everything she was a part of was destined to end badly. She ended up putting Blossom in a bad mood and then working herself up, too.

Concord Qin's wife's older sister had gotten wind of his mysterious illness and had decided to come to visit. She had spent a day in the village but had to hurry back to Xijing, where she had moved after getting married. Concord Qin's wife had come to ask Thunder if he could give her a seat on the bus.

Blossom took Concord Qin's wife's hand and asked, "How is Concord Qin doing? It's not fair, is it? Spark cut his thing off, and he's already doing just fine. But Concord Qin is such a fine man, and he still hasn't recovered."

"That's why my sister came to see him."

"Thunder and I keep saying we have to visit, but we've been too busy. But if your sister is leaving . . . Could she maybe find another way to get to the city? I'm not sure how to explain this . . . You know, Concord Qin used to always hitch a ride with him, and it was no problem, but the company has gotten strict about the regulations. If the company finds out that a driver is taking unpaid passengers, they take the cost of the ticket out of their paycheck. On the second offense, they'll suspend the driver's license. So, you see . . ."

Concord Qin's wife's expression darkened. "She's a worker. She doesn't have much money. When she came down, she bought a bunch of things for us, so she doesn't have any money left to buy a ticket back. You know how things are for our family. Ever since Concord Qin got sick, it's all money going out and nothing coming in."

"Oh dear! If Thunder owned the bus, it wouldn't be a problem to take passengers. It would be fine if he was short three or four hundred on tickets for a run. But the bus company is state run. It's just like Concord Qin, in a way. He can't play fast and loose with the village money, right?"

"That's right."

Concord Qin's wife was silent for a moment and then took out a roll of money bound with a red string. There were only small bills in the roll.

Blossom said, "So you do have money."

"I've got forty yuan here, so I'm still short twenty-six yuan."

Thunder said, "How about this: you tell her to show up at the township offices tomorrow, and I'll take care of the twenty-six she's short."

Blossom said, "You'll take care of it? You work all day for twenty yuan."

"We owe it to her. We should have gone to see Concord Qin already." Concord Qin's wife thanked him, and he sent her away.

Blossom said, "You shouldn't have let that twenty-six yuan slide. She could have had another roll of cash in another pocket."

Thunder ignored his wife.

After Concord Qin's wife saw off her sister the next morning, she went home and saw that Concord Qin was already awake. She told Concord Qin what a good man Thunder was to help her out, and she went into the kitchen to fix poached eggs for her husband. After she brought him the eggs, she went out into the yard and took off her shoes and began poking her corns and blisters with a needle.

Meanwhile, Concord Qin was struggling to eat the poached egg. He cut it into slices with his chopsticks and tried to pick them up, but they kept falling. He managed to get a big chunk of the yolk, but it ended up on his nose. He said, "Why can't I manage to get this in my mouth?"

"Are you a baby or what? You need me to come feed you?" She popped the final blister on her foot and went back into the house. As soon as she saw the egg hanging from his nose, she got suspicious. "What the hell is wrong with you?"

"My hand isn't working right."

She told him to try again, and he still couldn't pick up the egg. His expression changed suddenly, and he moaned involuntarily. When the neighbors heard him in pain, they came running, and when they saw the situation, they went for Big-Noise Zhao. As soon as the old barefoot doctor saw Concord Qin's condition, he told them to take him off to the county hospital as fast as they could.

After being checked out at the county hospital, Concord Qin was diagnosed with a brain tumor. Big-Noise Zhao, who had accompanied Concord Qin there, didn't have the heart to tell him. He called Concord Qin's wife aside and told her what the situation was. She burst into tears. Big-Noise Zhao and Concord Qin's wife asked how much it would cost to hospitalize Concord Qin.

The doctor said, "There's no way to say for sure. We had a patient that died yesterday, in the room right beside your husband's. The family has already spent twelve thousand yuan." Concord Qin's wife staggered out of the doctor's office and collapsed in the hallway. She had no idea what to do. She could only listen to Big-Noise Zhao's advice.

Big-Noise Zhao said, "This is a dark day! You'll be throwing away money, when there's no way to cure what ails Concord Qin. You need to prepare yourself for what's coming. You have to trust me. We can take him back home, and I'll prepare some plasters for him. We can pray and maybe there will be a miracle, but that's all we can hope for."

Concord Qin's wife kowtowed to Big-Noise Zhao, her head knocking the hospital floor. She wailed, "You have to save him! I would do anything to save him. In our next life, Concord Qin and I will be reborn as a tree that shelters your front gate. You can tie your donkey and your dog around our trunk. We'll give you shade all year-round." They carried Concord Qin back to Freshwind.

But let me return to the story of Thunder's birthday. Rain Xia bought three rolls of fire-crackers and strung them from Thunder's courtyard gate out into the road. Third Aunt was hard of hearing to begin with, but after Rain Xia's firecrackers went off, she was completely deaf. Thunder's wife had set up fifteen banquet tables that ran from the central room of the house through Rites Xia's rooms and then out across the yard, but there still weren't enough places for all the guests, and she had a few more set up outside, running along the road. In previous years, the kitchen had been a hive of activity, with everyone packed in, washing and chopping, but Thunder's relatives had come out in force, and they made quick work of the preparation.

Around that time, Thunder's eldest daughter, Grace, had gotten engaged to a boy sur-named Wang from over on West Street. The Wang family had always been poor, but they were honest folk. Their son was more than worthy of Thunder's daughter, and he had found work as a laborer with Excellent Li's construction firm. In fact, Thunder and Blossom had at first opposed the marriage but couldn't dissuade their daughter. Besides, the Wang family was somehow related to Third Aunt's family, and she'd done her best to push for the marriage, too. Thunder and Blossom were finally convinced. After the engagement was formalized, the parents of the boy had been to visit Thunder and Blossom nearly every day. They never came empty handed, always bringing some eggs or potatoes or yams from their garden. They happily pitched in around their future daughter-in-law's house, mucking out the pigsty or pushing the stone roller. They worked hard without any complaints.

Third Aunt eventually told Blossom to stop letting them work so hard. "You can't let your future in-laws root around in the mud like hired hands."

"I didn't ask them to do anything. That's just how they work. I told them to take a break, but they didn't even slow down."

The day before the birthday, the Wang family came over to help slaughter the pig, and after the skinning was done, they had eight *jin* of leaf lard and three *jin* of belly fat. Third Aunt told them to take home the belly fat, but they refused. They'd brought along their younger son, who was still wetting the bed, and they agreed with Third Aunt's suggestion to let the butcher rub the pig's tail around their son's mouth—the butcher explained that it was supposed to cure bedwetting.

When they poured hot water over the pig to scald it, the mother of the Wang family caught the runoff in three basins: one for Rites Xia, one for Third Aunt, and one for herself. Third Aunt had bound feet, and the runoff from scalding pigs was supposed to help heal cracked and dried-out skin. She soaked her feet and picked the lice out of her socks. She looked down at Mother Wang's feet. "Those cracks in your feet are as big as a baby's fist. That's got to hurt!"

"Not at all."

"After you wash your feet, you should rest for a while. Come back for the banquet tomorrow."

When they showed up again at dawn the next day to start washing radishes and carrying water, Third Aunt found their son and future daughter-in-law and started to lecture them. The Wang son carried a load of water, but Grace disappeared immediately.

The afternoon of the birthday banquet, some people were saying that Concord Qin was being brought back from the county hospital. Rumor began to spread that he had a brain tumor, and the news could be traced from table to table by the sound of moans as people learned of his condition.

Justice Xia heard the news and set down his chopsticks. He chewed a mouthful of food, rolling it from cheek to cheek—crunch! He bit down on something hard and spat it out. It turned out to be half of a button.

Wealth Zhao said, "Who washed these vegetables?"

Hearth grabbed the broken button and was about to rush to the kitchen when Justice Xia waved him off. He told Hearth to go find Big-Noise Zhao. Justice Xia wanted someone to go and ask about Concord Qin and make sure Big-Noise Zhao came to the banquet. Hearth sent Tongue-Tied to the Great Qing Hall in his place.

On their way back home, Big-Noise Zhao wanted them to go through the market, but Concord Qin wanted to take a different road off Highway 312. The road Concord Qin chose was so rough that he fell off the stretcher. As he was being pulled back up, he heard the firecrackers.

"Where are those firecrackers coming from?" he asked.

"It's Thunder's birthday."

"Oh." That was all he said.

Once Concord Qin was safely at home, Big-Noise Zhao left, but Concord Qin's wife caught up with him. She said, "Are you going to the banquet?"

"Everyone knows I'm back from the county hospital. It would be rude not to go."

"Should I go, too? Maybe I should send a gift."

"Don't worry about that. I'll tell Thunder you asked about him." Big-Noise Zhao went back to the Great Qing Hall to change his clothes and ran into Shifty out front with White-Moth.

Shifty saw Big-Noise Zhao and said, "Big-Noise, I heard that Concord Qin has a brain tumor."

"News travels fast, huh?"

"He won't be around to eat the autumn rice!"

Big-Noise Zhao turned away from Shifty. White-Moth was at the pharmacy to buy bandages to cover up the blisters from her new shoes. Shifty bent to help her take her shoes off and put the bandages on.

Big-Noise Zhao said, "Buy her bigger shoes next time."

"I bought these a long time ago. If she can get her feet into them, then she can have them. I didn't think she had such big feet."

Shifty let White-Moth leave first; then he leaned across the counter and said to Big-Noise Zhao, "Women change fast. When I first got her, she was dead wood; now she's a firecracker. All I had to do was learn how to play her. Hit the right notes, and she'll do anything I want."

As he watched Shifty leave, Big-Noise thought to himself, *They say evil is repaid with evil and good is repaid with good. If that was true, then why do good men die early while evil men seem to live forever?* He pondered the question and came to this conclusion: *Evil men are shameless. They don't have a guilty conscience. Good men are governed by ethics. They torture themselves over every decision they make.*

He picked up his brush and wrote, "He shared for his entire life the joys and sufferings of the people. With his life cut tragically short, the villagers beat their chests and cry tears of sorrow. He devoted half a lifetime to serving the collective without complaint or rest. Through all the trials of office, he was an honest bureaucrat. The elders lament that his lofty aspirations could not be realized."

When he was done writing, he was surprised to read what he had written. *What have I done? Concord Qin is still alive, and I'm writing his funeral scroll.* As he wiped a finger across the ink, he looked up to see Tongue-Tied and Lucky. Tongue-Tied moaned and waved his hands around; Big-Noise Zhao understood. He took fifty yuan from a drawer and followed the mute and the dog.

Big-Noise Zhao and Tongue-Tied ran into Clerk's wife on Middle Street. He asked where she was going, and when he learned she was going to the banquet, too, he said, "You better fix yourself up before you go over there."

She tried to stamp the dirt off her shoes, but they still had a layer of grime on them. "What's the problem? You think Blossom would kick me out for not being dolled up? Clerk is already there. He brought a gift for Thunder. I just want to get a plate of food."

Lucky had gone ahead of everyone and was waiting for them, wagging his tail. Tongue-Tied saw that Lucky had lain down in front of Star Chen's place. Looking in through the window, Tongue-Tied saw a pair of legs sticking straight in the air. He wasn't sure what he was looking at, exactly, so he leaned in for a closer look. He saw Emerald lying on the kang and Star Chen standing in front of her. They were both completely naked. Tongue-Tied staggered back and grabbed Lucky by the ear to pull him away from the window.

Big-Noise Zhao said, "What's going on?"

The mute moaned, spit bubbling at the corners of his mouth.

"What did you see? What's wrong with your mouth?"

Tongue-Tied blocked his way and stuck out his little finger and spat on it.

When he arrived at the banquet, Big-Noise Zhao made the formal announcement that Concord Qin had a brain tumor. Nobody had the heart to drink after hearing the news. Thunder's wife had gotten three cases of liquor, but only one was opened. After the meal, Justice Xia and Pavilion went to see Concord Qin, and Blossom packed up some leftovers for them to bring with them.

They stayed at Concord Qin's home for a short time, and on the way back Justice Xia said to Pavilion, "Give it three days and then visit him again. At this point, you have to put aside any disagreements between you two."

"There is no disagreement between us."

"That's good to hear. Just think: today you're alive and well, and tomorrow you find out that your days are numbered. Concord Qin's family isn't wealthy, and this is going to bankrupt them, if it hasn't already. Not to mention, this kind of illness . . . is . . ."

"If Big-Noise can help out, I'll tell him that I'll take care of any expenses."

"Patches and plasters don't cost much, but he'll need more than that."

"The village should help pay for some of it. But with the market being built, there's not much in the coffers to spare. Maybe we can start a collection for him?"

Justice Xia thought for a moment and said, "Taking up a collection is fine, but we need to make sure Concord Qin doesn't get wind of this. He's too proud to take charity. If we do it in the name of the Two Committees, some people won't be willing to donate. There are plenty of villagers that have gone through natural disasters and man-made tragedies. If we take up a collection for Concord Qin, it won't look good. I was thinking, since his birthday's coming up, we could help put together a banquet for him, just like Thunder. Instead of a collection, we can put together whatever people bring to the banquet."

"Perfect! Great idea!"

Justice Xia turned around and went back to Concord Qin's home. Concord Qin was already asleep. His wife said, "You have to come and see him as often as you can, Second Uncle."

"I will."

"But when you come around, please don't bring Pavilion with you."

"I have to disagree with you and Concord Qin on that. What is it between the two of them that's worth not even seeing each other? As a village cadre, you have to soak up all the shit that rains down on you. If you can't handle that, you end up like Concord Qin. You must let it go. I want you to tell Concord Qin the same. Do you understand?"

"Fine."

"Now, Concord Qin's birthday is coming up, isn't it?"

"It's not until the twelfth month. On the thirteenth."

Justice Xia told her about the plan. They agreed to move up the date of his birthday to three days from then.

Everyone in Freshwind knew that Concord Qin had an incurable disease; only Concord Qin was unaware of his fate. As far as he knew, he was suffering from a circulatory problem that was affecting his brain. When his wife told him about the plan to move up his birthday, she explained that she hoped it would help improve his circulation. Concord Qin reluctantly agreed. The banquet was arranged by Justice Xia, and five tables were set. The villagers came, one by one, to pay their respects. Concord Qin was reluctant to get out of bed to greet them, but he eventually relented and emerged for a short time before returning to the kang.

The villagers didn't bring the usual gifts of cigarettes, liquor, dried noodles, and steamed buns. The only gifts given were in the form of cash. Pavilion took the money, and Goodness made a note of each contribution. The final total handed over to Concord Qin was 13,420 yuan. Concord Qin asked, "Did you make a mistake? Where did all this money come from?"

Goodness said, "Just think how many years you served as a village cadre. You helped plenty of people. When they found out you were sick, they wanted to repay your kindness. Just think, Thunder got over ten thousand yuan, too."

"I can't compare myself to Thunder. I don't feel right taking the money."

"You don't feel right? You need to worry about getting better, not how much money you got for your birthday. Once you're back on your feet, you can repay them however you want."

Tears ran down Concord Qin's cheeks as he got down from the kang. He went out into the yard and bowed to each of the villagers. He humbly apologized for the meager banquet. It was only the heads of each household who stayed for the banquet. The rest of the villagers made an excuse and left. Concord Qin's wife saw them off.

I gave twenty yuan. Bounty told me it wasn't enough, but it was more than I'd planned to give—I wasn't going to give anything. When I went through the list that Goodness had kept, I saw that there were at least ten families that hadn't bothered to come. Some of them didn't come because they were working out of the village, and a few had had disagreements with Concord Qin in the past. Concord Qin had never treated me well, and I'd still brought twenty yuan. Even with all that Concord Qin had done for Mid-Star, Mid-Star's father hadn't bothered to come. I couldn't figure it out.

I went looking for Uncle Glory, to ask why he hadn't gone to the banquet. I told Roughshod Ding where I was going, and he said, "You always have to go poking your nose where it doesn't belong." But what about a bee? That's what I was like, a bee flitting from flower to flower. When I got to Uncle Glory's place, I saw that he had lost weight. He was mixing up a medicinal tea on his stone table. Sitting in front of the stone table was Emerald, looking worried.

I said, "Why didn't you go to Concord Qin's place, Uncle Glory?"

"I wasn't feeling well. I went up to the Tiger Head Cliff shrine and got some spirit medicine."

"Why not just go to Big-Noise? What do you need spirit medicine for? What are you boiling over there?"

"Each kind of medicine has its own use. You wouldn't understand."

Emerald said, "Stay out of it! I came here to get my fortune told."

"What do you need your fortune told for? You're about to get married."

"Fuck off!"

"Your fortune is not clear. If you go, you will be fine. If you don't go, you will be fine."

"What the hell are you talking about? Should I go or not?"

"Go where?"

"You know Virtue's daughter is coming back soon . . . She wants some people to come with her to the city. Xiao Qin wants to go, and so do I."

"It doesn't matter if Xiao Qin wants to go, but there's no way you can go."

"Why not?"

"Star Chen won't let you."

Emerald lost her temper and said, "Quit spreading rumors about me, Spark! Star Chen can do whatever he wants, but I'm my own person. Understand? I know you tried to blackmail him. Now you're worried about whether I go to the city? What's wrong with you?"

I didn't want to tangle with her when she was angry, so I said, "Get him to tell your fortune again then." I took Uncle Glory's notebook and flipped through it.

The notebook had ten more pages filled in since I'd last looked at it. On one page, he had written, "Calling on the masters and begging for offerings. The fortune was read on the 15th day. I called on the master at the cultural center on the 16th. My condition has worsened, and I have already expended four hundred yuan on medicine. I will persevere and continue to expend all necessary funds. I called upon Epoch Gao at the cultural center to earnestly implore him to offer me one of his horse paintings. I will sell his painting to subsidize my treatment. Fortune divined on page 39. Great success! Miracle! I have requested of the master a painting: the first time with success, but I was refused when I went to him again. Gao's wife regards me with contempt. I was disrespected when I visited the master's home. She made no motion to offer me a seat and refused me a cup of tea. She swept around my feet as if I was not there, hoping to hurry me out. Epoch Gao was more hospitable. Now that Mid-Star has taken the reins of the opera troupe, I know that Gao's wife dare not ignore me. Whatever her disposition toward me, Epoch Gao might still fulfill his earlier offer.

"Epoch Gao mostly stays home, rarely visiting his office at the cultural center, but I hope to catch him there. I managed to slip inside without the gatekeeper noticing me. I asked after the master and heard conflicting reports—one person responding that he had not been to his office, and another speculating that he might even then be on the grounds. I was overjoyed to come across him in his quarters. It was truly a miracle. When I spoke again about the horse painting and my treatment, he generously agreed. He said he would paint three horses on a large scroll. My happiness was indescribable. We agreed that I would go to his home on the 17th. I spent the night at the home of an old friend named Moss-Green Yuan. On the 17th, I ate breakfast at the home of Moss-Green Yuan and on the way to meet Epoch Gao, I met another old friend—Omen Han from over in West Mountain Bend—in front of the Bureau of Forestry. He asked me to tell his fortune. He gave me three yuan, and we stood beside the bureau's wall. Han's donation was disappointing, but just then rain started coming down and Han passed me an umbrella. I went then to an alley restaurant and ate noodles. In the afternoon, I returned to Epoch Gao's home. The rain continued and I was worried that it might have kept Gao's wife at home. What should I do? I was on tenterhooks, waiting for the door to be answered, but I thanked Heaven when I saw that his wife was out. The painting was complete and hanging on the wall. Once again, my happiness was indescribable. The great master Epoch Gao had blessed me! He told me that if I fostered the talents of my son, Heaven would bless me with longevity. He promised that people in high places (meaning himself) would look after me. I was sure then that my illness would be cured. I was consoled and comforted. Epoch Gao truly is a cultured and heroic man. I must stop here. The sun is coming up. Could my sickness be ending soon?"

While I was looking through the notebook, Uncle Glory and Emerald had kept talking, but I hadn't been listening. When I looked up again, I saw that she was leaving, looking as unhappy as she had when I had arrived.

Mid-Star's father said, "She didn't listen to a word I said." He took the notebook back from me.

"She didn't even pay you," I said. "Why did you read her her fortune?"

He ignored the question. "How many people went to Concord Qin's banquet?"

"Everyone was there."

"Even Pavilion?"

"Yep."

"How much money did Concord Qin get?"

I told him.

"Seriously? How is he going to spend it all?"

"If you give a gift, you expect to get it back in kind someday. You wouldn't know about that, would you? You've never given a gift in your life. If you had a banquet for your birthday, nobody would come."

"I do feng shui. If someone needs to choose a day for a house to be built, or decide where to put a kang, they come to me."

I could tell that he was in a bad mood. He bent his head back to the medicinal tea he was brewing and ignored me. I asked him, "You went to the county seat a couple of days back?"

He ignored me.

"Did you see Mid-Star? Is the troupe done with rehearsals?"

He looked up at me. "If you get sick, you have to spend money. If you try to swindle people, you'll never get better, will you? I don't care what Concord Qin's done for the village. It doesn't compare to my one single act of raising Mid-Star. My son has brought real merit to the village."

I hurriedly agreed.

His mood brightened. "Rehearsals are almost done. Do you want to see a picture?"

He led me into the main room. On the table was a small photograph. It was a souvenir photo, taken at the troupe's dress rehearsal. My eyes immediately found Snow Bai, and I smiled.

"You see Mid-Star sitting up front?" he said. "That suit he's wearing cost five hundred yuan. Just think, a single suit!"

I studied Snow Bai. She was more beautiful than any of the other actors. I smiled at her. She was smiling, too. I knew she had a dimple on her left cheek when she smiled, but I couldn't see it in the photo.

Mid-Star's father suddenly jerked his head up from the picture and ran out of the room. I heard him out in the yard, cursing me. "It boiled dry!" While he was out of the room, I picked up the photo and pressed it to my chest. It was easy enough to slip it into my jacket. Actually, that picture is still sitting at the head of my kang. Every time I look at it, I wish that Snow Bai could walk out of it. I can see her moving, but she's forever trapped in the picture.

I read a story when I was in middle school about a guy who buys a painting of an immortal princess, and every time he leaves the room, the princess jumps down from the painting and washes his clothes and sweeps the floor. Every time I went home, I'd always run into the kitchen, hoping to see her working at the stove. But even if Snow Bai could jump out of the photograph, I shouldn't have expected her to be working in the kitchen. She was an artist, after all, an actress. After I took the photograph from Mid-Star's father and heard the news that the rehearsals were done, I started waiting for the opera troupe to arrive. I decided that while I was waiting, I would go to Goodness and ask him to teach me some opera. He was happy to help, but he didn't know many songs. He taught me a section of "Visiting the Judge Carrying a Child."

The lyrics suited me perfectly. I practiced until I could recite it word for word. Don't believe me? Here:

> They're calling out, calling out, calling out for you!
> Little baby girls and grandpas, too!
> Headed to the cornfield with a yoke and a plough,
> Bumping into stalks while looking for the cow.
> Switch the bomb with the carrot-top sprout,
> Blow you right across the sky like a waterspout.
> Dung beetle fell in the ol' pisspot,
> Eat it like a pickled plum, it's all you got.
> Dung beetle fell on the butcher's block,
> Take in the scene like a soaring hawk.
> Dung beetle crawled up the bamboo stick,
> Dance all day like a lunatic.
> Snake crawling around with its head lopped off,
> No worse than the maggots down in the trough.
> A snake comes coiling, twisted on the handle,
> Won't catch you unless you get caught on the handle.
> Snub-nosed dog scratching the altar with a paw,

The Shaanxi Opera

You come around here again, fighting with your grandpa.
Pumpkins growing along the temple walls,
Cursed to wash your grandpa's nasty balls.
Couldn't scrub you off as hard as they tried,
Don't look like much from any side.
Writing in the grease with an old scrub brush,
Can't read a word, you old dumb lush.
The rake lays down to sleep after a day in the grass,
When you wake you find it halfway up your ass.
Tossed you two fifty and that's enough money,
With that dick in your mouth, you look awful funny.
Some folks came round gave you a boot in the head,
When you finally woke up you done shit the bed.
Dinner was cold and so is your sheet,
Don't complain to me about the price of heat.
Slapped a pelt on a stool and called it a dog,
Turned around three times and leaped in the bog.
Pet the dead dog and call it your pal,
Turned around four times and fell in the canal.
Filthy old monster with hair on your back,
Called your dad your uncle and he gave you a thwack.
Buried a baby in the old graveyard,
Watched all night like you was on guard.
Quicklime for breakfast and indigo for dessert,
Squirting blue shit over your own nightshirt.
Saw you went up the hill and buried your pa,
Then sucked the widow's fart through a piece of straw.
Dung beetle scrounging in a heap of shit,
Try to pretend that you've got some wit.

Chapter 21

Every time anyone overheard me, they told me, "Your late dad would die of embarrassment. You look like you're eating a cake of soap! That's no way to sing local opera."

The Freshwind villagers had never respected me, but what did I care? I looked at the rays of light beaming from the tops of their heads and smiled at how weak they were. Huh! They'd better watch out for themselves.

I'm serious—I can see people's auras. When they're in good health, then the rays are big, and in a sick person, they're pea-size, flickering like an oil lamp that might blow out in a draught. Big-Eighth Zhang, the one with the stuffed-up nose, he had one of those. Auntie Wang had practically no light at all, but Mid-Star's dad wasn't doing too badly. Bright Chen was young, but his light was dim, and I asked him, "What's the matter?"

"I've had a cold for three days. It was a hot day, but I was shaking all over and I needed two bed quilts."

The weird thing was that Concord Qin's light looked as feeble as a candle flame the day he went to the hospital, but after he came back and Big-Noise Zhao pasted an herbal poultice on him for three days, his light brightened again. When he was able to get off the kang, he went for a stroll around the village, and his light stood up like a cockscomb.

One day, Concord Qin's wife made some *liang fen* noodles with pea flour, and Concord Qin got me to help him over to Justice Xia's house because, as he said, "The old village head loves *liang fen*."

While he and Second Uncle were talking, Tongue-Tied came in to get a new pair of pants because his old ones were split at the crotch.

"Where are you off to in such a hurry?" I asked Tongue-Tied.

"They're fixing the tiles on Treasure's new house today," said Justice Xia.

That was the very last stage, and they needed some help, so I left Concord Qin and went along with Tongue-Tied.

There were plenty of people on the site, and a lot of noise and chatter. Virtue's daughter had come home, too, and was pitching in and carrying tiles.

"Hello, Spark," she said to me. No one ever said hello in Freshwind. It was always "Had your dinner?" or "Are the old folks well and the young ones being good?"

So when Virtue's daughter said hello and in Mandarin, not dialect, I was flummoxed.

The girl was a schoolmate of Treasure's daughter Bodhi, and Bodhi said to me, "Spark, answer when someone says hello to you!"

"Say it again, with your tongue in the right place," I said.

"Have you had your dinner?"

Everyone burst out laughing.

"That's better," I said. "You've only been trash-picking in the big city; you haven't come down from heaven. You can still speak like us, can't you?"

Virtue's daughter swore and turned her back on me. Some of the young guys up on the roof were shouting down to her, "Forget Spark; he's not interested in girls. Come up on the scaffolding and bring us some tiles." But she didn't get up on the scaffolding or shift any more tiles. Instead, she fetched the teapot and refilled the workers' mugs. She wasn't wearing a lot, just a skimpy top that showed a waist so slender you could have put your hands around it. Then she and Bodhi found a couple of stools to sit on, and Bodhi asked her about life in the city. The girl was full of fine talk about city high-rises and highways, bars and internet cafés. One of the guys on the scaffolding was listening so hard he dropped a stack of tiles, and they all slithered down and landed with a crash.

"How much does a *jin* of old newspapers sell for?" I asked. "And how many cents for an empty wine bottle?"

The girl got out lipstick and applied it to her lips, then put some on Bodhi, too, so Bodhi's lips looked puffed up suddenly.

Bodhi answered, "Spark, you're a fine one to talk. You've never been to the provincial city. It's my friend's dad who picks trash, not her. And have you ever seen pants like my friend's got on? Just look at what you're wearing."

I admit that Virtue's daughter was doing better than me. I could see that from the plume of light at the top of her head; it was like a fireball. But I was annoyed all the same. Inwardly I said, *Virtue, you were such a useless farmer; why's your whole family lit up so bright?*

Bodhi was still trying to put me down when her mom, Chrysanth, interrupted. "You two girls, you go home if you want to chat. You're putting everyone off their work by sitting around here."

"No, don't go," the guy on the scaffolding called down. "Having women around makes it light work."

"That girl grew up in this village, and you never paid her any attention. What's so special about her now she's been in the city a couple of years?" said Chrysanth, and she turned on her daughter, Bodhi. "What have you got smeared all over your mouth? You look like a vampire!"

Virtue's daughter was so embarrassed that she got up and walked away.

"Aunt, you've upset her. She was only trying to help; fetch her back," said the young guy above them.

"She wasn't doing anything at all except distracting you from your work," retorted Chrysanth. She was so furious her freckles went all dark. She scooped up a pile of wood shavings left over from making the scaffolding and went to the kitchen. The tilers, meantime, stopped for a break and a smoke.

They all grumbled about Chrysanth. "What a bitch. No wonder Treasure can't stand her!"

"So who can Treasure stand?" I asked maliciously.

"Plump white flesh," someone said. "He likes fatty meat."

Everyone agreed that Black-Moth was fair and plump and had breasts like pig's bladders.

You had to mind your mouth in Freshwind 'cause you never knew who might be lurking around the corner—like, just then, who should come along but Black-Moth herself, wearing a pair of yellow rubber shoes. I gave a warning whistle and told them, "That's enough—we don't want to get into trouble."

"We were just talking about you, Black-Moth. What took you so long?" said someone above.

"I knew if I came earlier, I'd get a lot of work to do." And she rolled up her pants legs and started to shift bags of mud.

She certainly put her back into it, trotting to and fro, her big boobs jiggling up and down. The first time, when she got the bag to the foot of the house and heaved it up, the guy on the scaffolding didn't take it from her, and the bag dropped to the ground.

"Haven't you got eyes in your head?" Black-Moth said crossly. "Screw you. This bag's killing me!"

"Screw me? Don't tempt me. My wife's right over there."

Black-Moth threw a handful of mud up at him. "Wash your mouth out! Is that any way to talk to a woman?" The mud splattered all over his face, and there were loud jeers from the other men.

Just then, Chrysanth came back with a fresh pot of boiling water. At the sight of Black-Moth, her freckles went dark again, and she asked me, "Who told that bitch to come?"

"It must have been Treasure." I said, to wind her up.

"Couldn't he have asked someone else? Has everyone else died in the village?"

Forest Wu, who oversaw getting water and mud to the site, walked by and overheard her loud comments. "N-no one asked her. We-we're all just h-humble folk with itchy p-palms."

"Well, that bit's certainly true. And I bet that's not the only place you itch, either," Chrysanth said.

"D-don't t-talk so dirty," Forest Wu admonished her.

"You're a fine one to talk! You and all the dirty things you're doing."

Forest Wu was speechless with fury. As the two of them argued, the tilers above stopped to listen, and Black-Moth herself came over. "Who's been acting dirty?" she asked.

"I can see you really love Forest Wu," said Chrysanth. "You made sure he's got a nice green cuckhold's cap, even on a hot day like this."

"What are you calling me?" yelled Black-Moth and then whacked Chrysanth across the face. Her hands were all muddy, and her fingers left streaks down Chrysanth's cheek.

The two women began to grapple like praying mantises, grabbing and kicking with their arms and legs. Then they got into a clinch and pulled each other's hair, screaming shrilly, like stuck pigs.

The onlookers made no attempt to stop them, except to shout, "No scratching faces! No scratching faces!"

It made no difference; they scratched each other's faces anyway.

Someone shouted, "Move the teapot in case it breaks!"

Too late—Black-Moth hurled the pot to the ground, smashing it to smithereens.

Big-Noise Zhao turned up, soaked in sweat, and pulled the pair apart, getting his clothes streaked with mud and his hair all mussed up in the process.

Black-Moth, knowing most of the onlookers were backing her, laid into Chrysanth. "It was Treasure himself who invited me; that was the only reason I came. Do you think I'd put myself out to help a slut like you? If I saw you strung up in a tree, gasping your last breath, I'd hold a branch over my eyes so I couldn't see till you were properly dead and stiff!"

Having said her piece, she started working on the bags of mud again, but Forest Wu stopped her. "Off you go! Otherwise, who knows how it's going to end?"

Black-Moth stood her ground. "Why?" she demanded.

"Why should she go?" asked the men above. "She's going to be living in it."

"Am I? How come?"

Big-Noise Zhao flared up at that. He shouted at the tilers, "You're not helping, winding them up like that." And he beckoned me over.

"It was Chrysanth's fault," I said.

"You stay out of this," said Big-Noise Zhao. "Get off home!"

"But then I'll miss the fun."

And then Big-Noise Zhao told me, "I've just been in the Great Qing Hall. Mid-Star Xia called and said to tell you the troupe's ready to tour, and you've got to join them within three days at the latest."

"Wah!" I shouted in excitement. That was great news. As I shouted, Black-Moth and Chrysanth launched into it again. What did I care? Let them fight to the death if they wanted; I couldn't give a fig for them now. I ran off as fast as I could.

As I passed Treasure's home, Lucky ran out with a bone in her mouth, with Tiger tagging along behind. They took it in turns to stop and have a gnaw at the bone; there wasn't a scrap of meat on it, so they must have just liked the smell.

I'll be able to see Snow Bai every day from now on. Will she let me get closer to her? I wondered. I looked up at the sky. I'd gotten into the habit, every evening on my way home, of saying a little prayer. *If I can see Snow Bai again, just let a star appear above the house.* But the sky was always clouded over. Maybe there were stars up there, just not in the sky above my house. Now I looked up, but I'd forgotten it was still daytime, so of course there weren't any. At the entrance to the alley, I ran into Wisdom Xia. He'd been to buy some ladles and was walking along with them, belting out:

> He who finds a treasure is filled with joy
> See, the shining light of the midautumn moon!

I came to a sudden halt. I wanted to run away, but there were no side roads. *There's nothing to be scared of,* I told myself. And I stood at the end of the alley and looked at him. He looked back at me.

"Huh?" he said.

"Hello, Uncle. Have you been buying ladles?"

He grunted again and walked past. Once he'd gone, it was my turn to sing:

> He who finds a treasure is filled with joy,
> See, the shining light of the midautumn moon!

I got home and started to wash my clothes. I washed all the good stuff, and I unpicked the quilt cover and washed that, too. The weather was hot, and they didn't take long to dry. So that evening I spread the quilt cover out on the stone roller outside my gate and was sewing it up again when Favor Bai came by. "You poor man, having to sew your own quilt together."

"I do my own dinners, too," I told him.

"I got good news for you, but how are you going to thank me?"

"You've got good news for me?"

"I've found a wife for you."

I looked at him, touched by this kind thought.

"A beggar turned up in the village. She's only a bit over twenty; she's definitely not a looker, but she's in good health. I'll take you to see her."

Behind the big chinaberry tree, a woman's face appeared. She was in profile, and I could see she had a mouth that stuck out like a cucumber, and she was chewing on something. Her hair was dry as straw, tied up with a bit of red string, and it was full of barley husks.

"Favor Bai, you fucking dare match me up with an ugly beggar woman! Is that all you think I'm good for? Are you deliberately insulting me?"

"I told her you were poor, and she said a crow doesn't mind a pig being black. I said you weren't all there down below. She said she didn't mind; all she wanted was food to eat."

"Then she can eat shit!" I said.

I told Favor Bai to piss off, gave up the sewing, and went back indoors. I was so angry I didn't sleep a wink all night. At dawn the next day, Treasure turned up. He wanted me to help fix the tiles—a day should do it.

We were all busy at work when Pavilion came roaring out of the alley on his motorbike, spun in a circle, skidded to a halt, and yelled, "Bounty!"

"Yeah!"

"The market opens for business tomorrow. The work isn't finished on the archway, and you disappeared."

"It's just fixing a few carved stones in place. I left a couple of men on the job."

"They don't know what the hell they're doing. I want you there right away."

"He can't go," said Treasure. "He's the main tiler here. If he goes, who's going to fix the tiles?"

"Why should I care?" said Pavilion.

"People always said you were a hard man, Pavilion. Doesn't family mean anything to you? You took all the craftsmen in the village to the market site, so we've only worked on this house in dribs and drabs; the job's been going on forever. Finally, today we're tiling, and my own brother can't stay and help?"

"I'm talking to my contractor, not you. Bounty, if you want to be paid, you get yourself over there and make sure everything's ready for the opening ceremony, or else!"

Bounty came down off the roof and rubbed the mud off his hands with a bunch of grass. "Brother, you all get on with it, and if you don't finish, I'll be back tonight to help."

"You can't do tiling at night. You think I'm building a hen coop? Screw you. Go and earn money!" Treasure was so angry he aimed a kick at a stack of tiles that were soaking in water and knocked them over so they broke.

"Who are you lashing out at?" said Pavilion.

"I'm not lashing out at anyone. Can't I kick my own tiles? I'll kick them again!" And he trampled on the tiles and smashed them. Any that weren't broken he picked up and bashed against the stone so they shattered into smithereens.

There was such a racket down below that all the tilers stopped work. Tongue-Tied jumped down off the scaffold and ripped his pants at the crotch again. He held the rent together with one hand and hollered for Justice Xia. The old man came running and slapped Bounty across the face.

Bounty stood holding his hand across his cheek. "They're the ones fighting. Why are you hitting me?"

"What's more important, a private project or a collective one? You know what weighs heavier in the balance, don't you?"

"This market project is such bullshit," said Treasure. "Why's such good land being turned into a market? And selling what? Old bones?"

"Bullshit to you!" said the old man. "Do you think I'd have allowed you to get the market builders over to work on your house if I was against the project? You just listen to me. The Two Committees both agreed on the market project, so we all have to go along with it." And he shouted up at the workers, "Who's come from the market site?"

"Only me," said Bounty.

"You take him with you," Justice Xia told Pavilion. "What are you doing, standing here arguing?"

And Pavilion drove off with Bounty sitting on the rear carrier.

Treasure was still squatting on the ground. From some way away, Bodhi shouted, "Dad! Dad!"

"What?"

"Mom wants money from you. She says there's no food in the house, and no corn grits or noodles in the pot. She needs to go and buy some right away."

"Tough luck if there's no food," said Treasure.

"What's she been doing? She should have taken care of it earlier," said Justice Xia. "She can go and pick pumpkin leaves."

"Can you eat pumpkin leaves?" I asked.

"Of course you can. Not like a salad, but you can put them in the pot." And he told the workers to get on with their tasks. He climbed up the scaffolding and onto the roof himself and began to paste on mud and put the tiles in place.

Justice Xia kept the pressure up on everyone and made a point of showing he could do more than men half his age. The worst was that he kept his eye on the workers on the ground, too. Wearing sunglasses, with one of his dark rollies clamped between his lips, he kept shouting at me, telling me I wasn't trotting fast enough with the bags of mud. My shoes were full of it, and I kept slipping, so I thought I might as well take the shoes off and go barefoot.

I trotted back and forth under the blazing sun until I started seeing things, like feet everywhere—big feet, little feet, feet with big blisters, toes sticking up in rows, feet lined up like soldiers, marching along, climbing the walls, and running around on the roof rafters. The troops of feet scared me because that time I fell out of the mulberry tree, I'd seen lots of feet running everywhere, too.

"I'm going for a piss!" I shouted. I pulled someone's straw hat off a rafter and crammed it on my head so no one could tell it was me, then sprinted away.

The sky was covered in fish-scale clouds, the scales neatly overlapping each other. There must have been a fish in the sky; I could smell its fishiness. Just then a plane passed overhead, trailing a plume of white smoke that stayed there for ages. Then the sky was cut open, or rather, it split, and water leaked out and the fish disappeared.

I spent hours that afternoon gazing at the sky and didn't go back to work on the house, though Tongue-Tied did come and fetch me when the evening meal was ready. It was *mi'rm-ian*—corn grits—and noodles in which Chrysanth had cooked pumpkin leaves. It was pretty to look at and good and thick, but it tasted bitter from the leaves. I complained, and then everyone started complaining, and the craftsmen and the laborers all put their bowls down. In the kitchen, Chrysanth told Bodhi off and sent her to get a fresh bag of flour and make more noodles.

Justice Xia had exhausted himself. He lay flat out on a bench in the house and made Tongue-Tied pound his back and use a wooden club to tap the soles of his feet, too. He heard the fuss the workers outside were making about the food. "Pumpkin leaves aren't bitter," he said and then went out and helped himself to a big bowlful. I was watching him, and I saw him frown as he took the first mouthful.

"Bitter, right?"

"Not a bit," he said and then ate it all up.

"You don't taste the bitter, but you feel bitter inside, right, Second Uncle?" I said to him.

He stared at me and muttered, "That's a whole pot of food. Quit making mischief again." He went back for a second helping, but Chrysanth was already ladling the leftovers into a wooden bucket, clattering her ladle against the rim. "See how rich we are?" she said. "We can afford to waste food."

Justice Xia said nothing. He refilled his bowl and sat on the doorstep to eat it.

"Take the bucket home for the pig," Chrysanth told Hearth.

"If you're not going to eat it, I'll take it with me," said Justice. "I'll eat it tomorrow. I don't expect it'll kill me, but we'll wait and see."

I'd never seen Justice Xia be quite so stoic before. He finished his second bowlful and went back for a third helping. No one told him not to; they seemed to think it was a great joke, watching him dig himself into a deep hole. That infuriated me, and I went over and snatched the bowl out of his hand. "Stop it! A pot of *mi'rmian* isn't worth it."

"In that case, you finish this for me."

And I did, just to save Justice Xia's face. It was so bitter, it tasted like traditional medicine. Just then, Pavilion came past the gate, holding up Bounty, who was very drunk.

"How did you get so drunk?" I heard someone ask.

Bounty could hardly get his tongue around the words, and they came out all slurred, but the gist was that when he'd finished the arch, Pavilion had invited him for dinner at Clerk's wife's restaurant. She'd killed three cockerels, and they'd had five bottles of liquor. And they'd finished off a basket of steamed buns, too. "We had meat . . . and drink!" Pavilion exclaimed. Then the pair of them slumped to the ground.

The next day, the market had its grand opening. Pavilion oversaw all that, and he did it in style, of course. There were over a hundred stalls with goods laid out, and it even attracted passing traffic from Highway 312. The shoppers descended like locusts, snapping up this and that, and went away laden with bags of all sizes. Star Chen had a stall, too. He had no apples for sale, but he'd been up in the mountains, buying from the folks who foraged up there, and was selling wood ear fungus, day lilies, and edible ferns, as well as thirty-six free-range chickens and twelve rabbits. Emerald was helping him serve customers.

Star Chen was smart—he'd brought his guitar, which he strummed as he sang songs, and the customers came flocking around him. He sold everything. He was so pleased that he sat down to count his takings—a stack of small-denomination bills—licking a finger and flicking through them one by one. Then he rolled them up and handed them to Emerald. She refused to take them, so he got hold of her collar, pulled her to him, and stuffed the money inside her bra. Pavilion saw that, but he didn't get angry; in fact, he brought his VIP visitors over to Star Chen's stall.

"Star Chen here is showing us how it's done," he told them.

Mr. Lin, deputy head of the county and the biggest VIP, patted Star Chen on the head. "Smart guy. You did well!"

Star Chen, never one to let an opportunity slip, said, "Mr. Lin, tell me what song you'd like me to sing."

"Can you play local opera on that guitar?"

"Nope."

"Are you an opera fan, too, Mr. Lin?" asked Pavilion.

"I certainly am. It's my understanding that you have a retired teacher in Freshwind who's devoted to opera and paints opera masks."

"Her fourth grandad," said Star Chen, pushing Emerald forward.

"I'd love to meet him."

"He's my fourth uncle. I'll get him here," said Pavilion.

"No, no, I'd like to go and see him," said Mr. Lin.

So Pavilion sent Emerald with a message for Wisdom Xia. That would give him time to prepare, and Pavilion could take Mr. Lin over there after their meal. Emerald scurried away.

When Emerald turned up with her message, Wisdom Xia said, "I don't believe it."

"Well, that's up to you. I've done my bit," said Emerald, and she flounced off.

Wisdom Xia called her back. "Are you sure you're not putting your old granddad on?"

"I wouldn't do a thing like that. Cross my heart and hope to die!" exclaimed Emerald.

Just then, Blossom came into the yard, grabbed the broom from behind the gate, and hit her. "You're gonna die, are you? That's good. You can't bring shame on me anymore."

The barber shielded Emerald. "Don't take it out on her; she only said that because her grandad didn't believe her."

"People have been telling me all day that Emerald's been off at the market, getting customers to Star Chen's stall," said her mother. They were talking at cross-purposes; that much was clear to Wisdom and the barber.

Emerald burst into tears. "And what's wrong with that? I was only helping him sell his stuff, not moving in with him. I haven't shamed you."

"You've been sleeping with him!" cried her mother. "You're the biggest slut in the Xia clan for generations!" And she raised the broom again, but Emerald slipped out of the gate. Blossom ran after her, then came back and swapped the broom for a tree branch and ran out again.

"You've always spoiled her rotten. What's made you so fierce all of a sudden?" Wisdom Xia called after her. "She's a big girl now; you can't keep her cooped up all the time . . . Is the county head really coming?"

"That's what Emerald said," said the barber.

"Then hurry up and finish. What are you standing around gawping for?"

When the haircut was done, the old man looked in the mirror. "It's too short at the front. When a man gets old, his hair goes thin. If you cut it that short, what will I have to comb over the bald patch?"

"If it's long at the front and shorter at the back, then it makes the back look even shorter, Uncle," said the barber. "You can't see your hair at the back."

Wisdom Xia looked in the mirror again and mussed his hair, still dissatisfied. "This haircut looks stupid on me."

"All haircuts look stupid at first. Give it a couple of days, and you'll like it."

"A couple of days? The county head's coming now!" He fished out two yuan for the barber, grumbling as the man left, "Bamboo says your barbershop doesn't make money. No wonder, if that's the way you cut hair . . ."

After the barber had gone, Wisdom Xia called to his wife, who was in the kitchen, "Come and look. Does it look all right?"

"I heard you going on at that poor man about your haircut," said Fourth Aunt. "He won't want to cut your hair again. Since when did you stop being a peasant and turn into a teacher?"

"Even if I am a peasant, the county head's coming to see me." And he went and washed his head and fluffed his hair up a bit. "Sweep the yard, woman, and tidy up Wind Xia's room. We'll take the county head in there when he comes. The furniture's new; it's still shiny." And he displayed all the masks he'd painted and set out the paints and the brushes beside them, then sat in the rattan chair to wait.

Two hours went by, and Pavilion had still not turned up with the county head. Fourth Aunt wanted Wisdom Xia to have his meal, but he refused. It just wouldn't look good if he was eating when his guests arrived. Besides, Mr. Lin must have been a big fan of local opera if he was coming to look at the ladle masks. And when opera fans got together, there was sure to be singing, and you couldn't sing on a full stomach.

"Tell Goodness to come over," he went on. "Snow Bai's not here and Concord Qin's sick. But Goodness can sing a bit of *Going East of the River*."

"You're such a dignified man, but now the county head's coming, you've gone soft in the head."

The two old folks fell silent. Wisdom Xia sat in his chair, watching the sun dipping down over the eaves until the sunlight fell on the house steps and onto the yard. No one came. He suspected Emerald had been telling lies.

Fourth Aunt agreed. "That girl's always lying," she said. "How many times has she told her mom she was going to a schoolmate's house, and afterward, she was spotted in Star Chen's orchard? She was tricking you, for sure. Have some food. If you don't eat, your belly'll stick to your backbone." She brought the bowl out, and Justice Xia was just about to start when he heard beeping from a motorbike outside the gate.

"Big day for you, Pavilion," said someone.

"Not a big day for me, a big day for Freshwind Village."

"You're being too modest. Such a big day; have you been celebrating?"

"No, not at all." There was a crash, and the yard gate burst open. Pavilion and the motorbike lay in the entrance.

Wisdom Xia put down his bowl. "Coming!" he cried and then went to the gate and looked out. But there was no one else in the alley except a solitary cockerel sidling past, its head held high.

From his feet, Pavilion said, "Fourth Uncle, pull the bike off me, quick! My leg's trapped."

"What about the county head? Didn't you say he was coming?" said the old man.

"He was called away in the middle of dinner, a phone call to say that people from Dongxiang Township were outside the county offices, kicking up a fuss. I just came to tell you."

Wisdom Xia heaved a long sigh.

Pavilion slept at Wisdom Xia's house all afternoon. The market's success meant he could relax, and he'd had far too much to drink. Now he needed to sleep it off. Husband and wife managed to get him onto the kang and covered him with a quilt. Then they went to look at their vegetable patch. Pavilion was still asleep when they got back, and there was vomit on the floor beside the kang. Fourth Aunt cleaned up, grumbling at Pavilion as she did so. But Pavilion did not wake. In fact, he slept right through two days and nights.

Has it ever happened to you that you're on top of a mountain, a really high mountain, nothing and no one in sight, and you stop for a shit, and suddenly flies appear? Or you dig a pond and put water in, nothing else, and no more than six months later, there are fish in it? Maybe a miracle was going to happen to me; it was possible that after this trip I wouldn't be a peasant anymore. If so, I wouldn't be answerable to Pavilion.

Once I finally had my bag packed, ready to go and join the county opera, it occurred to me I should go and see him, but Pavilion was still sleeping off the alcohol in Wisdom Xia's house. I paced back and forth outside their yard wall, but I didn't dare go in. The west wall abutted Water Buffalo's home, and his grandma, an old woman in her eighties, was sitting at the foot of the wall, combing her white hair, bundling up the hairs that fell out and stuffing them into a crack between the bricks. An odd idea suddenly popped into my head. I took off my jacket and nabbed a louse. We didn't have many lice in summer, but I got one. Then I stuffed it into a crack in the wall and plastered it in with a bit of mud. Lice were ancient bugs, and I was going to leave this bug of mine behind me.

When I joined up with the county opera, Mid-Star Xia was as good as his word. He was going to take me along with them when they went touring and assigned me the tasks of looking after and displaying the ladle masks. But he laid down strict conditions: while we were in the townships and villages, I didn't leave the ladles and they didn't leave me, and I had to guarantee that they would not be damaged or lost. "Sure," I said. "I'll treat them as if they were my grandad and I was their grandson."

Mid-Star combed his hair, or the few strands that remained of it, smoothing them over the crown of his head and pasting them down. He grumbled, "I'm going bald."

"A spiritual man never has a full head of hair," I told him.

That cheered him up, and he began to sing:

> All the king's horsemen raise a yell
> Did you bite the master's dick?

Then he smiled apologetically at me, having remembered that I didn't have one anymore.

I wasn't bothered about that but about something completely different. "Does Snow Bai know I'm coming on tour?"

"Yes."

"Has she said anything?"

"No."

"Wah!"

"What's up?"

"Nothing, nothing."

Our first performance was in Zhulinguan Township. When we set off, I saw Snow Bai get into the truck, so I went to climb in, too, but Mid-Star pulled me out and told me I was riding on the tractor trailer, which was loaded with the props trunks and the masks. We rocked along the mountain roads for hours, and I suddenly thought of the louse I'd stuffed in the crack in the wall. It must have been starving hungry. But even if it was completely deflated, it would soon be puffed up again; deflated lice were like wheat bran—they floated away in the wind and sucked human blood if they landed on a human, or pig's blood if they landed on a pig. As we went along, I sent back commands to the louse: *Land on Roughshod Ding first, then Favor Bai, and finally Wisdom Xia.*

I imagined the old man feeling it bite his neck, putting his hand up there, pulling the louse off, and exclaiming, "Have I got lice?" Then he'd go to squash it between his fingers, but before he could do it, the wind would snatch it away.

When we got to Zhulinguan, we headed for the Traders Guildhall, built during the Qing dynasty as a place where traveling traders and their mule trains could stop over and make offerings. It was almost in ruins now. All that was left was the theater building, where we would perform, and a hall at the back, where I would exhibit the opera masks. I didn't see a lot of Snow Bai. They were rehearsing and staying in an old warehouse nearby. I was responsible for the masks, so I slept alone in the back hall.

We had one performance in the daytime and one in the evening. Mid-Star would start by going up onstage and giving a talk about how our local opera, Shaanxi opera, was quintessential to the national culture, showing popular traditions at their best. We should cherish Shaanxi opera, and everyone should come along and watch it. If we revitalized the art, then it would nourish our own internal energies. We were deeply grateful to the county Party Committee and government, under whose correct leadership and solicitous guidance the troupe had rehearsed meticulously and was now about to put on the best of local operatic art for the delectation of the general public. There was also a special exhibition of opera masks painted on ladles to accompany the performance, and he hoped everyone would leap at the chance to go and view them . . . et cetera, et cetera. Mid-Star Xia delivered his speech in the same vehement tones in which Pavilion read the newspapers and political documents in Freshwind Temple, but the few people who had turned up to listen were unmoved, and he got no cheers or applause. He finished with a "Thank you!" and got off the stage.

If few people went to the performance, even fewer turned up at the exhibition. The idea was that I would show them around and talk to them about the history of our local opera and explain why the masks were special, but I couldn't do that. All I could tell them was that the masks had been painted by a retired Freshwind head teacher, Wisdom Xia, and that he was the father-in-law of Snow Bai, the singer in our troupe.

When they heard Snow Bai's name, my listeners showed a lot of interest. She was such a good opera singer, her singing made you feel all soft inside; they wondered what it was she ate and drank that had made her grow up so cute; she seemed so pure, they couldn't believe she shat or pissed or even farted. I was annoyed. It was all right for me to say stuff like that, but not them. Their words sullied her name, the way someone would if they admired a rose in a garden and then pulled it up by the roots, or threw a handful of earth over it, or spat on it.

Of course I threw them out; in fact, I nearly got into a fight with some of them. So even fewer people came. But one man, an ugly-looking character, came three times. He spoke ever so precisely and had a ballpoint pen stuck in his breast pocket. He came first for the performance, then to see the masks, and when he found out that the masks had been painted by Snow Bai's father-in-law and that she and I were from the same village, he asked me endless questions about her. That put me on my guard.

"Who are you?" I asked him.

"I'm a big fan of hers."

Well, if that was the case, I needed to check whether he was really crazy about the opera or crazy about her. To my surprise, he said he'd seen every one of her performances and had even written a poem in praise of her singing.

"Recite it," I ordered him.

And he did. He recited it really well, and I memorized it. And I got into the habit of reciting it, too, when there wasn't anyone around. The poem went like this:

> The Opera Troupe on the River Zhou
> Has had one *dan* singer this last decade, oh!
> Snow Bai's age hasn't dimmed her reputation.
> She's graceful as a swan, her crescent eyebrows a sensation.
> She has dimpled cheeks, a willow waist, a face like peaches
> and cream.
> A radiant smile, an enviable frown, and her rear view's an
> artist's dream.
> She has a profile like a peony that kisses the wind and rain.
> She is the beauteous narcissus facing the surge,
> The pear blossom embracing the pale moon's urge.
> She is Chang'e descending to the Flower Pearl Palace,
> She is Concubine Yang, flat out drunk, alas!
> She weeps like Lady Xue, whose tears put cuckoos to flight.
> She paces like the wise Pan Jinlian, whose name means
> Golden Lotus.
> She dances as gracefully as the spring-green breeze,
> Her clear notes eddy skyward, like the oriole's *twee, twee,*
> *twees.*
> In the "Jade Tree Song," she is the bashful Zhang Lihua,
> In "Shadow on the Hand," she's the delicate Miss Zhao, ah!
> No artist's skill can capture her killer looks,

The Shaanxi Opera

Even the iron warrior sickens as his heart is hooked.
Let us talk about her starring roles:
In "Plum-Purple Snow," she laughs prettily;
In "The Emperor Abdicates," she dies pitifully;
In "Dragon's Beads," she is a princess royal;
In "The Jade Tiger Drops," she is Juanjuan the loyal;
In "Flying Leopard," she is female and male, too;
In "Double Impression," she rips foot bindings through,
And holds her jeweled sword with hands soft and true.
She dons a kerchief, and her eyes look weary;
But with a child in arms, she is a maiden merry.
They swoon who gaze at her, their eyes blaze bright;
Starry eyed and adoring, they're beaded with sweat.
She plays shades of feeling, so truly, so deeply;
The arts of battle she has mastered completely.
In "Mountain of the Beauties," she exchanges her man;
In "Matchmaker's Peak," she reads poems with élan;
In "Conquering Hong Prefecture," she is Mu Guiying;
And in "Attacking the Inn," she is Sun Erning.
At handling the gun, Snow Bai is the queen;
Knife skills such as hers are rarely seen.
Her whip is a whirlwind, her two swords pierce the moon,
Her feet lightning fast, she rides the peach blooms.
Her three-foot dagger streams out like shining silk,
But she is determined never to wilt.
When Monkey appears on his magic cloud,
She remains bold, bravehearted, and proud.
Snow Bai's performances drive people half-mad,
Scholars throw down their pens and feel sad,
Heedless, the boss pulls bills from his pocket,
The water carrier hefts a leaky bucket,
Daoists abandon their mountain retreat,
The tailor discards his sewing so neat,
The monk leaves the palace, his prayers gone awry,
The ill forget water, swallow their pills dry.

And men put their pipes in back to front, that's no lie!
Noble or lowborn, Hui or Han,
We even forget to eat while we can
We never get tired of singing her praise
Devoted to Snow Bai, our paeans we raise.

I recited this lengthy poem repeatedly in the back hall, under the suspicious gaze of the visitors to the exhibition. I looked at them, they looked at me, and I heard them say, "He's sick in the head, that one," and they fell over their feet to get back outside.

Mid-Star laid into me for that. "I told you to organize an exhibition, not act like a performing monkey."

"I'm promoting Snow Bai," I protested.

"Well, she doesn't need your promotion. Your responsibility is to show the masks. Just stick to talking about them."

"I don't know anything about them."

"You've got a mouth; go and ask the performers."

Ask which performer? The first one I thought of was Snow Bai, but I didn't dare approach her, so I went and asked Mrs. Wang, one of the singers in *Picking up the Jade Bracelet*. I didn't know who was more knowledgeable, Mrs. Wang or Master Qiu, but I decided on Mrs. Wang because Qiu was a man, and with Mrs. Wang, I'd get nearer to Snow Bai. But every time I went up to her, if Snow Bai was with her, she'd leave. Once, I saw Snow Bai with a bunch of the other players, setting off for the canteen with their bowls, so I took my courage in both hands and marched up to her. But she just doubled back into the warehouse dorm as soon as she saw me.

"Aren't you coming to eat?" someone said.

"In a bit. You go ahead," she said.

Obviously, she was avoiding me. All I could do was fill my bowl, spear two steamed buns on my chopsticks, and take my food back to the hall. There was no one there. It was so quiet I could hear the rats scurrying around and gnawing on things. I stamped my feet, and they stopped their noise, but as soon as I went quiet, they started again. I put my bowl down and lit a cigarette and listened to the distant chatter and laughter from the rest of them.

I could only get a proper look at Snow Bai during the evening performances. Tonight, it was "The Hidden Boat," and she sang:

I hear the fourth hour strike in the watchtower
I, Hu Fenglian, sit in the little boat,

Weeping that my old father has disappeared
He can only be found in Nan Ke's dream.

Onstage, it was the dead of night, while offstage, a sliver of moon hung high in the sky. I imagined a boat bobbing in the middle of the river, in it, a grieving woman singing her heart out, and my tears began to fall. Just then, someone patted me on the shoulder—it was Mrs. Wang. "Don't cry," she said.

"When I see Snow Bai in the boat, I can't stop crying."

"It's not Snow Bai, it's Hu Fenglian."

"Hu Fenglian . . ."

"I wrote this aria," she explained. "Hu Fenglian is grief stricken because her father has died, but she's conflicted, too. Prince Xia is with her, so the rhythm is peaceful, and the melody is gentle. Making you cry was exactly what I was aiming for."

She was so pleased with herself that I stopped and wiped my tears. But they kept trickling down, and soon I burst out crying again. Onstage, Snow Bai was still rowing the boat, taking little steps, as if she was bobbing on the water. I felt like the water was covering the whole stage. Suddenly, she staggered, put her hand over her mouth, and almost fell. The drums went wild. Obviously, something had gone wrong. No one else realized except Mrs. Wang, who gasped.

"What's all the drumming for?" I asked her.

"Snow Bai's pregnant; she's feeling sick," she said.

"Snow Bai's pregnant?" I exclaimed.

Mrs. Wang gave me a kick. "Keep your voice down!"

It was true. In fact, everyone in the troupe knew; she'd told Mid-Star when they did the dress rehearsal. But she was the star performer, and Mid-Star wanted her to go on for as long as she could.

After that evening, Snow Bai didn't play the main roles anymore, just bit parts. I wasn't quite sure what I felt about Snow Bai being pregnant. It wasn't true to say I was happy, but I wasn't sad, either. I kept my eye on her, and several times I saw her squatting in the distance, vomiting until there was nothing more to come out and she was just dry heaving. Then she would carry on sitting there, dribbling spittle. After she left, I went over to the spot where she'd been. The vomit looked like a puddle of rain, and I felt very sorry for her, but what could I do?

The next evening after the performance, I saw her with another woman performer. They were going out to buy roast chicken. Her companion wanted to get it with thick soy sauce, but Snow Bai wanted chili chicken. "Nothing tastes like anything anymore; I'm craving spicy chicken," she said.

243

"You want sour, it's a boy; you want spicy, it's a girl," said her friend.

And Snow Bai got herself a wing and a leg, and they walked away laughing. I went over and spoke to the guy with the roast-chicken stall and told him to take a bowl of chicken legs and wings to sell at the warehouse every evening after the performance.

With Snow Bai no longer taking the lead roles, fewer people came to watch. Mid-Star got so worried that he ordered them to go out and drum up customers every evening, two hours before the performance was due to start. Almost no one came to look at the masks, and even though I'd learned quite a bit about our opera from Mrs. Wang, it still wasn't enough to draw in the pundits.

"Mrs. Wang," I said, "can you write something down for me, and I'll copy it out and paste it on the walls? Maybe that'll bring more people in."

"You're a fine one," she said. "Where would I get the time to write stuff down for you?"

That wounded me, and I decided not to bring it up again. But before lunchtime that day, she came back and said she'd changed her mind, so I bought her a chicken leg as a thank-you.

After lunch the performers took a siesta, but I couldn't sleep so I went down to the stream that ran past the village to have a wash. To my surprise, there was Snow Bai, sitting in the shade of a tree. She was writing something, using a flat bit of rock as a table. I kept thinking I'd go up to her, then changed my mind. If I did, she'd just walk away. Best to stay where I was, so I could get a good look at her. She was bent over her writing, her hair falling forward. It was so jet black it made her face look dead white.

She wrote and wrote and carried on writing. Then she stopped and looked up. The sun came out from behind a dark cloud, and she chewed the end of her pen. What had that pen done in a former life to deserve such luck in this one? Then she retched and dribbled again and spat a few times into the river. The water was full of little red fish that swam over to her, turning the water red. I gazed and gazed as she raised her hand, turned her waist . . . I couldn't exactly put it into words, but I drank in the sight of her so that even after she left, I saw her spirit still sitting there and writing.

That afternoon, Mrs. Wang gave me some handwritten introductory notes on Shaanxi local opera. The handwriting was not beautiful, but at least it was clear and neat.

"Thank you. I'll buy some chicken thighs," I said.

But as I was copying out the notes onto poster paper back in the hall, I smelled a scent on the notepaper. It was the scent of Snow Bai that I remembered from way back. Then I knew that it was Snow Bai who'd written the notes, not Mrs. Wang. *You thought you could pull the wool over my eyes, did you, Mrs. Wang? Why would an old hag like you ever wear such a lovely fragrance?*

The notes explained that our local opera, more properly called Qinqiang—the voice of Qin—took its name from the ancient Qin dynasty and was the earliest form of Chinese opera.

> . . . Qinqiang began in the Ming dynasty and took off during the Ming and Qing dynasties, becoming one of the four main operatic forms. It is sung to the accompaniment of wooden clappers, which mark the beat and the tune and underscore the text. There are a variety of meters: the "slow beat," the "two-six beat," the "carrying beat," the "rolling beat," the "arrow beat," and the "rhythmic beat." There are also a dozen or so "color" tunes, with names such as "Hempen Shoe Sole." The clapper rhythms and the color tunes fall into two kinds: doloroso and allegro. The sad ones are very characteristic of this type of opera and have the power to move us deeply; the happy ones are robust and energetic. In Shaanxi opera, singing to the clapper beat is done with "true voice," whereas color tunes are sung in falsetto. The musical accompaniment consists of strings and wind instruments. The repertoire is very rich, and there are more than a hundred different tunes, including "The Opening Door," "Purple South Wind," "A Song to Heaven," "Wild Geese Descend," "The Willow Tree Buds," and "Stepping High." The percussion beat can be slow, medium-paced, fast, or irregular, depending on what function it has—as an introduction to a scene, to emphasize movement and action, or as accompaniment to melodies. Depending on whether the opera contains elements of combat, the main instrument that maintains the rhythm may be the huqin—a two-stringed instrument—or the clappers (for battle scenes). In accordance with Chinese tradition, and in order to provide the maximum enjoyment, realism and stylized expressions are interwoven. The actors use numerous stylized movements as a means of expression, as well as their own knowledge, experience, and creativity, to create a performance of unsurpassed mastery.
>
> In Qinqiang there are three main types of roles: *sheng* (male roles), *dan* (female roles), and *jing* (painted faces). Within these three, there are subgroups: bearded *sheng*, older *sheng*, young *sheng*, and warrior *sheng*; the *dan* lead, lively *dan*, minor *dan*, comic *dan*, warrior *dan*; and three grades of *jing* painted faces. More than three thousand operas have been preserved, most of which have a historical theme, with protagonists such

245

as emperors, generals, loyal ministers, heroes, learned men, and beautiful women. The best reenact "bachelor operas," where most of the roles are male. The leading roles are known as the "four main beams and the four pillars." The four beams are the bearded *sheng*, the main *jing* (painted face), the leading *dan* (female), and the young *dan*. The four pillars are the second bearded *sheng*, the second *jing* (painted face), the young *sheng*, and the clown. These actors must be skilled in singing, recitation, acting, and martial arts, and each one should also have their own specialties. The *dans* often sport a black turban and special false hairpieces. The clown's makeup includes motifs such as plum blossoms, bats, and copper coins, or is completely white. Makeup for painted-face roles is designed to represent a forehead positioned high in the face; different designs are known as patterned face, black face, red face, and painted face. The black color symbolizes determination and selflessness: for example, Judge Bao Zheng in the opera *Chen Shimei's Execution*. White faces symbolize arrogance, brutality, and scheming, as with Cao Cao or Pan Renmei. Red faces represent loyalty, steadfastness, and heroism, as with General Guan Yu. There are also several other special masks for the different roles, for men, and for women.

I was touched that Snow Bai had written me such a long piece and impressed that she knew so much. I understood now why she had not left the opera troupe for a new life in the city—in fact, why she lived for opera. *What a wonderful woman you are, Snow Bai!* I said to myself. But I was worried about her health. Her morning sickness meant she couldn't take the leading roles, and that, in turn, meant that the audiences were getting smaller and smaller. It was wretched. Once the evening's performance was over, we would all go out for a nighttime snack: a bowl of cabbage soup and tofu, and a big, steamed bun.

One evening, as we sat around in a circle eating and drinking, Mid-Star called me over. "How many visitors to the exhibition today?" he asked.

"Four," I said. "Two old guys, a woman with babe in arms."

"Spark, now you see we're just like beggars or tramps, wandering around with a bedding roll on our backs," said one of the actors.

"That's enough of that," Mid-Star chided her.

"Fine, fine. We have to go around butt naked, fearless, and shameless, just so we can revitalize the local opera."

I laughed and hurriedly changed the subject. "How many more days have we got in Zhulinguan Township?"

"Two more performances, then we move on to Guoyunlou. Audiences should be better there," said Mid-Star.

"I admire our troupe leader's revolutionary optimism," said another actor. "Before we came here, you told us how well it was going to go, but with just one play, how many people are going to come and watch? It doesn't matter how much effort we put into it."

"It's precisely because audiences are small that I made the township authorities book out the whole theater for us," said Mid-Star.

"We can't take more than four or five hundred yuan a performance, and that's not even enough to cover our sweat and tears. Even if we're running at a loss, we still need an audience. That extra performance we put on in the afternoon—I'm still red from embarrassment!"

"You're an actor and you can still get embarrassed?" I asked.

"When we finished this afternoon, I came down off the stage, and there was only one person left in the audience. And he was shouting something about having lost his money. He accused me of taking it, but I said I was onstage, acting. How could I have? He said he was the only one in the audience and I was the only one onstage, so with only the two of us here, who could it be except me?"

Mid-Star's face darkened with anger. "If you keep running down the opera troupe like this, I'm going to fire you." He stood up and said to me, "Don't listen to that shit. You and I are going to the back hall to talk."

When we got there, he went on, "Some of the actors have no culture; they're pig-ignorant. All they're worried about is where the next paycheck's coming from."

"Look, there's no one else here, so be straight with me," I said. "Now, you've been head of the troupe for a while. What do you think—does the opera have a future?"

"What do you mean?"

"Do you think there'll come a day when the troupe has to break up?"

"The troupe at least gives people a place to eat."

He was going to go on, but suddenly we heard a rumpus outside. A woman rushed in to tell Mid-Star that the props people had gotten into a brawl with the villagers. The villagers were saying that three families used the area where we'd set up the stage to store their straw, and they'd had to clear it all away for the performances. Now they wanted compensation.

"We had a contract with the township government to put the stage there. Why would we pay other people as well? Tell Wang, the logistics manager, to sort it out."

After they'd gone, he turned back to me. "There's all this talk about passing our cultural heritage down to future generations. Well, Shaanxi opera is quintessential cultural heritage, so those who work in arts and literature should take responsibility for revitalizing it. Besides, without it, the only cultural activities left would be drinking and mah-jongg, right?"

"The problem is that no one comes to see it. People prefer pop songs and dancing. You know we've got a good singer in Freshwind Village, Star Chen?"

Someone came running in again. "You'll have to come, boss. Wang can't deal with it; there's a big fight going on!"

"Can't they talk about it? Why are they fighting? Just because there's a bit of wind doesn't mean it's raining. Tell Zhang to take care of it; he can stop them." Mid-Star turned back to me. "Pop music? Do you think we're going to turn the opera into karaoke?"

"When Star Chen sings, all the youths in Freshwind go and listen," I said. "Emerald got together with him just because he sings so well."

Another runner arrived. "Boss, Zhang's lost control of them; people have been injured. If you don't come, someone's gonna lose their life!"

"Then go and call the police," Mid-Star commanded. The runner disappeared, and Mid-Star asked me, "Emerald? You mean Thunder's daughter . . . ?" Then he exclaimed, "Someone's gonna lose their life? I'd better go and see!"

Nobody lost their life that evening, but the fuss didn't die down so easily, and it affected me, too. I not only lost my chance to follow the traveling players around but also was completely humiliated, and Snow Bai saw it all.

This is what happened: Mid-Star left me kicking my heels in the back hall while he went to the theater. After the actors' pitched battle with the Zhulinguan folk, Mid-Star sent them back to the warehouse and ordered them to be locked in. No one was allowed out. If they wanted to shit, they had to hold it in. If they wanted to piss, the men were to piss out the window in the corner of the north wall, and the women were to piss by the partition door. But that didn't mollify the villagers. They gathered around outside the warehouse, yelling obscenities. Some even threw stones and tiles at the iron door.

I stayed in the hall like a good boy, but then I started to worry about Snow Bai. Had she been there during the fighting? Even if she hadn't been fighting herself, she might have been caught in the crossfire. She was pregnant, after all. If you're carrying a basket of eggs across the street, you're worried about getting caught in a crush, not because of the person you bump into but because of yourself.

I began to daydream someone would hit Snow Bai. Not too hard, though; I'd see it and I'd hurl myself into the fray and pummel whoever it was who'd hit her. I'd be a hero, and

Snow Bai would warm toward me. So I ran off to the warehouse, forgetting to lock up or turn the lights off. A dark mass of people was crowded around the warehouse door, flinging stones and tiles at it.

I sneaked around to the back, stood under the window, and called softly, "Hey! Hey!"

All was quiet inside, and no one answered. The banging and shouting at the front door were beginning to die down.

I called again, "Boss! Boss!" I always called him "Mid-Star" when no one else was around, but in the troupe, I called him "Mr. Xia" or "Boss."

"Who is it?" he asked.

"They've gone," I said.

He came to the window. "Gone?"

"Are you okay?" I asked.

I heard him tell the others inside, "They've left."

Then all the lights went out. There was noise and confusion inside.

"No one's to go out!" Mid-Star shouted. "So they cut the electric cable; it's no different from you shutting your eyes."

There was silence inside, broken only by a loud fart.

Then I heard the chicken vendor arriving. "Roast chicken! Come buy your roast chicken!"

I shouted again, "Mr. Xia! Mr. Xia!"

"Go back and go to sleep," he ordered.

"Are you okay?"

"Yes, we're okay."

What I meant was, was Snow Bai okay? But I couldn't say her name, so I just repeated, "Really okay? The chicken vendor's here."

Mid-Star was furious at that. "Scram!" he shouted.

I set off back, and while I was still quite a way off, I was startled to see the hall door wide open. Had I forgotten to lock it? I hurried in and found a terrible mess: three of the ladles were smashed to smithereens, and the handles were broken on four more. My bedding was soaked, and my bowl was in the doorway, in three pieces. The fuckers! They couldn't break down the warehouse door, so they'd come here and taken out their fury on the exhibition and my things.

I started cleaning up. Out of 120 ladles, I counted seven broken and eight missing. I was suddenly furious. I grabbed a stool and rushed outside. I ran back to the theater, but there was no one there, and the streets were deserted, too. I howled like a wolf. "Where are you fuckers? You smashed those ladles, and I'll fuck your mothers for that!"

No one answered.

I whirled the stool around and brought it down on a stone roller. All four legs flew off. I flung myself to the ground and wailed loudly.

The next morning, two of the actors packed their bags and went off back to the county seat. They had already wanted to leave—they'd landed jobs somewhere farther south—but Mid-Star wouldn't release them. With them gone, everyone was unsettled. Mid-Star tried to stop them, but it was no good.

Then he laid into me, in front of the whole troupe. "Why didn't you take better care of the ladle masks? Why didn't you sacrifice your life? If you had, I could have reported you as a revolutionary martyr, but instead you let them smash up the ladles. What am I supposed to say when I report back to Fourth Uncle?"

"I'll pay Fourth Uncle back," I said.

"What with? You want to pay him back with balls? You haven't got any."

I didn't mind him cursing me out, but telling everyone about that—that was too much. Snow Bai was there, for starters, and maybe not all the members of the troupe knew that I'd mutilated myself.

"You're the leader of the troupe. How dare you talk to me like that?" I said.

"The trouble you've caused, do you expect me to be nice to you? Get out of my sight!"

And so I turned and left. I'd failed completely, but so be it. I should never have tried to look after Wisdom Xia's opera masks. I'd only gone a few paces when I looked around. Mid-Star thought I was coming back to settle the score with him, but I was scanning the crowd for Snow Bai. She was standing with the other actresses. She had a hair clip in her hair, and it caught the light and sparkled.

I made a deep bow to her, and as I bent down, the straw hat fell off my head. I didn't bother picking it up. I felt like my whole head had come off. They were all so astonished at my gesture that you could have heard a pin drop. After a long pause, I turned away and broke into a run. Tears poured down my face like rain.

I went back to Freshwind Village. That was where I had always lived, and that was where I belonged. As I passed the Zhou River, I stopped and gave myself a good wash. The sun was hot. I saw Tongue-Tied in the distance, jabbing at soft-shelled turtles with a prong. He was strong but clumsy, and he didn't manage to stick any. He yelled at me in angry frustration, but I ignored him. I reached into a crevice in the dike to tickle a fish—but luck was still not on my side, and what I brought out was a snake. I threw it up onto the bank, and Tongue-Tied ran over and chopped its head off, stuck it in his mouth, and sucked the blood. The rest of the snake was still alive, and its tail beat against his chest. I didn't want to be near anyone so savage, so I got out of the water and walked into the village.

Tongue-Tied was following me, and I turned on him. "Get out of my sight! Go!" That was a bit over the top, but if I couldn't be mean to Tongue-Tied, who could I be mean to? The pair of us found somewhere to sit down in Second Alley, over on East Street, and played hop squares.

You've probably never heard of hop squares. It's a Freshwind game, with the same rules as chess. Tongue-Tied might have been stupid, but he was good at hop squares, and I could never beat him. I was quick fingered, though, and I used to steal the pieces or move them. Tongue-Tied was paying attention today, staring at my hands. He had Lucky trapped between his legs. The dog struggled and he tightened his grip, and Lucky's tail thrashed madly.

"Is he driving you crazy, Lucky?" I said and then made a grab for one of Tongue-Tied's pieces.

He didn't seem to notice, just dropped a piece on another square. He realized he'd lost and scratched his head, looking puzzled.

I cackled with laughter, a nasty, spiteful laugh.

Tongue-Tied suddenly pushed all the pieces away and spat in my face.

I spat right back, and we carried on spitting at each other. Meanwhile Lucky wriggled free and ran off, barking furiously. Just then, Mid-Star's dad came out of the alley and stood watching us.

Chapter 22

I looked up and saw him. I was about to boast about my win, but then I remembered yester-day's disaster, so I slunk off.

"Spark," he called after me. "You're back from Zhulinguan?"

I didn't stop.

"Didn't Mid-Star give you something to give to me? Like their wood ear fungus?"

"I hate you!" I said.

"You hate me?"

"'Cause that bad man's your son!"

Mid-Star's dad gaped at me. After a good while, I heard him ask Tongue-Tied, "What's up with Spark?"

Tongue-Tied went, "Wah-lah, wah-lah . . . ," but the old man didn't understand. He walked along to Wisdom Xia's, three gates down the alley, but the gate was shut. Tongue-Tied was still going, "Wah-lah, wah-lah . . . ," and Mid-Star's dad asked him, "Are your fourth uncle and fourth aunt not here?" He rattled the door ring and heard footsteps. It was Rain Xia who opened up.

"Where's your mom?"

"Out with my dad."

"Why did you shut the gate if you're in?"

Rain Xia peered past the old man to the top of the alley, where Tongue-Tied and I were standing. "Because I didn't want them coming in and messing around."

Mid-Star's dad walked inside. Roughshod Ding was standing at the door and smiled at him. His face looked like a frosted potato.

"Roughshod and I are discussing important business," Rain Xia announced.

"What important business? Are you up to no good again?" said Mid-Star's dad.

"Uncle Glory, you shouldn't underestimate Roughshod. He doesn't make a big deal out of it, but he's the richest man in Freshwind Village."

"Don't exaggerate," said Roughshod Ding.

"Why don't you let me read the signs for your business deal?"

"'Cause we'd have to pay you."

"If you're worried about spending a few cents on 'important business,' then it's not that important."

"You tell Uncle Glory, Roughshod," said Rain Xia.

Roughshod Ding looked solemn as he explained what they were planning. He was a good speaker, got the pace just right, and his dark eyes gleamed. He started by saying what a great man Pavilion was—a humble farmer but still able to dream up a plan like the farmers market on that triangle of land. The market had only just opened but was attracting a big crowd of customers every day. Freshwind used to have only a weekly market. Now it was daily, and the markets at West Mountain Bend, Teahouse Village, and Liuxian were losing business. And Pavilion's market was cashing in on passing traffic from Highway 312, which was even better. Almost every vehicle stopped, and Freshwind had become as busy as a county seat.

Then Roughshod Ding talked about Clerk and his wife. They had complained about the new market, but they hadn't let the grass grow under their feet, either. They were already planning to build a public bathroom on some land that belonged to them alongside the highway. Mid-Star's dad laughed at that, but Roughshod Ding was serious. "I did the math. It doesn't cost more than three hundred yuan to build a public bathroom, and you can turn the piss and shit into fertilizer. They can sell it, big piles of it, and make loads of money. By the way, I haven't talked to them about the fertilizer idea yet. But just think, if they build a proper, good-quality bathroom and keep it clean, they can charge for entry. It costs thirty cents to use the public bathroom in the provincial city, and if they charge just five cents, that'll bring even more traffic from the 312, and how much would they earn in one day? But I'm not asking you to make a prediction; it might go belly up if you do."

"Roughshod, you're a born businessman," said Mid-Star's dad. "But after all this, you still haven't said what your important business is."

"You'll laugh at me," Roughshod said, but he carried on talking anyway. With the new market, there would be an increase in people passing through Freshwind. He'd checked up, and one-third were coming from surrounding townships. Not in great numbers so far, but it meant that Freshwind Village could grow into the biggest distribution hub for the whole of the east of the county. National policies provided support for this sort of thing, and Pavilion was playing an active part, too—he'd gotten the deputy county head, Mr. Lin, to come to the opening ceremony, which showed how the county was eager to help. That meant the market could expand. It was a farm-products market just now, but it could expand to sell herbal medicines and other merchandise, even agricultural supplies. With projects like this you couldn't look just at the first step; if you did, you might trip—you had to look three or four steps ahead.

"When I started selling clothing a few years ago," he went on, "Favor Bai from the dyehouse laughed at me for thinking anyone in the village would wear clothes like that, but I did good business. I did so well that everyone started selling clothes. They're copycats, like monkeys on Nanshan: one throws a stick, they all throw sticks. Of course, once they'd all started dealing in clothing, I stopped."

"Don't talk so much," said Rain Xia. "Tell him about the restaurant."

"I need to set the scene, to make myself clear. Uncle Glory, we're thinking of setting up a restaurant; what do you think?"

"A restaurant?"

"I know there are plenty in Freshwind, but they're all garbage. I wouldn't bother to set up another one of those; I want a classy one. We'd serve meat—chicken, duck, and pork—as well as fish, squid, and sea cucumber, and we could offer game, too. You've been to my home—our four rooms are at the back of the big yard that faces the street. I'd pull down the yard wall and build a two-story house in the yard, with a restaurant at street level and guest rooms above.

"And listen, I know Pavilion has a hotel in the farmers market, but the facilities are poor and there's nowhere to eat. We'd open a karaoke bar as well, so we could offer the whole package—food, accommodation, and entertainment. There'd be three sorts of customers: people from hereabouts, coming to buy local food products; travelers on the 312 and bus drivers—you only have to offer a dozen drivers commission, and they'll bring all their passengers for a meal; and staff from the township's state-owned companies.

"I know there aren't many of them and the companies have their own canteens, but they often have cadres visiting from the county seat or the city. For the last few years, they've been staying in the township and eating in local restaurants. They're not up to much, but last year, the Liu family's restaurant hosted the township officials, and in one meal they spent forty thousand yuan." And Roughshod Ding took out a sheet of paper covered in drawings of the restaurant, followed by line after line of figures. "If business goes well, we could clear 150,000 to 200,000 yuan in a year."

Mid-Star's dad didn't understand the drawings and wasn't interested in the figures. "How much will it cost to build?" he asked.

"That was what we were discussing."

"Go ahead and discuss it then."

"As you say, Uncle Glory. Well, now we're talking money, you don't need to hang around. It's going to be Rain Xia and me doing it, and we'll raise the funds. If we can't raise enough, then you'll have to tell Mid-Star to help Rain Xia out."

"Mid-Star hasn't got a bean to his name," said his dad.

"You make a prediction for us; will it work out?" said Rain Xia.

But the old man got up and said he was going to the bathroom.

He squatted in the shithouse for a long time. Finally, the gripes in his belly eased. The shithouse was built onto the back wall of the main building, and there was a red toon tree next to it with a trunk so massive it would take both your arms to girdle it. Mid-Star's dad figured it would make a good coffin, or even two, if it was felled. Coffin wood went for two thousand yuan, or four thousand for two coffins.

Money attracts more money, he thought. *Wisdom Xia is so rich, he even has a big tree like this growing next to the shithouse!* He could hear Rain Xia and Roughshod Ding having a muttered conversation in the side house.

"I'm not going to read the signs for you," Mid-Star's dad said softly. "If you want to pour money into your restaurant, you go ahead."

A short while later, they heard someone come through the yard gate. It was Rain Xia's mom, with Wisdom Xia in tow. "We're back now; where are you off to?"

"I'm discussing business with Roughshod Ding," said Rain Xia.

"Business? What business? Everyone else is out harvesting beans and potatoes, and you never go near our land. In fact, you never come home at all."

"Why are you worried about a scrap of land with a few vegetables? I've got a proper business deal going on. You wouldn't understand even if I explained it to you. Give me five yuan," said Rain Xia.

"And where would I get the money from?"

"I'm borrowing it off you. Give me five, and I'll pay you back fifty thousand."

"Fifty thousand!" Wisdom Xia exclaimed. "Are you going to steal it? You make me so mad! Just look at your getup, arms bare, and what color do you call your pants? They're not black or white, they're rat colored. What happened to your black ones?"

"Why do you care what pants he's wearing?" asked his wife.

"Because you can tell a man from the clothes he wears. Black is good—a clear color like water, clear like virtue."

"You want him to look like a crow?"

Rain Xia broke in. "If you give me money for new clothes, I'll wear black from head to toe, Dad."

"I'll give you a kick in the ass!" said Wisdom Xia. "Aren't you ashamed to be asking for money, a grown man like you?"

At that moment, Mid-Star's dad coughed and stepped out of the shithouse.

Wisdom Xia greeted him. His wife jerked her chin toward the gate, to tell her son to see Roughshod off.

"I came to borrow a clay pot to boil up some medicine in; mine's broken," said Mid-Star's dad.

"Are you still sick?"

"It won't stop."

Fourth Aunt went indoors and found the pot at the bottom of the cupboard. As she gave it a wipe, she asked, "Was Roughshod Ding here to talk about that woman?"

"I don't know," said Mid-Star's dad. "I heard them talking about opening a restaurant." He took the clay pot and left. He really did hop along the alley just like a sparrow.

"Won't you stay for a bit?" Wisdom Xia called after him. Then he shouted, "Rain Xia! Rain Xia!"

"Dad, what's gotten into you? Have you come back just to cuss me out?" Rain Xia came back in from the alley.

"Your sister-in-law's nephew's dead, did you know?"

"You mean Pathway Bai?" Rain Xia was startled. "Wasn't he doing bits and pieces for the Excellent Construction Team? What happened?"

"They were building a high-rise in the county seat, the scaffolding collapsed, and he was crushed under it. He died later."

Rain Xia was silent for a while.

"They've brought the body back," his father went on. "Your mom and I have been to West Street to pay our respects. The dad's long dead, your sister-in-law's away, it's the busy season in the fields, and the whole family's in a mess. You go over and give them a hand."

"When's the funeral?"

"They need to settle the compensation first. I told Goodness to go over there. Leave everything else—you get yourself over there, too, and help with the fieldwork."

Rain Xia set off for West Street at a run. As he got nearer, he could hear wailing coming from the Bais'. He went into the back part of the mourning pavilion where the corpse was laid out. Pathway Bai's head had swelled up like a gourd ladle, and he didn't look human anymore. Rain Xia began to cry. Snow Bai's mom had collapsed and was lying on the kang in the east side building, surrounded by people who were attempting to console her and get her to drink a little water. There was a pile of pea stalks on the steps in the yard, still with their pea pods on. No one had spread them out to dry, and the pig was rooting around in the pile. Snow Bai's sister-in-law was sitting in the yard, wailing, ignoring the onlookers who were urging her to get up. Rain Xia went to the west side house, where Goodness and Snow Bai's second-oldest brother were talking. They seemed to have been talking for a while, and neither looked happy.

Snow Bai's brother greeted Rain Xia, then turned back to Goodness. "You represent the village Party Committee. What do you think about their compensation offer; can Excellent get away with five thousand?"

"I'm in a difficult position here, brother," said Goodness. "I was sent here by Fourth Uncle, and Pavilion, too, to settle the compensation on behalf of the Party Committee. But I've got to keep both parties happy, bump up an offer that's too small, reduce a claim that's too big, so we can arrive at a reasonable figure."

"But I've lost a brother! What's the money to Excellent, anyway? Can't he pay more? He's built a big brick-and-tile courtyard house and earned a pile of money in the last few years. If he won't pay any more, then fine, I'll take him to court. From what I heard, even though Pathway Bai was seriously injured, his life could have been saved if Excellent had driven him to the hospital right away. But he refused. He said Pathway Bai was going to end up crippled and his treatment would cost the earth; it would be pouring good money after bad, and he'd be better off dead, because then they could pay once and that would be the end of it."

"Do you have any evidence for that?" said Goodness.

"That's what I've heard."

"Well, if you don't have any evidence, then don't go spreading ridiculous rumors. Pathway Bai died in the hospital, don't forget. Two other men from West Mountain Bend died instantly when the scaffolding collapsed, and Excellent even took them to the hospital. Pathway Bai's from Freshwind Village; of course Excellent would have taken him, too."

"So is five thousand all we're getting?" asked Snow Bai's brother. "Is that all a man's life is worth?"

"Excellent says he's more or less settled on five thousand for the other two families."

"Well, that's their business. I'm not accepting five thousand. I want ten thousand, not a cent less! And if Excellent refuses, then we're not burying Pathway Bai; we'll take the corpse to his house!"

Finally, Rain Xia understood what was going on. "If I could butt in here," he said. "Five thousand's too little. The village committee should put a bit of pressure on."

"Well, that's typical of a man like you, isn't it, Rain Xia?" said Goodness. "Fine-sounding words, but all you're doing is fanning the flames. You go and speak to Excellent yourself."

Rain Xia was annoyed at not being allowed to say his piece and left. He hung around for a bit in the yard, driving the pig away from the peas, but he knew no one was going to pay any attention to anything he said, so finally he grabbed a basket and a sickle from by the gate and went off to the field to cut more peas.

As he cut, he remembered Goodness's peremptory instructions, so he stopped and headed straight for Excellent Li's house. On the way he prepared his words carefully, but when he got there, he found himself unable to say a single one of them. Excellent, a white-haired old man, was busy shifting a sofa and two armchairs into the yard. Next, it was the turn of a bed, but it stuck in the front doorway, and Excellent cursed and swore at his wife. She didn't answer, just got underneath the bed and heaved it upward. Excellent elbowed her out of the way and gave the bed a hard push. His hand got trapped between the bed and the doorframe, and when he pulled it out, he scraped a layer of skin off, making his hand bleed. His mother was inside, clearing out a cupboard, her tears running down her cheeks. Once she'd finished that, she lit a stick of incense and placed it on the offerings table in the main room, then rolled out her prayer mat and fell to her knees. Shifty was out in the yard, walking around the furniture and patting the back of the sofa till the dust rose and got into his eyes.

"You can have the TV, too," said Excellent. "I'll take twenty thousand for it."

"That battered old TV? No thanks. I'll give you ten thousand for the sofa suite, the bed, and the chest of drawers."

"Ten thousand? They cost me thirty thousand!"

"It's all old stuff."

"But I've only had them a year."

"Well, if you split up with your wife after a day, it's still divorce, isn't it? And how much is a secondhand woman worth?"

Excellent's mom had come out and was standing very still. "Give us a bit more. We'll take fifteen thousand."

"I'll give you two thousand more, just because it's you," said Shifty.

"All right, take it away," said Excellent.

Shifty got a couple of guys to load the sofa suite and the bed onto a wheelbarrow outside the gate, accompanied by Excellent's wife's sobs.

"What are you crying about? Huh?" demanded her husband. The back of his hand was still bleeding, and he picked up a chicken feather and stuck it to the broken skin. Rain Xia beckoned to him.

Rain Xia took Excellent over to the henhouse and spoke to him. "Why are you selling your furniture to Shifty?"

"I need the money badly."

"You're not just doing this for show then?" Rain Xia asked.

"You think I want people to see me selling stuff worth thirty thousand for twelve thousand?"

"Everyone says you're rich. What have you done with all the money you earned?"

"I built this house, right? And then I bought furniture for it. And I'm still owed tens of thousands of yuan on construction projects I've done elsewhere and not been paid for. I've been waiting for two years."

"I've just been with the Bai family," said Rain Xia. "Their world's fallen in on them; can't you give them a bit more?"

"Five thousand," said Excellent.

"Too little. No one wants accidents like that to happen, but it did happen, and they need to lay him to rest as soon as they can. Five thousand's too little. Give them ten thousand. I'm representing my dad here."

"You're related to the Bais," said Excellent. "I'm grateful that Fourth Uncle asked you to come on his behalf, and I'm grateful to you, but I'm not budging. If I pay ten thousand for Pathway Bai, then the other two families will want ten thousand, too, and I might as well off myself in that case." He turned to his wife. "And you stop your tears. Get out some cigarettes for Rain Xia. He's come on Fourth Uncle's say-so."

"I don't smoke," said Rain Xia. Excellent got him a stool and made him sit down.

Excellent's daughter ran into the yard, shouting, "Dad! Dad! They're here! They're here!"

"Who's here?"

"The West Mountain Bend people."

"Then invite them in. Don't make such a song and dance about it."

"There are two groups, a dozen of them. They're standing out in the street, shouting that they want at least twenty thousand, not a cent less."

Excellent turned as white as a sheet. He said to Shifty, "Do something for me, brother. Go and stop them at the top of the alley."

"If there's going to be a brawl, then I want to watch," said Shifty, setting off down the alley.

"See? See?" Excellent said. "Now they want twenty thousand!"

They could hear shouting in the distance. "Rain Xia," said Excellent suddenly. "This is embarrassing, but nowadays I get diarrhea as soon as I get stressed. I can't hold it in. Stay here; I'm going to the bathroom."

Excellent disappeared around the gable end into the shithouse and didn't emerge. Meantime, a bunch of people dressed in mourning garments burst into his yard, bawling, "Excellent Li!"

Rain Xia hurried to the shithouse, but he wasn't there. There was a stepladder leaning against the wall, and a single cloth shoe—Excellent's—lying at its foot. The intruders were hopping mad that he had escaped them and getting more and more raucous. Someone gave a stool a mighty kick into the main room, and it landed on the screen that stood on the offerings table. The screen glass smashed to smithereens, leaving pockmarks on the face of the photo of Excellent's dad.

Excellent's mom was furious. "Vandals, the lot of you! Bandits!" she shouted.

"You're the bandits!" they shouted back. "It runs in the family. Like father, like son!" And they began to smash the whole place up.

A ceramic pot full of salt on the chest of drawers was toppled, spilling gleaming white salt all over the floor; the brass washbowl was trampled and dented. They were going for the TV, too, until Excellent's mother threw herself on it.

"Let's have a bit of order!" shouted Rain Xia. "You won't get anything if you smash the place up. We're all here to sort this problem out. Excellent Li's taken off, but he can't run far. The village committee will deal with him, or if they don't, there's the township committee. This is a matter for the local government."

"Who are you?" someone asked.

"I'm Wisdom Xia's son, Rain Xia, so Pathway Bai was family."

Silence fell.

Rain Xia managed to pacify the West Mountain Bend families, and after they had all swarmed off to Freshwind Temple to find Pavilion, he left, too. Outside, he bumped into Shifty.

"Rain Xia, you're as imposing as your dad. Congratulations!"

Rain Xia sped away in a hurry, the tears running down his cheeks.

He didn't say a word all afternoon. He cut Snow Bai's brother's peas and brought them back and spread them out in the yard to dry. He did not ask whether Excellent Li was going to pay five thousand or ten thousand in compensation; he asked nothing at all. He left the Bais' feeling low and tired. He dragged his feet. There was nothing heavier than tired legs—not gold, not even stone.

He met Clerk coming from the direction of the township government offices, carrying two buckets of slop water balanced on a carrying pole.

"Rain Xia, Rain Xia, gimme a smoke, will you?" Clerk called out as soon as he'd spotted him.

"I don't have any. If you're so addicted, I'll do you a rollie with tree leaves."

"You sound just like my third uncle. Here, let me give you one." And he pulled out the one he had tucked behind his ear and handed it over.

"This is a Hong Zhonghua," said Rain Xia, inspecting it. "You didn't really want one off me. You wanted an excuse to show off what you had."

"Where would I get the money to buy smokes like this? Just one cigarette would cost you a bag of wheat. We had some of the county officials visit today, and one of them liked my food, so he gave me this. I'm a canteen cook, Rain Xia, and the only good thing about that is you come into contact with government officials. What they eat, I eat, and my pigs get to eat it, too. Half of the slops I've got here is leftover food."

"How many pigs have you got now?" asked Rain Xia.

"A sow and twelve piglets. You want to see them?"

So Rain Xia went along with him. The place where Clerk and Forest Wu lived was originally an old-style tiled house with five rooms standing in a big yard. Then, ten years ago, Clerk coughed up some money and split it into two dwellings, right down the middle, separated by a brick wall. Clerk's family didn't own any furniture to speak of, so everything lay around on the floor—baskets of vegetables, bits of old netting, a mixing bowl for noodle dough, dirty socks and shoes, all jumbled up together. The sow wasn't penned up; she roamed around the courtyard, grunting and snuffling, rooting and pawing, and her twelve piglets tagged along behind. Then one wandered into the house, and they all followed and squeezed onto some straw bedding by the kang flue. Rain Xia hadn't been there very long when he felt something scurrying about in his pants. He rolled up his pants leg, and out jumped two fleas.

"Have you been bitten?" asked Clerk. "You must have tender flesh to get bitten when you've only just gotten here." He got out some fireworks powder. "Here, sprinkle this in your pants." Rain Xia refused it, so Clerk unbuttoned his jacket and put some on his chest. "What do you think of the piglets then?"

"Nice and fat," said Rain Xia.

"What do you see when you look at them?"

"Piglets."

"I see money on legs!" And he grabbed one and held it up by the hind legs. "Here, feel the weight."

But Rain Xia refused again. They heard sounds next door.

"Forest Wu, Forest Wu!" shouted Clerk. But there was no answer. "Odd, I'm sure I heard someone." He tried again. "Forest Wu, Forest Wu! Have you got dog hair stuffed in your ears?"

"There's no one there; what are you shouting for? Forest Wu's a sad old man. He's aged a lot this summer," said Rain Xia.

"Yup, he's sad, and he's annoying, too. He's clumsy. I got him to dig the trench for the new bathroom by the 312 for me, said I'd give him twenty yuan for it, and you know how long he took? Three days, and he still hadn't finished. I told Black-Moth yesterday, and she reamed him out."

Clerk started scooping the solids out of the slop bucket into a willow basket. Sure enough, out came bits of rice, noodles, green leaves, and sliced meat. The sow came over and stuck her snout in, smacking her lips. For himself, Clerk got a bit of flatbread out of the cupboard and a fresh chili, which he sprinkled with salt. "As soon as the sow starts eating, I get hungry, too. You want some?"

Rain Xia shook his head, and Clerk chomped alternately on the bread and the chili, making more noise than the pig. "Do you listen to opera?" he asked. He got out the radio and fiddled with the knob.

An aria sung by the painted-face lead filled the room. Rain Xia had a sudden vision of the singer, puce in the face, purpling veins standing out on his neck, spittle flying as he bellowed out the notes. He could almost feel the spittle spurting out of the radio. "Turn it off. I can't bear it!" he exclaimed.

"Don't you like it? I studied opera with Fourth Uncle. You really don't like it?"

Suddenly Rain Xia had had enough. He got up to go, but Clerk suddenly said, "Did you hear something?"

"He sings like he's having an argument."

"Sit down a moment." Clerk went into the back room, then came out and beckoned to Rain Xia. Rain Xia was puzzled but he followed. Clerk made him climb the ladder placed against the partition wall. Rain Xia looked over the partition. On the kang on the other side, Black-Moth lay naked on her front, with Treasure thrusting into her from behind like a dog. The pair were drenched with sweat but going at it hammer and tongs. Every now and then, Black-Moth looked around, clenching the pillow towel between her teeth.

Rain Xia shot down the ladder. "What are you making me look at stuff like that for?"

"I bet you've never seen . . ."

"Keep your voice down."

"I'll make them scream, just you wait!" Clerk turned the radio up to full volume, waited a couple of seconds, then switched it off. There was no more local opera, just moans and cries from next door. A few seconds later that, too, stopped.

There were people in Freshwind who would steal anything—grain, daikons, chickens, even the long tiles that covered the tops of Freshwind Temple's walls. But this was the first time Rain Xia had seen a man steal someone else's woman. He was furious with Treasure and sorry for Forest Wu.

It was evening by that time, and I was in the temple with Forest Wu, watching as Pavilion sorted out the compensation claim against Excellent Li. There were a lot of villagers there, first to see how Pavilion dealt with it, and second to back him up in case the West Mountain Bend folk got up to their tricks again. Forest Wu stayed for a bit but then said he wasn't feeling well and wanted to go home. I tried to stop him, but then I saw he was a bit green around the gills. Suddenly, his hair all stood on end, like a prickly chestnut or a hedgehog. He looked scary. The West Mountain Bend people exchanged glances and suddenly quieted down. In the end, they agreed to accept another one thousand yuan, making six thousand in total.

Once that was settled, Snow Bai's brother sent a grave-digging party to Bowed Ox Ridge the same night. Obviously, they needed Forest Wu, and Goodness wanted me to go, too.

"Will they let me?" I asked. I knew Snow Bai's brother couldn't stand me. He'd kicked me once.

"You should go. It'll be a chance to make up for past misdemeanors," said Goodness.

We spent a whole night digging the grave, and it was ready by the time it got light the next day. But that very day, Freshwind was invaded by bugs. I'm sure you know what I mean: those tiny bugs with wings, but they don't fly far; we get a lot of them in summer. For some reason, we got a swarm of them that morning, filling the air like drops of rain, landing in the trees and on the roofs, then pitter-pattering to the ground. By breakfast time they were in the houses, too, and all over the ground, in the threshing circle, along the base of the walls, on the cookers, and even wriggling around in the cisterns. They stank.

What on earth was going on? Was it Pathway Bai's spirit being spiteful? But why was he still hanging around like a restless ghost? His parents had been paid the compensation, after all. Obedient Zhang's farm store was soon clean out of insecticide powder, but the bugs were still alive. So then everyone let their poultry out to eat them up. When the hens were full to bursting, they squatted in the dust, and then they had bugs crawling all over them, too.

I'd been looking forward to going home to catch up on some sleep, but the house was too full of bugs for that, so I went down to the field to do some work. The fields were full of people harvesting peas and corn. The family had buried Pathway Bai. Not many others went. A few firecrackers were let off, and then the soil was heaped up in a low mound on the grave. Something odd happened, though. Pathway Bai's mom wept inconsolably at the grave, there was a gust of wind, and suddenly all the bugs were swept up into the air and hung in a black cloud over the village. Three times they moved first one way, then the other, then they flew west and disappeared.

If Pathway Bai had just died with no fights over compensation, then the villagers would have said, "Well, Pathway Bai's dead," or "Poor kid, cut off in his prime." But there had been a fight over the compensation, and that threw Freshwind into turmoil for a while. All the same, once he'd been laid to rest, the village quieted down. The sun continued to shine and turn the corn and the paddy rice golden. Snow Bai's brother bought a sledgehammer and went off to Zhoucheng City on a demolition job with three other men. But Snow Bai's mom was still sick, so Snow Bai cut short her tour with the opera troupe and came home to look after her. She brought with her Wisdom Xia's collection of opera masks.

I don't know how the old man took it when he learned that eight of them were missing. At any rate, he didn't come complaining to me. And Snow Bai was back in Freshwind, with her mom. I could see her every day, and I smiled with happiness at anyone I came across.

One day, Bright Chen, the stutterer, saw me smiling at him and rubbed his face, as if maybe there was soot on it. Then he said, "D-dickhead, wh-what are you sm-smiling for?"

I carried on smiling and set off in the direction of the market, singing a snatch from the opera *The Thirteen Hinges*.

I had moved on to *The Cry of the Water Dragon* when a cloud appeared over Yijia Ridge. I thought the bugs were back, but when I looked carefully, I saw it was a real cloud, one shaped like a cat's tail, hovering over Middle Street.

"Come down, cloud!" I shouted at it.

And it came down and landed on the steps on the Earth Shrine. The Earth God and the Earth Goddess were the most important Freshwind spirits right then; they knew all the village's stories and even my innermost feelings. I stopped singing and put my palms together in a prayerful gesture. Pavilion put-putted past on his motorbike, spraying me with muddy water, but I didn't get annoyed. I smiled at him, and he smiled back at me.

"Why are you smiling?" I asked him.

He stopped in front of the shrine and parked, and the cloud enveloped him. He thought it was smoke and batted it away. "Smile, Spark!" he said. "If you're happy, you gotta smile." And he slung his jacket over his shoulders—it was a silky one that made a breeze as he twirled it—and walked off down the street.

Chapter 23

After the market was finished, there was a lot of wrangling among the villagers about who was going to rent a stall. Auntie Wang and Dog-Scraps's widowed mom even got into a fight and almost scratched each other's eyes out. All the same, Pavilion was proud of the fact that Freshwind Village was doing well and raking in substantial rents and admin fees. Whenever he strolled along the village street, the snacks vendors called out solicitously, "Had your dinner yet, Mr. Party Secretary?"

"Do you have any red-cooked pork? Put a bowl aside for me then," Pavilion would answer.

One day, Clerk's wife was about to throw out the water she'd been using to rinse the rice when she suddenly realized Pavilion was walking by. She tried to stop, but too late—she tripped over the threshold and tipped the water all down her front.

"The street's a real mess in front of your shop," Pavilion reproved her. "If you keep tipping slops out, you'll have to repair the roadway."

"Oh, but I wasn't tipping water out. Had your dinner yet?"

"No, I haven't. What have you got that's good?"

"You really haven't eaten yet? It's a hard life being a cadre. Pavilion, I didn't call you 'Mr. Secretary'; you don't mind, do you? You know what they say—our bodies are our capital. It seems to me your body doesn't belong to you anymore, Pavilion."

"What are you talking like that for?" said Pavilion. "And what's Clerk doing? Hasn't he finished that bathroom yet?"

"Yes, it's in use. You can go and use it, add some shit to it for us."

But Pavilion had already walked away and was exchanging a joke with the young woman at the dyehouse. It used to be that the dyehouse took in cloth the villagers had woven at home, dyed it, and handed it back again, only charging for the dyeing—but not anymore. Nowadays, they took in the local cloth, dyed it, and sold it in the market. Cars passing along the 312 stopped every day, bought the cloth, and took it home to make sheets and tablecloths. The most they'd sold to a single customer was forty-eight pieces. Pavilion suggested that they package each piece of cloth in plastic and print the packaging with a history of the dyehouse and a list of their products.

"Oh, what a good idea!" exclaimed Favor Bai's wife.

"So how are you going to thank me?"

"How do you want to be thanked?"

"You leave your door off the latch tonight."

The woman choked with laughter, then grabbed a clothes pole and took a swipe at Pavilion with it. Pavilion skipped out of reach, hopped onto the dyehouse steps, and peered in through the open door. Four people were playing mah-jongg, making no attempt to hide from him. Shifty's wife sat on the east side of the table. It looked like a worm was crawling from under her skirt and down her swarthy leg.

"Look at your leg," said Pavilion.

The woman looked, exclaimed, wiped it with a bit of paper—her period had come, and the worm was a trickle of blood. "What do you think you're looking at?"

"You spend so much time playing mah-jongg, you wouldn't stop even if you turned into a dragonfly carcass."

"And why shouldn't I play, at my age? What else do I have to do? I don't have any land to work, I can't trade, I don't have any family, and no sweetheart. We're only playing it for fun, Mr. Pavilion. We're not playing for money."

Pavilion flushed. He went off to the farm shop and bought a carton of cigarettes, then headed for the Great Qing Hall.

Big-Noise Zhao and Mid-Star's dad were there and jumped to their feet when they saw him.

"Haven't you been to the market, Big-Noise?" said Pavilion.

"Of course I have. Everyone's saying what a good thing you've done for the village."

"Is that so? Then why haven't you written some couplets for the decorative arch?"

"I did, a long time ago. Tell me what you think of them." And he bent down and pulled out two rolled-up scrolls. One read, "If I cheat you, may my head be scraped along the ground; if you cheat me, may heaven deal with you."

"You can't write that! It doesn't matter if the cat's black or white, so long as it catches mice. What business is it of yours if the traders cheat?"

The second scroll read, "Pay less heed to your home life; pay more heed to profiting from others."

"Not bad," said Pavilion. "The market's full of stallholders and customers. It's a feast of local delicacies every day, and that's the way I like it. What really sticks in my craw is people going on about right and wrong. Add a couple of political slogans, and that scroll would be even better."

"I don't know any political slogans. I've never been a government cadre."

Pavilion thought for a minute, then said, "'To develop economically, you should pay less heed to your home life; to attain prosperity, you should pay more heed to profiting from others.' How about that?"

"Fine," said Big-Noise Zhao.

"By the way," said Pavilion, "I went past Roughshod Ding's house just now, and he has couplets hung on his gate, too. On one side, it says, 'Go places by using your legs; keep the peace by using the dog.' And on the other side, it says, 'Make yourself clear by using your voice; amuse yourself by using your hand.' Did you write them?"

"His idea; I composed the couplets," said Big-Noise Zhao. "I'm a bit worried they might reflect badly on the village, though."

"He's ambitious, that man," Pavilion commented.

"Do you know he's talking about building a restaurant now?"

"Right, and the Two Committees will back the proposal. You'd never believe it of the little short-ass, would you?"

"Don't judge by appearances; you can't tell how deep the sea is by looking at it," said Big-Noise Zhao. "Yesterday he got into a fight with that devious bastard Shifty and hit him on the head with a brick."

"What were they fighting about?" Pavilion asked anxiously.

"Shifty despises him. Yesterday he caught up with him in the village street and made a point of walking alongside him, pretending to have bandy legs. People laughed and Roughshod Ding got angry. Shifty was clearly out to make trouble—he sees Roughshod Ding as a threat."

Pavilion grunted. Then he turned to Mid-Star's dad and said, "Uncle Glory, I need your help with something."

The old man straightened up. "You want my son to go and talk to one of the county seat cadres?"

"You're proud of that son of yours, aren't you?"

The old man looked embarrassed. "Or you want me to make a prediction for you?"

"No, not that, either. If I don't want to do something, I can always find an excuse, and when I want to do something, I'll find a way." And Pavilion got up, clapped his hands together, and took himself off.

If there was one thing I admired about Pavilion, it was his self-confidence. Whenever I looked at him, even from a distance, I could see his aura shooting up from the top of his head. Nowadays, he rode his motorbike faster and faster, its wheels churning up clouds of dust. The way he was doing so well for himself, it occurred to me that all he needed was a piece of cloth around his shoulders to sail right up to heaven.

When you separate the wheat from the chaff, you make sure to wait for a gust of wind before you throw a few more shovelfuls in the air. Pavilion had that gust of wind—he'd no sooner completed his market project than he'd started drawing up new plans. Most of the villagers had no idea what he was planning, but he couldn't fool me. I saw the way he was all buddy-buddy with Shifty to his face, laughing and talking and patting him on the back, and I also saw how sober he looked as soon as he turned his back on him.

I understood that things were looking bad for Shifty. I have a good reason for saying this. Twenty years ago, the reservoir was built, partly for irrigation, and partly as a fish farm. But it was too far from Freshwind, and hardly anyone bought the fish. Four fishponds were dug in the village instead, for the county seat cadres to come and do a bit of fishing on Sundays. During festivals and holidays, the fish were caught and given out as gifts to local government officials.

At first, both the fishponds and the brickyard were managed by the township government. But the staff changed from day to day, and the management was slipshod. Far from turning a profit, they didn't even make ends meet. So finally, the brickyard was handed over to the village, and the township government kept the fishponds. Shifty was put in charge of the day-to-day running of the brickyard and somehow ended up managing the fishponds as well. He'd always been tough, and with his new powers, he really began to throw his weight around in Freshwind. If he didn't get his way, he shouted and yelled until he did, and he argued with the Two Committees, too. In the end, people were so frightened of him that if any kid cried in the night and wouldn't settle down, the mother would threaten, "If you don't shut up, Shifty will come and get you!" Shifty had become the village boogeyman, the way the local bandits were before the revolution.

When Pavilion first became a village cadre, he'd needed Shifty's backing to push through his ideas. But as soon as his projects were up and running, he proposed that the local government either take back the brickyard or that Shifty sign a formal lease on it. He received strong support from everyone except Shifty, who refused either to hand it back or to lease it. He mounted a counterattack, plying the township government with gifts and accusing the Two Committees of corruption. As a result, the proposal was put on the back burner, and instead, there was an investigation into the accounts of the projects my dad had overseen—selling the trees on the river embankment and the roadworks. They obviously found no irregularities, but if you piss on someone, the stink hangs around, and Dad's reputation suffered.

Now that Pavilion was Party secretary, he raised the question of Shifty's lease on the brickyard again, but the feeling in the Two Committees was that it wasn't worth getting on the wrong side of Shifty—he was still useful, and you needed someone nasty in the village. He could get things done that the rest of them couldn't handle. And the more you fought demons, the more they multiplied; best to show them proper respect.

Pavilion realized that he couldn't get rid of Shifty so easily, so he started working out ways to undermine his power. I was on Pavilion's side, but I didn't like how he went about it. His first step was to take back the fishponds. He knew the reservoir management would veto that, so he used Seven Li Gully as a bargaining chip. That got their agreement. The gully could be part of the "green belt" around the dam, which they planned to make into a tourist attraction. Pavilion submitted the proposal to the Two Committees. Half the members opposed it, arguing that it wasn't cost-effective to swap four fishponds for the whole of Seven Li Gully. The village could afford to build ten fishponds if they sold the gully instead.

Of course, Pavilion couldn't be up front about his real purpose, but he stressed that the gully was wasteland, of no use to anyone except the reservoir. His opponents carried on, insisting that even though the gully was useless, it still couldn't be swapped for the fishponds because Freshwind villagers had put money and labor into the gully-filling project and it was always possible that the project might be restarted and completed one day. As soon as the gully-filling was mentioned, Pavilion flew into such a rage that the meeting came to a halt.

For a few more days, he mulled over his options. Then he met with Mid-Star's dad. He was of two minds whether to ask him to make a prediction, to help him weigh up the potential gains and losses, but the fact was that he just didn't like the old boy's manner. He made Pavilion feel uneasy.

A few more days went by, and they were all busy bringing in the autumn harvest and spreading it out to dry. Then Roughshod Ding knocked down his old yard wall and began to dig the foundations for the new restaurant, and Rain Xia rented a truck and brought steel and cement from the county seat and started making prefabricated, reinforced concrete beams on the flat ground in front of the theater.

Pavilion went along to have a look. "How much is that restaurant going to cost you then?"

"It's gonna make me money, not cost me money."

Pavilion put an arm around him and gave him a friendly punch. "Short-ass: small size, big spirit!" he exclaimed.

And at that instant, he made up his mind. He was going to swap the gully for the fish-ponds, and to hell with the naysayers! You couldn't cross a marshland without making the frogs croak, after all. It was just like when you appointed new cadres: beforehand, everyone had objections, but once they were in the post, it was like the village was full of dogs joyously wagging their tails. That very day, he took Goodness and Lotus to the reservoir, and they signed the agreement with the management.

Chapter 24

One afternoon, New-Life Liu asked Justice Xia to come and look at his fruit trees. Something was ailing them; many leaves had shriveled and gone yellow. Justice Xia discovered grubs hiding in the soil beneath the roots, the kind that you couldn't see by day, but at night they crawled out and up the trunk and chewed the tree bark. He suggested that Liu paint the lower part of the trunks with lime. New-Life Liu and Star Chen weren't on speaking terms, and Justice Xia was worried that New-Life wouldn't pass on his advice, so after that, he went straight over to Star Chen's orchard, where, sure enough, trees were dying, too. Star Chen was at his wits' end as to what to do. He was touched that the old man had taken the trouble to come and give his advice, and grateful that he didn't bring up his relationship with Emerald, either, so he pressed him to stay for a drink. Justice Xia was soon roaring drunk and staggered home, singing some lines from the opera *Crashing the Imperial Chariot* at the top of his voice:

> When the eight-man sedan came to rest in the back street, hey!
> Judge Bao descended from his palanquin for a full inspection.

He sang with such vigor that he dislodged a front tooth. He retrieved it and wrapped it up, but now he couldn't articulate the words properly, so he just had to hum the tune.

When he got to the smithy, he noticed a crowd of people around the Earth Shrine.

"Mr. Xia's here!" someone shouted.

Justice Xia stopped humming and went over to the shrine. He was walking lopsided, and folds of swarthy flesh jiggled and rippled on the back of his neck.

A sheet of paper covered in black lettering had been stuck to the wall. Justice Xia quivered at the sight and instantly sobered up. "Who stuck that there?" he demanded. "The Cultural Revolution's been over and done for years; why's someone stuck up a big-character poster?"

"It's not a big-character poster," said someone. "The writing's very small."

"Well, it makes no difference whether it's big or small," Justice Xia said, reaching out to tear it down.

Someone stopped him. "Mr. Xia, read it first."

Justice Xia was farsighted, and the light was fading by then. He couldn't read it. He felt in his jacket pocket, but he hadn't brought his glasses, so someone else ran over to the smithy, grabbed the glasses off the blacksmith's face, and passed them to Justice Xia. When he was village head, he used to read the newspaper or local government notices out loud.

Now he began, "'The village's own Mao Zedong thinks he's number one. The frogs in the pond and even the insects dare not make a sound. Forget democracy; it's all about power and making big bucks in the future. He won't fill the gully, he just wants to swap the gully, he eats roof tiles and shits bricks, and General Li Hongzhang was his ancestor. He rears the fish to gift to his superiors, so he can rise in the ranks himself. Ordinary folk have a hard life, they live off scraps and grain husks so they're all skin and bone. They earn a cent here, spend ten cents there. Some want to get contracts and screw around; the real nasty ones are very popular. Is this really what the Communist Party is about, I ask myself? I've signed this with my real name: Spark Zhang wrote this, and I'm not afraid you'll bite my balls.' Did Spark really write this?"

"Spark has no balls. Of course he's not afraid someone'll bite him in the balls," someone said.

Everyone laughed.

"Do you think mutilation is a laughing matter? Anyway, what does it mean?"

"He's talking about the Seven Li Gully swap; haven't you heard? Pavilion's taking over the four fishponds in exchange."

"Bullshit," said Justice Xia. "The reservoir's the reservoir, and Freshwind's Freshwind. You can't give away the village land; what kind of nonsense is that?"

"You're not on the committee anymore, so you wouldn't know."

"But I'm still a villager," the old man retorted. And he tore the poster down. He did not, however, tear it to bits as they expected, but folded it and tucked it away inside his jacket.

"Off you go, all of you, get moving," he said.

Confession: it *was* me who wrote the poster. I'd been doing a bit of work for Roughshod Ding and Rain Xia, smashing a rock with the eight-pound hammer, when I overheard Roughshod Ding say, "You're looking good today."

I turned around because I thought it must be Snow Bai, but it was Lotus. She was wearing a short-sleeved T-shirt that showed off her high breasts.

"Keep your eyes to yourself and carry on with your hammering," Ding said to me. "I'm the only one who's allowed to look."

I did as I was told, but I thought to myself, *What a slut!*

Lotus bounced over and said to Roughshod Ding, "Looking good, am I?"

And they started talking. I wasn't trying to eavesdrop, but then Lotus began to talk about Pavilion and about how they'd signed the contract with the reservoir management, and I couldn't help butting in: "Giving away the gully for some fishponds—that's like General Li Hongzhang selling off bits of China to the imperialists."

"Wash your mouth out! You're talking a bunch of shit," said Lotus. "Who said they're giving away the gully?"

"You did," I said.

Lotus rolled her eyes in exasperation. "When would I have said that?"

"Roughshod," I said, "you're my witness. Did she or didn't she just say that?"

"What? I didn't hear anything."

How can there be people like that in this world? "Roughshod," I said, "I'm not helping you anymore."

"Fine. Then I don't have to give you dinner."

I wrote "Pavilion is a tyrant!" on the wall with a bit of charcoal, but Roughshod Ding scraped it off with his spade. "If you want to write, do it on your own wall."

"Roughshod Ding," I said, "I thought you were rock solid, but you're just a clod of earth. What are you scared of?"

"I'm just scared," he said.

"I'm not."

"Yeah, but you're crazy. Of course you're not scared."

I left Roughshod Ding and headed home. On the way, I passed the Great Qing Hall and saw Big-Noise Zhao pasting new couplets around the entrance. The new pair read, "Would that the bag was full of money," and "Would that the body was free of sickness."

"Hypocrite," I muttered. "You think you'd have a bag full of money if you weren't sick anymore?"

"What's that, Spark?" asked Big-Noise Zhao.

I didn't answer, but I had the germ of an idea: I'd write a poster. So I went into the courtyard and told Big-Noise Zhao about the plan to swap Seven Li Gully with the fishponds.

His eyes grew round as copper coins. "Are you talking crazy?" he exclaimed.

"You think I'm sick in the head again, Big-Noise?"

"Look at that light bulb inside; is it round or square?" he said.

A light bulb hung from the ceiling. I looked straight through and out the back, where I could see morning glory plants climbing in a neat row up the wall of the building in the rear yard. They'd already gotten to the top of the wall, and a bird was hopping along, taking a peck at the flowers, hopping again, and taking another peck. "Round," I said.

"You're not sick," Big-Noise Zhao said. Then he took another look at me. "It's too bad you get so easily worked up, Spark."

"I don't just get myself worked up; I can get other people worked up, too," I said. "Let's write a poster about what Pavilion's up to."

"A poster? You can write it."

"I don't write as well as you," I protested.

"You write, I'll correct it." And he passed me the brush, paper, and ink stone.

So I did. I wanted to explain in detail why swapping the gully with the fishponds was a bad deal. And I strongly suspected that there was some dirty business behind it, but in the end, I wrote some paired sentences. It was more important to write something in a formal literary style. I didn't want Big-Noise Zhao laughing at me. I asked him to correct it, but he said, "It's fine," and didn't change anything. Then I asked him to come with me and stick it up outside the Earth Shrine, but halfway there, he sneaked off, saying he needed the bathroom, then climbed over the back wall of the shithouse and took off. Big-Noise Zhao always insisted he was so cultured, but how could someone who was cultured be such a coward?

Now it seemed like my paired sentences were no good. They were too literary and didn't explain enough. Still, I'd written the poster. All those people in Freshwind Village, but only I had written anything. Just the thought of my heroism almost moved me to tears.

I'd been hiding behind the gable end of the smithy, watching as everyone clustered around and argued over the poster, and Justice Xia got really angry. This was the first time since my dad died that anyone had paid so much attention to me. Now they really had to give me respect! I got so excited that I grabbed a white cat and threw it up the smithy chimney, and by the time it squeezed its way out, it had turned into a black cat.

Justice Xia set off toward East Street, his hands clasped behind his back. At the first alley off East Street, he bumped into Bamboo and asked her straight out, "Are you planning to swap Seven Li Gully for the fishponds?"

"There was no agreement at the last Two Committees meeting; I thought it was shelved," said Bamboo, her cigarette still clamped between her lips.

"So how come it's happening?"

"I dunno."

"You're head of the East Street Residential Group. If you don't know what's going on, how can you represent their interests? You know how to smoke a cigarette; why don't you try smoking big stuff like opium?" And Justice Xia stomped off, puffing and panting, without waiting for a reply.

Bamboo gaped in astonishment, then called after him, "You been drinking again?" She hurried home to tell Hearth.

Hearth was in their yard, running the stone roller over the bundles of just-harvested rice. Without pausing, he said, "He was drunk. You better go and see what's going on. Mom can't see well enough to look after him."

Bamboo went to see her in-laws, but strangely, Justice Xia hadn't arrived home. After a little while, Lucky came running in, barking furiously, then ran out again. Bamboo followed the dog out and down the alley until she came to Pavilion's. Before she got close, she could hear Justice Xia and Pavilion yelling at each other.

Justice Xia's face was red and puffed up with anger. He had rolled the poster out on the table and was thumping his fist on it. "Look what the masses think of you. All these years, there's never been a whisper of protest in Freshwind Village, and as soon as you take over, someone's written a wall poster in great big characters denouncing you!"

"Those characters are small, not big," said Pavilion.

"And you think a small-character poster's something to be proud of?"

"You're bound to get birds tweeting in a forest of any size. Spark's crazy; don't listen to his crazy talk."

"So you don't listen to Spark. What about all those people on the Two Committees? Will you listen to them?"

"Democracy's got to be centralized. Otherwise, how would we get anything done? When you started the gully-filling project, you didn't carry everyone with you, did you? So how come you went ahead and did it? Let's not beat around the bush. You're the retired village head, and you're my uncle, so it's right and proper for you to speak your mind. But you're taking all this too much to heart. You were against the market before it was built, and now you're throwing a tantrum over this deal."

"Taking it too much to heart, am I? Let me tell you, I'm not thinking of my reputation. It's Seven Li Gully—I don't want to let it go. Just because we never finished filling the gully last time doesn't mean we won't do it one day. And that'll be over a hundred *mu* of extra farmland. You think you can become a cadre and say no to that? The population's expanding all the time, and the land area is shrinking. All you care about is what's right in front of your eyes; you're not looking to the future. You were prepared to ruin eighteen *mu* for the market, and now you're throwing away over a hundred. By the time you die, there won't be any land to bury you on."

Cutie, who had been trying to calm Pavilion down, took exception to this last comment. "Uncle, you shouldn't be bad-mouthing your nephew; it's not right in an old man of your age."

Justice Xia got even angrier. "Why shouldn't I bad-mouth him? And who told you to butt in, anyway? Get lost!"

Cutie began to cry. "You'll be the death of Pavilion."

Tongue-Tied had been standing by the gate, holding on to Lucky, but now he rushed over and howled at Cutie.

Pavilion slapped his wife across the face. "Quit talking bullshit! What does this have to do with you, anyway? If I die and there's no place to bury me, you can sew me up in a dog's stomach instead."

"If you're so good at beating me, you go ahead and kill me!" Cutie screamed at him and then offered herself up to be beaten.

Pavilion gave her another pair of slaps, and then Bamboo hurried over and pulled her away, though Cutie resisted. Then Bamboo shoved Pavilion so hard he sat down on the ground, and Justice Xia, meanwhile, turned on his heel and disappeared through the gate.

During the quarrel, Justice Xia's five sons had turned up and were standing under the elm outside Pavilion's gate like a pack of wolves on the prowl, ready to take on Pavilion and his wife if they became too unpleasant or threatened to hit the old man. Everyone on East Street who did not belong to the Xia family stood watching from a safe distance, whispering among themselves, not daring to move a step closer or raise their voices. They understood quite well that even though the argument was over village business, it was still a family fight, and there was no point trying to figure out the rights and wrongs of it. When all was said and done, the Xias were the Xias and always would be.

Wisdom Xia was the last to hear what was going on. By the time he arrived, Justice Xia had gone and only Gold, Treasure, Bounty, Hearth, and Halfwit were left outside Pavilion's.

"What are you hanging around here for?" he admonished them. "Are you planning to start a fight? Be off with you! Go home!"

Once they'd gone, Wisdom Xia muttered, "Outrageous." And when the other villagers heard that, they hurried away, too.

Just then, fiery red clouds boiled up and poured across the sky, looking and sounding like a raging torrent.

The next morning, Justice Xia got up very early and headed up the alley, going north. A broken *baijiu* bottle lay in the road, and as he kicked the bits of glass to one side, he suddenly heard a torrent of abuse coming from someone nearby. It was Cutie. Who was the mother-fucker who'd cut down her gourd vine? She'd slash them with a knife if she found out who it was; she'd shoot them; she hoped they'd fall off a mountain and into the river, or get water on the brain when they were asleep.

Justice Xia saw Mid-Star's dad on his way home with a load of manure and asked, "What's she swearing about?"

"She planted a gourd vine by the screen at their gate, and it did really well—produced a dozen gourds. But this morning, when Cutie came out to water it, she noticed that the leaves were wilting, and when she lifted the plant, the vines were all snapped off. Or rather, they'd been neatly snipped off. Seems someone cut them with a knife, right at the roots."

He'd hardly finished speaking when she started again. "I'll fuck your mother, whoever you are. And you can come here and cut off my head, and Pavilion's, too, if you think you can do it!"

People started to gather in the alley, but no one said anything. The only sound to be heard was barking as Lucky and Tiger raced by, one after the other.

"Pavilion!" Cutie yelled. "Pavilion! You've brought shame on your ancestors, and you've ruined my life, too. You've sacrificed me for the collective!"

Just then, Justice Xia came along the alley.

"Justice, don't go down there," warned Mid-Star's dad. "You'll set her off again."

But Justice Xia stomped stubbornly on. Lucky and Tiger scattered in alarm, the ants fled, and the sparrows in the trees flew off. A clod of earth too slow to escape was crushed under the old man's shoes.

He got to Pavilion's gate, and Cutie saw him. She fell silent, went inside, and shut the gate. *You carry on shouting,* Justice Xia thought to himself. *What's a red mouth and white teeth like yours made for?* He stomped on past and headed for the township government offices.

The township head had just washed his face and was tipping the contents of the basin over the flowers next to the gate when he saw Justice Xia and shouted, "Hello, Mr. Xia!" Then he went in and put on the kettle. Justice Xia settled down at the concrete table in the yard, scowling. There was a chessboard etched on the table and a pile of chess pieces, which he scooped to one side. Then he spotted Lucky and Tiger both cocking their legs and pissing against the yard wall.

"Lucky!" Justice Xia shouted. "Lucky!" Lucky ran toward him, then came to a halt, looked at her master, and suddenly turned tail and ran out of the gate.

The township head came out with the teapot and smiled. "So is this a visit from the morality police? You know Lucky's here every morning to see her gentleman friend."

But Justice Xia was serious. "There's something I want to report to you as township head."

"Of course," said the head. "You wouldn't come to the township government unless you had something on your mind."

"I'm not village head anymore," said Justice Xia. "In fact, I'm worried that people will accuse me of meddling."

"They wouldn't dare. I certainly never heard Pavilion say anything of the sort. After all, he needs your support. He took over from you, and he's your nephew, isn't he?"

"We're not uncle and nephew when it comes to work. It's because of him that I'm here today."

"Not the market project? That's going well, isn't it? The village is doing good business; the market's really put the village on the map."

But Justice Xia had something else on his mind. "I want to ask you one thing. Is there a national policy that states that a township or department has the right to exchange land for other types of property with another township or department?"

"You need to tell me what exactly this is about."

So Justice Xia explained that Pavilion had arbitrarily decided to give Seven Li Gully to the reservoir management in exchange for the ponds. He pointed out that the Two Committees had not agreed, and he showed the township head my poster as proof that the villagers were against it, too. The head looked thunderstruck.

"It is my duty as a long-standing Party member and a villager myself to report this to our leaders," said Justice Xia. "I hope the township officials will put a stop to it and ensure that the village doesn't lose any land."

The township head read the poster. Then he looked around and shouted, "Li! When will the Party secretary be back?"

A head popped up above the shithouse half wall in the corner of the yard. "He said he was going to stay two days in South Gully Village and then go on to Dongbaochuan."

"Did you know that Pavilion has given Seven Li Gully to the reservoir in exchange for their fishponds?" the head asked.

"He mentioned something once, yes," the young man answered.

"So why didn't you inform me?"

Li came out, buttoning his fly. "I thought it was Freshwind business."

"So if Freshwind Village sold off all its land, that would be village business, too, would it?" Justice Xia said.

"I'm only a junior," said Li. "Talk to my boss; he's here."

Justice Xia poured himself a cup of tea. It was very hot, but he swallowed a gulp anyway and felt it burn its way down to his stomach.

The township head smiled. "You are a very responsible person, Mr. Xia. We younger officers should take a leaf out of your book. Refill his cup, Li." He paused. "But go wash your hands first."

After the young man had gone, Justice Xia said, "What can be done?"

"Leave it with me; I'll look into it. If it really is as you say, I'll have to go through government documents first and see if such a policy exists. Then I need to discuss it with the Party secretary. But no matter what the outcome, I must say I'm touched at how conscientious you are, and at your age, too. You should take care of yourself. Li! Go and tell Clerk to cook a few more dishes today. Mr. Xia needs lunch, and it's on me."

Justice Xia knew he was being dismissed. "No, no, no. I have to go home," he said.

Just getting to his feet made him feel giddy. Everything seemed to spin, and he had to stand still for a few moments before his head cleared and he could walk out of the gate.

As he crossed the 312 back to the village, the giddiness returned. He slapped his forehead and swore, "Fucking dizzy spell!" He looked around and noticed that his shadow seemed to be dangling from a jujube thorn bush by the road. Then he saw Rites Xia coming toward him, a pack on his back.

"Did you go to the township offices and report Pavilion?" Rites asked his brother.

"No, I just told them what was going on."

"And what was the point of that?" Rites Xia grumbled. "Pavilion's the village Party secretary; he can do what he wants. If he was corrupt and building a luxury house for himself and living a life of debauchery, then you'd have every reason to report him. But Pavilion's not like that—he's committed to the interests of the collective."

"If Pavilion really was corrupt, the Xia clan would pull him into line themselves. It's precisely because he does things in the name of the collective that the township government needs to know about it."

Neither of them was enjoying this conversation, so they changed the subject.

"Where are you heading?" Justice Xia asked.

"To the market in Zhaojialou Township."

"Freshwind has a market every day now. What do you want to go to Zhaojialou for?"

"I need to get out of the house. A walk does me good."

Rites Xia was waiting for the bus on the 312 when Treasure came by pulling a cart full of lime. A sudden gust of wind whipped a cloud of the stuff, and it got into Treasure's eyes.

"Blow it off for me," he said.

Rites Xia did as he was asked. "Are you doing some whitewashing? Those mud-brick walls'll take all summer to dry out; why are you in such a hurry to paint them?"

"I'm getting the materials in place."

"You've been home for days. You should be paying more attention to your schoolwork."

"You think that'll make me into a Wind Xia?"

"What nonsense you talk," said Rites Xia, and he stopped blowing the lime from Treasure's eyes.

Treasure rubbed them himself. "I saw Shifty just now; he's looking for you. You better watch out. Fighting with Pavilion is one thing, but don't let Shifty use you to get one over on Pavilion."

"What do you mean, 'get one over' on Pavilion?"

"He's had a falling out with Pavilion, too. Pavilion's using this fishpond business to undermine Shifty, isn't he?"

"I have no intention of seeing him."

Justice Xia went home, stripped off, and sat down in his underpants for a smoke. Second Aunt was on the kang, holding a long conversation with herself. Justice Xia pondered the township head's words. Local government cadres were too young, nowadays, and didn't know how to weigh the relative importance of things. If they waited to step in until they'd had a meeting and investigated, the gully-fishponds swap would be a done deal.

Suddenly he felt hot all over and helped himself to a scoop of sour broth from the jar. "Stop reciting the scriptures; it really bugs me!" he exclaimed to his wife.

She said nothing, but she got off the kang and felt her way along the wall and out into the yard. To make up for having been sharp with her, Justice Xia moved the pans out of the way so she wouldn't fall over them. As he did so, it occurred to him that he might be able to use Shifty. Yes, he could! After all, you could make use of someone without liking them.

He put his clothes back on and took a fan out to Second Aunt, who had settled by the gate outside. Then he went to find Marvel, to ask him to find out how much electricity the brickyard consumed. Marvel didn't need to look it up—the brickyard had run up arrears of at least ten thousand yuan. "Don't bother chasing the payment," said Justice Xia. "Just cut his electricity off."

Marvel duly disconnected the brickyard's power supply. Then he went home and made some tea for Justice Xia. They finished the first pot. There wasn't a sound from outside, not even from the hens dozing on the gate sill.

"Do you really think he's coming, Uncle?" Marvel asked.

"Drink your tea," said Justice Xia.

Marvel looked at the gate. "Shifty's never been to my house."

"If I tell you to drink your tea, you drink it."

Marvel sat up straight, and they started on the other pot of tea. Suddenly the hens flew up, startled, and they heard a motorcycle.

"He's here," said Marvel and got up.

Justice Xia gave him a hard look and said quietly, "Drink your tea."

Marvel already knew that Shifty had high cheekbones, but this was the first time he'd realized that his face was a mass of wrinkles, too, ones that radiated out from the central feature, his nose. That was because Shifty was smiling broadly at him.

"Put the electricity back on," he begged.

"When you've paid off what you owe."

They argued back and forth, wheedling and bullying, until finally they were both red in the face and furious.

Justice Xia just sat there and drank his tea—a good tea, slightly bitter but with a sweet aftertaste. Several times he saw Marvel's mother in the yard, but she didn't come into the house, and Justice Xia didn't go out and greet her. Once the teapot was empty, he added more water and carried on drinking.

By this time, Shifty was frothing at the mouth. "Marvel, my pal," he implored him. "I've never asked anyone for anything before, but now I need your help."

"Don't beg," said Marvel. "I don't want to beat you, and I don't want to be beaten by you, either. Pavilion ordered me to turn off the electricity if the bills aren't paid. It's not the first time it's happened, you know that. You can go talk to Pavilion. It's not me who decides; I'm just the electrician."

"I'm not going to talk to him," said Shifty. "I'm going to report him. Uncle Justice, you're here. Tell us, how did it go when you went to report Pavilion to the township government?"

Justice Xia tipped his remaining tea away. "Your affairs have nothing to do with me, and you can keep your nose out of my business, too."

"But Uncle Justice, everyone knows that you put the interests of the village first. I support you in that."

"It was in the interests of the village that I disconnected you."

"What's more important, for the village to lose Seven Li Gully, or for me to owe ten thousand?" said Shifty. "The money will be paid, but when the gully's gone, it's gone for good. And there was no point you going to complain to the township head, Uncle Justice. He's too highbrow; there's no way he can keep a wolf like Pavilion under control. You need a dog to bite a wolf, and that dog's me. I'm going to put in a complaint to the county government."

"You go right ahead," said Justice Xia. "But you've put in complaints your whole life . . . and you've never once won a case. It hasn't done your reputation any good, either. No one will care whether you're right."

Shifty fell silent. He sat down, poured himself a cup of tea, and gulped it down. "Marvel, you're acting very cocky. You never even offered tea when I turned up."

"What's that you're drinking then?"

"Uncle Justice," said Shifty, "if I write a report, will you sign it?"

"Why not, as long as you're in the right?"

"Excellent! I'm putting your name on it, too, Marvel."

Someone knocked on the window, and they could see Marvel's mother's head outlined against the window paper.

"You can't add wind to a fart," said Marvel. "My name being on it isn't going to tip the scales."

"You don't want to get your nose dirty," said Shifty.

"I told you, I'm just an electrician."

"You're Pavilion's gun!" said Shifty.

"You flatter me," Marvel said. "You mean, I'm Pavilion's dog?"

"I never said that." He wheedled again. "Please turn on the electricity. The brickyard's made huge losses, and if I'm without electricity for another ten days, I'll have to take rat poison."

"Marvel," said Justice Xia, "I am not a village official anymore, and I shouldn't get involved, but now that Shifty's explained the situation, I think you can turn on the electricity again. The brickyard's in debt because it doesn't have money, and without electricity, it'll never pay what it owes to the village."

"That's right," said Shifty. "Uncle Justice can see the bigger picture. I always tell people that when Uncle Justice was in the post, I was too stupid to understand how good he was. I was always complaining. I didn't appreciate him until he'd stepped down. It's like kids fight with their parents all the time, and it's only when they themselves have children that they understand how much their parents loved them."

"Stop trying to pour wine into me," Justice Xia said. "I don't get drunk that easily."

"Okay," Marvel agreed. "I'll do as Uncle Justice says. But one thing I want to make clear: if Pavilion insists on cutting you off again, I'll do it."

"Just wait until we put in our complaint, then he may be out of a job," said Shifty.

Shifty really did write out a complaint. He did it in the brickyard, and when it was finished, the three of them signed and put their fingerprints on it. Then he told White-Moth to take the last page home to Forest Wu to add his fingerprint.

White-Moth, who was in the middle of washing her feet, said, "What's this all about then? Read it to me."

Shifty read it out in his garbled Mandarin Chinese, sounding smug.

"Very grand," said White-Moth when he'd finished. "But why does it sound like a mess of daikon and noodles?"

"If I wrote as well as Wind Xia, I would have been married to Snow Bai. I'd never have ended up with you," said Shifty. "The only good thing about you is your big tits."

White-Moth flicked her dirty foot-washing water at Shifty, and he jumped out of the way. She flung a sock at his head and scored a hit.

"You're bad news, you are!" he exclaimed, and he kicked out at her chest. The water spilled, and White-Moth fell over and burst into tears. Then she got up and went back to her sister's house and refused to go back to the brickyard even after dark.

The brickyard was dreary without White-Moth, and Shifty quickly got fed up. He went off to Forest Wu's house. Forest Wu was grinding soybeans, the stone roller creaking and groaning as it turned. Pure white soy milk flowed out the bottom. Meanwhile, Black-Moth and White-Moth had tipped more beans from a bag into a basket and were picking out the stones.

When Shifty arrived and hung his straw hat on the door post, Forest Wu greeted him, "Ah . . . it's . . . it's you, Sh-Shifty. Have . . . have you ea-eaten?" White-Moth got to her feet and disappeared into the bedroom. Black-Moth followed.

"He's come to fetch me back," said White-Moth.

"You get yourself nicely dolled up," advised her sister. "Then go out and ignore him."

Shifty sat down on the doorstep. Forest Wu called out, "White-Moth, White-Moth, Sh-Shifty's h-here."

White-Moth emerged and pulled the door curtain back. She had her best clothes on, and Shifty smiled at her. She turned her back on him and carried on picking over the soybeans.

"What . . . what can w-we do for y-you, Shifty?" asked Forest Wu.

Shifty had had enough by then. "I've come for some tofu," he said. And he bought two *jin* and left.

That night, in bed at the brickyard, Shifty couldn't get comfortable. He ended up with the pillow under his feet. When day broke, he went back to Forest Wu's. Forest Wu was busy filtering soy milk into a pan, and the room was full of smoke from the cooking fire. "Shifty, h-have you eat-eaten?" he greeted him.

"Is White-Moth here?"

"White-Moth . . . White-Moth!" Forest Wu called toward the bedroom.

White-Moth knew perfectly well it was Shifty and didn't respond. Instead, she sat at the mirror, trying on a new top. A few minutes later, she came out in a short-sleeved jacket that showed off her white neck and arms. Still ignoring Shifty, she walked past him and went to light the stove. Shifty picked up a stick and poked her in the back with it, until Forest Wu looked around and asked, "Wh-what can I d-do for you, Sh-Shifty?"

"I've come for some tofu," he said. And he bought two *jin* and left.

That evening, when Shifty came back again, Forest Wu asked, "H-have you come b-back to buy m-more tofu? I-I n-never knew y-you liked it so m-much!"

"It's all I ever eat! All that tofu I bought, it's to entertain brickyard visitors. This lot's got to go through the accounts. I've written out a receipt; put your thumbprint on it, will you?" Forest Wu had to leave his mark because he couldn't read or write. He dipped his thumb into the tin of red ink Shifty had brought with him and pressed it firmly on the receipt, once, then again. Shifty pulled back the curtain to the bedroom, where White-Moth was sitting barefoot on the kang, eating pumpkin seeds.

She crossed one leg over the other. "Did you make him put his thumbprint on it?"

"Aren't you coming back to the brickyard?"

"I'm not Snow Bai. What would I do in the brickyard?"

Shifty puckered his lips in a kiss. White-Moth spat out a pumpkin husk that hit him in the face.

That was too much for Shifty. He went in, pushed the door closed behind him, pulled White-Moth into his arms, and covered her face with kisses.

Outside, Forest Wu called, "Shifty, come and see if these thumbprints are okay, will you?"

Reluctantly, Shifty went. "They're fine," he said, and retrieved the paper and the ink tin. "I'm off!" He picked up his two *jin* of tofu, glanced in through the door curtain, twitched it, and called again, "I'm off!" And finally left.

As soon as he'd gone, White-Moth came out. Forest Wu looked at the livid round mark on her cheek. "What happened to your face?"

"Nothing."

"You . . . you have a j-job in the br-brickyard, and when . . . when the b-boss turns up here, you don't even say h-hello."

"That's my business, not yours. And do you know what you just put your thumb-print on?"

"What?"

"Shifty's made a complaint against Pavilion, and you've just put your thumbprint to it. That means you're complaining, too."

Forest Wu looked horrified. "Why didn't you say . . . say s-something?"

Ashen faced, he stopped what he was doing and hurried off to Pavilion's.

Pavilion listened to Forest Wu's story. Things were looking serious, but he told Forest Wu, "There's no need to cry; I'm not blaming you. Just don't go talking about this to anyone else, right?" He sent Forest Wu off home and went to find Goodness and Lotus. They needed to discuss their next move.

The night passed quietly enough, and come daybreak, Goodness ordered Forest Wu and Bright Chen to go with him to the county forestry plantation to buy some redwood saplings. This was the first time Forest Wu had been given such a task by the village committee. He was happy, but he didn't want to go with Bright Chen, who talked too fast and bullied him, in his view.

"You hopeless man!" Black-Moth yelled at him. "Don't you know you get a top-up for going on a business trip? Besides, you'll have the bookkeeper with you. Why are you afraid of an outsider like Bright Chen?" Then she asked Goodness, "Will you be back this evening?"

"Probably not."

"So you're spending the night away?"

"You don't want him to be away even one night?" said Goodness.

"He's good at it," said Black-Moth.

"Huh? I've almost forgotten how to do it," said Forest Wu.

The three men went to catch their bus. As soon as Forest Wu had left, Black-Moth pegged out a checked sheet on the clothesline by her gate. Treasure saw it and set off for the brickyard with his cart to collect a load of bricks.

"Have you brought the money?" asked Shifty.

"I want this lot on credit."

"The brickyard owes for the electricity, and Marvel cut us off for half a day. I can't give you credit."

"Don't sound so unfriendly, brother."

"I'm not your brother. You're a Xia and I'm a Chen."

"Well, but we're brothers through those two girls."

Shifty looked around him. "You're bad! But you don't scare me. You're not such a model of virtue yourself."

"Forest Wu's gone on a business trip today. Will you be dropping by?"

"You mean, Forest Wu's not there?"

"Black-Moth hung the checkered sheet out."

"She fucking doesn't miss a trick!"

He gave Treasure a load of bricks, grumbling, "If you carry on like this, my brickyard won't have any bricks left."

"I don't know what I'm turning into. The King of Hell sticks his tongue out when a pimp dies!"

Toward evening, Shifty set off for Treasure's, carrying a bottle of liquor. He called out when he got to the gate, and Treasure told his wife he was off for a drink.

"We haven't brought the corn in yet. Why are you going out drinking?"

"I've been loading bricks and tiles all day. Why can't I have a drink?" And he went, leaving his wife to go to the field on her own.

First, Treasure and Shifty went to see if Forest Wu's neighbor Clerk was home. It so happened he was back early from the township offices. "What are you doing here?" he exclaimed.

"We're parched," said Treasure. "We need a drink and something to eat."

"I have some persimmon liquor at home," Clerk said. "Come and drink some with me." They followed him into the yard, but it turned out that he didn't have any left, so they had to drink what Shifty had brought. Clerk brought out a single saucer of pickled cabbage to go with it. "Got any fried eggs?" asked Shifty.

"No," said Clerk. "What a shame. If you'd come this morning, you could have had as many eggs as you wanted, but I sold them all at lunchtime. But the pickled cabbage is good. You don't get so drunk."

"Chilies are for getting hot and liquor is for getting drunk, and drunk is what I'm getting today," said Shifty. "White-Moth! Black-Moth!"

White-Moth did not respond, but Black-Moth called back through the wall, "Is that Shifty? What's up?"

"Treasure and I are drinking next door, but Clerk's only got pickled vegetables. Do you have any eggs?"

"No eggs," said Black-Moth. "But we have tofu."

After a bit she came over with a plate of freshly fried tofu. Clerk's wife and Black-Moth sat enjoying a good gossip, laughing and crying by turns, while the three men drank. Clerk loved to drink but couldn't handle much, and soon he was slurring his words. Still, Shifty pressed toasts on him until finally, when he couldn't swallow any more, his wife drank them for him. Before the bottle was finished, the couple were out, stone cold. Treasure and Shifty slipped next door. At first White-Moth didn't want to open the door to Shifty, but the window was ajar, so he pushed it open and climbed in. There on the kang lay White-Moth, stark naked, except for a cotton cloth covering her down there.

In the middle of the night, Goodness came back to Freshwind with Forest Wu and Bright Chen. As soon as they'd arrived in the county seat, Goodness called the forestry farm, but the saplings were too expensive, and the three men ate dinner in a restaurant and then took the night bus home again. First, they went to the village offices, where Pavilion and Lotus sat, watching TV. Goodness reported back, and Pavilion told him they wouldn't get their expenses paid because they hadn't bought the saplings. That upset Forest Wu—if he went home empty handed, Black-Moth wouldn't believe he hadn't been reimbursed.

"We can come with you and confirm you're telling the truth," Pavilion offered. They duly set off for East Street. They passed the brickyard on their way and shouted for Shifty, but there was no response. Then they passed Treasure's, where Chrysanth, just back from their field, said that Shifty had taken Treasure somewhere boozing. Pavilion shot Goodness a glance, and they headed straight for Forest Wu's. They found the front gate bolted, so Forest Wu climbed over the wall and opened it up. They could see a light on in the side house, but suddenly it went out.

"S-so now y-you put the light out when y-you hear me come home?" Forest Wu shouted. "Get . . . get out of bed!" He tried to open the side house door, but it was bolted, and no matter how hard he knocked, nobody opened it. Then he peered in through a crack in the wall below the window and came back to tell Pavilion, "Treasure's in there."

"What's he doing in your house?"

"W-w-what do you think he's d-d-doing, you fathead!" Bright Chen said. "He's f-f-fucking your wife, Forest Wu! Forest Wu and I have only been gone half a day, and meanwhile, the pair of them have been screwing their heads off!"

By now, Clerk and his wife had sobered up enough to come over and see what was going on. The door of the side house opened, and there stood Treasure and Black-Moth, disheveled and silent.

"Shifty's here, too, so where is he?" said Clerk's wife. "Now I get it. Those two came here to fuck the sisters, and they got us drunk first so we wouldn't hear anything."

Lotus Jin knocked on the door of the main house, and finally Shifty came out. "I must have drunk too much and got the wrong house on my way home. Well, so here we are. What d'you think we should do about it?"

Forest Wu was shaking with anger. He rushed at Black-Moth and smacked her across the face. It wasn't a very hard blow, and he was shaking too much to go on, so then he banged his own head against the wall.

"Now you're really l-letting the f-family name down!" Bright Chen shouted at him. "Wh-what are y-you doing th-that for?"

"Keep your voice down, Bright Chen," said Pavilion. "Isn't this bad enough already without you waking up the neighbors to come and get an eyeful? That's enough. No need to wash your dirty linen in public. Treasure and Shifty, get out of here, quick. Otherwise, the villagers will make a fuss 'cause Forest Wu hasn't beaten you up, and we'll have to put it before the Two Committees at the next meeting."

Treasure and Shifty were just slinking off when Goodness asked, "Is this public now or just a private matter?"

"You two! Wait a moment!" Pavilion shouted. Treasure and Shifty stopped. "This business is a public matter and private, too. Do you have any money on you? You can each give Forest Wu a hundred yuan of injury money."

Neither Treasure nor Shifty had any money on them.

"Then bring me the money tomorrow," said Pavilion, "and I'll give it to Forest Wu. And nothing that's happened here tonight goes any further, got that? Off you go, all of you."

The next day, Treasure gave Pavilion a hundred yuan. Shifty did the same and then asked, "Is that the end of it, Pavilion?"

"You paid up, so what else is there?"

"I don't know how to thank you for sorting this out," said Shifty. "I'm wild; you're the only one who can keep me under control. And I've done something else bad to you, too. I don't know if you know about it?"

"About what?"

"I put in a formal complaint about you."

"I don't think so," Pavilion said. "I fell out with Spark, not you."

"I complained that you swapped Seven Li Gully for the fishponds."

"Were you upset about that?" Pavilion said. "Wouldn't you be better off running them under contract from us?"

"I heard you were going to give the contract to Lotus."

"Who said that? You must have a screw loose. If I were going to replace you, wouldn't I talk to you first?"

Shifty pulled the written complaint from his pocket. "I'm such a dickhead to have complained about you, Pavilion. Do you want to read it?"

"What for?"

And without further ado, Shifty tore the document into smaller and smaller pieces until all that was left were fingernail-size scraps.

Chapter 25

When news spread that Forest Wu was being cuckolded, White-Moth had to stop working at the brickyard and stay home with her elder sister. But she also needed to earn her keep, and Forest Wu wasn't providing. White-Moth decided to head out with the shoulder pole and two buckets of tofu to sell. On the street, behind her back, the villagers called her a slut and tried to sneak a peek at her breasts. Someone came to ask about the tofu and, when she took the pole off her shoulders, pinched her ass. White-Moth said nothing. She took out the scale and weighed the tofu out for him.

He said, "Looks fine." He took the tofu and left.

White-Moth managed to sell out of tofu much faster than Forest Wu, so he decided he'd stay back and make tofu while she went out on his usual rounds.

That day, I was at the dyehouse watching Favor Bai brushing the donkey. As he was brushing, the donkey brayed and shook its head, and its penis shot out of its sheath. I looked up to see White-Moth standing in the doorway with her tofu.

"Oh, was it her?" Favor Bai said.

White-Moth asked if he wanted to buy tofu. He bought two *jin* of tofu from her.

Favor Bai took the tofu and asked her why she was selling it. White-Moth explained that she had to find some way to earn her keep. She said that if the dyehouse was looking for someone to do some work, she'd be willing. She was sick of her brother-in-law.

"What could you do here?" Favor Bai asked. "The outlet on that dye tank over there is blocked up. If you can open it up, I'd be happy to give you a job."

White-Moth set down her pole and went into the dyehouse. The tank was very large, and the liquid lapped over the edges. She rolled up her sleeves and reached down for the outlet, but she couldn't figure out how to unblock it. She leaned farther over the tank and yanked hard at something, almost sending herself splashing into the tank.

Favor Bai's wife came over from the cloth house and stood at the front door, watching White-Moth work. "Look how round her ass is," she said.

White-Moth kept working, trying to open the outlet, not making any sound. Finally, the blockage was cleared, and water began to run out of the tank. She straightened, her face red from exertion. She turned back to look at Favor Bai's wife and flashed a smile.

Favor Bai's wife said, "Come over here. There's something I want to ask you." White-Moth went over, still smiling. "Be straight with me, White-Moth. Did something happen with you and Shifty?"

White-Moth's smile faded, and she said in a quiet voice, "He raped me."

"He raped you? How many times?"

"Five or six."

"Then let me ask you, when he raped you, were your eyes open or closed?"

"Closed."

"Five or six times, huh? If you enjoyed it so much you had to shut your eyes, I don't call that rape. Get the hell out of here and don't come back!"

White-Moth stood for a moment, stunned. Tears began to run down her cheeks. She left the dyehouse.

White-Moth had done plenty wrong, but that was no way for Favor Bai's wife to treat her. I had always thought Favor Bai's wife was a good woman. I'd never imagined she could be that cruel. After that, I never went back to the dyehouse again, and I ignored her whenever I saw her in the street.

White-Moth was humiliated and decided to leave Freshwind. She went back to her family's place up in the mountains. But Shifty was Shifty. He heard some people chitchatting who stopped as soon as he came near. "Were you talking about me?"

"We heard you raped White-Moth."

"Yeah, so what? You know my wife can't give me a kid. If the land's no good, the farmer's gotta plant his seeds in another field."

When the villagers heard that, they thought, *This is a real man! Treasure doesn't even come close.*

Treasure refused to admit anything. Two days after the affair, when rumors started to spread, Chrysanth asked him what had happened. He was completely calm. "Some people are spreading stories."

"Out of everyone in Freshwind, why did they choose you?"

"I went from a farmer to a teacher, and now I'm on the government payroll. We just finished our new house. Everything is going well for us, so of course they're going to be jealous."

"I'm not going to try to argue with you. If you didn't sleep with Black-Moth, you won't have a problem giving me my share." She pulled him down to the kang.

Treasure couldn't get hard. He tried to force it, but it was hopeless.

"How can I believe you now?" Chrysanth pinched his dick between her fingers and said, "Is this all?"

They began to fight. It wasn't the first time, and Chrysanth had learned a thing or two. As soon as he squared up with her, she leaped like a cat toward his crotch and got a firm grip on his balls. Treasure grabbed her by the hair, and she tightened her grip until he fell back onto the kang, writhing in agony. When she saw that the fight had gone out of him, she picked up a shoe and hit him hard across the face. His cheek immediately swelled up big as a pig's bladder.

When she heard Chrysanth screeching like a stuck pig, Fourth Aunt came running over from next door. When she saw the door was closed, she called out, "Treasure! Treasure! You're gonna kill her!"

From inside the house, she heard Treasure saying, "I can't take it anymore. I want a divorce!"

Chrysanth took her chance to get away from her husband and ran from the room, a bed sheet wrapped around her lower half and her breasts swinging. "If you want a divorce, you can have it," she said. "You're going to end up killing me one of these days."

"What are you two talking about in there? I'll say this: you say something once, you'll never be able to stop saying it." There was silence from inside the house.

She was right. Once a couple starts talking about divorce, they usually don't just stop there. For the next few days, Chrysanth and Treasure kept arguing. The final solution was always divorce. There was no flour in the house, so Chrysanth mixed up a pot of barley and green beans and set it out on a mat to dry. As she worked, she kept cursing her husband. The curses came rough and mean at first, but then settled into a steady rhythm like a child reciting from a textbook.

Chrysanth got herself a bowl of sour broth and drank it, cursing between sips. Treasure was out in the yard, beating clay with a stone hammer. He carried the hammer inside. "You still running your mouth?"

"Fuck that Black-Moth. Her mother was a whore and so is she! She can eat her mother's cunt!" Chrysanth tried to shoo away a chicken that had come over to eat the barley and green beans, but it only came closer. She took off her shoe and threw it at the chicken. "The only thing you think about is fucking. Why don't you take that hammer and smash your dick? Take that thing and stick it in a rat's nest."

"Keep running your mouth. See what happens."

Chrysanth took a sip of sour broth. "I hope a flower grows out of your cunt, Black-Moth. You . . ." He raised the hammer, and she went silent for a moment. "Go ahead," she said. "Go ahead and crush me. Nobody would even care if a son of the mighty Xia family murdered lowly old me. Go ahead!"

"I want a divorce!" He brought the stone hammer down on the table and reduced it to a pile of lumber.

He went to find a sheet of paper to write a divorce contract. He came back and bit his middle finger to draw blood to make his print at the bottom. Treasure wanted Chrysanth to come with him to the village administration office to make it official.

"Fine, let's go!" She didn't want to show any weakness. As they went by Wisdom Xia's yard, she called out, "Fourth Aunt! Don't let the chickens eat my barley. I'm going to divorce your nephew."

Fourth Aunt ran out of the yard, ripped the contract out of Treasure's hand, and tore it up. "What the hell are you two doing?"

Chrysanth started sobbing and ran to Fourth Aunt.

They didn't manage to get divorced on their first try, so they tried again. On their second try, it was Bamboo who stopped them. Things continued to be icy between Treasure and his wife, and they fought often. The threat of divorce was always hanging in the air.

The Xia family stopped offering their lectures and concluded, "She's stubborn. The more you push her, the harder she pulls. Leave the situation alone and see if they really want to divorce." The next time they went to divorce, nobody stopped them. Fourth Aunt saw them passing by as she was working in the yard, tying a hempen rope to the gate's knocker. A group of people out in the lane watched a rooster and a hen fighting and let the couple walk past them without even looking up. It was only when somebody heard Chrysanth wailing and saw Treasure packing up his blanket and a pot to move to the new house that they knew the couple had finally ended it.

Treasure only spent a few days in the new house before Chastity saw Black-Moth go over with cabbage, onion, and garlic, picked from her field, to make *jiaozi* for him. Chastity went to tell Gold, who was digging a hole in the sand by the riverside.

He had already dug out plenty, so he decided to take a rest. He started a game of cards beside his plot, with Hearth and Halfwit. They were gambling for a few yuan a hand, but after Gold lost, he wouldn't pay up.

Hearth wasn't going to let it go. "You're making money, big brother. Don't hold out on us."

Chastity arrived right around then and wasn't happy with Hearth and Halfwit. "You think he's got money? He just bought clothes for your mother yesterday, and three *jin* of salt. You think he's holding out on you?"

"What are you telling them that for?" Hearth said.

"Why shouldn't I tell them? Your parents had five sons, not one. Your brothers are all building new houses now, and they're still worried about how much you're making?"

Hearth and Halfwit rose to leave. Halfwit looked back to say, "You still owe us, though. Get back to digging. You can come back here to farm after you retire. This is good land. Toss some beans in the dirt, and you'll have them to harvest soon enough. Bury some potatoes, and you'll get a good crop. Maybe if you plant some cash, you can grow a money tree for your wife."

After his brothers had left, Gold turned to his wife. "You didn't have to interfere with our game. I wasn't going to lose that much anyway."

"I thought you might be hungry, so I made you some *jianbing*. I didn't think you'd be out here gambling. You've been working out here for days now, and this is all you've done?"

"I don't have it in me. I could work my whole life, but if I can't get this plot of land in order, everyone will ridicule me. I'm not even going to bother."

She squatted beside him, seeing he was in a bad mood. "You were wasting your time at home. Your dad told you to find something to do. I didn't force you. You've had enough for the day. Come back in. Get back to it tomorrow. Did you know Black-Moth and Treasure are together?"

"Don't get involved with that."

"I think he planned to get divorced. I knew it as soon as I saw Black-Moth go over there to make *jiaozi*."

"Don't get involved. If you're worried that a pile of manure stinks, you don't go stir it up to find out."

Chastity managed to go the rest of the day without mentioning it, but she cracked the following day and told Fourth Aunt and Bamboo.

Justice Xia called Treasure over and asked him, "You want to marry Black-Moth?"

"Of course."

Justice Xia kicked Treasure and sent him sprawling in the dirt. "I thought you and that wife of yours were going to make up. You don't know what you're doing."

Treasure looked up at his father. He'd split his lip when he'd fallen, and he let the blood trickle down his chin as he spoke. "We're getting a divorce, and that's final. You know we are, don't you? It's almost every day now, bickering and fighting . . . Back in the old society, before Liberation, her family were all bandits. She comes from a long line of them—what do you expect from her? You think she's going to dutifully stay at home doing the mending? You think she's going to come over here and do the laundry?"

"You think Black-Moth is any better? Did she ever wash clothes for Forest Wu's mother? Was Black-Moth cooking for her? When she was stuck in bed during those last days, was Black-Moth there to bring her meals and take away her bedpan? Forest Wu is an honest man. If you want to know what happened, you can ask him. You think you can trust her now, but if she's with you, she's bound to do the same thing to you she did to Forest Wu."

"The difference is, I'm not Forest Wu. With me, she's met her match."

Justice Xia looked at his son, gave a deep sigh, and then took out a cigarette. As Treasure struck the match, Justice Xia pulled the cigarette from his lips and said, "You have a son and a daughter. Culture is a boy, so I'm not worried about him, but your Bodhi has been over here a few times already, crying her eyes out. She told me she's planning to leave. She's going to work in the city. Do you realize how much you hurt her? Let me put it this way: I know marriage isn't a walk in the park, so if you decide to end it, I can live with that. But forget about Black-Moth. How would it look if you married her now, after you already went around denying anything happened? How would our family look?"

"Like I said, nothing happened. But if we get married now, it will prove to everyone that we have real feelings for each other. What can anybody say about that?"

"Have you told her your plans? You definitely want to marry her?"

Treasure didn't answer. "Or is she trying to force you into something? If that's the case, I'll have your brothers go over and put a scare into her. If a dog gets a piece of turnip caught in its teeth, it has to shake it out, right? Is that what's going on here?"

"I was the first one to bring up marriage."

"So you really proposed." The words caught in Justice Xia's throat, and he found the cigarette again and pressed it to his lips. He tried to strike a match, but his hands were shaking.

"Father . . ."

Justice Xia tried to calm his anger. "You're over forty now," he said, "and I try my best not to interfere with your life. But I'm not dead yet. You might not care what other people think of you, but I care what they think of me. If you cuckold Forest Wu, there's no way he'll be able to live with himself. You take a man's wife and bring her into your home, you think that man is going to just let it go? In a village like this, you're bound to end up running into Forest Wu. He's not a class enemy . . ." Justice Xia paused and then asked, "Can Black-Moth even divorce him?"

"It's happening, whether he agrees or not."

"You're full of shit. You're the bandit, not that wife of yours. I pleaded with you, and you didn't listen to a word I said." Justice Xia wound up and sent his son to the dirt with another hard kick.

Treasure scrambled to his feet and started to leave.

His father called after him, "Get the hell out of here!" Then Justice Xia fell backward off the stool and lay there for a long time.

Things kicked off after that. Justice Xia didn't see Treasure for a couple of days; Black-Moth and Forest Wu started fighting over a divorce, Forest Wu promising her that the only way she'd be rid of him was if he died; almost every day, Treasure went over to the dike or down to the pit under Bowed Ox Ridge to meet with Black-Moth. To me, the whole thing was like an opera.

When I ran into Treasure, I sang to him in a Qinqiang melody.

> When you're gone, the sky isn't blue
> When you're not here, the days are long
> My nights are sleepless, without you
> Without you, everything feels so wrong

Treasure picked up a clod of dirt and cocked back his arm, but I kept singing.

> When can I hold you in my arms again
> My beloved . . . money!

I looked at the clod of dirt and said, "I said 'money.' Are you still going to throw that at me?"

Treasure laughed. "You're fucking in love with money now, huh?"

When I ran into Forest Wu, I decided to rile him up. "Just because your life is shit," I said to him, "doesn't mean you have to make Treasure suffer."

"Th-that's right. Even i-i-if my w-w-wife is no good, at least I-I-I've got one. If I d-d-divorce, I-I-I'll only have the edge of the kang to rub against all night."

I told Forest Wu he should pay a bit more attention to Black-Moth, and that's exactly what he did. After he was done working in the field, he went home and cooked for her, washed the laundry, and started sweeping and dusting. But Black-Moth wasn't paying much attention. She fell asleep with her clothes on, and when he came to lay beside her, she turned her back to him.

Black-Moth started to wash her neck with scented soap that she told Forest Wu was a gift from Treasure. She threw away her old shoes and started wearing a pair that Treasure had brought back for her from the county seat. She told him in no uncertain terms, "I'm going to stay with Treasure. I don't care if you divorce me or not."

Forest Wu came to me for advice. I told him that he had to go straight to Treasure. Even if he was going to eat shit, he shouldn't let someone crap down his throat, right? Go find Treasure Xia. Forest Wu wanted me to go with him, so I tagged along to the yard out front of Treasure's new house. I told him to go ahead, and he took a deep breath and went up to the door. When he saw Treasure sitting in the doorway, he lost his nerve and sneaked around to the back of the house. There was a freshly dug cesspit, and Forest Wu waited there until Treasure came out to shit in it, then he picked up a big rock and tossed it in the pit so that piss and shit splattered up onto Treasure. Before Treasure could pull up his pants, Forest Wu had already beaten his retreat. It pissed me off.

Forest Wu went looking for Justice Xia. He shut the door in Forest Wu's face. "Open up, Uncle Justice! I have something to tell you." Justice Xia ignored him until he left. Once he was gone, Justice Xia lost his temper and cursed his son.

Justice Xia wondered how it was possible that, just as he was fighting over the swap of Seven Li Gully for the township fishponds and worrying over Shifty's complaint, Treasure had decided to go off the rails. He looked across the pond at the layer of duckweed floating on it. The duckweed was bright green in the daytime but turned rusty brown each night. Culture and Tongue-Tied were digging up some persimmons that they had buried in the black mud along the bank of the pond. They passed one to Justice Xia, who took a bite and said, "These aren't even ripe yet. I want them sweet."

He looked down at the persimmon and saw that it was stained red. For a moment, he thought it was from the fruit, but when he spat it out, he saw that it was coming from his teeth.

Bamboo rushed over. "Father," she said, "you're eating persimmons?"

"Is the harvest on the flood land done yet?"

"Up along the north side, some of the crops are still there. Is your tooth okay?"

"It's fine. I know the guy that should have harvested them. I want you to go over to the far alley and tell his mother to call him back. He's working in the city right now, but the crops can't just rot in the ground."

"It'll have to wait until tonight. Pavilion called a meeting."

"The neighborhood heads have to go, too? What are you going to get out of a meeting like that?"

"I don't know."

Justice Xia suddenly realized that the village administration must have gotten involved with the gully-filling project and the fishponds. He told Bamboo, "You'd better go then." He went out into the courtyard, rolled a cigarette, and paced as he smoked it. He looked over to the pond where Culture and Tongue-Tied were swimming. Tongue-Tied could only dog paddle, and he stuck to the edge, splashing water across the yard. Tongue-Tied kicked hard and sent a splash of water at Justice Xia, extinguishing his cigarette.

When Justice Xia arrived at the administration office, it was just as he'd thought: the Two Committees were meeting to discuss the management of the fishponds. There were five regulations that the management would have to follow, as well as a requirement that they open a stall at the market to sell the fresh fish. It was unclear who would take on the project. Some proposed Shifty continue as the manager, but others pointed out that the reason the fishponds were being exchanged in the first place was because Shifty refused to pay the fees asked by the reservoir management. Pavilion decided to put it to a vote.

There were five nominees. When the votes were counted, Lotus Jin was chosen. Lotus Jin signed the contract. After the meeting was over, Bamboo didn't tell Justice Xia how things had turned out. Shifty held court outside Roughshod Ding's yard, cursing Lotus Jin.

I didn't sympathize with Shifty, but I also knew that Lotus Jin taking over would mean that the exchange of ponds with Seven Li Gully was a done deal. It was bound to be a disappointment to Justice Xia. I should have gone to give him the news myself, but I forget about it completely when I saw Snow Bai and Fourth Aunt going toward the farm store. I couldn't control myself, even if I knew I was letting down Justice Xia. As soon as I saw Snow Bai, I let out a yelp and startled Auntie Wang, who was standing beside me eating a steamed bun, so badly that she bit her tongue.

"She's back!"

"What's wrong with you?" Roughshod Ding said.

"Let me help you carry stones."

The second story of the restaurant that Roughshod Ding was building was already completed. There were stairs leading up to the top floor, but I shimmied up a scaffolding pole instead. I had a special method, sliding up it, working my hands and my feet, without ever touching my belly to the pole. When I got to the top I did a Monkey King pose, crooking my hand over my brow like Sun Wukong surveying the seas.

There were no seas to survey—I was looking over at the doorway to the farm store. Someone called up to me, "Hang upside down, Spark." I looked down to where Snow Bai and Fourth Aunt were standing, talking. Fourth Aunt had bought two bags of powdered milk. I knew the milk must be for Snow Bai. I couldn't be sure from where I stood that Snow Bai was really pregnant. She was still as slim as ever. They left and walked along the front of Roughshod

Ding's restaurant. Snow Bai looked up at the second story, and I locked my feet around the pole and leaned back into midair, hooting down at her. Some people below yelled up, "Nice job!" Idiots. I wasn't performing for any of them.

I worked on the building site for two hours without a break for food or water. It was getting dark when I left, and I saw Justice Xia with his glasses on, sitting in Clerk's wife's restaurant, eating a bowl of *liang fen*. Justice Xia must have already heard that Lotus Jin had taken over the fishponds, and the exchange for Seven Li Gully was a sure thing. I felt a bit bad about going up to him right then, so I slipped off into the shadows. I saw Justice Xia ordering another bowl. The loudspeaker in the gingko tree in front of Freshwind Temple crackled to life with the sound of local opera.

"What are they doing, playing opera right now?" Justice Xia said.

"Lotus Jin got them to play it," Clerk's wife replied. "She must be in a good mood."

"Give me another bowl," Justice Xia ordered in a gruff voice. From the loudspeaker came the sounds of "The Smoking Cave."

When Shifty came out of the blacksmith shop, he saw Justice Xia and tried to slip away, pressing his straw hat tighter on his head.

Justice Xia called him over and said, "You motherfucker, you try to sneak away when you see me?"

"I don't want to see anybody right now. I'm not in a good mood."

Justice Xia lifted the brim of Shifty's straw hat and said in a low voice, "How's that complaint going? It's been a while now, hasn't it?"

"I never filed it."

"You think this is a game? Why didn't you tell me you didn't file it? Your mouth is as tight as your ass, huh?"

"You know what happened with me and Treasure, right?"

Justice Xia nodded, but he asked about it anyway.

"I don't want to talk about it. What good does it do, bringing it up again?"

"Just tell me what happened. I'm listening."

Shifty told him how Forest Wu, Goodness, and Bright Chen had gone to the county market to buy saplings.

Justice Xia said, "Since when is the village government sending Forest Wu out on errands? And if you're buying saplings, you have to contact the farm beforehand, right? So, why did Goodness only start worrying about the price afterward? And if they went out there and didn't buy anything, then what did they bring Forest Wu along for?"

Shifty clapped a hand to his forehead. "You're saying they knew I was going to file a complaint? They were trying to trick me then?"

"I didn't say that."

"They must have been trying to lure me into something. Now they've got the upper hand. Why didn't they give me the fishponds, Uncle? Tell me. I've had my issues, but is Lotus Jin so innocent? This is too much to swallow. I'm going to file that complaint. We're going to settle this."

"My name's not going on it," Justice Xia said. "You do what you want." He went back to eating his *liang fen*.

Actually, I don't know whether or not Shifty filed the complaint against Pavilion. But I wanted to say something about the fishponds being looted that night. That was the second case of looting in the history of Freshwind. Three years prior, an oil tanker truck had flipped over on the 312. The driver ended up trapped in the cab of the truck with his leg busted. People started to arrive on the scene to help the driver out, but then even more people arrived to collect the oil in basins and jars to bring home. Eventually the crowd of villagers scooping up oil was too big, and even those who were helping the driver raced home to get something to put oil in. When all the spilled oil was gone, Shifty opened the valve on the truck's tank and started filling a bucket with what was left inside. The entire tank of oil was spirited away.

The fishponds were raided around three in the morning. It might have been Old Zhang from the blacksmith's shop who discovered it first. He was on his way back from visiting family in South Gully and was coming around the south end of West Street, close to the embankment along the ponds, when he heard a loud thud. He was scared and knelt beside the embankment. He heard a few more thumps, and then a splash of water came up from one of the ponds and soaked him. He looked up to see three people around the pond. They had rigged up explosives from old liquor bottles stuffed with gunpowder and topped with a blasting cap. Each time they tossed a bottle in, he could see the water boiling with the explosion. The three shapes around the pond gathered the stunned fish into a burlap sack. At first, Old Zhang thought it must have been Shifty, the bastard—passed over for the job of managing the ponds, so he came back to steal all the fish. But when he got a better look, he knew that none of them were Shifty. Old Zhang figured they must have been professional fish thieves. He called out, "Who's there?" The thieves tossed the sacks over their shoulders and started to scramble. One of the men stumbled as he went and dropped his sack.

Old Zhang yelled, "Thief! They're stealing the fish!"

Some villagers over on West Street who were still up playing mah-jongg and drinking heard the commotion and rushed over. They saw the dead fish floating on the surface of the ponds.

Someone from West Street said, "Evil is repaid with evil. They weren't our fish anyway, so who gives a fuck?"

"They didn't let Shifty run it," Old Zhang said, "and Lotus Jin hadn't taken over yet."

"Good fucking time to strike."

They started to leave, and then someone said, "If the thieves are going to take them, we might as well grab a few, too."

They went down to the ponds and started scooping out fish. Everyone managed to take a couple, at least. More people arrived and started fighting over the remaining fish on the banks of the ponds. Eventually, a few jumped into the water, splashing around. Other villagers rushed home and came back with baskets to fill. I couldn't sleep that night and went over when I heard the ponds being looted. I never really liked fish, actually—too many bones—but I was happy to see everyone grabbing them. I hated Shifty and I hated Lotus Jin, too, so I jumped in to grab my share.

I stripped off my pants, held the cuffs shut, filled them up with fish, and hung them around my neck. Right around then, I heard someone yelling that Shifty was coming. I ran away from the ponds, tossing a fish into each yard that I passed. When I got to Snow Bai's mom's yard, I tossed in three, then paused and tossed in another three. If Snow Bai was pregnant, some fish soup would be good for her. I tossed in the last four fish.

It turned out that Shifty wasn't actually coming—it was Lotus Jin who got the news first. All the villagers scattered, and she was left alone on the banks of the pond, crying her eyes out.

When the police came out to investigate the robbery, they came up empty handed. Lotus Jin suspected Shifty, but he flatly denied it. He said he'd been at Roughshod Ding's place that night, playing mah-jongg. Roughshod Ding testified that Shifty was in fact there that night, but it was harder to prove that he'd had nothing to do with the theft. Pavilion decided to have Goodness look into the situation. He went through West Street, but it was hard to cast suspicion on anyone in particular since everyone had stolen fish from the ponds. Collective punishment wouldn't work, of course. The investigation was quietly dropped.

Pavilion didn't want news of the looting to spread. He was worried people would look down on Freshwind. The villagers didn't agree with him, though. They admitted that the looting of the tanker hadn't been their finest moment, but the fishpond—that was their fish in the first place, since the ponds were village property. Whether Shifty or Lotus Jin took over, they'd make out okay themselves, but looting the ponds satisfied everyone.

People in Freshwind never ate fish heads or fish maw, so small piles of heads and guts and scales appeared in every alley on West Street. The sun glinted off the scattered scales and roasted the guts, filling the village with the smell of fish and bringing hordes of blowflies.

Snow Bai's mother was happy when she found the ten fish out in her yard. She kept four for herself and brought six over to her daughter on East Street. Snow Bai went to gut the fish, not knowing where they'd come from. She ran into Justice Xia and Gold on the way—they were carrying loads of dirt up to their plot of land. Snow Bai offered the fish to Justice Xia, telling him that her mother had brought them over.

"So," he said, "she got involved, too, did she?" She wasn't sure what he was talking about and motioned for him to take the fish. "I'm not eating those fish," he said.

Gold told her about the ponds being looted. Snow Bai gasped and blushed. "There's no reason not to eat them, though, is there?"

Gold said, "If he doesn't want them, I'll take them."

He took the fish. Snow Bai turned to Justice Xia and saw that his jacket was soaked through with sweat. She told him to take it off so that she could wash it. He took the jacket off without speaking and handed it to her. He scratched his back against a tree. As far as he could remember, it was the first time any of the brides of the Xia sons had offered to wash his clothes—a simple act, but one that showed a sense of filial duty to their husbands' families. As he watched her wash the garment in the river, Justice Xia was moved. He leaned back and belched.

"Is everything okay, Second Uncle?" she asked.

"It's fine. Always start burping like this when the wind picks up. If I go down to the river and take a big drink, it usually sets it right again. Now, I haven't seen you in a while . . . You were in Xijing, huh?"

"I was in the county seat with the troupe; then we went down to the countryside for our tour. I couldn't find the time to go to the city."

"How has Wind Xia been? Is he writing another book?"

"He's working on one right now. It'll probably be published next spring."

Justice Xia sighed happily and then ripped a belch. He was lost in thought, thinking back to a long time before, when Wind Xia was young. He was still in open-crotch pants back then, with his hair parted down the middle in two waves that looked like garlic sprouts. Justice Xia told Snow Bai that, as young as he was, he came home each day with lumps of charcoal and wrote all over the house, on the walls, on the counter, on the table . . .

She beat the laundry as she listened. She asked him, "I heard that a fortune-teller told you that the Xia family was going to produce a famous man."

301

"You heard about that?"

"Wind Xia told me. I thought he was making it up."

"He wasn't. That day, I was sitting out front of the house, eating, when a fortune-teller came down the road. He pointed up at the elm tree and said it was growing well. He predicted that the family would produce a famous man. My wife asked him if he meant a village head. The fortune-teller said he'd be more important than a village head. I thought he meant your father—he wasn't your father yet, at the time . . . He was still teaching in the school then, but he loved singing opera. He got the other teachers together to put on a production of *Three Drops of Blood*. He played the magistrate. Always the magistrate, even though he only ever got to be an elementary school principal in his own life. But when Wind Xia ended up in the city, I knew the fortune-teller must have meant him."

Snow Bai chuckled. "You think he's more powerful than a village head?"

"It might not be official, but he's connected. You see how it is when he comes back to the village. Even the county heads come down to see him."

"That's the way you see him? His own family spoiled him too much. It wasn't good for him." She looked down at the basin, then reached in to get the wooden stick to continue beating the laundry, but instead of the stick she pulled out a snake. She dropped it and fell backward.

Justice Xia was just as surprised as Snow Bai. He ran over from the tree, picked up a branch, and poked at the head of the snake. When the snake was distracted, he reached down and picked it up by the tail. He cracked the snake like a whip, and it hung limp and dead in his hand. Justice Xia tossed the snake into some rocks along the river.

Snow Bai went looking for the wooden stick again. She couldn't find it. She looked back at Justice Xia and said, "Just opera, that's all it was. If my father had really been a bureaucrat or a magistrate, then maybe Wind Xia wouldn't look down on opera."

"Wind Xia doesn't like opera?"

"He says it's outdated. He says it's only for farmers."

"Outdated? Only for farmers? Horseshit! He's forgotten his roots."

"Father," Gold said.

"I've said my piece. He's only done good things for his family and the village. He didn't forget about his uncle. Every time he comes back, he brings me two *jin* of Sichuan tobacco."

That made Snow Bai giggle to herself.

Then something caught her attention on the small stone bridge. She looked up to see Bamboo, who had run into someone she knew from West Mountain Bend and was talking to her excitedly. "I never see you around here anymore. Everything's been good with you?"

"Fine, fine."

"And the kids?"

"Fine, fine."

Bamboo led the woman across the bridge and then caught sight of Justice Xia, Gold, and Snow Bai down by the river. She raced over and went right to Snow Bai. "How have you been? Look at all this laundry! And look at this guy, scratching around in the dirt like a hen."

"What's so funny about that?" asked Gold. "You should take a long look at yourself first. Look at who's washing your father-in-law's jacket. All of his five daughters-in-law combined aren't as good as Snow Bai."

"It's just a jacket," Snow Bai protested. "It's nothing."

"No, no. You're setting an example for us. Tomorrow morning, I'll go get Chastity and we'll do some laundry for them." She turned to Justice Xia and asked, "Did you file a complaint?"

Justice Xia had been watching them while dozing against the tree, but his eyes suddenly opened wide. "What?"

"I just went to the Two Committees meeting, and they settled the thing with Seven Li Gully and the fishponds."

"They should have done it sooner," said Justice Xia.

"So, you *were* the one behind the complaint . . . ," said Bamboo.

"That's right."

"Why didn't you say something before they signed the contract? You went to complain after everything was settled. Pavilion is furious and everyone is annoyed."

"You're saying I wasn't justified?"

"You're upsetting everyone," said Bamboo. "And did you ever deal with the floodplain?"

"What do you mean?"

"At the meeting," said Bamboo, "some people were saying we were dealing with things out of our jurisdiction, but the village administration gave the order, and we have to follow it. Anyway, there aren't any fish left in the ponds. The head of the Middle Street Residential Committee said that whoever made the complaint should fuck off to Seven Li Gully and die! He means you, doesn't he? I was going to lay into him, but Lotus Jin said—"

"You think that guy cursing me is going to do anything? Anyway," Justice Xia said, chuckling, "he's not wrong. My grave is already prepared over there." He stuck a cigarette in his lips and passed one to Gold.

Justice Xia had never passed him a cigarette before, and Gold could only stare at it. "Come on. This is good smoke." Gold reached for the cigarette and put it to his lips. "I was thinking," Justice Xia went on, "if you want some soil, we should go out to Seven Li Gully."

"Might as well just stay here, instead of heading out there to feed the wolves. Farming the land is more complicated than my job. You shouldn't be getting involved with this; you should be over playing mah-jongg with all the other old folks."

"Now I see why your work unit got you to retire early." He picked up his jacket from where it was drying on a rock. It was still damp, so he slung it over his shoulder. If he'd looked back, he would have seen Gold's face flushed red as a pig's liver.

"He thinks I retired early?" Gold asked Snow Bai. "I left so that Shiner could get in there."

Snow Bai looked up after washing the laundry and saw in the sky three streaks of red cloud and three streaks of black cloud. They were as vivid as greasepaint. She looked down at the ground, and at the trail her heels had left in the soft ground of the riverside. She remembered then the wooden stick that had turned into a snake, and her fear returned. She ran all the way home.

Fourth Aunt was out in the yard working on putting stakes in to support the peony branches. Wisdom Xia had gotten tired of painting his masks and was switching the couplet in the main room again. He settled on a scroll reading, "The flowers attend the woman / The book is the ancient teacher." He sat down and readied a cup of tea and began to sing.

Snow Bai gave the fish back to her mother-in-law and told her where it had come from.

"How was I to know?" Fourth Aunt said. "We live so far from the fishponds. If we lived any closer, I would have gone over and gotten some for myself."

"Does he know?" Snow Bai asked calmly, motioning to the main room.

"He said he doesn't want any. He said it stinks worse of thieves than it does of fish. That's fine with me, but if he tries to take some, I'll make sure he stands by his word." The two women laughed.

Snow Bai tried to bring up what Bamboo had said about the meeting, but Fourth Aunt brushed her off. From the main room, Wisdom Xia listened. He smiled to himself and then ripped a loud fart. Fourth Aunt peeked around the corner and narrowed her eyes at him. "You . . ."

"It's unhealthy to hold it in."

In the kitchen, Snow Bai grinned to herself as she sliced the fish and began chopping green onions and ginger.

"Did you know Justice Xia filed a complaint?" Fourth Aunt asked.

"About what?" Wisdom Xia asked.

"He didn't want the fishponds being swapped," Fourth Aunt said. "Someone was cursing him out at the Two Committees meeting." Wisdom Xia grunted, and the smile on his face froze. "You should go talk to him," she said. "At his age, he should be spending his time differently. The things people are saying about him . . ."

"If we force him to stay at home, it'll kill him," Wisdom Xia said. The old couple fell into silence.

From the kitchen, Snow Bai called, "Where's the clay pot?"

"Enough," she said to her husband. "Like the saying goes, if you've got fur, you run on the ground, and if you've got feathers, you fly in the sky. You go try to convince him, if you want. But you know how he is, getting involved with everything. There's no way for his sons to control him even. And don't get me started on the women those sons of his married. None of them are any good compared to Snow Bai."

"Once a phoenix is up in the *wutong* tree, it's hard to knock it down."

"Did you plant a *wutong*? You go back to painting your masks."

"It's because of these opera masks that we've got a singer in our family now. I'm telling you, when Rain Xia goes looking for a wife, he has to find one with a set of pipes on her. She has to be able to sing the local opera."

"Then I'll find me a wife who paints her face." It was Rain Xia, coming in from outside. He was soaked in sweat and immediately stripped off his jacket. He stood in front of the electric fan and let it blow over his belly.

"Don't try to cool yourself off like that," his mother said and pointed the fan away from him. "It's not good for your health."

"Look at this son of mine," Wisdom Xia said, suddenly serious.

"I just accomplished something big!"

"Oh yeah? What is it now? You rolled yourself up in your blanket and floated up to heaven?"

Snow Bai came out with a ladle of sour broth for her brother-in-law. As he was about to speak, she stuck the ladle to his lips, and he sucked it down. "I heard you opened a restaurant," she said.

"Once everything is set up, you're welcome to come by as often as you like."

"Don't listen to his boasting," Rain Xia's mother cautioned. "We'll see the sun rise in the west before he turns respectable."

"I'm not boasting. If I can't convince my own family, what hope do I have of getting any customers? Justice Xia worked his whole life, and that house he built ended up looking like a chicken coop. Pavilion is a capable man, but I can't stand what he did—he tried to turn his chicken coop into a house. Our restaurant is two stories already, and we're about to put the roof on it. I just came back from getting the interior decorations, and tomorrow I'm going to get the plates and utensils. You're only ever worried about my older brother. You never thought I'd amount to anything."

"I'll have to pay more attention to you after this," said Snow Bai, laughing. "We've got a tycoon in our family now."

Wisdom Xia frowned and headed to his room to continue painting.

"No need," said Rain Xia. "I'm the one who should be paying more attention to you. I have a favor to ask. I was wondering if maybe all of you could perform at the grand opening. Of course, there'll something in it for you, too."

"Who, though? Didn't you hear? The head of the troupe changed again."

"Isn't it still Mid-Star? He just took that position, didn't he?"

"As soon as he took over, he lit a fire under the troupe. He wanted to get people interested in the local opera again. We went out on tour, and as soon as we got back, they came and awarded us a silk banner. But they ended up promoting him to head up the County Party Committee's Publicity Department. Things fell apart after he left. The original company ended up splitting into three separate troupes. There's no way they could mount a big performance, the way things are now."

"It doesn't have to be a big performance then," Rain Xia said. "We'll get a few singers and have a small concert. The last performance, the village paid for it, and we just had the one show. What I have in mind is three separate concerts. I can pay each performer three hundred yuan."

"Three hundred a person?" Fourth Aunt asked. "That restaurant is going to be a money pit, the way you're spending."

"You have to spend money to make money," Rain Xia said.

"You have to have some money in the first place, though," Fourth Aunt said. "The restaurant hasn't made anything yet."

"You wouldn't understand, Mother."

"I'll get in touch with some people," Snow Bai said.

"You just ignore him," Fourth Aunt said. "You really think he can pay three hundred yuan? When they show up and he hasn't got the money, you'll be left holding the bag."

Before Snow Bai could answer, she was hit with a wave of nausea. She covered her mouth and ran for the bathroom.

When dinner was ready, Fourth Aunt sat in front of the stove and watched Snow Bai fill her bowl and then splash vinegar and chilies on top. Snow Bai went off to her room to eat. Fourth Aunt waited a long time for her daughter-in-law to return for another bowl, but she never came. She went looking for Snow Bai and found her sprawled on the bed with a pool of saliva on the floor below her. She asked, "Are you okay?"

"Fine."

"It's been a couple of times now that you've suddenly gotten nauseous. Are you pregnant?"

Snow Bai rolled off the bed and shut the door. In a whisper she said, "Yes."

"Unbelievable!" Fourth Aunt shouted. "Father! Father!"

Wisdom Xia came running, but Fourth Aunt pushed him out of the room, saying, "It's fine. You get out." She took Snow Bai into her arms and asked her how long it had been.

"Almost two months," Snow Bai said.

"Does Wind Xia know?" Fourth Aunt asked.

"I haven't told him yet."

"Have you told your mother?"

"I told her a couple of days ago," Snow Bai said.

"Then why didn't you tell me?" Fourth Aunt demanded.

"I thought I'd tell you before I left."

"Why not give me a few extra days to enjoy the good news?" Fourth Aunt asked.

"I just thought . . ."

"You kept it a secret for so long," Fourth Aunt said. "You're a tough girl. Look at how hard you've been working, washing clothes and carrying water. All that trouble for us!"

"I thought that's how you'd react," Snow Bai said, "but I'm fine."

"You just stay in here and rest," Fourth Aunt said. "You don't have to do any more work around the house. Just tell me, and I'll take care of it."

"You want me to boss you around?" Snow Bai asked.

"If that's what you want to think." She took Snow Bai's bowl and went back to the kitchen to fill it again.

When Fourth Aunt came back from Snow Bai's room, Wisdom Xia called her out into the yard. "What are you doing running food for her?" he asked. "You're going to end up spoon-feeding her, if you spoil her like that."

"What the hell do you know? She's eating for two now."

"Really?"

"I'm telling you . . . Now, I don't want you fighting with me anymore, no moping around, and don't do anything to upset her. I don't want you calling people around to smoke and drink here, either."

"I don't have to drink here, but you're not going to stop me from smoking."

"You can't give it up, can you? Take your pipe into the kitchen, if you have to smoke."

Snow Bai was eavesdropping from her room, and she giggled to herself.

Snow Bai had originally planned to take advantage of the troupe's disarray to sneak in a trip to Xijing, but Fourth Aunt told her there was no way she was going to let her daughter-in-law ride a bus while pregnant. It would wear her down, Fourth Aunt said, and the baby. There was another reason, too: if she went to the capital, the couple might have sex, which wouldn't be good for the baby. Snow Bai listened to her mother-in-law. She didn't go to the capital. She called Wind Xia and told him that she was pregnant. Snow Bai imagined Wind Xia whooping and shouting when she told him, making kissy sounds into the phone, but the truth was far from that. He told her to get rid of the baby.

She couldn't believe her own ears. "What did you say?"

"Get rid of it. You have to get rid of it!"

She lost her temper. "Why wouldn't I keep it? You think it's not yours?"

His tone softened. "That's not what I meant. It's just not the right time." He'd gotten her a new job, and he worried about what her new work unit would think when they found out their new hire was a pregnant woman. Even after she gave birth, she'd be breastfeeding for two or three years. It would be at least that long before she could return to work.

"I never agreed to work there."

"You think I got married just to have us split up?"

The call ended with Wind Xia hanging up and Snow Bai in tears. After she told her mother-in-law what had happened, she called her son and told him there was no chance Snow Bai was going to abort the child, and no chance that she'd go to see him in the capital. She shouted down the line at her son, "You get back here! Get back here right now!" But Wind Xia did not return to the village.

For me, it was another two days without sleeping—all because I'd seen Snow Bai. Whenever I ran into her, I couldn't rest. My mouth started watering and I couldn't stop swallowing. I got this feeling like there was a blast of heat coming up from the bottoms of my feet, up through my legs to my belly. My belly would swell up, and the heat would spread up through my palms to my forehead. When Star Chen saw me, he shouted that I looked like a pork liver. He said he'd been to see an execution once and that I looked just like the accused about to face the firing squad. The criminal had taken the first round and fallen to the ground, still pumping blood into the dirt. They'd had to put a second bullet into him to kill him.

I told Star Chen to quit messing with me, but I could feel my blood pumping harder than it usually did. If my brain looked anything like the inside of a watch, and you could have cracked it open, the gears would have been whirring as fast as a wasp beats its wings.

Now, if you remember, that time when Snow Bai came to Freshwind, I saw her for the first time at Roughshod Ding's gate, then alongside the river—and you remember when she lost the wooden stick? That was actually my fault. I was hiding under a willow tree downstream and I said, "Bring on a big rain! Let a big rainfall come and wash Snow Bai down the river to me. If you can't bring me Snow Bai, at least send some clothing floating down to me." I repeated it like a prayer. I thought about the bra I had stolen that day and felt a shiver of fear. I changed the incantation. "Bring me the stick!"

The river didn't quicken or swell, but the wooden stick slipped from her hand and fell into the water. I snapped it up. I looked down into the river and tried to figure out which drop of water might have touched Snow Bai. The whole river seemed to reflect her back at me. I dipped my hands into the water and drank a mouthful of river water. I kept drinking until I saw Snow Bai leave the riverside. I tucked the wooden stick into my waist and went home. After that, I was awake for two days and two nights.

The truth is that the wooden stick was keeping me awake. I lay on my kang, hugging it to myself. I stuffed it down the front of my pants and let it prop them up like a tent. The length and the thickness was just about right . . . I started to sing to myself. The thing about the local opera is, if you're in a good mood, the more you sing, the better you'll feel, but if you're in a bad mood, the more you sing it, the worse you'll feel.

I sang a bit from *The Sacrificial Lamp*:

> For my kingdom, I have fought battles on every front.
> For my kingdom, I have launched six campaigns from Mount Qi.
> For my kingdom, I sacrificed much in the Western Lands.
> I spilled blood and sweated and toiled.

Once I'd sang that much, I felt like singing some more. I sang my heart out, beating out a rhythm on the edge of the kang. I beat out a long, slow pattern of four beats.

And then I beat a rhythm of four soft strokes.

I beat a rhythm of four hard strokes.

I kept beating out the Qinqiang rhythms, "reverse four beats," "four head beats," "the big plate," each pattern pounded out with more force than the last. The whole time, I was howling along with the rhythm. Then I pounded out the "string of bells" pattern.

It was right then that Doubleday Yang came from next door and started pounding on my gate as hard as he could, shouting, "Spark! Spark! Are you ever going to let us get to sleep?" He peered in and watched me beating the edge of the kang, but I just ignored him. That's when he decided to try kicking down my gate. "If you keep it up," he shouted, "I'll burn you out!"

I thought he was only trying to frighten me, but the motherfucker lit a pile of barley straw. Black smoke started billowing up out of my yard, and flames lit up the sky. A few of my neighbors came over to fight the fire.

Once they got the fire out, I heard somebody say, "If it had gotten out of control, you might have killed Spark." But I was still lying on the kang. I had stopped drumming, and the wooden stick was still propping up my pants.

Doubleday Yang jumped over the wall into my yard and came into my room. He'd put a scare into himself with that fire, but it hadn't bothered me much at all. I knew that barley straw wasn't going to burn long enough to catch the house on fire. I knew the neighbors would come along to put it out.

As soon as he saw that I was okay, Doubleday Yang started cursing me out again. I told him, "You started a fire!"

"What? I came to save you. Why would you say I started a fire?"

Nobody believed that he'd set the fire since they'd arrived to find him trying to put it out. His eyebrows had been scorched off in the process. As he went out of my room, he called to someone in the crowd, "Who says Spark is lacking? You should see what he's got in his pants!"

Some people tried to get a better view, and someone asked if I'd somehow grown my cock back. I didn't say yes, and I didn't say no.

Around that time, there was a murder on Middle Street. That was the first murder in the history of Freshwind. Now, if you had to guess, you might speculate that it was the hotheaded Shifty, or maybe Forest Wu looking for revenge, but it was actually Clear-Spring Qu. I don't even want to bring him up. He's on the same level as Dog-Scraps, a disgrace to the village. But if I don't say something about him, you won't be able to follow the rest of this story. That's how stories are, all joined together, like links in a chain. If a tree suddenly withers, it usually means there was something wrong with the leaves.

Clear-Spring Qu's next-door neighbor was Lotus Jin's uncle on her father's side, River Jin. River Jin's wife was really upset because of the way Clear-Spring Qu's cat yowled when it was in heat. The two households fought almost every day. They'd gone to Pavilion and Goodness for help, but neither man could offer a solution, and the quarrel continued. Clear-Spring Qu ended up building a new house over by the east side of the opera theater. He kept the land beside his old house, where there was a cow pen and a garden. The cow pen was empty, but he was still growing onions and garlic in the garden. River Jin wanted to put a pigsty out in front of the cow pen, but Clear-Spring Qu refused. The two families began fighting again. In one scuffle, River Jin threw a handful of quicklime into Clear-Spring Qu's eyes.

The garden ended up being dug up several times, causing more trouble. Clear-Spring Qu's wife got injured in one of the fights, and he dragged her in a cart to Big-Noise Zhao's place, where she was put on an IV. River Jin showed up shortly after to cause trouble, claiming that Clear-Spring Qu's wife was faking her injury to get him in trouble. He told Big-Noise Zhao to disconnect the IV. He grabbed the blanket that Clear-Spring Qu had wrapped her in and tossed it into the street. Clear-Spring Qu went off to the village office to find Pavilion or Goodness. They weren't there, but he found Lotus Jin, eating fried eggs that she'd cooked over the office's kerosene stove. He made his complaint to her, but she said, "There's nothing I can do for you."

"You want your uncle to beat me up?"

"Fine with me," she said angrily.

Clear-Spring Qu went back to Big-Noise Zhao's and took his wife home in his cart. He looked after her at home, and after a month she had recovered completely and got a job as a cook, working in the city with Excellent Li's construction team. She told her husband to get a job in the city, too, but he wasn't willing. "If we both leave, they'll build that pigsty, right as soon as we're gone." He refused to leave. There was another argument over the garden, and this time Wisdom Xia came over to mediate.

Everyone thought that Wisdom Xia would be able to solve things once and for all. When he showed up, the argument ended, and Wisdom Xia went away looking very proud of himself. He was heard to say, "All these years and nobody's been able to get this sorted out, including the village cadres. It's a joke." But the murder occurred within a couple of days.

I was walking out front of River Jin's yard that morning when I heard someone crying. I saw River Jin's mother was sitting by the gate. She called to me, "Go get my son. His wife's in trouble." I saw Clear-Spring Qu standing in the garden, not far from their gate, holding an ax with blood dripping from its head.

"Where's your son?"

"Down by the river. Go get him!"

I picked up a heavy branch from the ground and called over to the garden: "Put down that ax, Clear-Spring!"

Clear-Spring Qu staggered as if drunk, but his eyes gleamed with murderous intent. "Spark," he said, "don't come over here. Take another step and I'll hack you to pieces."

He repeated it three times.

I took off running to the police station and came back to find Clear-Spring Qu gone and River Jin's wife collapsed in the main room of her husband's house with blood all over her face. I felt her neck for a pulse, but she was already gone.

The neighbors had gathered, and we went looking for Clear-Spring Qu. He wasn't at his new house, but written on the wall in charcoal was a message. "You promised Fourth Uncle that you wouldn't bother me anymore. Why did you cut down my family's tree? If you don't want me to live, I'll take all of you with me." Under the message, we found an empty bottle of pesticide. We went through the village looking for Clear-Spring Qu, but he was nowhere to be found. We circled back to River Jin's place. We noticed that the elm tree beside the cow pen had had its branches lopped off where they stretched beyond the boundaries of Clear-Spring Qu's land. We found Clear-Spring Qu's body leaned up against the tree. The pesticide hadn't been enough to kill him, and he'd cut his own throat with his ax. The ground around him was covered in blood and vomit.

Of course, this was an easy enough case for the police to solve, and the murderer was already dead. A file was drawn up by the Public Security Bureau and immediately closed. But the village cadres criticized the Two Committees for failing to act. The Two Committees agreed to buy a coffin for River Jin's wife. But since Clear-Spring Qu's wife was working out of the village, and his family didn't have any money to buy him a coffin, his body was still sitting in his home where they had laid it out. Some villagers from Middle Street asked the Two Committees to help buy him a coffin as well. After a brief meeting, they decided to buy Clear-Spring Qu's coffin. It wasn't very good quality, of course, fitted together roughly and not painted.

"Does he deserve better than that?" Pavilion asked.

That day, he went with Goodness and Lotus Jin to Guofenglou Township to see how they'd set up their market street. But Wisdom Xia couldn't let it go. He'd been the last one to try to mediate the dispute that had cost two people their lives. He felt as if it was an insult to his reputation. He refused to leave his house. Even when the head of Middle Street came looking for him to help set the date for the funerals, he stayed locked up behind his gate. The street committee head yelled for him to come out but got no answer.

On the day Clear-Spring Qu was buried, ten stone-faced people carried his plain wood coffin. None of them wore the hemp mourning robes and none of them wept. Ten minutes after they'd set out, his coffin was laid to rest, and his funeral mound joined the others at the base of Bowed Ox Ridge. The villagers stood along the road and looked over at the base of the ridge. They still couldn't figure it out—Clear-Spring Qu didn't like to kill his chickens. How could he have gone and killed one of his neighbors?

"Everyone said he was honest, and he kept his word, didn't he?" Shifty said.

That brought to Shifty's mind a story about Clear-Spring Qu and him. They'd gone together one time to the county seat. They had a couple of meals, and when it came time to pay for the first meal, Shifty went to pay and so did Clear-Spring Qu. Clear-Spring Qu put his right hand over his left hand and forced it into his pocket. What was the point of that? In the end, Shifty paid. The second meal, Clear-Spring Qu didn't want to pay, either, so they decided to take two empty bowls up to the counter and get two bowls of noodle-boiling water to wash down the black buns they'd brought in themselves. It was Clear-Spring Qu who had the idea to grab two bowls off the table once another customer left. That was another clever idea from Clear-Spring Qu. Shifty was completely wrapped up in the story, but I couldn't take it.

"He's dead," I said. "What are you in such a good mood for?"

"Why not? He's better off."

"You're heartless. What did he ever do to you?"

"If it wasn't for him, Lotus Jin's aunt would still be alive." He hated Lotus Jin.

I walked away from him and stood with another group, but Shifty came after me, saying, "That big-character poster you wrote isn't bad, Spark."

"It was a small-character poster."

"The calligraphy on it looks good. The villagers of Freshwind thank you."

"You're the only one who noticed."

"So what? Let me buy you a drink!" I decided to ignore him, and he suddenly broke into a honking laugh. I stared back at him, and he gestured behind me. "Look at Fourth Uncle. He hasn't got his copper pipe."

I looked back and saw Wisdom Xia looking stone faced up at the ridge.

"Clear-Spring Qu's ghost is going to haunt him," said Shifty. "If he hadn't gotten involved, nobody would have died."

Fourth Aunt and Snow Bai came down the alley from East Street, through the archway, and paused as if they were about to talk to Wisdom Xia, but he waved them off. He stood there for a moment and then squatted down with his head buried in his hands. When I saw Fourth Aunt and Snow Bai coming toward me and Shifty, I wanted to say something, but I knew I couldn't.

It was Shifty who spoke first. "What are you two up to?"

Fourth Aunt answered that Snow Bai was on her way to the county opera troupe's offices.

Was Snow Bai leaving again? My head started to buzz. I saw the road in front of me stretching upward until it rose vertically in front of me. The people who were on the road floated and spun in midair. I fell to the ground.

As I fell, my spirit floated up out of my body and took a seat up on an electrical pole. I looked down and saw myself, lying on the ground like a dead hog. My eyes had rolled up in my head, and there was spit bubbling up at the corners of my mouth.

Shifty said, "Spark must've run into Clear-Spring's ghost."

Fucking bullshit, is what that was. Some people came around to pat my face and pinch my upper lip, trying to wake me up. Eventually, they carried me off to Big-Noise Zhao at the Great Qing Hall. When I opened my eyes again at the Great Qing Hall, I looked around for Fourth Aunt and Snow Bai, but they weren't there. I started to wail. The villagers who had carried me over kept saying it must be Clear-Spring Qu's ghost, still haunting me.

One of them took a strip of peach wood and started slapping me with it, shouting, "Get out of there, Clear-Spring! Spark didn't do anything to you. Go bother Lotus Jin or Pavilion."

I tried to struggle to my feet and get away, but Big-Noise Zhao pressed me back down, saying, "He's lost it again. He's crazy." He deftly slipped a needle into me and injected a sedative.

I spent the rest of the day on my kang. For the next two days, I was paralyzed in that position, unable to move. It felt as if the marrow had been taken out of my bones. At the same time, Wisdom Xia was at home, too, with no appetite and racked by insomnia. People came by to plead with him to forget about what had happened with Clear-Spring Qu. Roughshod Ding stopped by my place to ask me to go with him to talk to Wisdom Xia, but I refused. All I cared about was Roughshod Ding's restaurant. Once it opened, Snow Bai would come back to Freshwind for sure.

Once the restaurant's opening day was set, Rain Xia took a trip to see the county opera troupe. When he came back, I was already at the restaurant, so I could hear him telling Roughshod Ding about the trip. I was confused by what I heard. Rain Xia said that the opera troupe had an impressive theater in the county seat, but a collection of stalls, wrapped in cheap felt, had just been put up around the main entrance. One stall was selling *jiaozi* and another had household goods and another was selling funeral wreaths, mourning clothes, and spirit money. Rain Xia recognized the sellers from his brother's wedding. The *jiaozi* seller recognized him, too. "It's Snow Bai's brother-in-law," he said. "When is the restaurant gonna open?"

"How did you know I was opening a restaurant?"

"Your sister-in-law told us. She said she wants us to sing at the grand opening."

Rain Xia felt a bit awkward as he asked, "Did you open this stall yourself?"

"You want to try the *jiaozi*?"

"Why aren't you guys busy performing right now?"

"You're opening a restaurant in the village, and I'm running a stall in the county seat . . . Is that any reason to look down on me?"

"Are you kidding?" he said as he went toward the gate to the theater's yard.

In the yard, there were three rows of low buildings, the first two rows serving as quarters for the opera troupe and the support staff and the final row of buildings housing the company's offices and rehearsal spaces. There were two cypress trees in the yard as well, their thick trunks topped with sparse crowns. The sun that day was scorching, and there was no breeze to cool things off. The courtyard was a mess, overgrown with weeds and ragged patches of grass. It was also completely deserted. Each dormitory had in front of it a collection of sheds and huts made from brick, mud, wood, and felt. As Rain Xia stood there longer, he saw a few of the women in the troupe padding around in slippers, their hair freshly washed, headed to the bathroom or to dump loads of ash scraped out of their stoves beside the courtyard walls. There were already piles of garbage along the walls, and as they dumped the ash over mounds of watermelon rinds, the flies flew up and started buzzing around.

Rain Xia hadn't expected this. He had seen these actors and actresses take the stage in pristine, immaculate costumes, but the courtyard was filthy. He had been nervous about going there at first, but now he started to despise the people who lived there. He had never been there before and wasn't sure where to find Snow Bai's dormitory. He didn't bother asking and just went down the row of dormitories, darting looks in doorways, until he eventually came to the rehearsal spaces. There were two people inside the first room. Rain Xia peeked in and saw a skinny, dark-skinned guy and his unexpectedly beautiful female companion, who was wearing a short skirt that showed off her long legs. It sounded like the man was reciting a dirty joke, and when he delivered the punchline, he smirked, and the woman leaned in and kissed him on his lips.

The man caught sight of Rain Xia outside the door, and his smile disappeared. "Hey!" he said. "What the hell are you doing?"

"I'm looking for Snow Bai."

"Who are you?"

"I'm her brother-in-law."

"Right, right, I heard that her brother-in-law is more handsome than Wind Xia." He turned and called, "Snow Bai! Snow Bai! Your brother-in-law's here, looking for you."

Snow Bai had been over in the dormitories, washing her laundry. She came over to the rehearsal space and led Rain Xia back to her dorm. She asked him to take a seat, then ran out to get him a pack of cigarettes. She rushed back to boil a pot of water and make tea for him. "It looks like there's not enough dormitories here," Rain Xia said.

"I was lucky to get this room. It was only after I got married that they assigned me this dorm," Snow Bai said. "So is the restaurant open yet?"

"Are you ready?"

"I've gotten in touch with about a dozen people, but three of them can't make it. It'll be hard to put together a performance with that many. We'd have trouble doing the opera excerpts we had planned. What do you think I should do?"

"You couldn't even do an excerpt?"

"I don't know what's going on here with the heads of the county. They brought Mid-Star up and then transferred him out. There's nobody in charge now. Everyone treats the opera as a springboard to promotion, basically. The salary was never good for performers, but now they've cut that by forty percent. A bunch of performers are making money on the side, playing at funerals and weddings, but that only pays about forty or fifty yuan a pop. I was thinking, if we can't do any excerpts, we'll just do a couple of songs, get a band, and then put up a few singers to do solos. As long as we've got the musicians, it'll be lively enough. I already got the players to stay here, although it wasn't easy. The drummer I got, he's selling *jiaozi* right now, but he can let his wife take over for a few days."

"The guy out front selling *jiaozi*?"

"He's very talented."

When Rain Xia told Roughshod Ding about the planned performance, Roughshod Ding frowned and asked, "Why not just have Star Chen do some pop songs? The way he sings, it sounds just like the songs on the radio."

"The opera troupe has professional performers. The opera performers lend a certain air of credibility. Anyway, I already invited them, and since they're not doing full excerpts, we can get them for an even better price."

I was quick to echo him. "What the hell is that Star Chen gonna sing? You think he sounds like the songs on the radio? He can't keep time, and he's always way out of tune."

"When the time comes," Roughshod Ding told me, "just make sure everything goes according to plan."

When the day of the grand opening came, I got up early, washed my hair, put on a new shirt, and then walked through East, West, and Middle Streets, beating my gong and announcing the event at Roughshod Ding and Rain Xia's grand opening. Twelve performers came from the county troupe, and a small stage was set up in front of the restaurant. Big-Noise Zhao had rushed to offer his talents, too, writing a couplet that was split between both sides of the stage. Roughshod Ding had glanced at it and told him to write something about getting rich. Big-Noise Zhao wrote a couplet that went like this:

Brother Poverty, cast out, never to trouble me again
If you deign, God of Wealth, please enter our domain

The crowd began to arrive around ten in the morning, spreading out along the road. Eight fireworks cannons were set off, and the show began. Because Snow Bai was pregnant, she wasn't performing, but she took the stage to announce the players and introduce the opera they were performing from.

The first performance was by three famous singers of the local opera, taking solos. The first sang a heartrending piece from *Third Mother Teaches Her Son*, the second performed an equally harrowing piece from *An Offering of Rice*, and the third sang from *Yellow Gown*.

The third singer had just begun to sing the opening of the piece, "How shall I speak to you when I enter the court as king," when his voice cracked. He pushed ahead, but the hoarse wailing was unbearable, closer to the crashing of gongs than a human voice. Snow Bai tried to get the audience to applaud, but most in the crowd ignored her. There was no getting one past that audience—Freshwind had no shortage of opera lovers and amateur singers. As the crowd grumbled, I looked up to see Snow Bai blushing and looking awkward.

When the performance ended, she went to the center of the stage to announce the next performer. "Next up, I'd like you to put your hands together for a renowned performer of the local opera, Bull Wang, and his performance of a section of *Down to Hedong*!"

A wave of laughter went through the crowd. Snow Bai wasn't sure what she had said to make people laugh. I held up a willow switch and addressed the crowd, "What are you laughing about? It better be your mother's cunt!"

"Spark," said Shifty, "I was laughing, too. Are you trying to start something with me?"

"If you were laughing, I am."

He spat in my face, and I did the same to him. I took a swing, and he came back at me, and we tussled until Favor Bai from the dyehouse stepped in between us. Shifty walked off, running his mouth the whole time.

"That guy can't stand anybody else making good," I said. "He started trouble on purpose."

I took up a post on the grindstone beside the stage, waving my switch menacingly. "Nobody else better cause any trouble!" I shouted down at the crowd.

As Bull Wang got back onstage, he motioned for me to get down off the grindstone and then turned to the audience, twisting his rubbery face into a grimace.

He pulled another face that made his nostrils and his eyes both dart to the right, saying, "Now, please don't laugh. My name is Bull Wang, not Balls Wang." The crowd laughed even harder than they had before. As a guttural roar came from Bull Wang's throat and he began his performance, the crowd applauded and shouted their approval.

Goodness arrived, and Roughshod Ding rushed over and offered him a cigarette. "Look at the mouth on that guy," he said, nodding toward Bull Wang. "I bet he could fit his whole fist in there."

"He should have kept that kind of talk to himself," Goodness said. "This is a grand opening. There'll be people from the village administration here, and plenty of folks just passing by. You know we always have to watch the guidelines on spiritual civilization. Make sure they aren't using any obscenities onstage. It sets a bad example."

"That's good advice," Roughshod Ding said. He went and whispered the message in Snow Bai's ear. When Bull Wang got offstage, she told him he should have kept it clean while onstage.

"Just trying to please the audience," Bull Wang said. "Nobody appreciates it if you aren't willing to have fun up there."

"A village cadre complained."

"What's the problem? I can't poke fun at myself?"

"We're representing the county opera company."

"So what? You still think we're artistic revolutionaries locked in some kind of a struggle? I'm just here to put food on the table." They went back and forth for a while, and when it was time for Bull Wang to take the stage again, he complained that his throat was sore and decided to sit out the second half of the morning's program. As the time came for the performance to start again that evening, Bull Wang still refused to get up onstage. He went for a second helping of the meal provided to the performers and was lining up for a third bowl right as I got to the kitchen. I dished him up a bowl of noodles and waited for him to look away, then spat a chunk of phlegm right on top.

The next day, once almost all the performers had sung their parts, the band was invited to perform. As they played, the crowd at the edge of the stage fell silent. Wisdom Xia had staked out a perch down a street that led at an angle to the front of the restaurant. He squatted on the steps of a courtyard there until the family saw him and brought out a chair for him to sit in. As he listened, his eyes slid shut and he beat a rhythm with his hands on the arm of the chair to accompany the band's percussion. Finally, his hands fell still, but he kept time with the tap of a toe.

Wisdom Xia hadn't noticed Big-Noise Zhao standing behind him. "Fourth Uncle," Big-Noise Zhao said, "you've really got the rhythm."

Wisdom Xia's eyes opened, and he turned back. "I know these tunes very well," he said. "Listen to this movement the orchestra just started. They're trying to mimic the sound of crying and wailing. If you really listen, it feels like your guts are being ripped out."

"It sounds like they're slaughtering a pig up there!"

Wisdom Xia turned back toward the stage and shut his eyes again. Big-Noise Zhao was tired of bothering Wisdom Xia, so he walked down and pressed himself into the crowd. He caught sight of Justice Xia approaching with his dark glasses on and his hands clasped behind his back. Big-Noise Zhao didn't greet him but watched silently as the crowd parted to let Justice Xia by. Years before, it would have been different. Wherever Justice Xia went, he always got a warm welcome. So what had changed? I couldn't tell you.

The welcome was so cold that even Justice Xia couldn't help but notice. He coughed dryly a few times and stood by himself. Halfwit's wife had brought her son to watch the performance, and he started crying. "Take that kid out of here," someone said. "How are we going to hear the music with him crying?"

She pulled her son out of the crowd and saw Justice Xia. "When did you get here?" she asked him. "Your grandson's crying because he wants to go in and get some melon seeds from Roughshod's restaurant. I can't go in, but maybe you could take him."

Justice Xia glanced up at the restaurant. "What does he need melon seeds for? Why can't you go in?"

"Pavilion and the other village cadres are in there, drinking tea. He didn't invite you?"

"It's too hot in there for me," he said and then turned and walked away. He headed down the street to a small restaurant on the road. In the doorway, he put his hands behind his back and turned back for a moment. The sun hit his dark glasses and turned them into two disks of white light.

Big-Noise Zhao called after him, "Uncle Justice!"

Justice Xia snorted.

"How are you, Uncle?"

"I'm fine. Why wouldn't I be fine?"

"And your wife?"

"Fine." He seemed, then, to snap back to life. "What the hell are they doing down there? No costumes. No makeup. Let's drink some tea instead."

"You're absolutely right," said Big-Noise Zhao, and he followed Justice Xia into the restaurant.

Justice Xia ordered tea but was told that they'd sold Roughshod Ding the last of their supply, so he asked for a jug of liquor and a plate of deep-fried chilies.

"What an honor," said Big-Noise Zhao, "to be treated to a meal by you. This is a big day for me."

"Just a jug of liquor. That's all." He turned toward the kitchen. "Have you got any fish? Bring us a roast fish."

"Where would we get fish from?" the shopkeeper asked. "Freshwind hasn't got any fishponds."

Justice Xia rolled his eyes and grunted.

"If you insist, Mr. Xia, I can go ask Shifty."

Justice Xia waved him off, tipped back his head, and drained a glass of liquor.

Even the jug of liquor didn't help the atmosphere. Justice Xia and Big-Noise Zhao spoke very little and mostly listened to the distant squeak and rattle of the orchestra. After a while, the sound of local opera was replaced by a singer doing pop songs. "Would you listen to that?" Justice Xia asked. "These performers nowadays, they barely get through a few opera songs and then start singing that shit."

"The young people like it."

"What a world we live in," Justice Xia said and sighed. "It's a goddamn mess. Tell me, this restaurant Roughshod Ding built—did you see the size of it? How many people in Freshwind are going to go there? All his land is going to waste, and he's worried about building a restaurant? The only customers he's going to have will be corrupt Party officials."

Big-Noise Zhao broke into a coughing fit. "Uncle Justice," he gasped. He stood and went to the doorway of the restaurant and spat in the dust, taking the chance to glance around to make sure nobody had heard their conversation. As he scanned the street, Justice Xia came to the door, too. "The liquor isn't done yet, Uncle Justice," Big-Noise Zhao protested.

"I've had enough. I wouldn't want to get local luminary Big-Noise Zhao in any trouble."

"Where are you going?" Big-Noise Zhao called after him. "Uncle Justice! That's not what I meant."

Justice Xia walked west down the road without looking back.

He tucked his neck into his jacket and kept going until the road ended. He didn't know where to go and started to get annoyed. The sun overhead was a ball of pure white, and shimmering heat rose from the baked earth, making it look like the wasteland was full of waving patches of tall grass. About a quarter mile up ahead was where the fishponds were. The water was hot and still, with a few dead fish floating belly up on the surface. River Jin's wife was buried at the undercliff near the end of the street, rather than over at the base of Bowed Ox Ridge. The wreaths on the grave mound looked like they had just been laid. The breeze had not yet swept away the black ash of the burned incense and spirit money.

He walked to the front of the grave mound and stood for a while, his teeth bared in a grimace. The sweat beaded on his forehead and ran down into the corners of his eyes. He followed the trail around the undercliff and up onto the knoll. As he looked over at the apple orchard on the northwest side, a loudspeaker not too far away crackled to life with the sound of Snow Bai's voice. "Next up, let's welcome to the stage Freshwind's own Star Chen!"

Justice Xia heard Star Chen break into his version of "The Price of Love," by Li Zongsheng:

> Move on, move on
> For your broken heart, find a new home
> You once shed tears, your heart was broken
> But such is the price of love.

Over in the apple orchard, New-Life was cutting down a tree. It was a tall poplar with a nest up in its branches. The nest looked to be even bigger than the magpie nest in the gingko in the yard of Freshwind Temple. Three days earlier, New-Life had been plowing with his walking tractor and had lost control of it. The tractor went into the trunk of the poplar and punched a hole in it. That night, some of the leaves on the tree had started rattling. Everyone who heard them was afraid. The day after that, there wasn't a puff of a breeze, but the leaves kept rattling. It spread throughout the entire tree, and the leaves seemed to rattle even louder. The magpies in the nest flew away, too.

But Justice Xia had no idea what was coming. He had decided to relax up on the knoll, and he stripped off his jacket to air it out. That was when New-Life finally cut through the trunk and the poplar came crashing down, flipping over a few water barrels.

Justice Xia flew into a rage. "Who the hell cut down that tree?" he demanded. When the orchard was being planted, he'd made sure to preserve the poplar, and it was around then that the magpies had first arrived to build their nest.

When New-Life saw Justice Xia, he rushed over, looking like a scurrying monkey. He tossed down the ax and tried to smile while he explained the situation to Justice Xia, who shouted back, "The hell are you talking about? Are you trying to bullshit me now, too?"

New-Life's wife appeared to offer her own testimony. "It's true," she said. "I didn't sleep a wink last night, Uncle Justice. It scared the hell out of me."

New-Life had it in him to cheat Justice Xia, but his hunchbacked wife did not. "Really?" Justice Xia demanded. "How could it be?"

"I asked Uncle Glory about it," said New-Life. "He said it was the sound of ghosts clapping their hands. Bound to be trouble, once that happens."

"What a load of bullshit! You drove a tractor into it and killed it. This tree suffered. God damn it, New-Life, how could you drive into a tree this big?"

"Some evil was at play, I tell you. The tractor suddenly went haywire. Of course I know the tree suffered. That's why I had to cut it down. I couldn't bear to see it in pain."

Without speaking, Justice Xia squatted and ran his hand over the top of the trunk. For a long time, he stayed there, stroking the cut while crows gathered on the orchard's wall, cawing and squawking. He tipped his head back and looked up at the sky, which was sliced into segments by the branches of the apple trees. "What the hell is going on today?" he muttered to himself.

"Uncle Justice," New-Life's wife said, "do you think it might be a bad omen?"

"Shut your stinking mouth," said New-Life. "What kind of bad omen? Just look, this year, right as soon as these apple trees blossomed, they got hit by a late frost, but we had a bumper crop. Anyway, if Uncle Justice is here, how could it be a bad omen? Him coming here must be a good sign."

Justice Xia stood up. He looked hard at New-Life, but his expression softened. "It's cut down now, so let's leave it at that." As he said it, he felt a bit better. He looked around the orchard. Before they'd planted the trees, this had been just another dried-out dusty knoll. He felt proud of himself.

"Uncle Justice," New-Life added, "you should come here more often. I'm happy to see you in the orchard, but so are the apple trees." He picked up a clod of mud and tossed it at the crows; then he led Justice Xia into the orchard. "Stand up straight," he said to the apple trees. "Let's have a round of applause for Uncle Justice."

Right as he spoke, the wind picked up and the trees rustled in the breeze. Justice Xia's expression brightened. As he walked deeper into the orchard, he looked like a general inspecting his troops. "New-Life," he said, "I don't get much chance to stretch my legs anymore, except when I go down to that piece of land by the riverside, but I do need to come here more often. You need to look after this orchard. The soil is our destiny, New-Life. It'll never set out to harm you, but it'll always pay you back in kind. Back when they split up the land, nobody wanted this dusty old knoll, but I agreed to grow apples here. They laughed at me back then. But look at what became of the land. None of them could have imagined that there would one day be a great big apple orchard up here."

"I will always remember what you said."

322

"You never remember! Shortsighted, that's what you are. As soon as that spring frost came, you wanted to give up half the orchard. If you hadn't given it up to Star Chen, you could have looked out on this entire orchard and known it belonged to you. Wouldn't that have felt good?"

"No sense worrying about that now, Uncle."

New-Life's wife, who had been trailing the two men, butted in: "If you keep fooling around with those drums of yours, you'll end up losing the other half of the orchard."

"What are you running that stinking mouth again for?"

"I wanted to complain while Uncle's here. If I hadn't told you to get up here and cut that tree down, you would have taken your drum down to Roughshod Ding's grand opening."

"Why didn't you go to the performance, Uncle Justice?"

"What performance? What are you talking about?" Justice Xia reached into his pocket for a cigarette and lit it, ignoring New-Life's confused look. "What are you going to do with the poplar now?" Justice Xia asked.

"Guess I'll burn it."

"If you're going to burn it, let me ask you a favor."

"What do you want him to do?" New-Life's wife asked. "Whatever it is, just say it. He can't turn you down."

"If you're willing, I'd like to send Tongue-Tied up to take some of the wood out to Seven Li Gully to build a shack. If you aren't willing, that's fine, too. It just came to mind, looking at it right now."

"What are you building a shack over there for?"

"You didn't hear about the swap?"

"What's that?"

"Are you playing dumb?"

"Well, you know, Uncle Justice . . . um . . . Whatever they're saying, I'm still on your side. Believe me. I'll always be on your side."

"I don't need you on my side. Pavilion hung me out to dry, but that doesn't mean I have to give up."

"He hung you out to dry? How could he do that?"

"You can play dumb with me," New-Life's wife said, "but don't try it with Uncle Justice. That Pavilion is a wolf. You're the one who built Freshwind into what it is today, Uncle. All he can do is continue the work you already started. And he thinks he can treat you that way? When you build the shack out at Seven Li Gully, are you going to live out there? He forced this on you, didn't he? You're going to show him who's boss, aren't you?"

"It's about more than Pavilion," said Justice Xia.

"Then why do you have to do it?" asked New-Life.

"If you won't give me the wood, that's fine."

"You sure are stubborn, Uncle Justice," said New-Life. "That's your only flaw."

Justice Xia unexpectedly broke into laughter. "You know how long I've heard my wife muttering that under her breath? Now I hear it from you. There might be some truth in it. But the way I think, how much can one person really get done in a lifetime? If you aren't stubborn, you'll end up doing nothing."

"Tell Tongue-Tied to come get that wood then."

"What are you ordering Tongue-Tied around for?" his wife asked. "You can take the wood there and build the shack for him."

"You must have been a man in a past life," Justice Xia said.

"Maybe I was a village cadre."

New-Life laughed along with them. "Since you're in a good mood now," he said, "what do you want to do? Drink some liquor or beat the drums?"

"The drums," said Justice Xia. The three left the orchard and went up to the rooftop of New-Life's home, where his freshly oiled drum was resting on a straw mat.

Justice Xia picked up the mallet and gave the drum a hard slap. The drum made a pathetic crack, and the drum head immediately split.

Chapter 26

Everyone in the opera troupe was impressed by Star Chen's performance. For the rest of the day and into the evening, they all took their own turns at singing pop songs, and the younger villagers in Freshwind rushed to the hotel to watch, filling the road out front. When the performance was over, the troupe's *erhu* player took Star Chen aside and praised his musical talents, then asked him where he'd studied and what he was doing for work. Star Chen replied that he was from outside the village, was working as a bicycle repairman and shoemaker, and had also recently taken over management of part of the orchard. The *erhu* player thought it was a pity that his talents were being wasted.

Emerald was listening in and hastened to add, "He writes his own songs, too."

"Really? Sing one of your own compositions for me."

Star Chen began to sing. He put his entire being into it, his head moving in time to the beat and his eyes shut tightly.

When he was done, the *erhu* player asked him, "Can you read music?"

"I just hum the tune, basically. When I'm in a good mood or feeling low, I'll hum a tune to myself. If Emerald says she likes it, I keep that in mind. So, now when I hum a tune a few times, I try to remember it, then I can usually make a song out of it."

"And you are . . . ?" the *erhu* player asked, turning to Emerald.

"I'm his biggest fan."

"You've already got a fan club, Star Chen."

"You think he could do a concert in the county seat? Would he be able to make it as a singer?"

"He's got some natural talent. That's for sure. Of course, it hasn't been refined yet. But with some formal study, I'd say he's bound for something bigger than fixing shoes and picking apples down here in Freshwind."

Star Chen was only too happy to receive the praise and immediately began to call the *erhu* player his *shifu*. Someone called over that he ought to give his *shifu* a gift in return. Star

Chen immediately got down and kowtowed to his new master, saying, "And I'll make sure you get some apples, too." He stood and called for Roughshod Ding.

"Who wants your shitty apples?" asked Roughshod Ding. "You should get your *shifu* some liquor."

"Of course! Tonight, it's on me. That goes for my *shifu* and the rest of the troupe." He was as good as his word. When it was time for dinner, he returned from the shop with four bottles of *shaojiu* and two cases of beer. The troupe drank their fill, emptying every bottle.

After dinner, Snow Bai led the performers over to the home of her parents-in-law, which made Wisdom Xia unspeakably happy. He told his wife to make up some noodles and fried eggs. The performers told them not to go to the trouble, and Snow Bai stepped in to ask her mother-in-law not to bother, but Wisdom Xia wouldn't hear of it. "We'll make some anyway. Even if they don't eat any . . . It's the least we can do. This is a humble village." He turned to Snow Bai and said, "You're so good at singing the local opera; what are you doing, singing those pop songs?"

"It's always the same tunes, the same operas. After you sing them for a couple of dozen years, you end up getting sick of them."

"Do you even understand local opera, though? The only way you can get onstage and sing to an audience is to know these songs inside and out. The local opera has meaning. Those songs Star Chen is singing—what is that? It's weak! He's up there moping around like he's trying to find a rope to hang himself."

"I was a bit surprised myself to see all those people out there this afternoon just to hear Star Chen sing those pop songs," she said.

"You could put on a monkey show and get a nice crowd, too! If local people don't sing local opera, it's like one of the sons of the Xia family getting married and changing his last name." Then Wisdom Xia felt he'd gone a bit too far, and for a while he sat without speaking.

The performers ate their bowls of noodles and fried eggs. Eventually, Mid-Star's father showed up in the courtyard, calling for Snow Bai. When she went outside, he asked her if the performers were inside. "They're there," she said. "Why don't you come in?"

"Well, since Mid-Star's not here, I guess I should welcome them to the village."

She led him into the house and introduced him. "This is the father of Mr. Xia, the head of the company."

"Everyone working hard here?" Mid-Star's father asked.

"Mr. Xia is working even harder," they called back.

"I see everyone got a tan, huh?" Mid-Star's father said.

"Your son is darker than all of us," Bull Wang said, and everyone broke into laughter.

Mid-Star's father was at a loss for words. But the light mood was broken by a chicken that strutted into the room and pecked a grain of rice from his shoe. "Look at this chicken," Mid-Star's father said peevishly. He chased the chicken out and then went into the kitchen to talk to Fourth Aunt.

The party eventually moved out to the courtyard, but when the topic of the next day's performance came up, there was a disagreement among the performers. After some discussion, two factions formed: one that wanted to put on a pure opera performance and another that was pushing for them to include pop songs. They began to argue, and the argument became heated. Around then, one of the performers who happened to be from West Mountain Bend and had gone back home to see his family instead of eating with them returned and finally split the group in two. The performer from West Mountain Bend told them that someone in his village had died, and he wanted the troupe to perform at the funeral. The family would pay each performer sixty yuan. Some of the performers were quick to agree, pointing out that they'd be making ten yuan more at the funeral than they were at the grand opening. Some, though, said it would be showing poor character to ditch the performance in Freshwind. And, they asked, aren't we better than funeral performers? They shook their heads forcefully.

The head of the faction that wanted to keep singing opera said, "Since everyone in Freshwind wants to hear pop songs, why don't we go to West Mountain Bend? Even if it's a funeral, at least we can sing opera."

"I'd be humiliated," said someone from the other faction. "Singing at the grand opening of a hotel, now that counts for something."

Snow Bai tried her best to keep the group together, but the faction that wanted to sing opera at the funeral eventually elected to leave. "It's only ten yuan extra," she said angrily. "What about my reputation? If you're going to leave, then go. Everyone that's going to stay here, I'll see to it that Mr. Ding gives you another twenty yuan a day."

The two factions separated, with one group going directly to West Mountain Bend and the other heading back to the hotel to spend the night. The courtyard was suddenly deserted. Mid-Star's father, who had been in the kitchen chatting with Fourth Aunt, came out of the kitchen and saw Wisdom Xia sitting by himself on the clothes-beating stone. "Did everyone leave?" he asked Wisdom Xia, who seemed not to hear him. "It was a good idea for Mid-Star to leave the company. I've heard people say directing an opera is an infuriating experience. And—"

"You head home," said Wisdom Xia. "Take a rest."

"Hey, I guess it's pretty late already. Everyone's in bed." He left the courtyard.

The performance continued the next day at the hotel, and the performers received their extra twenty yuan. Star Chen, however, was not paid. When Emerald went to Roughshod Ding to ask for his fair share, he refused, saying, "I have to pay him, too? I helped him find a *shifu*, didn't I? He should be the one coming to see me—to thank me!"

"Just got into business, and you're already bilking people out of money," she said angrily.

By the time Emerald got home, everyone had already eaten their dinner. Thunder had already come back from his shift and was in the main room playing chess with Wealth. Blossom was using a moist rag and a wicker basket to winnow grain from chaff. "You're only coming back now?" she said to her daughter. "Eat your dinner; then I want you to grind this for me."

"You want *me* to grind that?" Emerald sneaked a couple of *baozi* from the steamer and put another two in her pocket to bring to Star Chen.

"If you don't grind it, we won't have any flour to make more of those *baozi*."

"I'm so tired. I'll do it tomorrow."

"You're always opening your mouth to get fed, but you won't lift a finger to work for it. Why the hell are you so tired? I bet you'll get your energy back when it's time to go find Star Chen. Give me those *baozi* back."

Emerald took the *baozi* out of her pocket and threw them into the wicker basket. Mother and daughter squared off in the kitchen.

Third Aunt, who was out cutting bunions off her feet with a razor, tossed down the blade and rushed in to break them up. She dragged Emerald into the side house. "She just got in a fight with your dad," she told her granddaughter. "So don't go stirring things up. Your dad isn't in the mood. Be a good girl and grind that grain for her."

Every house on Middle Street had once had a grindstone that was pulled by a cow. By that time, however, there were no cows, and the only grindstone left was on the roadside in front of Wisdom Xia's place. Blossom headed there with the basket of grain, a length of rope, and a pole. She dumped the grain in the top of the stone and began to work. She hadn't bothered to ask her husband for help again. Ever since they'd been married, he'd never helped with chores at home. Her simple request for help with the grain had caused the first fight of the night, and then her daughter had tried to get out of it, too, leading to the second fight. There was no chance she'd get them to help her. They would just grumble.

She decided to stop by Bounty's place. With the moon up high, the ground outside glowed white. The gate of the courtyard was shut, but one window was open a crack. "Third Aunt," she called. "Third Aunt, are you still awake?"

The voice of Bounty's wife came from inside. "Sun just went down; I'm not in bed yet."

"Come and help me grind some grain. Whenever you're ready to grind, I can help you out, too."

"Don't say you're going to help me out. Don't worry about that. Anyway, I twisted my ankle going down to see the opera this afternoon, but I'll get Third Uncle to help you." "Bounty! Bounty!" she called out. "Blossom needs somebody to help her with the grindstone. Give her a hand."

"When it's time to work, I'm first on the list," said Bounty, "but nobody ever comes to get me when it's time to drink."

"Thunder always helps everyone out," Blossom said, "but when his family needs a hand, everyone grumbles."

"He's never even given me a ride."

When I heard that, I opened the door and went out and found her leaning against the wall. "If you can't find anybody," I said, "then I can help you."

"Neighbors are more dependable than family these days," Blossom said. "Spark, if you ever need a ride somewhere, just let me know."

You see, I happened to be at Bounty's place that night. I'd gone over after the performance to bring him some hammer drills. He'd come up to me at the grand opening to ask to borrow them. I told him that since they were my father's, I couldn't just lend them out. I was willing to sell them for a fair price, though, I told him. I went back home, ate dinner, then went over with the three drills. When Bounty's wife heard me say I was going to help Blossom, she giggled and jokingly accused me of trying to flatter the wealthy families in the village. The truth was that I did have an ulterior motive, though that wasn't it. Since the grindstone was down Wisdom Xia's road, there was a chance I'd be able to catch Snow Bai coming back from the hotel. The idea of helping her turn that grindstone filled me with dread. I started to get dizzy after going around a few times, but then Emerald showed up and took the pole from me. Emerald didn't say a word, but Blossom wouldn't shut up, constantly cursing out her husband.

I didn't bother saying anything; I just kept my eyes locked on the front gate of Wisdom Xia's place. It was already very dark, but I still hadn't seen Snow Bai return. Emerald started singing in a low voice, the lyrics reduced to a mumble. I managed to catch a bit of it, though:

> Love you, love you, love you so much
> Asked the artist to paint your face
> Below the string of my guitar
> So I can stroke your gentle face

"Did Star Chen sing that for you?" I asked. Emerald opened an eye to look at me. "The lyrics are great."

"Huh," she grunted, then laughed, as if to say, *What would you know?*

Once the grain had been run through the grinder twice, Blossom began to sift it. Emerald and I stepped aside. She was still singing.

That little slut . . . She thinks she's the only one who's ever been in love? I looked away from her and up at the moon. It glowed like a silver dish in the sky. I thought back to that morning when I'd sat on the edge of the kang, thinking about the dream I'd woken up from. I had flipped over my pillow, looking for some trace of the dream.

Right then, Blossom finished sifting and dumped the grain back into the top of the grindstone. "Push," she commanded.

I didn't hear her. She picked up the brush that was used to sweep the grindstone. "What are you just sitting there for?" She rapped me over the head with the brush. And that's right when the eclipse started.

Have you ever seen an eclipse? It starts out with a dark edge on the east side of the moon, and the darkness sort of slides over the moon. The white part shines brighter then, even as it's disappearing. And then, finally, pop! Everything is dark. It was so dark that I couldn't see Emerald's teeth. I couldn't see my own fingers. I made my way to the grindstone and began to push, circling it in the darkness. I walked and walked but never came to the end of the path. By the time the moon was light again, the grain had already been put through four rounds.

"That's enough," said Emerald impatiently.

"Let your uncle Spark do it. If he's going to keep going, we might as well grind it even finer."

"You want me to treat Uncle Spark like the family cow?"

"Let's keep grinding," I said. It was already midnight, and I was worried that if I stopped pushing the stone, I might miss Snow Bai coming back. If I missed Snow Bai, all the work would have been for nothing.

Blossom kept driving us to push the grindstone. When there was only chaff left under the stone, the wheel was easy to push, but then Blossom swept the surface and poured in another round. Sometimes the chute got plugged up and the stone ground nothing at all and just rumbled noisily as we turned. Emerald dozed on her feet, her legs moving mechanically under her. I felt like my brain was full of paste. I kept my eyes trained on Wisdom Xia's place, waiting for Snow Bai.

"Watch what you're doing!" Blossom shouted. "You don't have to keep pushing when it's empty."

Emerald came out of her walking nap and angrily jerked the pole out of the grindstone. She was done pushing. A flashlight beam came down the road. I tried to clear my head, thinking it must have been Snow Bai. When the flashlight got closer, I could see it was Fourth Aunt holding it. "You're out here grinding grain in the middle of the night?"

"Where are you coming back from?" Blossom asked.

"Over at the hotel . . ." She went past us, toward Chrysanth's place, and started noisily knocking at the gate.

"What's going on?" Chrysanth said, opening the gate. "Oh, it's you, Fourth Aunt."

"You must have been sleeping pretty deeply. Shouldn't you get up for a pee?" Chrysanth smiled, and Fourth Aunt continued, "The opera performers were thinking of going back tonight, but we held them up until they finally decided to just leave tomorrow morning. Snow Bai's going with them. You know she's pregnant, right? She'll need somebody to look after her, cook for her, do the laundry, and whatnot. I really can't go along with her. You know how your uncle is, don't you? His whole life, he was waited on hand and foot. If I left him alone, he'd pout. Hasn't Bodhi been saying she wants to get out of the village and get a job in the city? So, I was thinking, why not send her with Snow Bai? I'll look after her expenses, of course. What do you think?"

"I thought there must be an emergency, the way you came knocking here. It's after midnight!"

"If you think it's okay for her to go, I'll need you to pack some clothes for her tonight. They're leaving early tomorrow for the county seat."

"You'd have to talk to Treasure."

"I just did. He said he doesn't care."

"He doesn't care about me? Is that what he means? He doesn't care about his own daughter? He spends all his time with Black-Moth—has he forgotten his own daughter? Does that bitch have flowers growing out of her cunt or something? Fourth Aunt, tell me . . ."

Fourth Aunt cast a glance in our direction. "Why don't you keep your voice down?" she asked. "If Treasure isn't going to make a decision, then it's up to you."

"She can't go. Roughshod Ding was just telling her that he was going to give her a job as a waitress at his hotel's restaurant. She'd be making five hundred yuan a month. If she goes into the city, she can't work at the restaurant, right?"

"Five hundred? Are you trying to shake me down?" Fourth Aunt turned and left, heading back toward home. Once she got inside the gate, I heard her sigh loudly and slam the latch shut.

"Spark," Blossom said, "has everyone got a black heart?" She dumped another load of grain into the top of the stone and motioned for me to push.

"Seems like it," I said, tossing the pole to the ground and walking away.

Early that morning, around the time the rooster started crowing, it started to rain. Maybe it was because I was tired from pushing the grindstone, but I slept soundly for a few hours. I dreamed I was in the crowd that had gathered to see off the performers. They were riding on a tractor back to the county seat. Snow Bai was sitting in a cart being pulled behind, with her legs hanging down. Lots of people had come out to see them off. I saw Wisdom Xia and Fourth Aunt and Emerald, but I was really watching Snow Bai. It seemed like she saw me, too, because she turned to face me. It turned out she was talking to Fourth Aunt, though. I watched her legs, kicking in midair. It felt like she or maybe just her legs were trying to communicate something to me. *Please let one of those shoes fall,* I prayed. *Just let one fall.*

And that's exactly what happened. I burrowed through the crowd and lifted the shoe up to her. "Snow Bai, you dropped this!"

I turned when Wisdom Xia gave me a nudge. "That's enough," he said. "It's time for them to go."

But the tractor's motor wouldn't seem to turn over. I hoped that somehow the tractor could stay where it was forever! Right then, I got the sudden urge to pee and started looking around for somewhere to go. I couldn't find a quiet place. I'd never get a chance to see off Snow Bai. I held it and held it and then—I was awake. It was already light outside, and the rain was still coming down. I jumped off the kang and rushed to the hotel, but I was too late. Snow Bai and the opera company's performers had left an hour earlier.

Some people said I'd lost my mind again. That wasn't true.

I followed the two tracks left in the road by the tractor. The rain was coming down like bullets. I was like Yang Yanding in the *Yang Family* opera—the brave fighter, falling on the battlefield with a thousand arrows in his back. The dusty road had turned to red mud. My shoes became two mud bricks, and I kicked them off and went running barefoot. Stones cut my soles, and my blood mixed with the rainwater on the road.

Suddenly Cutie appeared in the road, trying to block my way. She had been out picking green chilies. I pushed her to the ground. She shouted after me, "Stop him! Spark is crazy again!" Tongue-Tied seemed to appear out of nowhere ahead of me.

The mute's face was pale, and the growth of fuzz across his upper lip stood out even more. I tried to dodge him to the right, but he moved to block me. I headed to the left, and he moved to the left. I put my head down and charged. I didn't go down. He caught my head and held me.

"Spark," said New-Life, "where are you running to?"

"I have to catch up with the tractor."

"What are you doing that for?"

"Snow Bai left!" As soon as Tongue-Tied heard me mention Snow Bai, he gave my neck a twist and tossed me to the ground. He knew what had happened before with me and Snow Bai. I didn't dare say anything else.

Justice Xia, who was standing at the side of the road in a raincoat, came over to me, frowning. "Leave Spark alone," he said. He tried to pull me to my feet. "Get out of here. Go!" I crawled toward him, sobbing. "That's fine. Go ahead and cry. It'll scrub your heart clean."

My heart did feel cleaner once he'd said that. I regretted mentioning Snow Bai. I squatted, panting. I wasn't going to go home, though. "If you aren't going home," said Justice Xia, "you might as well come with me."

And that's exactly what I did. I went with him, and I never left him until the day he died. For his remaining time in this world, I served at his side, bringing him whatever he needed, even joking around with him sometimes. Justice Xia had two dogs: one was Lucky, and I was the second. Mid-Star's father said that whatever you do in this life is decided by your last life. Whatever decided our fate, my father and I both must have owed Justice Xia something—we certainly paid our debt.

I'll always remember that day. I followed him through the rain, carrying a roll of tarpaper, leading New-Life and Tongue-Tied, until we came to Seven Li Gully. The day before, the three had put up a shack in front of Justice Xia's grave. The shack was not much to look at, but it was strong. There was a low wall of stone at the bottom, held together with mud, and a long triangular roof that came almost to the ground, made of poplar branches and covered with straw mats. We stretched the tarpaper over the mats. The rain came down even harder, and we took shelter inside. Deep puddles formed in the red clay outside the shack.

Lucky came running over toward us. Had she followed her master's footsteps out to the gully, or was she tracking him by scent? It had been a long time since I'd seen the dog, and I'd never really liked her. I remember chucking a stone at her when she'd tried to mate with Tiger. Now, though, I felt a certain warmth toward the dog. "Lucky," I said, "where's Tiger today? I didn't expect to see you here without Tiger."

Lucky whimpered, and tears ran down her snout. Dogs can cry—did you know that? The tears were cloudy and left yellow tracks down her cheeks. She bowed her head and kept whimpering. I knew from experience that the ability to understand the language of animals was a passing thing. Lucky was talking to me. Lucky was telling me this: Secretary Li from the village offices had locked Tiger up, beat him, and wasn't letting him out. I stood over Lucky and stroked her head.

"What are you two talking about?" New-Life asked. I told him about Tiger being locked up, and he scoffed. "There are plenty of other dogs for her in Freshwind."

Bullshit! I raised my head and glowered at him.

Right then there was a crash, and I caught sight of something black right before it slammed into me. It seemed to have come from directly above. When I looked around, I saw that it was a bird, about the size of a hen. The bird had knocked a ceramic bowl from a hook on the ceiling of the shack and now lay on the floor of the shack, flapping its wings.

None of us could identify the bird. It had a black head and a red beak. It had long wings, but the tail was too long to be a pheasant. It was extraordinarily beautiful. I thought it must have been a good sign for a bird like that to fly into the shack. The bowl the bird had knocked to the floor was Justice Xia's; he'd won it as a prize when he was studying at an agricultural school in the 1960s. When Lucky saw the bird flapping around on the floor of the shack, she pounced on it and held it tight in her mouth. "Lucky! Lucky!" I bent down and pried the bird free.

New-Life kicked Lucky. "This is a phoenix!"

"A phoenix?" I asked. "What are you talking about?"

"It looks enough like a phoenix . . . Have you ever seen a bird like this before? The way it just flew in here and knocked Uncle Justice's bowl down, it's a good sign. Uncle Justice is a dragon among men, so this is a 'dragon-phoenix meeting.'"

"You can really fucking talk, can't you?" Justice Xia chuckled.

"I'm serious."

"If it's as auspicious as you say it is, then let's hope it's a sign this Seven Li Gully thing is going to work out."

I carried the bird to the doorway of the shack. I held the bird under the rain, and it seemed to regain its senses. The rain beaded on its feathers and ran down its sides like drops of oil. The bird lifted its curved, elegant neck, gave a long cry, and then flapped noisily up into the sky.

I started to think about what Justice Xia had said. "Uncle Justice," I said, "what did you build this shack out here for?"

"I'm gonna live out here."

"Bullshit. How are you gonna live out here?"

"Who says I can't? I lived in a shack just like this back when we were planting the orchard. I ate there and slept there. Are you with me?"

Of course I was with him. Except for my rice paddy, there wasn't anything tying me to the village. Once I planted it, I was free to go. If I stayed around the village, I'd just be loafing around anyway. It might be good for me, I thought, to spend some time out there with Justice Xia.

"I'm with you," I said.

The rain came down even harder. Looking out the doorway of the shack, it looked like we had been set down in a waterfall. "The year we worked on filling the gully, I brought three hundred villagers up from Freshwind with me. Now all I've got is you three."

"And Lucky," I added.

"Huh, and Lucky, too." Tears formed at the corners of his eyes.

"Are you crying, Uncle Justice?"

"I'm not crying," he said. He didn't turn away, but he leaned back into the rain, letting it wash over his face. Maybe he was crying, but I couldn't tell with the rain coming down. He was mumbling to himself, "If I were forty or fifty, there wouldn't be a problem . . . Now, I've got nothing left, nothing left to give . . . But I'm still here . . ." He opened his pants and, without turning aside, pissed in the mud.

New-Life and Tongue-Tied went out to join him, pissing alongside him in the rain. I went out to take a piss, too, but unlike the other men I had to jerk my pants down and take a squat. When Justice Xia caught Tongue-Tied giving New-Life a look, he gave him a kick.

I started to feel a sense of camaraderie out on Seven Li Gully. Apart from the smell of piss, it was a fine place. I forgot all about the pain that Snow Bai had caused me and how the villagers had bullied me. I bounced happily around the shack. After a while, we were all feeling hungry, so I offered to head back into the village and bring back some food. Justice Xia shouted after me, but I kept going.

There's a saying that summer rain won't cross a furrow. You can have rain coming down hard on one side of a field and the sun beating down on the other side. That's exactly what was going on that day. As soon as I got to the 312, I saw that half of it was wet and the other half was dry. The ditch on the left side was full of water, and the ditch on the right side was dry as a bone. The rain cut the sky in half. I didn't want to walk on the wet side or the dry side. I stayed right along that dividing line.

Mid-Star's father said that our world is made up of yin and yang, so you've got day and night, the sun and the moon, men and women, fast and slow, high and low . . .

As I ran down the borderline between rain and sun, at first I felt as if I, too, had been split in two, but then it felt as if I was completely whole. Does that mean I'm made up of yin and yang, too? What I mean is, you couldn't say I was a man, really, but I wasn't a woman, either. I'd always been ashamed of my body, but in that moment, I felt proud of it. I sang a snatch of a tune from *Creeping Peas*:

Yue Fei thinks he could put me in the eye of a needle,
Do you think you could measure the seas with a ladle?
I'm taller still than mountain peaks,
The Yangtze fades under sunshine streaks.
The *qilin* raises its magnificent head,
The sun sinks in its belly like a block of lead.

I thought I might as well go to Clerk's wife's restaurant, get some braised pig head and a bottle of liquor, definitely a plate of *liang fen*, too—I knew that Justice Xia loved *liang fen*. I'd have to get plenty of liquor, too. Justice Xia couldn't drink much, but when he got drunk, he liked to show off his drunken boxing. As I ran, I started shadowboxing. Both sides of my body, separated by the dark and light, rain and sun, were opponents pitted against each other. I threw *gongfu* attacks at my left hand with my right hand.

When I got to Freshwind, the rain was still coming down. Clerk's wife was surprised to see one side of me soaking wet and the other side completely dry. She was even more surprised when I ordered a bunch of pig's head. I didn't tell her anything.

Outside the shop, Rites Xia was sheltering under the eaves. He had on brand-new clothes, and his beard had been neatly trimmed. "Uncle Rites," I said, "where are you going on a day like this?"

"Grace and her husband are going to Xijing, and they insisted I come along. I'm catching a ride on Thunder's bus, so I'm waiting for him to come by."

"Headed to the big city, huh? Make sure you stroll around, get a good look at it."

"I could just stroll around Freshwind. I'm only going because they insisted."

I could tell he thought he was a big shot for going to the city with his granddaughter.

I grabbed the order from Chastity's wife and headed back to Seven Li Gully at a run. As soon as I went through the East Street archway, I had a thought. Justice Xia wasn't a young man anymore, and if he was going to be sleeping out in that shack, I should stop by his place to get a few blankets. I was proud of myself for having the foresight to pick up the blankets, but that moment of cleverness would come back to bite me on the ass.

When I arrived to pick them up, Second Aunt asked me what I was up to. I told her that Uncle Justice had put up a shack over at Seven Li Gully, and he planned to stay there. Justice Xia's blind wife passed me the blankets and then began to sob.

Her cries brought Gold running. He had come by to drop off a bundle of fresh scallions. He dropped his umbrella and went to her side, and she told her son that his father had gone to Seven Li Gully and planned to stay there. Gold was truly shocked. He went to find Hearth, and the two of them went to look for Wisdom Xia, who happened to be out.

Zhang Ba had called on Wisdom Xia for his help mediating a dispute between his cousins on Middle Street. The head of the Middle Street Residential Committee had once tried to settle a dispute between one of the cousins and his former wife, but there had been complaints each time he'd tried. And so this time Wisdom Xia had been enlisted.

Like Zhang Ba, the two brothers were not wealthy men. One of the brothers had his head shaved bald, and the other had long hair that had grown into a messy pelt. The two brothers were trying to divide their possessions. The younger of the two, still unmarried, insisted that, because the elder brother already had a wife, he should be given the larger of the two wardrobes. The older brother said that this was impossible; he was in charge of the household, and there was no reason he should have to give up the larger wardrobe.

Bashful, the older brother's wife, was looking on, sniggering. She was an ugly and feeble-minded woman. The younger brother suggested that if he didn't get the wardrobe, he should get Bashful instead. If he could leave with the wardrobe, the older brother could keep his wife.

"What kind of horseshit is that?" Wisdom Xia swore. "Even before the revolution, nobody split up a household that way." The two brothers fell silent.

"I'll tell you how it should be divided. The courtyard will be shared between the two brothers, with the older brother in the east side of the house and the younger occupying the west. The younger brother gets the shithouse and the big elm tree out back. The older brother can keep the big wardrobe. The younger brother can take a basket, three ceramic jars, and one glass jar. Both of them can use the potato cellar. What's left after that? Everything's divided, just as it should be." He sat down in the main room and sucked at his pipe.

"So that's all set," agreed the head of the residential committee. "But what about the odds and ends?"

"You need me to divide those, too?"

The residential committee head and Zhang Ba went through the items, beginning by assigning a small stool to the older brother and a ceramic basin to the younger brother. Both brothers continued to squabble until they were silenced by a grunt from Wisdom Xia. After two piles of shabby household items had grown in the yard, Wisdom Xia said, "I should be going now." He rose quickly and made for the door.

Right then, Dog-Scraps's widowed wife and her son came in. "I heard you were over here," she said. Since Dog-Scraps's death, Wisdom Xia had looked after the school fees of his son. The boy had scored 98 percent on his midterm exams. He followed his mother, carrying his exam paper and a pumpkin from their garden as a thank-you gift. His mother prodded him to give it to his benefactor.

Wisdom Xia's mood immediately improved, and he was no longer in a hurry to leave. He took the exam paper and examined it, saying, "Not bad, not bad. My investment paid off." He spotted a character the boy had written wrong but that the teacher had failed to correct. He pulled out his pen and made the correction, then directed the boy to write the character three times in the dusty ground of the yard.

"We'll never forget what you've done for us," Dog-Scraps's wife said. "I already told him, if he studies well, the first job he gets, he'll give his first month's wages to you. That's the least we can do to repay your kindness."

Wisdom Xia laughed. "I'm worried I won't still be around by that time," he said. "Come here. You should kowtow to your grandpa." The boy kneeled and smacked his forehead on the yard. "Now"—he turned to the boy's mother—"why haven't you done anything about those red bumps he's got?"

"He's a boy. He doesn't care."

"He's still young," said Zhang Ba, "but once he grows up, he'll blame you for not doing anything about them. What you need to do is get some bitter chinaberry, some pomegranate skins, and juniper berries, boil all that into a tea, and then wash him with it every night before he goes to bed."

"Don't talk nonsense," said Wisdom Xia. "Take the boy to Big-Noise Zhao tomorrow. Tell him I sent you. You won't have to pay."

There was a knock at the gate, and Gold appeared, beckoning his uncle over. Hearth had headed back to get his brothers together, but Gold had kept searching for Wisdom Xia. "What's going on?" Wisdom Xia asked.

"Trouble at home," said Gold. "You've got to get over there!"

"Just come in and tell me what's going on." Gold went to his uncle's side and whispered something in his ear. Wisdom Xia's expression suddenly became serious. "How come you've never got any good news to tell me?" he said. As he went out of the yard, he called back to the residential committee head and Zhang Ba, "Make sure you deal with everything here. I don't want to be blamed for anything again."

When they got back to Wisdom Xia's house, Bounty, Hearth, and Halfwit were already waiting for them. Wisdom Xia took a seat in his seat in the main room and said, "Now, what the hell is going on? Your father went to Seven Li Gully?"

"He asked me and Hearth to go up there with him," said Gold. "He said he was going to plant something up there, eventually, once he completed the gully filling. I didn't take him seriously. I didn't think he'd really go up there."

"The old soldier wants one last campaign," said Wisdom Xia.

"I suppose so," Gold said. "He's always worked hard. But he's always been a reasonable man, as well. This past half year or so, I don't know what's come over him. There's no talking sense to him, and he's dragging his own good name through the mud. You have to talk to him, Fourth Uncle."

"I have my own thoughts, but you're his sons; I want to hear your opinions before I speak my piece."

"It's disgraceful," declared Halfwit. "Even people outside the family have tried to reason with him, and he just spits right in their faces."

"Dad only cares about showing off his own accomplishments," said Bounty. "He never takes us into consideration. It was bad enough when he decided to plant on Virtue's plot, but now he's over on Seven Li Gully, farming on village land. I can't figure out what we should do."

"What is he going to grow out there?" Hearth said. "You know the story of Yugong, ninety years old and decides to try to move a mountain—even he wouldn't have the devotion to spend twenty years at Seven Li Gully, trying to get a bit of land to plant on. How does he think he's going to do it?"

"Mother said that New-Life built a shack for him over there. Tongue-Tied and Spark are out there with him, too."

"Spark's sick in the head," said Hearth, "but what the hell is Tongue-Tied thinking? I know we wanted him to look after the old man, but this is going too far. I don't even care if he wants to do something with the land at Seven Li Gully, but he plans to live there? When he gets rheumatism, who are we going to blame? Tongue-Tied?"

"What are you talking about now?" Bounty said. "Let's stick to the facts. Don't go off into the weeds now."

"Is this how you're going to deal with it, by arguing?" Wisdom said. "I just had to separate Zhang Ba's two cousins, and now I'm mediating for Justice Xia's sons. If you want to shout at each other, then leave me out of it."

Gold shot a look at Hearth. "How dare you say I wasn't sticking to the facts! You call this going off into the weeds?"

"Watch your tone—all of you," said Bounty.

"What's wrong with what I said?" demanded Hearth.

Gold gave an angry growl in response.

"Some tea!" commanded Wisdom Xia. "Bring me some tea." Fourth Aunt hurried in with a cup of tea for her husband. He took a sip and slammed it down on the table. "This is from this morning. Make a fresh pot."

Fourth Aunt brought in a fresh cup. Wisdom Xia took a sip and put his cup on the table. The room was silent except for the sound of rain dripping from the eaves. "Well?" he said. But nobody spoke. "Everybody's got their mouths shut now, huh?"

"What should we do about our father?" Gold asked.

"What should you do?" Wisdom Xia asked, suddenly furious. "His grave is in Seven Li Gully, isn't it? That's where he plans to be buried. Let him die up there, if that's what he wants. How does that sound to you?"

Gold froze where he stood. He tried to speak, but he couldn't form the words.

Halfwit stood and headed for the door, saying, "What's the use of talking? Our father will do whatever he decides to do."

"You get back here and sit down," Gold said.

"Keep going," Wisdom Xia called to Halfwit. "The rest of you might as well go with him. There's nothing I can do. I suppose my older brother thinks he still has something to prove. It's a shame, though . . . I don't really care what the rest of the village will say, but to see his own sons acting like this . . . Go!" He pushed Gold toward the door. "All of you, get out!" He pushed the other two brothers out, then slammed the door shut.

The four brothers stood in the courtyard, getting soaked by the rain. That was when Treasure arrived. "What did Fourth Uncle have to say?" he asked. He held an umbrella over the group while they talked.

"Shit!"

Wisdom Xia, who had been listening from inside, exploded, "Motherfucker! 'Shit'? That's what you call it?"

"Now, don't talk to them like that," Fourth Aunt said. "There's nothing to get angry about, is there? These are Justice Xia's boys you're talking to, not your own sons."

"Look at this family. Even when he failed, Justice Xia always kept his head held high. How did he come to have such worthless sons?"

Out in the courtyard, the sons were still arguing. After a while, they came to an agreement. They would settle any other arguments later, but first they had to get their father to come home. They headed straight for Seven Li Gully.

Meanwhile, I headed back to the shack and started drinking with Justice Xia. He didn't get drunk, but I did. I ended up taking a nap on the bed that I'd made up in the corner. I had a dream where I saw my father. In the dream, he was sitting in the shack with us, too. Somehow, even in the dream, I knew he shouldn't be there. *He's been dead for years,* I thought. My father ignored me and read from a small notebook, lecturing Justice Xia on the topography of Seven Li Gully. "Seven Li Gully is like an acupuncture point on the landscape. It's a particularly important one. Think of it as a woman's vagina. You know everything below it is gonna be filled in. So, you've got to build a dam down below here."

As my father spoke, I noticed someone else, crouched in one corner of the shack. Even though her back was turned, I knew it was Marvel's mother. She was cursing. I wondered what she was doing in the shack. What would have brought her out here? I turned back to my father to see Justice Xia laying into him, waving a finger that started to rap on my father's forehead. There seemed to be some disagreement about the plan.

My father kept laughing. "How come you're not saying anything?" he asked Marvel's mother. "What have you got to say?"

I was starting to get upset with my father—how could he just sit there and take Justice Xia's abuse? But right then, he ran toward the door of the shack. As his foot hit the mud outside, he turned into a giant bird.

I called after him. "Dad! Dad!"

That was when Halfwit kicked me awake.

The five brothers knelt in the shack, pleading with Justice Xia to return home. Justice Xia sighed. "My own sons don't understand me," he said. But he was genuinely moved by their attempt. He agreed to head back home with them.

Halfwit gave me another kick. "Get back to the village!" he shouted.

I would have preferred to stay asleep. I saw that Bounty had put a length of rope around Lucky's neck and tied her up in the shack. I looked out the door and saw, perched on an outcropping of granite less than a quarter mile away, the big bird with the black head and red beak that New-Life had called a phoenix.

"I'd rather stay out here. Why should I go back?"

"You must've gone feral already. You might as well stay out here with that bird."

"I know that bird. That bird is my father."

"He's sick in the head," said Gold. "Listen to this bullshit!"

"My dad said that Seven Li Gully is a power point. This area around here is shaped like a woman's pussy. He said that, didn't he, Uncle Justice?" Halfwit kicked me again.

Justice Xia looked at me and then looked out at the gully. The gully's two ends narrowed to points, and on each side, and up along the edge of the gully, there were tracks worn in the dust by villagers. At one end of the gully was the half-finished stone embankment that the villagers had built to fill in the gully. In front of it was a set of earthen steps carved out of the dark-red clay. Below the stairs was a patch of wetland, green with reeds. The entire gully, seen from above, was in the shape of a boat or a weaving shuttle—the shape of a woman's private parts.

I stood beside Justice Xia, looking out over the gully. I was surprised, too. My father was completely right. "You understand what this means?" Justice Xia asked me. "Did your father tell you about the feng shui here?"

"Yes."

"When did he say that?"

"Just now, he was saying it to you and Marvel's mother, wasn't he?"

"Who? Who did you say?"

"Marvel's mother."

Justice Xia was stunned into silence. He tried to speak, but nothing came out when he opened his mouth. He put a cigarette between his lips and struck a match.

"What are you and that head case talking about?" asked Halfwit. "You believe a word he says?"

Justice Xia took a drag off the cigarette. He exhaled, and the smoke didn't float up to the ceiling of the shack but hung thick in the air around us. "Spark," he said, "you head back, too. Too much rain today. If you spend the night out here, you'll get arthritis."

"I'm staying here," I said.

"Go home and spend the night there."

"The night'll be just as cold, just as dark, wherever I go."

"Go home," New-Life said. "Just go home. Anyway, the shack is already built."

And so we left Seven Li Gully. Out at the end of the gully, the rain was still soaking half the highway and leaving the other side dry. Everyone walked on the dry side, but I walked under the rain.

Everyone in Freshwind learned about Justice Xia's failed plan to live at Seven Li Gully, and how his sons had needed to go out there to bring him back. Everyone was discussing Justice Xia, whether he might be having a hard time in the village, or whether his sons were giving him trouble. Some villagers pitied him, and others were only too happy to see him fail.

Wisdom Xia wrapped up some young ginger in a handkerchief and set off to see his elder brother. He didn't go directly there but took a detour to the willow tree along the dike. He sat in its shade, took out the radio he had brought along with him, and tuned it to a station playing local opera. The radio was playing an opera called *Han Dantong*.

I won't complain when others stray,

For truly I know there is no other way.

Third Brother Xu was strolling in the road,

Found the seer's stall and had his fortune told.

The future is bright, brother, I'm sure you know,

To Erxian Village is where you must go.

All difficulties will be rewarded in your new home,

Build a courtyard, put up three rooms for a stately home.

Suddenly, the willow tree he was sitting under began to shake, tossing its branches like a flirtatious woman tosses her hair. The rain came down then and seemed to be falling horizontally. Wisdom Xia was completely soaked.

Second Aunt was crouched in front of the chicken coop, sticking her finger up one of the hens to feel for an egg. When she heard local opera, she called toward the window, "Wisdom is on his way." Justice Xia was sitting inside on his kang. "Why don't you come out and stretch your legs?" she asked. "I don't want you holed up in there, sitting on that kang when Wisdom gets here."

Even as she spoke, Justice Xia was already stepping out the door. He headed straight for the dike. Second Aunt never heard him come out, the sound of the rain having covered up his footsteps. She put the hen down again and rapped on the windowsill with her cane.

Wisdom Xia had a feeling that Justice Xia had come up behind him, but he didn't turn around. He beat out a rhythm to accompany the opera on the radio.

Justice Xia sat down on a rock beside the tree. Wisdom Xia said, "You know who's singing there?"

"Who?" asked Justice Xia.

"Goodyear Tian."

"They used to call him 'Scabby Tian,' right?"

"All these years and nobody's been able to copy his particular sound. It's been more than ten years since he died."

Justice Xia didn't answer. The rain suddenly picked up again, like a basin of water had been dumped over the village. The two old brothers wiped rainwater from their faces. Wisdom Xia turned to look at his brother for the first time and saw that Justice Xia's eyes were bloodshot, and his beard, shot through with streaks of gray and white, was untrimmed. "How about this rain?" Wisdom Xia asked. He didn't want to bring up what had happened at Seven Li Gully. He was happy to pretend that nothing had happened.

Justice Xia followed his lead. "We can use a rain like this. It's been a while."

"I knew it was coming when my knees started to ache."

"I've got some knee-warmers at home. Shiner's daughter is a good girl. She took her first paycheck and bought her mother-in-law a cane, and then came over with the knee-warmers for me."

"Why don't you use them?"

"I don't need them."

"I should go pick up a pair for myself. We're getting on in years, you know. It wouldn't hurt to look after ourselves. You should wear them. Last night, I had a dream that I saw our brother. It's been seven or eight years since he came into my dreams, but I saw him last night. He said the house was leaking. I think he was sending me a message. Maybe his tomb is leaking?"

"That worthless son of his, Pavilion . . . He never goes out to his father's grave."

"That reminds me; there's something I wanted to ask you. Why can't you get along with Pavilion?"

"I can't stand the sight of him," said Justice.

"What do you mean? He's in charge now. If you're going to disagree with him on everything, it's going to cause trouble for him. He doesn't have any power anyway. Everyone comes to you for advice."

"I don't want him harming the village. Look at him. He spends all day riding around on his motorbike like a wild man. He isn't committed to the job; it was never a vocation for him. And what experience can he bring? He thinks he can do whatever he wants."

"Who considers becoming a cadre a vocation?" Wisdom Xia asked. "If you think he's made an error, you should just tell him politely."

"Why do I have to be so courteous to him? What are you trying to say? You think since I was a village cadre, too, and now I'm out of the position, that I must be jealous of him? That's not it. You want me to show how magnanimous I am, even though I've left the job. I can't do it. I don't know what it is, exactly, but I can't stand the sight of him."

"I can understand that. There are plenty of things in this world that aren't easy to put into words. I've read before that some people just don't match. Maybe that's how it is with the two of you."

"Maybe I crossed a line."

"You're his uncle. Even if you slapped him, it's your right. How about this: I'll invite him over, and you two can talk."

"Don't bother. The second I see him, I'll be back in the same mood as always. Let's go over to big brother's grave instead."

The two brothers walked over to Justice Xia's home, and Wisdom Xia gave the ginger to Second Aunt. He told her to make some soup with it; she went into the kitchen and came out a short time later with the ginger brew. They drank it, sweating the whole time, and then Justice Xia grabbed a shovel and the two brothers headed for Benevolence Xia's grave. They saw that the rats had been at work, tunneling into the mound, and the rain had started to run into the holes. Justice Xia and Wisdom Xia spent a long time working there, plugging up the rat holes and redirecting the water. As they walked home, they went by Pavilion's place. Wisdom Xia called for him to come out, but Justice Xia kept walking.

It turned out that Pavilion wasn't even at home. Cutie was out in the yard, cutting weeds to feed the pigs. She heard Wisdom Xia yelling and came around to ask him what the matter was. Wisdom Xia told her not to worry and continued on his way. The next day, in the farmers market, he picked up some wooden ladles from a seller from Nanshan and was on his way home when he ran into Pavilion. "Have you been out to your father's grave?" he asked his nephew.

"It's been a long time," said Pavilion. "I heard from Culture that some kids came and cut down the cypress over there. I was thinking I'd go over there this winter and plant a few saplings."

"The mound is already full of rat holes. If you don't plug them up, it'll be washed out."

"Really? I'll go over there tonight."

"If we'd waited for you to go, the whole thing would have already collapsed. Your second uncle went out there yesterday to fix it up."

"Second Uncle went out to my father's grave?"

"If you don't look after us, we'll have to look after ourselves."

"What are you trying to get at?"

"You don't have to force your second uncle into anything."

"Are you talking about him going to Seven Li Gully? I heard about that . . . But what does it have to do with me?"

"Be straight with me."

"He went to the village administration repeatedly. I kept my mouth shut about Seven Li Gully. What is it now? He has a guilty conscience about Seven Li Gully? It's a wasteland. Not even a fly would take a shit there."

"A guilty conscience?" Wisdom Xia asked. "Why would he have a guilty conscience? He's not looking out for himself in this. He wants what's best for the people. You can say it doesn't have anything to do with you, but your whole attitude is what forced his hand in the first place!"

"Fine, fine, I'll stop talking and stop thinking altogether, all right? Now, have you had anything to eat, Fourth Uncle? The food at Rain Xia's restaurant is pretty good. Why don't you go over there and rest for a bit? I'll come by in a while, and we'll have a meal." Pavilion turned from his uncle and hurried off to a stall at the eastern end of the market, where he started arguing with the stallkeeper over unpaid fees.

Wisdom Xia didn't go to the restaurant. He turned and headed for the Great Qing Hall, saying, "Why wouldn't I have eaten already? He didn't even let me answer."

Justice Xia stayed holed up in his house for a couple of days. He shuffled around the place, mumbling to himself, and a blister grew at the corner of his lip as the fire in his body tried to escape. He grumbled through meals, complaining about grains of sand in his rice. He laid into Tongue-Tied for not putting up a bundle of tobacco to dry on the gable of the house. "It's sunny outside, and he's got that tobacco going moldy in here," he groused. He led Lucky out for a walk, and when the dog headed toward Middle Street, Justice Xia lost his temper again, shouting at her until she sat down in the street and whined pathetically. He regretted losing his temper. "Go on then," he said. "I'll follow you." He followed Lucky along the road, past the entrance to Middle Street and out along the stream and the stone bridge. When he realized Lucky was headed toward Seven Li Gully, Justice Xia was overcome with emotion. He hugged the dog to his chest. "You understand me," he said.

Although nobody noticed at first, from that day on, Justice Xia resumed regularly visiting Seven Li Gully. Like I said, Justice Xia had two dogs: he had Lucky, but he also had me. Somehow, I could feel that Justice Xia and Lucky had gone up there. But there was another reason I headed to Seven Li Gully: it was my fate. It was my destiny to follow Justice Xia.

Right around then, though, I was extremely bored. I found myself wandering around Freshwind, and whenever I saw a crowd, I'd go over and have a look. When they started arguing, I'd drift away again. I overheard someone say, "Spark must have worms up his ass, can't sit down." I went over to East Street and chased a flock of chickens over to Mid-Star's father's place. Mid-Star's father was lying on the ground outside the walls of his yard, huffing and puffing and poking in a sewer pipe. He was skinny and black as a stick of charcoal.

"What the hell are you doing, Spark?" he asked.

"Chasing chickens."

"Help me out with this pipe."

"You should have come out and cleared it when it was raining. Why are you doing it on a day this nice?" He started to tell me that his illness had gotten worse. He'd read his own fortune, and it looked like he might not see out the year. "I'm willing to help, Uncle Glory. You don't have to try to scare me."

"Pretty soon your ol' Uncle Glory won't be around anymore. Last night, I went out to take a shit, pushed as hard as I could, and nothing came out. I had the runs before, but now I'm completely blocked up. It hurt so bad I was crying from the pain. I stuck a finger up there and started fishing around and managed to pop out a chunk about as big as a walnut. I took some phenolphthalein tablets, and they did nothing. I got a glass syringe and put five shots of vegetable oil right up my ass, too, then I took some glycerin tablets, but I still couldn't shit. My belly was all swollen up. It hurt like hell. I was cursing and swearing, but the only thing I wouldn't do is curse the gods. I decided to make one final push. I counted to a hundred and then grunted out four or five pellets. After that came a couple of bursts of diarrhea. I woke up this morning, asking myself what I'd done to deserve this illness. That's when I remembered this pipe. This is where I always dump my shit and piss. I was worried the illness had something to do with the pipe. I went and checked my fortune again—and it was just as I'd guessed."

It put the fear in me. I didn't want him to suffer anymore. I got down on my belly, started poking around in the pipe, and pulled out a busted straw sandal, a bunch of weeds, and some steel wire. Mid-Star's father took the steel wire from me, pulled it straight, and put it up on the windowsill. "You're a good boy, Spark," he said. "If you hadn't done what you did to yourself, I could have set you up with a nice girl."

I didn't want to hear that. "You need to find a woman for yourself first," I said, "so you'll have somebody to look after you."

He was silent for a while, and then he said, "Can I ask you something? You went down to the countryside with the opera troupe, didn't you?"

I didn't want anybody in Freshwind to know about that. "What did you say?" I asked.

"Now, that's your secret to keep. Nobody else is going to find out, but you had to have known I'd catch on. So, Mid-Star—"

"Hasn't he been back to see you yet?"

"He's too busy. Once someone gets in a position like his, why are they always so busy?"

"Busy, busy . . ." I stood and made to leave, but Mid-Star's father gave me a tug.

"Would you be willing to help me with something?" he asked. "If you can help me out, I'll give you a secret recipe of mine. You'll never have to worry about making a living for the rest of your life."

"You promise? What's this recipe, anyway?"

"I'd never give it to you if I was healthy. If I had any money to look after myself in my old age, I wouldn't give it to you, either. Before I give it to you, you have to promise to never reveal it to anybody—especially Big-Noise Zhao."

"What the hell is it? You're making it sound like a miracle."

He turned to a page in his notebook and motioned for me to look. At the top of the page was written:

> The prescription contained within these pages, handed down from immortals, gives divine healing to women suffering from chronic blood stagnation. It was used by an elderly woman of the Southern Liu clan, a lifelong imbiber of opium smoke who never lacked for money to spend and was blessed, through this recipe, with unimaginable gifts. On her deathbed, she passed the secret to her daughter. The daughter's nickname was Sunwa, and she lived in the village of Xiaofan. From the end of the Qing, through the founding of the Republic of China, and after the revolution, she kept it safe. If a woman is weak during menstruation, this medicine should be ground to a fine powder, divided into three portions, and sewn with white silk into three bags. Each bag should be fitted with a long string. Each bag should be exposed in turn to the sun, left out for one day. Each bag should be pushed into the woman's womb through the vagina and then pulled out by the string. The first time, there is often no reaction. The second time, a yellow discharge should appear. The third time, menstrual blood will flow, and the illness will be cured. If there is no reaction on the third attempt at inserting the bag, the patient is incurable and will die. The prescription can only be used for patients suffering from stagnant blood. Use by those without the condition can cause excessive bleeding and death.

"Believe me now?" he asked.

"So what's the recipe?"

"Are you going to help me?"

What he wanted me to do was go up into the mountains and find a jujube tree that had been struck by lightning. Once I found a tree that had been hit by lightning, he wanted me to take some wood from it and bring it to him so that he could carve an ink stamp from it. The symbols and characters, matched with the lightning-struck jujube wood, would carry power. "Find it and bring it to me. I'll trade the recipe for the wood."

I went to Yijia Ridge first to hunt for the wood, then I headed to Seven Li Gully. Justice Xia happened to be over there, too. Actually, I saw Lucky first—she was headed down the gully with two watermelon-size rocks lashed over her back with a length of rope. I thought that Justice Xia must have been trying to punish the dog for something or other, but then I saw him coming along the trail that ran alongside the gully—he was carrying a rock, too. He was bent over at a right angle and clasped the big rock behind his back, balanced on his tailbone. It looked like he couldn't carry it much farther. I couldn't see Justice Xia's face, but I could see the beads of sweat running off the top of his head.

"Uncle Justice!" I hollered and then ran over to help him. He saw me coming down the narrow path and yelled for me to get out of the way. The path went right along the edge of the gully, and there was a steep drop on one side and a wall of rock on the other. I tried to squeeze over to the edge of the path to let him pass. I sucked in my gut and motioned for him to go past me. It looked like he had lost his nerve and wanted to rest for a moment, too, but there was nowhere along the edge of the path to set down the rock. He picked up his pace instead, jogging awkwardly down the path. It was pretty funny, but he was making me nervous, running like that with the rock. If he wasn't careful, he'd end up falling into the gully. I hollered at him again. "Uncle Justice! Uncle Justice!"

He kept his mouth shut and plowed ahead on his skinny legs. I called for him again, and without turning he swore back at me, "Shut your fuckin' mouth!" His panting curse threatened to take the last bit of energy out of him. I didn't dare call him again.

He finally made it to a point in the path where he could set the rock on a ridge of rock. "Why the fuck are you still standing over there?" he said, struggling to roll the rock off his tailbone. I rushed over to help, and once the rock was settled, he sat down hard on the path, panting and wheezing. I could see his legs were trembling.

"What the hell are you carrying rocks around for?"

"I was headed up to the embankment, so I figured I might as well take some rock up. What the hell are you doing here?"

"If I didn't come, how do you figure you'd get that rock up there?"

"That's what I want to hear. Go ahead, take it."

As soon as I started lugging the rock over to the embankment, the hunt for the lightning-struck jujube wood fell by the wayside. There really are things that go on between people that are impossible to explain. Mid-Star's father was promising to give me a recipe that would guarantee I'd never have to worry about making a living again, but I couldn't stand him. I knew I'd be happier at Seven Li Gully with Justice Xia, even if he was cursing me out.

"I want you to get Tongue-Tied up here tomorrow. We need to get that embankment built up. We'll do it slow and steady," Justice Xia said.

"What is your family going to say?"

"I do as I please," he said, glaring at me.

That caught me off guard. "The dike on the river, the flood lands, the reservoir canal," I murmured to myself as I hefted the stone. "Doesn't he ever get sick of this?"

"What are you mumbling about over there? Let me ask you this: How many meals are you going to eat in your lifetime? Plenty. But you still get hungry at suppertime, don't you?"

He couldn't have put it better. "All right then," I said, chuckling. "I'll sneak up here every day and help you."

"Fuck, we're like a pack of bandits now."

We made a secret pact to continue building the embankment needed to fill in the gully. Justice Xia slipped away from his wife each day, telling her he was going to play mah-jongg at New-Life's place. At breakfast on the third day, she asked him, "Are you going over to play mah-jongg with New-Life?"

"There's money to be won," he said.

"Every day you come back here saying you won again."

"What can I say? I have a knack."

"You should bring over a bottle of liquor. Games like that drive people apart, but liquor brings you closer. If you keep winning every game, nobody's gonna wanna play with you."

After breakfast, Justice Xia went off with Lucky, and Second Aunt went out to the chickens and felt for eggs about to drop. She put the hens with eggs together in a wicker enclosure and then went out, bolting the gate of the yard behind her. Leaning heavily on her cane, she headed toward Marvel's mother's place.

Marvel had come over a few weeks before to invite Second Aunt over. When she'd finally gone to visit, Marvel's mother had welcomed her warmly, sat her down for a meal, and even given her a bit of fabric as a gift. Back in the day, Marvel's mother was a landlord's wife—not somebody to get close to—but now that they were both old, the distance between them was gone. The two women had kicked off their shoes and sat together on the kang.

"How are your eyes?" asked Second Aunt.

"When the wind blows, I start tearing up," said Marvel's mother. "And I can't see to thread a needle anymore."

"Still better than mine. I can't see a thing," Second Aunt said. "Have you been out to see the market yet?"

"These days, I just don't have the energy," Marvel's mother said.

The two old women laughed.

"Sister," continued Marvel's mother, "tell me, what's the heaviest thing in the world?"

"Stone."

"That's not it."

"Grain then. Grain is the most valuable thing in the world."

"That's not it. It's your legs. When you can't get your legs to go, you can't move an inch."

"Back when we were young, we went around like we were floating on air," said Second Aunt. "Now we can barely walk." She reached out to put a hand on Marvel's mother's leg, feeling its thinness and loose skin.

The two old women gossiped away, wagging their toothless jaws. They could talk about things long past without worrying about what side each was on at the time. Whether it was land reform or the Four Cleanups or even the Cultural Revolution, they could come together, finally, and mourn the dead. There were not many left alive who had escaped those days and lived long enough to tell about them.

"How is Justice doing?" asked Marvel's mother.

"Don't even ask! He goes running around all day, then rolls around in bed every night complaining that his back hurts."

"Has his stomach been okay?"

"It's gotten a bit better since he retired, actually."

"Back when he was young, he used to belch up bile," said Marvel's mother.

Marvel's mother thought back to the things that had happened between her and Justice Xia. She didn't bear a grudge. She actually felt a bit pleased with herself. She shut her eyes and leaned back on the kang.

"Why did you go quiet?" asked Second Aunt.

"I was thinking about someone."

Second Aunt was surprised. She breathed a long sigh. "That's good," she said. "You've got someone to think about. I'm shut up at home all day, trying to think of something—and my head's completely empty!" Both women giggled. Second Aunt suddenly put a hand over her mouth and tilted her head to listen for something. "What the hell are we saying? If someone else heard us . . . What's that sound out there in the yard?"

Marvel's mother stood and peered out the crack between the window and the frame. "It was just a cat," she said. They went back to gossiping.

When Second Aunt got there that morning for her second visit, she heard Marvel's mother talking inside the house. She rapped on the door with her cane. Marvel's mother came out to lead her inside. "Who were you talking to?" Second Aunt asked.

"Marvel's father."

"Marvel's father?"

"But I'm done with him now. That ghoul, he put me through hell my entire life. I won't say another word to him, even if he beats me."

"He beats you?"

"We used to chat, every now and then. But yesterday afternoon, when I was on my way out, I smacked my head against the side of the door. It must have been that ghoul. Feel it," she told Second Aunt, leaning down toward her. "There's still a bump there. I told Marvel as soon as he got up to go out to his father's grave and burn some spirit money. I want that ghoul to take his money and go. Can you believe he'd attack me like that?"

The two women suddenly started laughing. Neither of them really believed the story. They sat down together, and it was almost an hour before Second Aunt broke the silence. "Is the sun coming down yet?" she asked.

"Must be afternoon already."

"Finally. The days are so long."

"I still haven't bothered to fix something to eat," Marvel's mother said. "What's the point? We spend all day waiting. We're either waiting for a meal or waiting to die."

"The meal has to come first, at least today," Second Aunt said. "I better get back home and make something. Justice Xia can't stand a meal being late. He'll fly into a rage if the food's not on the table when he's hungry." She left Marvel's mother's home and felt her way home. When she got there, Justice Xia still wasn't home. "That damn mah-jongg!" she swore. "How can he still be over there?" She went over to the steamer to look for a bun to heat up, but the steamer was empty. Justice Xia had taken the buns with him when he left.

We were working in Seven Li Gully, clearing broken stones and weeds off the rock wall to build up the embankment. We'd managed to clear a space about as big as a dinner table in the rock wall and were pulling stones that we'd then carry down to the embankment. Justice Xia told us not to worry about how much work it looked like we'd done.

"Rock by rock, day by day, month by month, we'll get it done," he said. "Imagine how it will look in a year, in ten years . . . This gully will be farmland someday. If you believe in it, you can make it happen."

"You mean I can get a wife for myself?" I asked.

"Sure." He pointed at me. "Everything that gets planted here, where there used to be a gully, it'll be a testament to our hard work. When you see those plants growing on this land that used to be waste, you'll completely forget about finding a wife."

Maybe Justice Xia didn't really mean that, maybe he was just trying to comfort me, but I took him completely seriously. I looked around for something to plant. I thought about dragging one of the trees down from the edge of the gully, but I knew it wouldn't work. I went over to the shack, pulled one of the poplar branches out of the roof, and planted it in the mud.

Tongue-Tied laughed and pointed at my stick. He wanted to know what I was doing, planting a stick in the ground and expecting it to grow into something.

"You're going to grow into a tree!" I said to the branch. "Remember! You must live. Snow . . ." I was about to call her full name, but knew I shouldn't. Tongue-Tied smirked and pointed at my crotch, making the same gesture repeatedly. I knew he was mocking me, and I couldn't stand it.

I ignored Tongue-Tied for the rest of the afternoon. I worked on the east side moving stone, and he worked on the west side moving stone. "Bad blood is good for work," said Justice Xia when he saw us. He took out two steamed buns and gave us each one, and when we were done, he brought out another two.

"Aren't you hungry, Uncle Justice? Why aren't you eating?" I asked.

"I just want to watch you two eat."

"Doesn't that make you even hungrier?"

"It makes me feel good."

Tongue-Tied squeezed out a silent toot, then bent down and strained to let out a string of loud farts.

When Justice Xia got home that night, his back itched something fierce, and he called over his wife to scratch it. He immediately started complaining about his aches and pains. It didn't take long for Second Aunt to figure out that her husband must have been over at Seven Li Gully again. She wasn't happy about it and let him know. But Justice Xia kept his cool. He brought her around to his side, eventually, and she agreed to get up early and prepare some steamed buns and pickled cabbage for him, as long as the trips to Seven Li Gully remained a secret from the rest of the village.

"I'll be fine," Justice Xia told her. "After all these years, I know how to look after myself."

Justice Xia kept working at Seven Li Gully, but finally Second Aunt revealed the secret to Bounty. Bounty was upset, and he focused his anger on Tongue-Tied.

If Justice Xia was going to Seven Li Gully, then Bounty knew that his father would have his mute grandson working for him. Tongue-Tied came home that night to change his pants. He was already a head taller than his father and had red spots across his cheeks. His pants had split, and his black ass was hanging out the back. He took off the pants and called for his mother to mend them. She was busy rolling out noodles and told Tongue-Tied to get his father to help.

Bounty took out a needle and thread and started roughly mending the split in the pants, grumbling the whole time that his son had become a bandit. "Just bought pants, and three months later they've got a rip in them," he said. "Have you got teeth growing back there?" Tongue-Tied sat in the doorway, his legs straight out in front of him and Lucky at his side. He popped steamed buns in his mouth and chewed them with cheeks bulging. The smell of his feet wafted through the house. "You went over to Seven Li Gully with your grandfather, didn't you?"

With his mouth stuffed with steamed buns, Tongue-Tied couldn't have said a word, even if he'd suddenly been given the power of speech. Lucky answered for him. "Woof!"

"Have a heart," Bounty said. "You should be trying to stop him."

"Woof!"

"What the hell did you just say? Who asked you?"

Lucky barked a response again and then rushed at Bounty, who chased her out of the house.

"You're forbidden from going to Seven Li Gully. You understand me?" he asked Tongue-Tied. "If I catch you going out there again, I'll break your legs." Tongue-Tied stood up and looked like he was about to leave. "Where are you going? I'm not done with you yet!" Bounty made a clumsy grab for his son, but Tongue-Tied wrapped his arms around his father and squeezed him hard. Tongue-Tied lifted his father clean off the floor, and Bounty's feet kicked in midair. He set his father back in his chair with a thud and then walked out of the house.

Bounty told Gold and Hearth about his son dropping him in his chair after he'd forbidden him from going to Seven Li Gully. Both brothers sighed. They knew that their father was stubborn, and it would be even harder to bring him back from the gully if he had Tongue-Tied at his right hand. They decided to go to the gully and ask him to come back. But short of putting him in chains, they knew it would be tough to keep him away.

The three brothers went to Halfwit's wife and asked her to look after Second Aunt. Halfwit's wife had a mouth on her, but she wasn't much of a worker. By the second day, she'd already left her post to go up to the shrine at Tiger Head Cliff, tying her three-year-old to the door latch with a rope around his waist. When Justice Xia got home from the gully, Halfwit's wife still wasn't back. The child had pissed his pants and mixed it with the dirt in the yard, spreading filth all over himself. When Halfwit's wife got back, Justice Xia scolded her, but she only smiled and changed the topic.

"I want to talk to you about something," she said.

"What is it?"

"I would've been back sooner, but there were a bunch of people over there waiting to worship Master Clear-Bright's remains. He was a great holy man. I ended up staying longer than I thought I would."

"I heard that his body is preserved somehow. It won't rot . . . ," Justice Xia said.

"Of course not; he was a great master. When you see him, it just looks like he's asleep. So I was thinking, if you're going to Seven Li Gully every day, I should go along with you. I can make sure you have hot meals while you're working."

"You want to turn Seven Li Gully into a temple, too?" Justice Xia asked.

Halfwit's wife turned without speaking and went into the kitchen to wash rice. As they ate dinner, she broke her silence. "Do you think Mid-Star's dad is a good man?" she asked Justice Xia.

"He's your elder. Call him Uncle Glory."

"Is Uncle a good man?"

"What do you mean?"

"He told me that when he dies, his body is going to be preserved."

"You're talking nonsense," Justice Xia said.

"He said he wants to build a coffin," said Halfwit's wife, "and then get nailed inside. He plans to starve to death. He says he wants to leave his body for the people of the world to see . . ."

"He wants to die, is that it? He plans to kill himself? That guy is more scared of death than anyone." He told Halfwit's wife to take her child and go and focus on her own problems.

Chapter 27

Mid-Star's father might have claimed his body would somehow be preserved after his death, but he never really built a coffin and kept on making his predictions. His claims didn't amount to much, but mine did. When I planted that poplar branch I'd taken down from the roof of the shack, I said, "You must live!" And that branch grew, and the green buds on it sprouted into leaves. I sat under my tree and sang a few lines from *A Chance Meeting*.

As I sang, I looked up out of the gully at the sky overhead where the big bird glided, and the clouds seemed to float up and away from it. But while I was singing, the gingko tree in the courtyard of Freshwind Temple was weeping. That's the truth.

Lotus Jin, who was sitting alone at a desk in the village government offices drawing up Freshwind's family planning program, heard clattering and went out to look. There wasn't a cloud in the sky, but the gingko tree had a layer of moisture on its bark. She looked closer and saw that the source was the leaves on one branch of the tree. She found it unusual, so she called over some people from the dirt yard in front of the opera house. They frowned and agreed that this tree was suffering from the same haunting as the big poplar out at New-Life's orchard. The rattling poplar in the orchard was a ghost clapping its hands, and now the gingko was weeping. Someone asked if it might be an omen that it was going to be a bad year for Freshwind. Lotus Jin was stunned. At first, she decided not to tell Pavilion about it. But the tree kept weeping for three days.

The gingko had stood there for several hundred years. Villagers relied on its feng shui when they planned where to build their houses. When the tree started to weep, there was inevitably talk that this was a bad omen for the most recent session of the Two Committees. Pavilion, Goodness, and Lotus Jin decided that they must do their best to preserve the ancient gingko. The folk remedy for saving ancient trees involved watering the gingko with vegetable oil. The village government didn't have the fifty *jin* of vegetable oil required, and it would be yet another expense that they could not afford. It was Goodness who came up with the idea of collecting the oil from the villagers.

Goodness went looking for Mid-Star's father, who had begun spreading his own ideas about the tree. An ancient gingko in a temple yard must have long ago become a spirit, so if the tree spirit was sick, it would certainly repay everyone who donated oil to save it, whether they gave one *liang* or ten *jin*. Mid-Star's father was the first to donate, giving half a *jin* of oil and tying a red string around the trunk of the tree. When the villagers saw a stingy bastard like Mid-Star's father donating oil, they pitched in, too. West Street gave twenty-one *jin*, Middle Street gave twenty-five *jin*, and East Street enthusiastically gave their share as well.

That night, a wind blew through the village, and Justice Xia was up at dawn. He went out and saw that Forest Wu was already out picking up shit. He had a basket partly full, but he had another basket that was loaded not with fertilizer but with a few tree branches. Among the branches was a bird's nest about the size of a bowl. Justice Xia noticed that Forest Wu had hung a small bottle of oil at the end of his carrying pole.

"Uncle Justice," Forest Wu called when he saw the old man, "you're u-up early."

"Not as early as you."

"E-even if I get up early, th-that's no guarantee I'll be a-a-able to fill my baskets."

"What are you collecting, shit or firewood?"

"The wind blew i-i-it down, so I picked it up. Uncle J-Justice, have you donated any oil o-or not?"

"Hearth donated my share," Justice Xia said.

"I'm g-g-going over to the vi-village government in a while, gotta give my share."

"How much oil is there in that bottle?"

"O-one *liang*."

"One *liang*?"

"I borrowed it fr-from Clerk's wife. T-told her I wanted half a *jin*, but uh, sh-sh-she's cheap. She only g-gave me one *liang*."

"You don't have any oil at home?"

"W-we haven't had a-any for a few months."

"Is that any way to live?"

"I h-had a good year, not a bad month, but every d-d-d-day is a s-s-struggle. Uncle Justice, w-wasn't there a pro-program before to help people out with some relief, f-for the elderly? Wh-where's it been th-these last couple of years?"

"You got used to eating for free, huh? We've had bumper crops out here. Don't expect a handout. What happened to the grain and oil you had saved up?"

"Black-Moth, that wh-whore, made off with all of it. That wh-wh-whore!"

Justice Xia's words caught in his throat. "You bring shame to your ancestors," he finally said, then walked quickly away. He turned back suddenly toward Forest Wu. "Give me that nest," he said.

"Cook it up and it'll be r-r-real tasty," Forest Wu said, passing Justice Xia the nest.

Justice Xia had no plans to cook the nest. When he'd seen the nest, he'd thought of the tree I'd planted. He wanted to put the nest up on it and attract some birds. He went over to the bridge where Tongue-Tied and I planned to meet him. But I was running late that day and so was Tongue-Tied. Justice Xia assumed that Tongue-Tied was lazing around somewhere and that I must have gotten busy with something at home. He went by himself toward Seven Li Gully.

When he entered the gully, the morning's mist still lingered. He sneezed, and the fog flowed away from him like water so that he could suddenly see the black-and-white stones and the wolf fang growing between them. Justice Xia put the nest up on my tree and then squatted beside it, trying to call a bird to settle on the nest. No birds came; there was no response to his calls.

He reached out and tried to grab the thick fog that clung to the trunk of the tree, but when he opened his hand, it was empty. From his fingertips came trails of steam. He looked out over the gully—he could imagine what it would be like if it was filled in, if this fog was instead silt turned to soil. He could picture the fields of corn, paddies for rice with flowers growing between the beds, tall sunflowers and sesame and lilies below them, fireflies darting among them.

Wow! Look at the size of those fireflies! Suddenly glowing green! Abruptly, he realized that they weren't fireflies at all; he was staring into the eyes of a wolf. He gave his head a shake. He knew his eyes weren't deceiving him—it was a wolf! It had been twenty years since he'd seen a wolf. The last time had been during land reform, one afternoon when he'd been planting trees up on the river dike. Back then, he'd had to beat the wolf off him. It had pounced on him, and he'd ended up putting his fist down its throat and gouging its eyes with his other hand. He went and told the other villagers about the wolf attack, but nobody had really believed him. He could barely believe it himself—had he really jammed his fist down a wolf's throat? But that was what had happened. They ended up finding the wolf's paw prints and droppings below the dike. At least for a while, the story of Justice Xia and the wolf became legend in Freshwind.

Justice Xia told me later that it was fate. Perhaps it was the same wolf he had faced all those years before, or maybe this was the son or grandson of that wolf . . .

But this was not the same Justice Xia who had faced the wolf on the river dike. He was old and his joints creaked. He was no match for a wolf. He quickly looked around for a position to retreat to, but there was nowhere to go. He stayed completely still and cautioned himself, *If there's nowhere to go, just don't move; don't let the wolf know your weakness.*

Justice Xia stood motionless for a long time before there came the faint sound of Tongue-Tied coming down to the ravine. The wolf lowered its head and then turned suddenly. The last sight Justice Xia caught of it was of its tail disappearing into the thick mist.

After the encounter with the wolf, Justice Xia behaved nothing like the Justice Xia of decades before, who'd beaten back the wolf and then immediately told the story. It was twenty days later that Tongue-Tied and I finally heard of it. At first, I only half believed him. I knew Justice Xia wasn't in the habit of bullshitting, and judging by the way he'd told the story, he was clearly ashamed. But I was skeptical because I'd never seen a wolf around there. Tongue-Tied and I had been through every inch of Seven Li Gully, up every cliff and through every stand of brush, but we'd never seen a wolf.

But then I thought back to the day that Justice Xia said he'd seen the wolf. Lucky had barked and run to him. Justice Xia struggled to his feet, looking pale. His expression seemed to be frozen, like his face had been carved out of wood.

"Uncle Justice," I said, "when did you get here?"

He didn't say anything. He didn't even look at me.

"What's wrong, Uncle Justice?" I reached out to steady him, but he immediately keeled over and fell to the ground.

"What happened to my legs?" he asked.

I gave his legs a pinch, but he couldn't seem to feel it. Once he'd recovered a bit, Tongue-Tied and I led him into the shack. I noticed that the crotch of his pants were wet. I realized he'd pissed himself.

Tongue-Tied and I didn't suspect anything else; we just worried that Justice Xia must have been really sick. But around noon, Justice Xia came out of the shack completely transformed. He stood in the doorway of the shack and gave three mighty roars. Three pheasants roosting along the cliff took flight. I began to tremble. I cast a hesitant glance in his direction, and he waved Tongue-Tied and me over. He wanted to arm wrestle with us.

As soon as I took his hand, he gripped mine so hard that it felt like he could turn my bones to powder. He quickly forced my hand down. Tongue-Tied stepped up next and locked hands with Justice Xia. The mute was stronger than I was and battled Justice Xia for a full two minutes before finally being beaten. "I beat both of you," he said. "Two young bucks can't stand up to the old man."

"Were you older than my dad? If he was still alive . . ."

"Your dad was three years younger than me. He didn't have as much heart as me. He passed early."

"You're going to live to a hundred. You almost broke my hand just now," I said. I was only trying to compliment him, maybe give him a laugh, but he didn't even crack a smile.

He turned away from me. "You notice anything different?" he said, pointing at the top of his head.

"It's white up at the front and still dark at the back."

"Half-and-half, right? That means half my life is already over. I'm seventy-five this year, so I've got seventy-five more years to go. Let me tell you this, when land reform came, I handled all of it as a village cadre. I settled things for all the rich peasants and the landlords, big and small . . . I never let anyone down, and I never allowed myself to be swayed. I split up every plot of farmland, whether rice paddy or dry field, every slope, every gully . . . I built the river dike with my own hands and worked the marshlands. Back then, Spark, you were just a twitch in your father's nutsack. The calluses I got on my knees took three years to wear away. These red marks on my neck are from carrying a shoulder pole back then. I pushed the power plant project, even though they ended up pulling power from the Hubei grid. Our plan for a power plant came to nothing, but the canals we dug down from the dam are still being used to irrigate crops. With my own hands, I terraced the fields. With my own hands, I built the dam.

"Then, we were told to reform, right? Society was changing, they said. So with my own hands I set up the brickyard, and with my own hands I planted the orchard. I was the one who won all those awards and banners on the walls of the government office. They had classified Freshwind as a poor village—not anymore! That was because of me, too. So you tell me, did I do the right thing?"

Tongue-Tied and I listened intently. It felt like we were listening to one of the lectures he used to give when he was still leading the village. He'd stand up in front of everyone, his jacket open, a cigarette in his hand, and launch into his speech. I used to interpret for my father all the impressive language Justice Jia tossed at him. My father was never much of an orator, either, especially compared to Justice Xia. He used a type of repetition to make his point, setting up parallelisms, one after the other. My father tried it, too, but he could never quite master it. When he talked, nobody paid attention.

When Justice Xia came to his final question, I answered, "You did the right thing, Uncle Justice."

"Bullshit I did the right thing," he said. "I was a failure. Seven Li Gully is where I was defeated. But I refuse to accept it. I know that what I am doing here is right. As an old village cadre, it's my responsibility to stick with my assessment. As an old village cadre, it's my duty to use my insight. This gully will one day become farmland. If you two believe in me, then work with me on this. If you don't believe in me, feel free to go. You understand me?"

Tongue-Tied moaned his response.

"I understand," I said.

"So, are you leaving or not?" Justice Xia asked.

"If you're staying, I'm staying."

"Fine. In that case, I need you to go to Concord Qin's house and get that old musket of his."

I followed his order. At the same time, Tongue-Tied was sent to the edge of the gully to dig out a channel for mud to run through, and Justice Xia headed up to the reservoir to lay into the reservoir manager for taking the fishponds in exchange for Seven Li Gully. He was going to force the reservoir manager to hunt through every cupboard and filing cabinet in the office to find the original plan for reclaiming the gully.

When I got to Concord Qin's place to get the musket, he asked me to take him over to Seven Li Gully. I didn't want to—what would he accomplish by going to the gully? He'd just end up slowing me down. He gave me a pickax to take to Justice Xia, but the musket was nowhere to be found. It turned out that Big-Noise Zhao had borrowed the musket on the day that Wind Xia was married and still hadn't returned it.

When I went to get the musket from Big-Noise Zhao, he wanted to know what we needed it for at Seven Li Gully. He decided to go there with me. When we got there, the big bird was sitting on a rock preening, burying its head under its wing to peck at the feathers there. Big-Noise Zhao shouldered the musket, but I caught him with a kick that knocked him back a step.

"What do you want to shoot it for?" I asked. "What'd that bird ever do to you?"

"Protecting a wild bird like your own father, huh?"

"That's exactly right. That bird is my father."

"Your father? Your father! You've really lost it."

"My father told me that the gully is like a woman's pussy."

"You ever seen a pussy before?" Big-Noise Zhao asked.

I was about to kick him again when I heard a dog barking. I looked around, but Lucky was nowhere to be found. "Tongue-Tied!" I yelled. There was no answer. But the dog appeared, barking again as she squeezed out of a pile of stones. I ran over to look at the pile of stones. I

361

peered into a crack and saw that under the stones was a dark crevice. "What were you barking for?" I asked Lucky.

Lucky kept barking, and I looked in the crevice again. I finally saw Tongue-Tied down inside.

"What the hell did you crawl in there for?" Big-Noise Zhao asked. There was no answer. "He must have fallen in there!"

We rushed over and slid down into the crevice. Tongue-Tied had passed out, but I revived him with a pinch under his nose.

When he saw Big-Noise Zhao, Tongue-Tied rubbed his eyes. Once he'd regained his senses, he got to his feet and spat an egg out of his mouth. I thought it was odd for Tongue-Tied to have a wild bird egg in his mouth, but after a bit of gesticulating from the mute, I realized he had picked the egg from a nest that he'd found while working on the edge of the gully. He'd planned to put the egg in the nest Justice Xia had put in the tree I'd planted. He didn't want the egg to break while he made his way down the side of the gully, so he'd popped it in his mouth. He'd ended up stumbling and falling down the side of the gully and into the crevice.

I had to give him a hug, I was so grateful. I took the egg up out of the crevice and put it in the nest.

"You're insane," Big-Noise Zhao said, pointing at me. "But you must be retarded," he said to the mute. "You could've cracked your head open, all for an egg."

"The feng shui must be good in Seven Li Gully! Tongue-Tied fell all that way, but he's fine."

Big-Noise Zhao turned and looked up the gully. "It does look a bit like a vagina," he said. "The gravesite Uncle Justice's plotted out is right where the clit would be. He must have come out here to protect his grave."

Right as he said that, Tongue-Tied clenched his fist and knocked him over the head.

Big-Noise Zhao rubbed the lump that was already growing on his forehead. "You ungrateful son of a bitch," he said. "How could you do that, after I just pulled you out of that crevice?"

Tongue-Tied cocked his fist back again, jabbering and moaning unintelligible curses at Big-Noise Zhao. I jumped between them and held Tongue-Tied back. "Get the hell out of here, Big-Noise Zhao. I don't know if I can hold him back."

Big-Noise Zhao took off running. Before he got very far, he saw Justice Xia coming down from the gully ridge. "Uncle Justice!" he called.

"You trying to start a fight here?" Justice Xia said as he came down in the gully. Tongue-Tied saw Justice Xia's frown. He moaned something to his grandfather. I didn't understand much of it, and Big-Noise Zhao didn't understand any of it. "You're telling them I want to fill the gully to protect my grave?" Justice Xia asked Big-Noise Zhao.

"It was a joke. Tongue-Tied took it the wrong way."

"Did he hit you?"

"He hit me right here," Big-Noise Zhao said, pointing at his forehead.

"Serves you right," Justice Xia said. "You really think that's what kind of person I am?"

"Uncle Justice," Big-Noise Zhao said, "if I didn't believe in you, I wouldn't have come here. You think I came to Seven Li Gully for my health?"

"That gravesite was picked out by Forest Wu's father-in-law, at Treasure's request. Once he picked out the site, I started preparing the gravesite. If it's a good spot, according to feng shui, then it'll be a blessing to the descendants of the Xia family. If we succeed in filling up the gully and reclaiming the land, that will be a blessing for the people of Freshwind."

"Oh, I see. So if you want to protect the gravesite, you have to reclaim the land, and if you want to reclaim the land, you have to protect the gravesite . . ."

"That's one way of putting it," Justice Xia said. "But what brings you out here?"

"I was sitting at home trying to put together a couplet about Seven Li Gully."

"Well, you've come to the right place."

I was perplexed by Justice Xia's mild treatment of Big-Noise Zhao. "Uncle Justice," I asked after Big-Noise had left, "did you get some good news?"

"How did you know?"

"I saw how you treated Big-Noise Zhao."

Justice Xia took some documents from under his arm. "Look what I've got here," he said. "Have a look. Your father and I planned everything."

Here is what the document said:

1. Preliminary situation

Freshwind is located to the southwest of the Miaogou Reservoir. The main reservoir canal runs north of Freshwind (flow rate 12 m3/s). The village contains one thousand *mu* of arable land, with 300 *mu* on alluvial soil, 500 *mu* located atop plateaus, and 200 *mu* of sloped land. There are 410 households in the village, with a population of 2,120 people. There is roughly 0.5 *mu* of arable land per villager.

2. An analysis of irrigation conditions for gully reclamation

a. Terrain conditions

The plan calls for diverting the reservoir's main canal, north of Seven Li Gully. The middle section is 1,200 meters long, at an elevation of 38 meters above sea level, while Seven Li Gully is at 30.5 meters. Because of the higher elevation of the canal, it should be feasible to send water to irrigate the land.

b. Inflow and drainage

This plan calls for a dam to be set up along the irrigation canal. The dam will be approximately 200 meters wide and have a slope of 1:1500. From the reservoir, a sluice will be installed with a length of 1,200 meters and a slope of 1:1200.

Timing for irrigation of the area and discharge from the dam must be staggered. The people have high hopes for the project and faith in Party cadres so, apart from financial contributions, can certainly be counted upon to offer voluntary labor.

3. Plans for reclamation

a. After three years, 500 *mu* of land will be reclaimed. There will be biannual flooding of the gully, each session lasting 200 hours. The silt content of the irrigation water is approximately 40 percent, which will add 60 centimeters of soil to the gully. The water will reach an elevation of 200 meters during that irrigation process.

b. The irrigation canal diverted from the main canal will be 2,000 meters long and 200 meters wide, with edge slopes of 1:1, and an overall slope over its run of 1:1500. 20,000 m³ of soil will be excavated.

c. The sluice gate system will have a gradient of 6.5 meters and have three lock gates, each 2 meters wide. There will be 3 apertures in the gate, with a diameter of 2 meters.

4. Economic benefits

Following reclamation of the gully, the land will be used mainly to grow corn. A harvest of 500 kg per *mu* is expected. The expected harvest for grain is 500 kg per mu, along with 500 kg per *mu* of stover. The current price of corn is 0.6 yuan per kilogram for the grain and 0.02 yuan per kilogram for corn stover. Revenues will be 138,000 yuan a year.

As I read, two red-winged birds flew above me. They must have been husband and wife. They sang to each other as they flew, sometimes paired together and sometimes flying apart, floating toward the ground and then suddenly soaring upward . . . It was as if they were putting on a performance. The two birds finally sank slowly down out of the sky and perched together on the nest that Justice Xia had put up in my tree. The two birds were happy with the nest, but even happier to find the egg that had gone missing from their own.

"Uncle Justice," I shouted, "come have a look!"

But Justice Xia was busy showing Tongue-Tied how to shoot the musket. The mute fired two shots at the old dam site, and the sound echoed down the sides of the gully and back again. It was so loud that it felt like the earth was shaking. I reached over to steady my tree. I was worried the birds would get spooked, but they didn't even move as they bent over their egg.

"Get over here, Spark," Justice Xia called. "Come pull the trigger a couple of times."

I went over and shouldered the musket, and Justice Xia leaned in the doorway of the shack, scratching his back against the frame. The entire shack shook with each rub of his back as he smiled with satisfaction. Big-Noise Zhao, standing not far from the shack, seemed to be deep in thought. "Did you finish that couplet?" Justice Xia asked.

"I'm not sure yet," said Big-Noise Zhao. "Let me write it down and see what you think." He took a branch and wrote in the dirt:

> Suffer and work to make something better,
> And pass it down to bless your ancestor.

"Not bad," said Justice Xia. "You read my mind."

"I know you better than the worms in your belly," said Big-Noise Zhao.

"Oh? What am I thinking of right now?"

"You're thinking, 'I better treat Big-Noise to a drink.'"

"You clever son of a bitch," said Justice Xia, chuckling. "I'll treat you, but you'll have to settle for some *liang fen* instead."

When we were done with work for the day, Justice Xia really did take Big-Noise Zhao out to eat *liang fen*. I didn't understand Justice Xia—couldn't he see what Big-Noise Zhao was up to? Justice Xia's one failing was that he fell for flattery too easily. He went weak in the knees as soon as anyone buttered him up.

Tongue-Tied and I tagged along, too. The mute ate the *liang fen*, but I refused; I had principles. I went and sat down on the steps of the Earth Shrine.

The late harvest was already in, and down every street and alley were heaps of corn and rice straw. Someone had laid a bundle of sesame stalks in the doorway of the temple. I kicked it out of the way. I'd gotten half the straw down the stairs when Rites Xia came walking over from the west. "Who put that there?" he asked me.

"Must've been blind to put sesame stalks in a temple doorway."

"Are you looking for trouble, you crazy son of a bitch? Someone's gonna lay a beating on you."

"Fine with me. They better be looking for trouble, too, if they're messing with me."

"Forget it, forget it," Rites Xia said. "You should have some pity."

I didn't understand what he meant. As he walked away, I asked him, "Weren't you going to the capital, Uncle Rites? How come you're back?"

"You wanted me to stay there?"

"How'd you get back? Did you get a ride on Thunder's bus?"

"Wind Xia brought me back in his car," said Rites Xia.

I had no response to that. I thought to myself, *Does that mean that Wind Xia is back?*

I stood up straight, brushed the dirt off my clothes, and shot down the alley toward home. There was a brilliant sunset that night, and the donkey at the dyehouse brayed for an entire hour after.

Chapter 28

Wind Xia really had come home in a company car with a driver. When they turned off the 312 and drove into the village, they were hailed by some of the villagers who had spread pea stalks out in the roadway to dry and were hitting them with flails.

"Wind Xia! Wind Xia! Can you run over our peas a few times?"

So Wind Xia stepped out of the car and told the driver to drive back and forth over the stalks.

Meanwhile, Rites Xia was on his way home. He popped into someone's yard and took a freshly grilled corncob, which he gnawed on until his lips and teeth turned black.

Wind Xia stayed two days in Freshwind Village. He'd planned to help with digging a bit of riverside land, but Wisdom Xia wouldn't let him. Rain Xia had paid Forest Wu and Doubleday Yang, a neighbor of mine, to do the job, and they were getting five yuan a day, Wisdom told Wind Xia. Instead, Wisdom wanted his opinion on his opera masks.

He got out the masks that the troupe had brought back from their tour and arranged them all over the room. Wind Xia came up with the idea to photograph them, and then he would get his publishers to publish an illustrated book about the painting of opera masks. This put Wisdom Xia into a tizzy of excitement.

He tapped Wind Xia on the temples with his finger. "I raised you right, you little rascal! Why didn't I think of that myself? Find me a publisher, and if I really get to publish that book, I want a copy in my coffin as a headrest!"

They fetched the camera and began to photograph the masks. In fact, they took the task so seriously that they locked the gate and told Fourth Aunt not to let anyone in; they were not to be disturbed on any account.

At lunchtime, Forest Wu and Doubleday Yang came back from the fields and had to knock because the gate was bolted. Eventually, Fourth Aunt answered their shouts and came out of the kitchen, grumbling to her husband, "Why couldn't you or Wind Xia open the gate?"

"Can't you see I'm busy?" Wisdom Xia said.

"You and Wind Xia better go and do some of the digging this afternoon. You can't pay men to help and leave them doing it all themselves. What do you think they are, hired hands?"

"I'm not sending Wind Xia out digging. He's much more useful compiling a book for me than turning over the soil!"

Fourth Aunt unbarred the gate, and Forest Wu and Doubleday Yang tumbled in, covered in mud and sweat. They watched with fascination as Wind Xia photographed the masks, picking up first one mask, then another, commenting on how this one was well painted and that one wasn't, until they'd daubed the ladles with muddy fingerprints.

Wisdom Xia hurriedly urged them to "Sit yourselves down; you deserve a rest." Then he called, "Get a basin of water, wife, so they can wash their faces. And bring them my water pipe."

Fourth Aunt did as she was told, and lit a cord to start the water pipe as well.

"What are we eating?" Wisdom Xia asked her.

"Porridge with dumplings."

"No *luomo* pancakes?"

"Why are you shouting like that? We're almost out of white flour. I haven't got enough to make even one pancake . . ."

"These men have been hard at work, and if you don't feed the workers well, how can they get the job done? You make some small *luomo*, just for them, and Wind Xia and I will have porridge and dumplings."

"Are you done with the masks?" Fourth Aunt asked that evening.

"Yup, all the photography's done, but compiling the pictures into a book is gonna take some time. A few days at least. What's up now?"

"What's up? What d'you think is up? Has Wind Xia only come back to put together a book for you? You know perfectly well he's quarreled with Snow Bai. Why aren't you sending him to the theater to see her?"

Wisdom Xia slapped his head as if he'd completely forgotten, then called Wind Xia in. "You go see Snow Bai first thing tomorrow morning," he ordered him. "And take some of that freshly milled rice to her as well."

Before Wind Xia set off the next morning, his father asked, "What else do I need to do on the book?"

"Write a foreword that explains the history of Shaanxi opera and its importance. And write about how you paint the masks, too."

"Anything else?"

"Yes, raise some money. This book's not gonna be a bestseller, and the publisher won't want to lose money on it, so you'll have to cover the costs."

"Don't you earn money writing books? How come your dad has to pay to publish a book?" asked Fourth Aunt.

"What do you know about anything?" Wisdom Xia snapped.

"How much money?"

"About twenty thousand should do it."

"Twenty thousand? Are you sure you haven't got that wrong?"

"Never mind the money," said Wisdom Xia. "I'll get the manuscript ready for you, and you take the book back with you." And he stalked off, his head held high until he got to his room, where he slumped on the bed.

Fourth Aunt grumbled to Wind Xia, "Why do you get him in such a tizzy? What use is this book, anyway? When Snow Bai has the baby, you'll need every cent you've got. Where will you get twenty thousand for a book? Don't give it to him!"

Wind Xia said nothing. He picked up the bag of rice to take with him, but his mother held him back. "Snow Bai's not been feeling well. You make sure you take good care of her." Then she called after him: "And another thing . . . she's a few months on now, so you stick to separate beds."

Wind Xia did as he was told. All the time he was with the opera troupe, he and Snow Bai had slept in separate beds, and he did her washing for her and made her rice porridge and washed her feet and rubbed her back. But he was only there two days, and part of that was taken up with an argument.

The way Wind Xia saw it, Snow Bai should have respected his wishes and gotten rid of the baby, but now he'd found out that she hadn't. He'd thought that by going to see her, he might still persuade her, but when he arrived, he realized that she was too far gone, and also that the pregnancy was affecting her badly—her face had broken out in freckles. He did what he had to do, in a state of gloom, then spent the rest of his time in the county seat renewing old acquaintances and drinking with them.

There were not many people left at the theater. The splitting up of the troupe and its assets had created a lot of bad blood, and there was no money to put on new productions, so all that was left were small groups of half a dozen to a dozen friends who put on the occasional performance, singing and dancing in the county dance halls or at weddings or other celebrations in the local villages or townships. Snow Bai was too pregnant to go with them.

Mrs. Wang, who used to sing in *Picking up the Jade Bracelet*, stayed behind, too. She'd been a famous singer, but she was old now and had become rather odd. She and Snow Bai spent their time in the theater gossiping, Mrs. Wang pouring out her heart to her friend. She told Snow Bai that she had recordings of her own performances and she'd like them put out as a CD, but it was going to cost too much. At this, she broke down in sobs.

Snow Bai tried to comfort her. "Mrs. Wang, you're one of our great performers. Of course you should put out a CD. Mid-Star said he wanted to revitalize local opera, but he didn't put his money where his mouth was. And now that he's gone, there's no one else to turn to. But if we don't save these recordings, in a few years . . ." Snow Bai trailed off, and taking the handkerchief, she wiped Mrs. Wang's tears for her.

"Well, soon I'll be dead and gone, and that'll be that," said Mrs. Wang. "But then who'll be here to put on a good show in the county seat?"

"I could get some of the performers together and go and talk to the county head," offered Snow Bai.

"Don't bother. I've been trying to get the county head to pay my medical bills, and I'm still hoping he'll agree to reimburse me. If you raise the business of the CD with them, he'll just say no to both."

Snow Bai couldn't think of anything to suggest, or even any words of comfort, so she poured Mrs. Wang a cup of tea and added some sugar.

"Out of all the performers, you're the only one I respect," Mrs. Wang said. "If you really want to help, why don't you ask Wind Xia if he'll talk to a recording company in the provincial city? His word carries more weight than the county head's."

"What a good idea!" exclaimed Snow Bai. "How come I never thought of that?" And she went home to wait for Wind Xia.

But when she suggested to him that he might help Mrs. Wang with a CD of her singing, he said, "Dad wants to publish a book of his opera masks, and now your teacher wants to bring out her songs. What on earth gets into these old folks' heads? How much can she pay?"

"If she could pay anything, she wouldn't be coming to you, would she?"

"Well, she needs to pay even if I help her."

"But she's been a singer all her life, and she sings really well. The CD's the least we could do—something for her and for the township and the county seat, too."

"But she's a nobody! Okay, she's well known in your troupe, and maybe in the county seat, too. But she's nothing in the province. Much more famous performers have put out CDs in the provincial city, but even they don't sell. Why should the recording company lose money on her?"

"Let me get Mrs. Wang here to have a chat with you."

"What is there to chat about? I don't want to see her!"

Snow Bai looked disconsolate, and her freckles stood out more than ever.

"It's stuffy in here. Why don't we go out for a stroll?" said Wind Xia.

"I don't want to go for a stroll. Mrs. Wang's waiting for me to call her back. What am I going to tell her?"

"Who asked you to meddle in her business, anyway?"

"Me, meddle? She's the one who thinks you can do anything. She doesn't know you're useless!"

They argued back and forth, then lapsed into a dismal silence until they heard the roast-chicken seller outside in the street.

"Go and buy us a bit of chicken," said Snow Bai. But when Wind Xia came back with a whole chicken, she said, "Who asked you to buy a whole one? I usually just buy a wattle and some claws for a snack."

"You wanted chicken. Why shouldn't my wife eat a whole chicken if she wants?"

"You're so generous! A whole chicken's expensive. I can't afford a dozen chickens a month on my wages."

"And whose fault is that? I wanted you to get a city job, but you wouldn't, and you knew you couldn't afford chicken on your current wages."

Snow Bai felt her mouth fill with acid and retched. "Well, I'm a low-wage actor, and you knew that, and you went ahead and married me all the same!"

Wind Xia grunted.

"What's the matter? Having second thoughts?" said Snow Bai.

"Forget it. Such is life; there's nothing more to be said. You're more pigheaded than me; I give in. Satisfied now?"

"So I'm pigheaded, am I? Do you have any idea how ill I feel? I'm not moving anywhere. I asked you to come home. I called you, your mother called you, but you didn't even take the time to visit!"

"I told you to get rid of it, but you wouldn't."

"Why should we get rid of our first child? When Dequan's wife got pregnant, he took care of her like she was his old granddad. But you didn't even discuss it with me; you just told me to get rid of it. I have no idea why!"

"Why? Because you won't move to town. You're always thinking of this or that excuse."

"It's because I want to perform!"

"Then perform!" said Wind Xia. "Isn't that what you're doing now?"

Snow Bai put her head on her arms and burst into tears.

"If you work long enough in a petty county-level job, you get to thinking petty, too," Wind Xia said. "If you carry on like this, you'll start to believe that what you do is art, something grand and noble. You'll turn into a narrow-minded hick, and then you'll never achieve anything."

"But I am a narrow-minded hick," said Snow Bai. "I'm a chicken living in the henhouse, not flying up to perch in a parasol tree!" And her sobs became loud howls.

The other women performers clustered outside their door and pushed their way in when they realized it was Snow Bai weeping. "What's the matter? Snow Bai, you shouldn't cry like that; it's bad for your baby!"

Snow Bai had always been careful to present a brave face to the world, and the others in the troupe had always seen her and Wind Xia as the perfect couple, so though there were some who were genuinely concerned, others took a malicious delight in the scene.

The fact that Wind Xia wasn't trying to put a brave face on it made Snow Bai even angrier. "None of you care about me and the baby. I wish I was dead!" The tears ran down her face.

"Wind Xia," said one of the singers, "what have you done to Snow Bai to get her so upset and angry? What have you got against Snow Bai?"

"Pig ignorance, that's what it is," said Wind Xia. It was, of course, the other performers he was referring to, but he didn't explain himself, just sat in a corner looking like a thundercloud and lighting a cigarette.

"Now that's enough," someone said to Snow Bai. "You have to be forgiving, too. All men get a little weird when their wives are pregnant, especially an educated man like Wind Xia. You know how the opera aria goes—a man of talent has his head in the clouds!"

But that just added fuel to the flames of Snow Bai's rage, and she almost choked she was crying so hard.

"Pay no attention; leave her with me and go home," said Wind Xia.

"Not if you carry on treating her badly!" was the general view.

So Wind Xia slammed out of the door and out of the theater, and then he went back to Freshwind Village on his own.

When he got back to his parents' house, Fourth Aunt didn't take the bag he held out. She stuck her head through the gate and looked down the street.

"What're you looking at, Mom?" said Wind Xia.

"Snow Bai. Isn't she with you?"

"What would she come back here for?" And Wind Xia stomped off to his room angrily.

Fourth Aunt stood irresolute for a moment, then hobbled into Wisdom Xia's room. There, she grabbed the ladle out of his hand. "Painting masks is the only thing you're good for! Did you carry pisspots or sell water in your last life?"

Wisdom Xia took off his glasses. His lips were daubed in every color of paint from the brushes. "Eh? Eh?"

"Wind Xia's come home alone. He must have had another falling out with Snow Bai."

Wisdom Xia flew into a fury. "They just got married! They can't be falling out now! How are they going to get on in the future?"

"You seem more upset than me," said Fourth Aunt. "You go ask him."

"No, you go."

Fourth Aunt hobbled back to Wind Xia's room, but when she stuck her head through the door, he'd already gone to bed. "Wind Xia!" she called anyway. "What was this quarrel with Snow Bai about? You're going to be a dad soon! You can't be arguing all the time!"

But Wind Xia didn't say a word, even though she repeated her question. The old lady went out into the yard and sat on the clothes-beating stone and wiped away her tears.

Then the gate flew open with a kick. Rain Xia was home.

"You'll break that gate the way you're kicking it!" his mother yelled at him. "You playing at being a bandit?"

"Why are you sitting alone and crying, Mom?" Rain Xia asked.

Fourth Aunt pulled him down beside her and quietly told him what had happened.

"You always take his side, Mom," said Rain Xia. "I have no wife at all, and you never worried about that. My brother's married and he's going to be a dad soon, and you sit and cry over him."

She put her hand over his mouth. "Don't talk so loud! What if he hears you?"

"If you can't get him out of bed, I'll go get him," said Rain Xia.

By dint of telling Wind Xia that he didn't want to go to the House of Treasures Hotel on his own, Rain Xia succeeded in getting him up and out of his room.

"Are you getting your brother into gambling now, too?" their mother protested.

"Love makes you forget betting, and betting makes you forget love!" Rain Xia told her.

In the hotel restaurant, two tables were occupied by diners playing raucous drinking games. Upstairs, at the east end of the building, Wind Xia and Rain Xia pushed open the door to a private room. Thick smoke billowed out, and inside four people were playing mah-jongg.

Wind Xia recognized Roughshod Ding, Goodness, and a man from West Street called Compliance. The fourth, a burly man with a swarthy face covered in a sheen of sweat, he did not know. They exchanged greetings, and Roughshod Ding said, "Here, you take my place, Wind Xia. I've had a run of bad luck the last few days. Stinking bad luck!"

Wind Xia sat down and played three rounds and won twice.

"See? I was right," said Rain Xia. "Unlucky in love, lucky at cards!"

"Unlucky in love?" Goodness asked.

But just then, there was a shout from the street below. "Goodness! Goodness!"

Goodness pushed open the window and looked out. "It's the head of the Youth League. Hey, come up for a couple of rounds!"

"You come down. I've got something to discuss with you."

Goodness went down, and when he came back up, he looked stricken.

"What did he want to talk about?" asked Roughshod Ding.

"He's getting married, and he's invited me to the feast. What'll I do?"

"Take your mouth with you and stuff it, that's what. You showing off or something?" said Roughshod Ding.

"You don't understand. If a township cadre gets married, you have to give them a red envelope full of money. And where am I going to get my hands on a hundred or thereabouts?"

Goodness was so gloomy that he no longer had the heart to play. He said his goodbyes and went off to the village offices.

Just as he walked in through Freshwind Temple's gate, Lotus Jin was coming out of the shithouse in the corner of the yard and gestured to him.

Goodness was momentarily puzzled. "You're looking nice today," he said. "Who bought that for you?"

"Where've you been?" she whispered. "They've been looking all over for you. There's a Two Committees meeting on right now."

"Dammit, I forgot!" Goodness spat in the dirt.

The two of them crept up to the doorway, and Lotus Jin went back in. Then Goodness slipped in behind her and took a stool next to the door. There was a newspaper lying on it, and he picked it up and sneaked a look at it.

Pavilion didn't break his stride, just coughed and went on. "Since we got the individual-responsibility production system going, people have fallen behind with their dues," he was saying. "Village-retention levies, payments for farm animals and machinery, and contract fees for arable land, reserve land, dikes, riverbank reed beds, the orchard, and the brickyard are all outstanding.

"Additionally, the triple-debt system that preceded the individual-responsibility production system hasn't been properly wrapped up. There's still money owing on plowing and water fees, agricultural taxes, and grain-price-equalization dues, and that money's still in private hands. That makes it impossible for us to carry out collective projects, to pay normal expenses, or to fund any kind of development.

"There are a number of root causes: First, people don't think collectively anymore. They put their own interests before those of the country or the collective. All that counts is getting rich; community duties go out the window. For example, there are families who have used communal property and funds for years without paying what they owe . . . Livestock and farm tools, they've used them for six or seven years and then sold them. They've benefited from the collective and enriched themselves, and not a cent of what they owe has gone back to the collective.

"Second, we cadres have failed to give enough weight to village projects; we've failed to take firm measures to see these projects through. We've been content to put out a call for contribution; we've let everything drag on. And now the village coffers are empty, and we've lost credibility. The volume of work's increased, but we've given it all to individuals, which has made it impossible to support village-wide activities like the communal school, the local militia, needy families, even cadres' salaries—all perfectly normal responsibilities for the village government, but we have no money to pay for them. The collective is poor while individuals have gotten rich.

"There's no food to put into the communal pot anymore. In line with the spirit of the township government's document number nine, individual debts of up to five hundred yuan are all to be collected within one year; debts of between five hundred and one thousand, within two years; and debts of more than two thousand, within three years. The debtors will pay in installments and will have to sign repayment plans with the village. They will also need to offer collateral in the form of personal property to guarantee the loan. We will levy interest on the debt, at the bank's maximum rate, to apply from the day the installment-repayment plan is signed, and those who default on payments will receive a penalty of thirty percent or be taken to court. If a debtor doesn't pay what they owe, or refuses to sign the contract, the village can seize their livestock or farm tools by way of payment, and as long as it does not affect the debtor family's ability to support themselves, the village can also seize their grain or take back the fields they have under contract.

"As I have already explained, we can also bring miscreants to court. If there are plowing and water fees, agricultural taxes, or grain-price subsidies that have not been paid in full, those debts, no matter whether they are big or small, must be settled before the end of the year. Those who still have not paid a cent for their animals or farm equipment will have them confiscated and will be liable to pay a ten percent surcharge for depreciation.

"As for people who have paid off part of the debt, we will set a final payment date— the end of the year at the latest. Defaulters will have their property confiscated. In the case of people who have sold agricultural equipment or animals that came from the collective, without paying the collective back, they will have to settle the debt as soon as possible. Failing that, we will apply the highest bank interest rate from the day they first acquired the goods, and they will have to pay cash, or we will bring the full force of the law to bear on them."

Pavilion was nowhere as good a speaker as Justice Xia. Justice Xia had the knack of phrasing his arguments in the language that the country folk themselves used. No matter how serious the topic, he could make them laugh. He entertained them. But Pavilion was a total loss. It wasn't that he talked nonsense; it was just that his speeches were mind-numb-ingly dull. By the time he'd finished, half his audience had their eyes shut. Some of the shut-eyes were still listening. Others really did nod off, at which point their cigarettes dropped from their lips, or they lurched forward and banged their heads on the edge of the table, which woke them up. They wiped the dribble from the corner of their lips and looked around them.

Pavilion carried on and on in his usual monotone. Without pausing for breath, he fin-ished: "Some people have not even turned up at this vitally important meeting. One wonders if they were not told, or were told and ignored it? Goodness, you're our bookkeeper. Never mind everyone else; you should have been at this meeting from the start."

Goodness was reading the newspaper and had almost finished it. He held the paper to the bridge of his nose and peered out over the top of the page. He could see a spider crawling up the meeting room wall; it seemed to have a pattern on its back. He had the impression Pavilion was still going on about taking collective property back for unpaid debts . . . the words were going in one ear and out the other. Then he thought he heard his name mentioned and came to with a start.

"Were you talking about me?" he asked.

"Yes, why were you late?"

"I was on my way here when I got called to the township offices."

"What did they want?"

"I'll report back to you after the meeting."

"They certainly know how to keep the pressure on us," said Pavilion, and then he started talking again.

Goodness stared at the spider again and wondered about that pattern. He got up and walked over to it. It looked like a face.

"This spider has a human face on its back!" he exclaimed. Several of the others got up and came to look.

"It's true!" they exclaimed.

Pavilion stopped his speech and came to look, too. It was very strange.

"Spiders are wise creatures," Goodness said. "It's probably understood everything you've said, Pavilion."

"Nonsense!" And Pavilion made a grab for the spider, which scuttled away up the wall and disappeared into the ceiling.

Let me tell you, that spider could have been me. Before the meeting of the Two Committees started, I passed the cultural center on my way to Seven Li Gully. There was a chess game going on inside, and I couldn't resist going in to have a look. Pavilion was at the gate, shouting for Goodness. He thought Goodness was playing chess, and when he discovered he wasn't there, he told me to go look for him and make sure he came to the meeting. I asked what the meeting was about, and Pavilion said it was about clearing old debts.

"Does that mean I'll get paid the subsidy owed to my dad?" I asked, but he went into Freshwind Temple without answering. If he ignored me, then, dammit, I wasn't going to look for Goodness. But even though I was physically in the cultural center, my mind was at the Two Committees meeting.

I saw the spider crawling up the wall, and I told it, "Spider, spider, listen to what they say at the meeting. See if they say anything about the subsidy owed to my dad." The spider didn't budge. "Spider," I said, "did you hear me? If you heard, climb higher up the wall!"

And then it really did. It went right up to the rafter where no one could see it. And even though I was standing next to the chess players, offering my opinions on the game, there was this loud buzzing in my head.

In the end, the players got annoyed and said I was talking too much. "A true man keeps quiet during a chess game; just stop talking out of your ass," they said. And when I couldn't keep my mouth shut, they got angry and threw me out.

I swore silently at the chess players as I walked to Seven Li Gully. *What a stupid blunder. If you'd attacked the soldier, you'd have scored, but instead you rode off on the horse!* As for the meeting, I knew Pavilion wouldn't raise the issue of Dad's subsidy. Your tea gets cold as soon as you leave, and Dad hadn't just left; he was dead.

At the east end of the small stone bridge, I came across Rites Xia, sitting in the shade of a persimmon tree. His eyes were half-closed. He saw me, opened them for a second, then shut them again.

"Taking a break, Uncle Rites?"

"Yup."

"Not going to market today?"

"Can't be bothered."

"Can't be bothered to make money?"

"Where are you off to?"

When I said Seven Li Gully, he beckoned me closer. "Spark, tell me, set my heart at rest. Do you really think that if the gully-filling project's finished, we'll get to live as well as the folk in the provincial city?"

I dodged the question. "When you went to the city, did you come back with a new head?"

"Before I went, I still thought there was a future for us here, but once I'd seen people there, I lost heart completely."

"Very strange. People go to the city and come back and throw themselves into making money, but you go and you lose heart."

"If I'd been your age, I might have been like them. But you know what? As soon as I saw all those city folk, I just wanted to die."

"In that case, why don't you give me some of your silver dollars, Uncle?"

"What silver dollars?" Rites Xia said immediately. "How do you know I have silver dollars?"

"There, that scared you, didn't it?" I said. "But I don't want your money. You sit here in the shade. I have to get a move on." And so I went.

By the time I reached the gully, the Two Committees meeting was over. Pavilion went to the shithouse and took a nice long piss, and then told Goodness to stay and report on his meeting at the township offices.

Goodness improvised. "The township head just wants to know how work's going in Freshwind."

"And what did you say?" Pavilion asked.

"I said everything's gone quiet. Uncle Justice's still busy with the gully business, but Shifty's not putting up a fight anymore. The hens are laying, the cat's in heat, and production and public order are exactly as they should be."

"And what did he say then?" Pavilion asked.

"He just said, 'Good.' As long as we have no problems, he's satisfied. It's not easy pushing through new projects right now; it's like herding sheep. It's as much as you can do to keep them going forward and stop them straying off the straight and narrow and having an accident."

"The current township head's better than his predecessor," Pavilion said. "Did he say anything more?"

"Yes, the head of the Youth League's getting married. He's invited you and me to the wedding feast."

"That poor young man. He was married less than a year, and then his wife died. Who's he found now?"

"Another girl from the same Zhou family on West Street."

"How come?"

"It was the eldest Zhou daughter who died; his new bride's her younger sister."

"So the brother-in-law marries the sister-in-law. Ask Big-Noise to write some couplets that we can take along with us when the day comes."

"The thing is, he's made a point of inviting us, so it's clear he wants us to bring a red envelope with money."

"Okay, how much, do you think?"

"That's up to you, but at least five hundred."

"Five hundred it is. Where do we get it from?"

"We've no money in the account," Goodness objected.

"Anyway, can we really get away with having the village pay?"

"It'll have to. No one else can afford that kind of money. He hasn't invited us as individuals; we're not relatives or close friends. The only reason is that we represent Freshwind."

Pavilion was silent for a while, and then he said, "So there's no money in the account? Haven't we had fees from the market stallholders?"

"Yes, but that all went to pay the community teacher's salary."

"Then can you borrow some cash?"

"I already borrowed two thousand for the village cadres."

All the same, they wrote out a voucher on the spot, and Pavilion authorized it. Goodness went and bought red paper for the wedding couplets and asked Big-Noise Zhao to write them. Big-Noise wrote:

> The one was the most beautiful in the city, the other the
> handsomest in the kingdom
> The first shared house and home, the other the pillow.

Goodness thought this was a bit too high flown for the villagers, so Big-Noise Zhao tried again:

> The Zhou family are the best in the village;
> The Youth League leader is the best in the township.

Wind Xia spent that night at the House of Treasures Hotel's restaurant playing mah-jongg, and he got quite pally with the fat, swarthy man sitting opposite him, whose name was Big-Guy Ma. Ma was from Henan, and he'd been staying in the market hotel while he purchased wood ear mushrooms from the Nanshan and Beishan Mountains for his boss. Then he realized that no one around here was growing shiitake mushrooms. Here was a chance to pass on cultivation techniques. He needed a partner, and he settled on Compliance, who had an oil mill in Freshwind, was a local, and was honest, too. Together, they got the folk from the Nanshan and Beishan Mountains into farming shiitakes. These went for four yuan a *jin*, and the farmers were soon selling all they could grow. Then a lot more families went into shiitakes, and Big-Guy Ma could afford to move to the House of Treasures Hotel.

Big-Guy Ma had a face like a bandit and a belly so big that he told them it was five years since he last saw the little guy between his legs. He was a jolly fellow who could charm anyone, from a two-year-old toddler to an eighty-year-old granny. He only had to appear for things to liven up.

At the mah-jongg table, Roughshod Ding was talking about shiitake cultivation. Was it easy to make a go of it without cheating other people and hurting oneself, he asked?

"There used to be four families pressing sesame oil in Freshwind. Now there's only me. You know why? Because I'm quite clear whether I'm doing a good thing or a bad thing, and I'm quite clear with myself and everyone else," said Compliance.

"Here's a businessman with moral standards!" Wind Xia said.

"Wind Xia's right!" said Big-Guy Ma. "I'm staying at the House of Treasures Hotel, but that doesn't mean I'm going into business with Roughshod Ding."

"What do you mean?" said Ding. "Are you saying I'm dishonest?"

"You're smarter than Compliance, but Compliance is more honest; you have to admit that. We've signed contracts with ten families to grow shiitakes, and I've given them video recordings to learn from. Plus, I've invited an agronomist from Henan to teach them. We reinvested the profits in that. So now they trust us not to exploit them. In fact, they see us as their saviors!"

"You've got the gift of gab, all right," said Roughshod Ding. "You could turn water into oil and burn it."

"Yes, I've got the gift of gab," said Big-Guy Ma. "But Compliance can't string two sentences together, and he does good business, too, right? If you want to succeed, you got to be friendly and honest. Not like you, Roughshod Ding. You've been fleecing me ever since I got here. You've raised the room charge already, and I've only been here a few days!"

"If you want a masseuse, you have to pay extra for her!" said Roughshod Ding.

"You've got masseuses here?" asked Wind Xia.

"They just do massage," Ding said.

"Of course we have masseuses," said Rain Xia. "You might as well ask if the hotel has flies. We don't go out and recruit these young women; they just come. As soon as they heard we were open, they came flocking."

"I'm a peaceable guy," said Big-Guy Ma. "Dammit, I'm even prepared to kneel down and beg for mercy if I have to. But if anyone gets me riled up, they better watch out. Blood will flow!"

"Well said!" said Roughshod Ding. "Everyone says you're friendly, but I can tell there's a bandit lurking behind all those nice words. Tell me, how much do you clear when you buy the ripe shiitakes for four yuan a *jin*?"

"I can sell a *jin* in Fujian for forty yuan."

"Fucking hell! You're bad!"

"Maybe I'm a bit bad, but no one else does it as well as me," said Big-Guy Ma. "I've got the distribution network, you see."

"Well, we're not going to steal your business," Ding said. "You eat the meat, and Rain Xia and I will drink the broth. Now, drink up! And hand over the money! Mr. Ma, I know you're not short of cash, so I'm not starting a tab for you!"

They played until noon, and then Roughshod Ding and Rain Xia invited Wind Xia to share a meal of palm civet meat.

Afterward, Ding muttered in Wind Xia's ear, "You must be tired. Let me fix you up with a massage."

"Who's the girl?"

"The one who was serving the drinks at lunch. You like her?"

Wind Xia did like her and booked a room. There, he took his shoes off and lay facedown on the bed. A few minutes later, the girl came in, shut and bolted the door behind her, and drew the curtains.

"It's too dark with the curtains drawn," Wind Xia objected.

"That's how I do it," said the girl. And she began to rub and pinch Wind Xia all over, paying no attention to the acupressure points. In fact, she might as well have been kneading dough.

"What kind of massage is this?" said Wind Xia.

"I can't do massage," said the girl.

"What can you do?"

"I can bring you off."

Wind Xia sat up with a jerk. "Out!" he said. "Out of here!"

The girl looked bemused. "You don't come from Freshwind, do you?" she asked.

Wind Xia put his shoes back on and went down to the ground floor, where Roughshod Ding was sitting on a stool at the foot of the stairs.

He smirked. "That was quick."

"Nothing happened!"

"I've been keeping an eye out for you; everything's okay. But didn't you like her? She's clean."

"If that was what I was looking for, I wouldn't come here." Wind Xia was furious.

At that moment, Rain Xia came in with Goodness, and Wind Xia took his chance to slip away. Roughshod Ding shouted after him, but he didn't look around.

"What's up with my brother?" Rain Xia asked.

"He's gotten picky now he's a city man. Not satisfied with the local birds."

Rain Xia was furious at Roughshod Ding. How was he going to face his big brother now? The whole thing was so comical that Goodness burst out laughing.

Wind Xia hadn't slept all night and was thoroughly depressed. He left the hotel, rubbing his face with his fingers, and headed home, hoping he wouldn't meet anyone on the way. There were not many people out in the streets, and when anyone looked up and saw him, he made sure to slip into an alley before they got near. He knew one or two well enough that it was hard to avoid greeting them, but he got by with just a "Busy today?" or a "Yes, I'm back!" and dashed on past, patting his pocket for a cigarette and finding nothing there.

Behind him, he heard someone shout, "Isn't that Wind Xia?"

And someone else answered, "Who else would it be?"

"Wind Xia, why are you ignoring everyone?" came the first voice.

"What do we have to talk to him about?" the other said. "He's got bigger fish to fry. I've never even had a smoke off him, let alone a meal!"

"Is that all you ever think about?"

"We humble folk need stuff to put in our mouths."

Wind Xia felt increasingly uneasy.

Then one of the villagers caught up with him. "When did you get home? How's life in town? If it's that good, why have you gotten so skinny? And what about Snow Bai? When's she due? It's sure to be a boy, and he's sure to be as smart as you!"

Wind Xia found himself relaxing, until the man went on, "My daughter just graduated as an infant teacher, but she can't find a job. Wind Xia, could you see your way to writing to the county officers, or calling them, and see if they can help her out?"

Wind Xia felt the stress beginning to build again. He explained that he didn't work for the county, and he didn't know anyone in particular there. Besides, the officers changed every three or four years, and he'd never even met the new bunch. His words had no effect. The man pleaded that his daughter was engaged to be married, but the boy was not happy that she had no job and was threatening to break it off. How could Wind Xia bear to see young love blighted?

Eventually, Wind Xia told him to find a workplace that might offer the girl a position. "And if there's a problem at that point, then I'll talk to the authorities." He got rid of the man and carried on, but then someone else stopped him. Would Wind Xia please lobby the head of the county's Department of Transport?

"But I don't know the head of the county's Department of Transport!" Wind Xia was puzzled.

"But he's always boasting that you're friends. Of course you know him!"

"Then he's lying."

"That's good. It shows he respects you, so you can tell him to promote my second son. He's worked under him for eight years, so he's sure to stay loyal if he's promoted."

"But how can I say something like that?" asked Wind Xia.

"Of course you can, and it'll work! But if I can't persuade you, I'll get my dad and my kid to come by tonight to beg you!"

"Okay, okay," Wind Xia muttered, and walked away.

Under the archway on East Street, someone else hailed him: "Hey, speak of the devil!"

When he looked up, he saw Snow Bai's sister-in-law. "How are you doing?" he greeted her.

"Not good at all. I'm going white haired with worry."

"Has something happened?"

"I heard that you'd come home, so I asked Mom if you'd been by, but she said no."

"I was going to go see her tonight."

"You do that. You're her favorite son-in-law. She loves you more than her own son!"

And she pulled him aside and whispered something in his ear. He couldn't make out what she was saying and had to ask her to repeat it several times. The gist of it was that when the responsibility system was introduced for land and farm equipment, Snow Bai's brother had taken over a tractor. After a while it had broken down, and now it was just a heap of rust, but he still owed the village money for the machine. He'd put the payment off for so long that he'd forgotten it, but now suddenly all these debts were being called in, the deadline was soon, and where would they get money for it?

"Can't you fix your brother-in-law up with a job in the city?" she finished.

"Where?" said Wind Xia. "He's got no skills, and besides, he has chronic stomach trouble. What's he going to do?"

"He can be a gatekeeper at a big company," said his sister-in-law. "He's dull and quiet; he can sit still."

"I can't get him a gatekeeper's job."

"Then you're sending him to his death!"

"What? How am I sending him to his death?"

"You don't know Pavilion. Once he gets an idea in his head, he's vicious. He doesn't care about people!"

"How much does he owe then?"

"A thousand yuan. I know that's nothing for you, just a single hair on an ox's hide. But for your brother, it's like scraping bones and pulling tendons."

Wind Xia pulled a thousand yuan from his wallet and handed it over.

She grabbed the bills unceremoniously and counted them one by one. "You saved your brother-in-law's life! I often say it's strange how things can work out so differently for two children with the same mother. One has work, makes money, and marries you, and the other's so poor he's just a bag of bones rattling around on the kang all day. Wind Xia, your brother-in-law may be dirt poor, but once he gets some money, he'll pay you back."

They talked for a bit longer. Wind Xia felt his head spinning and tried to get his sister-in-law to go to his parents' house with him, but she said she'd just bumped into Uncle Wisdom and Fourth Aunt on their way to Concord Qin's place. He should go to West Street himself.

"They've gone to Concord Qin's? Then I'm going home to catch up on some sleep. I'll go to West Street tonight."

There was no one at home, and he went to bed, slept until evening, and never did go to West Street.

Wisdom Xia and Fourth Aunt arrived at Concord Qin's, bearing a hen as a gift. His wife wasn't at home, and Concord Qin sat by himself on a stool, gazing into space. A small swarm of mosquitoes had settled on his head, but even though he had a fan in his hand, he just left them there. His arms and legs were covered with lumpy red bites.

"You're here?" he greeted Wisdom Xia and Fourth Aunt. He tried to get up, but Wisdom Xia pushed him back in his seat, got out his pipe, wiped the mouthpiece, and handed it to him. Concord Qin took it, but he gripped it in his hand without smoking it or saying a word.

"Smoke it!" said Wisdom Xia. Concord Qin took one puff and stopped again.

Fourth Aunt took the pipe off him and the fan, then began to fan the mosquitos away. "Where's your wife?" she asked.

"Gone to the fields."

"Have you eaten?"

"Don't know."

"What do you mean, you don't know?"

Wisdom Xia looked at Concord Qin, shook his head, and said, "He's turned into a pumpkin."

"When I was here a couple of weeks ago, he was a bit dopey, but he could talk and there was life in his face," said Fourth Aunt. "But now . . . It's like the herbal poultice has sucked all the life out of him."

"It's that poultice of Big-Noise's that's kept him alive. Otherwise he would have died long ago," said Wisdom Xia.

As they spoke, the gate creaked open, and Concord Qin's wife appeared with a big basket of firewood on her back.

"Oh," she said. "It's kind of you to visit!" The firewood stuck out on either side, so she had to wriggle and push to get through the gate. Then she almost fell into the yard. Fourth Aunt hurried forward to help, and finally she was in and let the basket drop.

"Sit down! Let me get you something to eat," she said.

"Haven't you eaten your lunch? It's late," said Fourth Aunt.

"If you've eaten, that's fine," said Concord Qin's wife. "I'm not hungry, and Concord Qin has no appetite anymore." She went over and patted him on the head and wiped the dribble from the corner of his lips. "Why are you looking so dopey, when you've got visitors?"

"He seems to be talking less, too," said Fourth Aunt.

"He just sits there, whether we have visitors or not. If you give him a bowl of rice, he eats it up; you give him two, he eats two. If you give him nothing, he doesn't ask for anything."

"That's terrible for you," said Fourth Aunt. "Where did you get so much firewood from?"

"Splendid cut down the parasol tree outside their yard wall. He gave me this."

"He cut down the parasol tree? Thunder wanted to buy it and make furniture with it last year, but Splendid refused to sell. He said he wanted the wood for his coffin. Why did he decide to fell it now?"

"He sold it to someone from West Mountain Bend, and he's planning to run off tomorrow morning." Then she whispered, "I've told you now, but don't tell anyone else."

"Why's he running off?" asked Fourth Aunt.

"You know the business about everyone's debts being called in? It was decided at a meeting of the Two Committees. Three people who couldn't pay have taken off already. Splendid figured the tree wouldn't last long if he went, so he cut it down."

"Everyone should pay back what they owe. That's right and proper," said Wisdom Xia. "What good does it do to run away? Are they planning to stay away from Freshwind forever?"

"You're right, but they've got no money to pay off their debts with. Anyway, a dead pig's not scared of a scalding. Anyone who wants to can come and take Concord Qin away with them!"

"Do you owe money, too?" asked Fourth Aunt.

Concord Qin's wife nodded. "Not very much, but I can't get my hands on even a hundred yuan right now. I'm looking after Concord Qin; he needs his food and drink, and he has to have his medicine every day. Money grows from grain, but we don't have a lot of grain."

Tears welled in Fourth Aunt's eyes, but she didn't want Concord Qin's wife to see so she said, "You keep him so clean and tidy!"

"And that's quite a business! Can you imagine? I have to put a bib on him every time he eats, like a baby; he shits and pisses himself, too. What did we do in a past life to deserve this? It's hard for him, and for me, looking after him."

Wisdom Xia said nothing. He sat down on the steps and smoked his pipe while Fourth Aunt and Concord Qin's wife went into the kitchen to warm up some leftover food. They put the bowl in Concord Qin's hands, and he ate his meal. When he was finished, he carried on sitting quietly with his head drooping.

Wisdom Xia, still sucking on his pipe, suddenly said, "Concord, can you still sing opera?"

"Yes," said Concord Qin.

"How can you ask him to sing?" Fourth Aunt protested.

"A person could die of sadness if they don't sing," said Wisdom Xia. "Sing us an aria if you can, Concord Qin."

Concord Qin opened his mouth so wide you could see it was still full of corn porridge, and sang:

> Sir Zhu plunges into danger for my sake
> With his twenty-pound hammer, he vanquishes the Qin army
> I return to the Wei capital with new hatred in my heart
> How can I bear to drive my team of four horses through its East Gate again?

"What's he singing?" said Fourth Aunt. "I can't understand a word."

"It's from 'Stealing the General's Orders,'" said Wisdom Xia. "The aria that Lord Xinling sings."

Concord Qin's wife was wide eyed with astonishment. "He remembers his opera!"

"Encourage him to sing then," said Wisdom Xia. "Anyone would go crazy if they don't say a word from morning to night."

But Concord Qin had stopped, and when Wisdom Xia urged him to continue, he just said, "It's over."

"Then I'll sing a new tune for you," said Wisdom Xia, "and you can carry on." And he did.

Concord Qin smiled foolishly but wouldn't sing anymore.

"Tomorrow I'll bring the radio with me, so he can listen to some opera, and we'll see if I can get him to sing some more," said Wisdom Xia. He got up to go to the gate.

Behind him, Fourth Aunt was still talking to Concord Qin's wife. "You have to try not to take it so hard," she said. "A road always opens up when the cart reaches the mountain. When you have time, make him walk a bit and try to make him talk. Mid-Star's father was sick for ages, but he got through it in the end, even though he was on his own, right? I met him the other day, and he was making predictions for himself. I asked him to make one for Concord Qin, and he said he'd be fine; he'll last for another four or five years."

At that, Concord Qin's wife burst into tears. "Then I want to die! How will I cope if he lives that long?"

"How can she say stuff like that?" Wisdom Xia said once he and Fourth Aunt were outside.

"She's having a rough time; she can't take any more. You know what they say: your children desert you when you're really sick, never mind your wife."

They chatted as they headed home. It was dark now, and there were no streetlamps. But lights flooded out of all the gates they passed. They passed Favor Bai leading her donkey, which brayed loudly. In front of them, Splendid was standing outside a shop as if he was about to buy something, but before Wisdom Xia could shout to him, he suddenly vanished.

"So Concord Qin owes money to the village, too?" Wisdom Xia said.

"Yes, I don't understand that. But you know how many people helped themselves to commune property," said Fourth Aunt, thinking back to when the government let villagers farm their land again.

Wisdom Xia sighed as he trudged along, his hands clasped behind his back. He and his wife never walked side by side when they went out; he always strode out in front while she scurried behind him.

"Why do you go so fast? Anyone would think you had a wolf at your heels! You know my feet hurt!" she complained.

Wisdom Xia stopped and waited for her, and as he did, he saw Mid-Star's dad and Wind Xia come out of their alley. Mid-Star's dad bowed. "You're back late, brother!" he said.

"Where are you two going?" Wisdom Xia asked.

"Mid-Star's back; he asked me to bring Wind Xia over."

"What's the hurry?" asked Fourth Aunt, who had caught up with them. "Why can't Wind Xia drop by tomorrow?"

"Mid-Star's an official now," said Wisdom Xia. "If he's sent his dad out on an errand, it must be urgent."

Wind Xia didn't get back till midnight. He knocked at the gate, and Wisdom Xia, who had been busy sorting out his masks, opened up. "What took you so long?"

"He wants me to go with him to the city tomorrow to see the mayor. They're setting up courses for county officials, and he wants a place. He thinks that'll get him a step up the job ladder."

"Did you say yes?" Wisdom Xia asked.

"I couldn't refuse," said Wind Xia. "Though I don't know how he found out that I know the mayor."

"He's only been chief of the Publicity Department for a few days, and he's already plotting his next move!" said Wisdom Xia. "And as for your uncle Glory, he's unbearable nowadays, all that mumbo-jumbo he spouts. And he seems to think his son is the emperor himself!"

"You do what you can to help him," said Fourth Aunt. "You helped him get his job in the county government, didn't you? How will you get there? He's got a car of his own."

"He's not driving. We might go with Thunder."

"Then you'd better get straight to sleep," said Fourth Aunt. "You'll need to be up early."

Though by the time the three of them were ready for bed, the cock had already crowed twice.

Chapter 29

Mid-Star Xia and Wind Xia took Thunder's bus to Xijing. When they stopped at Zhoucheng City, halfway there, two passengers were getting off and asked for tickets, but Blossom refused. They didn't particularly need their tickets since they'd paid their money and been given a seat, but they did find it strange.

"What do you farmers need tickets for?" Blossom demanded.

"Why not? Just because we're farmers, we can't get a ticket?"

She pushed the two men off the bus and shut the door. "What the hell do they need a ticket for?"

As Thunder pulled away, the two men picked up bricks and stones and hurled them at the side of the bus. None of the passengers were hurt, but two windows shattered. Thunder stopped the bus and got out, waving a tire iron. The two men ran off. "Why the hell didn't you just give them tickets?" he asked Blossom. "How much is it going to cost me to replace these two windows?"

"What good are you two?" Blossom grumbled, pointing at Mid-Star and Wind Xia. "You're riding for free, but did you two get up to stop those two thugs? Nope. Frozen like a couple of corpses, you just let them go."

When they got to Zhoucheng, Mid-Star asked Wind Xia, "Should we slip the mayor some cash?" Wind Xia told him it wasn't necessary, but Mid-Star insisted that they couldn't show up empty handed. Finally, Mid-Star tried to stick a roll of bills totaling five thousand yuan into Wind Xia's pocket, saying, "You can always rely on your reputation, but you should at least treat him to dinner, right?"

"I've never given him a gift before," said Wind Xia angrily. "It feels very strange to suddenly change my approach now! And if you've got so much money, why'd we have to catch a ride on Thunder's bus? You could have helped out Blossom, instead of trying to slip it to the mayor."

"You want to start negotiating with her now?" said Mid-Star and then slipped the roll of bills back into his own pocket.

They got to the municipal government complex and headed for a small building located inside. It was then that Mid-Star started shivering violently. "What's wrong with you?" Wind Xia demanded.

"I'm just a bit nervous." He excused himself to the bathroom, splashed water on his face, and slicked down his hair.

After Mid-Star had composed himself, they went in to meet the mayor, who greeted them warmly, passing them cigarettes and pouring cups of tea. He asked them if they were on their way back from Xijing or coming from Freshwind. "We're in from Xijing," said Wind Xia, although that wasn't technically true. "I decided, since we were passing through Zhoucheng, we ought to pay our respects to the mayor!"

From under his desk, the mayor produced two bottles of Maotai, saying, "I want you to bring these to your father, from me." Wind Xia tried to wave off the gift, protesting that it was too generous, but the mayor insisted. He waved over his secretary and ordered the bottles wrapped up. "And right now," the mayor said, "it's time for us to eat."

When they got to the restaurant, it was Wind Xia who excused himself to use the bathroom. Mid-Star followed obediently behind him. "I had no idea your name carried that much weight," said Mid-Star in a low voice.

"The mayor is a good man," said Wind Xia. "Let him get settled in, but speak freely. You can tell him exactly what you're thinking."

"Easy enough for the famous writer Wind Xia to say. You aren't intimidated by guys like that. Did you see the way he talks to his staff? He tore them to pieces. And you want me to just chat with him like we're old buddies? What am I supposed to say?"

"Try to save a drowning man, and I end up being pulled underwater with him . . ."

When they got back to the table, Wind Xia hesitantly brought up his companion. He formally introduced him to the mayor and told him what the situation was.

"Chief of the Publicity Department, eh? How is it that we've never met?"

"You might not remember me," Mid-Star said, "but I know we've met. I was taking notes at the meeting when you came into the county government. I was the one who showed you where the bathroom was. You probably don't remember."

"Oh, uh-huh," said the mayor. "Which one of you two is older?"

"I've got more lines in my face, but I'm actually a few months younger than Wind Xia."

"Wind Xia has the face of an intellectual."

Everyone laughed, and Wind Xia took the opportunity to interject, "He's got more lines on his face for a reason. He might be younger than me, but he's more mature. He's always been someone to count on. Look, he's even in the county government now. I want you to look out for him."

"They're doing good work up there," said the mayor.

"Didn't most of them get promoted out of the city government?" Wind Xia asked.

The mayor turned suddenly serious. Mid-Star noticed his expression and immediately proposed a toast. Mid-Star was still feeling nervous, and there was sweat pouring down his forehead. "So, Wind Xia," the mayor said with a laugh, "you want to be a bureaucrat now, too?"

"That's not it at all. I know talent, though. I can vouch for his ability and character. Whether you have any use for him, I'll leave that up to you and your staff to decide."

The mayor asked about Mid-Star's situation. "I understand," he said finally, and Wind Xia also dropped it, engaging the mayor in small talk on the weather, his health, and the skills of the chef. When the general manager of the hotel appeared with the restaurant manager to offer a toast to the mayor and request a photo with him, he pointed Wind Xia out to them. "You two," he said, "wouldn't recognize gold and jade if it fell in your lap. You want to take a picture with me, when there's a real celebrity right beside me? This is Wind Xia. You know who Wind Xia is?"

One of the managers said, "Ah, yes, Chief Xia." They smiled.

"'Chief'? You haven't got any idea who he is, do you?" the mayor thundered. Wind Xia looked uncomfortable. "Uncultured," the mayor said, "that's what you two are."

"I've heard the name," said one of the managers.

"Yes, I've definitely heard the name," said the other.

"Go get a brush and some paper," the mayor said. "The famous writer will bless this restaurant with his calligraphy. I want you to know, an opportunity like this doesn't come every day."

Wind Xia picked up the brush and wrote, "Full stomachs, good cheer."

"Very good," said the mayor, laughing. "It's hard to believe there are people who still don't know the name Wind Xia!"

"I like it better that way. A full stomach and good cheer is enough for me."

They talked for a while, and then the mayor excused himself, saying that he had to get to a meeting. He told his secretary to book them rooms at the hotel, but Wind Xia said it wouldn't be necessary. So the mayor had a car take Wind Xia and Mid-Star back to Freshwind.

Once they were back in Freshwind, Mid-Star seemed to be back to his old self again. He said that he had been so nervous around the mayor that he hadn't eaten a bite. Wind Xia hadn't eaten much, either, so Mid-Star offered to take him out for dinner—for drinks, most importantly. Mid-Star was in the mood to get drunk, and Wind Xia knew he couldn't turn him down.

"Let's go to the House of Treasures then," he said.

But Mid-Star insisted that they go to the dining room of the township government. His argument was that the House of Treasures was privately owned. Even if the township government's cooks couldn't turn out anything to compare to the cuisine at the House of Treasures, a government employee should eat at a government canteen.

"So you want the government to pay for your meals," Wind Xia said.

"I have to play by the rules. The money doesn't matter."

In the government dining room, the secretary and township head came out to shower their praises on Mid-Star and Wind Xia. "Let me tell you something," Mid-Star said. "That fancy restaurant in Zhoucheng . . . I tell you, the people running the place are completely uncultured. But you look around here . . ."

"You two really do bring glory to Freshwind!" the secretary said. "It's an honor to have you here as our guests."

The township head shouted for Clerk to go out and buy meat, eggs, and vegetables. "And a bottle of liquor," he added. "Get the good stuff, the twenty-year-old Phoenix of the West!"

Wind Xia was out in the courtyard, admiring the roses in the flower bed. Clerk was bent over, scraping the scales off a fish. "Listen to that," said Clerk. "The way they're hollering, you'd think the emperor was about to come for a banquet."

"It's not for me," Wind Xia said. "It's for Mid-Star."

"Who would go to the trouble for him? Ugly as a mule, and they're treating him like the belle of the ball."

"It's his title that matters. If you had a title, they'd fawn over you, too."

"You've never had my cooking, have you, Wind Xia? How about this? Whatever you want to eat, I'll make it for you."

The sun was already dipping behind the hills when the table was set at the canteen. There were four cold dishes, four hot, four meat dishes, four vegetable. As expected, the presentation was passable and the flavors decent. The secretary and the township head proposed a toast to Wind Xia and then turned their attention to Mid-Star, both downing a shot with him. Mid-Star could drink most men under the table, and the township head was no competition.

"Bring the soup!" the township head yelled. His face had turned a deep red from the liquor, his cheeks the color of braised pork. "Bring out the soup!" he cried again.

Clerk appeared, carrying a tureen of spinach egg drop soup. The tureen was filled right to the brim, and it dribbled down the side, onto the floor. When Clerk set it down on the table, his two thumbs went right into the soup.

"Watch what you're doing, Clerk," Wind Xia said.

Clerk sucked the soup off one of his thumbs. "So what?" he said.

"What do you mean, 'So what'? You had your thumbs in the soup. Who wants to eat soup that you've stuck your fingers in?"

Now that it had been pointed out, Clerk tried to play it off. "Well, you know," he said, "maybe my thumbs were cold! I was just warming them up."

"Oh, they were cold, were they?" the village head thundered. "Why don't you stick them up your ass? Get this off the table. Go make a new one."

"Ah, you know how Clerk is," Wind Xia said to the township head. "He's just joking around. Don't worry about it." He reached for the ladle and filled his own bowl.

"Well, if Wind Xia's having some, I might as well, too," Mid-Star said. "If it's good enough for a big-city guy like him, it's good enough for me."

"I've always said, the only area where Clerk is lacking is cleanliness. You know him better than me, though. He's from East Street, after all. I'll leave it at that," the township head said, going back to his meal.

After they'd finished, the township head wanted to walk Mid-Star and Wind Xia back to Middle Street, but Mid-Star told him not to worry. The township head saw them as far as the courtyard gate, and they stood for a while talking there. Clerk was in the kitchen washing pots and rushed out when he heard them leaving. "Take it easy!" Clerk shouted.

"Get out of here! Who asked you to send them off?"

"Just saying bye to my old classmate," Clerk said, nodding toward Wind Xia.

It wasn't that Wind Xia didn't drink, but he'd never really been drunk. On that night, though, he was close enough. As soon as he stumbled into his yard, he sat down hard on the flower bed, crushing a rosebush. Fourth Aunt was in the kitchen, pouring rice from a jar into a basket to sieve. She heard her son out in the yard.

"You're just getting back now?" she said. "You better get over to Third Uncle's place. There's trouble over there."

"What do you mean?" he said, a wave of nausea hitting him. Wind Xia jabbed a finger down his throat. He wanted to empty his stomach of the liquor.

"He's dead."

Wind Xia stood up from the flower bed. "What did you say?"

"Third Uncle is dead."

"He's dead?" said Wind Xia. His head was suddenly clear. "Third Uncle is dead?"

It was true that Rites Xia was dead. Human life is a strange thing. There are times when you feel as if you're invincible, as if you could never die, but there are other times when you feel brittle, as if death is right around the corner. The way I saw it, if anybody was going to die, it should have been Concord Qin—if not Concord Qin, then maybe Mid-Star's dad. Those two were barely hanging on. They were like a cracked ceramic bowl balanced on the edge of a table: one wrong move and they'd slip away, with no chance of surviving the fall.

But it was neither of them. Death had come for Rites Xia. There was no warning, either. Third Aunt told me later that they'd eaten rice porridge with wheat berries. He'd complained that there was no flatbread, so she went and made some for him. He ate it all.

Mid-Star's father told me once that the time of everyone's birth and the place of their death are predestined. For Rites Xia, the place was the riverbank. It made sense that I was with him right before it happened. I don't know who or what I was in my last life, but I definitely had some connection to the Xia family. Maybe I'd been a Xia myself in a past life. Or maybe I'd just been a tree in the courtyard of their family home.

The night before Rites Xia died, it had started raining a bit. When the sun came up that morning, I had planned to go over to Seven Li Gully. Justice Xia had told me we were going to make *baozi* for lunch in the shack. I was trying to decide what to stuff the *baozi* with when the thought came to me that since it had rained that night, I should be able to forage some witches'-butter from the riverbank. I could bring it over to Seven Li Gully, and we could eat witches'-butter *baozi*. I found some of the slippery green fungus growing in the mud along the river, started to pick it, and had almost picked my fill when I heard a sound like someone moaning. I looked around, but a fog had set in after the previous night's rain. I couldn't see anyone, so I decided it must have been the tree up the bank making the noise.

When the sound came again, I looked up at the tree and was just about to ask the bird perched on a high branch if she'd heard it, too, when the fog cleared enough for me to see a shoe in the riverbank grass. Why would someone throw away a single, perfectly good shoe? Farther down the bank, on the muddy slope down to the river, I thought I saw someone lying there . . . Was it Rites Xia?

"Uncle Rites?" I asked. "I thought you said you were tired, coming back from Xijing and all that . . . What are you doing down here so early? You should still be sleeping. Did you come down here to collect firewood? Who are you trying to impress, getting out here so early? Nobody else is out here working. You should take it easy."

Rites Xia didn't answer; he was motionless in the grass. I knew something was wrong. I rushed over, knelt beside him, and saw that he was barely clinging to life. His face had already turned blue. I tossed him on my back and headed for East Street. I thought there was a chance that he could be saved, but I suppose I couldn't change fate.

Thunder wasn't home, and neither was Blossom. The only one home was Third Aunt, who wailed and wept and yelled for Emerald to go find Wisdom Xia. She rushed out and brought him back. He took one look at his brother and told Emerald to find Big-Noise Zhao. For once, Wisdom Xia didn't bother shooting me a dirty look. As I bent to try to breathe life into Rites Xia, he wiped the sweat from my forehead with a rag.

Wisdom Xia asked Big-Noise Zhao if it had been heart disease. "Judging by those bruises on his face and down his back," Big-Noise Zhao said, "it looks like he was beaten to death."

"Who would do something like that?" Wisdom Xia said.

"It was because of those silver dollars!" I said.

If he was out on the riverbank in the middle of the night, I figured he must have been meeting a coin dealer. I couldn't think of any other reason he'd be down there at midnight. Since the dealer knew Rites Xia would be bringing the coins, he probably jumped him and just took them, instead of going through with the exchange. Maybe the coin dealer hadn't intended to hurt the old man that badly—just a few good kicks, some punches—but Rites Xia was too weak.

"You're saying he was selling silver coins? That's nonsense," said Wisdom Xia sternly.

"Uncle Rites was a coin dealer."

"He used to sell coins," said Third Aunt. "But once he came back from Xijing, he told me himself he was getting out of that business . . ."

She went looking for the silver coins he kept in a hole in the kang, but they weren't there. She eventually found a stack of banknotes in an old slipper. Rites Xia had collected money his whole life, but it looked like the collection had outlived him. The coins and bills would go back into circulation, but he would end up in a tomb.

Third Aunt began wailing again, thumping her head against the stone kang.

Wisdom Xia withered like a pumpkin blossom hit by early frost. He collapsed into a chair. I glanced over and saw he was looking at me. "Spark," he said.

"I should go get some water," I said, heading for the yard. "We have to clean up Uncle Rites."

"Get over here," Wisdom Xia said. I took a few steps in his direction. "You carried Third Uncle back here, didn't you? We should thank you. When Thunder gets back, I want him to kowtow to you."

"No, no . . ."

"Why not? It's only right. Now, we're going to find out what happened to Third Uncle, but before we get the facts, I don't want you going around talking nonsense."

"I won't," I said.

Wisdom Xia took a carton of cigarettes out of a cabinet, ripped it open, and tossed me a pack. I felt a sudden closeness to the old man. There was no more awkwardness.

Big-Noise Zhao called us back to Rites Xia's side, saying there was nothing else he could do for the old man and we'd have to bring him to the hospital.

Rites Xia was loaded onto a cart, and I started pulling. We got as far as Teahouse Village, and he stopped breathing. Third Aunt was crying, and so were Big-Noise Zhao and I. But Wisdom Xia told us to stop. He went into the village and came back with a white rooster that he tied to the cart; then he told me to turn around and start pulling Rites Xia's body back toward Freshwind. I kept pulling, but I never stopped crying. I felt bad for Rites Xia—the son drove a bus, while the father, even as he was dying, was heaved onto a flatbed cart and hauled down the road.

By the time Wind Xia got to Rites Xia's place, the mourning pavilion had been set up, and everyone in the family was already wearing their mourning clothes. Bamboo hastily took him aside and put a boat-shaped hat of rough white cloth on his head. Third Aunt was in the mourning pavilion, crouched beside the body of her husband, wailing hoarsely. Goodness had been put in charge of the funeral arrangements, but he was finding it difficult to arrange things without her. He kept asking her about candles and sending people out to grind flour—where was the key for the mill?—and collecting money—that was a must!—until she finally told him that she couldn't worry about things like that in the state she was in. She looked ready to faint.

"Thunder is out on his route," Goodness complained, "and Blossom is nowhere to be found, either. We're running around like chickens with our heads cut off here."

Third Aunt told him that Blossom had gone along with her husband, to sell the tickets. Goodness called Rain Xia over and told him to get over to the House of Treasures and put in a call to the bus company. "As fast as you can," Goodness said.

"He already called," said Wisdom Xia. The bags under the old man's eyes had swollen. "Thunder won't be back until tomorrow afternoon at the earliest. You must take charge here. If something needs doing, make sure it gets done. You just give the command. You're missing a key? We can force the locks if we need to."

"Excellent," said Goodness. He pointed over at the cabinets that held rice and grain, and at an iron trunk. The trunk had some money in it, all counted. The next thing he did was draw up a schedule, then called the family together to give them their marching orders.

Bamboo and Halfwit's wife were to grind rice; Treasure and Hearth were sent to the market to get meat and vegetables; Pavilion was in charge of informing family and friends of the death; Bounty was sent out into the yard to ready the stove and prepare firewood; Culture, Shiner, and Emerald were told to stay at the house and help out with anything that came up; Rites Xia's wife would be looked after by Wisdom Xia's wife and Benevolence Xia's widow; Justice Xia and Wisdom Xia had nothing to do; and Gold was put in charge of greeting anyone who came to pay their respects.

Everything was set. Bamboo and Halfwit's wife took the rice out of the cabinet and filled two sacks. Halfwit's wife heaved one of the bags up onto her shoulder and headed for the flatbed cart outside the front gate. She was a small woman, and the bag was heavy. She sweated and grunted her way toward the cart. On her way out of the yard, Second Aunt, who was hobbling her way out of the gate, got in the way of Halfwit's wife.

"Where are you going?"

Halfwit's wife said, "You're in the way." It came out gruff.

"How can you talk to her like that?" Goodness said.

"You didn't see that I'm carrying this bag?" she asked.

"Yes, I saw. But how could Bamboo? The woman is blind."

"You know what I mean," said Halfwit's wife.

"Why don't you try to be more like Bamboo?"

"More like her? You don't see her carrying out sacks of grain, do you?"

"You can't just plough your way through things. If you want to show respect for your elders, you have to be a bit subtle sometimes. You have to show them that you care, through your words and your expressions. Make them happy . . . You might have it in your heart, but it has to come out in your words, right?"

Halfwit's wife grunted, tossed the sack on the cart, and left.

Everyone in the yard laughed. "You have a point," one of the younger relatives said to Goodness.

"I should come around every so often and give you daughters-in-law a lesson in respecting your elders!"

Right then, Marvel came back from the store with a bundle of incense, spirit money, liquor, and cigarettes. "That's enough talk for one day," Marvel said. "Open up," he said, sticking a cigarette in Goodness's mouth.

Goodness was just about to light his cigarette when the sound of weeping and wailing came from outside the gate. "How did the relatives get here so fast?" he asked. The gate opened and he saw Blossom, followed by Rain Xia and Wealth Zhao.

Rain Xia had found Wealth Zhao at home; he had the day off. Rain Xia wanted to know who to contact at the bus company. The first time he'd called, they'd brushed him off, saying, "Thunder's out driving!" and then hung up. Rain Xia had put down the receiver and sworn loudly.

Wealth hadn't been much help, but he'd decided to go with Rain Xia to his place. On the way there, they ran into Blossom, who'd gotten a lift back to Freshwind on another bus. As soon as she saw Wealth, she broke down. "You're our only hope now, Wealth," she wailed. "You have to save our family!"

"You already know?" Wealth asked her.

"How could I not know! You have to go to the bus company tonight, Wealth. You and Thunder are good friends. He has nobody else to turn to!"

"Why would I go to the bus company?" Wealth asked, confused. "Ever since I found out your father-in-law died, I've been trying to get in touch with you or Thunder."

"My father-in-law—he's dead?" Blossom asked, then immediately ran toward her home, sobbing.

As soon as she got into the yard and saw her relatives in their funeral clothes, Blossom rushed into the mourning pavilion and knelt beside the bed where the body of Rites Xia had been laid out, wailing and crying out inconsolably. A few of the mourners tried to pull her away from the body and soothe her, but she clung to the side of the bed.

"Wouldn't even bring the old man a plate of food when he was alive," said Cutie, who was standing outside the mourning pavilion. "But now listen to how she's carrying on!"

Fourth Aunt put a hand over Cutie's mouth. "He never had a daughter," she said, "so if he has a daughter-in-law to cry for him, that's good enough." She turned to the others in the yard and said, "Don't try to pull her away. Let the girl cry. I haven't seen her like this before."

Blossom cried. She cried long, racking sobs that brought tears to the eyes of everyone who heard them. They heard her calling out to the dead man, "How could it be? It's too soon!" But after a while, they heard something else. "How could you die, just when your son needs you most? This family is doomed! We're ruined! Why couldn't it be those people who hurt your son who died instead?"

"What is she talking about in there?" Goodness asked.

"People'll say anything when they're emotional," Justice Xia said.

Goodness looked back at the mourning pavilion.

"Did you hear anything from the police yet?" Justice Xia asked.

"They went to the scene already. They questioned a few possible witnesses or people involved. I don't know much more than that. But did you hear what she just said, about someone hurting Thunder? Is Thunder in trouble?"

"You know, I thought it was a bit strange . . . She went out with him to sell tickets, didn't she? So why is she back and not him?"

Goodness walked into the mourning pavilion and pulled Blossom away from Rites Xia's body. "There's no use crying like that now," he said. "The old man's already dead. There's no changing what's happened. You're his only daughter-in-law. You have to look after things, now that he's gone." He led her out into the yard. "There's something I want to ask you . . ."

Fourth Aunt came over and pulled a mourning gown over Blossom's head as Goodness took her hand and brought her into the house where Justice Xia and Wisdom Xia were waiting.

"How did he die?" she asked.

Wisdom Xia told her what they knew.

"I knew he was selling those coins," Blossom said. "Too cheap to buy some candy for the kids in the village, though. I never thought that would be what killed him! Have you called the police yet? I don't want him to just die like that without getting justice."

"We reported it," said Wisdom Xia. "We want to get our hands on the killer. I want to see who it was! But it looks like this could be a hard case for the police to solve. I don't know if we're better off waiting for them or going straight to a fortune-teller to decide when we should bury him. We were just waiting for you and Thunder to get back. Where the hell is he?"

Blossom started to cry again.

"What are you crying for? Was Thunder in an accident or something? You were with him, weren't you? You seem fine."

"It wasn't an accident. We were on our way to Xijing, and we stopped in Zhoucheng. He got into an argument with a couple of passengers. They smashed a few windows on the bus. Wind Xia was there, too. It was no big deal, really. But about a half hour outside of Zhoucheng, some inspectors from the company waved us down, stopped us . . . I knew they had inspectors, but I'd never seen them. I knew if there was one day we couldn't afford to run into them, it was this day. But that's exactly what happened. Like the saying goes, a chain always breaks at the weakest point. They got on the bus and found six passengers without tickets. They asked why they didn't have tickets, and they told them, 'We paid our fare, but they didn't give us tickets.' Right away, they said Thunder had broken the company's rules. They told him he couldn't drive, that they'd get someone else to take the bus into Xijing. They brought us back to the office.

"After a while they let me go, but Thunder is still there. I don't know what they're going to do to him. As soon as I got back to Freshwind, I went looking for Wealth Zhao. He knows people over there. I wanted him to talk to them, intervene on Thunder's behalf . . . I didn't know anything had happened here. It's true what they say: misfortunes never come one by one."

Wisdom Xia, Justice Xia, and Goodness didn't know what to say. They sat in silence.

"We're ruined," Blossom said. "This family is doomed."

Justice Xia sucked in a ragged breath and brought his fist down on the table, knocking a ceramic mug to the floor. The mug broke into three pieces at Blossom's feet. She bent to pick them up.

Wisdom Xia grabbed his older brother by the lapels, but Justice Xia shook him off. "What were you doing on that bus?" Justice Xia thundered. "That's state property! You were taking the fares and pocketing them. If it wasn't for you—if Thunder had a good woman by his side—this never would have happened."

Blossom sobbed pathetically.

"What good will it do to scold her right now?" said Wisdom Xia. "The more you stir shit, the worse it smells . . . That's not going to help Thunder any, is it?"

"And what are you doing about it?" Justice Xia asked. "I warned Rites that his son was going to get in trouble. He didn't listen to me. Now, whatever happens, it's going to look bad for Thunder. That woman of his didn't help any, either. All we can do now is get Rites in the ground. We have to choose a day and get the funeral done."

"So," said Blossom, "none of you care about Thunder?"

"I oughta slap you," said Justice Xia. "You think we have time to worry about him now? The best thing for him to do would be to confess to the bus company what he did and let them deal with him!" He took a few hard puffs off his cigarette. "What do you think, Wisdom?"

"I think you have it right. Let the police figure out who killed Rites. If they can do it, that's fine, but I have my doubts. With their budget and their manpower, they won't be able to conduct much of an investigation. We need to keep this quiet. There's no sense in us asking questions about what may or may not have happened. We need to bury him as soon as possible. Let the man rest. As for Thunder, as of right now, only the people in this room and Wealth Zhao know about it, and it would be best if we kept it that way. You got that, Blossom?"

"I got it."

"We have to do things properly now," Wisdom Xia continued, "and make sure to keep things quiet. We'll just swallow this rotten tooth. We should keep our problems to ourselves.

Goodness will look after things here, and I'll go find Wealth Zhao. I'll have him go to the company and try to talk to them. If he can't help Thunder, all we can do is wait to see how they'll deal with him. Whether they just fire him or get the police involved, he'll at least be allowed to see his father buried, right? I'm going to ask Rain Xia to borrow Pavilion's motorcycle and run Wealth over to the office, just to be sure he gets there safe. And Blossom, what you need to do is get together five thousand yuan and give it to Goodness, so he can look after things."

"Five thousand?"

Justice Xia lost his temper again: "You can't get five thousand? I heard you going around, saying Thunder was making good money. How much did you make skimming the fares? Every other word out of your mouth was 'money'! That's why Thunder is in trouble now. And when you really need money, you don't have it?" Justice Xia stood and went out into the yard. "Burn the spirit money," he said.

Marvel called the Xia family to kneel before the mourning pavilion and lit the bundle of spirit money. As the money burned, Rites Xia's relatives wept. Justice Xia was joined by Wisdom Xia in the doorway of the house. Their eyes were wet and red.

"You two should be in the mourning pavilion," said Goodness, coming up behind them.

Justice Xia lowered his head and walked past the mourners, out of the gate, and back to his home at the tail of the scorpion.

Thunder came back to the village the next day. Goodness took him aside and told him that it would be best if no effort was made to solve Rites Xia's murder. He invited Mid-Star's father over to help him choose the most auspicious day for the burial. Mid-Star came along with his father but left after offering his condolences to Thunder—he had his own business to attend to. Mid-Star's father set about forecasting the right day to put Rites Xia in his coffin, and then the right day to bury him. Mid-Star's father also set about preparing the silk scroll with gold dust letters for the burial, but he had to run to the bathroom four times. Each time, he'd yell for me to bring him paper.

I couldn't find any wastepaper to give him; there was always a shortage in our village. So, I ended up asking Marvel for some. Marvel always wore a cap, and I knew that he used to stuff newspaper in it. The balls of newspaper gave it the right shape, with a high peak . . . But he didn't want to sacrifice any for Mid-Star's dad. I went and got some of the spirit money for him, ripping it into smaller pieces before passing it in.

"Why don't you just use one of the rocks in there to wipe your ass?" I asked Mid-Star's dad. "Are you that delicate?"

"After you've had the runs for a while, it hurts to use a stone or some dirt or whatever. Anyway," he said, "I'm still looking after Rites, right? I picked out the right day, made the scroll . . . His family can't give me some paper to wipe my ass with?"

"That's the spirit money for Uncle Rites!"

"I'll be with him soon enough. I can pay him back then."

"What do you mean by that?" I asked. "Did your illness come back? Uncle Rites was the same, always sick with something, but he used to say that even if someone looked sick, they might end up hanging on longer than anyone else. I never expected him to die so soon."

"What the hell do you mean? You thought you'd be at my funeral instead? I can tell you this: I was on my deathbed. This disease is a death sentence. But when your uncle Rites died, he went in my place. The quota was filled, for this year, at least."

While Mid-Star's dad and I were arguing, Thunder arrived home and offered his condolences to his uncles. Wisdom Xia asked him what had happened at the bus company. Thunder said that there wasn't much he could do but wait for their decision.

Justice Xia angrily cut him off. "It's all down to you. Of your generation, I only had hopes for you and Wind Xia. But you've become a stone roller around our necks! You betrayed the trust of the masses, profiting off them for your own gain. How can you live with yourself?"

"This whole thing was Blossom's fault."

"I've seen the way you let her behave," Justice Xia said. "You're lucky they let you burn incense for your father. If they turned you over to the police, you'd be in real trouble."

"That's enough," Wisdom Xia said. "We've already set the time—tomorrow at noon. The coffin and the graveclothes are ready. The grave is prepared. We still have to decide how many people should be at the funeral."

"The way he died, I'm sure his spirit is not going to be eager to cross over," Thunder said. "I won't be able to rest, either, if the funeral doesn't go well. I don't want to go around with a knot in my chest the rest of my life, worrying that I let down our ancestors."

"You won't be able to rest? What about me and your uncle Justice! What point is there in wasting a bunch of money on a big funeral now? The fewer people we have at the funeral, the better. We need to keep the circumstances of his death as quiet as possible. Let's spare your poor father the shame. The way I see it, we should send out invitations to some of the families on East Street and his former coworkers, and then maybe a few other relatives and close family friends. That's enough. We have to make sure to keep out everyone else, especially his old drinking buddies."

"I'll follow your lead on this," Thunder said.

Wisdom Xia sent Bamboo over to Middle Street and West Street to head off any potential uninvited guests. Pavilion was in charge of patrolling the township government, the police station, the post office, and the credit cooperative and dissuading any overenthusiastic funeral crashers or curious lookie-loos. Wind Xia called Snow Bai and told her to come back right away. She showed up, put on the funeral clothes, and knelt on a straw mat in the back room of the mourning pavilion, weeping.

Bounty, Hearth, Forest Wu, and I went up to the attic of the house to get the coffin. Everything up there was covered in a layer of dust and spiderwebs. I squinted against the dust and rubbed my eyes hard. Sticking my head out the window, I caught sight of Snow Bai on the straw mat. She was crying but without exaggeration, quietly . . . In her funeral clothes, she was somehow even lovelier than usual. I decided if a girl wants to be beautiful, she should dress in funeral clothes.

I took one corner of the coffin, and we began carrying it down, but I was too busy looking at Snow Bai's wet eyes. My grip slipped and Bounty swore at me. I put my head down and focused on our task. The coffin was surprisingly heavy, made from solid cedar. When we passed it down to the people waiting in the yard, they told us, "Take it easy. Slow down!"

I was distracted by Snow Bai again. She had pulled aside the sheet of hempen paper that covered Rites Xia's face. His eyes were wide open, staring up at her.

Several people had already tried to shut Rites Xia's eyes, but they seemed to be stuck open. In the village, we had a belief that a person's soul would be reborn twenty-four hours after their death. How and where they were reborn was more complicated—depending on how they had behaved in their last life. They might end up as a human or as a pig, maybe even a wild animal or a fish or a tree or a worm. That was for those who had died a normal death. But someone who'd left the world violently couldn't be reborn that easily. Their soul would wander, their spirit like a soldier without an army. The sign that someone's soul had been left to wander was that their eyes refused to close.

Snow Bai tried to shut the old man's eyes, but they wouldn't close. As she pulled her hand away, there was a sound from up in the rafters, a loud crack. I looked up, but there was nothing there. Bounty caught me looking. "You're not even lifting," he said.

"The coffin's too heavy. We should take it down in two pieces. Take the lid off and pass it down first."

Bounty agreed, so we set the coffin down again and lifted the lid. We saw that there was a small cloth bag inside, containing ten coins. Bounty passed the coins down to Blossom. She bit one of them, then flicked it and held it up to her ear. She looked over at Snow Bai, who was still trying to shut Rites Xia's eyes.

"Snow Bai," she said, "why are you worried about shutting his eyes? You're not scared, are you?"

"I was telling him not to be angry, that he could shut his eyes now."

"Put a couple of these coins on his eyes," I said. "That'll close them."

As soon as I spoke, everyone turned to look at me. They thought I'd lost my mind again, that I was just ranting. But Snow Bai took a pair of the silver coins from Blossom and put them over Rites Xia's eyes—and they shut. She looked up from the body and over at me. Her expression seemed to say, *How did you know that would work?*

To be honest, I couldn't tell you. You could call it heaven's will, I guess. And maybe it was heaven's will that she should look up at me like she did, too. I was proud of myself and looked right back at her. I even wrinkled my nose and gave her a wink. She got down beside the table again and started crying.

Fourth Aunt was in the kitchen, giving instructions to Chastity and Cutie as they fried slices of dough to make sesame twists. You know what sesame twists are? They're a type of fritter made from dough, shaped like flowers. Before everyone had a rosebush out in their courtyard, the flower-shaped fritters stood in for actual flowers. Fourth Aunt was grumbling about Chastity's clumsiness—the fritters looked nothing like flowers.

Fourth Aunt suddenly fell silent, listening to the sound of Snow Bai crying in the mourning pavilion. "How come Snow Bai is back?" she asked.

"Not even worried about us, are you?" Chastity said. "You're only worried about your little Snow Bai. You'd never talk to her like you talk to us."

Fourth Aunt wiped her floury hands on her apron and went out to the mourning pavilion to see Snow Bai. "That's enough crying for now," Fourth Aunt said to her. "You should burn some incense and offer a cup of liquor."

Snow Bai followed Fourth Aunt's orders but then went back to the straw mat again.

"That's enough crying," Fourth Aunt said again. "You're pregnant," she reminded Snow Bai. "You should go home and rest for a while, at least. This is no place for a woman in your condition. Have Wind Xia take you home and get you some soup. If anything happens here, we'll let you know."

Snow Bai rose from the straw mat and went home.

When she got there, First Aunt, Second Aunt, and Wisdom Xia were sitting out in the yard talking. Snow Bai saw that their eyes were red. "You aren't going over to your uncle's place?" Wisdom Xia asked.

"I already went," Snow Bai said.

"Did you cry?"

"I cried."

"Snow Bai's a good girl," First Aunt said. "Came all the way back to cry for her uncle, even though she's pregnant. Better than that Blossom, at least. Blossom barely wept and then ran home. This generation of the Xia family didn't have any daughters, so there's nobody to cry for Rites Xia, only his daughter-in-law . . ."

"Blossom doesn't have time to cry," Wisdom Xia said.

"That's true," First Aunt said. "You know how Thunder is. He leaves everything to her."

"Bodhi's mother was crying, though, wasn't she?" Second Aunt asked.

"Chrysanth? What would she be crying for?" First Aunt asked. "She's not even part of the Xia family anymore."

"She and Treasure might be divorced, but it's not like she's moved out of the village. She's still living in one of the Xia family homes."

"She went to see the mourning pavilion," Wisdom Xia said, "and she went out this morning to pick a bundle of green onions to bring to Blossom. That's good enough."

Second Aunt let the topic of Chrysanth drop. "What about Black-Moth?" she asked.

"Why would she go?" Wisdom Xia said.

"We have to tell Blossom not to let her in," Second Aunt said. "That shameless little slut might show up, trying to claim she's part of the family."

Snow Bai stood listening to the conversation. She didn't understand what they were talking about, but she felt it would be rude to walk past them into the house. "It's a bit hot out here," she said. "Why not go inside and talk? I can plug in the electric fan."

"Did you have something to eat yet?" Wisdom Xia asked. "Wind Xia is still over there, isn't he? Go over and get him, tell him to make you something to eat."

"I can make something for myself. I can make some extra, if anybody else wants to eat."

"We've already eaten," Wisdom Xia said.

"Out of the four brothers," First Aunt said, "you're the only one who's had it good."

"I've had it, all right—good or not, it's hard to say."

"You might not say it, but I know you're happy. You ended up with Snow Bai as a daughter-in-law."

"Your daughters-in-laws are just fine," Wisdom Xia said. He seemed to suddenly remember something and rushed into the kitchen to look for Snow Bai. "When Wind Xia called you," he asked her, "did he ask you about getting some of your troupe down for your third uncle's funeral?"

"He didn't say anything about that."

"I'll ask Goodness about it," he said.

Wisdom Xia left, and when he came back, he told the aunts, "Justice says he doesn't want any opera at the funeral. That's not right, is it? We don't need a full performance, but it would be nice to have some of the musicians play, at least."

"You can't listen to him on this," said Second Aunt. "He's just worried that if the funeral is too big, there'll be a bunch of outsiders there, spreading gossip. What kind of funeral would it be without some musicians, at least? That'd make people talk, too. They'd say it was the sign of a guilty conscience, not even having musicians to play at the funeral."

"Has he said how Rites died?" Wisdom Xia asked.

"However he died," Second Aunt said, "it's not hard to guess that there was some foul play."

Snow Bai had come out of the kitchen to listen. This conversation was even harder to follow than the last one. "How did Third Uncle die?" she asked.

"Go finish cooking," Wisdom Xia said. "Once you've had something to eat, I want you to call the opera company and get a few performers to come down."

"It's usually the son-in-law who takes care of that," First Aunt said. "Rites didn't have a daughter, though . . . Who's going to pay for the musicians?"

"I'll take care of it," Snow Bai said.

"What a sensible girl!" said Second Aunt.

Since Snow Bai had come back to Freshwind, she hadn't had a chance to tell Wind Xia what was on her mind, and Wind Xia hadn't had much to say to her, either. They were too busy at Rites Xia's home to talk much. Wind Xia was a writer, a man of letters, and so even as he handled the arrangements for his uncle's funeral, he was accumulating material for his writing. He asked his mother how his uncle's clothes had been changed before his body was put in the mourning pavilion. His mother told him that Third Aunt had scrubbed her husband's face and then cleaned his body. But Third Aunt had a bad case of bronchitis, and as she worked on her husband's body, she cried and found it hard to breathe, so First Aunt had stepped in to help her. It had been Wind Xia's mother and First Aunt who had dressed Rites Xia in a fresh set of clothes. He wore three layers of quilted material and three layers of cotton, with a long robe on top.

The old man's funeral clothes had been prepared many years before, except for a pair of socks, which the two women sewed for him from some plain white cloth. Once he was dressed, Rites Xia was laid out on a door plank. Three sheets of hempen paper were laid down and smashed together by pounding them with a hammer, forming one large sheet that was laid over his body.

Wind Xia got involved, too. Goodness directed him to write the couplet to go on the spirit tablets. He got a sheet of white paper, wrote the couplet, and stuck it to the memorial tablet. Once the body was in the ground, the paper would be torn off the tablet and written over, Goodness explained.

"What's the point of that?" Wind Xia asked.

"That's the custom," said Goodness.

It was Marvel who had set up the mourning pavilion, and Big-Noise Zhao had written the couplets pasted in the courtyard and on the doorway to the hall. The first read, "We keep walking forward and always think / The weight of sadness is never too much to bear." The second read, "From the deep dream awaken / And return to the earth."

"These are quite good," Wind Xia said when he saw the couplets, "but I don't know if they're exactly right for a funeral."

Big-Noise Zhao asked Wind Xia to write his own couplets to replace them.

The first one he wrote to hang over the doorway of the mourning pavilion read, "You come into this world with nothing to your name / And leave it just the same." For the couplet to be pasted above the doorway of the house, he wrote, "One day you're here and the next you're gone / Where did you come from and where have you gone?" And the final couplet he wrote for the courtyard gate was, "In death there is comfort / And worries can be laid aside."

"Truly a son of the Xia family!" Big-Noise Zhao said.

Wind Xia put on mourning clothes and straw sandals and went out with Hearth to pay a visit to Rites Xia's relatives, to inform them of the death and pay their respects. When they got to the first house, they bowed before the ancestral shrine and kowtowed, knocking their foreheads on the floor three times. The relatives helped them to their feet, and Wind Xia told them when the funeral procession would begin. They offered to make something for Wind Xia and Hearth to eat. The two men ate their meal without much enthusiasm and then returned to Rites Xia's home.

In the alley outside, craftsmen were using a stone roller to crush bamboo stalks. The strips of bamboo were used to form the "mountains of gold and silver" funeral decorations. They cut up strips of paper and made a basket about as large as a bamboo steamer. Figures of a boy and a girl were formed from clay, and around the neck of the clay boy was hung a sign that read, "Beat the dog, protect the home." Around the neck of the clay girl was a sign that read, "Wash clothes, cook food." After the coffin had been brought down, it was lined with sheets of tissue paper set down in layers. Mid-Star's father had been charged with writing a banner for the coffin, but after a long time pondering the inscription, sipping tea, and dragging on a cigarette, he finally said, "Let Wind Xia write it."

Wind Xia wasn't sure what he was supposed to write on the banner, so he told Mid-Star's dad he should write it after all. After examining his work, he found five characters written wrong. "That's the way I was taught," said Mid-Star's father when it was pointed out to him.

Wind Xia went back to examining the banner. The final two lines read, "Parting from this beautiful world / Never again to feel the warm breeze of love."

"My uncle only cared about money," he grumbled to himself. "I never heard him mention anything about 'the warm breeze of love.'"

The musicians Snow Bai had invited arrived in the village on the day the procession was to carry the coffin to the tomb. All the musicians sat out in the yard, smoking cigarettes and drinking shaojiu—all except for one of them, Mrs. Wang, who Dog-Scraps had once called Jade Bracelet after her most famous role in *Picking Up the Jade Bracelet*. Mrs. Wang left the others to their liquor and cigarettes and pulled Snow Bai aside, whispering in her ear. The two women went together to Wisdom Xia's home, one alley over.

Wisdom Xia had gotten up early that morning and felt twinges in his chest. Fourth Aunt told him to sit in the chair and relax. She brought him a bowl of brown sugar and hot water, saying, "It's going to be crowded and noisy over there. Just wait until they get his body in the coffin; then I'll come over and get you." Wisdom Xia stayed in the chair for a while, but he started to feel anxious again. He decided to head over to the alley behind his home, where his brother's house was. Just as he was heading for the gate, Snow Bai arrived with Mrs. Wang. When Wisdom Xia saw Mrs. Wang, he yelped in surprise and led her into the house to sit down.

"I can't believe you came down for the funeral, too," he said.

"It was only right. It's a chance to see you and Wind Xia, too."

"They won't start the funeral for a while, and Mrs. Wang said she had to come and see you," Snow Bai said. "Where's Wind Xia? I haven't seen him anywhere."

"He said he was going out to the grave to make sure everything was ready for the burial," Wisdom Xia said.

"Well," said Mrs. Wang, "if Wind Xia's not here, perhaps now is the right time to ask you for a favor?"

"Ask me for a favor? What! You are the greatest opera performer of your generation. Who could turn down a request from Mrs. Wang?"

Mrs. Wang immediately began crying.

Wisdom Xia wasn't sure what to do and could only stammer, "This, uh, well . . ."

"She was moved by your speech, that's all," Snow Bai said. "Please, Mrs. Wang, sit down, here . . ."

Snow Bai went and fetched a stool for the singer, but she didn't sit. Instead she stopped crying and smiled at Wisdom Xia. "You don't know how happy I am to hear that. We always listened to the Party's commands, the Chairman's orders . . . As performers, we devoted our lives to bringing joy to the lives of workers, peasants, and soldiers. I've never been one to complain. What do I have to complain about? In the old society, 'actress' was a dirty word. It was the Party and the Chairman that raised us up. Our vocation was no longer a slur but an honor—we became 'revolutionary artists.' We treasured the local opera.

"Mr. Xia, look around . . . The local opera has been passed down from one generation of performers to another, hasn't it? Now, we're getting old, and it's time to give the tradition to a younger generation. But the world has changed. The opera company is virtually bankrupt, the younger performers are mediocre—they want to sing pop songs, not local opera. Can you call any of that music art? These pop stars lack even the most rudimentary talent. But their adoring fans don't care about that. Those singers can go out and make a fortune in a single night. What has become of this world? You don't even need talent or skill nowadays, do you?"

"Opera is sacred," Wisdom Xia said. "You can eat meat and drink liquor, Mrs. Wang, and you can eat fruits, vegetables . . . But can anyone live without rice and grain? No chance! We have someone in Freshwind who sings pop songs—Star Chen is his name. I don't care for it. The local opera, though, as soon as I hear it, I feel at peace, from the tip of my toes to the top of my head, in every bone in my body . . . Why do you think I paint those opera masks? It's love, isn't it? Not many people around here understand that. They ask me, 'What the hell are you doing that for?' It's our local opera, it's Shaanxi opera. How can you claim to be a local if you don't appreciate the local opera? Are you really from the land of Qin if you don't feel a sense of peace when you hear Shaanxi opera? As the saying goes, 'It's not lamb unless it stinks like lamb; it's not fish unless it stinks like fish.'"

"You said it, Mr. Xia!" Mrs. Wang said. "Snow Bai was telling me you plan to turn those opera masks into a book?"

"I'm just getting everything arranged now. When the book's done, I'll make sure you're the first to see it. I would love to hear your suggestions."

"Did Wind Xia set this up?"

"He knows a publisher in Xijing."

"You have a good son. Unfortunately for me, my son was born with cerebral palsy. Now, what little I make as a performer . . ." She sighed. "I've sung opera my whole life, but I've started to wonder how much longer I have. The day will come. All I've done will be nothing but a gust of wind, here and then gone, without a trace." She began to cry again.

"I was thinking," Wisdom Xia said. "You should record something. Even if the troupe disbands, everyone will still be able to hear your voice."

"Who's going to record me? The company is nearly bankrupt. I wouldn't even know where to go to record, and I wouldn't be able to afford it, even if I did," Mrs. Wang said. "Wind Xia is probably the only one who could help me with something like that."

"Exactly. He could help. I'll tell him."

"You see, Snow Bai? There was no reason to feel awkward about it, was there? Your father-in-law is a straight shooter."

"What is there to be awkward about?" Wisdom Xia asked. "Now—"

"They're putting the body in the coffin!" said Fourth Aunt, coming into the yard from the alley. "It's time to go."

Snow Bai and Mrs. Wang went back to Rites Xia's home.

"That poor old woman," Wisdom Xia said to his wife, "was once famous for *Picking Up the Jade Bracelet*. They knew her all over the county, all over the province . . . Now, when she wants to record a performance, who's going to help her? She came to ask Wind Xia if he might be able to."

"Wind Xia is too busy!" Fourth Aunt said.

"What the hell do you know?" Wisdom Xia said. The anxiety he'd felt on waking returned, and he went out of the gate and into the alley.

Shifty was standing in the entrance to the alley, and Wisdom Xia saw that his face was shockingly pale. "Fourth Uncle," he said to Wisdom Xia, "why didn't anybody tell me Third Uncle is getting buried today?"

"Thunder wanted a simple funeral. Nobody from Middle Street or West Street was invited."

"Whether they go or not, I don't care," Shifty said. "But I should be there. It's only right that I carry his coffin. There's something I need to tell Third Uncle."

"What do you mean?"

"He took three silver coins from me. He'd always say he was going to pay me back, but he's dead now. I don't care about the coins, and I just want to tell him that. I don't want him to worry about it, wherever he is now."

Wisdom Xia turned and walked away. When he got to Rites Xia's home, he saw the crowd gathered outside the gate, reading the couplet pasted above it. He looked up and read it, too.

He wasn't pleased. When he saw the couplet over the door to the house, he went and found Big-Noise Zhao. "Did you write those?" he asked.

"Wind Xia wrote them," Big-Noise Zhao said.

Wisdom Xia looked around for his son and saw him coming in the gate, just back from inspecting the gravesite. "You, come with me," Wisdom Xia said, turning and heading for the gate. Wind Xia followed his father out into the alley and around the corner. "You wrote those couplets?" Wisdom Xia asked.

"Yes, I wrote them."

"I thought you had some culture," Wisdom Xia said. "What are you doing, dragging your uncle's good name through the mud?"

"What do you mean by that? I was only being honest. They've been up since last night, and you're the first person who's said anything about them."

Wisdom Xia was silent for a moment. He was just about to catch his breath and begin lecturing his son when from the other side of the low wall, he heard voices.

"They're burying Thunder's father today, aren't they?" one of the voices said. "Why didn't you go?"

"What's the point in showing up when nobody invited me?" another voice said.

"That's no reason not to go pay your respects. You're as stubborn as Wisdom Xia!"

The speakers strolled out from behind the wall, and as soon as they saw Wisdom Xia, both stopped talking and headed off in the opposite direction as fast as their legs would carry them. Wisdom Xia's nostrils flared, and he turned back to his son. "It's fine," he said. "Forget about it. You should get back."

Wind Xia went back into his uncle's yard, where the band had begun to play.

The sons of the Xia family came forward as the band was ripping into the next number. Thunder was the first, burning spirit money, lighting incense, and offering a cup of liquor to his father. Gold led the other eight Xia sons in making offers. After them came Culture and Shiner to lead their generation in making offerings to their great-uncle. As each group came forward, the musicians played mourning songs. The band's *bangu* player sang along to the beat in a voice that was hoarse yet piercing. The drummer's face turned the color of pork liver as he sang, his eyes got wide as saucers, and with each beat of the drum, the thatch of hair on top of his head bobbed.

Everyone who made eye contact with him was forced to stifle their laughter. "What a drummer!" they said instead. That only made him more animated. Someone was overheard to say, "Even for this audience, he hams it up . . ."

When it was time to lay Rites Xia in his coffin, juniper tips and ash were laid over the bottom of the box, and the body was wrapped with a final layer of plain white cloth. As Goodness and Marvel settled Rites Xia, more ash was laid over his body.

"Is he going to be buried with anything?" Goodness asked.

Thunder brought over three painted vases that Rites Xia had kept in his bedroom. They were placed alongside the body in the coffin, along with a bottle of liquor and a pack of cigarettes. Marvel was about to add a pipe that he had found in Rites Xia's house, but Chastity stopped him. "That wasn't his," she said. "Fourth Uncle left it there."

"He died over some silver coins," Third Aunt said, weeping. "He might as well take them with him."

"Where are they?" Goodness asked.

"I have them," Blossom said.

Goodness took them from her and was about to put them in the coffin when Justice Xia grabbed them out of his hand and dumped them on the ground. "What good'll these do him now?" Justice Xia said.

Third Aunt realized her mistake.

Goodness intervened quickly. "That's right," he said, "best not bury him with anything too valuable. I heard that last year at Teahouse Village, they put a set of jade mah-jongg tiles in as a burial gift. Someone got wind of it, and not long after the body was in the ground, some grave robbers came and dug up the coffin to steal them."

Goodness motioned for the lid to be put on the coffin. The crowd in the yard moved in closer to get a last look at Rites Xia. His eyes had closed but his mouth hung open, showing a missing incisor. Third Aunt pressed her hand to his mouth, shouting, "Father of my children! Why did they do this to you?"

"Somebody get hold of her!" Goodness said.

Bamboo wrapped her arms around the old woman's waist and pulled her away so that the coffin could be closed. Once the lid was on, ropes were wrapped around the coffin and poles fixed for the pallbearers to hoist it onto their shoulders. The sound of weeping echoed through the house and filled the yard.

After the coffin was ready, it was time for villagers of Rites Xia's generation to make their offerings. The coffin was lifted, and Gold went around to each of its bearers, offering them cigarettes. Some lit them and smoked while they walked, while others tucked the cigarettes behind their ears. Thunder dumped a paper box of ash in front of the coffin, then went to get a portrait of his father to carry in the procession.

"Music!" Goodness called. The musicians began to play again. The pallbearers roared in unison and began to make their way out of the yard. Thunder followed the coffin, and then came Culture, followed by Gold, Pavilion, Treasure, Bounty, Hearth, Halfwit, Wind Xia, and Rain Xia. The other relatives followed, with Snow Bai walking in the rear of the family procession. The procession went out in the street and ended up in front of the opera house, partly so the pallbearers could rest, and also so the band could play "Worrying Through the Five Night Watches." The coffin could not touch the ground, so a bench was brought out to rest it on while the band played. A crowd formed to watch. As the band finished, the coffin was lifted again, and the crowd dispersed. The only trace of the coffin's visit was a layer of white spirit money on the ground outside the opera house.

Once the procession reached its destination, Goodness told Thunder to sweep the grave, and then a strip of firecrackers was set off. The sons and daughters of the younger generations knelt and burned three bundles of spirit money. The coffin was set down in the grave, the grave was sealed, and dirt was piled in a mound over Rites Xia's final resting place. The sticks that the Xia sons had carried in the funeral procession were stuck upright together in the mound. Goodness went around and made sure the sticks were not driven too deep into the earth. "It wouldn't be good if the branches take root and start sprouting," he explained. The Xia family's daughters-in-law left the grave mound first, followed by their husbands.

Before she left, Fourth Aunt gave a handful of dirt from the mound to Snow Bai. "Wrap it in your jacket," she said.

"What for?" Snow Bai asked.

"When you get home, put it under your dresser. It's good luck."

When Thunder was ready to go, Goodness gave him some, too, and told him to take it home with him.

I was one of those who stayed behind to build up the burial mound. By the time the mound was at about waist height, most of the others had left. I noticed that two of the men leaving were carrying sledgehammers. They planned to go over to the 312, hitch a ride into Zhoucheng, and get a job in the city. The funeral procession was going the same direction, so they'd decided to join in. I wondered what they were going to do in the city, carting around those eight-pound sledgehammers. They said that they didn't have any skills, but they figured they might be able to get a job doing demolition. They'd do whatever job they could find, they said, no matter how tough. They told me they were hard workers.

"You won't make any money working hard," I told them. "You make real money when you don't have to lift a finger. You really think you're going to make money swinging a hammer?"

"Well," one of the men said, "if we can't make any money, we'll cut our dicks off and sell our holes."

I couldn't tell you if they said anything more after that. I saw red. I grabbed a handful of dirt and threw it in their faces. They ran at me and landed a few kicks before Forest Wu stepped between us.

The story of the two men was not a happy one. They ended up in Zhoucheng, working on a demolition team just as they'd planned, but they never made much money. Later, they turned to robbing people. They eventually got caught and sentenced to fifteen years apiece. Before that, it had been fifteen years since anyone from Freshwind had been sent to prison. They brought shame to their names, so I'm not even going to bother saying who exactly they were.

After everyone had left, I sat alone on the tomb and cried. I wasn't crying about the fight or because of how hard the kicks had stung but for Rites Xia. Was it really true? Would Rites Xia sleep here for eternity? It seemed impossible. One minute a person could be full of life, and the next, put in the ground forever.

The tears fell from my eyes like pellets of goat shit.

Chapter 30

On the way home from the grave, Snow Bai told Wind Xia that Mrs. Wang, the opera singer, wanted to meet him.

"Is it about recording the CD?" asked Wind Xia. "If it is, I'm not meeting her."

"The old lady's really having a hard time. I wish you'd help her out," said Snow Bai.

"She's being childish!"

"She didn't see you at the theater, and now she's come all the way to Freshwind; it would be bad if she couldn't meet you here, either. At least talk to her. It'll make her feel better."

"She's given you crazy ideas; you've all got your heads in the clouds. What's the big deal if I don't talk to her?"

"Dad already promised that you would. If you won't do what I say, you'll have him coming after you!"

Once they got home, Wind Xia didn't go in but went straight to Justice Xia's instead.

Justice Xia had come home earlier than the others, climbed up the ladder to the roof, opened his coffin, and brought down a bundle of funeral clothes. He hung each garment on the clothesline in the sunshine to air.

"You get yourself all worked up," said Second Aunt. "Are you getting dressed in your funeral outfit just because you saw Rites in his?"

"I'm just airing them," Justice Xia said.

"It's not the sixth of the sixth month; it's not the right time for airing silk!"

"The gown Rites had on was a terrible color," said Justice Xia. "Ah-ya! This shirt's a bit too short for me, isn't it?"

"Which one?" She came over and felt it. "It's an undershirt. Of course it's short. If you think it's too short, we can swap. But you know mine's made of coarse cloth, and yours is silk."

"If you don't like your coarse cloth, get your sons to have another one made for you," said Justice Xia.

He hung up all the funeral garments. There were seven in all, three unlined and three padded, plus a long gown. They'd been in the coffin for a long time and had a few mold spots, but the mold was only on the surface of the silk and rubbed off, leaving no mark. There were also a pair of shoes, a pair of socks, and a skull cap, which he didn't hang up on the line.

"I don't want this; I made that clear. When the time comes, you make sure they know not to put that cap on me. Who wears them nowadays? If you want me to have something on my head, you can put a fur hat with ear flaps on me, the kind I usually wear in winter. A new one!"

"Since when did you get so fussy about what you wear? You're as bad as Wisdom. Who am I supposed to tell not to put the skull cap on you? How do you know I won't go before you?"

Wind Xia had come into the yard and was silently observing the two old folks as they hung the clothes. If they'd been talking about Third Uncle's death, he would probably have broken down in tears, but their bickering over the funeral clothes just made him melancholy. He wanted to say something but couldn't think of what.

Finally he greeted them and asked, "What's so special about the number seven? You and Third Uncle both have seven grave garments?"

"It's just as important to have good clothes and food and furniture in the underworld as it is in the world of the living," Second Aunt explained. "You can have one, three, five, or at most seven garments. And if you wear all seven, then the dog at the gates of hell won't bite you."

"Why do they have to be an uneven number?"

"In the world of the living, things come in pairs, but in the underworld, they happen singly. Have you ever seen an old couple die as a pair?" asked Second Aunt.

Wind Xia studied the clothes. They were the same style as wealthy folk wore during the Qing dynasty. The shirts and pants were all right, but the gown seemed ridiculously heavy. "This isn't very smart," he said. "Why not buy a woolen coat, more up-to-date?"

"I've been a farmer all my life. I'd look completely out of place in a woolen coat. People would laugh at me," said Justice Xia. "You carry a fountain pen in your breast pocket, and it looks good, but it would look ridiculous on me. You buy a wool coat for your dad—he's had a fancy kind of job."

"I bought one for him last year, and a pair of leather shoes as well. He wanted to wear them, but Mom wouldn't let him. She said, 'How would an old man like him look, dressed up in such fancy clothes in the village?' She said she'd save them for his funeral."

"Your mom talks nonsense," said Second Aunt. "He could use the coat, but not the leather shoes. They're made from pigs or cows—he might get reborn as a pig or a cow in his next life. And even if he doesn't, how's he going to get over the Hopelessness Bridge with leather shoes on? He'll slip and fall!"

Wind Xia laughed. "The Hopelessness Bridge?"

"When you die you have to cross the Hopelessness Bridge to get to the underworld," said Second Aunt. "It's two feet wide, thirty yards high, and the surface is covered with Sichuan pepper oil. If there's a wind, or even a breeze, it sways, and the dead fall off it. And then they end up in outer darkness."

"Don't listen to what your second aunt says," said Justice Xia.

"Generations of folk have all said the same thing," said the old woman. "And the darkness is very dark, believe me."

"How dark?" Wind Xia asked her.

"Pitch black, just like it is in front of my eyes. You can't see anything at all."

Wind Xia fell silent, and Justice Xia didn't know what to say, either. "Wind Xia, why do you want to know, anyway?" he finally asked.

"I want to understand so that I can use it when I write stories."

"Huh, you and your stories. You listen to me. Write about Seven Li Gully. We've been working there for a while now, from early in the morning till late in the evening. We take our meals with us, just like you did at lower middle school in Teahouse Village—a jar of pickled vegetables and some steamed buns. I've carried those jars back and forth so many times that I've broken three of them. And I've snapped seven carrying poles, too, but we've managed to add several dozen stones to the embankment, and we've dug out the cliff and added several feet of soil to build up the land. Why don't you write about all that?"

"That's for journalists to write up, either as news items or reportage," said Wind Xia. "I'm writing fiction. It's different."

Justice Xia looked disappointed. "It's all writing. Why wouldn't it be the same?"

"It's not."

Justice Xia stood in the sunshine, his mouth agape in confusion. He couldn't see the difference for the life of him. Just then, Wisdom Xia appeared at the gate. "Second Brother, why didn't you join in the funeral feast?"

"Did the guests leave yet?" Justice Xia asked.

"Half of them," said Wisdom Xia. Then he turned to Wind Xia. "You could have told us that you were coming here. We've been looking for you everywhere!"

"Is something up?" Wind Xia asked, though he'd guessed what his dad wanted.

"I want to talk to you about something." They went into the side building and closed the door. Justice Xia left them to it. He waited in the yard, but it was fully half an hour before they came out again. Wisdom Xia had a face like thunder.

"So . . . ," Justice began.

"Brother, do you have any eggs?" Wisdom Xia interrupted.

"Sure," said Second Aunt. "I asked Tongue-Tied to sell them and buy salt and mung bean noodles, but that deadbeat hasn't even bothered to go yet. We've got about thirty."

"Can I borrow all of them?" And he departed, carrying the eggs in a basket.

A long time later, Culture turned up.

"Have the musicians gone?" Wind Xia asked.

"Yup."

"And Mrs. Wang?"

"Yup, her, too."

"Good. I'm off home then."

Snow Bai hadn't gone with the other actors, and he found her in the bedroom, seething with annoyance. Wisdom Xia was sitting in the yard smoking his water pipe, and he was angry, too. Fourth Aunt pulled Wind Xia into the kitchen, jabbed her finger into his face, and said, "What are you thinking, upsetting Snow like this?"

"What do you mean?"

"Mrs. Wang said some terrible things about you. She was in such a state that Snow was worried she'd make herself ill. Imagine such an old woman having such a temper!"

"And why's my dad got such a long face?" Wind Xia asked.

"He wanted to give Mrs. Wang the basket of eggs, but he was embarrassed that there weren't enough of them, and now he's angry with himself."

Wind Xia wanted to laugh but didn't dare.

Wisdom Xia spent that evening in his bedroom, writing up introductions to the different kinds of masks, while Wind Xia sat under the tickle tree in the yard and sorted out his notes. With her son and her husband both busy writing, Fourth Aunt hardly dared open her mouth and tiptoed around the house like a thief.

When the fragrance of chicken soup wafted out of the kitchen, Wind Xia put away his pen, went in, and had a good sniff over the pot. But his mother didn't offer him any. Instead she filled two bowls and told him to take one to Snow Bai and then another to Third Aunt in the back alley.

Wind Xia went into their courtyard with a bowl to find Thunder hunkered down on the steps under the eaves, smoking a cigarette. Thick smoke poured from his nostrils and rose up his face to the top of his head so his hair looked like a heap of dried grass that someone had set fire to. Then the smoke enveloped the gourd frame under the eaves. There were three gourds hanging on the vine, each one with a hard, yellow rind.

"You're back," Wind Xia said.

The day after Rites Xia's funeral, Thunder had gone back to the bus company.

"Yes," Thunder replied. He didn't seem to want to talk. A fly buzzed stubbornly around Wind Xia, then settled on the rim of the soup bowl. Wind Xia looked up and studied the gourd frame. The three vines swayed in the wind as if they were talking to each other, but he couldn't think of anything to say to Thunder, so he took the bowl of soup into the side house where Third Aunt lived.

He found her sitting cross-legged on the kang in tears. Ever since Rites Xia's death, she'd been sitting there, weeping, all alone day and night, and her eyes were red and swollen. She'd also developed a peculiar nervous tic. She'd repeat everything twice—first out loud, then in a mumble.

"I told your mom not to cook for me. What have you brought that for? What have you brought that for?"

"It's chicken soup," said Wind Xia. "Mom says eat it while it's hot, and when you've finished, go over and have a chat."

"No, I better not. Your mom might get angry with me, get angry with me."

Suddenly they heard furious shouting and swearing coming from the main house. Blossom was cursing out Emerald.

"Get out!" she was shouting. "Get as far away as you can! Go get yourself a lover!"

Emerald rushed out of the room. Her tears had made her eye makeup run, and she looked like a panda. Thunder leaped to his feet, seized Emerald by her hair like an eagle grabbing a chicken, and began to thump her hard. Emerald screamed blue murder.

Third Aunt had just started on her soup. "Don't you think enough people have died in this house?" she shouted. Then she mumbled, "Died in this house."

Thunder didn't let up; he just punched Emerald even harder. Now Blossom came out and pulled Emerald away from him. "Are you trying to kill her?" she yelled. "You men are so heavy-handed. What did she do to deserve such a beating?"

Emerald saw her chance and fled out the gate. Blossom threw herself on the ground and bawled loudly. Wind Xia came out, but by then Thunder was back to normal, sitting on the steps and smoking. It seemed like beating Emerald had taken it out of him, because he was out of breath.

Suddenly Thunder yelled, "What are you crying for, you stupid cunt?" He slammed into the house and kicked an enamel washbasin out the door.

Wind Xia gave Third Aunt a piggyback ride home to his parents' place.

Third Aunt sat with Wisdom Xia, weeping bitterly for a long time. It was true what they said, that happiness never comes in pairs and troubles never come alone. But why should her family suffer all this? She couldn't get her head around it. Was heaven trying to wipe the family out?

After Thunder had gone to the bus company, they'd taken away his license and moved him to the back office, where he had nothing to do and wouldn't earn any bonuses. He'd come home last night in a terrible mood. And then Emerald had made things worse by suddenly saying that she wanted to go to the city. She claimed there was a man in the House of Treasures who'd promised to get her work in a beauty salon. Blossom said she couldn't go, and they'd had a huge fight. Third Aunt panted and wheezed as she told her story.

Wisdom Xia didn't know what to say. He picked up his pipe to have a puff but couldn't find a paper spill to light it so had to shout to Wind Xia to bring him one.

"We have matches," said Fourth Aunt. "Can't you use them?"

"No, I want my spill," said Wisdom Xia.

Fourth Aunt ignored him and talked to Third Aunt instead. "Now that Third Uncle's dead, how much worse can it get?" she said. "Stop worrying about your children. You can't do anything to help them. You're just wasting energy. Snow Bai's staying here for a few days, and you should stay here, too. Then we'll have time to talk."

"But I'll get in your way, get in your way . . . When's Snow Bai due? Snow Bai due?"

Snow Bai blushed. "Not yet."

"We'll have to see if you present us with a gold nugget or a silver nugget!" said Third Aunt. "Don't go back to the theater. You can give birth in the countryside just as well, and if your mom isn't here when the time comes, you have me . . . you have me. I helped Wind Xia into the world, right? Into the world, right?"

"She wouldn't be able to go back to the theater even if she wanted to," said Wind Xia. "She's been let go."

"Let go?" exclaimed Third Aunt.

"She has no work to do. She's not allowed to sing opera anymore."

"It's her own mouth; who's stopping her?" said Third Aunt.

Snow Bai gave Wind Xia a hard look and went back into her room.

"I told you not to say stuff like that, and you just don't remember," said Fourth Aunt. "She's upset enough already, and you go and treat it as a joke."

As she grumbled on, Wisdom Xia went into their bedroom to reread his introduction to the masks, and Wind Xia picked up a pen and notebook and settled back down under the tickle tree. Meanwhile, Fourth Aunt led Third Aunt outside the gate, and they chatted under the elm tree there, shifting their stools as the tree shadow moved around.

Wind Xia paused often in his writing, his pen between his teeth, his eyelids flickering. Wisdom Xia must have tired himself out writing, because he turned on the radio at low volume and listened to opera. The music flowed through the house and yard like water, the peony bush seeming to come alive and the five China rose blossoms glowing redder than ever. Two of the flowers clung together, another two leaned toward each other, and the remaining one faced the wall. The hen with the crested topknot had been crouched in its coop, but now it emerged and quietly pottered around the yard. Wind Xia did not notice any of this, because his head was full of his writing and his eyes sparked like lightning.

Under the elm, Fourth Aunt whispered something to Third Aunt, but she kept her eyes fixed on Wind Xia. She felt so sorry for him that finally she couldn't help herself. "Wind Xia! Wind Xia! Stop writing now. You'll never finish even if you sit there all day."

"Everyone else makes money by hard labor, but Wind Xia makes money by writing. By writing," said Third Aunt.

"Yes, but the money's never enough, is it?" said Fourth Aunt.

Wind Xia put away his pen and smiled. "I'm not doing this for money. I have nothing else to do, and it doesn't feel good to be idle."

He got up and went indoors. The two old women could talk louder now.

"Apart from Rain Xia, the other two spend all day sitting on their butts," Fourth Aunt said. "Their dad is stuck in his room for days on end with his ladle masks, and Wind Xia is always writing. I have no one to talk to. Hey, shall I get Cutie over? We can play picture cards."

"I'm too anxious to play cards," said Third Aunt. "I'm anxious all the time. Wind Xia says he's anxious if he's not writing. Do you think he's coming down with an illness? An illness?"

"No doubt about it, they've both got it bad! His dad's got the opera bug, and Wind Xia has the writing bug!"

"Heavens," said Third Aunt. "How about you?"

"I've got the eating bug. I've been eating three meals a day for years and years, and I'm not sick of it yet."

They both laughed.

When Wind Xia went into the room, Snow Bai was sitting on the bed, crying. "That's enough. Why are you still so upset with me after all this time?"

"I'm not upset with you," she said. "I was just so sad when I heard your dad playing opera."

"Hey, you love opera, but the opera doesn't love you. You should hate it now that you've been let go."

"Do you think I'll ever get to sing again?"

"Do you really think it will ever be revitalized?" he countered.

"I started at the theater when I was fifteen, and then I did another year's study. I've had to fight hard to get where I am. If I can't sing anymore, what else is there?"

"You had the chance of another job, but you didn't take it," said Wind Xia. "You can't blame anyone else."

"I hate Mid-Star Xia!"

"Why? You could have changed your job."

"I didn't want to change my job. Why would I? How would you feel if someone said you could never write another article, or even pick up your pen?"

That shut Wind Xia up. He sat beside her, silently. On the radio, the opera was still playing. The aria was from *Third Mother Teaches Her Son*, and Wisdom Xia was humming along to it. Snow Bai was in floods of tears again, and even Wind Xia began to feel sorry for her.

"Don't cry," he said. "Third Aunt's sitting outside the gate. You don't want her laughing at you. Finding work as a singer isn't easy. You can do like Dad and sing at home."

"I'm a professional," said Snow Bai. "I took first prize in the City Opera Performance Competition." And she burst into tears again.

This time, Fourth Aunt heard her. "Snow Bai! Snow Bai! What's the matter?" she called. There was no answer, so she called to Wind Xia instead. He went outside and she asked him, "Why are you upsetting Snow Bai? Haven't I told you, she mustn't get angry, she mustn't! You had a big argument with her a couple of days ago, and now you're at it again."

"I didn't," protested Wind Xia, and he kicked the elm tree so hard that some of the leaves came fluttering down.

Suddenly the light dimmed. The three of them looked up at the sky. A big black cloud had covered the sun. Where had it sprung from? A gust of wind came down the alley and blew off the kerchief that Third Aunt had tied around her head.

"That's a sudden change in the weather," she said, getting to her feet to head home.

But Fourth Aunt wouldn't let her go. "I'm making rice porridge for dinner. Come into the kitchen and help me rinse the rice." Before they'd finished that task, the heavens opened and down came the rain.

Chapter 31

It rained nonstop for three days. The weather got colder, the leaves yellowed and began to fall, and the cicadas' chirps became shorter and shorter. The fields that had been sown with wheat appeared to be covered with a thin film of light green, but on closer inspection, it turned out to be mainly bare yellow earth. Only a kind of spear grass grew fat stalks that people harvested and made into sour broth.

The work of calling in the debts was still going on. Some had paid up, others couldn't and were still in debt, and still others had left to get jobs as migrant workers or were thinking of doing so. Wind Xia was still at home, fending off people who came to pester him for a city job. Of course he couldn't help, and so he just shut the gate and dozed the days away indoors. But here, too, Wisdom Xia kept bothering him about his book and trying to get him to photograph the masks. Once they had a complete set of pictures in sequence, each one needed a caption. But Wind Xia knew nothing about opera, so Wisdom Xia called Snow Bai in, and they spent two days discussing the text.

When it was ready, he said, "Should the book have a preface as well?"

"What do you know about prefaces, Dad?" asked Wind Xia.

"Even someone who hasn't eaten pork has surely seen a pig trot past. All your books have a preface, so mine should have one, too. You can write it."

"Why are you bothering so much about a book like this?" said Wind Xia.

"A book like this, did you say? A book like this?"

"Okay, okay," said Wind Xia. "It's a very fine book. A very fine book. But I don't know anything about local opera, so you'll have to write the preface yourself."

So Wisdom Xia put on his spectacles and sat down to write. An essay like this was a pretty big deal for him. He made sure the gate was locked, ordered that no one was to disturb him, and had Fourth Aunt make him some tea and light the fire cord. He brought the cord to the pipe bowl and lit it; then he wrote one page, tore it up, dissatisfied, wrote another page, and tore that up, too. Soon the floor was covered in scrunched balls of paper.

"You're capable of anything. Why are you finding this so difficult?" said Fourth Aunt with a smile.

Wisdom Xia was irritated, but then he smiled, too. "I may not be able to write, but at least I raised a son who can do it." He thought of Water-Rise's dad, who had loved opera. Wisdom Xia had hopes he might find some reference material at his home, but when he went to look, Water-Rise said his dad had had an excellent memory but couldn't read or write, so why would he have had any books? Wisdom Xia came home discouraged.

"You know people in the city. Can't you find a big name to write the preface for me?" he asked Wind Xia.

Wind Xia thought he was being ridiculous but didn't dare to say so. "Let me get in touch with the publisher's editor and see what he thinks," he said.

If he was hoping that that would be an end to it, he was swiftly disabused—his dad forced him to make the call right away. His contact was an old friend who was only too happy to have an excuse for an outing, and a few days later the editor turned up in Freshwind.

Mr. Black was his name, which seemed odd because he was as fair skinned as they come. During his stay, Wind Xia and he were often seen wandering around the village. One day I'd caught a fish in the pond and was taking it to Seven Li Gully to wrap it in lotus leaves and then in clay and grill it for lunch. I was on my way to the small stone bridge, carrying the leaves, when I saw Wind Xia, Snow Bai, and that Mr. Black some way off. I put the leaf bundle on my head, as camouflage. That way I could watch them without them seeing me.

Snow Bai had a big belly on her nowadays and waddled along. What kind of baby would she have? I couldn't tell. Lucky was pregnant, too, and if I stared long enough at her belly, I could see the outline of the puppies. But I couldn't see Snow Bai's baby. "It would be good if it looked like me," I muttered to myself. That was a terrible thing to say. I was a scoundrel, but say it I did.

Suddenly Snow Bai came out with, "That . . ." She was going to say something about me, but then she spotted me and clammed up.

"What?" Wind Xia asked.

"Nothing, nothing. Can we go home now? I'm a bit tired."

But Wind Xia ignored her and carried on toward the bridge. I was in trouble, and I knew it. The lotus leaves hadn't made me invisible at all. Not only that, but I was covered in mud, and I didn't want to give Wind Xia an even worse opinion of me. So I held the leaves over my head and jumped down from the bridge onto the shore. I thought they'd act as a parachute and slow my fall. In fact, I didn't break anything when I landed, even though I got a big bruise on my thigh.

I stumbled up the steep-sided embankment to where the 312 passed Seven Li Gully. There I bumped into Justice Xia and Tongue-Tied. Justice Xia was annoyed because I was late, but when I explained that I'd caught a fish we could grill for lunch, he forgave me. By this time I had a stomachache, maybe because I'd been so nervous up by the bridge, and my intestines were squirming like I was getting a bout of diarrhea.

"If you're going to shit, do it in the gully," said Justice Xia.

We always had to hold on till we got to the gully if we were on the road, because piss or shit was fertilizer. So I held it in as best I could, but it was really hard. After a while I couldn't hang on any longer and squatted down by the roadside. Justice Xia told me I was useless; why couldn't I keep it in for a bit longer? He was angry, and he and Tongue-Tied went on ahead. I felt pretty depressed, and after I'd finished, I stood there for a long time. Finally, I threw a stone at the shit and made it splatter. If I couldn't give my shit to the gully, then no one else was going to collect it for their fields, either.

I collected more stones to splatter it with, and threw them one after another, and then suddenly it began to rain stones from the sky. It was hail, rattling down around me. It often hails in May or June, but I'd never seen a hailstorm in the autumn. Some of the hailstones were as big as kidney beans; others were like abacus beads. They were cold, and they stung when they hit me. I made a run for the gully, where far in the distance I could see Justice Xia and Tongue-Tied shifting rocks.

Justice Xia wasn't wearing his bamboo hat—it was on the ground, and he was bare-headed. The rocks were so big he could only manage to grapple one at a time, then roll it over. Grapple, roll, grapple, roll. I could hear his wheezing from way off; it was as if the whole gully was puffing and panting. Suddenly it felt as if all the boulders had grown legs and were shoving each other out of the way to make it to the embankment first, and Justice Xia was just one more boulder among them. The hailstones bounced off the rocks with a crisp ping but landed with a dull thud on Justice Xia's head.

I rushed toward him. "Uncle, why aren't you wearing your hat? You should be wearing your hat."

I was about to pick it up for him, but he threw himself on it and shielded it with his arms. Underneath the bamboo hat a tiny wheat seedling was growing, a lonely little sprout arching out of the soil, faintly tinged with green.

"I planted a kernel to see if it would grow," he explained. "I want to know if it'll get as thick as a finger and grow a spike a foot long!" As he talked, he was no longer the angry old man who'd cursed me out on the road; he wanted me to be as excited as he was. But then a hailstone hit him on the nose, and it started bleeding.

But young corn blasted by hail never grows thick or tall. As for Justice Xia's nose, it was a long time before it healed. He went around wearing a poultice that Big-Noise Zhao made for him, and I teased him and said he looked like one of those white-nosed county officials in an opera.

Another day, after more rain had come and gone, the sky filled with fiery red clouds. It wasn't hot, but everything was bathed in a lurid light. The clouds weren't drifting; they slanted downward, pointing right into Freshwind Village. That was the day Lucky gave birth to her litter of puppies, and Mr. Black, the editor, finished checking through all the photographs and captions for *Shaanxi Opera Masks*. He'd be leaving the next morning, and Wisdom Xia organized a dinner to say goodbye and to celebrate his upcoming book. He invited the township Party secretary and the township head, as well as the senior cadres on the Two Committees and New-Life Liu.

Wisdom Xia had drunk toasts to his son's books many times in the past, but this time he was celebrating his own work, and he was very excited. He got up early and festooned the house and yard with all his masks, took down the old calligraphy and hung new scrolls, and tuned the radio to a station playing local opera. Then he sat on a chair out in the yard and smoked his pipe. "Open the gate, wide open," he commanded.

Snow Bai pulled it wide open, and in came the chickens and the cats. A butterfly as big as the palm of your hand fluttered in, too, and circled around the tickle tree before settling on the peonies.

"Would you sing an aria during dinner?" Wisdom Xia asked Snow Bai. "The editor knows all about local opera. And New-Life and Goodness are coming. They know a few songs, and by the time they've had a few drinks, they'll want to sing, too."

"Sure!" said Snow Bai.

Wind Xia was in the kitchen, helping his mother pick over the vegetables, and smiled at his dad's excitement.

"This book you've been helping your dad with, he's over the moon. He can't let it go," Fourth Aunt said to him.

"Once the book is out, he won't bother painting any more masks. It's like trying to keep out a thief—you can't do it, however hard you try. Best to invite them in. Then they won't steal anything from you ever again."

"Mind your language. That's your dad you're talking about."

Lucky appeared at the gate with her five puppies and barked.

"Even the dog knows there's a party!" said Wisdom Xia with a laugh. He called her, and she rushed in and crouched with her belly to the ground, tail wagging frantically. The five puppies tried to clamber over the gate sill after her, but it was too high for them, so Snow Bai went and helped them. They looked like five fluffy cotton balls.

"There'll be a lot of guests tonight. Anyone who wants can have a puppy," said Wisdom Xia.

Snow Bai picked up one that was pure white and said she wanted to give it to her mother. There was a shout from outside the gate—"If you're giving away dogs, I want one!"—and Goodness walked in.

As it happened, I was right behind him. I'd bumped into him on his way over. He was carrying a bunch of pork ribs, and I asked, "Are you offering me any of those?"

"You're a glutton! Go lick a stone if you're hungry! These are a gift for Fourth Uncle."

"What's Wisdom Xia's big event?"

"He's 'Fourth Uncle' to you! And he's having a book published, so this is a celebration."

"First his son writes a book, and now the old man, too. What's it about?"

"Opera masks."

"Really? A book about opera masks?"

"You sound as if you think you can make them, too."

"Well, I can't. But I understand them."

"Huh, out of my way." And he walked on past.

"You better believe me; I've got an article about opera right here!" And I pulled the article Snow Bai had written out of the breast pocket where I always kept it and held it out.

Goodness stopped, took the paper, looked at it, and said, "Did you write this?"

"Don't you believe me?"

Goodness took the article with him, so I followed close on his heels. But when he went into Wisdom Xia's house, I didn't dare follow him into the yard.

I sat against the wall outside and was sorry I'd shown him the article. If he showed it to Snow Bai, she'd surely take it back, and I'd never get my hands on it again. I cursed Goodness, wrote his name in the dirt with a stone, and scuffed it out. I could hear Snow Bai laughing in the yard, though I couldn't see her. I suddenly had the urge to let her know that I was outside, so I began to recite the poem in her praise at the top of my voice. I knew it pretty much by heart by now.

Fourth Aunt had been delighted to see Goodness and his present of pork ribs. "Have a whole rib for yourself if you want. But where's Lotus Jin? You two are always together." Fourth Aunt was desperately hoping that Lotus Jin would come, but she didn't.

"Torrent Bai's wife is back on West Street, and Lotus Jin and some other women have gone to get her," Goodness told her.

"She didn't come when Wind Xia got married, either. She's a strange woman; she doesn't accept any invites!"

"Don't blame her, Aunt," said Goodness. "She asked me to make her apologies specially. It was just bad timing that Torrent's wife got back today."

"Torrent's wife?" Wisdom Xia said. "Hang on, who's that reciting?" Wisdom Xia was attuned to anything to do with opera, so he was the first to hear me.

Silence fell in the yard, and I made a point of speaking more loudly, and in standard Mandarin, too. My Mandarin wasn't very good, and the words sounded sour-sweet.

"It's Spark," Goodness said. "He's talking crazy again." He called over the wall to me. "Spark! Spark! If you want to recite, do it properly. You need to get your tongue around that Mandarin."

I felt proud that they were all listening to me and carried on. But then suddenly a slew of party officials from the village and the township turned up at Wisdom Xia's gate, and I didn't want them to see me reciting outside the courtyard wall, so I left.

I hadn't finished my recital, but Snow Bai didn't have to hear more than a few sentences to recognize the words. She said nothing, just turned and went into the kitchen to help Fourth Aunt with the food.

"Did you hear what Goodness said just now?" asked the old woman.

"What?" said Snow Bai.

"Is it true your sister-in-law's gotten pregnant again without permission?"

"Yes, that's what Mom says. It's Torrent's wife," said Snow Bai. "She's been hiding with her mom and dad in Nanshan."

"Well, your sister-in-law's in trouble. Lotus Jin's after her; she'll take her off for an abortion today," said Fourth Aunt.

"Really?" said Snow Bai. "Well, she already has two daughters, and with another mouth to feed, what kind of a life are they going to have? What will they live on?"

"That's peasants for you," said Fourth Aunt. "Sons are everything. You better go and tell her to stay hidden."

"No, I'm not going," said Snow Bai.

"If we didn't know, it wouldn't matter," said Fourth Aunt. "But how will you feel if you don't warn her now?"

So Snow Bai took advantage of the fuss as Wisdom Xia greeted his official guests and slipped away unnoticed to West Street.

After a while, Wisdom Xia shouted for Wind Xia.

"What is it now?" Wind Xia asked. "Are five bottles of liquor not enough?"

"I forgot your second uncle. He's got to come! Go see if he's at home. If not, you can borrow Pavilion's motorbike and go to Seven Li Gully. Make sure you bring him back."

On the way to Justice Xia's, Wind Xia passed Mid-Star's dad's gate. The old man was outside, pouring away the dregs of some herbal medicine. "Are you dosing yourself again, Uncle Glory?" asked Wind Xia.

"Yes," said Mid-Star's dad. "I'm not in a good way."

"You've been poorly all your life, Uncle," said Wind Xia. "You've always got pain somewhere or other, but you manage."

"Huh," Mid-Star's dad said. "Are you getting a book published for your dad?"

"How did you know that?"

"I know everything. You're a good son. Not like Mid-Star. I asked him to fix this house, but he refused. He says he's going to build a bridge over the Zhou River for the whole village."

"Well, that's good. That's a big project. He's earned that big promotion they gave him!" Wind Xia felt a spasm of dislike for Uncle Glory. He was going to invite him to the party, but now he decided not to. When he got to the scorpion's tail of the village, he saw a tractor parked outside Justice Xia's gate. In the yard, Third-Kid Li was talking to the old man.

When Wind Xia came in, they fell silent. He asked, "Didn't you go to Seven Li Gully today, Second Uncle?"

"No, I didn't," said Justice Xia. "I keep asking you to come and look at it, but you never do. Why not?"

"I promise to come one of these days," said Wind Xia. "Dad's got his book on opera masks ready, and the editor's leaving to go back to the city. We're offering drinks at home. Come over and have a few with us."

"Right, that's good," Justice Xia said. "Is it a thick book?"

"About two fingers, I guess," said Wind Xia.

"Your dad told me that when he dies, he wants that book for a headrest, instead of a stone pillow like me." He turned to Third-Kid Li. "That's how it is: winners or losers, we all come from the village. Tell me, don't I usually treat you well?"

"Usually, except when you belted me across the ear because of the trees on the river dike. I'm still a bit deaf in that ear."

Justice Xia smiled. "You're still sore at me, you fucker? You should be glad I didn't kill you. I told you then, you can fleece me all you want, but don't try and rip off the collective!"

"But the tractor is mine. I've had to sell three *dou* of wheat to pay for it."

"It's just a heap of rust," said Justice Xia. "You can see that for yourself."

"The bodywork is a bit rusty," said Third-Kid Li, "but the engine's good. Look at the state of this table of yours!"

"Listen here," said Justice Xia. "This is rosewood. Is there anyone else in Freshwind with a table like this at home? If the Bai family hadn't been landlords, you would never have seen anything like it, and nor would I. Just take a look . . . It's decades old, and can you see a single crack? And have you felt how heavy it is? Go on, try it!"

Third-Kid Li got to his feet and tried to lift the table. Then he squatted down and tugged at the table legs. "If you have a teapot, you have to have teacups, too," he said. "Is this table on its own really worth a tractor? It's just a heap of wood. At least my tractor's a heap of iron."

"Fuck you, Third-Kid," said Justice Xia. "You're just like your dad. Can't cross a river without trying to scoop out water. You think I can't see the way your nasty mind's working, huh? You want those two chairs off me, don't you?"

"And you, you'd hang on to the rope even if you'd sold the sheep," said Third-Kid Li.

"He can't have them," said Second Aunt from inside the house. "If we don't have a table and chairs, we'd have nothing left in the house that's worth anything."

"Butt out of this," said Justice Xia. He waved Third-Kid Li away. "Fine, fine. You can take it all. Leave the tractor crank here, and come over when it's dark and pick up the table and chairs. I'm off to Wind Xia's for a drink!"

"A drink again?" said Third-Kid Li. "You Xias are never dry. It used to be Thunder who drank all day, and now it's Uncle Wisdom."

"What are you talking about? Just because you fucking can't afford to drink. Tell you what. I'll buy you some drinks someday, and you can leave your money at home so it can grow in peace and quiet."

Third-Kid Li laughed.

Justice Xia turned to Wind Xia: "You go ahead; don't wait for me. I'll help Third-Kid Li push the tractor into the yard, and then I'll come."

By now, all the guests except for Justice Xia had arrived, but Snow Bai had disappeared.

"Where's Snow Bai?" asked Wisdom Xia.

"She went to the store to buy soy sauce," Fourth Aunt lied. Then she said to Wind Xia, "Where's your second uncle?"

"Is he coming, too?" Pavilion asked from inside the house.

"Yes," said Wisdom Xia.

"Then I better go," said Pavilion.

"Nonsense! You got a problem with him? When he turns up, you make sure you raise a glass to him."

"I haven't got a problem, but I don't think he's pleased with me."

"The Communists and the Kuomintang were mortal enemies, but when Chairman Mao and Chiang Kai-shek met, they still shook hands. You and your uncle both want the best for the village; you just have different ideas on how to go about it. Everyone else thinks it's a joke. He's your senior. If he spits in your face, you just keep smiling."

"Pavilion, is it true that Justice Xia has been going to Seven Li Gully to work all on his own?" asked the township head.

"Yes, he's been acting like the Foolish Old Man Who Removed the Mountain, and it's embarrassing," Pavilion said.

"But if he's doing it for the collective, that's quite something," said the township head. "When he needs support, you'd all better be there for him."

"As soon as Second Uncle went to work in Seven Li Gully, the villagers started blaming me," said Pavilion. "His sons have been saying that I forced him into it. Even Fourth Uncle criticized me."

"As the village Party secretary, you work for the people of Freshwind, and that includes the Xias," Wisdom Xia told him. "You mind what needs minding and take care of what needs taking care of. There's no need to prove your honesty to the other villagers by being hard on the Xias. Your second uncle is stubborn as a mule. You've pushed him out on a limb, but he's not a selfish man. You could show him some respect and be a good nephew to him. Your third uncle's dead, so he can't help you anymore."

"I haven't been trying to prove my honesty to the other villagers by being hard on the Xias, and I haven't forced him out on a limb, either," Pavilion said. "At the Two Committees meeting today, I took a unilateral decision to award him the contract for Seven Li Gully, since he's so keen on it. The village won't charge him a cent in rent for a place where not even a fly wants to lay its eggs, and it gives him status!"

"Well, that's a good thing," said Wisdom Xia. And he sent Wind Xia off to tell Justice Xia to hurry up.

Justice Xia hadn't set out. Third-Kid Li was still there, and now Tongue-Tied and Treasure had turned up, too, and Justice Xia and Treasure were having a furious argument.

"What's all this about?" Wind Xia asked Third-Kid Li.

"Justice Xia wants my tractor to haul stones and earth in Seven Li Gully, so I said I'd take his Eight Immortals table in exchange. Justice Xia agreed, but when Treasure got to hear about it, he wanted the table himself. Of course Justice Xia put an end to that idea. He said

Treasure and his brothers have their own homes now; they have no right to come and take their parents' furniture. Treasure said that in that case, when it came time to divide up the old folks' possessions, he would forego his share so long as he could have the table and chairs. Providing his dad kept it and didn't swap it for the tractor, he and his mom could keep using it until the time came; otherwise he wants to take it with him right now."

Wind Xia pulled Treasure aside and laid into him angrily for shouting and swearing at his second uncle for no good reason.

"Wind Xia, you've seen a lot of the world outside the village," said Treasure. "Tell me, how can my dad give this table away? You know Ma Dazong, who's living at the House of Treasures Hotel? When he saw the table, he said it was an antique and it'd go for twenty or thirty thousand in the city."

"I knew you wanted that table for the wrong reasons!" Justice Xia exclaimed.

"But haven't I said I'm not asking for anything else of yours?" said Treasure. "After all, I am your son, aren't I?"

"I'm not dead yet! Why are you talking about dividing things up?"

"We don't have to divide it up right now. Just so long as you don't give the table to Third-Kid Li."

"Are you going to buy me a tractor then?"

"Is the gully project so important that you're prepared to sell the family's stuff for it? It's just a bit of fun to you, but you'll never finish the project by yourself. It'll take eight or ten years . . . and think of your age!"

"You trying to drive me into my grave? I'm telling you, if I knew I was going to die tomorrow, I'd still go and work there today. Third-Kid, you can take the table with you now."

Third-Kid Li approached the table, but Treasure wasn't giving up and sat down on it.

"Get down off it!" Justice Xia yelled, then grabbed him by the arm and tugged.

Treasure shook him off, and Justice Xia staggered backward and sat down hard. Tongue-Tied had been standing aside and watching, but when Justice Xia fell, he lunged and pulled Treasure off the table.

"Get your hands off me, asshole!" Treasure shouted, and when Tongue-Tied roared in response, he whacked him across the face. Tongue-Tied grabbed him around the waist, hoisted him into the air, and dumped him on the ground as if he were a sack of rice—once, twice, three times.

Treasure lost his glasses, and without them he was as good as blind. He groped around for them, but Tongue-Tied kicked them away.

Justice Xia did nothing to stop him. "Third-Kid Li," he said, "take that table away. Have you gone deaf?"

Third-Kid Li put one chair over each shoulder.

Treasure, who couldn't get up, yelled, "Third-Kid, if you dare to touch those chairs or the table, I dare to throw your kid down the well!"

Li dropped the chairs, went and started the tractor, and drove off with a roar.

Justice Xia was so mortified he began slapping his own face. "This is so humiliating, not just to me but to our ancestors as well. I can see I'm not going to die in Seven Li Gully or falling off a cliff or hanging from a rope. No, it's you who are going to be the death of me, Treasure."

Wind Xia tried to push Treasure out of the yard, but Treasure refused to go. So Tongue-Tied got him by one leg and dragged him out as if he were a dog. Then he went back in and slammed the gate shut. Wind Xia found himself locked out, too.

Wind Xia shouted, but no one opened. He heard Second Aunt crying. He ran back and told the guests what had happened, and Wisdom Xia, Pavilion, and Goodness immediately hurried to the scorpion's tail.

"Brother! Let me in!" Wisdom Xia shouted through a crack in the gate. There was silence inside. Even Second Aunt's sobs had stopped.

"Tell him the township Party secretary and head are on their way here," said Goodness.

"Brother!" Wisdom Xia shouted again. "The township Party secretary and the head are coming. They want to talk to you!"

Still no response.

"Let me try," said Pavilion.

"Then he definitely won't open up," Goodness said.

"Call Tongue-Tied," said Wind Xia. "He's still inside."

Wisdom Xia called and peered through the crack. He could see Tongue-Tied come out of the house and stand in the middle of the yard, but he didn't open up. Wisdom Xia was so angry he rained blows on the gate until finally Second Aunt unlocked it. "Wisdom," she said and then started to cry again.

They crowded into the house. Justice Xia was sitting straight-backed on a stool, eyes closed and nostrils flaring.

"Why have you got yourself so worked up over a little thing like that?" Wisdom Xia said.

He had hardly finished speaking when Justice Xia leaped to his feet, grabbed the ax hanging behind the door, and rushed out into the yard, where he started chopping up the table. One of the legs gave way first.

There was a shocked silence, then someone tried to take the ax from him. But Wisdom Xia just said, "You're doing a great job! What are you going to do with it now?"

Justice Xia, savage as a lion, carried on until, in only a dozen blows, he had reduced the table to a pile of wood. Finally he threw the ax down. "It's my table. I'll chop it up if I want."

His visitors stood rooted to the spot. Second Aunt burst into loud tears.

"Why are you crying? Because we produced this devil's spawn?" Justice Xia roared, his face black as the bottom of a cooking pot. Then he said to them all, "Come and sit down," and he handed out his black tobacco rollies. Even Pavilion got one.

No one knew what to say, until Pavilion said, "It's a long time since you offered me a smoke, Uncle!"

"You've been keeping out of my way. I can't give smokes to a ghost," snapped Justice Xia.

Goodness tried to mollify him. "Well, what's done is done. Hey, Tongue-Tied. Haven't you got eyes in your head? Take these bits of wood away and bring a stool for your granddad."

Tongue-Tied did as he was told and got a stool for Justice Xia. Justice Xia passed it to the township Party secretary to sit on and got another one for the township head. Pavilion hurriedly brought one of the rosewood chairs for Justice Xia.

"Uncle Wisdom organized the dinner tonight so that you and Pavilion could drink and make up," Goodness said. "But the drinks haven't even started, and you've already healed the rift. I figure you didn't show up on purpose, Uncle Justice, just so you could get Pavilion to come knocking on your door!"

"There's no rift between me and Pavilion!" said Justice Xia. "Of course we argue about village business sometimes, but there's nothing personal in it. What I'm really upset about is this brat we've raised. There's all this talk about who's digging whose grave. Well, my grave-digger's Treasure!"

"Of course your son will be digging your grave," the township head said.

"I'll tell you this: even if wolves and jackals tear me to pieces, I'm not having him seeing me into the next world!"

"But what, exactly, happened?" Wisdom Xia asked.

"I don't want to talk about it," said his brother. "Go and have your celebrations. Don't let my family business spoil the party."

"We already know," said Pavilion. "Treasure didn't want him to swap the table with the tractor. So it didn't happen . . ."

"But Treasure was still out to get it, all the same!" said Justice Xia.

"That table was hexed," Goodness said. "Now that it's in pieces, you can relax."

"By the way, the Two Committees have decided to give you the lease on Seven Li Gully," Pavilion went on. "You can do what you want with it, and the village won't charge anything. And we'll let you have the old village tractor, too. As for your things, you shouldn't give them to Treasure; the village won't agree to that even if you do. As long as you live here, Uncle, no one's to take so much as a needle and thread from you. And even when you and Auntie are gone, it's down to the village cadres to decide how to divide it up. I expect it'll be me in the end."

The township head put his hand on Justice Xia's arm. "You heard what Pavilion's just said. Can't you manage a smile to show you're willing?" Justice didn't smile. "Not one smile?" the head coaxed him. No smile.

The head poked him in the armpit, and Justice Xia spoke. "I work in Seven Li Gully because I have to, but I'll never get the project done on my own, will I? You township cadres are all here; you agreed to give me the lease so you can put a plan in place for finishing the work!"

"Hah, Mr. Xia," said the township head. "We give you an inch, you take a mile! We still haven't decided about filling Seven Li Gully. Today we're here to drink! We have some guests from the city, too, and we mustn't keep them waiting."

They finally managed to bundle Justice Xia out of the gate. Wisdom Xia tried to get Second Aunt along, too, but she refused. She fussed over Justice and called him "a big baby," picking a clean shirt for Wisdom Xia to take with them, along with his big-framed glasses and a packet of his dark tobacco. But she refused to go herself.

Wisdom Xia jerked his thumb at Tongue-Tied. "Don't be so dopey. Didn't I tell you to open the gate for us?"

But the boy just smiled, scurried off to the shithouse, and did not reappear.

The argument was settled, but somehow no one wanted to drink anymore. There were five bottles of spirits, but they only finished two of them.

"We gotta drink more," said Wisdom Xia. "Wind Xia! Fill everyone's glasses. A toast to you all!"

"I can't drink any more, Fourth Uncle," said New-Life. "It goes straight to my head."

"What do you mean? It's good stuff."

"It's nothing to do with the quality of the spirits, Uncle," New-Life said. "It's very fine stuff. But I slept badly last night. That's why it's gone to my head."

"A well-covered man like you should be able to soak up at least half a *jin*."

"I really can't have any more. Look at my face." New-Life's face was as red as a monkey's ass, and when he opened the shirt, his whole chest was red, too.

"All right, fair enough. But if you're not going to drink, then you have to sing for us. Mr. Black was pretty surprised there was someone in this little backwater who could paint opera masks. He'll be even more surprised that there are people in Freshwind who can sing opera, too. It goes to show it's not that I've got special talents. What counts is that the art of opera is firmly rooted in village culture; it's what we grow around here. Every soil produces something different. Our leeks here grow a foot tall, but Mid-Star told me that when he did military service in Xinjiang, he saw leeks two feet tall. Sing something for Mr. Black, New-Life."

There were shouts of encouragement. "Sing, New-Life, sing!"

"What should I sing?" asked New-Life. "Let Goodness go first. I'll sing something after you, Goodness."

"All right, you start, Goodness," said Wisdom Xia.

Goodness ran his fingers through his forelock and said, "Sure, I can sing. I'm not shy. There's plenty to celebrate today. Like, it's the first time we've had the pleasure of Mr. Black's company."

"No need to call me 'Mister,'" said the editor immediately. "I'm junior to all of you; just Black will do."

"Mr. Black!" Goodness insisted, and he went on, "We meet you today for the first time. And Fourth Uncle's bringing out a book. And Pavilion and Second Uncle are friends again. And we have two of the township cadres visiting, too."

"That's enough of that," said the township head. "We all meet up often enough, don't we?"

"But it's the first time we've had dinner together. And in celebration of all these happy events, I'll sing one piece for you. All of you, get those drinks down you."

They waited expectantly, but he still wasn't finished. "What shall I sing? I'm the worst singer in all of Freshwind. Fourth Uncle said the art of opera is firmly rooted in village culture, and he's right. Just now, on the way here, we met Spark, and he's written an essay on opera." He pulled the article out of his pocket.

"Who's Spark?" the editor asked.

"The village crazy," said Wisdom Xia.

"The village crazy? Let's see what he's written." Mr. Black read through the article. "Huh!" he exclaimed, then again, "Huh . . . Huh!"

"Goodness, we asked you to sing, not to talk," said Wisdom Xia. "Quit fooling around and get on with it!"

"This really is well written," put in Black. "We have no preface to the book yet; we could use this."

"What?" said Wisdom Xia. "Can I see?" He read the article. "Did Spark give this to you?" he asked Goodness.

"Yes."

"Where did he get it from? Can he really have written it himself?"

"Maybe Big-Noise wrote it," suggested Goodness.

"Who's Big-Noise?" asked the editor.

"The Freshwind doctor," said Wisdom Xia.

"This is an amazing place! Normally, we try and get a big name to write the preface, but we could use someone local. Why not? Remarkable!" He waved his hands enthusiastically.

Wisdom Xia was delighted. "Perfect! Like people say, *xian bing* pastries landing right onto our plates. Let's drink to it. Cheers!"

"Are you so happy you forgot you asked Goodness to sing?" said the township head.

"Right, right, Goodness. Sing!"

Goodness was still slapping his forehead, muttering, "What to sing?" He finally opened his mouth and recited in a monotone:

I am the school watchman, and I love beef and strong spirits. It's nearly the New Year, and the teachers at the school have told me to give old Master Lü a new cap and gown, as well as ten ounces of silver to get him to the capital so that he can take the imperial exams. But when I arrive at his gate, there is no one. Master Lü! Can he have starved to death? Mrs. Lü! Has she frozen to death? I go to the back of the house and cry, "Wake up, Master Lü! The God of Wealth has brought you treasure!"

And he slammed his wine cup down on the table.

"What are you doing with your cup?" said Pavilion.

"It's not a cup," Goodness said. "It's silver coins!" And then he began to sing:

Ye poor, no longer fret
Ye rich, do not boast
Poverty and wealth never last forever
One day the winds of change will blow
One day, you'll don the official's cap, stuck with fresh flowers.

Mr. Black clapped his hands. "Fantastic! Fantastic!"

"Do you know what he was singing?" Wisdom Xia asked.

"I'm afraid I don't."

"It's from an opera called *Munan Temple*. A poor student, Lü Mengzheng, and his wife, Liu Ruilian, are starving in their miserable cave home. Liu Ruilian's mother wants to help her daughter and sends over a maid with some rice for them. The school watchman recites and sings."

"Oh, I see, he plays the clown!"

"Goodness always sings the comic roles," Wisdom Xia said. "Or villains, of course."

"Are you saying I'm not a man of honor, Uncle?"

"You are a prodigy!" Wisdom Xia said with a smile. "Freshwind can't do without you! New-Life, now it's your turn. Goodness played the clown; give us something more serious, will you?"

"What from?"

"Choose something from *Weeping at the Ancestral Shrine*. I can beat the rhythm for you." And then he began to tap out the beat on the edge of the table, first a gentle opening that he hummed along to, then building up to the *erdaoban* beat. New-Life Liu began to sing:

Armed with his three-foot sword, the late great emperor annihilated the Qin and the Chu and set new boundaries for the kingdom. But Wang Mang overthrew Emperor Ping, dispatched him back to heaven by means of poisoned wine, and usurped power from the Han. Emperor Guangwu traveled south and restored the Han, with the aid of the Yuntai Twenty-Eight generals. Under Emperor Ling's rule, the Yellow Turbans rebelled. My imperial ancestor Liu Bei formed an alliance with Guan Yu and Zhang Fei in a peach grove, and they sacrificed a white horse and a black ox to heaven . . .

Wisdom Xia left the room. In the yard, Fourth Aunt sat dozing by the kitchen door.

"How can you sleep with him singing so loudly?" he asked.

"How long are you going to go on?" she asked. "The food's gone cold!"

"There's no hurry. Everyone's concentrating on drinking. Where's Snow Bai? She promised she'd sing for us. Where is she?"

"You can't make her sing with a belly on her like that! Are you going to take the blame if she does herself an injury?"

Wisdom Xia couldn't quarrel with that. He stood there for a while as New-Life Liu sang on:

. . . When Cao Cao arrived at Dangyang Bridge, the enemy tied branches to the tails of the horses, raising clouds of dust, and Zhang Fei challenged Cao Cao by roaring three times. This scared Cao Cao and his men so that they immediately withdrew. Men trampled men, horses trampled people. When a careful tally was made of the losses, twenty thousand generals had died and the deceased foot soldiers were too numerous to count . . .

Wisdom Xia went back in, and Fourth Aunt hurriedly got hold of Wind Xia and told him what was going on at Snow Bai's mother's house. "Go and check up on her," she told him.

A lot happened that day, especially among the Xias of East Street. Things were pretty lively at the Bai home on West Street, too, what with Lotus Jin on the warpath because she was the family planning officer and she'd found out about Torrent's wife, who lived at the Bais'. I had been on my way to Seven Li Gully, but Justice Xia told me he was going to swap his table for Third-Kid Li's tractor and asked me to go to the smithy and buy a shovel, so I did that instead. As I left the smithy, I bumped into Lotus Jin leading a posse of villagers to West Street.

I laughed at her, and she said, "What are you laughing at?"

"There are two flies doing it on your back!"

"Beat it!" she snarled.

But it was true, two flies were stuck, one on top of the other, on her back.

"Sure, I'll beat it," I said. "But those flies are going to make a mess of your clothes." I stood on the smithy steps and watched as Lotus Jin shook the flies off. They flew up, still stuck together.

Maybe Lotus Jin thought she had been too hard on me, because she said, "We're off to enforce family planning. Come with us."

"Why should I?"

"Because you can't have a family."

I said something rude, but then I asked, "Who are you going after?"

"Torrent's wife."

So I went along because I hated Torrent. The time I stole Snow Bai's panties, he'd been the keenest to beat me up, the first to throw himself on me. A true man can wait for ten years to take revenge, and now I finally had the chance to teach him a lesson, or at least make him a laughingstock. What I didn't expect was that I'd bump into Snow Bai at her mom's.

When Snow Bai got there, her mom wasn't there. Her niece, who was skipping in the yard, told her, "Gran's out the back."

That's where Torrent had his house. When Snow Bai got there, there was her sister-in-law Switch, sitting on the front steps, her big belly sticking out in front of her. Snow Bai's mom said something to Snow Bai's aunt, and they both burst out laughing.

Snow Bai passed on her news, and Switch went pale and rushed into the house.

"How does Lotus Jin know she's home?" said Snow Bai's aunt. "Who's been gossiping? Fucking Keeper, she'd love to see our family die out!"

Keeper was married to Ox-Tether, who also lived on West Street, and the two families had argued before about land boundaries.

"Why are you cussing Keeper? You should stop interfering!" said Snow Bai's mother.

"Keeper's the only person Switch met on her way home from the mountains. Who else could have gossiped? Switch, what are you hiding in there for? They'll be into every nook and cranny."

Switch came out carrying a bundle. "I'm going to the river. There's a reed bed I can hide in."

"That's no good. You can't spend the night there! Snow Bai, get a coat on your sister-in-law and make sure she covers her face, then take her home to your mother-in-law. Lotus Jin will never look there. Even if she finds out, she won't dare go into one of the Xia homes!"

"The only reason I know about Lotus Jin is because some village cadres are at home with us right now," said Snow Bai. "We can't go there!"

"She just needs to hide; it doesn't matter where. She can stay with me," said Snow Bai's mom.

They opened the gate, checked no one was around, and then slipped like thieves through to the front yard. Snow Bai's aunt cleared away the bowls and chopsticks, moved the loom onto the porch outside the gate, then peered down the alley toward the main street.

Snow Bai's mom settled Switch in a small room in their side house, told her to rest on the kang, and brought her a piss bucket. "Whatever you do, don't come out. It doesn't matter what's going on outside. When you need to pee, make sure you pee down the side of the bucket so it doesn't tinkle. If you get a tickle in your throat, swallow, don't cough," she instructed her.

She locked the door behind her and chased the niece out of the yard.

"Mom, I have to go!" called Snow Bai.

Only then did her mom ask, "When did you get back? How have you been feeling? You make sure you look after yourself and your baby." And she finished, "Now you can see how hard it is to bring a child into this world in a village!"

"The family planning rules are really strict."

"That's right. The village working group doesn't let any extra births past them. That's why Switch had to take off as soon as she got pregnant. She should have gone as far away as she could and not come back till the baby's born. But then she got this bee in her bonnet about coming back. Torrent is off working in town; what did she do that for? She's just making trouble for herself."

"And why does she want so many kids, anyway? I don't even want this one," said Snow Bai.

"Spit upward!" her mom exclaimed. She spat upward three times herself and made Snow Bai do the same. Snow Bai's spit landed back on her face. "You better never say anything like that at home," said her mom. "Don't you forget it!"

Snow Bai smiled but said nothing. They heard shouts coming from the backyard. "This has got me all in a tizzy!" said Snow Bai's mom. She climbed up the stepladder that leaned against the courtyard wall, pretending to tidy the rows of the corncobs drying up there, and peered over the other side. Lotus Jin was coming in from the alley with a group of people. "Lotus Jin, isn't it? Where are you off to?" she called, but then she climbed down without waiting for an answer and whispered to Snow Bai, "They're here! They're really here!"

"Then I'm off," said Snow Bai. "We have guests."

"Don't be in such a hurry. You keep watch here, and I'll go to the backyard and see what's happening."

Snow Bai's aunt heard the shouts, too, and hurriedly sat down at her loom, pedaling with all her might and slamming the shuttle back and forth. We were already in the yard, but she stayed right where she was at her loom. By the time Snow Bai's mom turned up, Lotus Jin had already gotten into an argument with Snow Bai's aunt, who was adamant that Switch had never come home. She waved her arms around and rolled her eyes with great scorn, but Lotus Jin wasn't having any of that.

"Violating family planning rules and hiding someone who's violated them are both offences against state law," she proclaimed. And the search began. The searchers included Hero Liu (a village cadre), a policeman called Zhou, Big-Noise Zhao, and me. We went through every single room, up into the roof space and down into the cellar where the sweet potatoes were stored. Lotus Jin even uncovered the big storage jars and bent down to peer into the hen coop. But we didn't see hide nor hair of Switch. Then Snow Bai's mom came into the yard. I panicked and grabbed a straw hat and pushed it down over my head.

"Thief!" shouted the aunt. "He's taken my hat!" She tried to grab it back, and I hid behind Hero Liu.

But Snow Bai's mom ignored me. "Lotus Jin, Lotus Jin, what taxes are you collecting this time?"

"Do you know if Switch's back?" Lotus Jin asked her.

"I haven't heard anyone say that."

Snow Bai's aunt, back at her loom, muttered angrily, "You've checked the hen coop. Why don't you stick your fingers up the hens' backsides while you're at it and see if Switch's in there?"

"Don't take it out on me," said Lotus Jin. "I'm only carrying out state policy. Last time she was home, you lied to me, too. You said she wasn't here. You can do that twice, but not three or four times. This time she's been seen. Where've you hidden her?"

"That's malicious gossip! You don't care if my family dies out. You'll never have a child of your own; that's why you're jealous of me. You're picking on me because I haven't got a grandson. If I did and he was as big as this"—she gestured to the door—"would you dare shoot your mouth off like that?" She burst into tears and banged her fists on the loom.

"Don't be like that. This is government cadres you're talking to! You haven't even offered them water," said Snow's mom.

Snow's aunt, still crying, said, "Pour them some water from the kettle." And she let out another loud wail. As Snow's mom fetched half a dozen bowls and filled them with water, she added, "Put some sugar in. It's in a pot in the cupboard." And she carried on crying.

Lotus Jin refused the water. All of us did, but we still couldn't find that big-bellied girl.

Then Snow's mom said, "Switch isn't an ant. If you can't find her, she's not here. I know you have a difficult job with this family planning business; why don't you come to my house and put your feet up for a bit?"

She was just being polite, but Lotus Jin actually accepted. Before she left, she muttered in Constable Zhou's ear, "You stand guard. You stay here one day, ten days, however long it takes! Freshwind's not going to lose its Family Planning Success Award because of her!" As she followed Snow Bai's mom to the front yard, she called me over.

"You want me to go, too?" I asked.

"Of course. Why not?"

So I went with Lotus Jin. But as soon as we got to the gate, there was Snow Bai. I stood rooted to the spot. She looked at me, too, then looked away again. Heavens, in that glance I saw fear and uncertainty, embarrassment and indignation. It was as if she'd thrown a bunch of grain stalks at me, and the bristles prickled and made me come up in a rash all over my body. I turned and ran.

Lotus Jin called after me, "Spark! Spark! Don't you want a bonus?"

But I ran all the way out of the alley, not even stopping when one of my shoes fell off.

The farther I ran, the closer my soul came to Snow Bai. There I was, in the form of a stick bug perched on Snow Bai's shoulder, not that she'd noticed.

The horrible Lotus Jin saw me first. "Surely there aren't stick bugs at this time of year?" And she flicked me off.

Snow Bai squealed. She said she hated bugs with long arms and legs. Then she called one of the hens. "Chook, chook, chook!"

It scurried over, pecked at me, and carried me away. It didn't eat me; it carried me out through the gate, where I struggled free and flew away.

Snow Bai and Lotus Jin had been classmates in high school, and good friends before Snow Bai married Wind Xia. After their marriage, Lotus Jin had cooled toward Snow Bai, but now she was suddenly very friendly. "What a pretty top you've got, and nice shoes! And where did you get that hair clip? It's so pretty."

She said nothing about Snow Bai herself being beautiful, just her clothes. I was suddenly so furious with her that I turned myself into a green-headed fly and buzzed around her head to annoy her. She tried brushing me off, but I just dropped some shit, which landed right on her face. She already had a collection of freckles the same color as fly shit.

"You're the one with nice clothes, Lotus Jin!" said Snow Bai's mom. "And how's your father getting on?"

"He was ill for a while in spring. He didn't throw it off for ages, but then he recovered and now he's pretty good."

"You should take good care of him. He only has you. A daughter is like a cozy vest for her parents!"

"But I'm busy all day. How am I going to have time to look after him?"

"That's true. And as a government cadre, you have to play good cop *and* bad cop. You're good at both." She paused, then added, "You could be a little more easygoing, a little less harsh, though, couldn't you?"

"Did you think I was too hard just now?"

"Yes, but you had to be."

"It's not like I wanted to be like this, neither like a man nor like a woman. But I'm a cadre; I have no choice. I have to be hard to get the work done. Switch's had two kids already, and now she's going for a third. That's against the country's interests, but never mind that. She's messing up the family planning quota. If we don't fulfill the quota, then the county will blame the township, and the township will blame Pavilion, and he'll blame me. What can I do? I'll tell you one thing: the village cadres have already decided that if Switch doesn't come home, then her family'll be fined."

"You'd fine the old woman?" exclaimed Snow Bai's mom. "Her son's gone to work in the mines and might never come back. If Switch runs off again, there'll be no one to farm their land, and what will she do then?"

"In West Mountain Bend, one couple had a second child, and the family planning team confiscated all their possessions, right down to the doors and roof tiles," said Lotus Jin.

"See? You can really fly off the handle!!" said Snow Bai's mom.

Lotus Jin laughed. Snow Bai got up and poured some tea for her. "Why did you invite her home?" she whispered to her mother.

"I was just being polite. I didn't think she'd take me up on it."

"I'll be off then."

"No, don't go! Stay and talk to her for a bit. She has no idea Switch's here."

Just then Hero Liu came into the yard and beckoned to Lotus Jin. They went into a huddle and whispered, and Lotus Jin smiled. Then she took the tea Snow Bai gave her and sipped. "What good tea! You're spoiling me with tea this quality, Auntie! I don't suppose Switch's here, is she?"

Snow Bai's mom's smile slipped, and she looked upset. She went over to the side house and fetched a broom that was lying on the windowsill. "What are you saying, Lotus Jin? This is my home. What would Switch be doing here? You're scaring me." She put the broom down. "Snow Bai, sit and talk to Lotus Jin for a bit. I'm going to fetch some water."

"You're going to get water? Let me do it for you," said Lotus Jin. She took the shoulder pole and buckets off the older woman. "Come with me, and we can chat," she said to Snow Bai. Snow Bai's mom, calmer now, winked at her daughter, who followed Lotus Jin unwillingly to the West Street well.

As soon as she was gone, Hero Liu and Constable Zhou, who had already searched the buildings nearby, pressed up against the side house from the outside and peered in the back window. There was someone lying asleep on the kang—Switch, judging by what they could see of her hair. They banged on the window and shouted, but there was no response, which convinced them it was her. They pushed a stick through the window frame and poked her with it. There was a slight movement, and they poked again, and then again, and finally managed to push her off the kang. Now they could see it was Switch for sure.

The pair of them ran into the yard and told Snow Bai's mom to open the door. When she refused, they forced it open, grabbed Switch, and dragged her away to Big-Noise Zhao's treatment room in Freshwind Temple. Snow Bai's mom was so furious that her legs gave way under her, and she slumped to the ground. Snow Bai's aunt didn't dare to cry or make a fuss, but she did run along behind them with her arms outstretched.

As soon as they'd all gone, the cry went up in the alley. "Switch's been caught! She's off for an abortion!"

Lotus Jin put down the carrying pole and buckets of water. "Snow Bai, I have to go," she said, and turned and ran. Snow Bai couldn't carry the water, so she left the buckets where they were and went to her mom's. She found her in the yard, sitting mute and blank eyed. There was a cat, too, curled up in a ball, looking up at the sky with big round eyes. And there was a hen craning its neck and tiptoeing carefully toward the cat.

It seemed as though the cat had tears running from its eyes, and the hen was wondering what the matter was. At that moment, Snow Bai realized that Lotus Jin had deliberately drawn her away. She was annoyed at her mother . . . How had she managed to mess it up so badly?

There was nothing unusual about women being dragged off for abortions in Freshwind, so when people heard the news, they just said, "Well, Switch only had herself to blame. Whatever made her come back home?" And they carried on with their lives.

All abortions performed on women who had violated the family planning rules were done in Freshwind Temple. Big-Noise Zhao used to say that the treatment room in the backyard was haunted by three hundred babies whose ghosts could be heard wailing in the middle of the night. So he hung couplets on either side of the door. "We found nowhere better, So we built this little hut here." A little later he had added the lines, "Society doesn't want you, why are you here? Poor babies, find yourselves other wombs and be reborn."

When they arrived with Switch, it was almost completely dark outside. Snow Bai's aunt was still following, and now she slipped quietly into the woodshed next door and hid. The place was full of mosquitoes, but she didn't dare slap them away. She just wiped her hands over her face and arms, and they came away covered with stinking blood. Lotus Jin went home, of course, but Hero Liu and Constable Zhou sat guarding the entrance to the temple. Big-Noise Zhao went in to perform the abortion, then came out to tell them that it was too late. Switch had gone into labor.

"Then deliver the baby and get rid of it," said Hero Liu.

"I can't kill it once it's been born!"

"Then call me when it's out!"

Hero Liu and Constable Zhou stayed in the pharmacy at the front, knocking back the booze until they were staggering on their feet. Big-Noise Zhao came for the sterilizing equipment and returned to the treatment room, and no more than an hour later, Switch had given birth. She'd had two kids in the past, and this time didn't cry out once. It was no different from having a crap. But the weird thing was the way it was born: the baby and the waters spurted out together, and the infant slithered over the sheets of oiled paper protecting the bed and plopped like a fish to the floor. And at exactly that moment, the lights went out. Big-Noise Zhao thought the switch must have tripped, and fiddled with the circuit board behind the door, but the lights wouldn't come back on.

"Dammit, a power cut!" he swore. He groped around on the floor for the baby but couldn't find it.

Hero Liu shouted from the pharmacy, "Big-Noise! Big-Noise! What's happened to the power?"

Big-Noise Zhao, his hands covered in blood, rushed in and found a candle but couldn't find the matches, and when he did manage to light it, he tripped in the yard, and it went out again.

Eventually, he was back in the treatment room, where Switch lay exhausted on the bed, but the infant, and even the afterbirth, were gone without a trace.

"Where's the baby?" shouted Big-Noise Zhao. "Where is it?"

"You've thrown my baby out without even letting me have one look!" Switch sobbed.

Big-Noise Zhao bellowed for Hero Liu and Constable Zhou.

In fact, it was Snow Bai's aunt who'd snatched the child away. She was a fey woman, and as she sat in the woodshed and peered at a star through the cracks in the wall, she prayed, "Let the lights go off when our baby's born!" And so they did.

Quick as a flash, she slipped into the treatment room, picked the baby off the floor, and felt between its legs. There was its little penis. She didn't make a sound in the darkness, but the tears came, and she mouthed, "Oh God!" She had terrible rheumatism in one leg and heavens knows how she managed it, but she tucked the baby with the afterbirth under her jacket, nipped to a corner of the yard, clambered onto the hen coop and over the wall, and hurried down the alleyway toward the 312.

In the meantime, Wind Xia had gone to fetch Snow Bai from her mom's on West Street. As he stepped out of the gate, he bumped into Tiger. The dog stared at him for a while, wagging its tail, and ran off. Wind Xia thought it must have gone in search of Lucky and shouted after it, but the dog didn't stop. Along the alley it ran, out into the street and off in the direction of the township government offices. Wind Xia followed—he had nothing better to do. Outside the gate of the offices, he met Clerk, who was dusting off his clothes and preparing to go home.

"Wind Xia, did you have a party today? You must have given them something good to drink. The Party secretary and the township head were so drunk they fell asleep as soon as they got back here." He aimed a kick at Tiger. "Was the dog there, too?"

"It wasn't a feast for dogs!"

"That wasn't what I meant," Clerk said. "Tiger's a strange dog. It doesn't matter how many bitches are after him, he only has eyes for Lucky. Even dogs seem to want to choose a mate from a nice family!"

"I'm not interested in dogs," said Wind Xia dismissively, and carried on along the main road. When he came to the brickyard and the turnoff for West Street, he spotted a dark shadow. It ducked out of sight, and he called, "Hello? Who is it?"

The figure emerged on top of the field dike. "Is that Wind Xia?"

Wind Xia went closer and realized it was Snow Bai's aunt. There seemed to be a big bulge in the front of her jacket. "What have you got there? Here, let me help you."

"Meet your nephew!" she whispered, and without waiting for an answer, she dragged him a hundred yards along the dike, knelt down, and showed him. Under her jacket she had a newborn baby, skinny as a little rat, with the cord still attached. "They snatched Switch," she said. "But she gave birth before they could abort her and put an end to my family's line! Can you help me cut the cord?"

Wind Xia looked helpless. "Find a stone!" the old woman instructed him. "Two stones!"

Wind Xia laid the cord over one of the stones and hit it with the other. The umbilical cord was soft and rubbery, and simply slipped off.

"Don't be so useless, hit harder!"

Wind Xia whacked the cord twice more, and it finally broke. Snow Bai's aunt tucked the baby into her jacket again. "Quick, go and tell your mother-in-law," she said. "Tell her to meet me in Star Chen's orchard." Wind Xia ran. Behind him he could hear the baby mewling. It sounded like a sickly kitten.

Wind Xia never imagined he'd be involved in something like this, and it made him feel energized and excited. By the time he'd finally fetched Snow Bai home, it was the middle of the night and both Wisdom Xia and Fourth Aunt had gone to bed. Wind Xia and Snow Bai lay awake, however, talking about Switch and the baby. "Your sister-in-law wanted a boy, and now she's got one," said Wind Xia. "What are you going to have?"

"What do you want?" Snow Bai asked.

"I don't mind. Boy or girl, but I'm guessing it'll be a girl."

"Why?"

"Because the poorer people are, the more they have boys, and better-off families have more girls. That's the way I see it."

"I still want a boy," said Snow Bai.

Wind Xia started laughing, and she asked, "What's so funny?"

"When you said that, I remembered a dirty joke. Some pregnant women were at the hospital to check if they were going to have sons or daughters. The doctor asked the first one, 'Who was on top when you had sex, you or your husband?' The woman said, 'My husband.' 'Then it'll be a boy,' said the doctor. Then it was the second woman's turn. 'Who was on top, you or your husband?' asked the doctor. 'I was,' she said. 'Then it'll be a girl.' When it was the third woman's turn, she began to cry before the doctor had even asked her the question. 'What are you crying for?' he asked. 'I might be having a puppy. He did it doggy-style!'"

Snow Bai felt a sudden cold draft blow over her, and she shivered. "Don't tell jokes like that!"

Wind Xia realized it probably wasn't the right time for dirty jokes and was just about to say something conciliatory when they heard a sound from the room next door. It was Fourth Aunt getting up for a pee. When she saw the light still on in their room, she called, "Snow Bai, aren't you asleep yet?"

"Yes, Mom," said Snow Bai.

"Hurry up and go to sleep. You need your rest."

"She's worried we're doing it," Snow Bai whispered to Wind Xia. "She dropped a few hints today, saying that I shouldn't let you get your way, that it's not good for the baby. I asked if it might make me miscarry, but she just said the baby will come out unclean."

"You're making me horny just talking about it!" said Wind Xia.

"Well, you'll have to sort that out yourself!" said Snow Bai.

"But it can't do any harm!" whined Wind Xia and then carried on pestering her. But Snow Bai wrapped her arms around her pillow and went to sleep with her head at the other end of the bed.

Chapter 32

That night, neither Wind Xia nor Snow Bai slept well. They weren't alone. Lotus Jin was still angry about the disappearance of Switch's baby, and she had reassembled the search party—Hero Liu, Constable Zhou, Big-Noise Zhao, and me, too. We knew the baby had been taken, but we had no idea where it might be. We went out to search, but we came back to Lotus Jin empty handed. She first directed her anger at Big-Noise Zhao but quickly turned on me. She wanted to know why I'd run off on her during the search for Switch. She said I was unlucky. Anything I was involved with was bound to fail, she told me. How do you think I felt about that?

I thought to myself, *Lotus Jin was the one who asked me to help; I didn't just volunteer. Why is it my fault that we weren't successful?*

The sun was coming up, and I was standing out in the street, arguing with her, when I saw Tongue-Tied pulling out of the yard of Freshwind Temple on a tractor. I said to her, "Lotus Jin, do you know the name of the worst kind of ghost?" Before she could answer, I said, "The ghost's name is Fucked Up. That's exactly what you are!"

As soon as the words were out of my mouth, I jumped onto the back of the tractor. Tongue-Tied pinned it, and we roared off.

Driving around on that tractor, I felt a sudden power. It was like putting away the musket and pulling out a cannon. We drove over to the Earth Shrine, and I told Tongue-Tied to get off. "You kowtow to the Earth God and the Earth Goddess," I told him. The mute climbed off, and I roared away on the tractor. I rolled past Third-Kid Li's gate and gave him a fright. He'd just opened his chicken coop. He called after me, but I just kept going, singing as I went: "I come from the Yang household with no protector, to turn myself in / Brandishing spears and throwing hands, a weak man I've never been."

"Watch out for my chickens," Third-Kid Li said.

I saw the chickens, but I didn't slow down. I went directly through the flock, sending the clucking chickens scattering, flapping away from the tires of the tractor. All that was left in my wake were feathers.

That morning, when we got to Justice Xia's home, Second Aunt was boiling rice porridge with broad beans, soybeans, cubes of tofu and daikon, potatoes, lotus seeds, red dates, and walnuts. Justice Xia called it Eight Treasure Porridge. Before we got our share, he poured a bowl that he set on the hood of the tractor.

"Uncle Justice," I said, "I was so excited to see this tractor, it was like meeting some long-lost relative. We should give it a name, shouldn't we?"

"Excited to see it, huh? Then let's call it Exciter."

It should have been me driving Exciter, but Justice Xia was worried that I'd have another episode and pass out, so Tongue-Tied was given chauffeur duties. Tongue-Tied might have been clumsy, but he knew his way around machinery. He drove Justice Xia and me out to Seven Li Gully every morning and brought us back in the evening.

With each trip out to the gully, each day that went by, the weather was turning colder. The people of Freshwind started wearing their hats and belting up their jackets. There wasn't much work left to do in the fields, but the farmers market was booming. When people saw Tongue-Tied ripping around on Exciter, they'd give him a thumbs-up and tell him how good he was at driving that thing. He was quite pleased with himself. He went to his dad and asked him for money to buy a pair of tinted driving goggles and wore them while driving the tractor, with the flashlight hung from a rope around his waist.

I spent quite a few days that fall pouring the piss I'd collected out over my fields, and Justice Xia, too, was fertilizing the fields he'd leased. And while we were at work, Tongue-Tied was racing around the village on Exciter, helping everyone else with their work.

He had been asked by a family on Middle Street to help their son out. The son, the eldest of the family's boys, had been working in Teahouse Village, finishing apartments for half a year, but the foreman hadn't paid him for his work. Tongue-Tied ran him over to Teahouse Village on the tractor and parked outside the foreman's home. Tongue-Tied sat on the tractor outside the home, eating the steamed buns that the family's son had given him. He inhaled five of them and was just about to start on his sixth when the foreman appeared. He handed the money over to the family's son, saying to Tongue-Tied, "You're scaring me to death, brother." Tongue-Tied hadn't intended to be intimidating; he'd just been hungry.

The next request came from the Han family on West Street. Their daughter had gone to Xijing and made out well, then come back to Freshwind and had built a new house. She wanted Tongue-Tied to take her over to the county seat so she could buy some furniture. But Tongue-Tied had heard rumors about what the girl had been up to in the city, so he turned her down.

The girl cursed him out, but he wouldn't give in. When she insisted, he made a vulgar gesture. The entire Han family came out of their yard, ready to beat him up, and he jumped on the tractor and roared off, racing blindly down the lane. He wound up crashing into the corner of Roughshod Ding's House of Treasures, putting a dent in the gas tank of the tractor. When he drove over to Justice Xia's home, hoping for his grandfather's sympathy, the old man cursed him out, too. He wanted to know why Tongue-Tied hadn't helped out the Han girl. I cut in to say that it wouldn't be right to help her, since she'd been working as a prostitute in Xijing.

"How the hell do you know she was a prostitute?" Justice Xia asked.

"How do you think a single girl, alone in the city, could make enough money to come back to the village and build a house?"

"If somebody's down, everyone's there to kick them, and if they manage to do all right for themselves, everyone'll talk about them behind their back."

"We all know what she was up to. You ever see the way she goes around, with that makeup on? Looks like a demon woman. She looks just like those whores over at the House of Treasures. You can tell by those high heels they wear what they're up to."

"Is that what's going on at the House of Treasures?" Justice Xia asked.

As soon as I'd said it, I knew I shouldn't have. Justice Xia stared me down. "Well," I said, "maybe they just look like whores."

Justice Xia went silent. When he spoke again, it was only to order me to fill up a sack with some of the leftover corn in his yard to take over to Concord Qin.

Treasure was furious when he learned that his father had sent the corn over to Concord Qin. The plan had been for the five brothers to send rice and corn to their parents after the harvest. Treasure was proud of his position as a teacher and went around with a pen stuck in his breast pocket. But he wasn't a paragon of virtue, to be sure. He'd already given over his share of rice but vowed not to give that year's share of corn, since his father had given away the previous year's contribution.

When Gold's, Bounty's, and Halfwit's wives heard about the situation, they decided they'd follow Treasure's example. If their father-in-law had enough corn to give some away to Concord Qin, they reasoned, then he was doing just fine without their contribution. Bamboo was the only one who stuck to the original plan. When Tongue-Tied came to pick up her family's share, she had the corn ready, and she also sent along an extra sack of soybeans.

When Tongue-Tied got to Halfwit's place, he received a very different reception. As soon as Tongue-Tied came into the house, Halfwit locked up the chest where the grain was stored. Tongue-Tied use the heavy scale rod he was carrying to smash the lock off. Halfwit pounced on his nephew, and the two began fighting. The younger man could have had his way with Halfwit, but Tongue-Tied wasn't prepared to beat up his own uncle. Halfwit had the benefit of family seniority. He was like a Pekingese barking at a mastiff from the top of a dung heap, and he gave Tongue-Tied a slap upside the head.

Tongue-Tied charged at his uncle and held him against the wall. Halfwit rained blows down on Tongue-Tied's wide back, but there wasn't much point. He could have kept at it all day without Tongue-Tied going down. But in the struggle, Tongue-Tied's pants had slipped down. Halfwit reached over the mute's back and jammed a finger up his ass. Tongue-Tied took off running for the yard with his uncle trailing behind him, his finger firmly trapped.

Halfwit yelled for his wife to grab a stick. "Smack him in the head," he said. Tongue-Tied's asshole unclenched, and Halfwit fell backward, landing in a heap in the yard.

Quite a few people outside the walls of the yard heard the fight. They muffled their laughter but didn't bother going in to break it up.

Second Aunt and Marvel's mother were in her side house, chatting while they shelled pumpkin seeds. Marvel's mother eventually started addressing her dead husband. "Who did you give my bracelet to?" she asked him. "The noodle factory should be giving you two hundred yuan a month, but this month you only got a hundred and twenty. Who did you give the other eighty to? I got that bracelet from my mother. You think you can just give it away to that slut?"

"Who are you talking to?" Second Aunt asked.

Marvel's mother seemed to regain her senses. "I was talking to Marvel's dad," she said.

"Nonsense."

"My old man is gone."

"So what? I've still got one, and I'd probably be just as happy without him."

"You're never as hungry when you've got steamed buns in the house, even if you don't eat them, as you are when you've got none."

Marvel's wife had come into the side house and heard them talking. "He's been dead for years already," she said, "but I hear you talking about him day and night. What do you need from me and Marvel that we aren't giving you?"

"I've got plenty," Marvel's mother said.

"Ask Second Aunt how much corn her sons gave her this harvest."

"How did you know about that?" asked Second Aunt.

"Everyone knows about it. Tongue-Tied is going around, trying to collect the corn right now. He beat the shit out of Halfwit."

As soon as she heard that, Second Aunt rose and hobbled out into the alley, leaning on her walking stick. The walking stick slid in a puddle of pig shit, and she fell to the ground. She sat in the dust, crying.

Wisdom Xia's splayfooted walk caused his shoes to wear in a peculiar way, with one half of the heel pristine and the other half ground down to nothing. He was on his way home from Star Chen and Bright Chen's shoe repair shop, where he'd had them fix a pair of rain boots for him. He came across Second Aunt, sitting in the alley and crying. He asked her what was wrong, and she told him about the issue with the corn and Tongue-Tied fighting with Halfwit.

"All right," he said, helping Second Aunt to her feet. He took off in the direction of Gold's home. The gate was open, and he hung the rain boots on the bolt, then went straight into the house and sat down in a rattan chair in the main room. The family's cat came and wrapped itself around his leg. He kicked it away. A chicken wandered into the room and pecked at his foot. He kicked the chicken away, too.

Gold came out of the side house, hearing the racket from the cat and the chicken. "Fourth Uncle!" he exclaimed. But when he saw the expression on his uncle's face he froze, his arms hanging limply at his sides.

Wisdom Xia, unlike Justice Xia, didn't have much of a temper, but when he did lose it, it was just as frightening. Wisdom Xia didn't look at his nephew but through him. He had his gaze fixed on the scar on the poplar that stood outside the wall around the yard.

"What's the problem?" Wisdom Xia asked, focusing on his nephew again.

"What do you mean?" Gold asked.

"I'm talking about Tongue-Tied and Halfwit fighting. You don't think that's a problem?"

"It's all Treasure's fault," said Gold, and he tried to explain the situation to Wisdom Xia.

"If Treasure told you to eat a bowl of shit, would all four of you rush to get a spoon? If someone starves to death in the county, they'll give the township head the boot. If someone starves to death in the county, they'll fire him. You're the oldest son, so you should take responsibility for not giving your parents their share of the harvest. How can you sit peacefully at home while your parents are in this state?"

Gold reddened. "Don't tell them about the fight," he pleaded with his uncle. He promised he'd sort out the issue of the corn and deliver each family's share as soon as he could.

Wisdom Xia rose and walked toward the door, saying, "I'll be waiting at your father's house!"

"Fourth Uncle," Gold called after his uncle.

But the tea that Gold had poured went untouched.

Before Wisdom Xia went out of the gate, he called back to his nephew, "And make sure you bring those rain boots with you when you come."

When Wisdom Xia got to Justice Xia's home, he discovered that his older brother was out. Second Aunt was sitting on the kang, crying. Wisdom Xia's feet had started to hurt, and he sat down, took off his shoes, and rubbed his feet, telling Second Aunt, "That's enough. What are you crying for?" He told her to comb her hair, then sit on the kang and eat her pumpkin seeds. He went over to the window and opened it, hoping to get rid of the sour smell in the room. A flock of ducks sent up a chorus of quacks from the fishpond. Bounty's wife came into the yard, carrying her family's contribution of corn in a sack.

"Ma," she said. "What are you going to do with all this grain you've got? There's no way you're going to eat it all." When she saw Wisdom Xia was sitting there, she stopped talking.

Hearth had already delivered his share of grain, but he came by again to drop off a basket of carrots. Treasure still hadn't come. Hearth asked Bounty's wife, "What about Treasure? He still hasn't brought his share yet, has he?"

"As the saying goes, a soft persimmon is easier to pick."

"Huh?" Wisdom Xia grunted.

"I'll go see what he's up to," Bounty's wife said. She headed for the gate and ran into Halfwit, whose arms were full. There was an open cut on his forehead, and blood was smeared across his face like an opera singer's makeup. The two baskets he carried were filled with his share of corn.

"If everyone is giving their share," Halfwit said, "you can count on me, too. Even if I have to drag it here on my hands and knees, I'll give my share. I pay my taxes to the government, so how could I not give a share to my mother and my father? I'd cut off my own flesh to feed them, if that's what they asked for. So what did Tongue-Tied think he was doing, breaking that lock? Let him finish the job next time and beat me to death—I can't stop him. I'm always the victim. If it's not Tongue-Tied doing the beating, it'll be Culture who does it, and if not him, it'll probably be Shiner."

As soon as the words were out of Halfwit's mouth, Shiner appeared, coming through the gate with a sack of grain and Wisdom Xia's rain boots. "I've never hit you before," he said to Halfwit, "and I don't plan to."

"Wipe that blood off your face," Wisdom Xia said.

Halfwit wiped the blood off his face without saying a word.

Wisdom Xia turned away from Halfwit to Shiner and asked when he'd gotten back.

"I was there when you came over, but I was off in the side house. I'd just had an argument with my dad, and I didn't want to come out yet," Shiner said.

"A good boy like you, arguing with your father? He retired so you'd be able to take over his job full time. What are you arguing with him about?"

"It'd be better if he'd never bothered!"

"Ungrateful little bastard!"

"I've got to pay these damn fees, two thousand yuan a month. I lost money my first month! What I really want to do is grow shiitakes. But my dad doesn't want me to. It's fine if he doesn't go back to work, but I want him to pay for my losses."

"Where is he going to get the money?" asked Wisdom Xia. "All he's got is that pension . . ."

"Just because he's unlucky, do I have to be unlucky, too?"

Wisdom Xia softened. He thought about the talk he'd just had with Gold. He'd cursed him out, but Gold hadn't complained. He sat for a while without speaking, then said, "Tell your father to come over tonight."

When all the corn had been put away, Wisdom Xia motioned for Halfwit, Bounty, and Shiner to leave.

"We've given what we owe, but what about the rest?" said Halfwit.

"Treasure is not my son," said Second Aunt from the kang.

"He clearly is! Look at Fourth Uncle. He rules his household with an iron first, but here, the second eldest could get away with murder!"

"A gate only keeps the good people out; the robbers will find another way in."

He motioned again for them to go, then, turning to Second Aunt and patting the chest where the corn was stored, said, "Everyone's turned in their share, right? There's no way they could refuse."

"Wisdom," Second Aunt said, "you're a credit to the Xia family!"

Wisdom Xia went home, turned on his radio, and cranked up the volume. There was a broadcast on of an opera called *Wallowing on the Floor*. At that part in the opera, Wave Zhang and Golden Zhang were going back and forth, singing then speaking, the performers throwing themselves into their work:

> Wave Zhang: Hey, oh!
> I'm an old man of seventy,
> Without a tooth in my jaw.
> Tofu is too tough for me,
> Let alone peppers or beans.
> And as I sat in peaceful contemplation, my daughter called for me.
> I will ask what it is that she wants from the old man.

Golden Zhang: Ah, Father, you have arrived. Please sit.

Wave Zhang: I am comfortable here.

Golden Zhang: Your daughter is here!

Wave Zhang: Yes, my daughter, now, have you brought me here to eat or to drink?

Golden Zhang: Father, why do you only think about eating and drinking?

Wave Zhang: If it's not to eat or to drink, then what is the matter?

Golden Zhang: How could you not know, Father? My master told me, this year, this month, this day, at this time, that a great general will pass by. It is my destiny to be with him. I want you to wait for him in front of the home, to be there when he comes to propose marriage.

Wave Zhang: My daughter, I don't know what to say.
This master has taught you everything, even how to find a son-in-law for me.

Golden Zhang: My father, my dear father, you know that I respect your instruction, but I must also respect my master.

I've spoken now to my father dear,

And told him clearly what he must hear.

That my respected teacher on the holy ridge,

Has informed me clearly of my fate in marriage.

Father must now rush to the village gate,

Where for my prince he must patiently wait.

Once their discussion has reached conclusion,

My prince and I will join in union.

Everyone on both sides of the alley could hear the opera from Wisdom Xia's radio.

Third Aunt had gone over to First Aunt's home to borrow a basket. First Aunt had been suffering for the past few days with a headache that never seemed to go away. The pain wasn't bad, but she'd been uncomfortable. Third Aunt performed a ritual that she hoped would get rid of the pain, starting by balancing three chopsticks in a bowl.

"You hear that?" First Aunt asked. "Wisdom is playing his opera again. He's got a good life now, huh?"

"Hold the chopsticks," Third Aunt said. First Aunt held the chopsticks upright in the bowl while Third Aunt poured water over them. "If it's really you, then stand up. Stand up!"

"Who are you talking to?" asked First Aunt.

"Your husband," Third Aunt said. "If it's really you, stand up! You should already be in another body by now, dead all these years already. What are you bothering her for? This world

457

and the netherworld are not the same. You take care of your own business and let her look after her business. She wants to remarry. She's going to remarry!"

"What the hell are you talking about?"

"I'm trying to scare this ghost off!" Third Aunt poured water over the chopsticks again, talking to the long-dead Benevolence Xia. "If it's really you, then I command you to stop. Stop all of this."

The chopsticks began to quiver. First Aunt pulled her hand away, but the chopsticks stayed upright in the bowl. The two old women shivered and then went pale.

"Have you dreamed about him coming in the gate?" Third Aunt asked.

"I dreamed he came in, sat down on the rush cushion, and told me to get him a bowl of green bean soup! That's when I woke up. Right after that, the headache started."

"Did Pavilion go to his grave on the fifteenth of August to burn spirit money? Did he burn the spirit money for his father?"

"You think he'd remember something like that?"

"He must have come here to ask for something," Third Aunt said. "He wants something."

First Aunt brought a stool and went up into the loft to bring down a sheaf of hempen paper. She'd bought the paper at the New Year, then pasted a layer of it over her coffin with clear lacquer. The leftover paper had been sitting there for long enough that when she brought it down, a thick layer of dust floated through the air, catching in rays of sunlight. The women coughed and then went to work burning the paper in front of a framed portrait of Benevolence Xia.

In his final portrait, with his narrow forehead and puffed-up cheeks, Benevolence Xia looked like a calabash. When they were done burning the paper, the chopsticks in the bowl were still standing. "He must still be here," First Aunt said.

Third Aunt went to the kitchen and came back with a cleaver. "Are you leaving or not?" Third Aunt said. She took a swing at the chopsticks and cut them into splinters, which rattled across the top of the cabinet and then fell to the floor.

"Get out!" First Aunt said, splashing the water from the bowl across the yard.

The water hit Chastity, who was just coming in the gate. The two old women rushed over to dry her off. They saw that her eyes were swollen and red as rotten peaches, and they asked if she'd had an argument with Shiner's fiancée. Chastity began to cry, a stream of tears running down her cheeks.

"So many tears," First Aunt said. "You're going to end up just like your mother. When Blossom was setting Shiner up with her niece, I knew she was trying to worm her way into your family, trying to get a comfortable life for herself. That woman looks good, but she's not the obedient type, and you're fighting with her even before she joins the family!"

"Her words are like a knife in my heart," Chastity said. "I went to talk to Blossom about it, but she got angry at me. She said that setting Shiner up with that woman would bring her a thousand years of bad luck. That niece of hers looked like a kitten at first, but now I can see she's a ferocious tiger."

Third Aunt came to the defense of her daughter-in-law. "Don't talk about Blossom! Don't talk about Blossom. What's the problem? What is it?"

"Ray is losing money," Chastity said, "every single day he's working. He's started talking about quitting. He wants to come back and grow shiitakes. He can't be serious, can he? He got a steady job, and now he wants to come back to be a farmer?"

"How can you call it a steady job if he's losing money? Thunder had a steady job, too, and his rice bowl was always full. But it broke—just like that! Just like that."

"You think he can really make a living growing mushrooms?" Chastity asked. "Treasure and I told him not to get involved with it. That's when Blossom's niece started fighting with me. She even said she wants to go to Xinjiang to work. She has a classmate out there who told her that the oil fields are always looking for workers. What the hell kind of place is Xinjiang? I'll tell you, as soon as you squat for a shit, the mosquitoes'll bite your ass raw. What the hell do they think they'll find there? And just think, with them all the way out there—and my health isn't good, and Gold isn't as energetic as he used to be—who's going to look after the fields?"

Third Aunt sighed. "Since your third uncle died," she said, "we've had nothing but bad luck. It seems like the entire Xia family is unsettled! Unsettled."

"Gold is so worried he just mopes around all day. When the issue came up about giving our share of corn and grain, Fourth Uncle even cursed him out."

"Your father-in-law isn't doing much better," Third Aunt said. "He's obsessed, going up to Seven Li Gully early in the morning and coming home late at night. Fourth Uncle has to keep the entire Xia family together now."

"He can curse out Gold, if he wants," Chastity said, "but that doesn't help us any. What are we going to do? I came by to see if you two had any advice."

Third Aunt turned to First Aunt. "Is your headache any better? Any better."

"I kinda forgot about it."

"Then it must be better. Must be better."

"You were standing chopsticks?" Chastity asked. "Can you do it for me, too? I must have a ghost haunting me, too, the way things are going."

"It won't help," said Third Aunt. "You should go get your fortune told. If the prediction is that Shiner can make money, then let him leave that job. If it doesn't work out, and Blossom's niece starts trouble again, you have to live with it. You're a mother-in-law now, and that isn't an easy job. It isn't an easy job."

"I always treated my mother-in-law well."

"That's right. You didn't run your mouth, but you didn't handle your family's business like you should have. Like you should have."

"I'm sorry for coming to you with this, Third Aunt. So you think I should go see Mid-Star's dad?"

"Call him 'Uncle Glory'!" First Aunt said. "Have you heard the news? Mid-Star got promoted to vice deputy of Yangqu County."

"Really?" Third Aunt said. "I saw his dad three days ago. I just caught a glimpse of him in passing, but I haven't seen him since then. Haven't seen him."

"It looks like our family's in decline, while everyone else is doing well," First Aunt said.

"We've lost the spirit that held us together before. That held us together."

"Is Mid-Star's dad going to want to read my fortune?" Chastity asked. "You know, his son's been promoted . . ."

"Go and talk to Halfwit's wife. She can take you to Tiger Head Cliff in South Gully to talk to the spirits."

"I'm not talking to her. She's free to believe in whatever spirits she wants, but look at what's become of her family. Look at how Halfwit has turned out. With a wife like that, there's no doubt he's headed for a bad end."

"You live your life and let her live her life," First Aunt said. "What's it to you how she chooses to live? The way I see it, she's a good, caring person. Not like you, walking around with a handful of leaves, acting like they're as heavy as Mount Tai."

Chastity began to cry again. She walked out of the gate, weeping.

"Except for Bamboo, that entire generation is spoiled. None of those women can look after their families. They're so bored that they go looking for trouble, and when they find it, they start blubbering. They'll lose everything, standing around blubbering like that."

"Is your headache better? Better?"

"Just a bit."

"Sickness comes in a tidal wave and leaves in a trickle. Trickle."

"Maybe it's for the best if this headache just kills me!" First Aunt said. "What's the point of getting so old? I'm nothing but a burden now. I'm not happy about it, either. The King of Hell must have misplaced my file. You tell me . . . ," she started to say, but suddenly went silent.

Cutie came in the gate, carrying a bundle of freshly dyed cloth, and dumped it with a thud on the table. "Ma," she said, "did your son get back yet?"

"He's busy in the village," First Aunt said. "I haven't seen him."

"What's he so busy with? He's probably down at the House of Treasures, sleeping with one of those girls they've got there."

"Don't talk like that!"

"Why not? That's the rumor at the dyehouse, at least, and they've got no reason to lie. They don't have anything against our family."

"Why would you believe them?" Third Aunt asked. "Pavilion isn't like Treasure. Pavilion's got more things to look after than a cow has hairs on its back. Even if he wanted to, he wouldn't have time to do anything like that. Plenty of people in this village bear grudges against Pavilion. Let them gossip, but you need to keep your mouth shut! Keep it shut."

"In this house, I have to take care of all my work, and then take care of all his work, too. If I ever catch him over at the House of Treasures with those whores, I'll bash my brains out right in front of him!" Cutie picked up the cloth and went into her bedroom.

The two old women exchanged glances but did not speak.

When Chastity got home, she was too flustered to do anything, so she decided to visit Mid-Star's dad. On her way out of the yard, she picked a few eggplants to take to him. When she got there, however, she found his gate locked. A few sparrows pranced across the threshold and left a mark in the dust shaped like an arrow. She decided to take the eggplants to Halfwit instead and found that he was out, too. His wife was there, though, and Chastity decided to ask her about Tiger Head Cliff. Halfwit's wife told her to wait for her at the south end of the village. "I have to wash my face," she said, "but I'll meet you there."

Chastity waited a few hours at the south end of the village, but Halfwit's wife never came. Chastity went back into the village to look for her and found her standing on a stone roller. She was craning her neck, looking into the distance. "What are you looking at?" Chastity asked.

"I'm watching all the people that came out to see Wind Xia off," Halfwit's wife said.

"What are you worried about that for?"

"You'd think Wind Xia would stick around, seeing how far along Snow Bai is. I guess a working man has to make sacrifices, too."

"Halfwit is always at home, isn't he? Did he look after you when you were pregnant?"

"Everyone's different."

"You think Snow Bai's worried about you? Look at those pants you've got on. The ass is almost worn through. If she really cared, she'd buy you a new pair."

"Almost worn through?" Halfwit's wife said and patted the seat of her pants. "I've got underwear on, anyway."

The two headed off to South Gully, talking along the way about the sons of the Xia family. The previous generation had worked heroically to build the Xia clan's legacy, but the only ones in Gold's generation worth a damn were Wind Xia, Thunder, and Pavilion. The way things had turned out, though, Thunder was like a lame horse, ready to be put down. Pavilion still had some fight left in him, but he was a farmer at heart, and he'd made too many enemies while climbing to his position. If he stumbled, there would be nobody to catch his fall. The only one from Culture's generation that anyone could be optimistic about was Shiner. But now Shiner was talking about leaving. The road ahead for Shiner led to great promise, but it was a road fraught with peril.

When they got to the shrine, they burned incense and then knelt in the main hall and pulled out the divination strips. Each strip had four sentences written on it, which were supposed to tell the fortune of whoever pulled the strip. All four sentences on the strip they pulled seemed positive, but neither woman really understood them, except for the one that read, "Peace and quiet at home."

"That means he shouldn't go," Halfwit's wife said.

"Indeed," said Chastity. "He'd be better off staying home. The god of this shrine really knows his stuff, huh?" Chastity knelt, mumbled her own questions to the shrine's god, and then pulled a few more strips, hoping to get an answer to her own and Thunder's problems and a solution to Shiner's issue with losing money. All the strips predicted a bad future. Chastity was unsettled and started to sweat.

She reached to pull more strips, but Halfwit's wife cautioned her, "You can't just keep pulling them out. It stops working if you do that."

She led Chastity out of the shrine. Out front, they ran into a worshipper who seemed to recognize Halfwit's wife. "Ah, you came for a visit!" said the worshipper. "And how much money did you donate?"

"You mean to Master Clear-Bright, to fix the pagoda? I gave fifty yuan."

"Only fifty? Mid-Star's dad gave two hundred!"

"He gave two hundred?" said Halfwit's wife, suddenly embarrassed.

When Halfwit's wife got home, her husband was in the main room, playing mah-jongg with a few people. The room was full of smoke, and the floor was covered in cigarette butts and gobs of phlegm.

"Where the hell have you been?" Halfwit asked. "Go boil some water for us."

"There's no firewood," she said. "Go down to the strawstack beside the field and bring back some straw."

"Who do you think you're talking to, telling me to go fetch straw? You're still running that goddamn mouth of yours, huh?"

The mah-jongg players didn't bother to intervene. They tried to wind her up even more. "My wife," said one of them. "Let me tell you, every time I come home, first thing she says is, 'Did you have something to eat? I'll make you some noodles!'"

"No matter what hour I show up at home," another said, "my wife is ready to go. She's got a bowl of noodles in one hand, and she's working my noodle with the other. She says to me, 'First eat, then fuck, or the other way around?'"

That just made Halfwit even angrier. "Why are you still standing there?" he roared at his wife. He kicked off a shoe, picked it up, and flung it at his wife's head. When the mah-jongg players saw that Halfwit was really upset, they told him to calm down.

"That's enough," one of them said. "At least wait until we've gone!"

"What's wrong? You lose money again?" Halfwit's wife asked.

"What do you give a damn whether I win or lose?" Halfwit said.

He leaped up, ready to go at his wife again. She rushed out and came back with some straw, then started boiling water. While the water boiled, she went to the chest and started filling a bag with grain. When the bag was full, she called out in a loud voice to the empty yard, "Forest Wu! Brother! Why don't you sit down and rest? Okay, okay, sure. I'll bring it over in a while!"

When she brought the boiled water into the main room, Halfwit asked her who she'd been talking to.

"It was old Forest Wu the stammerer, on his way to the market to sell some grain. He couldn't manage it all, so he left a bag here and asked me to take it for him."

"Who is he to show up here and order you around?" Halfwit said, then turned back to his game.

Halfwit's wife went back into the kitchen, grabbed the sack, and brought it over to sell to Big-Noise Zhao. She'd already sold a few bags of grain to Big-Noise Zhao and always at a more than fair price. "You can't tell my husband about this," she reminded him. "If he finds out I was making a bit of money on the side, he'd take it off me and lose it playing mah-jongg."

"You can trust me. I know it's Snow Bai's aunt that's hiding Switch's baby. But I haven't breathed a word of it to anyone."

"I heard it was a boy."

"You didn't hear that from me."

Halfwit's wife stuffed a roll of bills into her bosom, smiled, and left. When she got home, the game was still going on in the main room. Halfwit's wife didn't know where to put the money. First, she stuffed it into a bag of grain in the chest, but then she went back, took it out, and put it in an old cardboard box that she found behind an earthen jar of rice chaff. She worried that the money might get moldy in the cardboard box, so she grabbed a plastic bag and wrapped the box inside it before putting it back behind the earthen jar. The plan was to wait for a day, then head back over to South Gully and donate it to the pagoda project.

From the main room, she heard Halfwit yelling, "Hey! Hey!" She realized he must have been calling for her, but she ignored him. "Have you got your ears stuffed full of donkey hair?" he asked.

"What are you barking for?" she asked.

"Make us some *jianbing*. Get some leaves off the pepper bush at my big brother's place. Nothing better than pepper leaves in *jianbing*."

"No way. The last time I went over there to pick some leaves, Chastity got angry at me for taking them."

"What's she worried about? It's just a couple of leaves. Go!"

"If you want them, get them yourself."

Halfwit slammed down the mah-jongg tiles and went off to Gold's place to pick the pepper leaves. When he came back, he shouted at his wife, "You brought Chastity up to that shrine in South Gully?"

"She wanted to know her fortune, so we went to pull some strips. She wanted me to take her up there. You think I should have just refused?"

Halfwit slapped his wife. He was too short to reach her, so he had to jump. "It's a waste of goddamn time," he said. "Shiner is already on a bus headed for Xinjiang! If you hadn't brought her out there, she would have been in the village and stopped him from leaving. Now she's threatening to kill herself! It's all your fault."

"Heavens!" cried Halfwit's wife, then she turned and went out.

Halfwit aimed one final swipe at her as she left, saying, "Where are you going? Haven't you done enough already? Why not just stay home?"

She took the slap without crying, then sat down out in the yard for a while before returning to the kitchen to start making *jianbing*. Halfwit's wife couldn't sew worth a damn, but among the five daughters-in-law, she made the best bread.

Her mother had died when she was still young. Starting at four years old, she had dragged a stool over to the table and began learning to make the various breads, cakes, and other doughy staples of the village. She'd been married long enough to know what her husband was like and what their life together would hold. She was resigned to her fate.

She didn't bother crying anymore or making scenes. She knew what she had to do and did it. When the *jianbing* were cooked, she felt twinges in her breasts. The baby was still at her mother's place, so there would be no chance to use the milk. She pulled her full, tender breasts out of her shirt and squeezed the milk out over the fire. She put the *jianbing* out on a plate, then filled four bowls with vinegar and chili oil. She closed the kitchen door, went out into the yard, and called, "The *jianbing* are ready!"

With her work done, she prepared to go out to pick up the baby. As she was headed for the gate, Cutie appeared, coming in from the alley, her face green as a cucumber. With her breasts bouncing like two sacks of water, Cutie couldn't run very fast. Halfwit's wife couldn't help but laugh. "Is there a wolf chasing you or something?" she asked.

Cutie kept running, making it another three steps before she finally said, "What are you doing right now?" She squeezed the bridge of her nose and blew snot across the wall.

"I'm going to get the baby. She's at her grandmother's place."

"Then come with me," Cutie said.

Halfwit stumbled along behind her, heading out to the alley and then into the street without knowing where she was being led. "Did you know Shiner went to Xinjiang?" she asked Cutie.

"Good for him. What is he going to do, stuck here?"

"His poor mother's saying she's going to kill herself!"

"She's still better off than me," Cutie said.

Halfwit's wife didn't think that was true, but she wasn't going to tell Cutie that. She put her head down and kept following her, focusing on putting one foot in front of the other. She suddenly noticed that Cutie's head seemed to have a big red rooster's comb on it. "Sister," she said, "why do you have a rooster comb on your head?"

"If I was a rooster, I'd peck someone!"

When Halfwit's wife looked back again, she saw that it wasn't a rooster's comb but a ball of flame. She rubbed her eyes, and the flames were gone, too.

The two women were headed for the House of Treasures, kicking up dust on the road along the way. When they arrived, Roughshod Ding was sitting on a stone roller out front, eating a bowl of noodles that he had heaped with chilies. He tilted his head down toward the bowl and was just sucking in a mouthful of noodles when he saw Cutie. He hurriedly swallowed the noodles and jumped down from the stone roller. "Hey, Shorty," Cutie said. "Is Pavilion in there?"

"What's wrong?" Roughshod Ding asked.

"He hasn't been home in days. He's up there with some whore, isn't he?"

"Huh? What are you trying to say? I hope you're not casting aspersions on my operation. You think I've got whores working here?"

"Everyone knows those waitresses you hired are doing double duty. Shifty's been running around telling everyone. So when my Pavilion doesn't come home for a few days . . . Does he even remember he has a family?"

"Brother Pavilion is a village cadre," Roughshod Ding said. "That's just the way it is with these guys. You think a big deal cadre like him can just rush home whenever he wants?"

"Big deal? He's not even bigger than my fingernail."

"You don't consider him a big deal? Fine. I wouldn't expect you to understand. The way I see it, he's Freshwind's own Chairman Mao."

"I know he's up there," Cutie said. "If he isn't, why don't you let me go up and check?"

Roughshod Ding suddenly laughed and said, "I promise you Pavilion's not up there. What are you, a cop? Are you conducting a raid?"

"What are you yelling for? Are you trying to warn them?" Cutie turned to Halfwit's wife and said, "You watch the door. I'm going up to take a look."

Halfwit's wife had finally figured out what she had been brought along for. She wasn't particularly interested in this plot to catch a husband screwing around on his wife, and she thought it was better not to get involved, so once Cutie turned away, Halfwit's wife walked away. But as she went, she heard Pavilion yelling upstairs, "What the hell are you doing? What are you yelling about? Huh?" She decided to wait and see what would happen.

Pavilion came down the stairs with his shirt hung over his shoulders. Cutie was waiting for him at the bottom of the stairs. "Roughshod said you weren't up there," she said. "What the hell were you up to?"

"I have to report to you all of my official duties?" Pavilion asked. "Just go home. You're the only woman in the village who behaves like this. You think I'm going to get anything done with you running your mouth like that?"

He aimed a kick at Cutie's backside, but she scrambled away and headed up the stairs. From below, Pavilion heard a door being kicked open. Cutie had discovered the woman lying in Pavilion's bed. She leaped on the woman, pulled her out of the bed, and began slapping her. Roughshod Ding ran up the stairs first, followed by Pavilion. They came upon the two women, already locked together in combat, scratching and pulling hair. Roughshod Ding waded in to separate them, then grabbed them both by their hair and jerked them apart.

"That woman is a waitress here," Roughshod Ding said. "Who do you think you are, just attacking people indiscriminately?"

"What is she doing, lying around in bed in the middle of the day?" Cutie asked.

"She can't have a nap?"

"Why's she naked then?" Cutie pointed at the woman and said, "You want to prove you're innocent, spread that pussy open and let me see if he left anything in there." At that moment, Pavilion grabbed Cutie and gave her a slap. "You want me to make her bed for her?" Cutie wailed. "Is that what you want?"

"What are you screaming for?" Pavilion roared. "Scream one more time and see what happens!"

Cutie went quiet. Halfwit's wife had gone upstairs, too, once she heard the fight, and she pulled Cutie toward the stairs. Pavilion ran a hand through his hair and prepared to go downstairs, too, but before he went, he gave the woman who had been in his bed a final kick.

Chapter 33

The story of Cutie causing a ruckus at the House of Treasures spread through Freshwind, of course, but that didn't stop her from showing up there the next day. Her purpose in returning to the House of Treasures was not to start more trouble, but rather to apologize. She told the crowd of villagers who had assembled outside that she had wronged both Pavilion and the waitress. Of course, this was Pavilion's idea. If he had let the matter drop, there wouldn't have been an issue. But her little performance in front of the House of Treasures had made people think there might have been more to the story than they had first thought.

On one hand, you had to admire Pavilion's ability to deal with his wife. There weren't many men in Freshwind who were capable of controlling their wives. But I also discovered, based on my own observations hanging around Pavilion's place, that after the incident at the House of Treasures, Pavilion started arriving home like clockwork every evening to eat dinner and climb into bed. I also saw that Wisdom Xia had given Rain Xia a dressing down. Not long after that, the waitress disappeared from the House of Treasures.

When the woman disappeared, Shifty didn't go back to the House of Treasures for a long while. Finally, Roughshod Ding tried to lure him back with five dried donkey penises he'd gotten up north. He'd had the penises boiled in the runoff water from washing rice, then he went to find Shifty.

"Come and eat some donkey medallions," he told him. "You won't regret it. I only had them soaking for half an hour before they swelled up."

"I'm already all heated up," Shifty said. "If I eat those, I'll have blood gushing out of my nose." He took a seat out front of the hotel and called the barber over to give his head a shave. He took a piece of charcoal and wrote on the wall:

> You can drink your liquor and get some head,
> As long as you go back to wifey's bed.
> Yes, you can go out and get your rocks off,

But come home early or she'll cut your cock off,
And you'll live your whole life in dread.

Rain Xia knew who the doggerel was meant for. He grabbed a piece of roof tile and scraped it away.

After that, nothing seemed to happen in Freshwind for a long time. It was a dull period in the village. Every night when I came back from Seven Li Gully, Auntie Wang was sitting at her loom, the blacksmith's shop was closed, and the donkey at the dyehouse gave one final bray.

One night, I caught Obedient Zhang dozing on the counter at the farm store. I slapped the counter, and he woke up, saying, "Huh? What do you need?"

"You fine?" I asked him.

"I opened a new cask of liquor, but Bright Chen was around to give it a suck to get it started."

"Who says I'm hanging around for a taste of your liquor?" I said.

When I arrived back home, I got into bed. The brick I used for a pillow felt like it was flattening one side of my head. I couldn't sleep, so I sat up again. I was thinking about Snow Bai. I missed her.

I thought about that day when I had seen Bright Chen walking down the street with a load of apples from the orchard. Up on the carrying pole, he'd stuck a bouquet of roses. I grabbed an apple and was just about to take a bite when he said, "That'll be one jiao." I didn't have any money on me. I tossed the apple back into the basket and took the bouquet of roses instead.

"I don't have to pay for these, right?" I asked. As soon as I took them, I started to feel like I'd blossomed, just like the flowers.

That night, my mood suddenly got even better, and I knew it was the beginning of more good things coming my way. I grabbed the flowers and sang "Watching the Sun Sink into the Ocean."

Rain Xia yelled for me to shut up. He wanted to borrow our tractor, saying he was going to go to the opera company to bring back some of Snow Bai's stuff. Great, I thought, since that meant Snow Bai would probably come along, too, or at least it would be a chance for me to help her out. "Sure!" I told him. I looked over at the roses. The petals were so delicate. It looked like they were about to speak.

"Uncle Justice might not want me borrowing it," Rain Xia said.

"I said it's fine!"

"Fine, get it ready for me, then when I need it tomorrow, I'll just come by."

I went to find Tongue-Tied. I told him I needed the tractor, but I didn't say for what. I drove it back from West Street and parked it in my yard, then I started washing it. I was still working when the chickens were already settling in for the night. I hadn't even had time to eat. Suddenly, Rain Xia came rushing into the yard. "We aren't going tonight, are we?" I asked, jumping behind the controls of the tractor.

"First thing tomorrow," Rain Xia said, "but I'm going to park it over at the House of Treasures."

"You're gonna drive it?" I asked.

"Yes."

"You don't trust my driving? I'll drive it real steady."

"I'm borrowing the tractor, not hiring a driver."

That Rain Xia, the little monkey, what was he trying to do to me? Right away, I considered going back on my offer to lend him the tractor, but a promise was a promise. I slammed the tractor's control stick away and said, "Go ahead. You drive it then."

He took the controls and pulled it out of the gate, but I pleaded with him to wait until the next day to drive it over to the House of Treasures. I wanted him to leave the tractor at my place overnight, and then I'd drive it over in the morning for him to pick up. "Listen! Exciter's crying . . ." And if you listened to the tractor's motor, it really did sound like a choking sob.

"Have you lost it again, or what?" Rain Xia said. He dropped the tractor's controls and left.

That night, I made myself a bowl of noodles and split them with the tractor. I'd eat a mouthful, then offer some to Exciter. By the end, there were exactly thirty-two noodles hung from the hood of the tractor. "Exciter," I told the tractor, "when we head out tomorrow, you have to be a good boy. I don't want you being moody. Just remember, you'll be carrying Snow Bai, and you can't shake her around." I promised Exciter I'd give him a bottle of the best diesel oil as long as he got her there and back, safe and sound.

I used to thank my body, running through each limb and organ. I'd thank my eyes, my legs and my feet, my heart, my liver, my lungs, and my stomach . . . I'd even thank my asshole. They worked so hard for me. They let me see Snow Bai. Even if I was lacking a certain part of my body, I could still take a piss, at least. I could still live. I owed each part of my body a debt of gratitude. I had to thank Exciter for the same reason. To me, he was much more than a lump of iron.

The next day, even though I was in Seven Li Gully, I could still see what was going on aboard the tractor. That was because I had thanked Exciter. I could see everything, so I knew that Star Chen had hitched a ride, carrying two sacks of apples to the county seat to sell. On the way there, he plucked at his guitar, singing:

> You said our love was sealed,
> Why'd you go and leave me now?
> You must know how I truly feel,
> To you I've sworn a solemn vow.

While Star Chen played, Snow Bai lay motionless in the back of the tractor, her eyes red from crying.

"I wanted to ask you," Rain Xia said. "How are you and Emerald doing?"

Star Chen stopped singing. He looked out at the white poplars along the road, watching them pass, one by one. He didn't answer Rain Xia, and he didn't go back to singing.

"Do you know what she's up to in Xijing? You know what kind of work she's doing?" Rain Xia asked.

"Do you?" Star Chen asked.

"I don't know."

The tractor rolled over a chunk of stone in the road and bounced violently. Star Chen hit his head against the top of the tractor's cab, raising a red lump on his forehead. One of the sacks tipped over, spilling apples. The apples rolled around in the back of the tractor. Star Chen didn't cry out in pain. He didn't put his hand to his head. He looked as if he was about to cry.

Snow Bai picked up the guitar, but she didn't play it. "Have you written any new songs?" she asked.

"Yeah."

"Sing something for me."

"Okay."

He sang:

> Driver rolling down the 312
> Coming out of Xijing
> Tell me, did you see a girl with a red string in her hair?
> That's my little Emerald
> She carried my heart with her when she went
> She took my heart and lost it in the big city

Star Chen might not have been a local boy, but he had the power to move Snow Bai with his song. She didn't cry, but she came close. She inhaled deeply. "You've really got something there, Star Chen," she said. "Teach it to me."

"You want to learn from him?" Rain Xia asked.

"Keep your eyes on the road," Snow Bai said.

"You sing the local opera," Star Chen said. "What do you want to sing folk songs for?"

"Star Chen," Rain Xia said, "you must be confused. That's a pop song, not a folk song."

"That's where you're wrong," Snow Bai said. "Back in the day, folk songs were like pop music is now. And pop music now is like our folk music. I've been singing opera for ten years, but I still haven't made a name for myself. I want to be like you, singing whenever I feel like singing, singing what's in my heart. I want to be able to comfort myself with a song."

"Comfort yourself?" asked Rain Xia. "You know, there's a saying, when women are worried, they cry, and when men are worried, they sing . . . You should teach me the song, instead!"

"You're having girl trouble, too?" Snow Bai asked.

"Of course," said Rain Xia. "But the way I see it, if she wants to leave, she can go ahead and leave."

"Where does she want to go?"

"Xijing. There's no way to tie her spirit down in Freshwind."

The apples started to roll around again and finally came to rest in the corner. Snow Bai thought it was a good idea to change the topic. She looked at the apples and said, "You think you can sell these in the city?"

"Who knows," said Rain Xia. "I have to sell them somewhere, or they'll end up rotting."

Snow Bai lay down again in the back of the tractor. *What the hell is going on?* she said to herself.

While packing up all her things in the opera company dormitory, Snow Bai had come across a flute. Wisdom Xia had loved that flute very much, but he hadn't had the lungs to play it himself. He could blow a few notes through it, but he could never put together a melody. Every morning when he went out for his walk, he'd stand in the alley and listen to Snow Bai play her flute. She played the same song every day.

Fourth Aunt had said once, "When I listen to you play, it's like I can hear the sound of bamboo in the wind."

"Oh!" Snow Bai had exclaimed. "You really know your stuff. The piece I always play is actually called 'Bamboo in the Wind'!"

"I don't know anything about that," Fourth Aunt had said. "You can play now and then, but I want you to be careful. If you blow that flute too much, it could harm your child!"

"It should be fine. It's good for the child to hear music. It's a kind of prenatal education."

Snow Bai began to play the flute again. Wisdom Xia stayed in the alley for a while, listening, but he finally decided he should go into the yard. Snow Bai stopped playing.

"It was sounding good," Wisdom Xia said. He thought it was a pity that his daughter-in-law never played the flute or sang in front of him.

"No, it wasn't," said Snow Bai. She blushed and rushed off to her own small room.

Snow Bai could hear her mother-in-law saying in a low voice, "I've never seen a father-in-law behave like you do."

"She plays well, that's all," Wisdom Xia had said, then sat down in his chair in the main room, solemnly pulling on his pipe.

That night, after returning from the dormitory, Snow Bai had a dream about the flute. It was hanging on the wall and began to call in a soft tone: "I want to go home! I want to go home!" the flute seemed to be saying. Snow Bai told Rain Xia about it, and he told Roughshod Ding about it, and that's when I heard about it. After she woke up from the dream, she couldn't get back to sleep. She looked up and saw the flute hanging on the wall, bathed in an eerie light coming in through the window. She lay awake for the rest of the night, watching it.

The story of the flute is one that goes back very far. Among the opera troupe's members, only Snow Bai and Victory Bai came from the area west of the county seat. They were distant relatives who had known each other for ages. Snow Bai was from Freshwind, of course, and Victory Bai was from nearby West Mountain Bend. Victory Bai played two kinds of flute in the performances: a side-blown bamboo flute, and a vertical flute like the one Snow Bai had gotten from her father-in-law. In the past, Victory Bai had picked up Snow Bai from her dormitory every Sunday, and he'd dropped her off in Freshwind on the way back to his home village. He always carried his favorite flute—a vertical flute like Snow Bai's—in his bag. When he returned home, he liked to go up to the mountain range behind his house and play for the butterflies who flew around him.

Snow Bai told him that she didn't believe him, that butterflies would gather around him while he played, so Victory Bai invited her to come with him. She had always turned him down until one night, shortly before her engagement, she went up into the mountains with him. The sky overhead was full of stars, but there were no butterflies. "You were just bragging, weren't you? I don't see any butterflies."

"I see one," Victory Bai said. "One big, beautiful butterfly."

He'd given the flute to her that night. She hung it on the wall in her room. Even after Victory Bai was dead and gone, the flute stayed on her wall. Wind Xia didn't know where the flute had come from, and Snow Bai didn't tell him. He'd asked her once if she knew how to play it. She'd lied and told him that she couldn't play it but that sometimes, in the middle of the night, it would play itself. Snow Bai hadn't been serious when she'd said that. It wasn't until her dream that she heard the flute play itself. The day after she'd had the dream, she hadn't been thinking much about the flute, but that night she dreamed again that the flute was calling to her. "I want to go home! I want to go home!"

She had the same dream for three nights in a row. She was scared; anyone could have seen in her face that she was worried about something. She thought to herself, *Maybe it's Victory Bai's ghost trying to send me a message.* Was Victory Bai angry that she'd kept the flute and still played it every day? Four days after she'd had the dream the first time, she went out after breakfast, telling Fourth Aunt that she was going to her mother's house. "What are you taking the flute with you for?" Fourth Aunt asked.

"My nephew said he wants to learn to play," Snow Bai lied. "I'm going to lend it to him." She went out of the yard toward the West Street archway and turned onto the 312, heading northwest toward West Mountain Bend.

Now, I should probably mention what I was up to that day, or we can't get into the next part of this story. There are many parts of this story that may not seem to go together but in fact are closely connected. There was a haze covering the sun that day and dark clouds in the sky. When I looked up, it reminded me of a shattered pane of glass—or maybe a spiderweb, the sun being the spider in the web.

We were working over at Seven Li Gully, as usual. That seedling that Justice Xia had protected with his hat during the hailstorm had already grown twice as tall. Most of the time, a seedling planted at that time of year would only grow to about four fingers tall and then go dormant until the next spring. But that seedling was growing fast! I'd never seen anything like it, and Justice Xia, who was over seventy, had never seen anything like it, either. Not too far from the seedling was the tree I'd planted. The birds that had made a home in it still sang to us every day. These three things—the seedling, the tree, and the birds—were the three miracles of Seven Li Gully. We knew we had to protect them. There are many things that must be kept secret, because revealing them would be like divulging the secrets of the universe. I thought that must have been what happened with Tongue-Tied. He'd talked too much in a previous life, so he'd been struck dumb in this one.

Right then, as Tongue-Tied was driving down the gully, the tractor's motor died. No matter what he did, he couldn't get it started again. Justice Xia swore at Tongue-Tied, and I was sent into the village to find Marvel since he used to work on farm equipment. I looked all over but I couldn't find Marvel. When his mother heard that Justice Xia had sent me, she took my hand and asked me if it was still getting hot at midday over at the gully, and if it wasn't very cold in the evenings. She wanted to know if Justice Xia was looking after himself. She just kept going on and on. I didn't have time to waste answering all her questions.

I ran over to Middle Street and started asking if anyone had seen Marvel. It turned out he'd just been to Big-Noise Zhao's place to collect his electrical fees and was headed over to New-Life's orchard. As I was running past the House of Treasures, I suddenly felt a few drops of water on my head. I thought it must have been raining, but when I looked up, I saw that Henanese guy, Big-Guy Ma, standing up on a second-floor balcony with the tinker's wife. She was holding a baby out to piss.

"Watch where you're pointing that thing," I said.

She turned the child away from me. Big-Guy Ma gave a honking laugh that showed off his nicotine-stained teeth.

I was pissed off, but the tinker's wife said, "Spark, it's good luck to get pissed on! There're good things coming your way."

It's true there was a saying in Freshwind that it was good luck for a baby to pee on you, so I couldn't be angry at her. I bowed my head and walked away. I thought to myself, *What good things could possibly be coming my way?*

I got out to the brickyard along the 312 and saw Shifty squatting in front of the kiln, pulling on a bottle of liquor. He didn't call me over, so I just ignored him. I took the road leading toward West Mountain Bend, since it was a shortcut to the orchard. Looking down the road, I saw a figure in the distance. I realized it must be Snow Bai.

After Snow Bai reached West Mountain Bend, she stood for a while at the entrance to the village, unsure of whether to go to Victory Bai's grave or to the little house with the stone wall where Victory Bai's elderly mother lived. She paced back and forth and finally decided to visit Victory Bai's mother. On her way there, she stopped at a store near the village entrance and bought a bag of milk powder and two packages of cookies.

The years had not been kind to the old gate in front of Victory Bai's mother's house. The tiles that ran over the top of the gate were sprouting grass, and there were still tattered remnants of the white paper pasted up for Victory Bai's funeral. Snow Bai felt a pang of sadness as she stood in front of the gate. She closed her eyes and tried to gather her thoughts. Finally, she reached up to the iron knocker on the gate—bang! bang! bang! Before she finished knocking, she could hear footsteps, but it sounded as if someone was rushing out of the yard and into the house, rather than coming to open the gate.

Snow Bai knocked again, calling out, "Auntie! Auntie!" She heard a rustling in the yard. She peered through a crack in the gate and was surprised to see a pair of eyes staring back at her.

"Is that Snow Bai?" the old woman asked. The gate swung open with a creak, and the old woman dragged Snow Bai into the yard before shutting the gate behind her.

The old woman's hair had gone as white as frost, and there were wrinkles across her nose. She felt Snow Bai's face with her hands. As she rubbed at Snow Bai's cheeks, Victory Bai's mother saw that she was carrying the flute. The wrinkles on the old woman's face deepened, and her face seemed to shrink. She looked like a walnut. She began to cry, the tears running through her wrinkles instead of sliding down her face.

Snow Bai hugged her, and both women shivered. The old woman relaxed her grip and stepped back. "Did you come to see me, Snow Bai?" she said. "I said to myself, I couldn't be that lucky, to have Snow Bai come and visit." ·

Snow Bai began to cry, too, and Victory Bai's mother wiped her tears away. As they went into the yard, Snow Bai noticed a bamboo pole hung with an old rag with a shit stain the size of a hen's egg on it. She didn't think too much about it and pushed upon the door. The first thing she saw inside the room was Victory Bai's faint smile in his framed funeral portrait. She bit her lip and took a few steps forward, feeling as if she were being pulled toward the frame. She took the flute and set it down in front of Victory Bai's portrait.

She did not dare say it out loud, but she thought, *Victory Bai, here is your flute. I know you wanted it back.*

From the doorway fluttered a black butterfly that came to perch on Victory Bai's portrait. The butterfly flapped its wings a few times, seemed to bow, and then stayed motionless. Snow Bai shivered. She went weak in the knees and had to lean against the cabinet to stop herself from keeling over.

The old woman had turned away before seeing Snow Bai's reaction. She pulled back the door curtain covering the entrance to the room on the eastern side of the house. "It's fine," she said; "it's just Snow Bai."

Snow Bai was surprised to see Switch come into the room, holding her baby in her arms. "What are you doing here?" Snow Bai asked.

"Auntie and my mom were always close. I thought you knew. When Victory Bai was alive, I used to tell him we should get married so our families would be related for real."

Victory Bai's mother cut her off, saying, "Look at the baby. You helped to save this baby."

Snow Bai took the baby into her arms. She was surprised by its weight. "You weren't supposed to be born at all," she said, "and now look at what a plump baby you are."

476

Snow Bai had only been planning to return the flute and see Victory Bai's mother; she hadn't planned to run into Switch. She stayed longer than she'd expected, and the old woman made them each a bowl of fried eggs. After Snow Bai left, she felt a sense of peace at having returned the flute to its rightful owner.

She walked for a while along the river and then scrambled up onto the plateau where the road back to Freshwind ran. Both sides of the road were lined with embankments planted with persimmon trees. The fruit and the leaves had been picked, and the trees were skeletal and black, their bare branches clawing the sky. The branches could never have reached the clouds, but the wind puffed them away, just in case.

I was right; the figure in the distance was Snow Bai. My body suddenly felt hot, and I felt a twinge of anxiety. I wanted to go right up to her, but I wasn't actually headed for West Mountain Bend, so I'd have to pretend I was going that way originally and just happened to run into her. I was trying to work up the nerve to move, and to stop myself from blushing. I started walking again, awkwardly, not sure what to do with my hands. How come that dog Shifty could be so brazen with women? I mean, I could be brave with other women, but not with Snow Bai.

I patted my face. *Don't worry,* I told myself. *Just go. Lift your head up and go!* I took two steps. But I wasn't sure what I would do when I finally got up to her. I was worried that I was going to scare her if I just rushed up to her. I gave a loud cough, hoping to let her know that I was there, but she didn't hear it. She turned away and looked up at the persimmon trees. What would I do if I did get her attention? Give her a nod? A smile? Say something to her? I started getting nervous again. I sighed. If there was anybody else around, I could be more natural, but it was just me and Snow Bai out there. I couldn't work up the nerve. I jumped off the road and into the trough behind the embankment. I watched her walk by, and I immediately regretted letting her go. I pounded the dirt with my fists, then smashed my forehead into the dust.

Somewhere nearby, a crow ridiculed me, saying, "Caw! Caw! What an idiot!"

I wanted to tell that crow, *This is the best way. Secret, unrequited love is the safest. It's like a key that you can use to open every room in your house.*

That day, Snow Bai was wearing a floral jacket and black pants with really wide legs. Instead of her usual high heels, she wore flats with a little ribbon across the top and leather uppers that showed off the white of her ankles. As she passed by, I could see her neck and her breasts and the curve of her lower back above her ass. I couldn't control myself. I had a bad problem. No matter what I told myself, I couldn't overcome it. My hand slid down the front of my pants. There was only a little nub left, a ruined little remnant of what had once grown there. It was useless. But from it shot a load of liquid that fired out across the grass, hitting a locust. The locust was knocked from its blade of grass and rolled around in the dust before finally hopping away. I had no idea how it had happened. How could my body still have that function? It wasn't me who was the pervert—my own body had betrayed me. I floated up out of my body, leaving it below me like a petrified snake lying in the ditch, and watched Snow Bai going down the road.

Snow Bai hadn't seen me. She stepped off the road and down off the plateau. As she crossed the 312, she didn't notice the ashy brown moth that had settled on her shoulder. When she got home, the moth rose from her shoulder, flapped up to the tiles across the gate, and disappeared.

Chapter 34

It got colder still. The hens began to molt until they'd lost all the feathers from their necks and tails. Second Aunt worked on the persimmons she had picked and brought home; she pulled off the stems and packed the fruit in a jar to ferment. After a couple of weeks the vinegar was ready and the whole house smelled sour. There were fewer mosquitoes but more flies, drawn in by the smell and now squatting all along the electrical wiring.

Justice Xia collected thirty-seven cicada shells from the willow trees by the pond and three snakeskins from the embankment. Ground down into a powder, they could be used to treat middle-ear infections. Shiner had had ear infections as a child—they leaked a stinky pus. But just as Justice Xia was going to give the shells to Second Aunt to put away, he remembered that Shiner had left Freshwind Village, so he put them on the windowsill instead.

He dug in his pocket and offered Second Aunt a sour date. "Try this." And he sat down on the doorstep and rolled up his pant legs, scratching so furiously that the dry skin fell like fish scales.

Second Aunt put the date in her mouth, then spat it out. "You know that I've lost half of my teeth. I can't eat this stuff!"

"I'll make sure you get some false teeth," said Rites Xia. "Favor Bai's brother-in-law has a set, and they're very good."

That very day, a letter from Shiner reached Freshwind, and Justice Xia, just this once, didn't go to Seven Li Gully. Instead, he moped around his yard all afternoon. Shiner and his fiancée had gone to Xinjiang, and the letter was the first news they'd had of them. Gold had been dropping by the post office to see if there were any letters for him, but when this one finally arrived, it was addressed to Justice Xia. There was a small package, too, containing an extendable back scratcher in the shape of a hand. On the back of the hand, it said, "Shiner's hand," and on the palm, "Your dutiful grandson."

Justice Xia felt sad, but instead of saying something nice about his grandson, he tossed the scratcher aside. Of the younger generation, only Wind Xia had achieved anything. None of the others had brought honor and glory to the family name. Justice Xia believed in the old proverb: the only good people were faithful ministers and filial sons, and the only paths to success were through doing well at school or tilling the land. Good school results could get you a secure government job, but Gold, Treasure, Bounty, and Thunder had either done badly or dropped out without finishing. If you flunked out of school, you should be a good farmer instead. Rain Xia could have been one, but unfortunately, he'd chosen to hang around with Roughshod Ding.

The grandchildren were even worse. Justice Xia felt mortified. Emerald had left, followed by Shiner. Both had gone to get jobs in the city after falling out with their family. Justice Xia couldn't understand why these young people refused to settle down and work the land. The land was the one thing that never let you down, and yet they'd left it. As he sat glumly in his yard, the gate was pushed open a crack and Lucky slipped in, followed by Tiger and a tumble of small puppies. Justice Xia did not notice until Lucky picked up the back scratcher to carry it into the house and knocked it against the door.

He looked up and shouted, "Scram!"

Lucky cringed in terror, and Justice even found himself frightened. But his terror came from the sudden realization that it was all over for the Xia clan. Now that Emerald and Shiner were gone, they were likely to be followed by Pavilion's son and maybe Culture. None of the younger generation liked farming, so they would all leave Freshwind, but not for government jobs. They were going to end up as not-quite-peasants and not-quite-workers, not-quite-villagers and not-quite-townsfolk. Were they going to float through life as rootless as pondweed?

Justice Xia sighed. The fault lay with Pavilion as the village head, with Freshwind Village itself, and, most of all, with the Xias. They'd all failed.

That evening, he went to Clerk's wife's restaurant, but for perhaps the first time in his life, he didn't touch his bowl of *liang fen* noodles. Instead, he carried the bowl over to the Earth Gods' shrine on the opposite side of the street. He made an offering of the noodles to the statues of the Earth Goddess and the Earth God. Then he stomped hard with his foot so that the flock of hens pecking in the dirt at the gate took off, squawking loudly.

Justice Xia sat in the shrine until it grew dark. Eventually, Clerk's wife got worried about her noodle bowl and came over to retrieve it. "What are you doing sitting here in the dark, Uncle?" she exclaimed.

Justice Xia said nothing, just got up and left. At the end of the alley, he met Rain Xia coming toward him. "Rain Xia, do you remember the stone slab in the eighteen-*mu* field?" he asked.

Rain Xia looked confused. "Stone slab?" he queried.

"It had characters written on it, 'Blocking evil spirits like Tai Mountain.'"

"Oh, right, I remember."

"What happened to it after that?"

"I don't know what happened to it. Maybe it was used to cover the drains when the streets were done?"

Justice Xia opened his mouth, revealing a hole full of black-stained teeth. "Ah," he said. "Maybe it went for a drain cover."

"What made you think of that, Second Uncle?"

Justice didn't answer directly. "I want you to do something . . . Get a big piece of limestone and carve on it, 'Blocking evil spirits like Tai Mountain,' and put it at the top of the alley. Can you do that?"

"Easy as pie!" said Rain Xia. "But why there?"

"I got the last one carved and put in the eighteen-*mu* field during the land reform. We needed protection. And after that the rich peasants and landlords didn't cause us any more bother," said Justice Xia. "You can see what's happening to Freshwind Village now; we need something to keep the demons away . . . You young folk probably don't believe in that kind of thing anymore," he added.

"I believe, of course I do!" said Rain Xia. "I need to find a big slab of limestone."

He found one in the stream and got the characters carved on it. But he didn't put it at the top of the alley. Instead he placed it at the entrance to the House of Treasures Hotel.

That annoyed the hell out of Justice Xia, and his hopes for this nephew of his faded, especially now that he'd heard rumors of prostitutes at the House of Treasures. After that, when Rain Xia arrived while he was in Wisdom Xia's yard, he got up and left.

Once Wisdom invited him over for a drink and began to grumble that Rain Xia never lifted a finger at home. He was supposed to be digging a cellar for Lotus Jin's niece's house but had nothing to show for a day and a night of digging. "What kind of a son have I brought up?" he exclaimed. "The woman was all right about it for the first two days, but after that she got annoyed. Rain Xia's a lazy oaf, isn't he?"

"Of course he is," said Justice Xia. "He knows he can get away with it."

Fourth Aunt was not at all pleased when she heard this. "An uncle shouldn't badmouth his nephew, however much of a bad boy Rain Xia is," she said to Wisdom Xia in the kitchen.

"Well, you know what my brother's like."

"He's turning everyone against him." She ladled out the bowls of noodles for the guests, putting two fried eggs at the bottom for Goodness, who was visiting, and one fried egg at the bottom of Justice Xia's bowl.

Finally, Justice Xia summoned all the grandsons and granddaughters to Seven Li Gully. The sky was covered with clouds, and it was blowing hard, the gusts of wind ruffling the leaves of the willows, the pagoda trees, and the poplars, and catching the feathers of the hens so they seemed to roll like balls of yarn down the alley. Culture had been asleep and was reluctant to go, but he knew he had to all the same.

Justice Xia led them along, a scowl on his face and a rope in his hand. The wind mussed their hair and whipped dust up into their faces, and once they arrived and stood at the embankment, there was nowhere to sit, so they had to stand while Justice Xia delivered a long lecture about how the Xia clan had migrated along the Han River to escape war and starvation in Hunan, how they had crossed the Qinling Mountains and broken the first sod in this wild valley ringed by mountains. At first, the village had consisted only of East Street, but during the Qing dynasty other families began to move in, and it expanded to include Middle Street and West Street. His story made little impression on the young people; they grumbled about the miserable place their ancestors had settled on. Why hadn't they gone to the Guanzhong Plain, or even Xijing?

"Don't talk nonsense," said Justice Xia.

"But they didn't choose a particularly good place," Culture said. "At Guanzhong, the scallions grow two feet tall, but here they make a few inches at most. You can't deny that."

"How dare you talk like that about your ancestors?" Justice Xia said. "Where would you be without them?"

"Babies are just a by-product of having a bit of fun," Culture muttered, so quietly that it took a moment for Justice Xia to take in what he'd said.

He glared furiously at Culture but had to admit there was truth in it, so he let it go. He carried on with his narrative—how he and his brothers and cousins had turned the river mudflats into fields, and how there wasn't a man in the village who didn't end up with a great callus on each shoulder from the carrying poles. He told how they had terraced fields on the valley slopes; how, in just one winter, Marvel's mom had collected thirty-two hundred pairs of worn-out straw sandals from where they'd been working; how they'd brought the stones in to build the reservoir; how they only had toasted, ground-up rice husks for their lunch and not even any water to drink.

"Wasn't the river full of water?" Culture wondered.

"What? What did you say?" demanded Justice Xia.

Culture, abashed, went quiet, and Justice Xia continued his tale. So many people had been injured turning the mudflats into fields; so many more had fallen sick with exhaustion building the terraces. His eldest brother, their great-uncle, had died working on the reservoir.

The young ones already knew this part of the story, but they'd also heard that when he was a village cadre, he'd opposed the county's plans to take over some of the village land and build a coking plant in Freshwind, on the grounds that it would take arable land from the village, and finally the coking plant had been located eighty *li* away, in Zhaochuan Township.

"And now Zhaochuan's turned into a city," said someone.

"So what?" said Justice Xia. "It's nothing but coal there. It makes your piss black for years after."

"Shanghai was occupied by foreigners, and look at it now!" said someone else.

"You kids are just a bunch of scoundrels! There's nothing good about imperialist invasions. Whoever gave you that idea?" The old man was so angry that he stopped talking and put them to work instead in an attempt to reeducate them. He got Big-Noise Zhao to copy a rhyming couplet on the cliff face of the gully in red paint, then paint the numbers one to twenty onto stones and boulders in the gully. The young people then had to carry twenty marked stones each up to the embankment, where he stood waiting to inspect them. They had to earn three hundred work points in a day. Justice Xia told them that was the way it was done when they were building the fields, except back then they'd had to earn double that to get enough to eat!

The kids, naturally enough, goofed around, using their head wraps to dip in the still-wet paint and change a number two on a stone into an eight, or a twelve. Justice Xia didn't notice a thing. He was delighted with their progress and went into the shack to make a fire and bake potatoes for them as a reward. They got three each.

His daughters-in-law were none too pleased that Justice Xia had set their children to work laboring in the gully, but they didn't dare say anything. After Culture's parents divorced, he'd started skipping school, and his mom couldn't get him into class even though she came after him with the kang brush. So when, after several days' labor in the gully, he complained that his shoulders and legs hurt, she said, "Your granddad's teaching you a lesson. If you don't go back to class, hefting stones is what you'll end up doing for the rest of your life."

Blossom wasn't happy about her little boy working there, either, but she didn't try very hard to stop him. He was a disobedient little tyke, and at least Justice Xia was looking after him properly, and he could pick some pumpkins to bring back with him.

We'd planted pumpkin vines on the new land we'd made by filling the gully, and the pumpkins had grown huge, so Justice Xia used to cut one on his way home and give it to the first person he came across in the village, telling them smugly where it had grown. He'd chucked a few seeds here and there, he said, and the vines had grown fully three yards long, with pumpkins the size of sifting baskets. When Blossom's boy took pumpkins home with him, Justice Xia said nothing, but pretty soon those pumpkins were going to give him a bellyful of trouble.

It was Shifty's fault. His wife hadn't managed to get pregnant. Now that the fuss about his affair with White-Moth had blown over, Shifty had come back home and was behaving himself properly. He asked Mid-Star's dad to make a prediction whether they would have children. Mid-Star's dad told him to write a character, and Shifty wrote 牛, ox. The old man looked at it and predicted they wouldn't have any.

"Why not?" asked Shifty.

"Because you missed the bottom line. You should have written 生, birth."

"Dammit!" Shifty exclaimed.

Mid-Star's dad went on, "An ox only has value when it's plowing the land, but this ox has no land. It's not your fault; you can blame your wife."

Shifty cursed his wife. "Damn her, she's jinxed me! Is there anything you can do about it?"

"Come tomorrow, and bring her with you. I'll have to investigate."

But Shifty didn't. Instead he went to the Great Qing Hall to complain to Big-Noise Zhao. "The old scoundrel wants me to give him gifts. And why should I take my wife for an 'investigation' so he can paw her all over?"

That was when Big-Noise Zhao remembered the old custom. The Freshwind villagers used to sneak a pumpkin under the quilt on the kang on a married woman's birthday to help her conceive.

"Get someone to slip a pumpkin under her quilt when it's her birthday," he suggested.

"You do it."

"It should be a kid who does it. If you buy me some cigarettes, a decent brand, I'll make sure your kang's stuffed full of pumpkins."

So Shifty supplied him with a carton of cigarettes, and Big-Noise Zhao bribed Culture with a bag of walnuts and gave him instructions. The next day Culture and his buddies cut eight big pumpkins and took them to Shifty's. Shifty was at home, but he pretended not to notice as they put the pumpkins under the quilt, then gave them each a small bag of peanuts on their way out. When Justice Xia saw how many pumpkins were missing, he asked me. I told him what was going on.

"That man's nothing but trouble," he said. "And now he wants a baby? That'll mean even more trouble, won't it?"

He didn't bawl Culture out, but he did cut another pumpkin and give it to me with strict instructions to take it to Concord Qin's.

I took it over to him, and then I hurried back toward Seven Li Gully. When I got to the river at the end of East Street, I caught sight of Snow Bai, who was washing clothes. It must have been the river bringing us together . . . that was the second time I'd met her there. The water was much higher now in the fall than in the summer, and only the top of the rocks stuck out above the surface of the water. Snow Bai had washed everything in her basket by then and was trying to use the rocks as stepping-stones to get to the other side, but her big belly unbalanced her, and every time she tried, she got scared. I hopped down from the road above. I was feeling very brave and didn't hesitate for a moment. If I had, I would have lost my nerve. "I'll carry you on my back!" I said. And I waded into the water, still with my socks and shoes on.

Snow Bai looked startled, but she must have been touched to see me in the water, shoes and all, because she just said gently, "Don't worry, I can manage."

Then she turned to go downstream in search of a place where the river was narrower. I stood there, my cheeks flaming red, mumbling to myself, *Please, river, let there not be any narrower places!* And the water level did seem to rise a bit.

Finally, Snow Bai gave up looking for a better crossing place and came back. She took off her shoes to wade.

I stood on one of the stepping-stones, feeling sorry for her. "You don't have to wade. I can lead you across."

I was worried she'd refuse, so I hurried up the bank, broke off a branch, and handed one end to her. She brushed her hair off her face, looked around, and then grabbed hold of the branch. And so we crossed, with me holding one end of the branch and Snow Bai the other. Other people might have held a red cord or a silk ribbon between them, but we had a stick. My hands were trembling, and the shaking passed through the branch and made her hands tremble, too. She actually looked me in the face, and, overcome with shyness, I had to look down at the stones. There were far too few of them. If only there had been a hundred or a thousand and we could have gone on walking forever! But all too soon, we'd made the crossing. I heard her say thank you, and when I looked up, she was hurrying away. One of the garments she'd washed fell out of the basket, and I shouted after her, but she didn't look around, only sped up. When she started to climb the slope, there was a willow bush in her way, and as she brushed past, a duck skittered out of the bush, quacking loudly. I went and had a look at what Snow Bai had dropped. It was a small handkerchief.

When I got to Seven Li Gully, I found Justice Xia belting Culture with his rope. Culture was so stubborn that it didn't matter how hard Justice Xia whacked his buttocks; he stood ramrod straight, head held high, and didn't say a word. "Are you trying to be a martyr?" I whispered to him, and then I grabbed the rope and hustled Justice Xia into the shed.

The old man was furious. "If he'd just said a word or cried, I wouldn't have beaten him, but the rascal's so stubborn!"

When I asked what had happened, he told me that he'd picked the biggest pumpkin and was about to light a fire and cook it for the young ones, but when he cut it open, he discovered it was full of human shit. No one would own up to having done it, but finally someone snitched on Culture. He'd cut a hole in the pumpkin, dug out the seeds, crapped in it, and put back the cut rind. After a few days the edges had grown together, and the pumpkin was bigger than ever.

I was pissed, too, when I heard the story. "How could you?" I said to Culture.

He just glared at me.

"Are you going to beat me up?" I asked.

He raised his fists, but I wasn't scared. It wasn't just that I had Justice Xia at my back; I had Snow Bai's hankie on me, too. I sneaked behind him and kicked him in the back of the knees, and he crumpled to the ground. "Apologize to your granddad," I said.

Culture jumped to his feet and flew at me then, flailing his fists. We had a proper fight. He slung a punch, and I slung one back. Then we lowered our heads, took a couple of steps back, and charged like two rams about to lock horns. We slammed heads and both sat down, each with a big bump on our foreheads.

The kids shouted for Justice Xia, but he just sat there and watched without doing or saying anything at all. Finally, Culture got really mad. He couldn't beat me, so he grabbed one of the carrying poles and smashed it against a rock, breaking it in two, then turned and ran out of the gully.

"Why did you beat him up? Now he won't come back again," said Justice Xia.

Sure enough, Culture didn't appear the next day. None of the young ones appeared, so now it was just Tongue-Tied and me who stayed with Justice Xia. I teased Tongue-Tied that he must have been a dog in his last life because he was so faithful to Justice Xia. Tongue-Tied mimed that if he was a dog, then so was I; we were both dogs. But he had no idea why I was so full of energy today. I was hefting boulders that normally took two men to move. It was because I had Snow Bai's handkerchief! I didn't dare say a word to either Tongue-Tied or Justice Xia; I had to keep mum, and that was hard. Usually when you're happy or sad, you want to get it off your chest and tell other people. Finally I cracked, and on the third night, I told Big-Noise Zhao. "Big-Noise, I've got something to say."

"Say it then!"

I hesitated. "Maybe I'd better not say anything."

"Sure, it's up to you."

But I couldn't keep it in, and I told him.

He didn't sound very excited. "Is that all?"

"You don't understand!"

"No, I don't understand how someone with no cock thinks."

"Snow Bai must have left it behind specially for me."

"If she did, then that will bring you closer together."

"But what if she doesn't want that?"

"I know what you can do. But you'll have to pay . . ."

"Pay? I'll pay with my life if I have to."

"Okay, but you gotta keep it secret, and you gotta show me proper respect. I want to make a sign to hang over the storefront. Can you give me a plank from one of your parasol trees?"

What a brilliant man Big-Noise Zhao was. He gave me my instructions, and in return, I got the plank for him, and he carved the characters "For the good of all humanity" and hung it on the wall behind the pharmacy. That same night, I got the cat to piss on the handkerchief, and the next morning I took it with me to the gully and laid it out in a snake hole when no one was looking. I retrieved it that evening before I went home, and, sure enough, the snake had left sperm stains on it. I had to keep very quiet about this spell and not tell anyone else. Big-Noise Zhao said he'd read about it in an old book on traditional medicine.

I showed the handkerchief to him. "Is it really true that I can lure Snow Bai along with me by waving this under her nose?"

"Well, I haven't tried it myself, but it should work," he said.

"Is it against the law, or immoral?"

"I've only told you what to do. How you use it or who you use it on, that's your business. Like an ax can be used to chop wood or chop off heads—the ax itself is just a tool. Men all have a cock, but that doesn't mean they're all rapists."

I was over the moon with excitement. I yelled and rushed out of the pharmacy and hit my head on the glass door. It didn't hurt me, but the glass cracked, and Big-Noise Zhao chewed me out and said I had to pay him back.

I spotted Snow Bai near the gully. She was walking down the white center line of the 312, practicing not walking with her feet splayed out. I hurried toward her, ready to try out my plan, but I didn't want to scare her by running up behind her. So I ran like a madman through the fields that flanked the 312, dropped down onto the road after I'd passed her, and hid behind a bush. Snow Bai passed by, a smile on her face, walking as daintily as a cat, her butt swaying with every step.

I leaped out of the bush like a robber in a film, or rather like a warrior, landing in front of her with a mighty bound.

Snow Bai screamed in terror. It was really distressing to see how scared she was. Her mouth opened wide, and she flailed her arms to keep me back.

I fished inside my jacket and pulled out an old glove. I tried again and found the handkerchief. I waved it in her face.

"What are you doing?" I heard her exclaim.

I kept waving the handkerchief, and the muscles in her face went rigid and her eyes glazed over. "Big-Noise, I've done it!" I shouted.

I turned to go, and when I looked back, I saw she really was following me. She kept pace with me, speeding up or slowing down when I did, like she was my shadow or a puppet on a string. We walked through the village, end to end, and everyone stared at us. I scuffed some dead leaves so they flew in all directions, and then I kicked some more, though they turned out to be leaf-colored stones, not leaves at all, and kicking them lost me a toenail. I ignored the pain and carried on walking. We passed Favor Bai, and Roughshod Ding, Obedient Zhang, and Shifty, and none of them said a word. That was because they were too astonished to speak, and they were jealous, too.

I smiled and nodded at them all, as if I were the emperor. We got to my home, went into the yard and then into the house. Snow Bai went to the kang and lay flat out. But seeing her on the kang like that, I didn't dare lay a finger on her. I sat on the edge and gazed at her. She seemed as delicate as a flower that might blow away if I was rough with her. I reached out and stroked her foot. Her skin was as soft as a baby's bottom and cool as snow. I was burning hot from head to toe, and I was afraid that if I touched her, she'd melt. *Let her lie there sleeping quietly. Let her lie there forever, like Sleeping Beauty.*

I sat at the door and kept everyone out, even the flies. A bee from the elm tree did force its way in and stung me on the head, but when it pulled the stinger out, it lost half its innards in the process and died. For three days running, I didn't go to Seven Li Gully. Justice Xia was worried I was sick and dropped by.

When he saw me at the door looking fine, he said, "What are you doing at home?"

I didn't answer, just looked at the kang and smiled. Justice Xia went over and ripped off the quilt. There was nothing underneath. I jumped up and grabbed hold of him and pulled him away.

"Are you sick in the head again?" he exclaimed.

"Don't chase her away!" I shouted.

"Chase who away!" He slapped me hard around the face. I didn't move, but after a very long time, I came to my senses. Snow Bai had never been on my kang.

"Uncle Justice!" I wailed.

Justice Xia took me back to Seven Li Gully with him. I dragged my feet behind him like I was a kid who'd been caught skipping school, but he wasn't letting me go. When we got to the East Street archway, someone called him. "Second Uncle!" I looked up, and there was Snow Bai. Was it really her? I pinched my leg hard, and it hurt, so I wasn't dreaming.

"You been to your mom's?" asked Justice Xia.

"I've been to the shop for some dress material."

Suddenly I jerked free, rushed up to Snow Bai, and waved the hankie frantically under her nose. She shrieked and slumped to the ground. Justice Xia pushed me away and added a kick for good measure.

"You motherfucker!" he yelled at me, then pulled Snow Bai to her feet and told her, "You get off home; Spark's crazy!"

That was the second most humiliating thing to happen to me in my life, but I didn't hold it against Snow Bai, or Justice Xia. I loathed myself, and I loathed Big-Noise Zhao for being a double-dealing cheat! That night I went to the Great Qing Hall and demanded my plank of wood back, and he gave it up without protest. Then I landed a kick on his wall, as hard as I could. The muddy footprint is still there, a whole yard from the ground.

For a week, the sun was pitch black every time I looked at it. It really was. I wondered if Snow Bai saw it as black, too. One evening when it was raining heavily, I went to Seven Li Gully on my own. I'd move into the shack; I wasn't going back to Freshwind Village. You remember the wheat seedling? Well, it had grown into an amazingly sturdy plant almost a yard high, with a stalk as thick as a finger. I sat under the table and talked to the bird in the tree.

"Caw!" it said.

"What?" I asked.

"Caw! Caw!"

"Wawa?" I asked it. (That was our word for baby.)

"Caw! Caw! Caw!"

"Whose baby?"

"Caw! Caw! . . . Caw! Caw! Caw!"

I had no idea what it was saying. Then Justice Xia turned up with a pot of food for me. "It's just as well that you're not at home, you motherfucker," he said. "Otherwise Rain Xia would beat you to death."

"Why?"

"Snow Bai's given birth prematurely!"

I went white in the face with horror. My God, had I scared her so badly she'd gone into labor? How many months was she? Was the baby alive? How was Snow Bai doing?

"She's fine," said Justice Xia. "Both mother and daughter are doing well, but the baby's as skinny as a rat."

I heaved a sigh of relief, but my legs wouldn't hold me up anymore, and I slithered to the ground like mud.

After that, I worked my ass off carrying boulders, trying to punish myself by flogging myself to death, but whatever I did, I couldn't get the rat-baby image out of my mind. I imagined her skinny legs and arms, her outsize head, her little eyes, and sticking-out ears.

Snow Bai was as beautiful as a flower; I couldn't understand why I was imagining her daughter so ugly. But I did, and when I finally saw her, she looked pretty much as I'd imagined her. That was weird. But more on that later. First, let me tell you what happened with Snow Bai.

After Justice Xia had picked her up off the ground, she'd hurried home, her heart thudding in her chest. Then she'd thrown herself on the kang and fallen asleep. Fourth Aunt, meanwhile, was picking over greens in the kitchen. Wisdom Xia was in the bedroom, listening to the radio, and she listened as opera arias wafted out. First it was "The Wind in the Pines," followed by "The Impatience of Mothers-in-law." Then came a strange melody.

"What's that tune? It's horrible!" said Fourth Aunt.

"What's wrong with it? It's the 'Song from Ganzhou,'" said Wisdom Xia from the bedroom. "It's always played when there are ghosts onstage."

"Turn it off! Are you trying to bring ghosts to the house?"

But Wisdom Xia didn't turn it off. "Don't be dumb; this is art!" he said, and he hummed along with it.

Just then, Fourth Aunt heard footsteps out in the yard. *Snow Bai must be home,* she thought. But the moments went by, and Snow Bai didn't show up in the kitchen. "Snow Bai! Did you buy the fabric?" she called out.

No answer. That struck Fourth Aunt as odd, and she went to Snow Bai's bedroom. Snow Bai was lying on the bed with her hands clasped over her belly and her face running with sweat. "What's up?"

"I've got a bellyache." There was another sharp stab of pain, and Snow Bai doubled up so violently she banged her head on the kang.

"Is it really bad? Is it something you've eaten?" Fourth Aunt asked anxiously.

"I bumped into Lotus Jin, and she gave me a handful of peanuts."

"What were you doing eating something of hers? Do you need to go to the bathroom?"

"No."

"How does it feel? Is it a cramping pain?"

"It feels like someone's trying to tear out my innards."

At that, Fourth Aunt began to panic. "Oh Lord, what's the date today? I hope the baby's not coming early!" She raised her voice. "Stop that humming! Stop it!"

The radio in the bedroom fell silent, and Wisdom Xia came in. "What is it? Don't I have any rights in my own home nowadays?"

"Snow Bai's got stomach pains. Go and get Third Sister!"

Wisdom Xia didn't need telling twice. He hurriedly shuffled his feet into his shoes and stumbled out of the house. By now, the pains were bad, and Snow Bai got off the bed and tried to walk around the room. But all she could do was hold on to the edge of the kang and shuffle to and fro.

"Don't worry, Snow Bai," said Fourth Aunt. "It looks like it's starting, but there's nothing to be afraid of. Women give birth all the time in this world."

Snow Bai was breathing heavily. She tried squatting at the end of the kang. Suddenly, a fierce gust of wind blew the window open, and the pillow cover, a head scarf, some paper on the table, and a palm-leaf fan were all whirled into the air. The paper stuck to the mirror and hung there for a long time. Fourth Aunt rushed to shut the window. Outside the wind howled, and gouts of rain spilled against the windowpane.

Wisdom Xia arrived at Third Aunt's. "Snow Bai seems like she's gone into labor," he said.

"That's terrible! It's too early for that!"

"Right."

"Don't let her lose it! Lose it!"

They hobbled as fast as they could back up the alley, the wind buffeting them so they had to lean into it, and almost collided with the wall of a public bathroom. The tree branches were being blown horizontal, all pointing in the direction of Wisdom Xia's house.

A single cloud hung low over their heads, followed them home, and then dropped its load right there over the yard, soaking the old man as he pushed the gate open and went and huddled under the tickle tree. It was very odd. Inside the yard, the rain was streaking down in torrents, flooding the ground, while outside where Third Aunt was waiting, not a drop was falling and she was as dry as a bone. "Isn't this rain weird? Weird?" she exclaimed.

"Get yourself indoors, quick!"

Third Aunt plunged through the rain and into the house. Wisdom Xia waited until he saw her go into Snow Bai's room. "Call if you want anything," he said. He paced to and fro on the steps, as jumpy as an ant in a hot wok. Then he went to the shithouse and squatted down, but nothing came out. He could hear Snow Bai's screams. He came out of the shithouse, but he still didn't feel right and hurried back in again. Then he heard Fourth Aunt shout, "Go boil some water! Did you hear me? Boil some water!"

He went into the kitchen but had some difficulty lighting the stove. He poked inside with the fire stick, and eventually choking black smoke billowed up. The water boiled, but he could still hear Snow Bai's screams coming from her room. Calmer now, though still white as a sheet, he sat, puffing on his brass water pipe.

"Your water broke," he heard Third Aunt say. "You lie down properly for me. It'll be easy now; it's just like taking a shit. Wind Xia, now, he was coming down sideways, and he had to be pulled out, didn't he? Wisdom . . . Wisdom!"

Wisdom Xia, who had been concentrating on inhaling every puff of smoke right into his belly and keeping it there, emerged from his reverie. "You shouting for me?"

"You're not on the steps," said Fourth Aunt.

"I'm here!"

"Boil the scissors in the water!"

Wisdom Xia couldn't find the scissors anywhere, but he couldn't go in and ask his wife, either, so he turned everything out of the drawers in a frantic search.

Fourth Aunt came in. "I told you to boil the scissors; didn't you hear?"

"Where are they?"

"Where would they be?" And she got them out of the sewing basket on the kang.

"Do you want me to call Big-Noise?" he asked, but she'd already gone back into the bedroom. As Wisdom Xia boiled the scissors, the fire crackled merrily inside the stove and Snow Bai's screams grew louder and louder. When the scissors were done, he put them in a bowl and took them to Fourth Aunt, who was searching through the chest for a clean sheet and looking hot and bothered.

"Baby still not born?" he asked.

"Go away. Don't come unless I call you!" And she threw a bloodied sheet into the corner.

"Is she bleeding?"

"Hens bleed when they lay an egg!"

"Tell her to be strong!" he said. His wife stared at him. "I'll put some opera on for her; that'll ease the pains."

Fourth Aunt said nothing and went back into the bedroom. Wisdom Xia turned on the radio but couldn't find any stations playing opera. So he got out his *huqin*, sat outside on the steps, and began to play.

As the notes rose into the air, the wind and rain swirled in the yard, and the elms and the poplars outside leaned toward the wall. The old man played contentedly on, almost forgetting that he was playing for Snow Bai, who was having her baby.

Then he heard Third Aunt: "Wisdom, Wisdom, you've got a granddaughter! A granddaughter!"

He drew a long, trembling note with his bow, and at the very same moment, the storm quieted, and the rain stopped. One final crystalline drop fell, the size of his fingertip. It landed on the tickle tree and broke into a myriad of droplets that splashed up from the bark.

Chapter 35

Like I told you, everyone in Freshwind used to be there for me, but things changed. Everyone blamed me for making Snow Bai go into labor, and I didn't dare show my face in the village. I spent even more time at Seven Li Gully, but even there I wasn't safe. One day, I was digging a trench down the side of the gully when my shovel ripped open a wasp's nest. If those wasps weren't sent by the Bai family, then they must have been sent by the Xia family! I ended up getting stung all over my head. Luckily, I had my secret home remedy: I blew my nose into my hand and smeared the snot over the welts. Even Tongue-Tied thought it was disgusting.

That night, I couldn't help sneaking back into the village and asking Mid-Star's dad to read the fortunes of Snow Bai and her baby. He told me that the stormy weather the day of the birth had been a bad portent. I wanted to know more, but he said he needed to know the exact time the child was conceived. I had no idea. "What do you need to know that for, anyway?" I asked him.

"Human lives are influenced by yin and yang and by the five elements. Every life is different. But what's the one thing everyone has in common? Whether the person is rich or poor, highborn or low, they were all created the same way. To tell the fortune of the child, I have to know the circumstances of her conception. Was it during a storm or a clear night? What phase was the moon in? That's what I need to know. You know, the phase of the moon during conception could determine whether the child will be insane or blind or deaf or mute or as dumb as the pile of reject bricks down at Shifty's yard."

"You talking about me?" I asked him.

"Not at all. But in your case, it's your mother and your father who would bear the blame if they . . . Take Mid-Star, for example. I chose the perfect day and the perfect time. I had it planned for early in the morning, before the rooster crowed, when the sun was just coming up on the horizon."

I stood up and headed for the door. Mid-Star's dad kept going, but I didn't want to hear it. I'd gone to hear Snow Bai's fortune, not listen to the story of how Mid-Star was conceived.

Where did he get off saying my parents were to blame? He should blame his own parents for bringing a son as sickly and useless as him into the world.

On the way out, I grabbed one of the ceramic pots he used to brew his medicine. When I got out to the crossroads, I shattered it on the road. As I hurried away, I saw that the knocker on Wisdom Xia's gate had a piece of red cloth tied to it. The red cloth was a prayer for the safety of Snow Bai and her child. Fourth Aunt had tied the red cloth to the knocker after burying the afterbirth in the yard. The cloth was meant to bring safety to mother and child, but it served other purposes, too—everyone who passed by would know that a baby had been born to the family, and it would signal to strangers that they should think twice before rapping at the gate and disturbing mother and child.

The day after the birth, Rain Xia had gone to West Street to tell the Bai family the news. Snow Bai's mother had immediately set about preparing to visit her daughter. She'd thrown some flatbread on the griddle, making sure each one was at least two fingers thick; then she'd packed them up along with three chi of printed cloth, three *jin* of brown sugar, and twenty *jin* of eggs.

Fourth Aunt and Snow Bai's mother chatted late into the night. She spent the night there and woke up the next morning to go to the market for pig trotters. Braised trotters were perfect for making the milk flow. The trotters had just gone into the pot when Wisdom Xia, who was out in the yard watering his peonies, heard a ruckus in the alley and saw a plume of black smoke curl into the sky.

Wisdom Xia went down the alley to investigate and discovered that the strawstack at Lotus Jin's place was on fire. The pile of rice straw had been stacked up under a poplar tree behind the house. The poplar had burned up, but the fire hadn't spread to the cornstalks piled up against the back wall of the house. On his way back, Wisdom Xia saw that Snow Bai, her mother, and Fourth Aunt had come out into the alley and were talking to Forest Wu.

"Fourth Aunt," Forest Wu said, "Sn-Snow Bai . . . D-did the baby c-come?"

"It sure did," Fourth Aunt said.

"S-so w-was it a boy or a g-girl?"

"Guess!"

"W-was it a boy?"

"Wrong," Fourth Aunt said.

"A-a g-girl then?"

"Come on, Forest Wu," Fourth Aunt said. "You're really going to keep guessing?" She saw Wisdom Xia coming down the alley. "Where was the fire?"

"It was over at Lotus Jin's place," Wisdom Xia said. "Just the strawstack."

"She was just saying she'd had some chickens stolen out of her yard, and now this? You think it might be someone doing it on purpose?"

"That's horrible!" Snow Bai's mother said. She seemed about to continue but held her tongue.

Snow Bai's mother stayed until Jiang Mao's daughter came to take her home. Snow Bai's mother felt a twitch in her eyelid as she was saying goodbye. She plucked a blade of grass from the yard, ripped a piece of it, and stuck it to her eyelid. Fourth Aunt reached into the cabinet and came up with a dried persimmon that she gave to Jiang Mao's daughter.

The girl said, "My dad bought me some of these already."

"Your dad's back?" Fourth Aunt asked.

"Jiang Mao isn't working in the mine anymore," Snow Bai's mother said. "He's been back for a while. He's growing mushrooms now."

"Your dad might have bought you some, but this is a gift from me," Fourth Aunt. "Don't be so picky."

"It's a gift from the lady," Snow Bai's mother said. "Take it. You should kowtow to her."

The girl took the dried persimmon, stuffed it into her mouth, got down on her hands and knees in front of Fourth Aunt, and knocked her head on the floor in a deep bow. Snow Bai's mother and the girl left.

"Snow Bai," Wisdom Xia said, "what happened there? Your mother's expression suddenly changed."

"I think it might have been something with my sister-in-law," Snow Bai said.

"I heard they're looking for her to pay the family planning fine for breaking the one-child policy," Wisdom Xia said. "The way I see it, three or four thousand yuan is a small price to pay to have a baby boy."

"What's your mother so worried about?" Fourth Aunt asked. "It'll be Jiang Mao paying the fine, not her. What is she rushing home for?"

"They're the only other family we're close to. It's nothing like the Xia family . . ." As soon as the words were out of Snow Bai's mouth, she knew it was the wrong thing to say to her mother-in-law. "I just mean that my mother takes care of everything for them."

That seemed to satisfy her in-laws.

When Snow Bai's mother got back to West Street, she went straight to her daughter-in-law. Jiang Mao's wife, with her mouth agape and eyes staring into space, looked like one of the fish drying on a mat out in the yard. "The baby's good?" she asked.

"Baby's good," Snow Bai's mother said.

"Snow Bai is feeling okay?"

"She's fine."

Snow Bai's sister-in-law broke into a sob. "Auntie," she said, "it got out of control. I know you're going to be angry."

"Did Jiang Mao set that strawstack on fire?"

"I'm eighty percent sure it was him, but he won't admit it. A few days ago, when I heard that she'd had her chickens stolen, I asked him about it. He claimed not to know anything about it. Then a couple of days later, I go down to the root cellar, and there are feathers all over the place. So, I asked him about it again, and he still wouldn't admit it. He's a thug! He just sits at home all day, cursing Lotus Jin. It had to be him that set the strawstack on fire! Anyway, the police just came out here and took him away."

"They want him to pay the fine," Snow Bai's mother said. "I don't even care about that. I don't care if they come and take the mushroom shed. All I care about is that baby! I don't know why he thinks he can get away with attacking Lotus Jin. A flea can't hide on a bald man's head."

"What should we do? Do you think they'll send him to prison?" Her legs gave out from under her, and she slumped against the wall and slid to the floor.

"What's wrong with you? Huh?" Snow Bai's mother said.

"I'm fine. I just need to rest a minute."

"You have to face things calmly," Snow Bai's mother said, "no matter how bad it gets. We'll wait and see what Jiang Mao says to the police and figure things out from there. We already had one miracle, right? You made it home with the baby, didn't you?"

Snow Bai's sister-in-law nodded and heaved a sigh. The baby cried in the other room, sounding as if he was gasping for air with every sob. "What's wrong with that baby? Nothing seems to settle him down." Switch came out of the room, her son pressed to her chest. She opened her shirt and put a nipple in his mouth, but the baby kept crying. "What the hell is wrong with you," Snow Bai's sister-in-law asked. "Can't you even comfort your own son? We're in the middle of something right now. Are you trying to drive us crazy?" Snow Bai's mother took the baby from Switch's arms. She patted his diaper and felt that it was soaked through.

The anxious mood at the house continued until dinnertime. Jiang Mao still hadn't been released from custody. Snow Bai's mother told Snow Bai's sister-in-law to make a pot of noodles, bring it down to the station, and try to feel out the police as to what the situation was. She came back fifteen minutes later, bringing Jiang Mao with her. "I would've died before I told them a damn thing," he said. "They don't have any proof. They had to let me go."

"I'm happy to hear that," Snow Bai's mother said, "but I want to know what happened. Did you light that fire?"

"I sure did," he said.

"You just said you'd die before admitting anything, didn't you? What are you doing, confessing to it now?"

"You're family!"

"At this point, I don't care if the King of Heaven himself asks you; you better keep your mouth shut," Snow Bai's mother said. She was about to continue, but the sound of footsteps outside stopped her.

Some villagers came in through the gate, grabbed Jiang Mao's arms, and inspected them for marks. They said that a few days earlier, a guy from Middle Street had been nabbed after his wife had squealed on him for stepping out on her. The cops had handcuffed him to the window bars and then beaten him so badly they'd broken bones.

"Why the hell would they beat me?" Jiang Mao said. "I didn't set that fire!"

"I know," one of the villagers said. "Matter of fact, around the same time as the fire started, I saw a shooting star, and it looked like it came down around Lotus Jin's place. Then I come to find out there was a fire over there."

"A shooting star?" Snow Bai's mother asked.

"Yep. When I saw it come down by Lotus Jin's place, I was thinking to myself, 'Is that a bad sign? It could mean a death in the family.' Turns out, all they lost was a strawstack."

"You have to tell the police then. They're coming after Jiang Mao for setting the fire."

"You think I'd just show up there and testify?" the man said. "Why do you think the thing fell in Lotus Jin's strawstack in the first place?"

"You think the shooting star had it out for Lotus Jin, too? You want to protect it or something?"

Snow Bai's mother slapped Jiang Mao across the head. "If you're going to talk like that, you might as well just keep your mouth shut," she said. "Don't worry, nobody's going to mistake you for a mute."

The police dropped their investigation into the strawstack fire after hearing from other villagers about the shooting star. But Jiang Mao still had to pay the fine for breaking the one-child policy. The forty-two hundred yuan they were asking for was more than Jiang Mao could easily put his hands on. When Lotus Jin got tired of waiting, she assembled some men to go around and confiscate his mushroom shed. Jiang Mao had five days to come up with the cash, or the shed would be put up for auction. Whether he thought the threat wasn't serious or that they might come back with a lower figure, Jiang Mao didn't bother trying to come up with the money. The shed went up for auction, and that goddamn Shifty bought it. The thing was worth five thousand, but Shifty got it for four thousand, cash on the barrel. When Jiang Mao heard the news, he cursed Shifty and went looking for him, hoping to press him for some cash.

Jiang Mao showed up to demand a thousand yuan, but Shifty blew him off. Jiang Mao persisted, though, and when he showed up at Shifty's place for the fourth time, Shifty told him, "I bought this shed fair and square from the village. It's got nothing to do with you. If you come around here again, I'll assume you're here to take it from me. You know how I deal with thieves." When Jiang Mao showed up again, Shifty went at him with the thick iron rod he used to bar his gate. Of course, Jiang Mao was no match for Shifty. He ran home, crying. Finally, with no other option, Jiang Mao decided to leave the village to look for work. He ended up in the county seat, working on a building site, mixing concrete.

When Lotus Jin learned that the police had dropped their investigation, she felt sick to her stomach. Without the rice straw, she worried that she wouldn't have enough fuel for her stove. She went to ask Goodness for help. He managed the forested area along the riverbank and told her she was free to take four thousand *jin* of firewood. The men she got to do the job knew not to drag out any whole trees, but some of the branches they hacked down were big enough that they could have been used as rafters in a new house. Some villagers raised objections. And who did they raise those objections with? First, they went to the head of the residents' committee, but he wasn't willing to pass their complaints along to Pavilion, and he definitely wasn't going to tell Lotus Jin or Goodness, so three or four villagers ended up going to Wisdom Xia.

Wisdom Xia had been busy that day, so he wasn't around the first time they showed up. He'd bought five silver coins from Third Aunt and had taken them to the tinker to be melted down and made into a necklace for his new granddaughter. When he got home, the villagers who had gone to complain about Lotus Jin were waiting for him. Instead of getting into the topic right away, they told Wisdom Xia the latest gossip. Word around the village was that, around the grave mounds at the foot of Bowed Ox Ridge, they'd heard the head of the Peasants' Association arguing with my dad about something.

There's my dad coming up in the story again. I guess I need to explain what went on between my dad and the head of the Peasants' Association.

The head of the Peasants' Association was a Mr. Shou, who lived over on West Street. He died sometime in the 1970s, but when he was around, he was even more senior than Justice Xia. He and my dad used to argue a lot. As soon as they sat down for a meeting, they'd start going at each other and shout until they were red in the face.

One time, they were meeting to discuss the canal that was going to connect the village to the reservoir behind the power station dam. Progress had been slow, and the production team had added an overnight shift. My dad proposed that team members who worked overnight should get an extra five *jin* of steamed sweet potato. Mr. Shou disagreed. He said that class struggle rather than bribery would solve the problem. He kept quoting the line about class struggle being the key link, and once the key link is grasped, everything falls into place. He decided to call a struggle session and another round of beatings and public humiliation for anyone who had been classed as one of the "Black Categories," which included all the former landlords and rich farmers, and those who had been branded counterrevolutionaries, bad elements, or rightists. Following the old saying of "kill the chicken to scare the monkey," he figured this would motivate the production team.

When they went at it again, my dad accused Mr. Shou of abusing his authority. "You might be the head of the Peasants' Association," my dad said, "but my authority comes from— well, just flip your last name around and you'll know who I mean." What he meant was that Mr. Shou's last name 手 was written with a character that looked just like Chairman Mao's last name, 毛, except flipped to the right. Immediately, Mr. Shou started saying that my dad was being disrespectful to the Chairman. Back in those days, disrespect to the Chairman carried a death sentence. It was a very serious accusation!

Justice Xia stepped in and mediated the dispute, telling him not to bring revolutionary politics into a simple disagreement, and telling my dad not to stand in the way of Mr. Shou's struggle session. From that point on, the two men gave each other the cold shoulder. When Mr. Shou died, my dad didn't go to his funeral.

They were reunited soon enough, though. When my dad died, he was only the second member of the village government to pass away, and they ended up buried not too far from each other. For all eternity, they were destined to rest side by side at the foot of Bowed Ox Ridge, with only a drainage ditch and three persimmon trees to separate them. So according to what the villagers told Wisdom Xia, my dad's ghost and Mr. Shou's ghost were still arguing. They didn't know what the argument was about; they hadn't actually heard it, not exactly, but there were strange howls that seemed to whip back and forth between the graves. They weren't human voices, exactly, but the tone of each howl matched those of the two men.

Wisdom Xia didn't believe a word of it and only chuckled to himself. One of the men who had run to tell Wisdom Xia the news worried that maybe Freshwind had bad feng shui. "Nonsense!" Wisdom Xia said. "How'd the village produce a man like Mid-Star Xia then?" His choice of Mid-Star Xia rather than Wind Xia seemed intentional. "The feng shui is excellent."

"Not to mention Wind Xia!" one of the villagers said. "But just think, both of them were only successful once they left the village. Sure, you can find a few capable people in Freshwind, but they're only out for themselves, and sometimes they go too far!"

"What the hell are you talking about?" Wisdom Xia said. "Say it straight."

That was when they brought up the problem with Lotus Jin collecting firewood along the riverbank. As soon as they were done telling the story of her men cutting down the big branches, three more villagers came into the yard. They had come for the same reason: to get Wisdom Xia involved in the Lotus Jin situation. "What good is it going to do, complaining to me?" Wisdom Xia asked. "You should be talking to the village cadres."

"They're useless!"

"So you came to me because I'm Pavilion's uncle?" Wisdom Xia asked.

"No," one of the men said, "that's not it. There's an old saying: only the words of a righteous man stand firm. We need the words of a righteous man!"

Wisdom Xia took out his water pipe. He packed it with his tobacco blend enriched with flavored oils and fragrances, and the smoke filled the room.

"Smells great!" someone said.

Wisdom Xia set down the pipe. "I should be charging you all by the sniff."

Later that day, when Wisdom Xia went out to pick up the necklace from the tinker, he decided to stop by Pavilion's place. He checked in twice but each time was told Pavilion was out. Finally, Culture took Wisdom Xia aside and told him the truth. Pavilion was home, but every time he heard his uncle had come looking for him, he slipped out the back window. Wisdom Xia took a chair, packed his pipe, and parked himself in the alley outside Pavilion's gate. It wasn't long before he saw his nephew coming down the alley.

"Every year, the branches from the riverside trees get cut to give to elderly or disabled people in the village to use as firewood. How is it that Lotus Jin's been given the right to cut firewood down there? And why did her men cut down the thick branches? How can the village government have any legitimacy if the cadres are out to enrich themselves?"

Rain Xia had come up the alley while Wisdom Xia was interrogating Pavilion. "Dad," he said, "it's not the end of the world, is it? It's just a few villagers complaining. It's not like your older brother is involved. Shifty's not lodging complaints, and as far as I know, Spark hasn't said a word about it, either. So why are you interfering? I'm starting to think it's only because you don't approve of my relationship with Lotus Jin's niece."

"Stay out of it," Wisdom Xia said.

"If you keep carrying on like this, you're going to screw things up for me."

"I don't care!"

"You've always been like this," Rain Xia said. "You treat me like I'm not even your son. What's wrong with her? You don't like her because she can't sing opera?"

"Bullshit!" Wisdom Xia said.

A war of words erupted between father and son. Finally, Pavilion stepped in. "That's enough," he said. "I'm not going to try to tell you how to settle a family dispute, but you came here to talk about Lotus Jin cutting down those branches, and I can tell you that I already looked into it. Fourth Uncle was right to bring it to our attention. These types of complaints are perfectly valid, whoever they come from. It's the people of the village who supervise the local government, after all."

"Then why did you slip out the back window when I came to see you about it?" Wisdom Xia asked.

"How did you know about that?"

"So it's true?"

Pavilion chuckled. "Look at what I've become," he said. "I'm a village cadre, but I can't even go out my own front door. Of course I know all about the situation with Lotus Jin. But it's not as easy to deal with as you might think. In the course of carrying out her official duties, Lotus Jin offended someone. They came back for revenge and set her strawstack on fire. What am I supposed to do? She doesn't have it easy. None of us do. We're getting it from both ends: the higher-ups are breathing down our necks, and the villagers push back on every decision we make. We're like a rat in a bellows, either sucking smoke or getting crushed. Nowadays, nobody is willing to take these local government posts unless they know they can wet their beaks a bit. You can call it corruption if you want, but we have to live with a certain amount of corruption. That's the way I see it."

Wisdom Xia had nothing to say in response, so he tucked his pipe into his pocket, picked up the chair, and walked away down the alley. "You've never been in politics, Dad," Rain Xia said to him. "You don't know what it's like to be a civil servant. It's nothing like you see in your operas."

"Life is like opera," Wisdom Xia said, "and opera is like life! And where do you get off saying I've never been a civil servant? I was a principal, wasn't I? It was the same for me as it is for these village cadres. The higher-ups gave me targets, and I had to reach them. I was told to bring up the high school enrollment rate. The goal was for my school to be fifth in the county." He turned back to Pavilion. "Now, whether you're Party secretary or village head, I'd like to know what the hell you've got planned for Freshwind."

"Maybe I wasn't clear," Pavilion said.

"Clear about what?"

"I have my own dreams for the village," Pavilion said. "I'm just like the Zhou River. You look at the river, and no matter how many twists and turns are in it, it keeps running to the east, headed for the sea."

"I'm going to make sure you remember that," Wisdom Xia said. "The next time I come to talk to you, keep that in mind. If you're going to accomplish big things, you can't be jumping out of windows. And you better keep an eye on all the cadres working under you. If things get out of hand, if the village revolts, it'll be too late to get everyone back in line and put things right!"

Pavilion didn't entirely ignore what Wisdom Xia said. He didn't confiscate the firewood from Lotus Jin, but he told Goodness that he was no longer managing the forested area along the riverbank. After that, Lotus Jin stayed in her position but seemed to lose her enthusiasm for carrying out her duties. Goodness quarreled with Pavilion and then resigned his position. Pavilion had always thought Goodness was sneaky, but his passion for the job had made him indispensable. Pavilion used his knowledge of the dalliance between Lotus Jin and Goodness to strong-arm Goodness to return to work, but the relationship between the two men was never the same. That was when Goodness started going to Seven Li Gully.

Justice Xia was not surprised when Goodness came to see him—though he spent most of his time in Seven Li Gully, he knew everything that went on in Freshwind. "Uncle Justice," Goodness said when he saw Justice Xia at work, "you're like the great Su Wu, sent by the Xiongnu to tend sheep on the shores of Lake Baikal . . ."

"I'm up here because none of you are willing to work on reclaiming the gully," Justice Xia said.

"I was the one who suggested Pavilion give you the tractor," Goodness said. "That should count for something."

"The village has dynamite and blasting caps, right? I need you to bring me some."

"I don't have the authority to sign off on that," Goodness said. "You'll have to talk to Pavilion. But watch out—it's like dealing with Chairman Mao."

Justice Xia snorted. "What do you mean by that?"

"He's a dictator. His word is law."

"Freshwind is like a ship, and he's the captain. I don't know if I trust he's a firm hand on the wheel. I'll tell you this, Chairman Mao knew what he was doing. He struggled against heaven, against the earth, against anyone who stood in his way . . . You know how he kept his own forces in check? He divided them into two factions, one on the left and one on the right, then he set them both against each other. Do you think Pavilion is capable of that sort of leadership? If he was, he wouldn't have dealt with Concord Qin the way he did, and he wouldn't have let you and Lotus Jin get mixed up together. The man is soft!"

Goodness was temporarily struck dumb. "It's true what they say: wisdom comes with age," Goodness said once he'd recovered. "Pavilion was never ready to be the captain of the ship."

"That's a load of crap," Justice Xia said. "Nobody's ever ready. Look at you, happy to go along with the crowd when it's to your benefit, but when things go south, you can't handle the heat . . ."

"So, you heard what happened? Do you really think it was my fault?"

"Let me ask you—do you consider yourself selfish?"

"Everybody's at least a little bit selfish. I'm only human."

"That's right. If someone starts planting on your field, you look after your own patch. If someone insults your wife, you defend her. If someone borrows money from you, you have the right to demand they pay you back in full. If a meal isn't good, you have the right to complain. But as a civil servant, you have to be completely selfless. I ran the village for decades, and I can swear this to you: even though I made many errors, I never took advantage of the people. Selfishness is like a pond, and we're like ducks—that doesn't mean you can just head on in and splash around, does it?"

Goodness blinked several times and said nothing. I was glad I was there to witness Goodness getting dressed down. I had gotten sick of him flapping his thin lips all the time. As soon as Justice Xia got started, Goodness went stone silent.

"What are you so happy about? Go suck your mother's titty," Goodness said when he caught me giggling.

"I thought you could talk your way out of anything," I said. "How come you're not saying anything now?"

"Let me get a drink of water," Goodness said and reached for the canteen hanging in the doorway of the shack.

"That's not drinking water!" Justice Xia said. The water in the canteen was meant for the wheat seedling. Justice Xia took the canteen from Goodness. He began to moisten the ground around the seedling.

That was the first time Goodness had noticed the thick green blade poking out of the soil. Goodness being Goodness, he hoped to talk his way out of the put-down Justice Xia had delivered. "You've got wheat growing over here, in this season? And look at the size of it! You should put a fence around it and invite everyone over from Freshwind to take a gander."

I didn't expect Justice Xia to take Goodness seriously. He squatted down in front of the seedling and watered it from the canteen, saying, "Did you hear that? Even Goodness can see how big you're getting. You just keep growing. When you grow up, you'll be the king of the crop!"

The seedling seemed to come to life after drinking its fill of water. It fluttered in the breeze, and I almost thought I could hear it tinkle. Goodness seemed to have recovered, too. "Uncle Justice," he said, stripping off his jacket, "I didn't come here to talk about village affairs. I want to get a sweat on. Toss me a shovel, and tell me where to dig!"

"Is that right?" Justice Xia asked. "Well, how about you start by helping Tongue-Tied move those boulders." The original plan was to use the tractor to drag the dozen or so boulders over to the embankment, but Justice Xia clearly had something in mind. By the time the job was done, Goodness was lying, panting, on the ground. "Tired yet?" Justice Xia asked. "Maybe now you see what kind of work we're doing here. I'm not playing around."

"Don't blame me. I'm not the one who made the decision not to reclaim the gully. That was Pavilion."

"Heaven help us if you had any power. Freshwind would be even more of a mess!"

"Come on, Uncle Justice, how do you think it got to be a mess?" Goodness said. He paused. "Do you happen to know where Mid-Star's dad went?"

"You said you weren't going to talk about village affairs. What are you doing, bringing them up now? And what about Mid-Star's dad? You think I want to hear you flatter the man, just because his son is moving up in the world?"

"Flatter him? You've got completely the wrong idea. As soon as Mid-Star got promoted to vice deputy of Yangqu County, the township head was after me, saying that I'd better look after his family. So I went over there the day before yesterday, and Mid-Star wasn't around. I stopped by a few times yesterday; still not home. He's just never home."

"He can't have gotten far in the state he's in. If he didn't go to see his son, he probably went over to the shrine on Tiger Head Cliff in South Gully. You should ask Halfwit's wife. If that's where he's gone, she'd probably know it."

"Is she a Buddhist, too?"

"Even monsters believe they can turn into immortals," Justice Xia said.

"Maybe they can. Take Mid-Star. Who'd have thought he'd be a bureaucrat one day?"

"What about you?" Justice Xia asked.

"I'm just a village cadre. That doesn't count for much."

"Then what's stopping you from getting along with Pavilion? I'll tell you this: the more you fight him, the harder it's going to be for both of you. I can take out my anger on him, but you have to work with him. If you can't figure out how to cooperate, the road you're walking down together is only going to narrow. One day you'll find yourself out on a single plank, and both of you are going to slip. Just remember what I said. Pass the message on to Pavilion, too!"

Goodness nodded. He was listening to Justice Xia, but he was distracted by another noise. "Do you hear that?" he asked. "It sounds like someone singing opera?"

Justice Xia listened for a moment. "I don't hear anything. Now, don't take what I said to heart. I know how you are: just like a bell, you start tinkling as soon as the wind blows."

The truth was, Goodness hadn't imagined the sound. Wisdom Xia had stuck a loud-speaker up on the roof of his house and was playing local opera for the whole village to hear. Wisdom Xia had proposed to Pavilion that they put a loudspeaker up in the gingko tree outside Freshwind Temple. Since so many villagers had left to find work outside Freshwind, Wisdom Xia thought the place was getting too quiet. He told Pavilion that a daily broadcast of local opera would liven things up. Pavilion told him that the village government was short of money and staff, so there was no way he'd have the manpower or the budget to run the broadcasts.

That afternoon, while Goodness was over at Seven Li Gully, Wind Xia had returned to Freshwind with a bunch of baby clothes and a bundle of copies of *Shaanxi Opera Masks*, fresh off the press. Wisdom Xia was so excited he ran over to the village government office and brought back their stereo system and loudspeaker. Once the loudspeaker had been set up on the roof, he grabbed the microphone and asked Wind Xia to read the preface to his book. He wanted everyone in the village to hear it. "What's gotten into you, Dad?" Wind Xia asked him.

"He's drunk on success!" Fourth Aunt said.

"What do you mean, what's gotten into me?" Wisdom Xia said. "Just read it!"

Wind Xia turned and went into Snow Bai's room.

Wisdom Xia decided to read the preface himself, but he had to keep stopping to cough. Each time he stopped, he'd start again from the beginning. Once he'd managed to get through half the preface, Snow Bai turned to Wind Xia with a start. "What's he reading?"

"The preface to his book."

"Who wrote it?"

"I thought you heard about that," Wind Xia said. "When Mr. Black, the editor, came, he was worried the book had no preface. Goodness brought him that essay, said it was Spark . . ." Wind Xia trailed off.

"What?" she said, her cheeks turning red.

"I think it was probably Big-Noise who wrote it. It's quite good."

"What's good about it? Tell your dad to quit reading it. It's embarrassing."

"Embarrassing?" Wind Xia asked.

Snow Bai didn't answer. She looked down at the baby, sleeping on the bed beside her. She couldn't resist giving her a peck on her rosy cheeks.

When Wisdom Xia was done reading, he asked Wind Xia what opera he should play.

"What do you have?" Wind Xia asked.

"I've got all the twenty-four masterworks!"

"Really?"

"I arranged their titles into a little saying," Wisdom Xia said. "Would you like to hear it?"

"Let me drink my tea!" Wind Xia said.

"I'd love to hear," Snow Bai said from her bed.

"All right, here goes: *Across the Unicorn Bone Bed* are *A Chain of Dragon Pearls*, under *The Spring and Autumn Record* is hung a *Jade Tiger Pendant*, and *Wudianpo* has conquered the *Flood Dragon*, and *Purple Cloud Palace* will contain *The Iron Beast*, but *The Charcoal Iron* burns down *The Heavenly Gate*. While *Eight Pairs of Robes* are tied with *Silk Ribbon*, *The Black Book* is brought out to argue *The Case of Pan and Yang*, and we find *The Scholarly Matchmaker* who is *Going East of the River*; meanwhile *The Huai River Battalion* crushed the *Yellow River Army*, and *After the Sack of Ningguo* the fighters *Return to Jingzhou*, where *The Loyal and Gallant Warriors* are memorialized in *The Picture of Eight Righteous Men*, and at *White Jade Tower* they celebrate *The Joy of the Fisherman*. What do you think?

"I love it!" Snow Bai said. "You should play the '*Hanging Pictures*' section of *White Jade Tower*. I used to love singing that one."

The loudspeaker crackled to life with the sound of drums and strings.

Wind Xia didn't approve of his father playing opera from the roof. His first concern was that it would draw attention to their family. His second concern was that it was too noisy. He tried to take a nap, but it kept him awake. Snow Bai, however, threw her full support behind her father-in-law's plan. She spent the day on her bed, listening to opera, and slowly forgot all her worries. The baby, too, seemed to like the sound of opera. She stopped crying as soon as it came on and lay still, staring up at the world with her little eyes. The Xia family's cat, who was pacing on the roof, jumped down, appearing in the yard so suddenly it seemed to have fallen to earth from far above. The cat pricked up its ears as if it, too, was listening intently to the opera. The roses seemed to bloom at the sound, too. And Lucky appeared to appreciate it more than anyone. She sat out in the yard, gazing up at the loudspeaker, and howled along to the music.

Having heard about the birth of his child, Wind Xia was obligated to look after the child, but his relationship with his daughter had gotten off on the wrong foot and never recovered. As soon as he'd stepped in the door carrying his bags, the baby had started crying. When he finally got a look at her, he'd been startled. She was too skinny, he thought, and her wrinkled face made her look like an old man. "How are we supposed to keep that thing alive?" he'd asked.

When she heard that, Fourth Aunt picked up the baby and put it in Wind Xia's arms. "That's enough crying," she told her granddaughter. "Open up your eyes. Have a look at your daddy. This is your father!" When the baby cried, she shut her eyes tight, but she stopped for a moment and did as Fourth Aunt said. When the baby saw her father, she trembled and started crying even harder.

Wind Xia had returned to Freshwind to look after Snow Bai and the baby, since tradition dictated that his wife rest for a month after giving birth, but he wasn't much use. He had stopped picking up the baby after the first time Fourth Aunt had put her in his arms, he refused to wash diapers, and his mother didn't let him in the kitchen to help cook the five or six meals that Snow Bai ate each day. When Snow Bai ate, Wind Xia's bowl was always full, too. "I'm supposed to be the one resting for a month," Snow Bai said to Wind Xia, "but it looks like you're joining me!" Snow Bai pulled him over to sit beside her on the bed. She wanted to talk to him, but he seemed to have nothing to say.

"Why don't you say something?" she asked him.

"I'm waiting for you to talk," Wind Xia said.

"I want you to pick a name. What would sound good?"

"Troll."

"She already has an uncle named Halfwit. Isn't that bad enough?"

"Well, she's ugly, isn't she?"

"Why would you say that? I think she's beautiful!"

"That's your opinion," he said.

There was a long silence. "When you're out of the village," Snow Bai said, "you have plenty to say, but once you get back home, you're always like this."

"There's a new secretary-general of the United Nations . . ."

"You hate spending time with us, don't you? You can't stand your own wife, your own daughter? Why won't you talk to us?"

Wind Xia lit a cigarette. He took a drag, then thought that it might be bad for the baby, so he stubbed it out. "Why are you so goddamn chatty now?" he asked Snow Bai. "If I have something to say, I'll say it. If I've got nothing to say, I'll keep my mouth shut. Can't I relax in my own home?"

"This should be a happy time in your life," Snow Bai said. "We were all looking forward to you coming back. But ever since you got here, you've just moped around. I have to drag every word out of you."

"What do you want me to say? Every time you open your mouth, it's the same thing. What do you want from me?"

Snow Bai took a deep breath and exhaled slowly through her nose. Tears began to run down her cheeks. Wind Xia stood and leaned against the cabinet. "What are you crying for? You're supposed to be looking after yourself, especially now. I guess you don't care, do you? Go ahead and cry." Wind Xia jerked back the curtain over the door and went out, leaving Snow Bai to cry.

Clerk had just come into the yard, but he didn't go into the house. He was carrying a stone lion that he set down on the edge of the flower bed. He told Wisdom Xia that he'd asked Liu, the accountant from the township government, to get it for him when he went back to his hometown in Guanzhong. There was a custom in Guanzhong of giving newborn babies a stone lion, which was tied to the baby with a red string. The lion brought good luck and served as a guardian, but more practically, it helped stop the baby from slipping off the kang.

Wisdom Xia was overjoyed. He called for Fourth Aunt to put on some tea for Clerk, but Clerk said he had only come to tell Wind Xia that the township head had invited him for dinner.

"What delicacies are going to come out of your kitchen tonight?" Wind Xia asked.

"There's a VIP in town," Clerk said, "so the township head wants to take him out for a meal at House of Treasures. I've tried the food there. You didn't hear it from me, but it's not that great."

Wisdom Xia brought out a half dozen copies of *Shaanxi Opera Masks* and began signing his name on the flyleaf of each book. He told Wind Xia he wanted him to give them to the township head and his staff. "You don't even know if they like opera," Wind Xia said. "You can't just force your book on them."

"The important thing is that you'll be the one giving it to them," Wisdom Xia said. "Even if they never crack the spine, they'll make sure everyone sees they have it." He went back to signing the books, then called Fourth Aunt to take them inside and lay them out on the table so that the ink could dry. He held one of the books up to the sun and admired it. "What did you do when you published your first book?" he asked his son.

"You only waited a day before you started giving them out, but I sat with a pile of my first book for three days. I wrote a note inside each copy and gave them to my coworkers. Three days later, I found two copies at a used-book stall. I only had to look at the dedications to know who had sold them. I bought them back and wrote underneath the old dedication, 'I humbly present to you once again.' And then I gave the books back to those coworkers who'd sold them."

"You're just having a bit of fun with your old dad, aren't you?" Wisdom Xia said. "None of them would dare sell these."

Wind Xia and Clerk took the books and left.

First Aunt arrived, leading Second Aunt. Second Aunt hadn't been able to visit since Snow Bai had given birth, and she finally called on First Aunt to bring her over. "Where's my grandbaby?" Second Aunt called out. "This blind old lady has come to rub her cheeks!"

Fourth Aunt led her two sisters-in-law inside and called Snow Bai to bring the baby out into the yard. Before Snow Bai could wipe her tears and scoop her daughter up, Second Aunt came into the room. She took the baby in her arms, stroking her face. Second Aunt said the baby had the Xia family features—a big nose and thick ears. Second Aunt flipped up the baby's vest and rubbed her belly, then took out a roll of bills and tucked it into the baby's blanket. "Little one," she said, "your parents are civil servants, and your blind old great-aunt is just a farmer. I don't have much money, but I hope you'll accept this!"

"What are you giving her money for?" Snow Bai said. "It's not necessary."

"It's our custom," Second Aunt said. "I've given what I can. It's good luck!"

"Accept it on your baby's behalf," Fourth Aunt said to Snow Bai. "Tell her what a good heart her great-aunt has. When she gets older, she can buy a little present to pay her back!"

"I'm afraid I won't be around for that," Second Aunt said. "How many years have I got left? I'll just be happy if she comes to my grave and burns some incense."

"You think she's going to go all the way out there?" First Aunt teased. The three old women cackled. As First Aunt took the baby in her arms, the women heard a sound that they all recognized: the baby had filled her diaper. First Aunt set the baby down and peeled the diaper back to reveal a smear of diarrhea.

Snow Bai tried to take over. "You'll get dirty," she told First Aunt. They carried the baby out to the yard and set her down in the chair under the tickle tree.

"Since when am I worried about getting dirty? Changing a baby's diaper doesn't count as getting dirty." First Aunt wiped the baby's butt and then wiped between her legs. She noticed that the baby needed wiping farther up between her legs but that her butt was clean. Very casually, she said, "There's no hole back there."

As soon as the words were out of her mouth, First Aunt turned very pale. "How could that be?" she asked. Everyone bent down to take a closer look. It was true: the baby had no asshole. Fourth Aunt picked the baby up and pried its butt cheeks apart. She yelled for Wisdom Xia in a voice that sounded like she'd just been stung by a scorpion. Wisdom Xia came out, examined the baby, and immediately fainted.

Who'd have thought, huh? A baby born without an asshole! And it took everyone that long to notice! You'd have thought someone would have caught on that the piss and shit were coming from the same place.

In the history of Freshwind, there had never been a baby with this condition. It was something people cursed each other with, though. When people argued, they might say, "You filthy motherfucker, may your next child be born without an asshole!" But it was just a curse. Nobody expected it to ever actually happen!

The three sisters-in-law and Snow Bai got Wisdom Xia back to his feet and led him in to his kang. They pinched him under the nose and poured some sour broth down his throat. When she saw that Wisdom Xia was okay, Snow Bai ran to her room and broke down. She cried and pounded the bed until her fists hurt.

The three sisters-in-law were unsure what to do or how to react, but when they heard Snow Bai crying, they all started crying, too. Finally, First Aunt wiped her eyes and looked at Wisdom Xia. He was locked in the same position as before.

"Wisdom," she whispered. He didn't respond. "Wisdom!" she said, louder this time. He still didn't respond.

She got up and waved her hand in front of his face. She thought that maybe he was still unconscious, but then she saw the two rivulets of tears running down his cheeks. The tears dripped off his chin and soaked his shirt.

Wisdom Xia had never cried like that before. It seemed as if he was trying to squeeze every drop of water in his body out through his eyes. His face seemed to narrow as he cried, and his neck looked like it would no longer support his head. Finally, he stopped. The four women were still weeping. He stood and went to shut the gate. Then he told First Aunt and Second Aunt that the story could never leave the house. The Xia family's secret had to be preserved. It could never be revealed.

"You think we're animals?" First Aunt asked. "We know it can't leave this house."

Wisdom Xia told Fourth Aunt to go wash her face. The family had its shame to bear, and she couldn't give anyone else in Freshwind a hint of the pain they were suffering. He went out into the yard and looked up at the sky, full of white and black clouds, with no shades of gray. They were laid out like a mountain range to the horizon. A swarm of wasps landed on the top of the gate and then buzzed into the yard and hovered above the chair under the tickle tree.

There shouldn't be wasps in the middle of winter, Wisdom Xia thought to himself, *and definitely not a swarm of them.* He suddenly let out a gasp. It wasn't the thought of the wasps that had startled him—it was the baby! Nobody was looking after the baby! She was still in the chair. He went over and picked her up. "My little baby," he said, "what did you do in your last life to deserve this? Why did you have to be born into the Xia family?" He spanked the baby. She did not cry. She looked up at him with her bright eyes.

The sun set, and nobody went into the kitchen to make dinner. The house was dark. The wind blew over the roof tiles, and the tickle tree made its strange sound.

Out in the alley, Culture and a few boys from West Mountain Bend were talking. One of the boys said, in his thick mountain dialect, "There was a couple spurrows up i' the tree, one pretty spurrow an' one naughty spurrow. The naughty spurrow says ta the pretty spurrow, 'You move ower a bit,' but the pretty spurrow says, 'If I move ower, I'll fall aff the branch.' The naughty spurrow says, 'That's fine, I'll grab ye.' The pretty sparrow tells him off: 'Grab yerself, ya naughty cunt.'" They laughed until they were crying and gasping for air.

Wind Xia and the township head knocked at the gate.

Wisdom Xia jumped up from the kang. He reminded his wife and Snow Bai that they couldn't let on that anything out of the ordinary had happened. "You can't show it in your face," he said. "I don't want him to think that something's going on." They all took a deep breath, then Wisdom Xia flicked the lights on and went out to open the gate.

"Mr. Xia," the township head said, "I brought your son home safe and sound. He might've had a few too many, but it's nothing to worry about."

Wind Xia tried to focus his eyes. "I'm fine, I'm fine," he said. "Go boil some tea for the township head, Snow Bai. What is that baby crying about now?"

"I'll take care of that," the township head said, and reached down to pick up the baby. She stopped crying immediately and sputtered and hiccupped as if she was offended at being so abruptly lifted up. "Oh-ho-ho, you're angry at me for taking your daddy away from you, aren't you?"

Wisdom Xia looked over to see that his son had put his head down on the desk. "Why'd you drink so much?" he said angrily. "The township head is still here, and you can't even hold your head up. What's wrong with you?"

"Every man has his time and place. It's written in the stars. It's not my time to die yet."

"What the hell are you talking about?"

"Ask the township head!" Wind Xia said.

"It's true," the township head said. "Birth and death are both determined by fate. The time and place are not our own to choose. Did you hear about the strange event we just had in Freshwind, Mr. Xia?"

"You mean Lotus Jin's strawstack?" Wisdom Xia asked.

"Far stranger than that, I'm afraid. It's Mid-Star's dad. He's dead."

"What?"

"You didn't know?" the township head said. "I guess the word hasn't spread yet."

"How did he die?" Fourth Aunt shrieked.

"He'd been dead close to a month, it seems, but nobody knew. We just got word from South Gully. The village sent a few policemen up to check, and they confirmed it. Who would have thought? The word is, he died at the shrine on Tiger Head Cliff."

"So what exactly happened?" Wisdom Xia said. "He hadn't been well for a while . . . Did he take a turn for the worse?"

"It looks like a case of homicide."

"He was murdered?" Wisdom Xia said.

"I got the word this afternoon from the police," the township head said. "The culprit was caught and confessed to everything. It sounds like the murderer had also been worshipping at the shrine. I'm sure you've heard about Master Clear-Bright. After he died, his body didn't decay. The master's corpse was installed in the shrine, and pilgrims go to make offerings. Mid-Star's dad started saying he had done all the good deeds he had in him. That was why his son had been successful, he said. And he said that because of his good deeds in this life, his body would somehow be preserved after his death. He made a coffin and took it up to the cliff behind the shrine. Once he was in it, the murderer nailed him inside. It's always raining up there, and it's humid even when it's not raining, so the body decayed quite rapidly. The coffin started leaking. It was leaking down from the cliff, and somebody spotted it. They went to the police to report it."

Fourth Aunt pulled Snow Bai into the bedroom. Both women were horrified.

"How could this have happened?" Wisdom Xia asked. "He was always trying to tell his own fortune, always praying to live a bit longer . . . He was scared of death! Why would he do something like that?"

"Maybe the fear got to be too much," the township head said.

"Does Mid-Star know?"

"He hasn't been informed yet."

"We have to keep this private," Wisdom Xia said. "It can't spread."

"That's impossible at this point. Everyone over at South Gully is already talking. I'm headed over there tomorrow. I thought you might want someone from your family with me, to help out with the funeral arrangements."

Wind Xia lifted his head from the desk. "I'll go," he said. "I want to have a look."

"Have a look at what?" his father asked. "What the hell is there to see?" He turned to the township head and said, "You should talk to Pavilion. It might be best if someone from the village committee goes instead. We'll take care of notifying Mid-Star."

"You're probably right," the township head said and then rose to leave.

When Wisdom Xia noticed his son following, he dragged him back to the desk.

Wind Xia heard the sound of his wife crying in the other room. "What are you crying for?" he asked. "What a pain in the ass!"

"Go wash your face," Wisdom Xia told his son. "There's something I need to talk to you about."

Wind Xia looked at his father suspiciously but went to fill a basin. He stood with the basin held in front of him, dipped his face in it, and then lifted his head, sputtering and splashing water across the floor. As he dipped his head in again, Wisdom Xia told him about the child.

Wind Xia, facedown in the ice-cold water, did not move. He sucked in one mouthful of water and then another. Wind Xia didn't want to lift his head for air. Finally, his legs gave out from under him. The basin clattered to the floor, and he fell beside it. Nobody went to help him. Nobody spoke. The baby, sleeping on the kang, suddenly yawned.

Wind Xia sat up. He stayed for a long time in the puddle of water without speaking, and then he snorted and said, "So, she gave birth to a freak? We'll just have to get rid of it."

As soon as Snow Bai heard that, she reached for the baby and took her into her arms, crying.

"Then what do you think we should do?" he asked his wife. "Even if we didn't do anything, you think she'd survive? Now she's still breastfeeding. It's easy to push that out the wrong hole, but what about when she starts eating solid food? And when she gets older, what then? What about when it's time for her to get married? She'll suffer just as much as we will. Get rid of it. We can have another. Just tell everyone she got sick and died." Wind Xia looked over at his mother and father. They said nothing. "It's better we do it now," he said, "before we've gotten too attached. If we wait too long . . ."

"What do you mean by that?" Fourth Aunt asked. "Of course there's an attachment. You'd have an emotional attachment to a dog or a cat, even. But we're talking about a human being!"

"If you won't do it, I will," Wind Xia said. He stood up from the puddle and tried to wrest the baby from Snow Bai's arms. She fought back, but he overpowered her. He wrapped his daughter in a blanket. The baby woke up but did not cry. She looked up at her father with black, bright eyes. Wind Xia covered the baby's face with a rag. Snow Bai, Wisdom Xia, and Fourth Aunt watched as he put the baby in a bamboo basket and carried her out of the house.

Snow Bai wailed and sobbed. Fourth Aunt wept. The light bulb that hung over the desk suddenly burst with a pop. The two women stopped crying for a moment as the room went dark. Then they began to cry again, and Wisdom Xia, too, wept. When Wind Xia came back half an hour later, he was not carrying the baby.

"Why doesn't someone turn on the light?" he asked.

Nobody answered him.

When Wind Xia came back from the city, he'd set up a cot in the room at the back of the house so he could smoke and wouldn't have to hear the baby cry. He went into the room, shut the door, and lay down on his cot to sleep.

Wisdom Xia got up and wiped away his tears. He began to feel around in the darkness for a new light bulb. He gave up and decided to find a candle. He struck a match. "Where's that candle?" he asked.

"Behind the table screen," Fourth Aunt said.

He struck another match and another, and then the room was filled with a brighter light. The flame of the candle flickered like the heartbeat of a toad. "Wind Xia," Wisdom Xia called, "Wind Xia." Wind Xia didn't reply.

Fourth Aunt paced back and forth. "I can't stand it," she said. "Where did he go to do it? What did he do with her? Did he do it just like that, without even wrapping her in something clean?" She knocked on her son's door. "Where did you do it? Did she cry?"

"Down along the stream, where the castor plants are," Wind Xia said from behind his door.

"It's blowing so hard out there," Fourth Aunt said.

"You worried she'll catch a cold?" Wind Xia asked.

"I can hear her," Snow Bai said. She jumped down from her bed and ran outside. Fourth Aunt followed her. They went down the alley to the stream. There was nobody around. They looked through the castor plants, but the baby wasn't there.

"I don't hear her crying," Fourth Aunt said. "Maybe he buried her." Snow Bai started to sob. "You can't cry. What if somebody hears you?" As Fourth Aunt turned to go back home, she suddenly spotted the baby, lying down in a small depression along the riverbank. She could see in the pale moonlight that the baby was still alive. The rag that Wind Xia had covered her face with was gone, and she stared up at her mother and grandmother. Snow Bai knelt to pick the baby up and saw that she was covered in hundreds of black ants. As she reached for her child, the ants scattered.

They walked as quietly as they could but not quietly enough to sneak by Forest Wu. "F-Fourth Aunt," he said, "what are you d-d-doing out so late? And out w-with the b-baby?"

"She fell off the bed," Fourth Aunt said, "and she wouldn't stop crying, so we decided to take her out for a walk, calm her down. Call her soul back . . ."

"Easy e-enough, eh, for a baby to f-f-fall off the bed. Gave her a f-fright, huh?"

"Well, good night then."

"G-guess what I just h-heard over a-at Bowed Ox Ridge?"

"What did you hear?" Fourth Aunt asked.

"Couple ghosts arguing! It was Mr. Sh-Shou a-a-and Spark's dad, fighting o-over something!"

"What are you talking about, ghosts? Get out of here. Go home."

"W-well, if that's h-how you feel, I'll g-go!"

When Forest Wu left, Fourth Aunt spat in the dust. "I mean it, though," she said. "She must have gotten the soul scared right out of her. We have to get it back."

"Come back," Snow Bai called in a soft voice. "Come back!"

Fourth Aunt took the baby from Snow Bai and knelt beside the road. She rubbed dirt across the baby's forehead. "Come back," she said.

When they got the baby home, she started to cry again and refused Snow Bai's nipple. The baby's cry had become a high-pitched shriek. "She wasn't ready to be taken away," Wisdom Xia said, "and I'm not ready to have her taken away. That's just the way it is. We have to look after her."

"What the hell are you doing?" Wind Xia asked. "If you want to look after her, suit yourself. We're all going to suffer."

"Then just forget about her," Fourth Aunt said. "We can look after her just fine."

"I'm her father!"

"That's enough for now," Wisdom Xia said. "We need to discuss this."

Fourth Aunt, Wisdom Xia, and Wind Xia sat down together at the table. They talked until the rooster crowed out in the yard. They decided to take the baby to a hospital in the city. Medical science had made huge strides—a man could be turned into a woman, and a woman could be turned into a man, so why couldn't they make her a new asshole? Since the baby was too young to travel, the plan was for Wind Xia to return to Xijing and consult a doctor. When the time came, Wisdom Xia would bring Snow Bai and the baby into the city for the surgery.

That night, nobody under Wisdom Xia's roof slept peacefully, and neither did I. Right around the time the township head was telling Wisdom Xia about Mid-Star's dad, I was boiling up some potatoes for dinner. I guess I ate too many, since I got hit with a mean case of indigestion right after. Usually I could swallow a boulder and digest it just fine, so I didn't expect a few potatoes to keep me up with a stomachache. Since I couldn't sleep, I decided to go over to watch the mah-jongg game in the cultural center's activity room. Nobody was around except for Culture and some of his cronies. They played for a while, and then Culture started pushing them to go over to the 312 and make some quick cash. I'd heard about a couple of drivers getting held up on the highway, but I wouldn't have suspected Culture and his boys. I thought they might have been trying to avoid me, but Culture asked me to go out there with them. I didn't want to get involved.

"Culture," I said, "you're a son of the Xia family. This kind of thing is below you. You're not just some village gangster."

"Gangster? What do you mean by that?" Culture said. "I thought you of all people would be up for it! Suit yourself. But if you get in our way, you better watch out."

I wasn't often on the receiving end of that kind of talk. I was usually the one dishing it out! As soon as they left, I headed toward Pavilion's place, planning to tell him what his nephew had planned, but I ran into Forest Wu first. "T-talk to me th-that way? Tell me to g-g-get lost?" he was mumbling to himself.

"Who told you to get lost?" I asked.

"It w-was Fourth Aunt," he said, "a-and Snow Bai."

"Snow Bai told you to get lost? When was this?"

"J-just now."

I looked around. A firefly buzzed across my face. "Bullshit," I said. "Snow Bai is resting for the month. What would she be doing out so late?"

"F-Fourth Aunt said the baby got a f-fright, had to s-stick her s-s-soul back in her."

The sound of Forest Wu's voice was replaced by the sound of a baby crying. I guessed the baby must have gotten its sleep schedule reversed. She must be crying all night, keeping Snow Bai awake. I forgot about Pavilion completely and rushed home, leaving Forest Wu standing there. I got a piece of paper and wrote, "Lords of Heaven, Lords of Earth: my family's child is crying through the night. If you should read this, comfort the child until the morning light." That was the custom in Freshwind if a baby was crying at night. I wrote the same message on twelve sheets of paper and went out to stick them all over—one on my wall, one on the tree, one on a telephone pole . . . I didn't care about Culture and his cronies anymore. All that mattered was Snow Bai.

The next morning, I woke up to the sound of someone knocking at my gate. I opened it to see Pavilion standing there. "Why are your eyes so puffy?" he said. "You didn't sleep last night? What are you up to?"

"I was going to see you, actually, but I ran into Forest Wu and came back here . . ."

"You knew I was looking for you? Let's go!"

"Where?"

"I want you to come out to South Gully with me," Pavilion said.

I thought he had come to talk to me about Culture, but that wasn't it at all. I was relieved. He wanted me to go up to the Tiger Head Cliff shrine to help him bring back Mid-Star's dad's body. He knew I was up for anything, and I wasn't afraid of a little hard work.

We got up to the shrine and found the coffin. The body was like a pig trotter braised in soy sauce—the meat was falling off the bones. The flesh on his skull had almost completely rotted away, so I couldn't recognize his face. "Uncle Glory," I said, "is that really you?" I went and broke a branch off a tree and pried open his mouth to look for his two gold teeth. They were there, all right.

We laid the bones and rotten flesh on a sheet and carried them down from the cliff to the shrine, along with the coffin. When we got there, Pavilion kowtowed to the remains and burned incense. It was only right, since Mid-Star's dad was one of the Xia family patriarchs. We separated the pieces of the body into two bamboo baskets and brought them down the mountain.

Fifty years before, when Mid-Star's dad had been around my age, some bandits had come down from the hills and killed some villagers at West Mountain Bend, then cut their heads off, stuck their cocks in their mouths, and put them up on the stage at Freshwind's opera theater. They'd gotten Mid-Star's dad to carry the skulls in baskets just like this. Fifty years after that, I was carrying Mid-Star's dad's skull, too, in a basket hung on one side of a carrying pole over my shoulders.

"Uncle Glory, Uncle Glory," I said, "I guess I'll play the son in mourning for you." As soon as I spoke, the clay water bottle that the shrine had prepared for me slipped from the carrying pole where I had hung it and shattered on the ground. I knew it had to be Uncle Glory playing tricks on me. He was getting back at me for breaking his pot.

"What, did it just slip off?" Pavilion asked. I didn't want to tell him the truth.

When we got down from Tiger Head Cliff, some villagers from South Gully were hanging around waiting for us. I was surprised to see Fourth Aunt and Halfwit's wife, too, sitting on the stairs up to the shrine. What were they doing there? I thought Snow Bai might have come with them, but she didn't seem to be around. I assumed that they must have come because of Mid-Star's dad. I waved to them, and Halfwit's wife came over to me. Fourth Aunt stayed on the steps, muttering curses and spitting into the dust.

I didn't learn what had happened with Snow Bai's baby until a year later. When I thought back to that day, I wished I had gone up to the shrine to pray for her. I was so stupid; I just thought Fourth Aunt was muttering curses because she had seen me. I walked by their gate a few times after I got back to the village, hoping to see Snow Bai. Later on, I saw Fourth Aunt a few times, carrying water up from the spring. I always turned my back on her. "Huh," I said, "probably wants me to help her carry water . . . No way!"

Chapter 36

When it came time to bury Mid-Star's dad, his son didn't come home for the funeral. He was far away in Beijing, on a six-month training course at the Communist Party School. The funeral was simple: there was no memorial dinner, so as soon as the carriers had delivered the coffin to the grave, they dispersed. Fourteen days later—that is, what we called the "second seven"—Mid-Star turned up in a chauffeur-driven car.

His arrival coincided with snowfall in Freshwind Village. It wasn't much, a few flakes the size of wheat grains that scurried across the ground, blown by the wind, but it was followed by a cold blast fiercer than anything we'd had for three winters past. I hated winter, and this year I was unhappy as well as cold all over. All I could do was put my head down and shift stone in Seven Li Gully.

I was working my ass off, and Justice Xia was delighted. He figured I was a changed man. *How could you be so stupid, Uncle Justice? How can I make you understand?* When I thought about Snow Bai, I could forget that I was carrying stones, and when I was carrying stones, I could forget about Snow Bai. The hard work warmed me up, too, though my hands cracked all over and bled. Justice Xia told me to go to the store and buy mittens.

The village streets were deserted, except for Lucky and Tiger, who were glued together under the East Street archway. "Get lost!" I swore at them and threw a stone, but it had no effect.

Just then, Mid-Star and his driver passed by, laden down with baskets and heading for his dad's grave. Mid-Star called me over and told me he knew it was me who'd carried his dad down from Tiger Head Cliff. By way of a thank-you, he pushed a wad of bank bills at me, but as I went to take them, a gust of wind blew them away. I figured it was his dad's ghost trying to stop him from paying me. So when the driver had collected up the money and given it back to me, I refused it.

"If you really want to thank me, you can give me those leather gloves of yours," I said to Mid-Star.

And he did. He was much more generous than his father. One good turn deserves another, so I helped them carry the baskets, and at the grave I kowtowed to his dad. Mid-Star didn't cry, but he burned three whole bundles of paper and a stack of spirit-money bills stamped with "1 million" and "100 million." After they were burned down, he got ready to set fire to his dad's old clothes and bedclothes, and the double pouch the old man always took with him when he traveled around, making his predictions. One by one, he consigned them to the flames. "Dad, I've come home from Beijing. You know, doing the Party School course means I'll be promoted now I'm back!" he announced.

"Really?" I said. "Will you get transferred to Zhou City?"

Mid-Star glanced at his driver. "I'm just trying to keep his spirit happy."

I jumped in with, "Uncle Glory, Uncle Glory! Look at all the men in Freshwind. Wind Xia's just someone's pinkie, but Mid-Star's the thumb. I know you're down in the underworld, but I hope that puts a smile on your face!" I dragged the double pouch over to the fire. It was heavy, and I took a look inside. There was a roll of yellow paper, some cinnabar ointment, a stamp made from a piece from a jujube tree that had been struck by lightning, and the notebook I'd already sneaked a look at. He'd recorded all his predictions there, and his notes were very interesting. "Mid-Star," I said, "Uncle Glory spent a lifetime telling people's fortunes. He must have attended every wedding and every funeral in the area. Now that he's dead and gone, you should keep some mementoes of him."

"Then you take that notebook," Mid-Star said.

I put it in the inside pocket of my jacket.

Later that night I sat on my kang and read the notebook. When I got to page eighteen, there was a bit where he was cussing me for talking and joking with people outside the Earth Shrine. But I shut up as soon as he passed by, which showed I didn't trust him, and, to top it all, I'd been passing out cigarettes to the others, even to Forest Wu and Bright Chen. And he was the only one I hadn't given cigarettes to. He wrote, "Spark's pervy, he can't keep his eyes off Wind Xia's wife, he's worse than a dog. If I had a gun, I'd shoot him."

I turned scarlet in the face and was so scared that someone else might read it that I ripped out that page and threw it in the corner.

I went to bed, but I couldn't sleep, so I picked up the notebook again and carried on reading. There was no more cussing me, but he'd written a couple of dozen entries with predictions about his own health. According to these, he didn't have long to live and would probably pass on before the New Year. No *momo* buns made of freshly milled wheat flour for him then. He was angry that his life would be so short, angry that Freshwind owed him so much, angry that everyone was trying to run rings around him.

Five pages from the end, he'd written, "Last night I had stomach pains, and they were so bad that I was rolling around by the stove fuel opening. The rice in the pot wouldn't cook, and the flames licked out of the stove and set fire to the firewood stack. 'If I'm going to die, then just let me do it now,' I thought. 'Let the whole house burn down and me with it.' But then it struck me that I was leaving the house to Mid-Star, so I struggled up and smothered the flames, and poured a bucket of water over them so they went out." The fourth page from the end, he'd written, "I haven't got much longer, I know. But why do I have to die when so many of the villagers are older than me? Today I made some predictions to see what would happen to them. New-Life will die in water. Concord Qin will live to be sixty-seven. Justice won't be buried in a grave. Shifty will die on a rope. Wind Xia will never come back to the village. Next year, the apples and pears in the orchard will be laden with fruit, but the following year there will only be a single apple. Gold's mom will have a long life, she'll outlive her sons. Wisdom Xia's house will go back to the Bai family, Pavilion will crawl in the dust, Marvel's mother will be buried in Seven Li Gully, and Marvel will be village head. In twelve years' time, there will be wolves in Freshwind Village."

"That's ridiculous!" I exclaimed. "Ridiculous!" All the same, it made my hair stand on end. I looked up at the beams and almost imagined that I could see Mid-Star's dad's ghost hovering over me. I smoothed my hair down so hard that it crackled and spat with static electricity. Then I read the last bit again and looked for my name. I wanted to see what he had to say about me, but he said nothing at all. I looked for Wisdom Xia's name, but there was nothing about him, either. Most of all, I wanted to know about Snow Bai, but she wasn't there, either. Fine, but did the words "Wind Xia will never come back to the village" mean that Snow Bai would leave, too?

I cursed the old man. "I don't care that you died, but why did you have to let off such a smelly fart before you went?" I was so annoyed that I got off the kang and set the notebook alight in the pisspot.

The next day I didn't go to Seven Li Gully. I took my ax and climbed to Yijia Ridge. I had a heroic plan: I'd chop some stakes from one of the wild peach trees and knock them into the ground around Mid-Star's dad's grave so his prophecies wouldn't get through to the village. Well, I did that, but I never boasted to the other villagers about my good deed, because that day I shamed myself in Snow Bai's eyes and did something I still regret.

I'd chopped the stakes and was on my way back to Freshwind when it began to snow again, quite lightly. The flakes made me think of Snow Bai, and I stuck out my tongue and caught some. At the roadside there was a pile of corn straw. Someone must have built a shelter there to cover the melons in the fall, but it had half collapsed, and the straw was strewn all over the place. I sat down to give my feet a few minutes' rest. I stuck my tongue out as far as I could to catch the snow, and I said, "I'm gonna eat every bit of you up!"

Suddenly I heard a voice. "You're going to eat me up, Spark?"

That gave me a fright. There, at the roadside, stood White-Moth. Where had she sprung from? I thought she'd left the village long ago.

"Spark, what are you doing here?" she asked.

"What are *you* doing here?" I asked back.

"Can't I come back to visit?"

"Was it Shifty who asked you back?"

"No, it wasn't. There are other men apart from Shifty in the world."

She sat down beside me. I got up right away, but then she said, "Would you have gotten up if I'd been Snow Bai?"

So she knew about me and Snow Bai! I felt my face grow hot. "But you're not Snow Bai," I snapped.

White-Moth didn't get angry; she just smiled. "That's true. And there aren't many men like you nowadays."

Then she gave my nose a pinch. "Your nose is so cold it's gone red as a radish! Why aren't you wearing more clothes? Don't you have a thick sweater to wear?"

"I'm wearing it," I said, and I pulled up my jacket to show her. She pulled it up some more and looked and said there was a hole in it, and she could darn it for me if I wanted. That was kind of her. Ever since Dad died, people had looked down their noses at me. No one even asked if I had enough to eat. I felt quite friendly toward her. Then she moved closer to me. I was too embarrassed to get up again, but I shrunk away and made myself small.

"Shifty says you've got the guts of a thief," she said. "But you've sure got an ugly face."

I had no idea what to say to that.

"Let me see your nose," she went on. "Why's it got such a high bridge? I like noses like yours." I thought she was going to pinch my nose again, and if she had, I would have slapped her hand away. But instead she looked down and whispered, "I noticed you when I was working in the brickyard. I wanted to talk to you, but you ignored me. All you ever think about is Snow Bai. Fancy a man being so obsessed with one woman. I think she's really hard-hearted; she doesn't deserve you."

"Don't say bad things about Snow Bai," I said.

"Why not?"

"Because she's a good woman!"

"She's just a Snow White, that's all," said White-Moth. "You know what they say: whiteness hides a hundred flaws. And she's skinny as a rake."

Suddenly she leaned over me and picked a dry leaf off my head, and as she did so, her breasts pressed against my face. They were huge, and through the fabric I could feel how soft and warm they were. It was the first time I'd felt a woman's body, and it was like an electric shock, a flash of blinding white, then total blackness. I was falling, falling, down into a bottomless gorge, and I was shaking in terror.

White-Moth smiled. "Just look at you! Are you still in love with Snow Bai?"

She leaned over and looked at me, and her eyes glittered.

"Snow Bai!" I cried. I was so confused that I really thought it was her. I pushed my face between her breasts and squeezed them with my hands. She threw herself on top of me and squashed all the air out of me. But my hands were still moving, and she went wild. Her eyes rolled back in her head, and her lips trembled.

I really don't remember what happened after that, like, who was on top and who was underneath, which was my leg, and which was her arm. Then what was left of the shelter fell down on top of us, and if anyone had been looking, they would probably have thought we were a couple of pigs scavenging for food. I couldn't fuck her, but I pushed my fingers inside and kneaded her. She got very wet down there, and stuff spurted out of me, too. Afterward, she lay quietly beside me, her belly giving little flutters.

She brushed the corn leaves out of my hair. "You're a good man, Spark! Now I'm even more jealous of Snow Bai!"

That was like a smack in the face. I tried to get up, but my knees buckled, and I landed on the ground.

She was still saying, "Spark, Spark!"

But I struggled up again and walked away. I was overcome with remorse. Why had I done that with White-Moth? Why White-Moth and not Snow Bai? I felt so ashamed. I'd never be able to face Snow Bai again. The snow was still falling, and the wind felt like it was skinning me alive. I ran back to Mid-Star's dad's grave and started banging the stakes in furiously.

For four or five days straight, I was disgusted with myself. I refused to put any more clothes on and just let myself freeze. I spent the days silently shifting stones in Seven Li Gully and avoided anyone I bumped into when I got back to Freshwind Village.

Obedient Zhang from the supplies co-op wanted me to come and help siphon the grain spirits into bottles, but I said no. "Well, aren't you moral and upright? You've spent so much time with Justice Xia that you've turned into him."

"Fuck your mother!"

"Don't you swear at me like that!"

But I'd swear all I liked. And given half a chance, I'd have a go with my fists, too.

Forest Wu, who really felt the cold, had started wearing his padded jacket. It was the old one he'd been wearing the winter before, and there was cotton wadding poking out everywhere. He sat in the shoe shop, listening to Star Chen singing songs, while the wind whistled in through the entrance passage, so his back froze while the brazier toasted his front.

"Do you understand the words?" asked Star Chen.

"No! Why don't you sing opera?"

"If you w-want to hear op-opera, w-why don't you go to Tr-Treasure's?" Bright Chen said. "A-are you afraid of b-bumping into him?"

"Of course n-n-n-not!" said Forest Wu. "I just don't wan-want to get d-dirt in my eyes!"

Star Chen carried on singing regardless:

> Get drunk with me
> And be my friend forever . . .

His voice, and his eyes, were full of tears. Someone stomped past outside the shop. The street was surfaced with concrete, but it was covered now with a thick layer of mud and snow, and whoever was walking spattered dirty slush down the passageway, in through the door, and over Star Chen's legs.

"Wh-why are you in s-such a hurry? On your way to Bowed Ox Ridge, are you?" Bright Chen shouted angrily. The village burial ground was on Bowed Ox Ridge.

The person outside had stopped, and they heard a voice. "Aren't you going to buy yourself a market stall?"

"You-you want me to jump off a cl-cliff?" said Bright Chen.

Forest Wu laughed. "P-Pavilion d-doesn't know what to do now. The m-market looked like a fine meal for him, but now it's giving him indigestion! Star Chen! Y-you sing a-as if you're about to burst into tears. You got Emerald on your mind?"

Star Chen was so furious that the muscles in his neck stood out thick. "Wipe that snot away," he snapped.

Forest Wu blew his nose with his fingers and then wiped them on the bottom of his shoe.

The stalls in the farmers market were piled high with onions, potatoes, and cabbage. The buyer kept saying that he did not intend to buy more than he'd preordered, but the farmers weren't listening. They brought everything they'd harvested, lock, stock, and barrel, and they'd even bought more produce from the neighboring villages in the hopes that they could sell the whole shebang.

They waited for the truck, and waited, but the afternoon and the night went by, and then the next morning, and no truck appeared. Half a dozen families had brought their pigs to the square in front of the theater, but the buyer from the county bought only three until they surrounded him and argued, and he ended up buying more. Compliance's pig was the last to be weighed, and just as it was on the scales it crapped a load of manure.

Compliance was furious and gave it a kick on the rump. "Couldn't you have held it in one more minute? You've just crapped away my money!"

"The pig's more enlightened than you are!" said the buyer. "You'll make the sale even if it weighs a few *jin* less. Look at those vegetable vendors. They've been waiting for two days, but who's going to buy off them? The wholesale buyer they're waiting for has gone bust!"

The news spread to the farmer's market, and there was consternation. "They're not buying vegetables? Who says? Who said the vegetable buyer's gone bust?"

Goodness was collecting the fees for the market stalls as usual, and the farmers tried to get more information out of him, some of them with a quiet word, others noisy and abusive. By this time, the stalls had changed hands several times. But no sooner had one lot departed than another bunch of hopefuls took over. Those who'd given up figured the market was a bottomless pond that would drown anyone who jumped in, but the newcomers still hoped they could dip their fingers in and catch a few fish.

Clerk's wife was sorry she'd bought her stand and brought so much cabbage, and now she declared that anyone who took over the stall could take the cabbage, too. But no one was going to fall for that. When Clerk passed by on his way back from the township offices and asked how she was getting on, she said, "Getting on, my ass! I run a good restaurant. Why did you make me buy this stall? The sow might as well have had a litter of phantom piglets; it's throwing good money after bad!"

Clerk picked out a couple of cabbages that were rotting and threw them at an electricity pole, one after another, but didn't score a single hit. His wife picked them up out of the mud to feed the pig. "Why don't you try banging your head against the pole instead?" Clerk threw a handful of leaves at her back.

Big-Guy Ma stood at the gate of the House of Treasures and watched Clerk and his wife coming home from the market, having a furious fight. First, they grappled in the mud, then Clerk pushed her up against the dike at the edge of the road and belabored her with his shoe until Big-Guy Ma went and pulled them apart. They each complained loudly to him, and he listened to them with a smile on his face. Then he said something that silenced them. Clerk's wife went back to her stall, and Clerk brushed the snow and mud off himself and went into Star Chen's shoe shop.

"What did Mr. Ma-Ma say to m-make you quit ar-arguing?" asked Bright Chen.

"He said to go home and sleep in each other's arms, and the problem would go away."

Forest Wu laughed. "He's g-got you bo-both to a tee, h-hasn't he?"

"We might fight, but we'll never divorce, and that's because we have a good sex life!"

Star Chen, who was still singing, burst out laughing.

Clerk said, "What are you laughing at? What would you know? You've never been married. Anyway, Mr. Ma said that if the stall doesn't do well, we should start growing shiitakes instead. He can put in the start-up investment for us."

"He's generous!" said Star Chen. "I don't think he'll stay long in Freshwind."

"It's you who won't stay long here!"

"I'm a modest sort of fellow. I haven't made much on the apples, and I only get the odd customer to my stall from time to time, and now Emerald's gone, too. But do you see me leaving?" Star Chen said. "But Mr. Ma, now that's a man with big ideas, bigger than Pavilion. I heard Pavilion asked him to find some big buyers for the farmers market, and he refused. He acts more like a village head than a businessman. Is Pavilion gonna let that happen?"

Nobody answered. There was definitely something in what Star Chen said. They all turned their eyes toward the House of Treasures. Just then, Rain Xia pushed his motorbike out through the gate, with Lotus Jin's niece sitting behind him. The engine roared, and the pair shot off down the street. That started a few comments in the store.

"Women don-don't feel the cold! She j-just had a skirt on, and her legs looked like two wh-white d-daikons!" said Forest Wu.

"Mind your own business," said Bright Chen.

"Maybe Rain Xia's taken her into town to buy clothes," said Clerk. "Is she working at the House of Treasures, too?"

"Sh-she's head waitress. She oversees the other girls when they're at it," said Bright Chen.

"At what?" asked Forest Wu.

"Let it go!" said Clerk and whacked Forest Wu on the head.

Rain Xia had just bought his bike and was always taking Lotus Jin's niece around on it. He let her ride it on her own, too, so she could show off a bit.

Wisdom Xia was saving up for his granddaughter's operation and was being tight with his money, so when he heard there was a shop in Teahouse Village that sold the ladles he needed for his masks for fifteen cents less than in Freshwind, he asked Rain Xia to buy some for him.

Rain Xia delegated the task to Lotus Jin's niece. She was keen to get on the old man's good side and brought back a bag of Teahouse special steamed lamb for him, too.

"Was it you who went to Teahouse?" Fourth Aunt asked her.

"Yes."

"That's a long trip; you must be hungry. Stay and have something to eat."

"It was no trouble. It takes no time at all on the motorbike, and I had a bowl of noodles while I was there."

As soon as the girl had gone, Fourth Aunt said to Wisdom Xia, "Now look what's happened. Just because you wanted to save a few cents, your son sent that girl off on the motorbike, and she spent money on food as well as ladles. It's cost us at least twenty yuan! Radishes for the price of meat!"

When Rain Xia got back, Wisdom Xia ordered him to work the field they were leasing on the plateau behind the village. Spring was coming, and it was time to plant sweet potatoes.

"Why bother, it's not worth it!" said his son.

Wisdom Xia stared at him. "Are you going to live off farts and shit then?"

"Lots of the villagers have stopped planting their fields, and I don't see anyone dying of hunger. I promise to buy a sack of wheat flour for the family every month from now on. Will that do?"

"You could learn a thing or two from the ones who've stopped," said Wisdom Xia. "They're not farming because they've gone elsewhere to work. You're still in the village, so you'd better get on with it, and stop spending all day riding that girl around."

"Is she your girlfriend?" Fourth Aunt asked. "From what I hear, she's flighty, and a bit too friendly with Mr. Ma, too."

"Yes, well, that's why I wouldn't dare touch her," said Rain Xia. "Mr. Ma helped her set up an agency for people who want to leave the village and find jobs."

"Yes, I heard about that, too," said his mother. "And it's only jobs for women, not men. What's she getting these girls into?"

"Are you saying she's trafficking them, forcing them into prostitution? Both of you've been listening to too much gossip. If you won't believe her, you could at least believe me."

That shut the old couple up good and proper.

But Wisdom Xia remained anxious. He went looking for Pavilion and plied him with questions about what was going on at the House of Treasures and Big-Guy Ma's involvement. Pavilion simply told him, "That man thinks he's rich!" Which left Wisdom Xia none the wiser.

That night he didn't sleep a wink and got up the next day with a dull headache. His head felt heavier as the day went on, and eventually Fourth Aunt fetched Big-Noise Zhao to take his pulse. Zhao brought three bags of medicine with him. Wisdom Xia took traditional herbal medicine very seriously. First, he made sure that Fourth Aunt paid Big-Noise Zhao the full amount—he didn't want to run up any debts. Then he went personally to draw water at the well and brewed up the herbs. Chinese medicine deserved proper respect, he said. Before he drank the decoction, he washed his hands, meditated cross-legged for a while, and then slowly drank it down, one sip at a time.

Then he thought back to what Pavilion had said. What lay behind his words? he wondered. Could Rain Xia be up to something that he hadn't told his dad about? He urged Fourth Aunt to go and find Pavilion and get the truth out of him. But Pavilion and Treasure had left for Gaoba County.

Pavilion, meanwhile, was preoccupied with the farmers market. The produce just wasn't selling. So when Treasure came to discuss his and Black-Moth's wedding plans, Pavilion's responses were perfunctory. However, when Treasure happened to mention that Gaoba was home to a number of large, state-owned companies and there was a big demand for local specialties, he perked up.

It struck him that Mid-Star was now head of the Gaoba County government. Surely he'd be willing to do something for his old home village, especially as the village had taken care of his father's funeral in his absence. Pavilion decided to pay a visit to Gaoba. He also made a point of asking Treasure to come along, because he was the one in the Xia clan who was closest to Mid-Star.

Their visit quickly became the stuff of legend. The township head used to begin, "When Pavilion went to Gaoba . . ." at meeting after meeting whenever he needed to tell a success story. I'm not going to go into exactly how the visit enhanced Pavilion's reputation. Let's just say that Mid-Star received him and Treasure in his office with open arms, offered tea and cigarettes, and brewed two cups of coffee for them as well. Pavilion took one sip and left the rest in the cup. Treasure swigged the whole cupful in one sweep and then looked appalled, as if a cat had gotten into his belly and was trying to dig its way out.

There was a steady stream of visitors to the office while they were there, and Mid-Star's secretary told each one that they'd get no more than ten minutes. Pavilion and Treasure sat waiting until all official business was completed and Mid-Star turned to them, but he'd barely said more than a few words when the phone rang.

He signaled to them to keep quiet while he was speaking, and when he'd put down the handset, he said, "That was the provincial governor, Mr. Zhang. He's coming to inspect next week." More phone calls followed. First, it was Mr. Han the Party secretary, then it was Mr. Lei, head of the provincial agricultural bureau.

Pavilion was increasingly impressed. "I spend all day tripping over bricks with the peasants, while you're hobnobbing with the big boys!"

"It's nothing but a nuisance, you know," said Mid-Star. "The more higher-ups you know, the more work comes your way."

"I can see it now, Mid-Star. You'll go far!" was Treasure's verdict.

"Doesn't everyone want to go far?" said Mid-Star. "You ask Pavilion. I bet he spends all his time wondering when he'll get into the township government."

"No, not at all," said Pavilion.

"The soldier with no ambitions to be a general is a lousy soldier," Treasure pronounced.

"Then I'm a hopeless case," Pavilion said. "It's really never occurred to me."

"I believe you," said Mid-Star. "People want to go up the ladder one rung at a time. No village cadre dreams of becoming provincial governor; it is much too far out of reach."

"Mid-Star wants to be city mayor," Treasure said. "Just remember that a dozen years ago or so, everyone was saying, 'The bigger your ideas, the bigger the harvest.'"

"Let's hope so!" said Mid-Star. "I tell you, if I ever become mayor, I'll be sure to give Freshwind enough money to build it up into the biggest township along the 312."

"Never mind forking out for Freshwind in the future. All we're asking is for you to lift a finger and make a real difference to the village right now. Before we set off, Second Uncle and Fourth Uncle impressed on us that you're the most powerful man in the whole family. And by the way, they got us to bring you some apples as well."

"So they haven't forgotten me! Where are the apples?"

"At the hotel," said Pavilion. "We thought it might look bad if we brought them here."

"Oh, family members can bring me presents; that's nothing to worry about." Mid-Star clapped his hands, and the secretary popped in. "Go to their hotel and fetch the apples!"

Treasure and the secretary went off together, and after a while the latter called and asked if they should bring the fruit to the office.

"How much?" asked Mid-Star.

"Two cases," said the secretary.

"Put them in the mailroom," Mid-Star said. "Then everyone can help themselves."

Pavilion and Treasure had been worried about what to do with the apples they'd bought from New-Life Liu, in case someone saw them. Pavilion went red at the thought. But Mid-Star had sorted it out just like that. "It's just a few apples," Pavilion said.

"Oh, I know our villagers," said Mid-Star. "But you said you wanted me to help you with something?"

Pavilion told him that the farmers market wasn't doing well and asked if he could put them in touch with some of the big companies in Gaoba. He wanted to see if there was any possibility of getting sales for their fresh vegetables and other local products. Mid-Star grunted, then called in the office manager. "Have we approved Factory 707's declaration of expenditure yet?"

"We'll do it this afternoon," said the office manager.

"Then you can contact the factory head and just mention to him that he could send three trucks to Freshwind. His factory staff can do some good works there. The Freshwind wood ears, dried daylilies, and cabbages are famous throughout the province." He turned to Pavilion. "What else have you got?"

"Potatoes. Purple-skinned potatoes," said Pavilion.

"Yes, purple-skinned potatoes. When they're sliced and dried, they taste a bit like chestnuts."

The office manager nodded and went out. Pavilion stared at Mid-Star, his eyes wide. "You don't mess around, do you!" he said at last.

"You get a good name by doing things," Mid-Star said. "Right now, the main thrust is putting industry on a different track."

"Putting industry on a different track?"

"Yes, some state-owned industries aren't doing well, so we're selling them to private buyers. You know that distillery in Gaoba? Someone in Xijing's put in a bid to buy it for thirty million. Any buyer'll have to take over responsibility for the original workers as well, so that relieves the county government of a big burden."

"And you can sell it?"

"Well, it's not a simple process. In fact, it's a bit of a minefield. As a leader, you have to make quick decisions and be prepared to take drastic measures. But as soon as the distillery moves over to new products, the Xijing government will encourage other counties to go the same way."

Pavilion looked flabbergasted.

At midday, Mid-Star laid on a splendid restaurant meal for them and then made his excuses—he had a few meetings to attend—and said goodbye. His driver would take them home. However, Treasure was determined to stay. As soon as Mid-Star had gone, Pavilion asked him why he didn't want a lift.

"It's taken us this long to get here. Why not stay another day or two? Besides, Black-Moth's here; she's staying at the station hotel."

"So you two planned this in advance, did you? Well, I'm not paying your expenses for the extra days, that's for sure!"

"Black-Moth's not claiming, so why can't you pay mine?"

"All right, we'll both stay for the rest of the day. But I have to go back tomorrow, even if you don't."

"I'm staying two more days. But let's be clear. I've achieved something really big for Freshwind, and you're not paying me a cent less than I'm owed on my business expenses."

They got to the station hotel, and there was Black-Moth waiting for them. That night, Pavilion had the room next door to Treasure and Black-Moth. The two rooms were separated only by a wooden partition, and the lovers made a racket all night. Eventually, Pavilion gave up trying to sleep and got up to peer through a crack in the partition. All he could see was something white and finally realized that Treasure was screwing Black-Moth with her back pressed against the partition. Then Black-Moth farted.

Pavilion was furious, but there wasn't much he could say, so he got dressed and went out for a meal and a drink. As he ate and drank, he thought. What he was thinking about was Mid-Star's work in Gaoba to "put industry on a different track," thus off-loading a lot of the county government's overheads and solving the budget deficit. He was also thinking that there was an awful lot of untilled land just now in Freshwind. Why not take it back and bring in outside labor to farm it? The thought cheered him immensely, and he stayed out until after midnight.

Back in his room, he still couldn't sleep because, even though Treasure and Black-Moth were quiet on the other side of the partition, who was to say they wouldn't get up to it again and he'd get a rude awakening? Finally, when dawn was about to break and there was still no sound from next door, he closed his eyes and slept.

In due course, three large trucks arrived from Gaoba and bought up almost all the produce at the Freshwind farmers market. The villagers were overjoyed. Pavilion, dressed in his best clothes, sat on the stone bench under the market archway along with the buyers. "Go out and get some bottles of liquor!" he shouted to Shifty. "Let's give these gentlemen a drink." Shifty bought three bottles in the shop but no snacks, or cups, either, so they had to pass the bottles between them and take it in turns to drink.

"You've done good this time," said Shifty. "I should go and hang decorations around your gate!"

"I'll be happy just so long as you don't put in a complaint," said Pavilion.

"In a village this size, there's got to be someone playing the villain as well as the hero. But all anyone wants is to live well, right?"

"What's Big-Guy Ma been doing for the last few days?" Pavilion asked.

"Drinking and gambling, of course! And Lotus Jin's niece has found work for three more girls. She's doing well, that girl. She charges two hundred yuan for each placement she makes."

"Where did she place them?"

"Qinghai, or so I heard. Big-Guy Ma used to work there. Old Zhang at the post office says the day before yesterday, Lotus Jin's niece got a telegram from Osmanthus Li from West Street, who's just gone to Qinghai. It said, 'People dumb, plenty money, send girls fast.' Dammit, I guess she means the place is full of oil field workers, and they don't see a woman from one year to the next!"

"Big-Guy Ma is creating havoc in the village," Pavilion said.

"I know what you mean. You just wait and see. I knew he was up to no good from the start."

"Don't go stirring things up," Pavilion warned him.

"I'm not planning to get into a fight over this," Shifty said.

The next day it was colder than usual, and when the restaurants tipped out their swill, it froze on the pavement. Mrs. Wang slipped on her way to the dyehouse and broke her hip. Usually, a lot of villagers would have gone to see her, but not today. They were all clustered around a new poster stuck up outside the Earth Shrine:

> There's no treasure in the House of Treasure
> Only booze, mah-jongg, and hos,
> That Ugly-Mug has set up home
> He'd like to make himself village boss
> And the villagers are all in a tizzy.
> Wake up, people!
> Monkey, ride to the rescue!

Everybody knew who the Ugly-Mug was. Big-Guy Ma had been a heavy drinker for years, and he had a red face and a brandy nose. The trouble was that everyone thought I'd written the poster. I was aggrieved, because this time I was completely innocent. I'd been hard at work miles away in Seven Li Gully. Justice Xia was a slave driver—he had us carrying stones and digging, and digging and carrying stones all day long, and when I got home in the evenings, all I did was sit and sniff that little hankie of Snow Bai's. Speaking of which, I'd been furious with Big-Noise Zhao because he'd cheated me and made me betray Snow Bai. The bastard was still winding me up.

"Are you really in love with Snow Bai?" he asked.

"Yes!"

"She's not for you."

"Why not? I eat just like you do."

"People are different," he said. "Take Lucky. She goes after Tiger because he's from the township government."

"So, you're saying I'll never have a woman?"

"There are plenty of women to choose from. Like, White-Moth's back in Freshwind now."

That gave me a fright. For a moment, I thought he knew what we'd done. "Don't talk shit," I said. "There's nothing between me and White-Moth."

"I know that," he said. "But have you seen how that girl moves? Wriggling her ass, smiling, and throwing her arms around like a real slut. She's had Shifty, and if she's had one, she'll have two or three more. Now she's hitting on Big-Guy Ma. You're nothing compared to him."

"Right, I'm broke," I said.

"Big-Guy Ma's rolling in it, but his nose is disgusting! You try wagging your tail at her, and I bet she'll come after you. She might even share a bit of Big-Guy Ma's cash with you!"

"Huh!" I spat. "I might as well give myself a hand job."

"You're a handy man!"

I hated the way he talked. I'd made up my mind; I'd keep my body pure for Snow Bai. Still, that didn't stop me from calling her name at night when I was home and sniffing the hankie.

That handkerchief had a curious effect on me. Every time I sniffed it, I went into a daze. Roughshod Ding used to tell me that when you smoked dope, you got what you saw in your mind, and even though I didn't smoke, once I was in a daze, I could see Snow Bai in front of me.

Life was good for a while. I worked all day and sweated buckets; then I went home and conjured up Snow Bai; and when I was tired, I fell asleep. The next day I went to work again, and so on. I had no interest in the villagers and their petty concerns! Why would I? But on this particular morning, they came looking for me. The trees stood stiff on either side of Seven Li Gully, their branches knocking together in the wind. "Cold!" they whispered. "C-c-c-c-cold!" Then suddenly a bunch of men appeared in front of me. "Spark, you're a good man!" they said.

"I'm not so bad," I agreed.

"People are making out that Big-Guy Ma is the God of Wealth, but what's he ever done for us? The rich have gotten richer; the poor have gotten poorer. But we're all human, so why should he eat his fill when we're just left with rice gruel?"

"You eat your fill, too," I said.

"No, we don't!"

"Hard work," I said. "Work's the way to wealth."

"Hard work doesn't earn you much. You need luck to earn big money."

"What's the point of money if you're dead?"

"Very funny, Spark. We're supporting you, and you make fun of us. We're behind you, you know. That poster was great!"

"The poster? It wasn't me who wrote it."

"It must have been!"

"No, it wasn't."

"Yes, it was!"

They obviously weren't going to change their minds. Shit-eaters are not gonna let go of their shit. Just then White-Moth turned up, wearing a patterned scarf around her head. She stopped, gave a cough, and tried to catch my eye. I stood right where I was.

"Hah! The thief's here!" said one of the men.

"There are thieves in Freshwind?" I asked.

There was a lot of smirking, and a worker named Bull Wang said, "Of course there are. They steal men. Best make sure you keep your belt done up tight, Spark."

I realized they were taking a dig at White-Moth.

She scowled. "Who's a thief? Did I steal you?"

"That hole between your legs is so big, I'd need a roof tile to bridge the gap!" Bull Wang said.

White-Moth threw herself at him, her hands spread wide, ready to claw his face, but he pushed her so hard that she sat down on her butt. He'd gone too far now, and I hauled him off. "Bull Wang, stop bullying her. You're so heavy-handed. What's she done to you?"

"Didn't you see that she was trying to scratch me?" he said. "She can lose face if she wants, but I'm keeping mine!"

White-Moth sat on the ground and wailed. "You haven't got any face to lose! Remember what you said the day before yesterday, when you trapped me in the alley?"

"You don't give up, do you?" said Bull Wang. "If you fucking say another word, I'll rip your mouth open!" He tried to get back at her, but I put myself between them and pulled White-Moth to her feet.

"Get lost," I told her.

"Spark . . . Spark . . ."

"Don't 'Spark' me. I don't want anything to do with you ever again."

White-Moth was annoying, but the men were worse. I gave them all the slip and went to Star Chen's shoe shop. He was shaping a shoe on a cobbler's last and asked if I wanted some cloth shoes. I said no. Then Bright Chen came in and said that Goodness had spotted the poster, pulled it down, and shown it to Pavilion. Big-Guy Ma might be in for a rough ride. Meantime, Roughshod Ding was shouting and swearing at the House of Treasures gate.

I asked who he was swearing at, and Bright Chen said, "He's sw-swearing at y-you. He says you're trying to f-fuck them over, even though you d-don't have a . . ."

I got up and left. I'd gotten as far as the House of Treasures when Roughshod Ding stepped out in front of me. When I tried to get past on the right, he stepped left, and the same when I tried the left.

"A good dog doesn't block the road!" I said.

"Did you write the poster?" he asked.

"Was there something wrong in it?"

"What do you mean? Are you trying to drive Big-Guy Ma out of the village? Are you jealous of our business?"

"Jealous of you?" I said. "You must be joking!"

Suddenly, he pushed me to the ground. I wasn't paying attention; that's the only reason he succeeded. Of course, I had to hit him back. I'm quite short, but Roughshod Ding is even shorter. We grappled, and he tried to trip me up. I dodged and tried the same with him, and he dodged, too. We were just about equally matched.

A lot of people had gathered around by then. No one stepped in to break it up; in fact, they cheered us on. Finally, I got him down. He got on all fours like a dog about to take a shit.

Then he got hold of a broken brick and yelled, "I'm going to kill you!"

That scared the hell out of me, and I ran. Roughshod Ding followed me, still with the brick in his hand. The crowd got in my way so I couldn't escape, and the pair of us ended up chasing each other in circles.

"Tongue-Tied!" I yelled. "Tongue-Tied!"

I meant to bolster my courage and maybe scare Roughshod, too, but to my surprise, Tongue-Tied appeared. He'd been waiting for me at the top of East Street. He hadn't actually heard me shouting but was fed up with waiting and turned up on the tractor. When he saw the fight, he piled in, flinging his arms around Roughshod Ding and grabbing the brick off him.

I took my chance and landed a few hard punches. Roughshod Ding tried to bite Tongue-Tied's hand, but Tongue-Tied flung him to the ground. At that moment, Goodness came looking for Roughshod Ding and Rain Xia; they were wanted at the village offices. Roughshod Ding went, muttering, "I'll fuck your mom, Spark!"

"And I'll fuck yours!" I said.

"What with?" he replied. "Go on, pull down your pants and show us! I dare you! Go on!"

Everyone roared with laughter, even Goodness. I didn't mind Roughshod Ding being rude, but I couldn't stand all those people laughing at me. "Fuck you!" I said. They laughed even louder, and I got so angry that I started shaking and frothing at the mouth.

Tongue-Tied threw his arms around me so I couldn't move. Pinned against his chest, I suddenly felt like I was hovering up in the air, high enough to stamp down hard on their heads and shoulders. Then I flew higher and landed on Roughshod Ding and whacked him around the head.

When I came to, I found myself lying on the stairs of the Great Qing Hall. On either side of the door, new banners hung. They read, "I wish you were not sick / I wish I had more money."

"Wake up, you idiot!" Big-Noise Zhao was saying. "You got a beating from Roughshod Ding. Why take it out on me by going for my ass? You wanna eat shit and drink piss?"

I burst into floods of tears at that.

While I was crying in the Great Qing Hall, Roughshod Ding was sitting in the village offices, also crying. "What have I done to offend anyone? Even that cripple Spark thinks he can beat me up! Pavilion, you've got to see justice done and punish Spark!"

Pavilion paid no attention, just waited until he'd run out of steam. Finally, he said, "Is that all?"

"Yes, that's all."

"Then I'll tell you something! That poster's the last straw. The Two Committees have had a lot of complaints about the House of Treasures, and the township government's getting upset about it." The complaints weren't about the restaurant itself, he explained; they were about Big-Guy Ma. If Ma had stuck to shiitake mushrooms, he would have kept the Two Committees' backing, but this business of finding dubious jobs for village girls elsewhere was damaging Freshwind's reputation and upsetting everyone.

Rain Xia had kept quiet up till then, but now he put in, "Have you got something against my girlfriend?"

"The villagers do," Pavilion said. "But like I said, this concerns Big-Guy Ma. We look after our own."

"Do you have any evidence that those girls work as prostitutes?" Rain Xia asked.

"Do you have any evidence that they don't?"

"Okay, let's forget it. Let's not say things we might regret. So here's my question: If we want to kick Big-Guy Ma out of his room at the House of Treasures, what are we going to use as a pretext? If we let Star Chen lease the apple orchard and run a shoemaker's shop as well, what law can we hit Big-Guy Ma with to get rid of him? He's not a spy or an escaped criminal."

"I'm telling you the consensus among the villagers. If you won't listen to me, you have to take the rap, and don't come complaining to the Two Committees," Pavilion snapped angrily. "Right now there's at least twenty *mu* of land left fallow in Freshwind. Second Uncle's been haranguing me about it till he's blue in the face. He spends all his time at Seven Li Gully, sweating blood to turn it into new farmland, while we still have twenty *mu* or more lying fallow in the village. I'm not taking on responsibility for more development."

"Well, you can't blame the House of Treasures. People don't want to farm anymore; you can't change that. If we didn't have the restaurant, Roughshod Ding and I would have left long ago, and if you hadn't set up the farmers market, even more people would have left. I didn't object to the market. Can't you accept the restaurant?"

Pavilion didn't know what to answer. He sat in silence for a while, and then he smiled and said, "You're a smart one, Rain Xia."

"I understand what Pavilion's saying," Roughshod Ding added at this point. "You support the restaurant but not Big-Guy Ma, right? You leave Big-Guy Ma to me. Freshwind belongs to the villagers, and the village has to do what the Two Committees say. If Big-Guy Ma wants to stay in the village, then he'll have to stick to his shiitake mushrooms. Any bigger ideas, and he'll have to take them elsewhere. He won't be welcome at the House of Treasures, that's for sure. I can certainly understand Pavilion's dilemma . . . And Pavilion, I might be speaking out of turn, but I've got something else to say if you'll allow me."

"Roughshod Ding, you've got your head screwed on, you go ahead."

"Why not put all the fallow land under one management?"

"And who will farm it?"

"If you'll lease it to me, I will."

"You?" Pavilion looked at him. "The Two Committees would have to take a proper look at that proposal."

Pavilion didn't expect this one conversation with Roughshod Ding and Rain Xia to resolve anything, but in fact it did. As soon as Big-Guy Ma realized how precarious his position was, he put Compliance in charge of running the business and left Freshwind to spend some time back home. He kept his room in the House of Treasures, and White-Moth moved into it. She was supposed to be Compliance's assistant, but Compliance wouldn't let her do anything, so instead she did a bit of waitressing in the restaurant.

The Two Committees met three times and decided to take back the fallow fields and lease them out to Roughshod Ding. Roughshod Ding, in the meantime, did a deal with Star

Chen—the Chens would sublet the land. That way, Roughshod Ding could turn a nice profit without any effort on his part.

Once Big-Guy Ma was gone, Shifty owned up to having written the poster. He told me that I should pee on the ground and look at my reflection in the puddle; then I'd see that someone like me would never be able to write that kind of text. Meanwhile, he discovered that Roughshod Ding had sublet the fallow land to outsiders. That put him in a terrible rage, and for the first time ever, he went to Seven Li Gully to talk to Justice Xia.

He had brought a packet of tobacco with him as a gift for Justice Xia and put it down in front of the old man. I harrumphed and went back to carrying stones. Justice Xia told me to bring out the half bottle of *shaojiu* wine in the shack and pour Shifty a glass, but I didn't answer, so he shouted after me, "What do you think you're playing at, you shit-stirrer!"

"Are you talking to me?" Shifty asked him.

"You already know you're a shit-stirrer," said Justice Xia.

Far from getting angry, Shifty just smiled and said, "Now that you're not village head anymore, we need a shit-stirrer, don't we? This time, I'm going to make sure that Roughshod Ding doesn't turn into a landlord, and I want you behind me."

"You don't want Ding leasing the land, and neither do I. In a village of farmers like Freshwind, how will we ever have peace if the gap between rich and poor gets wider? But I'm not going to back you if you want the lease! I put in a report on you; this time I really did. My thinking is this: if some people let their land lie fallow and others don't have enough, then instead of taking it back, we should redistribute it and make sure every inch is used and everyone's got work to do. If you agree, then you put your signature to my report. If you don't, then you can take your tobacco back and take your complaints elsewhere."

"You want the land to be redistributed?" Shifty said. "I'm dead against that. My mom and dad are dead, and I still farm their land. If there's a redistribution, I'll be in trouble."

"You'll be in trouble? What about men with wives and kids and not enough land. Aren't they in trouble?"

Shifty got to his feet and began to head off. As he passed a patch of scallions, he swiped a handful to eat. Tongue-Tied went to grab some, too, but Justice Xia warned them, "I just sprayed them with pesticide this morning. Make sure you wash them before you eat them, Shifty!"

The weather was still so cold that the air felt like knife blades. But that one wheat stalk had an ear of grain on it that was two inches long. Astonishing! Tongue-Tied and I were worried that it would blow over, so we found three sticks and made a support with them. The bird's nest in the tree beside it was now home to a family of three fledglings, and they peered over the edge of the nest at us and chattered away.

"Have you ever seen such a long ear on winter wheat before?" I asked them.

"No!" they said.

"I bet there's a lot you've never seen," I said.

I jammed the teeth of the fork hoe into an old tree stump in the cliff hard so the handle stuck right up in the air. *Tomorrow maybe a miracle will happen,* I thought, *and this old hoe will grow shoots.* But it didn't. All that happened was that the birds spattered the handle with white droppings.

Justice Xia hadn't seen the wheat ear. He hadn't been to Seven Li Gully for a few days. He'd spent the time going around to every family on East, Middle, and West Streets, checking who'd left their land fallow, or dug sand or clay for concrete out of it, or dug trenches in it to make mud bricks in, or (as in Clerk's case) built a public bathroom or added new gravestones to old graves that had previously been flattened. He also made a note of families that had received a portion of land for a daughter who'd since married and moved away, or for someone who'd died or been absent for more than two years, or families who had a new daughter-in-law or a child.

He collated all his figures and wrote up a complaint. Then he went to talk to Wisdom Xia in the hopes he'd revise it for him. Wisdom Xia read it through and looked unexpectedly serious. His verdict: this was not something you could make a complaint about, but it was a great proposal. He got Fourth Aunt to cook them dinner, four dishes and a soup, and put the wooden chicken on the table. "A meal to build you up, brother, and to celebrate," as he put it.

After they'd eaten and wiped the table, Justice Xia said, "Then let's draft it as a proposal instead. You can dictate it; I'll write."

It was a lengthy process. They wrote one page and couldn't agree on a particular sentence, rubbed it out, rewrote it, wrote two characters wrong and corrected them, made an inkblot, crumpled the paper up, and started again.

Fourth Aunt stood watching them. "Good Lord, is that how you treat paper?"

"This is seriously important," said Wisdom Xia.

"Are you writing a prayer to the good Lord?" said Fourth Aunt. Then she started to grind chili peppers in the small stone roller in the yard.

They all loved chilis in that family. They never had plain noodles without sprinkling chili peppers over them. Clerk's wife came by to borrow a flat basket. To do this, she had to say a lot of nice things first. Fourth Aunt was so strong and upright; she hoped Fourth Uncle still had a brilliant appetite; how was Snow Bai getting on? And the little one? Then she chatted about the trees and the flowers, cats and dogs, just about everything under the sun.

Wisdom Xia couldn't concentrate on his proposal, so he came out to berate his wife, who chased Clerk's wife out and then hurried into the house and took the baby from Snow Bai. "Let's go out for a walk," she said. "Your granddad's got a big job to do, and if you start crying, he'll start shouting again!" And she went out and locked the gate behind her.

The gist of the brothers' proposal was that the Two Committees' decision to take back the fields that were not being farmed was a correct and timely one. (Those words, of course, came from Wisdom Xia.) But, they went on, it was not in the villagers' interests for the land to be leased and then sublet by the lessee to outsiders. To ensure that not one inch of the land went to waste and that each villager had land to till, and that it was fairly distributed without distinction between rich and poor, they suggested a redistribution. Once the proposal had been written out in full, Justice Xia added his name to it. Wisdom Xia was a retired cadre with no land allocation, so he signed on behalf of Fourth Aunt and Rain Xia.

For a few days afterward, Justice Xia went from house to house, hoping to get all the households to sign up to his proposal, but he was disappointed—half the East Street families turned him down. Some were against the proposal because their families had shrunk; others because, although family members were away doing jobs in town, they wanted to hang on to their land because one day the workers would come back to the village. Those who let out their land and took payment in kind were even less interested. By the time Justice Xia had visited the families in the first three alleys off East Street, the news of his proposal had spread to the rear alleyways, and some of those villagers made themselves scarce, heading for the West Mountain Bend market with their baskets on their backs or going to drop in on relatives.

At Clerk's home, his wife claimed her husband made these sorts of decisions, but Clerk had gone straight from the township offices to their Dongzi land to repair the field dikes. Justice Xia trudged off to find him, and Lucky followed. As soon as they'd crossed the river, Tiger came bounding up. The two dogs disappeared into the pussy willow that grew along the riverbank and didn't come back even when he called. Clerk had put his radio down at the field edge, and an aria from the opera *Golden Sands* was blasting out:

The king sits in the countryside, but it's his servant who tills it.
The servant is no different from a grazing ox, or the silkworm that eats mulberry leaves.
The ox is slaughtered when it has used up its strength,
The silkworm is fried when it's done making silk.
Those who eat beef or wear silk know nothing of their suffering.

It's all wrong that down the dynasties, the kings sit in the countryside, murdering their loyal ministers and generals.

Let us curse those vulpine traitors who bring disaster on the country.

One by one, they bury their consciences, and loyal ministers evaporate like dew on the grass . . .

Clerk spotted Justice Xia in the distance, put down his shovel, and sat down on the bank for a smoke. "Have you come to get me to sign?" he shouted. "I had to sign stuff during the Cultural Revolution, but we live in different times now. Why are you starting a mass movement again?"

"This isn't a mass movement," said Justice Xia.

"You're just like the Earth God, Uncle. If you're not collecting land up, you're sharing it out. Aren't you getting fed up with it?"

"We farmers live off the earth," said Justice Xia. "We're all earthworms at heart, aren't we?"

Clerk gave his pipe a wipe and held it out to Justice Xia, but the old man didn't take it. "Has Blossom signed? And Treasure?" he asked.

"They wouldn't dare refuse!" said Justice Xia.

"Maybe not, but I'm not going to."

"Why not?"

"Because if I do, our new public bathroom on the 312 will be no use, and that bathroom's going to bring in more than breeding a pig would."

Justice Xia looked stony.

On the radio, the singer had reached the lines:

> So, I go to the yamen to tie my son to the gate
> And what happens then?
> He's bound and beheaded!
> Beheaded? Is it true?
> Indeed it is!
> In line with the laws of the kingdom!

On the dike, the two men had begun to quarrel, each one of them shouting furiously over the other, till the veins in their necks stood out blue. At the noise, Lucky scurried out of the willows and stood staring at Clerk. Clerk took a step closer to Justice Xia, and the bitch gave a bark, and another bark as he poked a finger in Justice Xia's face.

"What are you barking at?" Clerk shouted. "Are you trying to force me to put my thumb-print on that paper?" The last was, of course, addressed to Justice Xia, and he and Lucky both knew it. The dog stood on her hind legs and barked furiously.

"Are you going to bite me?" Clerk said. "I work for the township, so you better leave me alone!" Lucky jumped up and put her paws on Clerk's shoulders, panting heavily, her tongue lolling. Clerk turned to flee but tripped and did a somersault off the dike.

The dike was three yards high, and Justice Xia was aghast when he saw Clerk fall. Then he ran down the path and pulled Clerk to his feet. As soon as he let go, Clerk fell over again. "My leg!" he said. "What's happened to it? I can't stand!" He grimaced in pain. Justice Xia was in a cold sweat. He squatted down and began massaging Clerk's right leg.

"The left leg!" said Clerk. "The left one!" But when Justice Xia tried to massage that one, it hurt so much that he wouldn't let Justice Xia touch it. Justice Xia realized that something must have been broken.

"Grit your teeth, Clerk," he said. "Grit your teeth!"

Then he put Clerk on his back and headed for Big-Noise Zhao's pharmacy in the Great Qing Hall. Clerk, meantime, was yelling and screaming. Justice Xia tried to calm him down, but when he carried on, he got angry. "If you make any more noise, I'm putting you down right here!"

Clerk stopped screaming but said, "My shoe, I've lost it!" One of his feet was bare, and Justice Xia told Lucky, who was running along behind, "Go back and fetch his shoe!" But instead of obeying, Lucky rushed up, took a bite out of Clerk's foot, and ran away down into the field.

At the clinic, Big-Noise Zhao told Clerk that his left ankle was broken. He wrapped it in a medicated plaster and fixed it in place with a piece of wood. Then he dispensed painkillers and three days' worth of herbal medicine.

"Will I ever walk again?" Clerk asked.

"Of course you will! Do you fancy being waited on for the rest of your life, is that it?"

Justice Xia was still anxious. "Big-Noise, why haven't you set the bone?" he asked.

"There's no need. He just needs to lie still on a bed board for three days and take the herbal remedy. I guarantee that in seven days, he'll be on his feet again."

"I'm a living person, not a lump of wood!" Clerk objected. "How can I stay still in bed? I can't piss and shit without getting up!"

"Make a hole in the board, and there's your problem solved!"

"And what if it heals crooked?"

"Then we break it and set it again!"

At that, Clerk began to panic. "Big-Noise, you can't do that to me!"

"If you go on like that, I won't treat you!" said Big-Noise Zhao, beginning to untie the piece of wood. Clerk hurriedly placated him. "Oh my Lord, these craftsmen are so fierce!"

There must have been some bad blood between Clerk and Justice Xia in their former lives, because Justice Xia had given him grief three times: Once, he'd cursed him out about looking after the ox; another time it was about irrigation, and he'd hit him; and now he'd made him break his ankle. But this time Justice Xia was in the shit because he'd have to pay Clerk's medical expenses. Even worse, Big-Noise Zhao was missing a key ingredient for the prescription—winnowing-fan bugs—and Justice would have to figure out how to get hold of them. Justice felt so dispirited that he delegated the search for the bugs to me.

I searched high and low in the village, through everyone's henhouses and sheds, but I couldn't find those bugs anywhere. They were a kind of ugly black beetle that hung around oxen and liked moist places. I took a look in a few of the sweet potato cellars, too, but still no luck. "Can't you do without them?" I asked Big-Noise Zhao. "Or use some other kind of bug?"

"No, the remedy's no use without it," he said.

"You substitute dog bone when the scrip calls for tiger bone," I pointed out to him.

"Who told you that? Did you ever see me do it? I always use genuine tiger bone!"

"But there are only a few dozen tigers in the whole country; how can you get hold of enough bone? Are you rearing tigers under your bed?"

He smiled. "Okay, you win! But remedies for traumatic injury absolutely need winnowing-fan bugs. Have you looked in any sweet potato cellar?"

"Yes, there weren't any."

"I tell you where there'll be some: in a sweet potato cellar where there's plant ash."

I went and told Justice Xia. Fourth Aunt happened to be there, too, and she said she didn't use plant ash to store the sweet potatoes. But she had a basket of regular potatoes left over from planting, and she'd sliced them and stored them in the cave, mixed with plant ash.

"Off you go with Fourth Aunt!" said Justice Xia. And that was how I ended up at Wisdom Xia's house.

It was the first time I'd been there since Snow Bai got married. As soon as I went into their yard, the peony shook on its stem and the China rose smiled at me. I suddenly understood why it was flowering that day, and what part of the China rose its flower was. This was my idea: the flower was its sexual organ and also the most beautiful part of it, and that was why it wore the flower on its head. A wire was strung across the yard, from the northwest corner to the southeast, with three white sheets hanging on it, and there was Snow Bai with the baby in her arms, amusing it by pointing up to the bird in the tickle tree. The bird had a long tail and a white beak.

"Look, look, it's a magpie!" Snow Bai told her daughter.

"No, it's not," I said. "It's a turtledove!"

Snow Bai looked around, saw it was me, and headed indoors with her baby. She stopped to pick up a diaper that had fallen to the ground and then vanished through the dark doorway.

Then I heard a cough. At one of the windows of the main room, I saw Wisdom Xia. He was wearing a pair of spectacles and following me with his gaze. I stood right where I was in the yard when I saw him watching me. He came out with his water pipe and said, "What are you doing here?"

"Hello, Uncle," I said, but he didn't respond. His expression hardened, and my legs buckled, and I began to sway. I tried to tell myself not to sway, but I just swayed even more.

"What are you doing that for?" Wisdom Xia said scornfully.

"It's the tickle tree that's swaying, not me!" I protested. And it did, too, after the turtle-dove flew away.

"He's looking for winnowing-fan bugs in the sweet potato cellar, for your brother," said Fourth Aunt.

Wisdom Xia sat down on the bench they kept on the house steps and lit his water pipe with a two-foot-long fire rope made of strands of corn silk twisted together.

The sweet potatoes were stored below the kitchen. I lifted the cellar cover and went down. The walls were wet and slimy—my foot slipped off one of the toe holes, and I fell the rest of the way. In one corner was a basket of seed potatoes mixed with plant ash, and I sifted through it. Sure enough, several winnowing-fan bugs skittered away from my fingers. I caught them and put them in a cloth bag I'd brought.

One, two, three . . . when I got to the eighth, it struck me how strange this sequence of events was: Clerk broke his ankle falling off the dike, and I'd found the winnowing-fan bugs he needed here, of all places. Was it fate that had brought me to Snow Bai again? "Oh, Snow Bai, Snow Bai," I murmured softly in the storeroom. I hoped she would somehow sense it, because if you thought of someone, they sneezed. I stood listening to the sounds of the earth beneath my feet.

Then I heard a sneeze, and Snow Bai said, "Mom, who's thinking of me?"

"One sneeze and someone's thinking of you; two sneezes and someone's cursing you; three sneezes and you've caught a cold," said Fourth Aunt. "Are you getting a cold?"

"Am I?" I heard Snow Bai say.

Down in the cellar, I murmured, "Don't worry, Snow Bai; it's only me thinking of you. And I'm thinking so hard I made you sneeze!" I felt pleased with myself and boldly took the little hankie out of my inside pocket and held it to my face.

That put me right into a daydream. I saw Snow Bai come into the kitchen, carrying her baby. She noticed steam coming from the opening to the cellar and laid her daughter down on a pile of straw by the stove. Then, steadying herself against the wall, she came down into the cellar. First, a left shoe appeared and rested in the toe hole. The right shoe hovered in the air. It was red leather. I grabbed the shoe, but the foot retreated, and I was left with the shoe in my hand. At that moment, the baby burst into loud wails, and I snapped out of my daydream.

I heard Fourth Aunt say, "You go and tidy up, and I'll hush the baby." The wails got louder and louder, and Fourth Aunt shouted from the kitchen, "Spark, have you found any yet? Why have you been down there so long?" I looked at the red shoe I'd tucked into my inside pocket, and it had turned into the cloth bag full of winnowing-fan bugs. Then I climbed up out of the cellar. Fourth Aunt was standing by the stove with the baby in her arms. "Did you find any?" she asked.

"Yup."

"Clerk really knows how to get under your second uncle's skin!" she said.

"Clerk was born in the Year of the Ox; it's like he's headbutting him," I said.

"Clerk was born in the Year of the Ox? Your second uncle's never gotten on with ox-year people. Either he gets into fights with them or they headbutt him."

"Why?" I wondered.

"Who knows?"

I looked at the baby and the baby looked at me, and I stopped talking about Justice Xia and Clerk. The baby was part of Snow Bai's flesh; she was a tiny version of Snow Bai. "Good girl!" I said, brushing her cheek with my lips. It felt a bit like the way birds feed their nestlings in the nest.

Just then she made a gurgling sound. I thought she was laughing, but actually, she was shitting. Fourth Aunt got a bit flustered. "Hurry up. I have to change her!"

So I had to leave. Fourth Aunt didn't come with me into the yard to hold the baby so she could shit on the ground; Snow Bai wasn't there, either. "I'll be off then!" I said. Still no Snow Bai. "I'll be off then!" I repeated. And I left.

The day Clerk started taking the winnowing-fan-bugs remedy, Wisdom Xia and Snow Bai left for Xijing with their daughter. No one had any idea why they were making the trip. Some of them even had a laugh at Wisdom Xia—they thought it was weird he'd sent his daughter-in-law so far away.

Every night, I visited Wisdom Xia's house in my dreams. To get there from the East Street archway, you went down an alley and turned three corners, but in my dreams, it was always just around one bend down the alley. I don't know why.

The next time I went to Justice Xia's and passed by Wisdom Xia's gate, I got such a strange feeling. There was no one there; the yard was empty . . . But maybe Snow Bai would come back? I looked for her footprints outside the gate and finally found one. She had stepped in some mud on a rainy day, and it had dried and preserved the imprint of her shoe. I put my own foot in it. Just then, Clerk's wife came by.

"What are you doing, Spark? It's too cold to go barefoot!"

"I got a stone in my shoe," I said.

She wanted to talk to Justice Xia about Clerk. Now that he couldn't work, the township government was looking to take on a new cook. They'd also found out about the fallow land in the village being taken back, leased out to Roughshod Ding and then sublet to outsiders. The township head put a stop to the subletting right away, but then Roughshod Ding said he didn't want the lease after all. So Pavilion shelved the land-redistribution plan on the grounds that there was too much opposition to it among the villagers.

Justice Xia had the wind taken completely out of his sails. He'd spent a huge amount of time and energy on his proposal, and all for nothing. Worst of all, Clerk's wife was demanding compensation for her husband's loss of income. Justice Xia was so upset that he stopped shaving. His beard grew long and tangled, and he lost a lot of weight, too. The next time Clerk's wife appeared, he asked her, "How much do you want? Spit it out!"

"Clerk's been earning four hundred yuan a month and getting three meals a day, and he gets the swill and leftovers to bring back for the pigs. We've got a sow and ten piglets," she said. "He's got the garden allotment to tend, and I have a stand in the market, too. And every day I'm not there selling, I'm out fifty yuan because I still have to pay the rental fee and charges even though I'm at home, taking care of him. He's going to be out of action for three months or so; you work it out for yourself . . ."

"Calm down and wipe those boogers out of your eyes," said Justice Xia. Clerk's wife rubbed her eyes, and Justice Xia went on, "How much does it add up to?"

"Give me five thousand yuan. That should do it."

"Only five thousand? Why not fifty thousand?" And he got up and went into the house.

After that, Justice Xia stopped sending snacks and drinks over to Clerk's, and when it was time for the patient to have a new ankle plaster, he told Tongue-Tied to take it to Clerk. Tongue-Tied banged loudly on Clerk's gate and disappeared, so that when his wife opened up, all she saw was the plaster lying on the ground. She cursed furiously. She went to Justice

Xia's with every intention of kicking up a big fuss. Justice Xia was at Seven Li Gully, so she had a go at Second Aunt instead. In fact, she wouldn't go away.

She helped herself to their food and drink, and had a nap on their kang, and then she began to wail, "I can't go on like this. I'm going to bring Clerk over here so you can take care of him!"

Second Aunt was a bit slow, and she couldn't see anything, either, so at first, she tried to calm Clerk's wife down. But the woman just got more out of control, screaming and shouting, crying and wiping her snot and tears all over the kang and the table. When Second Aunt put her hand down and felt the slime, she threw herself on the kang and started to cry, too. Finally, the neighbors turned up and put a stop to the commotion by taking Clerk's wife away with them. Later that evening, when the daughters-in-law found out what had been going on, they tracked Justice Xia down and told him.

"Well, I'd better give her some money then," he said.

"How much money?" Chastity asked.

"I have none," the old man said.

"How are you going to give her money if you don't have any?" Chastity asked. "Let her kick up a fuss. She can't do anything, can she?"

"But how'll she get by?" said Bamboo. "Why don't we all put in two hundred each and pay her off. At least it'll keep her quiet."

"You fork out if you've got money; I don't," said Chastity. "And it was Tongue-Tied who started all this. Why did he leave the plaster on the ground outside her gate like that?"

"After what you've said, I'm not going to pay, either," said Bounty's wife. "Let her come, crying and cursing, every day if she wants. We've got nothing to fear so long as Dad doesn't feel ashamed." And she slapped her ass and stomped off.

At that, Chastity went, too, and only Bamboo and another woman were left. Justice Xia was still sitting on the stool with his head in his hands.

He waved them away. "Go on, you two. Off you go!"

It was so unlike him to sound so meek that Bamboo said, "Dad, don't worry, I'll go and talk to Clerk. Even if we did his wife wrong, she has no right to come and abuse us like that. We have to put a stop to it. But however it gets sorted out, don't be angry with your sons."

Justice Xia, sunk in misery, suddenly started crying. "How did this happen to me? What's it all about? Everything I do goes wrong!" The tears poured down his face, along the furrows made by his wrinkles. The two daughters-in-law hastily tried to comfort him and then busied themselves making him a meal.

Bamboo bought a pack of cigarettes and went to talk to Clerk. She lit up one cigarette, then another, and told him, "Clerk, you fell off the dike. Justice Xia didn't push you, but he still paid your medical bills. And now you're opening that great lion's maw of yours, wanting five thousand yuan from him, and sending your wife to ask for it. Don't you have any conscience?"

"Give me a smoke," said Clerk.

"Why should I give you a smoke?" she said. "You can buy one off me; they cost five yuan each."

So Clerk changed his mind. "If Justice Xia hadn't tried to get me to sign that proposal, and if his dog hadn't bitten me, I wouldn't have fallen off the dike," he said. "I can put up with the pain in my ankle, but now I've lost my job and I can't do any farming, either. Of course I'm going to want compensation."

"And you'll get it, no question," said Bamboo.

"How much?" asked Clerk.

Bamboo put a cigarette between his lips. "If you'll just stop pestering us, we'll come up with something." For the rest of the afternoon, Bamboo sat with Clerk, playing nice, then nasty, then nice again.

Finally, she said, "About your job as a cook: I'll get Pavilion to speak to the township government for you. You'll be able to go back there as soon as your ankle's better, I guarantee that. And for the farmwork, Justice Xia's five sons can pitch in and help; I guarantee that, too. If those two things don't happen, you can ask us for as much as you want and we'll pay you, and you can spit in our faces, too, if you want. But there's one more thing I can guarantee—if your wife goes and harasses Justice Xia once more, I can't answer for what Tongue-Tied'll do. If he breaks her leg, you'll both be flat out on the board bed."

"Don't you threaten me," Clerk said.

"It's not a threat," said Bamboo. "Tongue-Tied's sitting outside your gate right now. Tongue-Tied!"

Tongue-Tied heard and grabbed one of the piglets and lifted it up by the hind leg. It squealed loudly.

Clerk looked dejected. "If you can't give us five thousand, maybe you can do two thousand?" he wheedled.

"And do you think two thousand's going to drop from heaven?"

"A thousand! And I'll forget the other thousand."

"You don't know when you're well off," said Bamboo. "You want the money, you go and ask for it." And she picked up the cigarettes and made to go.

"Bamboo!" Clerk stopped her. "You shouldn't come here and threaten me. I know the Xias are powerful and you're a big clan, but I've got three sons, and one fine day they'll be grown up, too."

Bamboo reported back to the five Xia sons and said she'd leave it to the men to decide. To her surprise, Treasure flared up. "He's not getting a cent!"

Then Gold muttered, "Dad's always poking his nose in where it's not wanted. And now that things have gone wrong, no one from the Two Committee has turned up to help. I blame the dog. If it hadn't bitten Clerk, none of this would have happened."

Bounty and Halfwit put the blame on the dog, too. Their dad spoiled it rotten; he treated it better than his own sons.

Just then, Lucky appeared at the gate. She'd been on her way to Seven Li Gully with Justice Xia, but halfway there, he realized he'd forgotten his matches and he'd sent the dog back to get them. When she got to the house, however, the gate was locked. Second Aunt was scared that Clerk's wife might turn up again, so she'd taken herself to Marvel's mom's. So Lucky went to Bounty's. When she saw the five men, she wagged her tail and snatched a matchbox from on top of the stove.

"Look!" said Treasure. "That dog's got a demon in it!"

Halfwit slammed the gate shut, caught Lucky, and began to beat her. The other brothers piled in, too, and the lot of them kicked and trampled the poor dog. Justice Xia waited a long while on the road, and when Lucky didn't come back, he was worried she might not have understood his instructions, so he turned around and went home to pick up the matchbox himself. As soon as he got into the alley, he heard the noise coming from Bounty's yard and went in. There he saw Lucky lying motionless on the ground with blood trickling from her nose and mouth. He was so angry that he started shaking all over.

"Is it the dog you want to beat up or your dad?" he yelled. "Come on, beat me up then!" His five sons let go of Lucky and stood stock still. "Hit me!" Justice Xia shouted. "Come on! If you don't, I'll hit myself!" And he punched himself in the face.

On the ground, Lucky started whining. His sons were so scared that they ran away. Gold headed straight for Fourth Uncle's house; he'd bring Wisdom Xia back to calm his brother down. But when he got there, he suddenly remembered that Wisdom Xia had gone to Xijing that day.

The sky was covered with lowering black clouds. Concord Qin's wife was on her way home from Bowed Ox Ridge with a load of firewood she'd cut from the sour-date bushes, and when she passed the cemetery, she heard my dad arguing with the chairman of the Peasants' Association again. She was so frightened she ran all the way back to the village, dropping her machete on the way. The dyehouse donkey refused his food for some strange reason, and his belly swelled up like a balloon. And the oxhide drum on the roof of New-Life Liu's house began to play by itself.

Chapter 37

Wisdom Xia spent ten days in Xijing, then returned home to Freshwind. His granddaughter's operation seemed to have been a great success. The surgeons had made an opening, and, once everything had healed, her bowels would work normally. So when Snow Bai's mother arrived with Treasure's daughter, Bodhi, to look after Snow Bai and her child, Wisdom Xia thought it was probably time to go. He went back to Freshwind with a box of cassette tapes of Shaanxi opera. He heard what had happened while he was away and went to the House of Treasures to ask Rain Xia for a thousand yuan, claiming that he needed the money to buy more copies of *Shaanxi Opera Masks* from the publisher. He took the money from Rain Xia over to Clerk's place to give it to him. When Clerk saw the wad of bills, he rose from the kang and limped over to pour some tea.

"Quit limping around," Wisdom Xia said. "Just walk straight."

"I can't!" Clerk said. "That goddamn Big-Noise Zhao fucked me up. All I can do is limp." He set a cup of tea down in front of Wisdom Xia.

"This is filthy!" Wisdom Xia said, noticing a ring of dirt around the edge of the cup. "I hope you were a bit more mindful of hygiene in the canteen kitchen!"

"Only the best for Fourth Uncle," Clerk said. "Even if you do yell at me, I'm only too happy to serve you. You're the most generous man I know. But speaking of the canteen kitchen, I was thinking you might help me out and ask the township government to give me my job back. You command respect, Fourth Uncle."

"You can stop flattering me," Wisdom Xia said. "Have you been over there to ask them yourself?"

"I sent my wife over to ask, but they said they didn't want me back. They're worried I'm a cripple now."

"What I heard is that they found out what a filthy bastard you are, and the broken leg was just an excuse to fire you."

"That's how it always is with those guys. What little power they have, they want to lord it over me," Clerk said. "One day, one of them called me to bring him some chopsticks, and he caught me wiping them dry on my sleeve. He said it wasn't sanitary. Does he think I've got shit on my sleeves?"

There was no way Wisdom Xia was going to intervene at the township government, but Clerk's wife went back again. When the staff saw her coming, they shut the gate and let her stand outside, pounding on it.

"How can a civil servant fear the people!" she shouted. The gate stayed shut. She yelled that she was there to pick up a pair of Clerk's shoes. "Are you corrupt bureaucrats going to take his shoes, too?" The gate opened a crack, and someone inside the courtyard tossed out a pair of beaten-up rubber boots.

As Clerk's wife left, carrying the rubber boots, she saw a few kids gathered around the edge of the brickyard, poking at Lucky and Tiger with sticks. The kids shouted for the dogs to quit mounting each other, but they were once again glued together. Clerk's wife went over and picked up a stick, too. They were still stuck together, and Lucky tried to drag Tiger away, but they weren't quick enough. Clerk's wife brought the stick down on the dogs until they whimpered, and she only stopped when someone came out of the township government courtyard and ripped the stick out of her hand.

"Why would you beat a dog?" he said. "It's a living thing!"

"I was only beating Lucky. I didn't touch Tiger."

"That's Tiger's wife. You think beating Lucky is going to send a message to the township government?"

"Oh, they're husband and wife?" Clerk's wife said. "So the township government is protecting Justice Xia?"

"Where do you get off?" the man from the township government said. "I'm done talking to you." He picked up the stick and went back to the courtyard.

Clerk's wife turned and aimed a kick at Lucky. While she'd been arguing with the man from the township government, the two dogs had come unstuck and were no longer defenseless. They lunged for the woman's pant leg. As the fabric tore, Clerk's wife turned and fled home.

That same night, Justice Xia started to feel ill. It started with a headache and then an incredible thirst. He got up, went over to get a ladle of sour broth, and crawled back into bed. Right then, he started to feel feverish, and his joints ached. The next morning at dawn, Second Aunt was surprised to see him still in bed. "Aren't you going to Seven Li Gully?" she asked. "What's wrong?"

"Do I have a fever?" Justice Xia asked.

Second Aunt leaned over and put a hand on his forehead. Justice Xia had broken out in a sweat. "You're on fire," she said. "You better have something to drink!"

Justice Xia shook his head.

"Do you want me to call Halfwit's wife over? She can take you over to see Big-Noise Zhao."

"It's just a headache and a fever. What use would it be, going there? Maybe it's because my hair is too long. Call Bamboo over to shave my head."

Second Aunt felt her way to Hearth's yard. Bamboo called over the young man who worked as an assistant barber at her hair salon, and the three went back to see Justice Xia. The old man's scalp was loose, and the young barber cut him three times in the process. Second Aunt stuck chicken feathers on the cuts to stop the bleeding.

With his head shaved, Justice Xia said he felt well enough to go for a walk, but he only managed a few steps before the world started spinning around him. He was seeing double. He looked at Second Aunt and wondered why she had two heads. He went back inside and got onto the kang and stayed there until the afternoon. When he woke up with a massive boil growing on the back of his neck, he'd never experienced anything like it before. The boil kept him awake for two days, unable to eat or drink. Second Aunt got worried and told her sons, who brought Big-Noise Zhao to see him. He laid a medicated plaster on Justice Xia's boil. "Is that your prescription for everything?" Gold asked.

"It's my specialty!"

"Why's the boil so painful?" Gold asked.

"Of course it's painful; it hasn't popped yet."

"Can you give him something for the pain?" Gold asked.

"I could put him on an IV to reduce the inflammation."

"An IV?"

"The plaster is free," Big-Noise Zhao said, "but he'll need five days on the IV, and that'll cost you."

Gold took his brothers aside to discuss the situation. They were unanimous: they had to look after their father.

"How much is it going to cost?" Bounty's wife asked.

"That kind of thing is expensive," Gold said. "At least a few hundred."

"It's just a boil, though," Bounty's wife said. "Shouldn't the plaster be enough? Give it some time to get better. What's the use of an IV?"

"He's an old man. Who knows what could kill him at his age?"

"He has to realize he's not a young man anymore," Chastity said. "Old people get sick— they die. That's just the way it is."

Gold gave his wife a slap upside the head. "How can you talk like that?" he said.

Chastity took her nails to Gold's face, leaving five scratches across his cheek. "You think you can hit me?" she said. "That's the way your family's always been, smacking people around. That's why you people live so long. Beating people up keeps you going. I don't have any obligation to this family; you do. Why don't you go out and beg for the money? You could knock on every door in the village, and you'd be lucky to come up with one yuan. You'd let me crawl around in the dirt . . ."

Gold went out without speaking and walked to the riverside. His stomach was rumbling, and he rubbed it while he paced. "That woman pisses me off!" he said. "She'll be the end of me, I swear."

Eventually, Gold's anger faded, and he started to feel sorry for himself. *She's right,* he thought to himself, tears coming to his eyes while he paced. *None of my brothers or their wives will be willing to put up the money.* He didn't want to talk to them anymore, but he didn't have the money to take the matter into his own hands. He headed straight to the blood bank at West Mountain Bend.

Gold paid for the IV, and Justice Xia recovered almost completely within a couple of days. But then it was Gold himself who fell ill. His skin took on a yellow cast, the smell of food made him nauseous, and whenever he sat down, he felt so tired that he would immediately fall asleep.

After Shiner went to Xinjiang, the farm-supplies store closed. Shiner still owed his management fee to the village, but someone had come up with the idea of collecting the fee by simply taking what goods were left in the store. Gold figured he could take a cut of the merchandise and open his own market stall. But he realized that there wasn't enough left in the store to settle the debt he was owed. Gold's anxiety was too much for him, and he fainted. When he came to, he took himself to the county hospital to get tests done. The diagnosis was cirrhosis of the liver.

Gold asked if it was serious, and the doctor told him, "Of course it's serious. You'll need to avoid getting angry or upset, get to bed early, quit drinking, and make sure you're taking liver-protection pills." Gold didn't bother picking up the medication. He didn't tell anyone what had happened, either. But after that, whenever liquor was being poured, he absolutely refused to drink.

It wasn't long before Làyuè came, the last month of the year. Gold was sitting in Wisdom Xia's yard, basking in the warm sunlight. Wisdom Xia took a drag from his pipe and looked over at Gold. His nephew and Lucky were both dozing. "You need something to perk you up," Wisdom Xia said. He went over and put on some opera.

"What song is this?" Gold asked. He didn't know much about opera.

"You don't recognize it? That sad melody, the slow beat . . ." He began to hum along.

"I was already feeling down," Gold said. "This is going to push me over the edge."

"Don't criticize what you don't understand! Let me put on *Ruoye Stream*. I'm just worried the lyrics are a bit too literary for you to follow . . ."

He put on the part in the opera where Xi Shi is found by Fan Li, a military strategist from the state of Yue, just defeated by the state of Wu, and Fan Li hopes to convince the great beauty to aid them in their campaign. Xi Shi sings:

A boat, a single boat, drifting on the current. The fisherman's daughter sits at the prow, while her father baits his hook. In this earthly paradise, the seagulls float overhead and the fishermen float below. What I wouldn't give for a life like that, to escape this spinning wheel and this thatched hut. My father is not here, and neither is my mother. All that remains is pain and grief. But the plum flowers will not blossom without snow.

Just as Wisdom Xia had expected, it had gone over Gold's head. "Someone's setting off firecrackers," Gold said.

Wisdom Xia tilted his head and listened. Gold was right: someone was setting off firecrackers. "Whose house is that coming from?"

"Treasure is getting married today, right?"

"Married?" Wisdom Xia said. "To Black-Moth?"

"He couldn't even tell me himself. I had to hear it from Bounty. He wanted to invite me over for a drink, Bounty told me. Is that what he thinks of me, that I can be bought off with some liquor? I'm his big brother, and he couldn't even invite me himself. It's not like he would've had to hike across a mountain range to get to my place."

"This is the first I'm hearing about it."

"He holds a grudge against you," Gold said. "He didn't invite his own father, either. While Bounty's wedding is on, he'll be over at Seven Li Gully."

"What is he doing over there, the state he's in?" Wisdom Xia said. "That brother of yours is a slippery bastard. Who did he invite?"

"I got a look on the way over. Pavilion was there, so was Goodness, and Lotus Jin, Shifty, even Roughshod Ding . . . Bounty said it's not going to be a big banquet, just three tables. It's just as well. Even if he laid on a gourmet feast, you couldn't find many people in Freshwind that would accept the invitation."

"I wouldn't have gone, even if he'd invited me," Wisdom Xia said. "Let's listen to some opera. Let's sing!" He put in a cassette and cranked the volume on the loudspeaker so the entire village echoed with the sound of opera. Lucky got up and howled along. The leaves of the tickle tree began to shake and fall to the ground. "People are going to think we're celebrating the wedding!" Wisdom Xia said to Lucky and switched off the PA. "Let me tell you something about opera. You know that singer who was with Snow Bai's group before he retired, the guy with scabies all over his head?"

"I've heard of him. I never saw him before."

"His head was covered in scabies. But he played the female roles, so he wore makeup and costumes. The way he walked, the way he sang, every smile, every frown—he was more feminine than any woman. He played Cao Yulian in *Walking in the Snow*. There's a scene where Cao Yulian has to cross a narrow bridge. At first, she doesn't want to cross, but finally the old man Caofu reaches out to her with a willow branch. She gets out to the center of the bridge and looks down. She's looking down into the abyss. She looks up again, but her legs begin to quake. She looks around. The color drains from her face. There's a line he sang in 'Sending Her Off' where he says, 'Everyone says a man must have a cruel heart,' then he reaches up and pushes Yu Kuan. He only uses one finger, but it's too much, and Yu Kuan stumbles and almost hits the ground, so he reaches out and pulls him back up.

"Amazing, isn't it? It really is. Hatred, fear, pity, tenderness . . . He expressed them all. And in one of the scenes with Yu Kuan, he's complaining to him . . . As he speaks, each word is more loving than the last, even as the complaints get more tragic. There's a part where he sings, 'As husband and wife, we shared the same bed,' and he blushes . . ."

Wisdom Xia was getting more and more animated, but he looked over and saw that Gold didn't seem to be listening. "You don't have anything to say?" he asked. Gold didn't respond. Wisdom Xia saw that he'd shut his eyes, as if preparing to take a nap. He gave his nephew's chair a kick.

"I'm listening," Gold said.

"Well, what did you hear? You're just angry that nobody invited you."

"I already forgot all about that. You're the one who keeps bringing it up. I'm tired."

"What the hell is wrong with you? Are you sick or something?"

"I probably haven't been getting enough sleep," Gold said.

"I was going to call you childish," Wisdom Xia said, "but you're already a retiree. Why don't you go play mah-jongg with Hearth and Halfwit? Your body can't even handle that?"

Gold gasped and ran for the shithouse. He squatted for a long time and finally squeezed out a finger-size, rock-hard lump.

I should probably talk about what I was up to around that time. I had managed to get an invitation to Treasure's wedding feast. The night before, I was on my way back from Seven Li

Gully when I ran into Clerk, limping back home from buying salt. I decided to follow him. His right leg was shorter than his left leg, so he slowly drifted over to the right side of the road as he walked. I decided to try it out myself. I copied his limp and found myself drifting, too. Forest Wu was sitting on the steps of the Earth Shrine and started laughing when he saw me.

Clerk heard his honking laugh and said, "What the hell's so funny? I'm glad I can be a source of amusement for you."

"I w-wasn't l-laughing at y-you," Forest Wu said.

I rushed up the shrine steps. I didn't want to give Forest Wu the chance to tell Clerk that I'd been imitating his limp. "Forest Wu," I said, "what were you doing over here?"

"Nothing, just h-h-having a smoke." He passed me a cigarette, but I waved it away.

"If you've got nothing better to do, why don't you get us a bottle of something?"

"I'm b-broke." He turned out his pockets and took out a one-yuan bill. That wouldn't get us any liquor. We were two broke bachelors. I figured Forest Wu must have been in the same situation as me. Neither of us had much to do, and nobody wanted us around. But the Earth Goddess and Earth God were just two lumps of stone—they weren't going to complain.

I suddenly had a wicked little idea. I took the one-yuan note from Forest Wu, we got some fishing line, tied one end to the bill, then hid in the shrine gate. I figured we'd be able to have a bit of fun with anyone who came along and tried to pick it up.

A short time later, a man and a woman came down the road. The woman had her head wrapped in a scarf, and the man had on a heavy coat, so it was hard to tell who they were. The woman saw the money first and bent down to pick it up. I jerked the line and sent the bill skittering down the road away from her. She chased the money all the way up the steps to the shrine before she stopped, lifted her head, and looked around. That was when I saw that it was Black-Moth. She looked embarrassed when she saw me. I wasn't exactly happy to see her, either.

"Spark," the man in the coat said. "Spark, what the hell are you doing?"

It was Treasure. Forest Wu scowled. He turned and stalked off, muttering to himself, "That pervert!"

Treasure didn't seem to mind, though. "Spark," he said, "I want you to come around for a drink tomorrow!"

"What are you talking about? You'd have me over for drinks?"

"I'm getting married tomorrow! You have to come. If you're there, it'll be a real party!"

Treasure and Black-Moth left, and I heard Forest Wu sobbing and beating his head against the shrine gate. "What are you hitting your head for? It's not going to hurt anybody but yourself."

Forest Wu looked up and stopped crying. "Spark," he said, "uh, S-S-S-Spark, those two animals are getting m-married." He spat on the ground. "You aren't going, are you?"

"I'll go drink, have something to eat . . ."

"N-no, please, don't g-go. I'll b-buy you a drink!"

"With one yuan?"

Forest Wu took off his cap and slipped out a fold of brown wrapping paper, stained black with sweat and grease. From the wrapping paper he took a fifty-yuan bill. "Please, don't g-go. It's my treat!" He went to the store and bought a bottle of *shaojiu*. I skipped Treasure's wedding banquet the next day. To tell you the truth, I wouldn't have gone, even if Forest Wu hadn't gotten me a drink the night before. A man has to live by his principles. I went to Seven Li Gully instead.

I didn't expect Justice Xia and Tongue-Tied to show up. I figured they'd be at the wedding banquet, but they arrived shortly after I did and didn't even mention Treasure and Black-Moth's marriage. I thought it was strange, but then I figured they might not have even known about it, and I wasn't going to be the one to tell them. That was the day we harvested the wheat. The ear of wheat was as thick as a thumb and about a foot and a half long. After we cut the ear of grain from the stalk, the three of us knelt in the dirt and kowtowed. We wanted to thank Seven Li Gully for giving us the stalk and its impressive grain.

Justice Xia put the ear of grain into a small wooden box he had brought with him that day, saying he was going to bring it to the county's seed bank. He figured they'd be able to clone it and develop a new breed of grain. I didn't agree with the plan—why would he give it to them? Would they pay any attention to our ear of grain? Even if they did, would they be able to use their technology to clone the wheat? I thought Justice Xia should take the wheat to show the people of Freshwind. It might even encourage the Two Committees to support the gully-reclamation project. Justice Xia agreed with me, but we couldn't decide on whether the ear of grain should be kept at Justice Xia's place or at the village government. We finally concluded that we should keep it at the Earth Shrine.

With the decision made, Justice Xia, Tongue-Tied, and I went back to the village. We hung a wire down from the rafters of the Earth Shrine and tied the grain to the end of it so it could hang in front of the altar. Have you ever seen the way people hang cured pork or cobs of corn from the rafters? It was just like that. To keep the rats from eating the food, you have to put a lampshade halfway up the wire. We didn't have a shade, so we used a straw hat. The Earth Goddess and Earth God watched over the land, so it was only right to offer the wheat to them. The shrine was a public place, too, so everyone in Freshwind could come and see. It was a beautiful scene, and Big-Noise Zhao perfected it with a pair of couplets. One side read, "Minor temple, mighty gods," and the other side read, "Skinny men, bountiful harvest."

"Are we skinny?" I asked.

I thought about it for a moment. It was true, we were skinny. But it wasn't something I ever paid attention to. I looked over at Justice Xia and noticed for the first time how much weight he'd lost since the spring—the rolls of fat on his neck had disappeared. Tongue-Tied, too, looked thinner. Even his whiskers couldn't hide the way his cheeks had hollowed out. His lips looked perpetually pursed. I couldn't see myself, but when I patted my belly, I realized that I'd lost weight, too. "It's true. I used to have a potbelly. Now it's more like a pit."

"We're not skinny," Justice Xia said. "Just hungry. Uncle Justice's going to treat you to dinner." He brought us over to the *liang fen* restaurant. "Two bowls each!" he shouted as he went in the door. "Load it up with vinegar, and make sure it's spicy as hell." After his second bowl, Justice Xia looked drunk. He closed his eyes in complete satisfaction. He staggered to his feet and had to grab the table to stop himself from falling backward. "Eat, Spark! I want you to get your fill. Treasure can have his banquet, but you're my guest!"

That was when I realized that Justice Xia knew about Treasure's wedding. I heard the sound of opera and called to Justice Xia. "Uncle, you hear that?" But right then, the loudspeaker went silent.

When Gold didn't come back out from the shithouse, Wisdom Xia started to get worried. He was going to go check on him, but Bodhi came into the yard and distracted him. Bodhi had been in Xijing, looking after Snow Bai's daughter, and Wisdom Xia wondered what she was doing back so soon. "How come you're back?"

Bodhi began to sob. She ran to her great-uncle and collapsed in his arms. Wisdom Xia tried to ask what had happened. "My dad," she said. "He married that slut, didn't he?"

"So," he said, "you heard the news and came back?" Wisdom Xia was relieved that nothing had happened to the baby.

"I heard it when I got off the bus."

"You're a big girl now. You'll be just fine without him. You've still got your mother, anyway, and your brother and your uncles and your grandfather, too."

"My poor mother," Bodhi said. She broke into tears again.

Fourth Aunt was sitting inside on the kang, sorting her needles and thread. When she heard Bodhi out in the yard, she rushed out to see her. "Have you eaten yet?" she asked. "Chrysanth, Chrysanth," she called next door, "are you over there? Your daughter's back!"

Chrysanth came over from next door, dressed to the nines, with her hair oiled and pulled back into a tight bun. She smiled when she saw Bodhi. "My little darling," she said, "what are you crying for?"

"Daddy . . ."

"Don't cry for him now. He's dead! Go inside and change your clothes. Put on something fresh. Life goes on, and we have to live well!"

Wisdom Xia shot a look at his wife, and Fourth Aunt led Chrysanth and Bodhi into the kitchen, telling them she wanted a hand pounding some potatoes into cakes. Chrysanth tossed the potatoes into a stone mortar and began pounding them with a wooden mallet. Standing out in the yard, Gold, who had finally come out of the shithouse, felt the pounding of the mallet shaking the ground and thought there was an earthquake.

"I want you to stick around, Gold," Fourth Aunt said. "Your aunt is going to make a special dinner for us tonight."

Bodhi started to feel a bit better once they had eaten. Wisdom Xia figured the time was finally right to ask her about what was going on in the city. "Why didn't your aunt and the baby come back with you?"

"They're waiting on another operation," Bodhi said.

"Who's getting the operation?" Gold asked.

"It's Wind Xia," Wisdom Xia said, hurriedly. "He's getting that hemorrhoid surgery. You know how it is with us northerners; almost everyone gets them. I don't know why he can't just paint some ointment on it. I don't know what he's thinking, getting surgery for it!" He stood and went into the bedroom, saying he needed to get some tea. "Bodhi," he called, "Bodhi, come in here and help me." She went into the bedroom, and Wisdom Xia reached into the sugar jar and rubbed a pinch of brown sugar on her lips. He licked his thumb. "I told you a hundred times, the baby's surgery is a secret! I don't want you telling your mother about it, either."

"It wasn't on purpose," Bodhi said.

"What's the second surgery for? I thought the first one was successful."

"As soon as you left, the opening they made started to get inflamed. The doctor said she was too young. She'll have to wait until she's twelve or thirteen. They can do the surgery then. Right now, all they can do is put a tube up there, so she can still shit."

Wisdom Xia's hands started to shake. The more he tried to stop them from shaking, the harder they shook. He fumbled with the lock on the cabinet. "Then what did you come back here for?" he asked Bodhi. "Couldn't you have stayed just a bit longer?"

"Snow Bai and Wind Xia won't stop fighting."

"Fighting? Isn't Snow Bai's mother there? What's the problem?"

"They made her so upset. A couple of times she was even crying. She had to leave, too. We came back together."

Wisdom Xia grunted and then went silent. "It's good you came back," he said, finally. "But no matter who asks, just say everything is fine with Snow Bai and Wind Xia. Make sure it stays a secret."

"I understand," Bodhi said.

They went out of the bedroom, and Wisdom Xia told Fourth Aunt to boil some tea. She was stingy with tea leaves but filled each glass to the brim. Wisdom Xia lost his temper. "Why did you pour the glass so full, for just that little bit of tea? You know what they say: pour a full glass of liquor and a half glass of tea. You think you're watering cattle or what? Dump it out, pour it again!"

"What's gotten into you?" Fourth Aunt asked.

"I'll get it, I'll get it," Gold said, and reached for the kettle.

After Bodhi, her mother, and Gold had left, Wisdom Xia told Fourth Aunt to finish the dishes and then come talk to him. Fourth Aunt ignored him, so after a while Wisdom Xia went into the kitchen. "I just want to talk to you, and you're acting like this? Do you have any idea what's going on? The baby's surgery failed. She has to have a tube stuck up her behind."

Fourth Aunt dropped the bowl that she was scrubbing, and it fell into a pot and shattered. "Oh no, a tube? How long will she have to use a tube?"

"I'm planning to go back to Xijing in the next couple of days."

"If you're going, I'm coming with you," Fourth Aunt said. "What did my little baby do to be cursed like this? She's just a baby . . . Why couldn't they fix it the first time?"

"What good will it do for you to go? You think that son of yours will listen to you? He spends all day fighting with Snow Bai, and it's gotten so bad that even Snow Bai's mother left. The baby's not better yet, and I'm worried that something's going to happen with those two."

Fourth Aunt sat down hard on the stool in front of the stove and started to cry.

But before Wisdom Xia could set off for Xijing, Snow Bai arrived back in the village, carrying her daughter. The plump, fair Snow Bai had become thin and dark. Her glossy hair had faded, and she had dark circles under her eyes. The three matriarchs of the Xia family arrived to see the child, and Snow Bai gifted them each a pair of rubber-soled cotton shoes. "These shoes are good for feet like yours," Snow Bai said. The aunts had all had their feet bound as children but unwrapped later in life. "They're light, but they've got good grip."

"They have shoes like that in the city?" Second Aunt said. The three women took off their old shoes and put on the new ones. Second Aunt couldn't quite fit her foot in the shoe. Her big toe was poking out. Snow Bai was upset, but Second Aunt comforted her, saying, "That's fine, that's fine. I'll still take them. I can be buried in them!"

The women passed the baby between themselves, trying out new nicknames for her, including "Puppy" and "Little Egg."

"Did you wean her yet?" First Aunt asked.

"Not yet, but I let her have some porridge."

First Aunt took a pinch of steamed bread, chewed it up, and stuck it into the baby's mouth on the tip of her tongue.

"Let me feed her!" Snow Bai said. She picked up the baby, discreetly plucking the chewed bread out of her mouth, then gave her bottom a pinch. When the baby started crying, Snow Bai passed her to Fourth Aunt, who passed her on to Wisdom Xia. He carried the baby out into the alley for a walk.

The tube inserted in her rear end solved the problem temporarily, but the baby still couldn't eat solids and had no control over her bowels. Her diaper had to be checked all the time. The baby was heavy, and it was tiring to carry her. Once Fourth Aunt, Wisdom Xia, and Snow Bai were alone again, Fourth Aunt began to cry. "Even if it's hard on us," Wisdom Xia said, "we have to keep it to ourselves. We'll get through it. If there's nothing we can do about it, we just have to accept it."

Wisdom Xia was speaking from experience. When he was around fifty, he had come down with a chronic stomach problem. He'd tried different treatments, but nothing worked. He spent every night negotiating with the illness. He knew there was no cure, so he made his peace with it. Wisdom Xia and the illness lived in peaceful coexistence—he made sure not to eat coarse grain and tried not to work too hard. He knew it would only make things worse if he lost his temper, so he did his best to be tolerant and kind, and to maintain good relationships with everyone. That was when he'd decided to start painting opera masks. The painting soothed him.

"It's been ten years already, and look at me now, I'm doing fine," Wisdom Xia said. He was doing his best to comfort Fourth Aunt and Snow Bai, but there was something weighing on his mind, something that he didn't dare bring up with his wife or daughter-in-law.

Seven days later, while Fourth Aunt was busy washing rice, the baby was down for a nap, and Snow Bai was sweeping the yard, Wisdom Xia was sitting in his bedroom, painting masks. Snow Bai stopped sweeping and paused to study the ants climbing up the tickle tree. A long line of ants was moving down the trunk, toward the roots of the tree, each of them carrying something, and she marveled at their orderly labor.

Wisdom Xia stood and went to the window. Watching Snow Bai under the tickle tree, he started to tremble, as if his flesh were going to shake itself off his bones. Wisdom Xia had wanted to ask seven days before, but he could wait no longer. "Why didn't Wind Xia come back with you?" he asked.

Snow Bai stared back at her father-in-law blankly, then lowered her head and went back to sweeping the yard. She kept her back turned to the window. Wisdom Xia realized that the thing he had dreaded most had come to pass: it was over between them. He opened his mouth, but he wasn't sure what to say. He looked up at the sky, where a single cloud was drifting down toward the yard. He was sure of it—a single cloud, drifting down toward them. Snow Bai whipped the broom across the dust, and when Wisdom Xia looked up again, the cloud was gone. When Snow Bai turned around, a tear dripped from her cheek and fell to the ground.

"It looks like it's going to rain," she said. "Should I bring in the tobacco you put up on the wall to dry?"

"Oh, are those rain clouds?" He went out into the yard, leaned a ladder against the wall, and started collecting the tobacco. As he came back down the ladder, he almost lost his footing and slipped off.

For the next several days, the loudspeaker was silent. The constant soundtrack of local opera had annoyed some people, but now that it was gone, even those people felt that something was lacking. It was too quiet. Lucky stayed away, too. The soup bones left for her at the gate went untouched until the chickens discovered them. When the chickens gave up on the bones, three bluebottles buzzed around them. The wooden sticks that held up the peonies at the foot of the wall snapped, and the bush came crashing down. Wisdom Xia went out and propped the bush up again, using the bamboo poles that they usually used to prop up the mosquito net in the bedroom. Fourth Aunt grumbled about it, and Wisdom Xia got annoyed. He went to inspect the planter and saw that one of the roses at the northeast corner had begun to drop its petals, as if an invisible hand were plucking the petals and letting them drop into the planter. Soon enough, the flower was bare. In her room on the west side of the house, Snow Bai hummed a tune from an opera, trying to comfort her crying baby. "Let your mother-in-law look after her," Wisdom Xia said.

Snow Bai passed the baby to Fourth Aunt. "Why don't you play opera on the loudspeaker anymore?" she asked.

"You want me to play something?"

"Sure."

Whenever opera played on the loudspeaker, Wisdom Xia would usually sit in his chair, nodding along with the tune, but this time, he went to pick up the baby. "I'll take her out for a stroll," he told his wife. "Do we have any silver-ear mushroom? You should boil some for Snow Bai."

"We still have the pork broth that I made. What does she need silver ear for? Don't worry about her!"

"What's gotten into you?" Wisdom Xia asked. "I don't want to ever hear you talking to Snow Bai like that."

Fourth Aunt snorted and prodded her husband out the gate.

The people Wisdom Xia passed on the road thought it was unusual to see the old man carrying a baby. "Hey," one of them said, "did you bring your copper pipe with you?"

"My granddaughter doesn't like me smoking," Wisdom Xia said.

A crowd formed around Wisdom Xia and the baby. They reached in to tickle and stroke the baby, but she didn't smile. Someone asked, "So what's her name?"

"No name yet," Wisdom Xia said.

The group that had come over from the dyehouse draped a length of floral fabric over the baby. One of them said, "You're a cultured man, Fourth Uncle. You'll pick a good name for her!"

"I flipped through the dictionary a few times, but I couldn't find anything with the meaning I wanted."

"She's plump, and she's got that kind of lucky face . . . Maybe call her Fortune Flower."

"I don't think so. It's not good enough to just have fortune; you need some money, too!"

"You know, there's a saying that peonies bring wealth and good fortune . . . Why not call her Peony?"

"Now, that's a good name!" Wisdom Xia said.

The man from the dyehouse was quite pleased with himself. He decided to push a bit further. "Does the baby have a godfather?"

"Quit while you're ahead," another man in the crowd said. "Just because you came up with the name doesn't mean you're fit to be the godfather. You know what kind of people Wind Xia and Snow Bai are. They don't want some farmer as the baby's godfather."

"I wasn't asking to be the godfather! But why couldn't a farmer be the baby's godfather, huh? It's not like the godfather has to raise her. A farmer might not have much education or money or power, but they're healthy. It might be good for the baby to have someone like that in her life."

"You aren't wrong," Wisdom Xia said. "The godfather should be a farmer!"

"Who's it gonna be?" the crowd started to ask.

That was the custom in Freshwind: when it was time to pick a godfather, you had to choose from the people around you at that moment.

When Justice Xia's fifth son was born, the baby had been as skinny as a sick cat. Second Aunt had taken the baby out to East Street to look for a godfather. She waited for a while, but nobody was around. Finally, a pig came waddling up the road. "My baby's godfather is going to be a halfwit sow?" But there was nobody else to choose from, and that was the custom, so she crouched down in front of the pig and pressed the baby's forehead against the road in a kowtow. They started calling the boy Halfwit Pig, but it was eventually shortened to just Halfwit. Halfwit grew up to be strong and healthy. Like his namesake, he'd eat whatever was put in front of him. He could eat just about anything without getting sick.

Wisdom Xia decided to carry Peony over to the Earth Shrine. He looked to the east, and so did everyone in the crowd. Who do you think he saw? That's right. It was me! It was fate. I would usually have been over at Seven Li Gully at that time, but I had to go back into the village. Tongue-Tied and I were moving loads of stone in baskets on the ends of a bamboo pole, but the pole had snapped. I was on my way to get a new pole when Wisdom Xia spotted me, coming under the East Street archway. The crowd roared with surprise. Wisdom Xia turned and started going in the other direction. One of the blacksmith's sons saw me. He had been busy out in his yard, swinging a sledgehammer, but he caught Wisdom Xia's eye and knew what he had to do. He rushed over to me and pulled me down an alley that ran south of the archway.

I couldn't figure out what he wanted. "What are you doing?" I asked.

"I lost some money playing mah-jongg. Lend me five yuan."

"It wasn't my money that you lost," I said angrily. "What are you doing coming to me for more?" I pretended to dig in my pocket. "Hold on, I think I've got something." I turned and ripped a fart. That's when I saw Wisdom Xia walk by the mouth of the alley with the baby. "Is Fourth Uncle out with Snow Bai's baby?" I asked.

"What do you care?" the blacksmith's son said. He walked off with his nose in the air.

I went out of the alley and got back on my way. The crowd in front of the Earth Shrine was laughing at me. I figured they must have been making the same old jokes about me, so I didn't bother paying much attention. I sang as I went:

> Since I left the Hanlin Academy
> I have been a judge in Gutian.
> Now that I must leave again,
> My heart is free and my gaze is distant.

I had no idea exactly what had happened that day, until the New Year, when I ran into someone at the Great Qing Hall who had been out front of the dyehouse with Wisdom Xia. After he told me the story, I lost my temper, huffing and puffing and cursing the blacksmith's son. But after I calmed down, I thought to myself, *It's a good thing he did stop me, because I don't know what would have happened if I had kept walking, right up to Wisdom Xia.*

Would he have even let me be the baby's godfather? There was such a big crowd, too. What would he have done? What would I have done? The way I figured, even if Wisdom Xia didn't actually choose me, I still would've considered myself the baby's godfather. I loved Snow Bai. It must have been fate that I arrived just as the baby's godfather was being chosen. That sounds like fate, doesn't it? I even started to think that maybe I had been the reason Snow Bai had gotten pregnant. I had been thinking about her so hard, after all. It was even possible that the baby was mine!

Anyway, let me get back to Wisdom Xia.

After he sneaked by the alley, he rushed home with the baby. Snow Bai saw the strange look on his face and asked what was wrong with him. "I've got a bit of a stomachache," he said.

"Carry the baby out for a little stroll," Fourth Aunt said, "and suddenly your stomach hurts."

Wisdom Xia wasn't exaggerating; he did have a stomachache. He went to his bedroom and lay down on the bed, holding his belly. It didn't get any better. He yelled for Fourth Aunt to come and rub his belly. She came in and saw that her husband was drenched in sweat.

"You're really sick!" she said.

"I must have sucked some cold air," Wisdom Xia said.

Fourth Aunt rubbed his belly and blew some hot air into his belly button. His stomach gurgled a few times, but he started to feel a bit better. "You didn't suck in any cold air," she said. "You're keeping something bottled up, aren't you?"

Wisdom Xia told her about what had happened in front of the Earth Shrine.

"If Spark's the person that you saw, then he should be the godfather," Fourth Aunt said. "Who cares? Halfwit's godfather was a pig."

"Don't talk like that! You know what Spark's like. You want him to be the godfather?"

"Well, he isn't the godfather, is he? What are you so angry about?"

Wisdom Xia didn't say anything. He reached for his pipe and took a drag.

"There's something I wanted to tell you," Fourth Aunt said. "I had a dream last night. Snow Bai and Wind Xia were getting married. When I woke up, I started thinking, 'Hey, that's not right; they're already married. Why would they get married again?' After the dream, I started to think . . . Did you realize, since Snow Bai got back from Xijing, she hasn't smiled once? Most of the time, she's just staring into space . . . That son of ours, he didn't bother to accompany Snow Bai and her mother back, and there wasn't a letter from him for the New Year, either. You don't think they might be planning to get divorced . . . ?"

"He wouldn't dare, that bastard. If he tries it, I'll go straight to his boss!"

Fourth Aunt was getting even more agitated. "But what if he really does it?" she asked.

"Why do you have to talk about that kind of thing now?"

Fourth Aunt took a rag and began to polish the pots and pans in the kitchen. Even when she could see her reflection in them, she kept polishing. She picked up a jar and rubbed it with the rag. Without making a sound, the jar broke into three ceramic shards, spilling rice out over the cabinet. She took a deep breath and glanced at her husband. Wisdom Xia wordlessly began sweeping up the rice.

"That bastard," he said again. "He can stay away as long as he wants. He's heartless. If he won't look after Snow Bai and the baby, we will!"

But Wisdom Xia was not a well man. His stomach had begun to hurt again. It came on every day at dawn, like clockwork. Fourth Aunt rubbed his belly and blew air in his belly button, but it didn't help. He went out into the yard to walk around until the pain subsided. One morning he kept walking and went over to Big-Noise Zhao's place. Big-Noise Zhao took his pulse and said it might be a stomach ulcer. Wisdom Xia went home and took the seven doses of herbal medicine that Zhao had prepared for him. After that the pain was less frequent, but he found he had no appetite.

After a few days, the pain got even worse, and the medicine couldn't touch it. Big-Noise Zhao was at a loss. He sent Wisdom Xia home with some poppy pods to boil into a tea. The poppy tea worked for two days, but then the pain came back. Wisdom Xia didn't want to risk getting hooked on the brew, so he stopped taking it.

When news of Wisdom Xia's illness began to spread, his neighbors were surprised. He had always been in good shape, and even after retirement he had rarely been ill. They couldn't figure out how he could suddenly come down with a stomach ulcer. Wisdom Xia was always good about paying a visit to anyone who was feeling under the weather, so plenty of people came by to repay the favor. Fourth Aunt's feet had been bound many years before, and while she managed to get around just fine once they were unwrapped, rushing around the house entertaining guests and well-wishers was doing a number on her.

A few days after his poppy experiment, there was a cold snap, so cold even the stones in the yard became brittle. A sheet of ice had formed across the plank covering the root cellar. Fourth Aunt took a pick to the ice and managed, finally, to crack enough of the ice to reach in and grab a daikon. She planned to make vegetable dumplings for her husband. As she was going back into the house, she saw Concord Qin, supported by his wife, coming into the yard. They had brought a few eggs wrapped in a handkerchief for Wisdom Xia.

Fourth Aunt threw down the daikon and went to lead Concord Qin to a chair. "What are you doing here?" she asked. Concord Qin stared back at her without speaking.

"When we heard Fourth Uncle was sick," Concord Qin's wife said, "we had to come over to see him."

Wisdom Xia was still in pain, but he got up, lit the charcoal in the stove in the main room, and sat down with his guests. He was worried about Concord Qin and tried to ask how he was doing. But Concord Qin just kept answering, "Sure, yeah."

Wisdom Xia went into the kitchen and came back with a few cold steamed buns. He toasted one over the charcoal and passed it to Concord Qin. Concord Qin ate it, and Wisdom Xia toasted another bun, which Concord Qin took, too.

"Don't bother, Fourth Uncle," Concord Qin's wife said. "He hasn't got any appetite, but he'll just keep eating. He doesn't know whether he's hungry or full."

One of the chickens jumped in from the yard and began to peck at the crumbs Concord Qin had dropped on the floor. While Concord Qin was looking in the other direction, the chicken pecked the last chunk of steamed bun out of his hand and carried it off to the corner of the room. "Shoo! Shoo!" Concord Qin said. He got down on his hands and knees and crawled over to the corner to grab the bun, then crawled back to his chair.

"What are you doing, crawling around like that in Fourth Uncle's house?" his wife said.

"This is how he gets around your house?" Wisdom Xia asked.

"He's like a worm! He's always crawling around on the floor."

"This is what the illness has reduced him to!" Wisdom Xia said. The pain in his stomach flared up, and Fourth Aunt noticed his grimace.

"If you aren't feeling well," she said, "you can go lie down in the bedroom. I'll stay with them."

Wisdom Xia went into the bedroom.

Fourth Aunt and Concord Qin's wife talked for a while; then a pair of old women from Middle Street came into the yard, walking hand in hand. They called loudly for Wisdom Xia. "We're here to visit you," they said. Fourth Aunt rushed out into the yard. The old women were village matriarchs, and she wanted to show them respect. "Is he doing any better?" one of the old women asked.

"He's still in pain," Fourth Aunt said.

"Why hasn't he been to see Big-Noise?"

"He's still taking the medicine. It doesn't seem to be working, though."

"If the medicine isn't working, it might not be physical. You need someone to lift the curse. Now that Mid-Star's dad is dead, it's going to be hard to find someone in Freshwind, though . . . Over in Guofenglou Township, there's a shaman by the name of Fu. He's supposed to be quite powerful. Why not take Wisdom Xia to see him?"

"He doesn't believe in that kind of thing," Fourth Aunt said.

"He should!" the old woman said. "How could he not believe in it? When Auntie Wang here twisted her ankle, some people went to see that Fu. He hadn't heard what had happened to her, but right away, he starts talking about the wall behind her yard, how a section of it was broken. He said that was the reason she had twisted her ankle. As soon as the wall got fixed, her ankle was fine. Strange, isn't it? How did he know about the wall? If Wisdom Xia doesn't want to go, I'll talk to him myself!"

"He's been in pain all morning. He managed to get out of bed for a while, but he just went down for a nap."

"Well then, better let him rest," one of the women said, lowering her voice.

"I don't want to disturb him," said the other. "He needs his rest." When the old women saw Snow Bai carry the baby out into the yard, their faces blossomed into broad smiles. "Bring that baby over and let me hold her!"

Snow Bai passed the baby over, and the old woman kissed her on the cheek. "Snow Bai's got good milk," she said. "Look at how fat this little baby is getting!"

"She's not fat," Snow Bai said. "You should see my sister-in-law's baby. He looks like Guan Yu! His cheeks are so fat they go out to his shoulders."

"That's the one they have to pay the fine on, right? I heard they cut the cord by smashing a rock on it."

"That's right," Snow Bai said, laughing.

"Snow Bai's baby doesn't have chubby cheeks," Concord Qin's wife said, "but she's plenty big around the middle."

Fourth Aunt's expression suddenly changed. She went over to take the baby.

"She's got a dirty diaper," one of the old women said. "I can smell it." She reached to lift up the baby's shirt, but Fourth Aunt swooped in, clutched the baby to her, and went into the bedroom. Fourth Aunt checked and the baby's diaper was indeed dirty, so she wrapped a fresh one around her and got her dressed again. "Are you still in pain?" she asked Wisdom Xia.

"They didn't notice anything off with the baby, did they?" Wisdom Xia said.

"No."

"Try to get them out of here. The pain is getting worse."

"You can't keep going like this. You should get Rain Xia to take you in to the county hospital."

"Have Concord Qin stop by the restaurant and tell Rain Xia to get over here then."

When Rain Xia got word that his father needed him, he jumped on his motorbike and rushed toward home. But on the way there, he was held up when he found the road blocked by Mid-Star Xia's car.

Mid-Star Xia had come back to Freshwind down the 312. His driver had turned off onto West Street and was driving toward East Street. It was slow going, since the street was full of people, not to mention the chickens and dogs. The driver laid into the horn while they crept through the village. In front of the farmers market, the driver managed to roll over some grain that had been laid out to dry. The owner of the stall rushed out, blocked the car, then went around to the driver's side and told him to get out.

"It's me!" Mid-Star said.

"Who the hell are you?"

"You don't recognize me?"

"You're talking to County Head Xia," the driver cautioned the stall owner.

"Yin-Yang Xia's little boy? It doesn't matter who you are, you can't be driving over people's grain."

Mid-Star got out of the car and apologized for the trouble. "The tarp the grain was on was halfway in the road," he explained, "and there was a chicken on the other side, so when we swerved to avoid it, we must have hit the grain."

"Oh, so you're saying I'm at fault here, for trying to dry some grain?"

"That's not what I meant, not at all," Mid-Star said. "Tell me how I can make it right with you. What do I owe you?"

"Make it right? Are you going to count every grain of wheat?"

That was when Rain Xia arrived on his motorbike. He stepped in and tried to resolve the situation, but the stall owner wouldn't budge. "He's out of control!" the stall owner said. "Your big brother has the right idea. I've never seen Wind Xia come back by car. If he did, he'd park it over at the township government and walk in. Yin-Yang Xia's boy came all the way over here, honking the horn the whole time! If he wants to show off, next time he should get a police escort!"

Mid-Star went red in the face with anger as the man lectured him. He told his driver to park at the entrance to East Street; then he climbed on the back of Rain Xia's motorbike, and they headed to see Wisdom Xia.

When Mid-Star found out that Wisdom Xia wanted Rain Xia to take him to the hospital, he offered the use of his car. Wisdom Xia didn't decline the offer. He went to pack his toothbrush, towel, and a change of clothes.

Mid-Star played with the baby and asked Snow Bai about the opera company. "It's been on its last legs for a while now," she said. "It's been a while since I've gone around to check on them."

"What happened, exactly?" Mid-Star asked. "It fell apart as soon as I left? Who's running it now?"

"Old Ma, the former stage manager."

"He knows how to direct an opera, but he has no business running the company."

"Nobody listens to him. He's too soft."

"That's not the issue," Mid-Star said. "The problem is that he hasn't got a head for politics."

"Politics?"

"Politics is pulling your own people to the top and dragging your enemies to the bottom. The quicker you separate the two sides, the better."

"Did you come up with that?" Snow Bai asked.

"Mao Zedong came up with it."

Snow Bai turned without speaking and rolled up a blanket for Wisdom Xia to lean on in the car.

Thunder and Blossom came over to see Wisdom Xia off, and they were followed by Gold, Bounty, Hearth, and Halfwit's wife. Gold bent down to lift his uncle and carry him to the car, but Wisdom Xia waved him off, saying he could manage by himself.

Before he went out to the car, Wisdom Xia looked at himself in the mirror and saw that his skin was gray. He put on his straw hat, pulled it low, and went out into the yard. "What'd you all come over here for?" he asked. "I'm just going for some tests. They're not going to keep me there. I don't need a final goodbye. You can all go home!" Only Rain Xia and Gold stayed in the yard, along with Fourth Aunt.

Life is strange, isn't it? All these stories about Freshwind, they somehow end up getting all mixed up together. You'd think I'd made them up, but they're all true. Right around the time Wisdom Xia was saying goodbye in the yard, on his way to the county hospital, Shifty had an accident.

Shifty had been down at the fishpond early that morning. He filled up a net bag with fish, but then he tossed it back into the pond. Goodness happened to come along around then. "What are you so angry about?" he asked.

"Some people are coming from the county government, so the township head sent me over here to get some fish. Why should I be at their beck and call?"

"So you aren't willing to listen to the township head, either? You're the type of guy to smash someone's rice pot after he invites you for dinner."

"I didn't smash your pot; what do you care? Where are you off to?"

"I'm going down to the riverbank to trim some branches. Since Dog-Scraps died, the family's got no firewood. The village decided that they had to step in!"

"Didn't Pavilion take the riverbank away from you?"

"You think he cut me out completely?" Goodness asked angrily. "I'm still part of the village government."

"I'll go with you!" Shifty said.

When they got to the riverbank, Shifty wouldn't let Goodness climb into the trees. Shifty worked quickly and soon had a pile of branches for Dog-Scraps's family, and he'd even found a stout branch that he could carve into a shovel handle.

As he went back up into the tree to keep cutting, he said, "Don't be angry with me, Goodness. That poster wasn't an attack on you. Pavilion used the situation to his own advantage. He made me the scapegoat!"

"I don't care about that."

"You know I'm more than a little rough around the edges, Goodness. I say what's on my mind, but this heart of mine is as soft as tofu. Pavilion took advantage of both of us. From now on, you can count on me, but I want to be able to count on you, too!"

"You really don't get it, do you?"

Shifty came down from the tree and passed a cigarette to Goodness. Shifty smoked better cigarettes than Goodness. After he had finished his smoke, Shifty went to lay down on the riverbank for a rest and drifted off to sleep while Goodness went to work tying up the branches.

Goodness was just about to leave when he heard an "Ah!" from Shifty. There was something very strange about the sound of it. When Goodness looked back, he saw Shifty had a snake halfway down his throat. Shifty had his hands wrapped around the tail of the snake, stopping it from going deeper.

In that moment, the first thing Goodness thought was, *It's the middle of winter; snakes should be hibernating. Where did this one come from?* Shifty's face was turning purple, and his grip on the snake's tail seemed to be slipping as it writhed in his hands. Goodness was frozen with fear for a moment, but he regained his senses, dumped the load of branches, and rushed over to try to pull out the snake. It was no use; the snake was too strong.

"Hold on to it! Hold on to it!" Goodness said. He ran with Shifty toward Big-Noise Zhao's shop. When they got there, Big-Noise Zhao knew at a glance that he couldn't help Shifty; he had to be taken to the county hospital. They went out to look for a tractor. And that was when they ran into Wisdom Xia. Shifty and Goodness quickly climbed into Mid-Star's car, and they took off for the county hospital.

When they got to the hospital, Goodness led Shifty in. The doctors cut a hole in his throat and ripped the snake out. It turned out to be a king rat snake; Shifty's life had been saved.

Rain Xia stayed with his father. Before being led in to have his stomach scoped, Wisdom Xia insisted on brushing his teeth—he was worried the doctor would laugh at him if he went in with bad breath. He went into the examination room, and Rain Xia waited outside. When Wisdom Xia came out again, he was crying. "Is having your stomach scoped that painful?" Rain Xia asked.

"It's humiliating. Absolutely humiliating. I threw up twice. Get in there! Help them clean it up."

Rain Xia led his father to a chair in the hallway and then went in to clean up. When the doctor noticed him, he said, "Are you the patient's son?"

"Yes," Rain Xia said.

"Your father has stomach cancer," the doctor said.

Rain Xia was at a loss for words. He forgot all about the cleanup and didn't realize he was standing in the puddle of puke. He motioned for the doctor to lower his voice. Rain Xia looked back into the hallway. "Are you kidding me?"

"Kidding you?" the doctor asked. Rain Xia's forehead beaded with sweat. "He can't leave here," the doctor added. "In this situation, the earlier we can operate, the better. I'll start the procedure to have him admitted."

"Admitted . . . admitted . . . Okay, but when I bring him in here, I don't want you to tell him how serious it is."

"I understand."

Rain Xia took a deep breath, steadied himself, and went out to see his father. "Dad," he said, "it's not looking good. The doctor is saying it's a very serious ulcer. You'll need surgery. They're going to admit you."

"I figured it might be an ulcer," Wisdom Xia said. "Surgery won't be necessary. An ulcer can heal by itself."

"The doctor says this is a serious case. If you don't get it operated on, it could turn into cancer. But you might be right; maybe we should wait. A county hospital isn't the right place for an operation like this. It might be better to go to Xijing. Wind Xia's there, anyway, and it'll be easier. We can get the best doctor. That way, we'll have nothing to worry about."

"I wouldn't go to Xijing even if it was cancer!"

"Well then, let's just get it done here," Rain Xia said after a long pause. "Let's go see what the doctor has to say." Father and son went back into the exam room. As he'd promised, the doctor kept the true diagnosis between himself and Rain Xia. He told Wisdom Xia that his ulcer had grown so large that an operation was necessary.

"Well, go ahead," Wisdom Xia told the doctor. "Once you're my age, you can't run from the knife."

Rain Xia filled out all the forms, and Wisdom Xia was admitted. Goodness and Shifty, with his neck wrapped in bandages, came to see him. "Fourth Uncle," Shifty said, "you've got nothing to worry about. Compared to what they just did to me, it'll be a breeze!"

"You're doing okay?" Wisdom Xia asked.

"Absolutely fine."

"You're a mean bastard, Shifty," Wisdom Xia said, laughing. "Anybody else, they would have been scared stiff, but you grabbed the thing by the tail."

"The snake got lucky. If he'd been just a bit smaller, I would have chewed him up and had him for breakfast," Shifty said.

"We're never going to hear the end of this, are we?"

"The real story is how lucky it was that you were passing by," Shifty said.

When he remembered the car, Wisdom Xia called the driver over and told him to hurry up and take the car back to Mid-Star in Freshwind. He figured Mid-Star would probably need it, and there was no reason to wait around for him, since he was going to be admitted.

The driver took Goodness, Shifty, and Rain Xia back to Freshwind. When Rain Xia got back, he went to get some money together, then returned to the county hospital with Fourth Aunt, Snow Bai, Gold, and Thunder. "Why didn't you bring my radio?" Wisdom Xia asked.

"You're only going to be here for a few days," Rain Xia said.

"Go back and get it," Wisdom Xia said. "If I'm going to be stuck in here, I need my opera."

By the time Rain Xia got back to Freshwind to fetch the radio, it was already getting dark. He held the radio to his chest, unable to stop himself from crying. He stood for a moment at the entrance to the alley and thought to himself, *Will Dad get through this? The operation might solve the problem, but who knows how long he'll have after that? Cancer is complicated. I'd be happy if he got a few more years; even one or two more years would be fine . . . I need a miracle. Give me some sign that it will be a success. Show me some stars. If the sky is dark, I'll know . . .*

He looked up and saw that there wasn't a star in the sky. Rain Xia shuddered. He blinked and scanned the sky again. Suddenly, a single star winked down at him. He looked for its light again, but there was only darkness. Finally, the star shone again. Rain Xia fell back, steadying himself against a tree, trying to catch his breath. At that moment, Pavilion and New-Life appeared in the alley. Pavilion was lecturing New-Life about something, but when he saw Rain Xia, he jogged over and asked, "Is Fourth Uncle still in the hospital?"

Rain Xia told him about the diagnosis. Pavilion seemed to shrink. He stood for a long time without speaking. "Keep it to yourself, though," Rain Xia said. "If anybody asks, it's just an ulcer. I don't want my dad to know how serious it is."

"I wish I could go visit him," Pavilion said as he took out a roll of bills, "but I just can't. I'm trying to deal with the township government's new tax program. You know how tough that is." He passed the money to Rain Xia. "I won't have time to buy him anything, either. I just picked up my salary for the month—that's the whole thing. Pick him up some vitamins or something. Make sure you let me know when he goes in for the operation."

"Why are they collecting taxes at the end of the year? Everyone's getting ready for the New Year. Nobody in Freshwind is going to have any money to pay them."

"If there hadn't been a drought, we would have collected after the harvest. We put it off until later in the fall, but it never got done. Now, it's coming down to the wire. We have to collect before the end of the year . . ."

New-Life came over. Rain Xia stepped away and got on his motorbike. "Where are you off to, Rain Xia?" New-Life asked.

"Fourth Uncle is in the hospital."

"What's wrong with him? Is it serious?"

"No," Pavilion said.

As Rain Xia pulled away on his motorbike, he heard New-Life call after him: "Rain Xia, if there's anything I can do, let me know!"

Chapter 38

I had no inkling that Wisdom Xia was in the hospital. By the time I found out, he had just had the operation. There was a balmy breeze that day, the balmiest so far that winter, soft as countless babies' bottoms tumbling around in the air. Justice Xia didn't go and wait at the hospital for news, but after he heard that the operation had been successful, he went and spent the afternoon sunning himself in Seven Li Gully, his jacket unbuttoned, picking out the lice. He caught seven.

He didn't want me to go and visit his brother, either. "You'll make him worse!" he said, and that made me cry, because it was true.

I didn't know at that point that the cause of his illness was getting angry with Wind Xia. I thought it was because I was always getting into trouble, so I had to accept a share of the blame. I prayed that he might have a few more years of life left. In the dead of night, I used to be able to see my own internal organs. If I shut my eyes tight, the intestines made a picture in my mind. I tried to turn my belly into Wisdom Xia's belly, but I couldn't; the belly has its own feelings. His had always liked chilies, while mine had liked onions ever since I was a kid. I had to chew onions at every meal—it livened up my guts and got them moving. Otherwise, they wouldn't digest and I just kept farting.

I thought wistfully of Mid-Star's dad. He'd known how to make people live longer, but now he was dead himself. So I tried to be like him and ask the trees to keep Wisdom Xia alive. For three nights in a row, I kowtowed to all the trees in Freshwind. *You're all over a hundred years old,* I told them. *You'll live hundreds of years, even a thousand—can't you spare a year, or even a few months, to give Wisdom Xia? Helping him live a few more years wouldn't cost you more than a hair off an ox's hide, but it would settle the village down, and it would settle me down, too!*

On the third day, a gale blew up from Yijia Ridge and howled over Freshwind, whirling soil into the air and knocking tiles off the roofs. The stone roller that Doubleday Yang's uncle used for grinding up reeds to sell for papermaking, the one he kept at the entrance to West Street, actually bowled along ten yards in the wind. I was worried that my old well (the first in Freshwind Village, back when my dad was alive) might be blown out of my yard. It wasn't, but thirty trees were damaged in the gale. Branches snapped off and clattered to the ground, some lost their tops, others lost bits as thick as a rake handle. Not many were actually blown over, though some leaned and roots were split. I knew this was the trees responding to my prayers. They were offering themselves to Wisdom Xia.

The tree that suffered the most damage was the gingko outside Freshwind Temple. It used to have five branches the diameter of a rice bowl. One broke clean off and ended up stuck between the yard wall and the shithouse wall. It happened while Goodness was squatting inside and scared him half to death.

Goodness had called everyone to a general meeting of the Two Committees at the Great Qing Temple. Pavilion chaired the meeting, read out the township's directive regarding the collection of the yearly taxes and charges, and pointed out that, as before, the following were to be collected: land tax; livestock tax; retention for provident funds, welfare funds, and the overall plan; road tolls; and charges for additional educational expenses, police and security, social welfare, sports and culture, and sanitation.

The Middle Street Committee head spread a piece of paper on his knee and rolled cigarettes, muttering, "And a long, long life to Chairman M . . . !"

Pavilion didn't hear, but the man's neighbors did. The village cop sitting on Goodness's left kicked him in the shin and said to Goodness, "He's talking fucking nonsense again."

Goodness pretended not to hear, scratched his bald head, then got up and went to the shithouse. He squatted there for a long while as the wind whirled and tumbled overhead. It was freezing, and his balls went numb with cold. He put his hand down to check; they were still there—it almost felt like the wind had sliced them off. Just then, he heard a gigantic crash above his head, and before he could react, something heavy and black had collapsed on top of him. It felt like the sky had fallen in. He yelled and tipped backward into the pit.

They heard the crash and Goodness's cry from inside the building and figured it was an earthquake. Some sat frozen to their seats; others shot under the table. Pavilion stayed right where he was and stared up at the light bulb. It wasn't swaying.

"This isn't an earthquake," he said, and rushed outside.

The others followed, to find a branch from the gingko tree stuck between the yard wall and the shithouse wall, and Goodness slumped in the pit with his hands covered in shit. They were relieved to see him alive. "Goodness! Goodness! Get out! Doesn't it stink down there?"

Goodness's eyes rolled in his head, and he came to. "What happened? How could such a thick branch snap like that? Is heaven angry with me?"

"You must have done something to offend it," said the village cop.

Goodness wiped his dirty hands on the wall of the shithouse. "Good thing it was me in here. If it had been anyone else, they'd have been killed by the branch or the wall falling on them."

"And it happened right when we were having the tax and finance meeting!" someone exclaimed. "What incredible luck that no one got hurt and the walls held up."

They tried to pull the branch free, but no matter how hard they tried, it wouldn't budge.

"Forget it!" said Pavilion. "We can use it, put some cornstalks over it so the shithouse has a roof. Back inside, everyone. Time to carry on with the meeting!"

"Really? Carry on with the meeting?" said Bamboo.

"Whyever not?"

Goodness went to the pond to wash his hands and wipe the shit off his pants. The village cop went with him to blow his nose on his fingers. "How much meat can you cut off a flea's leg?" he muttered to Goodness.

"You watch your mouth where other people can hear," Goodness said. "Don't let your mouth run away with you in the meeting."

"Did you hear what I said in there?" said the village cop.

"The township government gets pressure from above when it comes to taxes and charges," Goodness said. "If we get it wrong, it blows the township cadres' career prospects and salaries out of the water, and our bonuses, too. No one likes paying taxes, but you can't talk like that when you're a cadre. Take care Pavilion doesn't hear you!"

"Did he?"

"I don't know."

"I speak as I see, and I've upset plenty of people in the past. Still, you'll smooth things over for me when the time comes, won't you?"

"Huh! You think I will?"

The meeting went on. Of course, Pavilion emphasized how crucially important tax collection was. He also pointed out that Freshwind was already deeply in debt and that was having a serious impact on the village's routine work, drawing down heavy criticism from the township. The township head had issued a stern warning to Pavilion and had almost banged his fist on his office desk to make his point.

The debts came in three parts. First, there was the money that former cadres had borrowed to fund the gully-filling project and to build village-grade gravel roads. Not only had that debt not been repaid, but interest had accrued annually. Second, village income didn't cover its expenditures on, for example, the "three deductions" (for public reserve funds, public welfare funds, and management costs) and the "five charges" (charges for rural education, family planning, militia training, rural road construction, and subsidies to entitled groups). The village government was allowed to collect and keep the "three deductions," but in the past year, it had spent thirty thousand yuan and had paid another twelve thousand yuan or more to the township, while the villagers either paid their taxes late or not at all. Of the money paid into the township, you got nothing back, for the fact was that the township was overspending its budget, too.

The result was that the village had to borrow to pay what it owed to the township, and these loans, which could run to several hundred thousand yuan a year, attracted a high rate of interest. The thirty thousand yuan the village was supposed to collect was not enough to cover expenses. Over the years, the backlog of tax payments had become a vicious circle. It happened like this: The poorest households could not pay, and a few who had been forced off their land refused to pay. So then those villagers who obediently paid their taxes got fed up and they, too, refused to pay.

Pavilion stressed that it would be difficult to collect the money, but they would have to get tough. If they let things slide as the previous village cadres had, Freshwind would go under. He organized for every street committee head to go door-to-door and extract payment. The Two Committees cadres would join forces, too, and he, Goodness, and Lotus Jin would back them up by taking on East, Middle, and West Streets. To avoid any accusations of partiality, he decided that they would each go to the streets where they had no relatives living.

The meeting went on and on until it was nearly dinnertime, but still Pavilion would not let them go. He even sent someone to the township government offices to fetch Studious Zhang, who was head of the tax group. Zhang came, bringing with him First-Field Li and Thrice Wu.

Studious Zhang had been transferred from the County Party Committee. He was a forceful young man who immediately made his views clear: the Freshwind cadres had been delegated the task of collecting taxes by the township, and they had to do it. He understood the difficulties, given the poverty of the villagers, but there was nothing the township could do; county finances were crucial. This year, the finance officers had declared that tax collection would be key to evaluating the township cadres' performance; in the future, they would have their salaries docked if they did not fulfil their duties. The township had similarly decided to tie the salaries of village cadres to tax collection. On completion, they would receive an annual bonus of up to 40 percent, depending how much they'd collected of what was due.

Studious Zhang explained that the township tax group was concerned about Freshwind's taxes. After looking at the situation, they had decided to appoint himself, First-Field Li, and

Thrice Wu to support the village cadres. If these three were not successful, they would have their salaries stopped, too.

Finally, he thumped the table with his fist. "Comrades! We are like ants on a rope . . ." He suddenly stopped and stared out the window. A shadow wandered past and vanished. "Who's there?" Studious Zhang shouted. "Quit wandering around outside. No one's leaving the meeting!"

"Did anyone go out?" asked Pavilion.

"No," Goodness said. "Everybody's here."

"Who is that then?" Pavilion said.

Goodness went out to look and found Big-Noise Zhao standing under the gingko tree.

Big-Noise Zhao needed gingko leaves for his potions and remedies and reasoned that, although it was winter, he should be able to find a few on the gingko in the Great Qing Temple courtyard. The gate wasn't bolted, and he went inside. But before he could get to the tree in the corner, he heard Studious Zhang bang the table and figured he must have been arguing with someone. When he realized the meeting was about collecting taxes, he slipped past the window and headed for the gingko. Goodness waved him away, but Big-Noise Zhao was staring in shock at the broken branch.

"We're having a meeting," Goodness whispered. "What are you doing here?"

"I know you're having a meeting. I just came for some gingko leaves; I'm not making any noise. But what's happened to that branch? Why's it broken?"

"The tree doesn't want you picking its leaves. Get out of here. You're disturbing the meeting, wandering around like that!"

Big-Noise left. His parting shot was, "It's only a tax meeting." He was annoyed, though. Did they think that holding a big meeting was going to bring in the taxes? Taxes fell due every year, but they were never collected in full.

He picked up a clod of earth and used it to scrawl on the left-hand gate post: "Asking the fish about water"; on the right-hand one he wrote, "Asking the tiger for its skin."

When Studious Zhang finished speaking, Pavilion added, "You've all heard what's been said. The township government is laying down the line here. It doesn't matter how hungry you are; no one's leaving the room. We've got to use last year's experience to do things better this year and get those taxes in."

No one spoke. No one met his gaze. Some looked down and puffed at their cigarettes; others gave dry coughs but seemed unable to clear their throats, as if they had a feather stuck in there. Mostly, they looked out the window. A sparrow landed on the windowsill, hopped back and forth, and then flew away.

"Has no one got anything to say?" asked Pavilion. "Well, you can all stay hungry then."

Goodness bent down and picked up the thermos to refill his mug, then sniffed suspiciously at his hand. He hadn't managed to wash off the stink. "Every year when it comes to collecting taxes, I fall out with everyone. The rest of the time, I tiptoe around people, always helping them out, and then tax collection comes around, and any popularity I've built up is swept away. But it can't be helped. You're always gonna offend someone, and no one forced us to be village cadres."

"You've got nothing to complain about," said the head of the Middle Street Committee. "We get it in the neck day in, day out. We're treated like dogs!"

"My mouth works in my favor," Goodness said. "That's why I say that tax collectors have to have the gift of gab. If someone's a soft touch, then you don't play the tough guy with them, and if someone's aggressive, you can't be too soft on them. Let's be clear: you've got to adapt your approach to the person you're talking to. You use human language with humans and devil language with devils."

His words lightened the mood, and the leader of the West Street Committee head piped up: "You're saying I'm supposed to sell my ass?"

There was loud laughter, and Bamboo said, "Stinking lowlife!"

"You're right, I do stink," said the West Street head. "I've always tried to learn from Goodness, but there's only one of him in Freshwind. He can fall into a cesspit and come out smelling of roses. But me, I stink even if I don't go into the shithouse all afternoon!"

There was more laughter.

Pavilion tried to call them to order. "Can we be serious, please."

Then Lotus Jin spoke up. "I've been thinking. We need a slogan to help the tax collecting go smoothly. What about, 'Collect year on year; organize collection squads; share collection responsibility; collect according to the law.'"

"But you're not saying anything new," objected the village cop. "That's what happens every year. Only it's obviously more difficult this year—there's the drought and yields are down, and the farmers thought they could pay last autumn, but now prices have gone up, so where are they gonna get the money from?"

"Stop being so defeatist!" said Zheng Xuewen.

"I'm not being defeatist," said the village cop. "I'm just telling it like it is."

"Even if that is how it is, you shouldn't put it like that."

"So I won't say anything at all!" And the village cop bent over his pipe.

"There's another problem this year," Bamboo put in. "A lot of families have left their fields fallow. If they're not farming their land, should they be paying all those taxes and charges? If they bring that up, what are we supposed to say to them?"

"Of course they have to pay. Why aren't they farming?" said Studious Zhang.

"Because," said Bamboo, "one *mu* of land doesn't produce much grain, a *jin* of grain sells for almost nothing, the tax on it still has to be paid, and the costs of fertilizer, pesticides, and seeds keep going up. Farming isn't cost-effective. If things go on like this, we'll see a lot more land being set aside next year, too."

"Every year, we have nothing but trouble collecting taxes from the farmers, from start to finish. Why don't we petition the higher-ups to reduce taxes a bit?" said the village cop.

"And who are you gonna petition? The prime minister?" retorted Studious Zhang.

"Me and my big mouth," said the village cop. "Pity I'm not a mute!" He smacked himself on the mouth.

"You're quite right in what you say, but we don't get to decide on the rules," Pavilion said. "China's a big country, and the policies are the same everywhere. If other places can do it, Freshwind should be able to, too. As for us taking back fallow fields and getting other people to lease them, we've gotten nowhere on that front. We'll carry on looking into it, but in the meantime, we have to operate under the current rules, and everyone has to pay their taxes. People who go and work in the city need to be told they must come home and pay. If they don't, we'll force entry into their houses and confiscate their furniture, just like we did last year."

The village cop stiffened.

"You want to say something?" Pavilion asked.

"I'm not saying any more."

"Pavilion is right when he says we have to go on previous experience," Goodness said. "We have plenty of experience in collecting taxes, and we've learned a lot, too. Let's put it like this: As soon as we notice someone's sold a pig or a basket of eggs or a lot of vegetables in the market, we don't waste any time. We go and demand they pay up what they owe. If we find out someone's got a lot of cash at home, we don't wait until they've spent it; we go and demand payment. They make a cent, we take a cent. They make a yuan, we take a yuan."

This was a concrete proposal, and everyone jumped in with their own ideas. Lotus Jin added a new proposal: The shiitake growers got their money from Compliance, so the tax could be deducted at the source before he paid out. The post office could be required to inform them about remittances from laborers or businesspeople, and they could be at the door as soon as the money arrived. Plus, every street committee had its informers, and they could act the moment they were told something was going on. If you heard news in the morning, you shouldn't wait until lunchtime, and if you heard at night, you shouldn't wait until dawn.

"So we've all got to be spies?" Bamboo asked.

"There's nothing wrong with being a spy," Lotus Jin said. "A spy's a special agent, someone who performs special services for the state. Collecting village taxes is a special service."

"That's news to me," said Bamboo, and she fell silent.

Then they talked about the families who might give them particular problems, and also how they would go about taxing people like Shifty, Star Chen, Bright Chen, Roughshod Ding, Rain Xia, Compliance, and Favor Bai: that is, the lessees of the apple orchard, the brickyard, the restaurant, the hotel, the dye-shop, the smithy, the pharmacy, the paper shop and the general store, and the labor contractor. Finally, the meeting came to an end. There were loud grumbles about being so hungry they could hardly move. "Pavilion, where are we going to get lunch from?"

"You want to be dining at public expense? Sure, just as soon as we've collected all the taxes, I'll stand you all a meal at the House of Treasures, with squid and sea cucumber! For today, you can each have a bowl of mutton *paomo* soup and count yourself lucky."

On the way out, someone noticed the words written on the gate. "Who did this?" Pavilion demanded. "'Asking the fish about water.' What does that mean?"

"It means it's stupid to ask fish about water, because they live in it," Lotus Jin said.

"It's like a thirsty person asking the fish where to find water," the West Street Committee head added.

"I see," Goodness said. "It's an insult to our tax-collection work."

"How do you mean, insult?" Bamboo asked.

"A fish can't live out of water. Now even the fish are thirsty, and then people come and ask them for water."

Pavilion studied the second sentence, "Asking the tiger for its skin." Then he said, "Big-Noise Zhao wrote this, didn't he?" He wiped the characters off with his hand. "Don't let Big-Noise Zhao rile you. He's just itching for a chance to make trouble for us. And the fucker sure knows how to express himself elegantly!"

I won't say any more here about how the village cadres ate their fill of mutton *paomo*, or how Pavilion went to make his report to the township government cadres. Let me say a bit about how the taxes are collected. You had to strike while the iron was hot. The village cadres, normally so high and noble, turned into sons of bitches. Still, in three days they only managed to collect taxes from two families on Middle Street. Goodness was a smooth talker, but the Middle Street residents knew exactly how to wear him down by stringing him along. Goodness never wanted to offend anyone, so he spent nearly a whole day chatting with one family, apparently forgetting he was there to collect taxes.

They made better progress on West Street, and Pavilion told the street committee head to carry on on his own while he, Pavilion, went to back up Goodness. On East Street, everything went pretty smoothly, because most were nonlocal families with members working in the city and earning decent money. Only the women were left at home, and Bamboo and Lotus Jin worked them together, one with reason, the other with sympathy, and everyone paid up. Except for Shifty. He was courtesy itself; he would pay as soon as he'd been to West Mountain Bend and collected on a consignment of bricks and tiles, he told them. And then he vanished in a puff of smoke.

When they got to Clerk's, he said, "Have the Xias paid yet? I'll pay when they do."

So Bamboo, Pavilion, and Rain Xia paid the taxes they owed. Clerk then paid a third of what he owed and asked for a few more days to pay the rest.

Bamboo and Lotus Jin went to Forest Wu's next. Forest Wu was the poorest man in the village, and he told them that Black-Moth had stolen the three hundred yuan he'd hidden in his dad's photo frame, and that had cleaned him out. He begged them to wait till he'd sold some grain. Lotus Jin's response was to tell him to sell a sack of wheat in the market right then and there. So Forest Wu shouldered the bag and trudged off, but the wheat price was too low, so he brought the wheat back and said he'd try again the next day.

"Stop giving me the runaround," Lotus Jin snapped at him.

"I'm not g-giving you the run-run-runaround!" Forest Wu protested.

At that point, Bamboo took Lotus Jin home for a meal.

Forest Wu sat there, racking his brains, without coming up with a solution. It was obviously Black-Moth who'd landed him in the shit, so he gathered his courage and went to Treasure's to talk to her. Luckily, Treasure was not at home. "G-give me m-my m-money," he demanded.

"What money?" Black-Moth said. "I took what I was awarded in the divorce, that's all. I even left you those three hens that were mine by rights. I don't fucking owe you anything."

"And wh-what about the three hundred I hid in Dad's ph-photo frame? How c-come i-it's dis-disappeared?"

"So it's disappeared! Can you prove I took it? If you don't have any proof, then don't go calling me a thief."

Forest Wu shook his fist at her in frustration and yelled, "I'm gonna kill you, you fucking slut!"

But before he could lash out further, Treasure came into the room and laid Forest Wu out flat with the stone roller's handle. Forest Wu scrambled to his feet and fled, and Treasure chased after him, shouting, "Show your face here again, you fucker, and I'll break your legs for you!"

Forest Wu hurried home, swearing at Treasure and Black-Moth as he went. He was still furious when he got there, so he picked up a shovel and rushed back again. The yard gate was bolted, so he went to the shithouse and came back with a shovelful of shit, which he threw down in the gateway. He'd just gone to get more when Treasure rushed out the gate and kicked Forest Wu into their cesspit.

The piss and shit in the cesspit reached waist high, and Forest Wu nearly got a mouthful. East Street erupted in confused shouting. Lotus Jin and Bamboo came running to find Forest Wu sitting drenched in Treasure's gateway, yelling, "Black-Moth! If you don't give me my three hundred yuan, I'm not moving from here. You'll have to kill me first!"

Lotus Jin bawled Treasure out, and then she went and told Forest Wu, "You don't need to pay on the spot. Go on home."

Treasure, on the other hand, had to pay all his taxes immediately. He was a community teacher, and the township would withhold his wages until he did. He had no excuse not to, so he paid.

Next, Bamboo and Lotus Jin went back to Clerk's, but he was a harder nut to crack. "Forest Wu got more time. Why can't I have more?"

"You're not in the same position as Forest Wu," Bamboo said.

"Treasure stole Forest Wu's wife, and Treasure's father messed up my leg."

"What kind of nonsense is that?" said Bamboo. "You've got to pay. I'm sitting here, and I'm not going until you give us the money." She sat down on his doorstep and lit a cigarette. Lotus Jin could see that she had the situation under control and went along to the next house. When she got to Halfwit's, he clasped his head between his hands and squatted on the ground. "I have no money!" he wailed.

Lotus Jin flew into a rage. "You mean you haven't got any money to pay your taxes, but you've got plenty for a game of mah-jongg, is that it? Well, if you don't have cash, we'll take your grain or your gate or your roof tiles instead!"

Lotus Jin was in such a foul mood that Halfwit's wife rifled through the grain chest and pulled out fifty yuan. Before she could hand it over, however, Halfwit snatched the money from her. "Why are you so eager to pay up?" he shouted. "If she wants to take our grain or our gate or the roof tiles, let her try."

As Lotus Jin left, she said, "Halfwit, you're the rat droppings in the Xia family soup. Your sister-in-law is a street committee head, and your cousin is Party secretary. I'll get them to come and talk to you."

After Halfwit obdurately refused to pay, another four or five households followed suit. Bamboo went with Lotus Jin to report him to Pavilion. Pavilion shouted and swore at Halfwit, and Halfwit gave him the fifty.

"Look and see if there's any more," he told Pavilion. "Feel free to take it if you can find it."

Pavilion told Lotus Jin to pull the kang mat off, but there was nothing underneath. They went through the wheat and rice in the grain chest. Nothing. They even took down a basket hanging from the rafters, but it contained only some old cotton coverlets. "Stand up!" Pavilion ordered him.

Halfwit stood up and emptied his pockets. Nothing. Then he spread his legs wide so the crotch of his pants split. Nothing in there, either.

"You sad old prick," said Pavilion.

After seven days, they'd only collected one-fifth of the money, and when the payers realized that most of the villagers weren't cooperating, they came and demanded their money back. Pavilion called a new meeting, where all the street committee heads complained that the taxes were far too high and most villagers really couldn't pay. They wanted Pavilion to explain this to the township government and make their case for a reduction or waiver, or at least a postponement of the deadline. After all, the New Year holiday was coming up in a few days. The original idea of the meeting had been to encourage people to pay up, but instead it turned into a litany of complaints.

Pavilion gave in and went and put their petition to the township government. That earned him a rebuke from the township head. When he came back, he, in turn, rebuked the three street committee heads, who then said they were going to resign, and promptly downed their tools.

Pavilion discussed the matter with Studious Zhang, who said, "It's the East Street folk who started all this. Are you trying to protect your own?"

Pavilion was furious. "You're telling me I'm protecting the Xias? I've already offended every single one of them with my work for Freshwind Village. Go and do your own tax collecting!"

Studious Zhang set off for East Street, taking with him First-Field Li, Thrice Wu, and two of the local village cops. The first house they came to was Shifty's. Shifty abandoned the meal he was eating and vanished out the back window. Studious Zhang was enraged. He grabbed the bowl Shifty had just put down and hurled it to the ground, smashing it. "The monk can flee, but the temple stays put!" he yelled after him. "You better not show your face in Freshwind ever again, Shifty!"

Then they split up into two groups and started on the stickiest cases. If they could collect from them, it would put the frighteners on everyone else—"killing the chickens to scare the monkey." Studious Zhang, First-Field Li, and one of the police went to Halfwit's, while Thrice Wu and the other village cop went to Forest Wu's.

Halfwit was sitting indoors making straw shoes. He heard heavy breathing outside the back window, looked up, and saw the officer. He didn't give it much thought until Studious Zhang and First-Field Li came in through the gate. "Are you collecting taxes?" he asked.

"Why haven't you run away?" asked Studious Zhang in his turn.

"I've got a clear conscience; I've paid up!"

Bamboo just happened to be passing the gate, and Studious Zhang called, "Bamboo, Bamboo! Come in here!"

"Don't you shout at me. I'm not head of the street committee," Bamboo responded, and walked on.

Studious Zhang turned to Halfwit. "So you paid, did you? How much?"

"Fifty yuan."

"Who to?"

"Pavilion!"

"And Pavilion thinks that wipes the slate clean? You still have more to pay."

"But I haven't got any money!"

"Is that right?" He turned to First-Field Li. "Grab his grain!"

"Grab his grain?" asked Halfwit.

"Grab his grain!" Studious Zhang repeated. And First-Field Li took the lid off the grain chest and began to fill the bags he had with him with wheat, first one then the other. A few grains dropped on the floor, and the hens scurried indoors and began to peck them. Halfwit's wife wailed and chased them away and began desperately to collect the grains up.

Halfwit swore at her. "What are you fucking cleaning up grains for? The bandits get to eat our wheat and our hens don't?"

"Who's a bandit?" said Studious Zhang.

"You are. You're all bandits!"

"And you're a bad lot!"

While the argument went on, First-Field Li tied up the neck of the bags.

"Have some more!" Halfwit told him. "Are you sure you have enough? Look, there's some more in that chest!" And he pulled the chest out and tipped it over so that the remaining grain spilled out. Then he grabbed handfuls and scattered it all over the floor.

Just then, Thrice Wu and the other cop arrived with Forest Wu. He'd refused to pay, so what should they do?

"Grab his grain!" said Studious Zhang.

"He has no fucking grain!" said Thrice Wu.

"Then we take the gate and the roof tiles."

Thrice Wu said, "We tried that, but he threatened to burn down the house. And if he did that, we'd take the rap."

"Take him to the township offices and put him in political-education classes."

Thrice Wu tried to drag Forest Wu away, but Forest Wu locked his arms around a tree outside the gate. The village cop couldn't pry his fingers off—as soon as he lifted one finger, the other gripped the tree trunk. He tried hitting Forest Wu's hands, and Forest Wu yelled, "Help! Help! Tell the township officials! They're beating me up! Save me, save me!"

As soon as he started yelling, he completely lost his stutter. People began to cluster around the gate, and Halfwit, emboldened, said, "Is this how you go about collecting taxes? You're no different from the Kuomintang press-gangs!"

"Don't think you can get nasty just because there's a crowd of people here," said Studious Zhang. "You're a nasty piece of work; you only understand force. Take his grain away!"

First-Field Li got Halfwit's barrow, which was in a corner of the yard, and put the bags on it. Halfwit jumped to his feet and blocked the gateway. "You've got my wheat, isn't that enough? Leave my barrow alone. You can carry the bags on your back. If you touch my barrow, I'll kill myself right here!"

Studious Zhang shoved him to one side, and Halfwit went to push him back, but he was shorter than Studious Zhang and ended up with a handful of Zhang's jacket. He hung on, and when Studious Zhang shoved him again, there was a loud rip and the jacket tore. Inside, you could see his red sweater and the white collar underneath.

"Don't you dare lay hands on me!" shouted Studious Zhang. "He's attacking a tax collector going about his lawful business! Handcuff him! Handcuff him!" One of the officers pulled the handcuffs out of his waistband, fastened them on Halfwit, and dragged him away.

In the alley, the villagers began to protest. "You're collecting taxes. Why are you handcuffing him? Where does it say in Party regulations that you get to imprison people who don't pay taxes?"

Someone went and told Bamboo, who came running. "What are you doing?" she demanded.

"Can't you see? He ripped my jacket!" Studious Zhang said.

"So what?" she said. "Why are you using the handcuffs on him? Would you have shot him if you had a gun?"

"Bamboo, you're a village cadre. That's not the right attitude to take."

"I'm not a village cadre anymore. I've had enough."

"Well, if you've stopped being a village cadre, then you can make yourself scarce," said Studious Zhang and then shoved her aside.

The alley was filling up with people. There was nothing the Freshwind folk liked more than a good ruckus. It didn't even have to be fisticuffs; just a loud argument drew the crowds. And if people really came to blows, no one bothered to try and calm things down; they were more likely to fan the flames.

With the alley so full of people, there were a lot of raised voices, and someone in the nearby farmers market heard. That one person came running, and as soon as one person runs, ten more follow. And they came from West Street, too, and soon the alley was chockablock.

When they realized the fight was about collecting taxes, their sympathies were all with Halfwit against Studious Zhang. As Halfwit was put in handcuffs and hauled off to the township offices, there was a roar of disapproval. Studious Zhang was worried Forest Wu might take his chance to take off, so he put handcuffs on him as well. But they couldn't make any progress through the crowds.

Studious Zhang had a face like thunder. "Out of the way! Move!" he shouted. But no one budged. Zhang pushed forward and accidentally stepped on someone's foot.

"I've already paid. What are you stomping on my foot for?"

"Scram!"

"I live in Freshwind," said the man. "Where am I supposed to scram to?"

The ones at the back of the crowd started yelling and pressing forward, and those at the front were pressed against Studious Zhang. "Who's pushing?" Zhang shouted. "Stop all this noise. The next person who starts yelling, I'll handcuff you and take you, too!" Finally a gap opened up, and they could move toward the top of the alley. And there stood Justice Xia.

I'm going to say some more about Justice Xia, because his appearance turned what was happening into a major incident that reverberated through the entire county. Years later, I was talking about what happened that day with Big-Noise Zhao, and I said, "However did a village like Freshwind produce a man like Justice Xia?"

"Tell me this," he said. "Was it Freshwind that produced Justice Xia, or Justice Xia that produced Freshwind?" Big-Noise Zhao talked like the newspapers.

"Talk like a villager," I said, but he didn't repeat himself, just shouted at me, "You're pig-ignorant!" Maybe I was, but the only person in Freshwind who meant anything to me was Justice Xia, and anyone who said bad things about him was my enemy.

That morning, we were working as usual in Seven Li Gully. It was a dull day; there were no dark clouds, but thunder rumbled around us. Thunder without rain was unusual for winter, and we thought it was strange. Halfway through the morning, Big-Noise Zhao turned up to dig some licorice root to make a remedy for Marvel's mom's asthma. He mentioned Wisdom

Xia and made Justice promise to take him along, too, if he went to visit him in the county hospital.

After he'd gone, Justice Xia told me he was having terrible palpitations. "I dunno what's making me so anxious," he said.

"It's not like Tongue-Tied or me are goofing off," I said.

Justice Xia stared at me, then he said, "Do you think something's happened to your fourth uncle?"

"Fourth Uncle got through the operation fine. Nothing's gonna go wrong now," I said.

"True . . . Was Big-Noise making up a remedy for Marvel's mom?"

"Her asthma's chronic. She has it every winter."

Justice Xia said nothing more to me. He just looked up at the sky, then told Tongue-Tied and me to carry on digging up rocks; he had to go back to look at something, and he'd be back with some rice for our lunch later.

"What else to go with the rice?" I asked greedily.

"Pickled cabbage."

"Fine, but stir-fry it in some oyster sauce," I said.

And Justice Xia went off to the village, his heart still thumping hard in his chest. But at Wisdom Xia's house, the gate was bolted, and Snow Bai and the baby weren't there, so he couldn't ask how Wisdom Xia was getting on. He was wondering if he should go to Marvel's instead when he heard the ruckus at the end of the alley. He knew the village cadres had been collecting taxes in the last few days, and that was bound to upset people, but he was astonished by the big crowd and the pushing and shoving when he turned into the alley.

"What on earth's going on?" he asked Auntie Wang.

She thumped her walking stick on the ground, hard. "Second Uncle, why's it taken you so long to get here? The township cadres have handcuffed Halfwit and Forest Wu, and they're taking them off to the township offices!"

"What nonsense is this?" exclaimed Justice Xia.

Just then, the crowd fell back, parting before him the way the wind flattens a path through the corn, and there was Studious Zhang and his posse advancing toward him, pushing Halfwit and Forest Wu before them. Halfwit's left wrist was cuffed to Forest Wu's right one. Halfwit had slender wrists, but Forest Wu's were massive and he was complaining loudly that the handcuffs were hurting him.

Halfwit didn't want to go, and he was walking stiff legged, so First-Field Li gave him a kick behind the knee, and he tumbled to the ground. Forest Wu was dragged down with him and hit his face on a clod of earth. Blood flowed from his mouth, and he cried, "M-my t-tooth! M-my f-front t-tooth!" And he started looking around for it.

Everyone came to a halt—Justice Xia and Studious Zhang and his posse, too.

Justice Xia was dressed in black pants and a black padded jacket, and his face was as black as a thundercloud.

"What the hell's going on here?" he demanded.

Halfwit cried, "Dad! Dad! They've got me in handcuffs!"

"You keep your mouth shut."

Halfwit tried to drag himself to his feet but couldn't, so Studious Zhang yanked him upright. That pulled on Forest Wu's arm, and he yelled in pain, "Ai-ya! Ai-ya!"

"What crime have they committed?" asked Justice Xia.

"Mr. Ex–Village Head, please stay out of this," said Studious Zhang. "I know Halfwit's your son, but he's refusing to pay his taxes. Move out of the way; we don't want things getting any uglier than they already are."

"So you know I used to be village head!" said Justice Xia. "Well, in that case, let me tell you, I've been a cadre here since 1949, and I've collected taxes for decades. But I've never come across your method of tax collection, never even heard of it. A young guy like you, you've never been through the mill the way we have. What do you mean by coming here and getting everyone up in arms? Aren't you supposed to be working in the township?"

There were shouts and cheers at his words. Then they heard Second Aunt wailing at the other end of the alley, and Halfwit's wife came along with her baby in her arms. The child was screaming shrilly, and Lucky followed behind, snapping. In fact, all the East Street dogs were snapping at the crowd. At the entrance to the alley, people were pushing and shoving, trying to squeeze in, but the ones in front couldn't move their feet. Only their bodies were bent forward. Someone pulled a tile off the alley wall and threw it to the ground, where it shattered with a loud crack.

"What are you doing?" said Studious Zhang. He wore his hair parted down the middle, and when he looked up, the two sides flopped over his temples. "Mr. Xia," he said, "don't incite them! I have great respect for you as the former village head, but you're trading on your seniority now. The village isn't the same as when you were its head. If we don't get tough, how are we going to collect the taxes? Anyone who refuses to pay what they owe is breaking the law; that's why I'm taking them away!" And he gave Halfwit and Forest Wu another shove.

Justice Xia could see he was making no headway with Studious Zhang, so he just stood right where he was, in the middle of the road. Things got more chaotic, and someone pushed the barrow to the side of the alley, where its wheels got stuck in the gutter.

"Who pushed that?" shouted Studious Zhang. "Who pushed it?"

Thrice Wu got hold of it and began to pull it forward, but someone behind was pulling it backward. Studious Zhang came over and began to push it from behind, and some of the bystanders got their feet crushed under the wheels. There were shouts and screams, and someone grabbed the side of the barrow, and it ended up in the gutter again.

The gutters were actually ruts made by car wheels when it rained and the roads became muddy. Once they dried up, the ruts set hard as concrete. Studious Zhang heaved the barrow forward with all his might, and its wheels rose out of the gutters, sending it cannoning straight into Justice Xia. The old man didn't try to dodge and was knocked to the ground. The barrow just happened to catch him on his right collarbone. Studious Zhang hesitated a moment, then charged out of the alley, pushing the barrow. There was a rush to help Justice Xia. Although he wasn't bleeding, the bone was obviously broken, and he fainted from the pain.

"They've killed him!" someone shouted.

Bamboo was behind and couldn't see, but when she heard the cry go up, she shouted, "Don't let Studious Zhang get away!" And like a swarm of angry bees, they all set off in pursuit. Studious Zhang panicked and dropped the barrow. Then he and the men who were dragging Halfwit and Forest Wu ran as fast as they could for the township offices. On the way, Halfwit took his chance and grabbed a tree by the roadside, but the village cop who had hold of him drew his baton and struck his hand. Halfwit let go of the tree, but the officer's cap fell off. The officer was bald, and when he lost his cap, he turned back to pick it up, but then set off running again when he saw their pursuers were about to catch up with them. Bamboo picked up the officer's cap and hunkered down by the side of the road to get her breath back. She looked down a side alley and saw Shifty coming out.

"Where are you going, Shifty?" she asked. "Was it you who made Studious Zhang so angry with Halfwit and Forest Wu?"

Shifty didn't answer her. Instead he said, "I heard they hurt Second Uncle!" Then he raised his voice. "The township fuckers have beaten Uncle Justice to death!"

"Don't talk nonsense!" said Bamboo. "He's just injured."

But Shifty was still proclaiming, "The township fuckers have beaten Uncle Justice to death!" He turned to Bamboo. "If the villagers don't all go, they really will beat someone to death. Go and call people to follow them, quick!"

So Bamboo went into Wisdom Xia's yard. She found only Snow Bai and the baby. Snow Bai had no idea what all the commotion outside was about until Bamboo shrieked at her, "They're taking people away in handcuffs, and they've knocked your second uncle unconscious!" She rushed into Wisdom Xia's bedroom and turned the loudspeaker on. Then she made an announcement: "The township tax collectors have handcuffed some villagers! They've taken our wheat and our yard gates! They're beating people up! They're going to kill someone! What way is this to collect taxes? Are these people tax collectors or the King of Hell come to claim your lives? Go and get them! Get the murderers! Down with Studious Zhang!"

The East Street folk heard the loudspeaker, and so did the folk from West Street and Middle Street. Dry firewood crackles and spits when it bursts into flame. Gongs started up on West Street, and people started banging enamel basins and kettles on Middle Street. The news spread from one to another, and amid loud cursing and shouting, people flooded toward the township offices. Almost everyone grabbed a shovel, or sticks, as they ran out of their yards, or they armed themselves with a brick that they picked up as they ran along the road. "Moth-er-fuck-ers! Moth-er-fuck-ers!" the cry went up as they ran down the alleys and into the village streets, from the village streets to the 312, and from the 312 to the township government offices.

Some of the faster runners from East Street had already caught up with Studious Zhang's posse by the time they got to the offices. Studious Zhang squared up to them and roared, "You dare come any closer and I'll put handcuffs on you!"

The front runners stopped, but those behind pressed forward, shouting, "The law can't punish us all! Who are you gonna stick the handcuffs on? Go ahead, try it!"

Studious Zhang retreated a few steps, but one of the village cops rushed forward with his baton raised, and the crowd backed away. One step forward, one step back, one step forward, one step back. They repeated this three times, by which point the West and Middle Street contingent had arrived. Someone flung a clod of earth that didn't hit anyone but smacked down at First-Field Li's feet. Studious Zhang dragged Forest Wu and Halfwit in through the gate of the government office compound. "Shut the gate! Shut the gate," he shouted.

The pursuers threw themselves forward to stop the gate shutting, and First-Field Li and Thrice Wu laid into them, fists and feet flying. Some of those at the front were hit on the head by the closing gate, and the blood began to flow.

"They're beating people up! They're bleeding!" cried someone. And countless hands wiped over their comrades' bloodied heads and smeared the blood on the gate. A volley of shovels and sticks and stones and bricks clanged against the metal. By this time, several hundred people surrounded the township offices.

It so happened that the township head had received a gift of a bear's paw from someone in Yijialing North Gully that day. It was done on the sly because of the national ban on hunting bears, but the township head told the chef to cook it with a lot of soy sauce and pass it off as dog meat. "How do you like the dog meat?" he asked once they'd finished their meal that day.

"Delicious," said the Party secretary.

"Yes! Damned delicious!" the other cadres chorused.

Just then, Thrice Wu came running. "Chief! Chief!"

The township head hurriedly put the dish out of sight and shouted through the window, "What's up? Your balls on fire?"

He pushed the window open to see a tug-of-war going on around the gate. Studious Zhang was trying to pull Forest Wu and Halfwit inside, while the villagers outside were pulling them back out again. Then the gate banged shut, and they heard a roar out in the street. The Party secretary went ghastly pale and collapsed into his chair. "I knew something would go wrong! Well, that's put an end to my job!"

The township head went out into the yard, but before Studious Zhang could report to him, the head kicked him to one side and went to the gate. He opened it a crack and shouted, "Public disturbances are against the law, and so is besieging government buildings! Disperse, everyone! Disperse!"

The people outside shouted, "Let them go! Let them go! Hand over Studious Zhang! Hand over Studious Zhang!"

The gate slammed shut again, and stones and broken tiles rained down from the other side of the wall. The township head and Studious Zhang retreated a few steps until they reached the shelter of the eaves. Most of the missiles landed in the flower bed, but one broke a windowpane, and bits of glass flew in all directions. The Party secretary was still sitting inside, unable to get out of his chair, when the township head rushed in to phone Pavilion. It rang, but no one picked up. Through the window, he watched Studious Zhang shielding his head with a galvanized iron pan as he went to the stone table to retrieve a set of chess pieces. Something flew through the air and spattered against the pan. It was a bag of shit.

The township head dialed again, cursing, "Where the hell have all the Freshwind cadres gone? Is there no one in the village office?"

In fact, Pavilion and Goodness had been there the whole time. They already knew that the villagers had surrounded the township offices, but they had stayed where they were because they didn't know what to do. They were in a dilemma. Anything they did might actually make things worse, adding fuel to the flames, as it were. Besides, they didn't really know which side they were on.

When the phone rang, Pavilion went to answer it, but Goodness stopped him. "That'll be the township head, for sure!"

"If we don't go out, it could really blow up in our faces," Pavilion said.

"But if we do go out, who are we speaking for?" said Goodness. "The village folk or the cadres? If we side with the township cadres, the villagers will have our guts for garters."

"But this can't go on!"

"Studious Zhang went too far, and he got people's backs up. There's not a lot we can do about it. At least now they know how difficult it is to run things in the village. Now maybe they'll stop throwing their weight around."

But Pavilion couldn't let it go at that. "The villagers have gone completely crazy, and they're sure to do something stupid. If they carry on besieging the township offices, or even break in, the police will have to intervene. We can't sit here and pretend we're not responsible."

"This is what we'll do," Goodness said. "You make yourself scarce for a while. Go to West Mountain Bend. I'll go to the township and see what's going on. Whatever happens, they won't be able to pin the blame on you."

Pavilion gave it a moment's thought and then agreed. On his way out, he said, "You be careful, too." Then he put his head down and slipped out the temple gate and down a short alley that ran beside the theater. It was deserted, except for a sow waddling along, its big belly swinging. At the end of the alley, Pavilion emerged onto the riverbank and followed the path.

During the half hour after his departure, the phone rang three times. Goodness stared at it, smoked a cigarette, and drank half a cup of tea before strolling slowly down the street. When he got to the Earth Shrine, he bumped into New-Life Liu, Star Chen, and Smooth-Stepper, a lame man from West Street. New-Life Liu was saying, "Has someone dyed them red?"

"Who?" Smooth-Stepper said. "It's obvious they've gone red by themselves!"

Goodness coughed and began to sing an aria from *The Golden Bowl and the Hairpin*:

> What an adorable girl
> No one more witty, and
> Clever and pretty
> She sees my desires
> She knows where I come from,
> She's a real lady of learning
> No wench from a humble home . . .

The three men looked around at Goodness, and he said, "What are you going on about? Aren't you freezing out here?"

"Fancy you singing the *dan* role!" Star Chen exclaimed.

"When women are upset, they cry; when men are upset, they sing," Goodness replied.

"What are you upset about?" Star Chen asked.

"My wife nagging at home, and dogs nipping me when I'm out."

"Quit babbling," New-Life said. "Star Chen, show Goodness what's happened."

"What's happened?"

"The eyes of the Earth God and Goddess have gone red!" said Star Chen.

"Nonsense!" said Goodness. "They're made of stone; they're not people." He went a bit closer and peered at the statues. It looked like their eyes were a bit red, though he couldn't be quite sure of it. "It's you who've got red eyes, and that makes everything you look at appear red," he finally said.

"Why aren't you at the township offices?" New-Life asked him.

"I don't go currying favor. If no one calls me in, I don't go. I like to stay out of trouble."

"Don't you go even when there's trouble?"

"What trouble?"

"It's fantastic! Our folks have been trying to break into the township offices, and the cadres inside are so scared that not one has dared come out."

"Good heavens, what a mess!" exclaimed Goodness Li.

The four of them went there together. Outside, a seething mass of people were shouting and yelling. Amid the uproar, Shifty, Bounty, and half a dozen others were ramming the gate with a felled tree stump. Boom! Boom! With every blow, the gate rattled and shook on its hinges, and tiles from the gate porch fell off and shattered in the street.

Shifty shouted, "One! Two!" and the next blow left the gate tilting at an angle.

"What's . . . going . . . on . . . here?" Goodness shouted, drawing out the question long and loud. When he raised his voice, he sounded like a cockerel.

The township head heard him from inside the yard and shouted back, "Is that Goodness Li? Comrade Li, make the mob disperse!"

Goodness didn't answer; he just repeated, "What's going on? Tell me, what is going on?"

Someone said, "Goodness's here! Goodness, you're strong; help us batter the gate down!"

"But these are the township government offices," protested Goodness. "I can't do a thing like that!"

"We're all doing it. Everyone has to! If one person breaks the law, then we all have to!"

"I'm a village cadre," Goodness said. "How can I cut off the branch I'm sitting on?"

"The village cadres are the township's lapdogs. None of them care if we live or die," someone said. "Goodness, did you just come to see who's ramming the gate?"

"The gate? What do you mean? I haven't seen anything."

"Goodness is a wolf in sheep's clothing. He's not a real peasant; he'll never be with us," Shifty said. "Come on, batter it down! One, two . . ."

They hefted the log again, took a few steps back, then launched themselves forward as one. This time, when they rammed the gate, they made a big dent in it.

"Why are you using brute force?" Goodness asked. "If you've got a problem, let's talk about it. Why are you taking it out on the gate?"

He had hardly finished speaking when Tiger appeared on top of the yard wall, baring his teeth and snapping.

"What's the point of talking? Who listens to us?" said someone. "Studious Zhang was as fierce as a tiger when he came and took my grain. And now they've set the dog on us!" Some of the men reached up with their shovels and hit Tiger; he flew down from the wall and bit one of them on the leg. The others backed away so fast that some of them fell over.

"Motherfucker!" Shifty swore. "Even the dog treats us like shit. Beat it!" He dropped the log, grabbed a stick, and began to rain blows on Tiger. Tiger turned on him and took a flying leap at the stick. Midair, the stick hit the dog on the head, and he dropped to the ground. His hind legs scrabbled in the dirt before he got purchase and managed to get on all fours. He spun around and leaped at Shifty again, collapsed again, got up and leaped again. This time, he was panting, and his hackles stood on end. Shifty dodged sideways and landed another blow on Tiger's back. The dog's back went soft as tofu, and this time he did not get up again. The crowd rushed forward and beat him with sticks and stones till blood splattered all over the ground.

There were cries of "We've killed him! We've killed him!" but Tiger regained consciousness and started twitching.

"A dog won't die lying down," said Shifty. "You have to hang him up. String him up!"

Someone had a hemp rope with them and threw it into the circle of bystanders. Shifty made a noose at one end and tightened it around the dog's neck. He put the other end through the gate ring; they pulled the rope tight, and Tiger hung suspended in the air.

"His cock's hanging down! Strangle him! Strangle him!" people shouted.

Tiger scrabbled frantically with his front paws and then went limp. They heard a gurgling in his throat, and his eyeballs bulged.

"He's still breathing!" shouted someone. "Pour water over him, and that'll stop him."

"Get some water!" ordered Shifty. But there was none. The man who'd been bitten in the leg, one of the Ran family, pulled down his pants and tried to piss in the dog's mouth, but he couldn't piss high enough. Just then, Tiger's eyeballs burst from their sockets with a pop and hung suspended from nerve threads from the dog's head.

Goodness had backed out of the crowd, and now he was clasping his stomach and saying, "The shithouse? Where's the shithouse?" He trotted back toward the 312 and into the bathroom that Clerk's family had built. Inside, he didn't squat or piss—he leaned against the wall breathing hard, until he heard the police sirens. Then he peered out over the shithouse wall and watched as three police cars sped to the scene. He instantly squatted down. He was staying right where he was.

The police cars were from the county police station, responding to an urgent call from the township government. No sooner did they appear than most people threw down their sticks, shovels, stones, and bricks and ran away. They also left behind three caps and a dozen unmatched shoes. The police arrested the eight who had attacked the township offices gate and strangled the dog, and those inside pulled open the gate.

Chapter 39

The incident at the township government offices went down in history as the "Year-End Storm." It was the Year of the Dragon, too, and it's never too peaceful in a dragon year.

There were five major events in the county that year. The first was a village committee election in Guofenglou. The two big families in the village went to war, and eventually a couple of hundred people were out in the street, fighting it out. The next event happened in Dayoumen. The police station wanted to raise money to build a new dormitory, so they instated quotas for the collection of fines for all their officers. One officer, trying to fill his quota, arrested a woman, charged her with prostitution, and fined her three thousand yuan—but instead of paying, she went and complained to someone further up the chain of command. She got checked out by a doctor, who testified that her hymen was intact. That summer in Yong Township, they built a new classroom building for the school, and it wound up collapsing, killing six children. A few months after that, a bicycle-theft ring was cracked in Eight Li Village, Dongchuan Town. Out of 207 households in Eight Li Village, 198 were involved in bicycle thefts in Xijing and Zhoucheng, earning Eight Li Village a reputation as a den of bicycle thieves. The bicycle-theft cases made headlines, but it was nothing compared to what happened in Freshwind during the Year-End Storm. Our village was the real story. It was like comparing the rest of the fingers to the thumb.

That night, after the scene had been cleared, it started to snow. The snow came down in big flakes, like white flower petals falling from the sky. The snow hit the ground and didn't melt; it didn't take long for a thick layer to collect. A pure-white blanket was laid over the rooftops and yards, and over the roads and alleys and the highway. Anybody coming upon the village that way couldn't possibly imagine what had just taken place there.

Eight people were locked up in the township police station, including Forest Wu and Halfwit. The streets of Freshwind were empty. Everyone had returned home. The arguments were done. There was no crying. But Tiger's spirit still haunted the township government gates. Lucky was there, too, scratching around in front of the township government, as if looking for her lover. When she couldn't find him, she sat down under the hemp rope that still hung from the tree and howled pitifully.

Big-Noise Zhao went over to visit Justice Xia. He suspected he'd have to set the old man's collarbone but was relieved to see that it was only a hairline fracture. Big-Noise Zhao applied a medicated plaster, then pulled his jacket on and headed home. Trudging in the snow, he looked like an old man. When he came across Lucky, he called her over, but the dog stayed where she was. Big-Noise Zhao bent down and picked up a shoe that had been lost in the snow. It was a cloth shoe with a hole in the toe and one half of the heel worn away to nothing. Big-Noise Zhao couldn't guess whose shoe it was.

The iron gate of the township government creaked open, and a man shouted, "Stop right there!" Big-Noise Zhao didn't move. "Who are you?"

"Who are you?" Big-Noise Zhao said back.

"I'm from the special investigation team! What are you looking at over there?"

"I'm Big-Noise Zhao, the village doctor. I wasn't involved in the disturbance. Thrice Wu—Secretary Wu, are you in there? Tell them I had nothing to do with it."

Thrice Wu came out of the gate. "Don't get mixed up in this," he said. "Get out of here!" Big-Noise Zhao tossed the shoe into the snow and walked off, waving his hand in front of his nose and muttering about foot odor.

The special investigation team had been dispatched to Freshwind immediately after the disturbance and spent three days investigating. When they were done, they jailed the eight men who had been arrested by the police, charging them with breaking down the gate and hanging the dog. Their sentence was fifteen days of administrative detention. Of the eight, two were from the Xia family: Halfwit and Bounty. The investigators had gone looking for Bamboo, too. She hadn't been directly involved, but she had stirred up trouble on the loudspeaker.

Bamboo knew that since she was a village cadre, her punishment would be more severe, so when she got word that they were looking for her, she made herself scarce. Forest Wu and Halfwit hadn't been directly involved in the disturbance, either, but they had been the cause of it. They were fined two hundred yuan each and had to send for their family members to pay it off before they could leave.

The search for Bamboo continued, and Hearth was ordered to inform the investigators immediately if his wife showed up. Since the tax-collection situation still wasn't resolved, Pavilion went to the credit cooperative, borrowed 320,000 yuan, and submitted it to the township government, along with a letter of self-criticism. Forest Wu's tax bill was paid off by the village committee, and Halfwit got Snow Bai to lend him the money. The day after Forest Wu was released, he went looking for Star Chen, wanting to know if there might be some work for him in the orchard.

"It's the middle of winter," Star Chen said. "I don't need anybody. You want to freeload off me?"

"If y-you d-don't, uh, let me work for you, I'll h-h-have to go beg for food," Forest Wu said.

Seeing that Forest Wu wasn't going to leave, Star Chen offered him a job helping Bright Chen. The salary would be a hundred yuan a month, and meals would be provided. Forest Wu knelt down and kowtowed to Bright Chen.

"No need for all that," Bright Chen said. "D-don't worry about all the c-c-courtesy; you better l-listen to me. W-whatever I tell you to do, y-you better do it. I don't want any t-trouble, y-y-you hear me?"

"I, uh, I-I'll l-listen to you. There won't be any t-t-trouble. Don't worry a-a-about anything!"

Justice Xia had used up the three plasters Big-Noise Zhao had given him, so he went off to the pharmacy to get more. The wind was wailing through the village, and his baggy padded jacket flapped around him in the wind as he walked, making him look like a scarecrow. He leaned against the doorway of the pharmacy and noticed a new couplet. "For my diagnosis, I need to see your face / For the treatment, drop your drawers." Justice Xia went in and saw Clerk, who was also waiting for a plaster. By his side was the bamboo pole he was using as a crutch.

"I got my leg broken," Clerk said, "and you got your collarbone crushed. For what?"

"We deserved it," Justice Xia said.

Clerk laughed, and his eyes turned into tiny black specks in his face. "Uncle Justice," he said, "I don't hold it against you. Take a seat. Can you still lift your arms?"

Justice Xia turned his back on Clerk and went up to the counter. He asked Big-Noise Zhao to change his plaster.

"Uncle Justice," Clerk said, "you haven't given me a chance to thank you."

Big-Noise Zhao ran his hand along Justice Xia's collarbone, and the old man winced. "If you hadn't broken my leg, I would have wound up locked up along with the rest of them."

Justice Xia turned and kicked Clerk's good leg. "You want me to break that one, too?"

Clerk fell to the ground, moaning. "Why'd you have to kick me there, Uncle Justice?"

Justice Xia fixed him with a look that immediately shut Clerk up.

Big-Noise Zhao started laughing. "I've got a joke," he said. Before they could respond, he launched into it. "This is something that happened last month on Middle Street. The township head was at the barbershop getting a haircut from Zhang Ba. The two of them got to talking. He started talking about Deng Xiaoping's idea of the 'moderately prosperous society.' The township head asked if he'd heard Pavilion talking about the 'charge toward moderate prosperity' slogan. Zhang Ba said he had, so the township head asked what he thought 'moderate prosperity' meant. Zhang Ba explained it like this: You have liquor to drink during the day and a pair of tits to grab at night. Favor Bai's wife, who was sitting outside the barbershop, got angry and asked why he had to be so crude. So, Zhang Ba says to her, 'You're living the good life yourself: mah-jongg during the day and a pair of balls to slap around at night.'" Justice Xia and Clerk didn't laugh. "What's wrong with you two?" Big-Noise Zhao asked.

Justice Xia turned and walked out of the pharmacy.

Clerk watched him go. A low winter sun had emerged after the snow, and Justice Xia cast a long shadow on the steps.

"How is that a joke?" Clerk said. "Zhang Ba was telling the truth."

"You're a crude man," Big-Noise Zhao said. "But actually, that's even funnier than what Zhang Ba said."

As Justice Xia stumbled along the road, he ran into the tinker and Tied-Dog Zhang outside the dyehouse. They were both drunk, and the tinker was laughing. When he laughed, he opened his mouth wide and hooted like a barn owl. The tinker fell into the snow, and Tied-Dog Zhang walked off and came back with a branch. He ran from gate to gate, knocking down the icicles, which fell from the eaves with a crash. Finally his luck ran out, and a rain of icicles came down on top of his head. Two trickles of blood ran down his forehead like a pair of earthworms.

Justice Xia suddenly got a hankering for some *liang fen*, but all the restaurants were closed. Since he couldn't get his *liang fen*, he decided to walk over to Wisdom Xia's place on East Street. Once there, he stood for a while outside the gate, listening to a baby crying inside. "Snow Bai," he called. "Snow Bai, is Wisdom Xia back yet?"

"Is that Second Uncle?" Snow Bai called back. "Come in and rest for a while! He's not back yet, but Rain Xia says it'll only be a few days more."

"I know he'll come home safe and sound . . . Is the baby being good to you?"

"She is."

"How is your mother-in-law?" Justice Xia asked.

"I went to visit her yesterday, and she was doing fine. It's hard to sleep in the hospital, though."

"Oh. Well, I'd better be going."

Justice Xia tried to lift his arms but found he still couldn't. There was some foxtail grow-ing on top of the wall around his brother's yard, and he thought he might pluck some of the downy white grain from the ends of them—they were as pretty as flowers—but there was no way he could reach them. Right then, Bamboo appeared from the outhouse with a cigarette in her mouth. "Dad!" she shouted to her father-in-law.

Justice Xia was surprised to see her. "What are you doing here? When did you get back?"

"Early this morning," Bamboo said. "How's your collarbone? Damn, look at how thin you're getting!"

"Did the cops come looking for you?" Justice Xia asked.

"Nobody knows I'm back yet."

"You can't buzz in like a fly without anyone noticing. Someone must have noticed you're back. If I were you, I'd think about turning myself in . . ." Justice Xia was about to continue, but before he could speak, a cloud seemed to move across the sun, and a harsh smell stung his nostrils. At first he thought it might have been smoke from a stove, but he looked around and saw a cloud of fog rolling across the wheat fields.

"The fog came in early tonight," Justice Xia said.

Bamboo looked then, too, and saw the clouds rolling over the field. A cat ran past them, as if racing to get ahead of the fog, or as if it were pulling the fog behind it. The fog was sud-denly upon them like a wall of damp, and the cat disappeared.

"Turn myself in?" Bamboo said. "Bounty and the others aren't even out yet."

"That means that they haven't resolved things yet. All the more reason for you to go down there. You know how the Party works. You can hide for a while, but your number'll be up eventually."

Bamboo reached up and tried to snatch a handful of the fog that had filled the alley. She opened her hand—it was empty. "Dad," she said, "I just don't know what to do!"

Justice Xia sighed. "I'll go with you," he said. "Let's go."

Justice Xia and his daughter-in-law headed for the police station, with her in the lead and him in the rear. Neither of them had much enthusiasm for the task at hand, and they dragged their feet as they went.

Meanwhile, Roughshod Ding was working out front of the House of Treasures, skinning Tiger. A group had come from the township government earlier, carrying the body with them. They wanted a feast of braised dog. After he'd peeled the skin off, Roughshod Ding realized the dog's body hanging from the rope looked just like a human corpse. The cleaver fell from his hand and clattered to the ground. From somewhere nearby came the sound of someone singing local opera. He picked up the cleaver and went back to work again. Tiger was gutted, broken down, and then tossed, piece by piece, into a pot to braise.

The singing wasn't very loud. Roughshod Ding heard it, and so did Justice Xia and Bamboo, but that was about it. "Who's singing opera?" Justice Xia asked.

"You hear that, too?" Bamboo asked.

The fog was rolling in, and it was impossible to see farther than ten paces. Justice Xia and his daughter-in-law looked like they were walking through cotton. "I don't want you to go with me," Bamboo said. She couldn't stand seeing him like that. "I'll go myself."

"You think I'm too old, don't you? I'm not up for it?"

"I know you're going to heal up just fine, but right now you're hurt."

"I am too old!"

Whoever it was singing opera switched to another tune.

Justice Xia stopped walking. He stood and listened. The tune changed again.

I guess I can admit it now: I was the one singing. My throat was shot, so I couldn't really sing, but I wanted to offer some comfort to Tiger's soul. I felt bad that I hadn't joined the Year-End Storm. If I had, I would have been able to brag about it now. Instead, while all of that was happening, I was over at Seven Li Gully with Tongue-Tied. We didn't go back to the village until that evening. I was on my way to gripe to Justice Xia—little did I know that he'd already had his collarbone crushed. I found him lying on his kang. After that, I went everywhere with a cleaver. I even staked out the front gate of the township government a few times, waiting for Studious Zhang. *Fucking Studious Zhang,* I thought. *You hurt Justice Xia, and I'll have your blood on this knife!* But I never even caught sight of him. When I found out the township government was putting on a banquet over at the House of Treasures, I figured it must have been Studious Zhang who'd arranged it. I drank some liquor and headed straight over.

It turned out I was wrong. I went in and asked where Studious Zhang was, but I was told that he'd already left the village. I slammed the blade of the cleaver down on the stone table and said, "That son of a bitch escaped, did he?"

"What do you think you're doing with that cleaver? If you're planning to use it on somebody, you should know the special investigation team is still here."

"I'm just cutting up the table! I'm just chopping it up a bit!" Every whack of the cleaver sent up sparks from the tabletop. I kept going until the blade was ruined, then I left.

I found Roughshod Ding out in the yard, skinning Tiger. "They raised that dog themselves," I said. "How can they eat him for dinner?"

"They can eat him if they want," Roughshod Ding said. "It's their dog."

With the skin off, it really did look like a human body hanging from the rope. The only difference was the fierce canines in the jaw. That was when I started to feel bad for Tiger—was this all his life had amounted to? I started singing for him. I wasn't really in the habit of singing opera, but at that moment, I had to sing.

Studious Zhang wasn't at the banquet that night, but everyone else seemed to be there: the township Party secretary came, so did the township head, and even Wind Xia was there. Nobody in the village expected Wind Xia, except for Bamboo. She heard the news long before I did, at least—she found out when she got to the police station.

The cops slapped cuffs on her, and the chief sent someone to go and tell the township head that Bamboo had turned herself in. The township head didn't go to see her, but the cop who had carried the message to him whispered his own message to Bamboo when he got back. "Wind Xia is back from Xijing. The township head is treating him to dinner!"

I'm locked up over here, and Wind Xia is being treated to dinner over there, Bamboo thought to herself.

Not long after that, the phone rang, and the chief picked it up. "Now, Township Head, this is . . . ," he said. The chief glanced over at Bamboo, turned around, and continued in a low voice that Bamboo couldn't hear. When he hung up the phone, he went over and took the handcuffs off her. The chief explained that since Bamboo hadn't been directly involved in breaking down the gate or killing the dog, and in light of the fact that they had already collected fines from two of the eight perpetrators who had been arrested, the case against her was being dropped. The only condition was that she write a letter of apology and read it over the loudspeaker. Bamboo was going out the door of the station when the chief stopped her.

"You're just leaving?" he said.

"What else do you want from me?" Bamboo asked.

"How about a thank-you? We're being very lenient."

"I think I'll save the thank-you for Wind Xia."

Wind Xia had gotten back to the village at the perfect time without even realizing it. He had only made the trip because of a call from Snow Bai about his father. He'd had no idea that his father was even sick, and nobody had told him about the surgery, but Snow Bai worried how it would look to the village when people heard Wind Xia hadn't gone to see Wisdom Xia in the hospital. They didn't know the full story, so they would assume Wind Xia wasn't being a loyal son. Finally, Snow Bai decided that she had to let Wind Xia know what was going on. As soon as he got back to Freshwind, he ran into the township head, who invited him for dinner—helping Bamboo had never been part of his plan.

After he'd secured her release, he went to look for Justice Xia and found him on his kang. By that time, I had left the House of Treasures, and I was helping Tongue-Tied chop wood for Justice Xia. I'd already let Justice Xia know that I was going to spend the night, but I slipped out when I saw Wind Xia.

The greatest tragedy of my life was that I had to be born into the same lifetime as Wind Xia. Even worse, we had to share the same village. It's like the line Zhou Yu sings in the opera: "Why did I have to be born if there was already a Zhuge Liang?" I asked Big-Noise Zhao about it once. The next line goes, "Zhou Yu's mother called for the earth and Zhuge Liang's mother called for the sky." He laughed for a long time about that.

"Let me explain it to you like this," Big-Noise Zhao said. "Why does Freshwind need a Spark if we already have a Wind Xia?"

That night, when I slipped out of Justice Xia's yard, I was once again the lesser man.

I headed out into the fog, which swirled around me so that only my head was visible above it. If anyone had been out in the road, they would have seen only a disembodied head floating toward them. I didn't run into anyone except Lucky. She whined at me, and I saw that she had managed to climb onto the wall around the public bathroom beside the House of Treasures. She jumped for the House of Treasures gate, fell to the ground, and went back to the public bathroom wall to try again. I couldn't figure out what she was trying to do until I looked over at the gate and saw that Tiger's skin was still hanging there.

I took Lucky in my arms. "Lucky," I whispered, "Lucky!" I cried, and she did, too. It was bad enough Tiger was dead; what were they thinking, hanging up his skin like that? I carried Lucky over the back of my neck, like I was carrying a kid. We went and knocked on the door of the supplies co-op.

Obedient Zhang opened the door. "Give me a bottle!" I said. He looked me over suspiciously. "The two of us are drinking tonight!"

"Pay up."

"Give it to me on credit."

"No credit!"

"I'll help you siphon again."

"I don't need any help right now," Obedient Zhang said.

I pleaded with him, I begged, I negotiated, I told him how much I needed a drink, I told him that I'd give him my hat, I told him I'd work off the debt, and eventually he cracked. He was a soft touch when it came right down to it. He said the bottle was on the house, but he wanted to split it with me. We cracked the bottle and started drinking right there at the supplies co-op. I forget what we were talking about, but Wind Xia's name came up.

"Don't even say his name," I said fiercely.

"You hate him?" Obedient Zhang asked.

"I hate his guts!"

"He doesn't hate you. What have you got against him?"

"What do I care whether he hates me?" I asked.

"For Snow Bai's sake," Obedient Zhang said, and I started blubbering. "Spark," he said, "are you fucking drunk?"

"I'm not drunk. I could kill another bottle and still be fine." I stretched out on the counter and vacuumed up the droplets of liquor spilled across it. Obedient Zhang sprinkled a few more drops out onto the counter for me to suck up.

"Spark," he said, "you really love Snow Bai, don't you?"

"Have you ever seen a prettier girl? Her face shines, doesn't it? Her eyes are so big. And her thin little waist . . . And that voice, whether she's singing or just talking . . . When she laughs, you get a look at those pearly-white teeth. She's so clean, too. I doubt she even farts!" Obedient Zhang started laughing. That pissed me off. "What are you laughing about?" I said.

"None of that matters," Obedient Zhang said. "She's another man's wife. You're lucky I'm the only one here. If certain other people heard you talking about her like that, you'd get a slap."

"I love her," I said. "I'm going to say it: I love Snow Bai! I love Snow Bai!"

"Well, I've got an idea. I know how to make you stop thinking about her."

"I don't want to hear it! I'm not listening!"

"You're fucking drunk!" Obedient Zhang said.

Really, I wasn't drunk at all. Obedient Zhang, on the other hand, wasn't doing very well; when I looked up again, he was gone. I found him passed out under the counter. I woke up under the counter, too, early the next morning, with Obedient Zhang still passed out. Lucky was just waking up. She had been rooting through our vomit the night before and still had it all over her muzzle.

"Lucky," I said, "why were you eating our puke? You wanted to get drunk, too, didn't you?" I hugged her and we both cried.

While Obedient Zhang and I were passed out, Wind Xia was already getting ready to leave. He had gone to see Justice Xia to ask how all the trouble had started. Justice Xia dodged the question and asked why Wind Xia hadn't been to see his father yet.

"I didn't know anything about it," Wind Xia said. "I just got a call from Snow Bai last night. She's the one to blame here. She tries to hide everything from me."

"Don't blame her," Justice Xia said. "Since he's been in the hospital, she's been going back and forth to see him. She has to take the baby with her, too. It's been hard on her. Didn't you notice how much weight she's lost?" Wind Xia said nothing, and Justice Xia continued, "Did you get something to eat? I can have Second Aunt make something for you."

Second Aunt slid off the kang, but Wind Xia motioned for her to stay put. "I ran into the township head," he said, "and we had dinner at the House of Treasures."

"Ah, I see now," Justice Xia said. "I was wondering how your sister-in-law got out so quick. Wind Xia, you're the best the Xia family ever produced, but it doesn't do us any good if you're always busy in Xijing and never come back to see us."

"Uncle," Wind Xia said, taking a roll of bills out of his pocket, "I came back in a hurry this time." He set two hundred yuan on the edge of the kang. "I didn't have the chance to buy you anything. Go pick yourself up some snacks or something."

"You're giving us money now, huh?" Justice Xia said. He didn't turn it down, though. "Don't think because I worry about you that I'm not thankful. Those cigarettes you brought me last time, I still haven't cracked the carton yet. Look, look!" Wind Xia saw that the cigarettes that he had brought his uncle were still sitting unopened on a shelf over the kang. Justice Xia picked up the money and handed it to Tongue-Tied. "A hundred of this goes to Big-Noise Zhao, and use the rest to get us some steel wire. You got it? We'll need the thick stuff, for moving rocks."

After he left Justice Xia's place, Wind Xia didn't bother going home. He went straight out to the highway to hitch a ride into the county seat. He didn't expect to run into Snow Bai and Bamboo at the crossroads. Marvel was over there, too, and Wind Xia overheard them talking as he walked up. "You're back already?" Marvel said.

"That's right!"

"You're not in any trouble?"

"Nope." Bamboo caught sight of Wind Xia. "My little brother is a very powerful man!"

"Not as powerful as my sister-in-law," Wind Xia said. "If this was the Cultural Revolution, you'd be running around with the Red Guards."

"Couldn't you compare me to one of the earlier revolutionaries instead? I see myself as more of a Liu Hulan type." She took out a pack of cigarettes and offered one to Wind Xia. "I was waiting for you at your place, but Snow Bai told me you'd probably go from Second Uncle's straight out to the highway to catch a ride. Turns out she was right. She knows you like a tapeworm knows a colon."

Wind Xia glanced at Snow Bai and said, "I figured my dad would already be back at home . . . So, I'm on my way to the hospital."

"You think you're really going to catch a ride in at this time of night?" Bamboo asked. "Snow Bai, get Marvel back over here. He can give him a ride in on his motorbike."

"Thank you, Marvel," Wind Xia said.

"Don't mention it! I can tell everyone I chauffeured Wind Xia."

Snow Bai giggled but held her tongue.

"Marvel," Bamboo said, "let's go grab your bike and make sure you're ready to go. These two haven't had a chance to catch up. Let's give them some time alone. They don't want us staring at them."

Snow Bai passed the baby to Bamboo. "We have nothing to talk about!" she said.

Bamboo passed the baby to Wind Xia, saying, "Hold your baby for a while!"

As soon as the baby was in her father's arms, she started to kick and cry, until Snow Bai finally went to take her back. "You and Marvel go ahead," she said. "The fog is thick, so make sure you take it easy!"

Wind Xia stood awkwardly for a moment, looking at Snow Bai, then went to get on the back of Marvel's motorbike. As they pulled off, the fog started to lift. A rooster crowed in somebody's yard. The motorbike and its two passengers disappeared slowly into the mist.

Snow Bai began to cry. The tears slid across her cheeks without leaving a trace and dripped onto her daughter's tiny hands.

Chapter 40

By the time Wisdom Xia finally got out of the hospital, it was already the twenty-eighth of Làyuè. Wind Xia asked for the county Party committee to arrange a car. The Party secretary sent someone from his office to arrange New Year gifts for Wisdom Xia and see him off. Fourth Aunt sorted through the gifts, exclaiming, "Meat! And liquor, too! Fish, chicken . . . Just look at how much they gave us."

Wisdom Xia tugged at his wife's sleeve. "You have to thank them," he said in a low voice.

"Thank you!" she said.

"The Party secretary wasn't able to come today," the Party secretary's man said, "but he wanted me to tell you, if you need anything at all, if Wind Xia can't help, just let us know."

"Did you bring any copies of my book?" Wisdom Xia asked Wind Xia.

"No," Wind Xia said.

"I want to sign some for the committee. I want you to bring them around to them."

"You're an author now, Mr. Xia?" the Party secretary's man asked.

"I'm chasing after the dreams of my younger years, now that I'm getting up there." Wisdom Xia started to get light-headed, and there was sweat beading on his forehead. Wind Xia shushed him and settled him in the car for a rest.

The car dropped them off at the East Street archway, and Wind Xia offered to carry Wisdom Xia home on his back. Wisdom Xia insisted on walking himself. He made his way slowly down the road, his hands pressed to his lower back. He struggled to muster up a smile for everyone who greeted them along the way, but when he saw Justice Xia waiting for him, hunched over at the entrance to the alley, he broke down in tears. "Second Brother," he said, "I'm really in trouble now."

But Wisdom Xia made a quick recovery. He went out the next morning to walk around in the yard and play opera on the loudspeaker. As soon as they heard the music, the villagers knew that Wisdom Xia was home and started to arrive at his gate. When each guest arrived, Fourth Aunt rushed to the kitchen to get them water and cook something for them. Wisdom Xia sat out in the yard, talking to his grandkids. He told them about his ulcer and how they had cut three-fifths of his stomach out. He said that after a year or so, his stomach would expand back to its former size and his appetite would be just as big as before. The past few days, he'd eaten five times a day, a half bowl of rice each time.

The guests out in the yard reacted to the story first with nervous surprise, but soon everyone was repeating the truism that what doesn't kill you makes you stronger and saying he must have been saved for something bigger. The kids started giggling. They kept laughing until they were rolling in the yard.

"You little turds," Wisdom Xia said, "what are you all laughing about?"

Wisdom Xia started laughing, too. Fourth Aunt came out with fried eggs and hot water. "Where's the meat?" Wisdom Xia asked. "What about some liquor?"

"Wind Xia went out to get some, but he said all they had was some sow's meat. He didn't want that."

"What about the New Year gifts from the county Party secretary? Wasn't there some meat in there?"

Fourth Aunt nodded and went into the kitchen. "Your father-in-law really knows how to make me look stupid," she said to Snow Bai. She took the basket of gifts into the main room so that the guests could watch her open it. There was some meat wrapped in butcher paper. Across it was written, "Wind Xia." The package was ripped open to reveal a donkey penis.

"Look what the county Party secretary sent Wind Xia!" said one of the guests.

"Well, it ended up here," Wisdom Xia said, "so we might as well eat it." He told his wife to take it into the kitchen.

"I wouldn't even know how," Fourth Aunt said. "We need to get Clerk over here."

"That's fine," one of the guests said. "We don't need it. It's too much!" He picked up the donkey penis and put it back in the basket.

One reason for Wisdom Xia's quick recovery was that Wind Xia was there. Wisdom Xia hated to see Wind Xia and Snow Bai not getting along. He hadn't told his son that he was in the hospital and had been furious when he'd shown up there, but when he got out of the hospital and saw that his son and daughter-in-law were getting along better, he figured things must have improved. That made him feel much better. When it was time to eat, he made sure everyone was gathered around the table. When Rain Xia, Wind Xia, and Snow Bai were settled, Wisdom Xia called over his wife, but she didn't want to join them. "It seems strange to sit down at the table for dinner," Fourth Aunt said. "I'd rather eat over the stove."

"Look at this woman," Wisdom Xia said, "too good to join us at the table." He went on and on until Fourth Aunt finally settled down beside him at the table, chuckling to herself. "This illness made me realize how important it is to eat together. If I hadn't made it out of there, I'd never get to experience this again, everyone sitting down for a meal . . . It's wonderful, isn't it?"

"You don't know this," Fourth Aunt said to Wind Xia, "but the night before his surgery, your dad was preparing for his funeral. He told me of everyone who owed him money, everyone whom he owed money to . . . He said he wanted this house divided between his two sons. He said that if I get remarried, I can have my new husband move in here but that the house has to pass to you and Rain Xia."

"You agreed to that?" Wind Xia asked.

"I'm not that stupid. I told him I knew the house had to go to the two of you!"

"I forgot about that . . . ," said Wisdom Xia. "What you should have said is that you'd drop dead before getting remarried!"

"You know I can't promise that!" Fourth Aunt said.

"She was already looking for a new guy," Snow Bai said, "but you had to go and recover completely."

Everyone at the table laughed.

"Maybe I'm getting a bit slower in my old age," Wisdom Xia said.

"You're right about that," Wind Xia said.

"I was trying to test her," Wisdom Xia said, "but she outsmarted me!"

There was more laughter.

Before they ate, Wisdom Xia took out a pack of cigarettes and passed one to his son. "Really?" Wind Xia said. "You've never offered me a cigarette before."

"You're an adult, aren't you? If I hadn't retired when I did, I'd be just like one of your older coworkers. You should be calling me 'comrade.'"

"You're so funny," Snow Bai said.

"I was always the funny guy in the office!" Wisdom Xia said.

"Why can't you be the funny guy around here?" Rain Xia asked.

"You drive me up the damn wall, and you expect me to be cracking jokes?"

"What did I do?" Rain Xia said.

"Rain Xia was working hard when you were in the hospital," Snow Bai said.

"He was a good boy, this time! When you get older, nothing makes you happier than seeing your family getting along. If your family is at peace, you stay healthy!" Wisdom Xia turned to Wind Xia and asked, "Are you going to spend the New Year here?"

"Of course!" Wind Xia said.

"Good to hear. We'll have a good New Year. You go out in the afternoon, Rain Xia. I want you to get us everything we'll need. Get plenty of meat. Make some tofu, if you can, but buy whatever else you need. I want you to stay here tonight and help your mother steam some buns and start cooking."

"Forget about that," Rain Xia said. "Everything is ready at the restaurant. I'll get them to deliver some food."

"They've got it all ready?"

"I'll get them to send over some of the clay pots they're steaming. They can spare it. They made plenty. They won't struggle to turn a profit over there this New Year."

"Fine," Wisdom Xia said. "And send some over to your second uncle and his wife, and some for Third Aunt. Did you go over to visit your second uncle, Wind Xia?"

"I went there as soon as I got back."

"You should be spending more time over there. Since I got back from the hospital, I noticed he's lost a lot of weight. He's not the same. He just got through that illness, and then he managed to get his collarbone broken. He's in a dark mood. I'm starting to worry about him . . ."

"His daughters-in-law aren't much help," Rain Xia said.

"That's why I'm telling you, the two of you have to look after your second uncle and second aunt. You can't ignore what's going on in Freshwind, Wind Xia. You need to talk to the township government—the county government if necessary—and get them to release Bounty and the others. If you can't get them out, their families are going to be celebrating the New Year without them."

"Right," Wind Xia said.

"That's enough for now," Wisdom Xia said. "Let's eat."

Wisdom Xia only ate two mouthfuls before he started complaining about Rain Xia sounding like a pig when he ate, and his hair was too long, and there were no wool blankets at the store, so he'd have to go all the way to West Mountain Bend to get one for the baby. "Where did my leather shoes go?" he asked suddenly. "I need to shine them up. I've got to wear them for the New Year."

"Just eat," Rain Xia said. "When we're done, I'll dig out the shoes and shine them for you!" He took his father's bowl and went into the kitchen to refill it.

Snow Bai followed him and ladled more soup into her bowl.

"He won't shut up, will he?" Rain Xia said.

Snow Bai smiled.

"He's a changed man since his surgery. He still loves his opera, though."

Snow Bai said nothing but continued to smile.

After they ate, Wind Xia went over to the township government offices. Bounty and the others had been released. Wind Xia's prestige and power in Freshwind had grown in the years that he'd been away. As he walked toward the Great Qing Hall, he was greeted by everyone he met. New-Life Liu held him up, saying that he was going to play him "The Qin Emperor's Winning Move." He didn't have a drum, so he ripped off his shirt and started drumming on his own belly. By the time the song was halfway done, New-Life Liu's belly was as reddish brown as soy sauce, and Wind Xia pleaded with him to get dressed before he caught a cold. Leaving New-Life Liu, he hurried toward the Great Qing Hall. Big-Noise Zhao was standing at the gate, laughing at the scene.

"Look at you, just look at you," Big-Noise Zhao said. "You're a hero to these people, the hope of Freshwind!"

"I'm a greenhorn," Wind Xia said.

"You sure stuck your horns in over at the township government, though."

"What the hell is going on around here? I'm hearing about it from across the province, farmers refusing to pay their taxes . . ."

"I thought Freshwind was the first," Big-Noise Zhao said.

"Forget about that," Wind Xia said. "Are you ready for the New Year?"

"What do you mean, 'ready'? Little kids look forward to the New Year. For old folks, it just means another year has flown by and we're another year older."

Big-Noise Zhao apologized for misdiagnosing Wind Xia's father. "I never imagined it could be stomach cancer in his case." Wind Xia waved him off, saying that even the best doctors made mistakes. He changed the subject to the number of senior citizens over the age of seventy in the village.

Big-Noise Zhao counted on his fingers. There were five on East Street, seven on Middle Street, and the old folks of the Xia family over on West, as well as Marvel's mother. There had been more before, but many had died over the past several years, including eight from stomach cancer.

"It's been that many?" Wind Xia asked.

"I investigated it, actually. At first, I thought it might be a problem with the groundwater, but it was only affecting the elderly. People your father's age lived through hard times; that was hard on their stomachs. It changed the way they eat, too. Everyone that age lives off pickled vegetables—I've heard that can increase the risk of stomach cancer."

"You're saying it's because they went hungry when they were younger, and nowadays they stuff themselves with pickled vegetables? But what about Uncle Justice? He never left the village, but his stomach is just fine!"

"Let me ask you this: Have you ever seen him moping around? A fiery temper'll save you from stomach diseases."

"Is that right?" Wind Xia asked. He felt his heart skip a beat.

"You know, he's the man I admire most in Freshwind, your uncle Justice. He's been through it all, and he's kept his head held high. I borrowed a copy of the township records a little while ago and saw how many times they mentioned him. People our age, we only know half his story. We know he was a village cadre for years, but we have no idea what he really went through. I'd compare him to a bell, actually. You strike a bell, and no matter how long it's been hanging there, the sound is still pure. It's like breathing. Everyone breathes, day and night, all the time, but have you ever really thought about it? The only time you think about it is when you have trouble breathing."

"You're absolutely right," Wind Xia said. "Do you still have that copy of the township records? I'd like to take a look."

Big-Noise Zhao went into his bedroom and came back with the records. Wind Xia flipped through the pages. They recorded all the major events of the township. It wasn't long before Wind Xia came across his second uncle's name. The first entry concerned an engineering project started in 1958:

> In the eastern districts of the township, a labor force of fifty thousand was mobilized under the leadership of vice township head Zhang Zhen, with Justice Xia as deputy brigade leader, and put to work on a river diversion project in Hui Ravine. The project's goal was to divert the Zhou River at Red Plains Ford to flow into the northern districts of the township. Due to a lack of funds, the project was abandoned in 1961 and the diversion of the Zhou River was not completed.

> In August, following the "People's communes are good" directive from Mao Zedong, Chairman of the Central Committee of the Chinese Communist Party, the entire township was converted to people's communes in the space of ten days.

> In the first week of September, ahead of a visit by central water and soil conservation inspectors, the township mobilized a labor force of fifty thousand to carry out a water and soil conservation project

along the 160-*li* length of the roadway between Huajia Ridge, Liuxian Plateau, and Peach Bend. The team built twenty-four drainage canals, of which eighteen collapsed, resulting in three deaths. This had a negative impact on the autumn harvest.

Agricultural quotas in the township were set high, with high estimates of agricultural yield and high estimates of requisition from farmers. This was due to demands from the central government and overconfidence from lower levels of government. Actual production of grain was 150 million *jin*, while yields of 260 million *jin* were reported. In total, approximately 415,000 *jin* were requisitioned from farmers, amounting to approximately 36 percent of total yield. The average per capita shortfall was thirty *jin*, forcing many to turn to eating grass roots and tree bark. Cases of edema began to appear in Freshwind.

Between 1961 and 1963, the price of grain rose. The price of a market-standard *jin* of wheat in 1957 was 0.7 yuan but rose to five yuan by the end of 1963. The price of potatoes rose from 0.34 yuan per *jin* to 1.20 yuan per *jin*. The price of a deep-fried bun reached two yuan.

In October of 1961, a labor force of twenty-five thousand was once again mobilized to undertake water and soil conservation projects in Huajia Ridge, Yijia Ridge, and Jigong Mountain. A meeting was held for the township to select model workers. Legs Bai of Chengguan, Noble Wang of Liuxian Plateau, Third Li of Guofenglou, and Justice Xia of Freshwind were selected for the designation.

Between January and May of 1962, wolves wreaked havoc across the township. Thirty-five deaths and 106 injuries were reported. Casualties among livestock included forty-four hogs and 1,020 chickens.

In 1963, 90 percent of the workforce of Freshwind was mobilized to work on reinforcing the Zhou River dike, recovering eight hundred mu of arable land. The township head congratulated model worker Justice Xia and awarded him a red silk sash and a red flower. There was a three-day festival of lights.

In 1964, a campaign was launched to plant walnut trees. Xigu Commune planted six hundred *mu*, Nanyou Commune planted five hundred *mu*, and West Mountain Bend Commune planted eight hundred *mu*. Planting was not completed in Freshwind, Teahouse Village, and Liuxian Plateau.

In 1965, as part of the "Socialist Education Movement," village cadres worked on raising their revolutionary consciousness. Provincial Party Committee Secretary Upright Tan arrived In the township and led an inspection alongside his working group. Eighty percent of production brigade cadres were censured, including three arrested and nineteen fired from their posts. The head of Liuxian Plateau's East Gully production brigade killed himself by hanging.

In 1966, the Great Proletarian Cultural Revolution swept the nation . . .

In 1970, Lofty Liu was elected as the township Party secretary, Cascade Li was elected as township head, and a group of veteran village cadres returned to their roles, including Upright Liu of Chengguan, Talent Wang of Guofenglou, and Justice Xia of Freshwind.

In August of 1970, thirty thousand workers in the eastern districts were mobilized to build a reservoir at Black Mountain Ridge. In the western districts, twelve thousand workers from two communes were mobilized to assist in the reservoir construction project at Seedling Gully, later reinforced by seventeen thousand workers from three other communes.

In 1971, there was widespread starvation. The price of rice and grain rose. Nearly all wild plants were consumed, and bark was stripped from every tree.

In November of 1971, an earthquake hit the eastern half of the township.

In August of 1972, there was torrential rain for three days. Dikes along the Zhou River burst. A breach of three hundred yards was reported at Freshwind. The entire village was mobilized to reinforce the dike. Eighty villagers from West Mountain Bend arrived to assist them. Three hundred *mu* of farmland was destroyed, along with one thousand trees. Three people were swept downstream. Their remains have not been recovered.

In October of 1972, the dike at Freshwind was rebuilt.

In 1973, a forty-thousand-strong labor force was mobilized to build a reservoir at Tiger Mountain. Expounder Yan of the township Party committee led the team, with the assistance of Cannoneer Liu of West Mountain Bend, Justice Xia of Freshwind, and Clear-Skies Han of Teahouse Village.

In June of 1973, an oxhide-covered shack at the Tiger Mountain reservoir construction site caught fire, burning three workers alive.

In August of 1973, the cotton plants had three stamen on each flower. This was first reported by farmers in Freshwind. Journalists interviewed the farmers, and the story was published on the front page of the newspaper on August 28.

In 1974, shooting stars filled the sky. They appeared to be traveling from the northwest to the southeast. The phenomenon continued through the night. As part of the "In Agriculture Learn from Dazhai" movement, Township Head Magnanimity Wang arrived in

Freshwind to learn from village cadres as they prepared to convert Bowed Ox Ridge to a Dazhai-style terraced field. Workers leveled 420 grave mounds on Bowed Ox Ridge, built thirteen terraces, and dug two drainage canals.

In 1975, the township was involved in counterattacking the rightist deviation of reversing guilty verdicts. In March, dark haze and high temperatures. In July, there was a plague of rats. During the day, they moved about in the hundreds; at night, the sound of them kept everyone from sleeping soundly. In Freshwind and Guofenglou, the rats killed sleeping children.

In 1976, shooting stars fell like rain.

Wind Xia was fascinated and wanted to continue reading, but right then a wedding band went by the door, blaring horns and beating drums. The groom came past on a bike, with the bride riding on the back. A crowd followed them, carrying a red lacquer chest and cabinet, a TV set, a sewing machine, a radio, and blankets for three or four beds. A woman with the group, carrying a washbasin, saw Wind Xia and called out to him. "Wind Xia! Wind Xia!"

Wind Xia didn't recognize her.

"Ah, you're too important to remember all the little people, I suppose," she said. "I'm Success's wife!" His old elementary school classmate's wife had put on weight since he'd last seen her.

"Someone in the family's getting married?" Wind Xia asked.

"It's my nephew."

"It's all well and good to have a band playing," Big-Noise Zhao said, "but why are you giving away all your furniture? You're going to bankrupt the family."

"I don't think so. The bride's family contributed more than their share!" She turned back to Wind Xia and said, "Since you're back, there's a favor I want to ask."

"What is it?" Wind Xia said.

"My second-oldest daughter is working in Xijing. She was working for a big company, but her boss over there was a real asshole. He was trying to cheat her, so she left, but he held on to her wages and her ID card. The money, we can take the loss, don't worry about that, but without her ID card, she can't even get another job. She was crying on the phone."

"If you're going to fight him over the ID card, you might as well get the money, too," Wind Xia said.

"She's a trusting girl," his classmate's wife said, "fresh out of the village. I told her to go talk to you. I said you'd help her. Go talk to him for us. I bet you'd scare the shit out of that asshole boss of hers."

"Tell your daughter to come and talk to me," Wind Xia said, and he wrote down his address and phone number on a slip of paper.

"How can I ever thank you? I'll tell Success to have you over for drinks!" She turned and waddled after the wedding party.

"How many people from Freshwind are working in Xijing?" Wind Xia asked Big-Noise Zhao.

"Probably a few dozen at least. Some are working in restaurants, but most of them are selling charcoal, working as trash collectors, or dealing in herbs, or they're working construction. There are others, too, who nobody knows quite what they're up to. They end up coming back in body bags, missing an arm or a leg."

Wind Xia was silent for a moment, unsure of what to say. Once he'd recovered, he invited Big-Noise Zhao for dinner. Big-Noise Zhao agreed enthusiastically, saying he owed Fourth Uncle a visit. He wanted to bring a gift for the old man, so he snipped a square of paper and prepared to write one of his couplets.

"If you're going to write him a couplet," Wind Xia said, "it should be, 'To achieve peace and tranquility / Elevate yourself from jealousy.'"

"He won't understand that. Now that he's feeling better, I want to write something to celebrate that." He took out his brush and wrote, "Love and peace flows / Spring has come to this home." Above the couplet, he wrote, "Sow virtue, reap happiness."

As they walked, Wind Xia was once again stopped by villagers asking for favors. A woman from the Bai family stopped him along West Street and told Wind Xia that her son worked at the grain bureau. In the past, whenever Snow Bai had gone to buy grain, her son had switched the rough grain for wheat flour. Now, the grain bureau was going out of business, so she wanted Wind Xia's help to get her son transferred. She asked him to talk to the township head and have him send her son to the tax bureau. Another woman stopped to ask for Wind Xia's help in finding a wife for her son, who was a security guard at the provincial forestry-management office. He was almost thirty and had had no luck. The son was willing to take his wife's name, if that would help. "I just don't want him coming back to this damn village," she said.

As they walked farther down the road, Big-Noise Zhao turned to Wind Xia and said, "In the city, people are coming up to you to get your autograph, but in the village, they want you to do them a favor."

"They think I'm going to save them. They don't realize there's not much I can do. Nowadays, everything is a trade-off, but all I have to trade is my name. I can go in and see if my name holds any weight, but it's up to that person to decide whether knowing me is of any value to them."

As they walked down West Street, they saw Blossom's head pop up over the wall of a public bathroom. "Wind Xia," she said, "did the two of you eat already?"

"Worry about yourself," Big-Noise Zhao said. "Who peeks their head out of the bathroom to ask people if they've eaten?"

"So what? You know how I am—rough around the edges." Blossom stepped out of the bathroom and into the street. "Little brother," she said to Wind Xia, "your sister-in-law has a favor to ask."

"What is it?"

"I need you to help your nephew out."

"Didn't he take over from Thunder?"

"That's what I'm talking about! You know how Thunder is, though. He's an honest man. He gets upset easily. He wanted to retire, right after the incident. The rule is that the son or daughter can take over. But now that your nephew's taken over, the company has started contracting out the business, and they don't give him regular shifts. They won't put him to work, and they won't pay him. He was in love with a girl, but now that he's just sitting on his ass, she's saying she wants to dump him! You've got the power; go and talk to them. What you say will carry more weight than anything Thunder says. Tell them the boy needs to eat."

"Ai-ya!" Wind Xia said. "I do know the mayor, but nowadays, every company is under pressure to reform their business. They're all carrying too many employees . . . And I was just there to talk to him about Mid-Star. I can't just keep going in to ask for favors."

"You were willing to help Mid-Star out," Blossom said, "but you can't do anything for your own nephew?"

"Well, how about this: I'll write a letter. You send him to the mayor with it. I can't promise it'll work."

Blossom made Big-Noise Zhao and Wind Xia follow her home, where she took out a sheet of paper and told him to write the letter immediately. Once the letter was written, Thunder came into the yard with a hog's head. He greeted the two men and insisted that they stay for dinner.

"I told you to go buy meat," Blossom said. "You were gone all afternoon, and now you come back with a pig head! You haven't done anything to help your nephew. I'm worried that by this time next year, we'll be eating pig tails instead." She sliced some meat off the neck of the hog's head and went into the kitchen.

"It's for the New Year," Thunder said. He passed out cigarettes to Big-Noise Zhao and Wind Xia, then went to heat an iron in the stove. He came back and started burning the hair off the hog's head. The two guests stood awkwardly for a while, unsure of what to do. Eventually, they decided they might as well help Thunder with the hog's head.

That night, every home in Freshwind was busy braising pork, making tofu, steaming buns, and boiling carrots. The rare perfume filled the village. Out in the alleys, children shouted and ran around with candle lanterns. When the candles inside tipped over, the lanterns burned up, and the kids fought between themselves, then cried. Someone was setting off firecrackers—pop! But no string of explosions followed; maybe it was someone testing out their arsenal. A dog with a bone in its mouth was chased into the yard by another dog.

"Get the hell out of here!" Thunder yelled.

The dog with the bone headed out of the yard, but the dog without the bone had its eyes set on the hog's head. Thunder tried to scare it off, but the dog stood its ground and let out a fart. The stench was incredible. Thunder picked up the hot iron and threw it at the dog. He missed the dog and smashed an earthen jar set along the wall.

By the time dinner was served, it was already dark. Big-Noise Zhao thought it was too late to visit Wisdom Xia, so he took out the couplets and passed them to Wind Xia, telling him to give them to his father, along with his best wishes for the New Year. When Wind Xia got home, the house was completely dark except for the light in his own tiny room.

Snow Bai was changing the baby's diaper. "How come you're back so late?" she asked.

"Something came up."

"Did you eat?"

"I ate at Thunder's place."

"Pass me the dry one."

Wind Xia took the dry diaper from the bed and passed it to her. The baby, naked and clean on the bed, looked like a frog.

Snow Bai took the dirty diaper and went to dump it out in the yard. When she came back, Wind Xia was still staring at his daughter. "She's just lying there naked. Why didn't you pick her up or put something over her?"

Wind Xia took the baby's blanket and wrapped his daughter in it. He didn't do a very good job, so Snow Bai picked her up, took the blanket off, and wrapped the baby again.

"I'm going to bed," Wind Xia said. Snow Bai sat beside him for a while, then switched off the light and went to sleep.

While everyone slept, a rat emerged and began gnawing at a chest. Wisdom Xia got up three times, but not to scare away the rat—he wanted to take a pull off his pipe. He got up early the next morning, as he usually did. He wasn't well enough to take his usual walk down the road to the riverside. Even walking out to the stone roller at the start of the alley was enough to make him break out in a sweat. He headed for home, knocking on each gate as he went. Wind Xia and Snow Bai were up, too. One of them was sweeping the courtyard, and the other was watering the flowers. Wisdom Xia sneaked a glance at them. They seemed to be in a good mood, so he went and played some opera over the loudspeaker. Freshwind was filled with the sound of *A String of White Jade*:

> Ai-ya! The trees are all in bloom,
> The butterflies sip from lotus flowers
> Sprouts thread between the jasmine
> I sit beside the mountain lake
> And set my long dark hair.

But once breakfast was done, Wind Xia was ready to leave. He said he planned to buy some things for the New Year. He came back the first time with some potato starch noodles, then went out again and came back with some garlic sprouts and soy sauce. While he came and went, Snow Bai sat without speaking beside the clothes-beating stone, staring into space.

"I think she went in her diaper," Wisdom Xia said. "Sure smells like it." Snow Bai snapped out of her daze and began changing the baby's diaper. "Snow Bai," Wisdom Xia asked, "what's wrong?"

Snow Bai smiled quickly and said, "Nothing's wrong!"

"We're going over to your third aunt's place for a visit. Do you want to come?"

"I have to wash these diapers. You go on ahead."

"Let Mother wash them. There's no wind today. Take the baby and go out for a walk with Wind Xia. You should see all the lanterns. Maybe you can buy one for her, too."

"Okay," Snow Bai said.

After Wisdom Xia and Fourth Aunt left, Snow Bai left the baby where she was and waited for Wind Xia to finish his cigarette. He was about to leave again, but she shut the gate. She told Wind Xia that they needed to talk. She wanted to know why he couldn't stay home. She asked if she and the baby disgusted him.

"Why are you talking like that?" Wind Xia asked. "Can't you keep it to yourself?"

"Keep it to myself? I want to find a solution. Are you saying you won't talk to me, you won't communicate with me? Even if the baby has a problem, she's still your child. I don't understand how you can be so hard-hearted."

"What did I do? Tell me."

"Have you ever held her when she cries? Even once?"

Wind Xia sighed and sat down in the yard, looking as if all the air had been taken out of him. He seemed to have shrunk.

"You haven't even asked how I've been; you didn't ask about the opera company; you didn't ask if they're still going to pay me. I know I'm not like those girls in the city. I know I'm not even a legal resident in the city. I know you only wanted me because I was pretty. Maybe I shouldn't have said yes to you, but I wasn't thinking clearly; maybe I was just being vain. Maybe I wanted to attach myself to someone like you. I know the old saying: a chicken doesn't belong in a parasol tree.

"But now I've got a baby, the opera company has fallen apart, I'm not pretty anymore, and I'm not good for anything. You look down on me, don't you? You don't care about me and the baby anymore, do you? I just want to hear you say it. I can't live like this. We're just drifting along like two strangers—no, if we were two strangers, we'd probably get along better!"

Wind Xia reached for his cigarettes but found the pack empty. He crumpled it up and tossed it into the yard.

"Just say it," Snow Bai said. "I want to hear you say it!"

Wind Xia said nothing.

Snow Bai began to sob. When Snow Bai started to cry, the baby started to cry, and she filled her diaper. Snow Bai set the baby down on the steps. "Go ahead, go ahead and piss and shit. Shit yourself to death. At least then I won't have to worry about you anymore!" The baby cried even harder and seemed on the verge of choking. Snow Bai picked her up. Mother and child fell in a pile together, both crying.

Wind Xia shivered. "Is this how we're going to live?" he said. "This isn't any goddamn way to live!"

"Then divorce me!"

"You said it first!"

"That's right. You were just waiting for me to say it, weren't you?"

"If you want a divorce, you can have it. You think I'm worried?"

"Write up the contract then!"

"You wanted to divorce," Wind Xia said, "so you write it."

Snow Bai carried the baby into the house and began to write. When she was done, she called to him, "I'm finished. Come and sign it."

Wind Xia went in, took the pen, and wrote three strokes, and three tears dropped from his cheek onto the page. He corrected a character she had written wrong. Then he finished signing his name.

When she saw how fast he'd signed, Snow Bai started to cry again. She didn't wail or moan, but the tears streamed down her cheeks. "Wind Xia," she said, "you got your way. Are you happy now? You can tell everyone it was my idea. You can tell them I wrote the contract." She went out of the yard, carrying the baby. Her final words were, "Go make it official."

Snow Bai went to her mother's home on West Street. Forest Wu was the first person to see her leave. Forest Wu had quit selling tofu, but he and I had gone halves on twenty *jin* of soybeans, and we planned to make a batch at his place. He saw Snow Bai when he was on his way to the well. "Bai, uh, Snow Bai," he said to me when he got back, "went back to her mother's h-house."

"So what?" I asked.

"Sh-she was crying."

I ran out to look for her in the alley, but she was already gone. I knew Forest Wu wasn't lying, but I couldn't imagine why Snow Bai would be crying her way back to her mother's house. I bent down and looked for her teardrops in the dust but couldn't find them.

I went back inside to work on the tofu, but my heart wasn't in it. I was supposed to be holding up the cloth to filter the soybean milk from the tofu, but I let it go and the whole mess went splashing down into the hot pan, covering my arms in boiling-hot soybean milk. Forest Wu got mad and called me a useless bastard, but he knew I needed something for the burns, so he told me to go down the alley to Wisdom Xia's place. He said they'd have some ointment over there. I didn't want to go, so he went himself while I waited outside.

White-Moth came strutting down the alley. She said, "What are you looking at?" I just ignored her. "Did you see your little Snow Bai, running home to her mommy, crying her eyes out? She hasn't been the same since that baby."

"What do you mean by that?" I asked.

"She used to have such perfect white skin," White-Moth said, "and it's all gone now. She's withered away."

"Look at yourself, so ugly you'd have to use a puddle of dog piss as a mirror."

She was about to come back at me, but Forest Wu showed up with the ointment. She turned to go but not before reaching out to tousle my hair.

"You, uh, you, a-and her h-have something going on?"

I spat in the dust in front of him.

Forest Wu told me that when he got to Wisdom Xia's place, the old man and his wife had just gotten back, too. While Wisdom Xia was getting the ointment, Fourth Aunt asked Wind Xia, "Where are Snow Bai and the baby?"

"She went back to her mother's place," Wind Xia said. He sounded angry.

When Wisdom Xia heard that, he exploded. "Why the hell would she be going back to her mother's place, at a time like this? Did you two have a fight?"

"I can't live like that anymore!" Wind Xia said.

Wisdom Xia kicked his son and knocked him to the floor. As he fell, his shirt caught on the corner of the table and ripped. Wind Xia hadn't expected his father to hit him. He stood up without saying anything and went off to his room, shutting the door behind him.

"He's too old for you to be beating him," Fourth Aunt said.

"He doesn't know what's good for him."

Fourth Aunt went and knocked, but Wind Xia ignored her. "It's normal for a young married couple to fight," she said through the door. "You have to go and get her back! Women are delicate. She can't just come back by herself. You have to give her a way out. It's not going to kill you to give in on this."

Wind Xia didn't open the door. From his bedroom, Wisdom Xia yelled, "He's completely unreasonable. He's pigheaded. That girl isn't good enough for you? She didn't treat you right? She looked after your parents and gave birth to your child. And right in the middle of the New Year, you send her back to her mother's house. Do you have a single decent bone in your body? We never told you who to marry, did we? You chased after that girl like you were starving. Now, you married her—and how long has it been? You're already ready to give her up? I've seen the way you go around here. You don't even look at the two of them. That's your wife. That's your child! How can you call yourself a husband or a father? Huh?"

"Just save it," Fourth Aunt said. She knocked at the door again. "Wind Xia, you've got your father upset now. Is that what you wanted?" Wind Xia opened the door and headed for the yard. "Where are you going?" Fourth Aunt asked.

"I'm going to West Street!" he said.

Fourth Aunt fluttered around him like a mother hen. "With that face on?" she said. "You look like you're going to commit a murder!" She followed him out into the alley. "You better not upset her more. Be nice to her. That's what she needs to hear. Are you listening to me?"

Wind Xia walked away down the alley.

When he got to the main road, he still wasn't sure whether he should go over to West Street. As he walked through the crowd that was out to buy and sell New Year gifts, he ran into a few people he knew. Eventually, he found himself walking into the Great Qing Hall, where Big-Noise Zhao was washing out some pork intestines. "Wind Xia," he said, "get over here. I just heard a funny little rhyme." The rhymes had gotten popular first with people who had gone to work in the city. Eventually, they flowed back to Freshwind.

"How does it go?" Wind Xia asked.

"I heard it from Big-Guy Ma. He just came by, said he was going to spend the New Year here. It goes like this—and if you like it, maybe you can put it in your book:

> The Party smokes the finest cigars,
> The rest of us sit around and cough up tar.
> The Party drinks till they get their fill,
> The rest of us fill bowls with the same old swill.
> They steal all the pretty broads,
> And we're lucky just to find a maid.
> They build a life off deceit and fraud,
> But only because our bribes are paid.

"What do you think?"

Wind Xia didn't have the chance to answer. Out in the street, a crowd had appeared, coming from West Street. At the head of it, a man pushed a motorbike, followed by a man lugging a TV set and a few others dragging wardrobes and sofas. Big-Noise Zhao and Wind Xia watched the scene in complete bafflement. A bit farther down the road, Bright Chen asked the man carrying the sofa, "Did you g-get it for ch-cheap?"

"Of course."

"Do they have a tri-tri-tricycle o-o-over there?"

"What do you need a trike for? You haven't got a wife. But maybe they're selling one of those, too."

Big-Noise Zhao called Bright Chen over and asked him what was going on. "Y-y-you really don't know, or are y-y-you just playing d-d-dumb?"

"I r-really don't kn-know. Dammit, now you've got me stuttering, too. What's going on?"

Bright Chen finally managed to stutter out the story. Four years earlier, Excellent Li had borrowed fifty thousand yuan from the credit union. He built a new house but refused to pay back the money. The credit union kept going after him for it, but he ignored them, so they eventually took him to court. The court stepped in and ordered that all his things be auctioned off. Excellent Li figured nobody would be interested in his furniture, but news spread, and the auction went ahead. Later, his wife refused to give it up, but it already technically belonged to someone else. So, eventually, a crowd formed outside the house and started taking things. They had to pry her off her furniture.

"They're tearing up the house?"

Shifty came by, pushing a wheelbarrow loaded with wood and singing a tune from *Zhou Ren Returns to His Residence*:

> Sister, please don't go to the Yan home,
> Even Zhou Ren would struggle to survive.
> If you must go, I'll know it's true,
> Zhou Ren truly is a monster.

"You're the monster," Big-Noise Zhao said. "Where'd you get that wood? Those are railroad ties!"

"Excellent Li is a clever son of a bitch," Shifty said. "I've got no idea where he got these old railroad ties, but I'm sure he never dreamed he'd be off-loading them on me for a third of the price. Should be able to make a coffin out of these."

"You're taking advantage of those people."

"Well, Wind Xia's here; let's hear what he has to say. All I'm doing is collecting on a bad debt. They owe that money to the state."

"Excellent Li must hate your guts," Wind Xia said.

"And I hate him. We're all farmers, right? Where does he get off, going and building that house of his, two stories, all concrete. It's the only one in Freshwind. Have you seen his bed? He thinks he's too good to sleep on a kang."

Wind Xia laughed joylessly. "You're right, those are perfect for a coffin."

Shifty left, pushing the wheelbarrow. He turned around to say, "Wind Xia, you were the one who got me out of trouble. Second day of the New Year, instead of going to pay my respects to my own father, I'll be going to see you."

Once Shifty was gone, Big-Noise Zhao turned back to Wind Xia. "Would you look at that . . . Maybe another one of those rhymes . . ."

"What's the point?"

"Oh? Maybe you're just in a bad mood. Tell me the truth. Did you do something to Snow Bai?"

"What would I do?"

"I saw Snow Bai on her way to her mother's house," Big-Noise Zhao said. "She had the baby with her. I tried to talk to her, but she was crying too hard. I see Snow Bai going home, carrying the baby, sobbing . . . You must have done something to upset her!"

"You're a clever bastard! I might as well tell you. We're going to call it quits."

"Are you kidding me?"

"As the saying goes, the foot knows best if the shoe is giving it a blister."

Big-Noise Zhao became suddenly serious. "Wind Xia," he said, "there's nothing wrong with blowing off some steam, but divorce is going too far! When you two got married, everyone in Freshwind said it was a match made in heaven. I remember the band, the opera . . . Your wedding was the biggest event in years. And you've got a child now. You've got it made! This is the good life! If you and Snow Bai get divorced, all the blame will be on you. Nobody's going to have a single bad word to say about Snow Bai."

"You're talking like it'll be the end of the world."

"You've done a lot of good for this village. You can't walk down the street without people coming up to pay their respects. But if you do that to Snow Bai, you won't be able to hold your head high in Freshwind anymore. You know the story of Chen Shimei, the poor man from the countryside who made it big in the city, then tossed his beloved aside to marry up. You'll be no better. Just tell me, what's going on? What's the real reason?"

"I guess it's true what they say," Wind Xia said. "A husband and wife need to be from the same social and economic level."

"What do you mean? Your family is from East Street and her family is from West Street. Your family is wealthy and powerful now, but the Bai family was even wealthier and even more powerful. You've got a government job, but she's got her own work, too. Sounds like a match to me."

"That's not what I mean," Wind Xia said. "When I went looking for a wife, a few friends introduced women in the same line of work as me, but I wasn't interested. I didn't care that she wasn't educated or that she didn't understand my work. That has its benefits, too. But now that we're married, I realize that we just think differently. We can't get on the same page."

"Marriage is about getting along," Big-Noise Zhao said. "Forget about love. What are you talking about? What is it that you can't get on the same page about?" Wind Xia laughed bitterly. "What is it? I'm a vault. Whatever you tell me stays with me. Did I tell anyone about Snow Bai's sister-in-law?"

"You told me, right?" Wind Xia asked.

Big-Noise Zhao laughed. "If you don't want to tell me, that's fine. How about a drink?"

"Get us a bottle."

The two men cracked the bottle and drank together until evening. When the chickens roosted and the dogs returned home, they were still at it. They kept drinking until Wind Xia passed out in the Great Qing Hall.

Chapter 41

On the morning of the last day of the old year, Fourth Aunt set to work frying cakes and doughnuts and tofu. The rest of the New Year meal was already prepared, and now she was steaming two baskets of buns. One basket held buns made of sweet potato flour and okra, which she made for herself because she liked simple country food. When the buns were ready, Rain Xia and Roughshod Ding arrived with a carrying pole laden with a variety of steamed dishes. Roughshod Ding looked at the buns and smiled. "Are you trying to remind us how hard the old days were?"

Just then, Chrysanth came to borrow their sieve, and she tasted one. "They're good!" she said. A couple of the neighbors, including Gold and Cutie, happened to be passing and overheard. They came in, too, and took a bun each. Fourth Aunt told Rain Xia to take the steamed dishes to relatives who lived nearby, and then she steamed the second basket of buns. But these were different, shaped like white rabbits. She was going to stick candles in them for her granddaughter on the first day of the New Year. They were going to have peas for eyes, so she climbed up the steps to where strings of pea pods had been hung to dry under the front eaves. At that moment, Rain Xia came running in to tell her that Wind Xia had left the village in Wealth Zhao's car, headed back to the city. What on earth was he doing, leaving on the morning of the thirtieth, on New Year's Eve? Fourth Aunt got such a shock that she fell off the ladder.

Although the four Xia brothers had moved out of the family home and into their own houses a long time before, they always came together to celebrate the New Year, especially the New Year's Eve meal, each hosting the others in turn. In the old days it always happened like this: First, Justice Xia, Rites Xia, and Wisdom Xia went to Benevolence Xia's. After they'd eaten and drunk there, they went to Justice Xia's because he served the best pork belly strips. Then it was Rites Xia's turn, and he served his specialty, "gourd chicken," steamed, then deep-fried. He'd learned to make it when he worked for the township government, and he only prepared it once a year. Finally, Wisdom Xia told everyone to hurry up and get themselves to his house, where the food had probably been warmed up several times over by now. There they lingered over their meal until well into the afternoon, after which the food was cleared away and they washed it all down with tea. Often, they were still drinking their tea when the sound of the gongs and drums carried from the opera stage on Middle Street, and the children ran to watch.

Wisdom Xia always knew long beforehand which opera pieces would be performed. The afternoon percussion was only intended to drum up business. By the time darkness fell and the gas lanterns were turned on, Justice Xia would be at the theater and stepping out on the stage to say his piece about the past year's work and the coming year's spring plowing. That took at least an hour. In the meantime, Wisdom Xia ordered Wind Xia and Rain Xia to remove the paper that covered the windows. The windows had wooden lattices in them, and they pulled off the paper one square at a time, then pasted on new paper. Then they wrote out the New Year couplets.

Wisdom Xia made both brothers write the couplets so he could see who had the better hand; then he pasted them around the gate and the front door to the house and on the doors to the kitchen, the henhouse, the pigpen, and the shithouse. Next, Fourth Aunt chopped and minced the meat for the *jiaozi* stuffing with rapid strokes of the cleaver, and the whole family gathered around the basin of dough to roll out circles and fill the dumplings. Wind Xia and Rain Xia quickly lost patience, and their *jiaozi* got bigger and bigger.

"The drums have got you hooked, haven't they? Off you go," said Wisdom Xia.

So Wind Xia and Rain Xia would go to the cupboard and stuff their pockets full of dried persimmons and peanuts and disappear. Once they were gone, Wisdom Xia got restless, too; he pulled on his sheepskin-lined serge coat and set off for the opera house.

This routine didn't change even after Benevolence Xia died and there were only three brothers left. They still visited First Aunt, Benevolence's widow. They didn't eat there, but they took her with them to the other three houses. This year was different, though. Rites Xia had also passed away, Justice Xia was still recuperating from his injury, and Wisdom Xia had only just been discharged from the hospital. So Wisdom spoke to the four aunts.

Things had not gone well for the family this year, but they would still prepare plenty of New Year goodies. They could rely on him for the celebrations—he and Fourth Aunt would host them. They had received a gift of food from the county Party secretary, and Rain Xia had brought the ready-cooked steamed dishes, but still they bought a cockerel, ginseng, and chestnuts to cook chestnut chicken; pork ribs to make crispy pork slices; and a pork joint to make red-cooked pork shoulder. They gathered lotus leaves from the pond to make pork "cigars" and bought pork heart and lungs, lotus root, wood ear fungus, and dried daylilies to make pepper soup. Fourth Aunt fried sticky-rice cakes, and there were sweet dishes of glutinous rice wine, dates, gingko, walnuts, and raisins. And cold dishes of smoked tofu from Nanshan, soy-marinated bamboo shoots, ginger and bean sprouts . . .

Everything was ready and waiting, yet suddenly Wind Xia was gone. Wisdom Xia took refuge in the bedroom and refused to go to the store to pick up the *baijiu* and *choujiu* rice liquor he had ordered. He couldn't even be bothered to mix himself his usual shredded tobacco flavored with oils and spices. Luckily, Fourth Aunt didn't break anything from falling off the ladder, though she did end up with a purple bruise on one arm. She shed a few tears but didn't complain about the pain otherwise and carried on making the rabbit-meat buns. Then she asked Wisdom Xia to wash the daikon for her.

"You can wash them yourself," he said. "You've got hands."

"You've been stuck in your bedroom for too long. You should get out for a bit."

"Get out?" he said. "I'll never be able to get out and show my face again. Better for me if I just stay here in bed."

Fourth Aunt felt this was such an unlucky thing to say that she spat upward into the air. But she didn't dare say any more and decided to wash the daikon herself. Wisdom Xia lay on his back on the kang and stared up at the ceiling. He stared and stared, but nothing suggested itself to him, so finally he got down, found his razor, and scraped the hairs off his chin. Then he came into the kitchen.

"Just because Wind Xia's gone doesn't mean we're not having New Year. We're gonna have a great celebration!" And he hunkered down beside the washbowl and washed the daikon.

Once they were clean, he cut them up and put them on to cook. The pair of them worked away for two whole hours, without a break, until Fourth Aunt fetched his water pipe and put water on for tea. But Wisdom Xia told her, "Go and get Snow Bai and the baby back from West Street first." Then he took the window lattices out, tore the old paper off, and pasted new squares on.

And that was how they celebrated New Year's Eve. This year there was no carnival parade or opera performance in Freshwind, not even any drumming; it was just like any other day. For men on their own like me, New Year was no fun. It didn't matter where you went; you didn't fit in. When Forest Wu and I were making tofu, he asked if I had any plans. I knew he was hinting he wanted to come to my place, but I didn't answer. I was better off alone than with him. He couldn't talk properly, and he smelled bad, too.

I shut my gate behind me, and early that evening I fried a dish of pork, steamed a plate of tofu, and boiled some rice. As I carried my bowl to the table, I thought of Mom and Dad. "I'm eating this for you!" I said as I took the first bite. Of course, my next thought was of Snow Bai. "Snow Bai," I said, "this bite is for you!" The third mouthful was for Justice Xia.

But after that, I had no one else to eat for. I tried to think of someone who was worthy, maybe Tongue-Tied, or the Earth God and Goddess, or Second Aunt or Fourth Aunt, Pavilion or Big-Noise Zhao. And then, of course, there were the trees: the tree in my yard, the gingko tree at the Great Qing Temple, the tree that had grown out of the stick we stuck in the ground in Seven Li Gully, Wisdom Xia's tickle tree, and all the other trees in Freshwind. Or Lucky, maybe? I should include Lucky. And the donkey at the dyehouse, the tabby cat at the House of Treasures, and the peony bush at Wisdom Xia's. And . . . and . . . How could I have forgotten the stones? All the boulders in Seven Li Gully! The great boulder in front of the theater that was covered with moss and changed color four times a year, as if the moss were its clothes. And the rock underneath the market archway, a large square marble block where I'd seen Snow Bai sitting with her baby. The stone never said anything, but a trumpet flower vine grew out from beneath it and twisted and twined around the archway.

When I thought about it, there were so many creatures and things I needed to thank for helping me get through the year, and I had nothing to pay them back with, except this food I was eating for them. But I couldn't eat enough for all of them, so I put half a bowlful on the ground and said, "Bring on the birds, the wasps, and the flies. This bowl of food is for them!"

Believe it or not, no sooner had I said the words than six sparrows fluttered down and flew away with a rice grain each. Then a swarm of wasps and moths and flies followed, and a long line of ants marched down the yard wall and came and helped themselves to a grain of rice each. Finally, there was only one rice grain left in the bowl. I stuck it to the tip of my nose and then licked it off with my tongue and swallowed it.

Let's get back to Wisdom Xia. When Fourth Aunt brought Snow Bai and the baby back from West Street, he complained that she hadn't brought the rest of Snow Bai's family along with them.

Snow Bai answered, "My big brother's come home with his family, and my mom can't leave them."

"Your brother's an engineer, right?"

"Yes, he's chief engineer now."

"A good man, and an educated one," Wisdom Xia commented. "Right, let's do it like this—the second day of the New Year, you go and spend it with them, and the third day, bring your mom and dad and brother and sister-in-law over there! Right now, go and tell your second uncle and their family not to cook; they can come here and eat. And First Aunt and Third Aunt, too."

He turned to Fourth Aunt. "Should we ask Pavilion and Gold as well?"

"Of course, but then we have to invite the whole lot of them. And Snow Bai should leave the baby here. If she takes her, it'll look like a big hint that she wants people to give the girl New Year's money."

"They're supposed to present gifts for the baby to me," grumbled Wisdom Xia. All the same, Snow left her behind when she went to issue the invitations. But then First and Third Aunts complained that she hadn't come with her daughter and pressed five yuan each on Snow Bai.

Snow Bai tried to refuse the money, and that upset them even more. Was she turning it down because it was too little? She should realize that an old woman and a blind woman had no earnings! Justice Xia gave Snow Bai twenty yuan, and so did Gold. Pavilion was not home. Hearth and Halfwit each gave five yuan to Snow Bai, and she went on to Bounty's. She found him standing at his gate. But when she said that Fourth Uncle wanted them to come by for the midday meal, he was upset.

"Oh, dear me! We never invited Fourth Uncle, and now he's invited us! Right, let's have them and you to lunch, and then I'll come to you."

"There's no need!" Snow Bai protested. "It'll be fun if we all eat together."

Finally, Bounty gave her thirty yuan for her daughter. While they were talking, she'd spotted Treasure sweeping just outside their new house nearby, but by the time she got there, they'd locked up. She knew he was trying to avoid her, so she said loudly to Bounty, "Where did Treasure go?"

"He was just here. I don't know where he disappeared to. When you come over, can you bring him with you?"

Then she went to Thunder's. When she arrived, Blossom had just come back with a bucket of hot water that someone had used to scald the pig and was making Thunder soak his feet in it.

Thunder greeted Snow Bai politely but complained, "Why's Fourth Uncle telling us to come over? The uncles always used to go to each other's houses, and we younger ones got the food ready and ate the leftovers when they finished. Of course, it's always cold by then, but hey, what's New Year without cold dishes. Snow Bai, it's your first New Year with the family; I hope they've welcomed you with some good liquor."

"Our dad bought some bottles, but I don't know what brand it is," said Snow Bai.

"It's bound to be good," Blossom said. "It's only your family that drinks the good stuff these days. But why didn't you bring the baby? I'm her fourth aunt, aren't I? So I have to give her a New Year's gift!" She cuffed Thunder and said, "Let me have ten yuan." Thunder pulled a fifty-yuan bill from his jacket pocket.

"Have you got nothing smaller?" Blossom asked.

"No," said Thunder.

Snow Bai turned to go, but Blossom stopped her. "Don't go. We always do it this way. I give her a gift as her aunt, and when she's big, her light shines on me!" And she popped into the next-door neighbor's yard and got them to change the fifty-yuan bill for five tens, one of which she gave to Snow Bai.

Thunder, his feet still soaking in the bucket, asked her, "Has Wind Xia gone again?"

"He's on call at his office this New Year," said Snow Bai.

"But he was back here! Why couldn't the office have arranged someone to cover for him? You used to be able to rely on companies to look after their workers—not anymore. But they still rely on him!" said Blossom.

With the turn the conversation was taking, Snow didn't feel like hanging around any longer. She simply said, "Does water with pig's blood in it really cure cracked feet?" and then she hurried away.

Once I'd finished eating, I thought I'd have a snooze, but then suddenly Tongue-Tied appeared and invited me to Justice Xia's for a New Year's Eve meal. I didn't feel like going, but Tongue-Tied wasn't taking no for an answer. I had no idea they'd invited Wisdom Xia and his family, too.

When we got there, Tongue-Tied fetched water from the well, and I sat down by the stove and fed straw in through the little door, making the flames crackle inside. "What are you so cheerful about, fire?" I asked. "If you're so clever, make me see Snow Bai." To my astonishment, the gate banged open and in came Wisdom Xia, Fourth Aunt, and Snow Bai. I jumped to my feet in a panic but then hovered at the kitchen door without a clue what to do.

"Spark, Spark," said Justice Xia. "It's New Year! Make a bow to your fourth uncle!" I flung myself down on the ground and kowtowed.

Wisdom Xia was taken aback by my fervor, and he muttered, "There's no need to go that far," and went straight into the house. Fourth Aunt was standing in front of Snow Bai with the baby in her arms.

"Get up, get up!" she said. "You're not a kid. Why are you banging your head on the ground like that?" I was still sprawled on my front, from where I could see Snow Bai's feet. Meantime, the little one took her chance and reached out and grabbed the woolen hat off my head. I didn't protest, and Fourth Aunt didn't notice until she was halfway up the front steps to the house. Then she turned and saw me lying on the ground outside the kitchen, bareheaded.

"Oh, for heaven's sake, Spark!" she said. And she came back with my hat.

"Sweet baby," I said, but Fourth Aunt wouldn't let me play with her.

Then Justice Xia told me, "Go and bring the food in." And he turned to the others. "Spark and Tongue-Tied have worked for months with me at Seven Li Gully. That's why I invited them here tonight."

I brought the dishes of food in and laid them on the table. It was simple fare, only one dish of stir-fried pork, braised shredded tripe, and deep-fried tofu. There were sticky-rice cakes and meatball soup, too.

"Say the name, Spark!" Justice Xia told me.

So when I brought the shredded tripe, I announced, "Spark!"

"The name of the dishes!"

I brought the soup. "Soup with meatballs and Spark!"

Snow Bai laughed, showing her shiny white teeth. Then she stifled her laughter and bent down to pick up a chopstick that had fallen under the table.

"What d'you think you're doing?" Justice Xia hissed at me. "I asked you to announce the dishes. Everyone here knows you're called Spark!"

I'd behaved like such a clown. When I went back to the kitchen to get the rest of the food, I gave myself a proper slap across the face. When all the food was on the table, Justice Xia called Tongue-Tied and me to come and sit down. I sat down at the north end of the table, which happened to be right opposite Snow Bai. I didn't know where to look. I didn't dare look straight at her, or at Wisdom Xia, so instead, I stared at the food. But that didn't feel very good, either, so I studied my hands.

"Why aren't you eating?" Justice Xia asked me.

"I am, I am," I said. Then I saw that Wisdom Xia's glass was empty, so I got up to refill it.

"Spark, wish your fourth uncle and aunt a Happy New Year," Justice Xia instructed me.

I clinked glasses with Wisdom Xia and emptied my glass, refilled it, and clinked glasses with Fourth Aunt. I was going to empty that, too, when she stopped me. "You're not well, Spark; you shouldn't drink too much."

"I'm fine!" I said and poured the liquor down.

"He drinks like his father!" she said, and I relaxed a little bit then. *Should I clink glasses with Snow Bai?* I wondered. *What will I do if she refuses? What if Wisdom Xia gets annoyed?* I took the risk, got up, and said, "Happy New Year, Snow Bai!"

Snow Bai blushed and said, "I don't drink."

"It's New Year," I said. "Have a sip!"

"You can have a sip," Fourth Aunt told her.

So Snow Bai got to her feet, but her hand shook when she held her glass up, and when we clinked glasses, I saw a flash of light. She took a sip and was overcome by a fit of coughing.

She hurriedly made her excuses. "Second Uncle, Second Aunt, I've got to go get the dinner ready. Don't eat too much; come over soon!" And she left with her baby in her arms.

This was the first time in my life that I'd shared a meal with Snow Bai, and as she went out, I said to myself, *Please, give me a sneeze!* And sure enough, she did. That was good. That meant that the bit of liquor she'd drunk with me would warm her guts for a long time to come.

In due course, Wisdom Xia and the others finished their drinks and set off for his house. That left just Tongue-Tied and me at the table. The clouds above the courtyard turned red, blue, and white, like bedcovers. Tongue-Tied was still gobbling the leftovers, but I'd stopped eating. He grunted and waved his arms to try and get me to eat more. Poor guy, he had no idea just how much a woman's beauty gladdened the heart.

When Wisdom Xia and Second Aunt arrived home, a single white bird was perched motionless on the roof ridge. Wisdom Xia was the first to see it. He flapped his arms at it, but it didn't fly away. It stayed right where it was. Wisdom Xia wasn't giving up. He shouted to Rain Xia, who came with his slingshot, but by then the bird had disappeared. Meanwhile, the house was filling up with guests—first, the seniors, First and Third Aunt; then Gold, who brought with him a bottle of liquor and a thermos; he was followed soon after by Bounty, Hearth, Halfwit, and then Thunder and Blossom, and Bamboo, too.

"You invited your nephews, Fourth Uncle, but not their wives. Are you worried we'll eat too much?" Blossom teased him.

"We came anyway!" said Bamboo.

Fourth Aunt laughed. "Blossom, you're Thunder's tail; if we invite him, then of course the invite includes you. And Bamboo, you're head of the street committee; you don't need an invitation. Snow Bai, give your aunt Bamboo a cigarette—she's desperate. But where are Pavilion and Treasure?"

"I went and called them," said Rain Xia. "But Pavilion's not home. Maybe he's at the township offices. Treasure said he'd already eaten. He refused to come."

"He's an odd one, that boy," said Fourth Aunt. "He's a loner. Please, help yourselves to the food."

Wisdom Xia brought the dishes to the table himself, one by one. "Are they good?" he asked. The older guests were seated at the table, while the younger ones stood around the edge and leaned over, chopsticks at the ready to help themselves to morsels.

There was a chorus of, "Very good! Very good!"

After the meal had been going on for a while, Bounty's youngest daughter turned up outside the gate with Chastity and called to Bounty and Gold that the food at home was going cold. Snow Bai went and tried to persuade them to come in, but they refused.

"Chastity knew we were coming here; she was just annoyed that she hadn't been invited," Bamboo said to Snow Bai when she came back.

"Gold, go and invite her," said Fourth Aunt.

"Oh, never mind her!"

So Fourth Aunt went to the gate herself, but Chastity had gone. Blossom turned to Snow Bai, suddenly very chatty. "How does your family celebrate New Year's Eve? The Xia family's like this every single year. The men take turns going from house to house eating, while the wives and kids sit at home waiting. We never get to eat a hot New Year's meal."

"We don't make such a big deal of it," said Snow Bai.

"In the past, before we brothers set up our own homes, we were a couple of dozen people around the same table," said Wisdom Xia. "Now that we have separate houses, this is the way we do it. We're the only ones in Freshwind who do it like this."

"I don't think it proves you're especially close to each other," Blossom said. "Everyone should eat in their own home."

"What nonsense you talk!" Wisdom Xia exclaimed. "Eating together shows we're family."

"You like things formal, Uncle," said Bamboo.

"There are some things that have to be done properly," said Wisdom Xia. "Like the People's Consultative Congress in the county seat every year. The delegates have to report to the county head, but it isn't just a matter of giving a report, is it? The report is a formality, but it shows we're all taking things seriously. Don't you think?"

"I don't know! I only know how to eat," said Bamboo. She helped herself to a large bowl of rice and said to Blossom, "You have some more, too! Fourth Aunt's rice is delicious." But Blossom and all the younger ones said they were going. "You old folks take your time; enjoy yourselves!"

The atmosphere wasn't nearly so lively once they'd left, and a mountain of food was left over. As she was clearing away afterward, Fourth Aunt grumbled, "No one's eaten a proper meal; look at the leftovers. We'll be eating it for days to come."

Wisdom Xia grumbled about Blossom and Bamboo. "They don't know how to behave themselves, or how to make proper conversation."

"I can't imagine we'll all be eating a big family meal next New Year's Eve," said Fourth Aunt. "They all care less and less about celebrating together."

Wisdom Xia tried to warm his mug of tea over the brazier, but it wouldn't come to the boil. He blew on the flames but got soot in his eyes, so he gave up. Turning on the loudspeakers, he asked, "Is there no procession in the village this year?"

"Pavilion never said anything about one," said Fourth Aunt. "It's always been so lively over the New Year, but this year I can't hear a single drumbeat." Just then, there was a burst of opera music from the loudspeakers.

As the notes rang out, the sky suddenly darkened, and the wind picked up and shook the treetops. Wisdom Xia looked upward doubtfully. "There's a change in the weather. Do you think it's going to snow?"

Just then they heard a volley of drumrolls and gongs, and Wisdom Xia exclaimed, "They're drumming in the New Year! I knew it wasn't right for the New Year to be so quiet! Take the baby and go look. If there's really a procession, let her sit on a carnival float for a bit. I did that as a kid; I was 'Guan Gong of the Peach Garden Brothers.' Wind Xia did, too." But mentioning Wind Xia reduced him to silence.

Snow Bai was talking baby talk with her daughter. "Who would you like to be then, huh? . . . My daughter's going to be the hero Chenxiang, who split open the mountain when his mother was trapped inside," she announced. Wisdom Xia had been taking opera masks out of the cupboard. Suddenly, the acid rose into his throat. But he didn't spit it out. He simply stiffened and forced it back down again.

Snow Bai went out to look, her daughter in her arms. It was blowing harder out in the street, and the hens were scuttling along the foot of the wall, their feathers fluttering wildly, until finally they tumbled head over heels. Culture, Zhang Li, and his buddies emerged from the alley opposite, carrying large chunks of ice they had smashed and brought back from the pond. They were using them as skateboards, throwing them on the ground and sliding along on them. Zhang Li was out of control and almost crashed into Snow Bai, forcing her to jump out of the way, before he ran straight into the wall and fell flat on his face. His ice block was triangular in shape, and there was a fish inside, frozen as if caught in midswim.

At the farmers market, the stalls were empty, and bits of straw and plastic bags rolled along the ground. Dogs played among the piles of garbage, or perhaps they were fighting; it was hard to tell. Lucky was standing some way off. Snow Bai had heard Wisdom Xia saying that she'd howled all night, and as soon as it was light, she'd run to the township offices. Now she wasn't joining in the other dogs' play-fighting, and they didn't try to involve her. Instead, she lay on the ground, licking her leg.

"Lucky! Lucky!" Snow Bai shouted, and the bitch approached. She was limping, and Snow Bai saw blood trickling down her leg. "It's New Year's Eve!" exclaimed Snow Bai. "Who's been beating you?"

Big-Guy Ma was standing at the gate of the House of Treasures. He was wearing two sweaters under a checked suit and a scarlet tie. "It was Clerk," he said.

"Clerk?"

"When the dog saw him, she attacked him and tore a hole in his new pants. So Clerk got a stick and laid into her."

Snow Bai sighed. Then she ordered Lucky, "Go on home, go on." But Lucky refused to move and howled into the wind.

Bright Chen and Star Chen came out of the shoe store. They rubbed their hands and stamped their feet, then went to stick up New Year's couplets on either side of the gate.

"Have you eaten?" Big-Guy Ma shouted at them.

"Yes!" Star Chen said. "How about you?"

"Yes, thanks," said Big-Guy Ma. "Hasn't Emerald been home to see you?"

Star Chen looked around at Snow Bai, who avoided his gaze. He didn't answer.

"Did Big-Noise Zhao write those for you, or did you do it yourself?" Big-Guy Ma asked.

"Big-Noise Zhao wrote them," Star Chen said. "The first one reads, 'Incomers need a leopard to turn into a scholar,' and the second one, 'Leavers need a fish to be wise.' Clever, huh?"

"Freshwind is a strange place," said Big-Guy Ma. "The peasants write couplets that are so clever you can't understand them."

"The first one is about outsiders like you and me," Star Chen said. "The second is about people who leave the village. All you understand is money!"

"I don't think they're very well written," Big-Guy Ma said. "Look at the ones we've got on the House of Treasures. 'Once you dreamed of millet gruel and pumpkin soup, one wife and one child. Now you have white rice and turtle soup, one kid and a harem of wives.'"

"He must have had you in mind when he wrote that," Star Chen said.

"Of course he did. Nothing wrong with that!" Big-Guy Ma gave a belly laugh. He turned around to see Snow Bai approaching and bowed deeply. "Happy New Year, Snow Bai!"

"Happy New Year!" said Snow Bai.

Big-Guy Ma took out his wallet and extracted three hundred yuan, which he held out. "Here's a New Year's gift for the baby."

Snow Bai backed away, but Big-Guy Ma pushed the bills into the baby's blanket. "Take it! It'll bring her luck."

Star Chen and Bright Chen both spat on the ground and retreated into the shoe store.

"Don't you go home over New Year?" Snow Bai asked Big-Guy Ma.

"Everywhere's home to me."

"Well, now you're settled here in Freshwind, why don't you bring your wife and kid, too?"

"I've gotten used to living alone, and they aren't interested in moving out of the county seat. Usually I spend the New Year there, but this year I decided to stay in the village and watch the fun. I didn't think it would be this dead on New Year's Eve!"

"I heard drums and gongs, so I thought there was a procession," said Snow Bai.

"It was New-Life Liu, Compliance, Tongue-Tied, and their buddies. They played a bit here, but no one invited them in, so they went to West Street. They'll be back."

And a little while later, a crowd of people did turn up from West Street, following a tractor with the oxhide drum loaded on behind.

It was me driving the tractor. I was so happy that I really wanted to do some drumming. After we'd eaten, Tongue-Tied and I went to try and persuade Pavilion to arrange a procession. But he'd just come back from the township offices, and he told us that, with the Freshwind villagers' attack on the offices, they weren't in the mood for festivities. They'd skip it for this year. But Tongue-Tied and I weren't giving up, and we went looking for New-Life, who got the drum down. The skin was damaged on the right side, so we had to turn it upside down. I was driving along from West Street, and to my astonishment, there was Snow Bai. The tractor leaped like a bull calf and veered toward her. She was talking to Big-Guy Ma and didn't notice until he shouted a warning. Snow Bai looked around, but instead of jumping out of the way, she froze, rooted to the spot. I froze on the tractor, too, and my hands and feet went stiff. But when the tractor saw it was going to knock Snow Bai over, it careened away and drove straight into the inscription on the boulder by the gate to the House of Treasures. There it stopped, puffing and panting. New-Life jumped down from where he was sitting next to the drum, swearing, "Spark, you fucker! Are you trying to kill someone, or get yourself killed?"

"Don't talk about death on New Year's Eve!" Compliance admonished him, but New-Life was still swearing. "Can't you fucking drive properly?"

"It was the tractor that wanted to go this way," I said. "I couldn't control it!"

The others laughed, and one of them said, "When Spark sees Snow Bai, he goes cross-eyed. Don't blame the tractor!"

I got down and muttered to Snow Bai, "Hope I didn't scare you."

When we were eating together earlier, she'd gone red but ignored me. Now, she looked ashen. She bent down and took a pinch of soil, which she dotted on the baby's forehead, in case she'd been frightened by the near miss.

"The tractor went off course by itself," I said. "It's true! It's got a soul!"

New-Life hit me on the head with the drumstick and said, "Rat-a-tat-tat! You're not driving us anymore. We'll play here!" And he started banging away.

After a while, people began to come out into the alleys. I saw Forest Wu at the fork in the road by the market, his hands tucked into his sleeves. Halfwit had been squatting at the foot of the field dike, taking a shit, and suddenly got up and scared him.

"Forest Wu!" said Halfwit. "Are you collecting shit today?"

"N-not to-today, it's N-New Year," Forest Wu said. "I'm gonna g-go and look at the pr-procession."

"In your dreams," said Halfwit. "What procession?"

Forest Wu was just about to answer when he looked to the north and saw Studious Zhang walking down from the 312. He crouched low and sneaked away.

"Forest Wu!" shouted Halfwit. "Forest Wu!" Then he saw Studious Zhang and hunkered down behind the dike so he couldn't be seen, either. "Studious Zhang," he muttered to himself. "You'll die by New Year's Day! And if not tomorrow, then on the fifteenth!"

Studious Zhang didn't see either of them. He'd made himself scarce for a few days and was doing a shift with the township head at the government offices over the New Year. But after a few games of chess, they were both bored, and he was going out to buy cigarettes. Whenever he met people coming out of the alleys, they came to a halt and then slunk back the way they'd come. New-Life was still banging on the drum, but he kept his head lowered and his eyes down. Around the tractor, no one said anything or looked at Studious Zhang, and even the drum fell silent as he passed.

"Why didn't the fucker go home for the New Year?" said New-Life.

"Did you see that he had a pair of handcuffs clipped to his belt?" Compliance said.

I grabbed the drumsticks and jumped down.

"What are you doing?" New-Life said.

"I'm gonna hit the bastard!" I said.

"Don't do that, old boy!" said New-Life. "It's the New Year. We don't want any trouble!"

"I've got itchy palms!" I said.

"You've got such a big mouth," Compliance said. "Where were you when we tried to get into the township offices? Miles away!"

"I was in Seven Li Gully," I said.

"I'm stopping," said New-Life. "No one's listening, and it's boring without an audience!"

Let me tell you, if I'd really wanted to beat Studious Zhang up, New-Life would never have been able to hold me back. The only reason I didn't was that Snow Bai was there, and I didn't want to do anything more to alarm her. I didn't look good when I was fighting, either. When New-Life said he was stopping drumming, I sneaked a glance at Snow Bai, but she was already on her way home with her baby in her arms. "Right, let's all go!" I said.

I started the tractor and headed for Justice Xia's, and when New-Life shouted after me to take the drum back to the orchard, I pretended I hadn't heard. As I drove under the East Street archway, I caught up with Snow Bai. I stopped the tractor. "Snow Bai! Jump up and I'll give you a lift!" But she ignored me. So I jumped off the tractor. "If you're walking, I'll walk, too." I trotted alongside, my hand on the steering wheel, with the tractor chugging along beside me.

Suddenly the wind picked up, and I heard a whistling sound. Snow Bai clutched her baby to herself and started running. "Jump up!" I shouted. "Get on!" Dust swirled up from the road and got in my eyes. The tractor veered off course again, and the front wheel got stuck in the gutter. The wind got worse and worse, and I could see a twister on the plateau on the other side of the 312. Who knows where it had come from, but by the time we Freshwind folk saw it, it was almost on us. It swept over Bowed Ox Ridge, almost flattening the trees and covering the burial mounds of the Peasants' Association, and my dad's and Mid-Star's dad's graves, with a layer of soil. It uprooted the stakes in front of Mid-Star's dad, swept past the farmers market and into the village, through the theater square, and then south, down to the river, where it blew up a pillar of water several feet high that looked like it was going to suck the river dry. Then suddenly it was gone. It had blown over thirteen trees, scattered two stacks of wheat straw and three of cornstalks, torn down the eaves of five houses, and killed ten hens and three cats. The dyehouse dog was whisked up into the air and broke a leg when it landed. A quilt and four pieces of clothing hanging out to air disappeared completely. I didn't know what was happening to me. I was just shouting to Snow Bai to run when I found my feet lifted off the ground, and then I was being held up in the air. The wind really could hold me up. It was like when you were swimming in the river and you grabbed the bank and burst out of the water. You couldn't see the wind, but you could get a grip on it if you tried. When I was ten yards above the ground, I looked down, feeling pleased with myself. I could see Snow Bai crouched over and running down one of the alleys. Her hair was standing on end. The baby's hat blew off the way a leaf blows up into the tree canopy. I made a grab for it but couldn't catch it. "Hat! Hat!" I shouted.

I started spinning around, first upright, then on my side, then twisted like a dough stick. Then I felt an explosion in my head and lost consciousness. When I came to, I was sitting inside the tornado. You might not believe me, but inside it was white and like a big hollow bamboo tube, with walls that were covered in a stripy pattern that sounded very solid when I patted them. If I'd tried, I would probably have been able to climb up the inside, but I was afraid I'd get up five yards and then slip down again and land with a bang. About three minutes later, I was swept up again and dumped on the ground, and the tornado whirled onward and was gone. I wasn't hurt, just a bit bruised on my ass where I landed. Away in Wisdom Xia's house I could still hear the loudspeakers blasting out opera.

Chapter 42

Nine times nine is eighty-one,
A poor kid leans against the wall,
She'll never freeze her butt off,
But she's worried she might starve.

This is an old nonsense rhyme we Freshwind folks learn from our grandparents, who learned it from their grandparents, who learned it from their grandparents. That springtime, the kids started singing it again, and I had the feeling that they were singing about me, so I took off my dirty old padded jacket and stopped walking around hunched up inside my collar. I put on a thin sweater and jacket instead. But I was still hungry. I must have had worms in my belly, because one meal didn't last me till the next.

The smell of steamed rice and stir-fried onions wafted through the alleys. A lot of families were going through their sweet potato and daikon and potato cellars and throwing out the bad ones—sprouting potatoes and daikons that were growing roots were cleaned up and laid down in store again. Some of the sweet potatoes in my cellar had black spots. I picked the good ones out and washed them and decided I'd eat them. I cut the spots out of the spotty ones and put them back into the cellar again. My neighbor Take-It-Easy had laid out a mat in his doorway and was mixing dried persimmons with toasted rice husks and barley, which he was going to grind up fine. He looked at me as I picked over the sweet potatoes. "You don't know what you're doing!"

"What do you mean?" I asked.

"You should eat the spotty sweet potatoes first."

"But then I'll never have any good ones to eat," I said.

Take-It-Easy didn't understand me. He thought he knew what he was talking about, but he'd never eaten a bowl of really thick and good porridge in his life.

"Why don't you make the husk mix I'm making?" he asked me.

"'Cause it makes you constipated, and I don't want to have to dig the shit out of my ass with a stick."

Then he thought he'd poke fun at me for not having a wife or a kid. "I'm not as lucky as you," he said. "I have four mouths to feed. You eat a meal yourself, and you've fed the whole family!"

"Sparrow!" I said.

"Sparrow?" Take-It-Easy had never seen the opera *Chen Sheng and Wu Guang*, and he'd never heard the line, "The sparrow doesn't understand the mind of the swan."

Tongue-Tied and I took a break until the fifteenth of the first month. We only went back to work in Seven Li Gully when the villagers who'd come home for the New Year put their bedding over their shoulders and went back to their city jobs. As we walked over the small stone bridge, we saw Gold and his wife planting potatoes on two mat-size bits of land where they'd cleared the stones on the riverbank. When Gold saw Justice Xia, he shouted, "Dad! Dad! You can't fertilize potatoes with chicken shit, right?"

"Chicken shit has bugs in it that burrow into the potatoes," said Justice Xia. "How many potatoes can you get in there? Come and plant some at Seven Li Gully!"

"You're still going there?" Gold said. "Are you fit enough for that?"

"I have Spark and Tongue-Tied. I just tell them what to do."

Gold stared after him and said to me, "Dad's gotten so much older this past year."

"You're looking old yourself. Haven't you noticed?" Chastity said.

Gold's dark skin had a definite yellow tinge to it. His liver had given him trouble for years, and when it hurt, he had to stop and push his fist against his lower back until it eased. Now he was concerned about his dad and told me I had to keep a proper watch over him and make sure he didn't take on more work than necessary.

"You're a good man, brother," he said. "If you weren't so obsessed with sex, you'd be the best man in Freshwind."

I wasn't gonna let him get away with that, but he stopped me talking by stuffing a cigarette in my mouth.

Justice Xia wasn't capable of carrying stones anymore or digging out the gully sides, either. Just walking up a steep slope started his legs shaking. We'd brought buns and cold sweet potatoes with us for lunch. Justice Xia always used to wipe the dirt off his hands and eat his potato, and when he was finished, he'd lie down on his belly by the spring at the bottom of the gully and glug down some water. Today, he just ate a bun and then sat watching me and Tongue-Tied eat. He started to talk about how, when he was young, he could eat six sweet potatoes and steamed buns at one sitting, how he could balance the stone roller on his belly afterward. He told us we weren't real farmers, because a real farmer eats fast, shits fast, and falls asleep fast.

"Why are you always talking about when you were young?" I asked. I sounded harsh, but Justice Xia didn't get angry. He looked me in the eyes. "Do you think I'm old?"

Then I said something really clever. "Second Uncle, do you love money?"

"What a stupid question! Everyone loves money. I like money, but the money doesn't like me."

"There are supposed to be three signs of getting old," I went on. "Fear of death, love of money, and insomnia. So you are old, Second Uncle! You just have to accept it. Sit here quietly and let Tongue-Tied and me do the carrying."

"Fuck it, you're just like your dad," Justice Xia said. It was the highest praise I'd ever had from him. The rest of the day he was good as gold, just sat watching us work. But three days later, he got Halfwit's wife to make him some knee protectors, three layers of sacking sewn into a tube, so he could kneel on the dike. From there he could pile up the rocks or shovel away any soil that fell from above. But after he'd been doing this for a while, his legs went numb, and he had to stop. He made Tongue-Tied and me thump and rub them, but we never managed to find the right place, and he cursed us and crawled on all fours to the shed to smoke a cigarette.

He looked so funny that I started laughing. "Uncle! You look like an ox, crawling along with your butt stuck up in the air!"

Justice Xia paused and turned his head. "Spark, have you seen Marvel lately?"

"I don't owe anything on my electric bill, so why would I see him? Why are you asking about him all of a sudden?"

"Why shouldn't I?" Justice Xia said. "You carry on with those stones!"

The next morning I had just gotten as far as the dyehouse on Middle Street when a minibus stopped under the archway. I thought it was probably Mid-Star or Wind Xia back for a visit, but half a dozen people got out and ran down Middle Street, with Goodness in the lead. At the first row of houses, they stopped, and Goodness knocked on Auntie Wang's door, shouting, "Goat Boy! Goat Boy!" The door opened a crack and the men stormed in, emerging with Auntie Wang's son, Goat Boy, his arms twisted up behind his back. "Mom!" he yelled. "Mom!" Auntie Wang rushed out, but the men pushed Goat Boy into the minibus, and it roared off. Auntie Wang collapsed to the ground, wailing loudly. Meanwhile Goodness patted the dust off his hands and walked away, his hands clasped behind his back.

"What's happened?" I asked. "Who took Goat Boy?"

"They came from the provincial police," Goodness said. "Goat Boy's killed someone!"

That gave me a shock. "That can't be right, can it? He's too short to kill anyone!"

"When you're really poor, you get brutal," Goodness said. "There were three of them with laboring jobs, and they wanted to earn a bit extra to take home for the New Year. But they couldn't find work, so in the middle of the night they broke into an old couple's house, and when they were discovered they shut the old folk's mouths for them . . . And you know how much money they stole?"

"How much?" I asked.

"Two hundred yuan! Goat Boy'll forfeit his life because of two hundred yuan! Did you see him being taken away?"

"I saw you bringing them here."

"I'm a village cadre. If the police come asking for help, I have to take them there. Wouldn't you have done the same in my place?"

"I'm not a cadre," I said.

"Just remember: of you ever break the law, I'll bring them to your house, too," he said.

His words sounded unlucky to me, so I hurriedly spat into the air a few times. Once Goodness had gone, I ran down to East Street, where Justice Xia and Tongue-Tied had been waiting for me for a while. When Tongue-Tied heard what had happened, he wanted to go to Goat Boy's, but Justice Xia grabbed hold of him. "If it hadn't been for Seven Li Gully, you would have gone to Xijing along with Goat Boy last winter!"

"Will he get the death penalty?" I asked.

"Well, if you kill someone, you pay with your life," said Justice Xia.

I could see Goat Boy in my mind's eye, see him on his knees at the edge of a ditch trussed up with a rope, a gun pressed against the back of his neck. I heard the bang, and I saw him fall into the ditch and lie motionless.

Poor Goat Boy. He'd tried so hard to get me and Tongue-Tied to go with him to Xijing. He said life was so much better there, that you could make money doing anything. It was only the hopeless cases who stayed behind, he said. As soon as he'd made some money, he'd be back to build a big house and get his mom fitted with new teeth—all hers had fallen out, and she couldn't chew anything. How had he ended up stealing? Worse still, killing the people who'd discovered him in their home?

"I don't believe he killed anyone," I said. "Maybe the other two did it, and he got arrested because he was with them."

"It doesn't matter if he did or not. He was with them, so he's implicated," said Justice Xia.

"But he never stole anything in Freshwind."

"Why do you think that Xijing is heaven, and the streets are paved with gold? It's a farmer's job to make crops come up from the earth, and all everyone wants to do is run off to Xijing!"

I couldn't settle down to work when we got to Seven Li Gully—my head was full of Goat Boy, with his persimmon-cake face and his stick-bug head, and I kept hearing his yells, "Mom! Mom!" when he was being bundled out of the house. It was his spirit inside my head, I figured. People left a spirit behind when they died, didn't they? People had a spirit when they were alive and when they were dead, and it was Goat Boy's spirit bothering me now. Justice Xia started yelling at me for not working properly and being a dope. I looked at him vacantly.

"I asked you, why are you being so dopey?" he repeated. I opened my mouth to speak, but countless Goat Boys came bursting out in a loud yell. Justice Xia looked shocked.

Tongue-Tied thought I was getting aggressive with the old man, so he came charging over to beat me up.

Justice Xia grabbed him. "I think he's having an attack," he said.

It wasn't true. After I'd yelled, I just wanted to cry. I jumped down to the bottom of the gully and rinsed my head in the cold water of the spring, then got out my handkerchief to wipe my face. It was Snow Bai's little handkerchief, and I thought of her. That made Goat Boy disappear completely.

The thing is, Seven Li Gully's a spiritual place. When it got dark and we were packing up to go home, Tongue-Tied took a piss, and I turned my back and pissed, too. Just then, I looked up to the hill at the top of the gully, and I seemed to see someone in the trees there. I felt sure it was Snow Bai. I didn't know what she was doing in the trees, but I was sure it was her. So I said, "Uncle, you two go on ahead; I'm going to take a shit." And I walked up the slope and went behind a large boulder.

Justice Xia and Tongue-Tied went, but after they'd gone about a hundred yards, Justice Xia sat down and waited for me. It really was Snow Bai walking down the little path from the top of the gully. Justice Xia rubbed his eyes and asked Tongue-Tied if it was her, and Tongue-Tied nodded. Justice Xia looked around to check what I was doing—I must have been pretty dumb not to realize that they would stay and wait for me. I hid behind the boulder and watched Snow Bai coming down the trail, and it seemed to me that she was floating on a cloud, descending from heaven. When she passed by, I gave a couple of grunts, and she stopped and looked around. She couldn't see anyone, but she increased her pace and began to run.

Justice Xia got to his feet and called out, "Snow Bai! Snow Bai!"

"Second Uncle! Haven't you gone home yet?"

"What are you doing here? Where have you been?"

"There's a wedding in Chenjiazhai, west of the reservoir," said Snow Bai. "I went to help out with the celebrations. But I have to get back before night because of the baby, so I took a shortcut."

"Oh? Who's getting married?"

"A man called Lu. This is his second time."

"Are they really having music and singers at a second wedding?" Justice Xia tut-tutted. And he sent Tongue-Tied off with Snow Bai and came up behind the boulder, where I was squatting with my pants around my knees. I blushed and tried to get up, but my legs were so weak I couldn't stand and pull up my pants. I didn't dare look Justice Xia in the face.

"Have you finished shitting?" he asked.

"Yes," I said and then scuffed some loose dirt over it.

Justice Xia said nothing more; he just turned around and walked down the gully. I followed behind, as if he were leading me on a string.

Down in the village, Tongue-Tied and I ate our meal at Justice Xia's like normal. But this time the old man prepared it himself. He made us sit in the yard as he rolled out the noodle dough and cooked one bowl for each of us. Tongue-Tied was in a high state of excitement. He hunkered down on the doorsill with his bowl in his hand, and I sat on the steps. As I got near the bottom of the bowl, I realized there were some bits of chopped grass at the bottom.

"Why have we got chopped grass in our bowls?" I asked.

Second Aunt overheard. "What are you talking about? You're not an animal. Why would your uncle give you grass to eat?"

I got a funny feeling in my head, as if it were splitting open, and saw countless Goat Boys with persimmon-cake faces and stick-bug heads, all circling around me.

I was sick again, but this time it wasn't as bad as before, when I'd had a burning ball of fire in my chest and the urge to scream and run. At that time, if I'd had a gun in my hand, I could have shot someone. This time my face swelled up, but then it was all over and done with. I met Hearth in the village, and when he asked if I'd eaten, I just looked expressionlessly at him, as if I hadn't heard what he was saying, which made him swear at me. I didn't care; swearing couldn't hurt me. I went to Roughshod Ding's House of Treasures to watch TV and sat there staring into space, even after Roughshod Ding got up and turned the TV off.

Justice Xia invited me over for some of their *jiaozi* dumplings stuffed with daikon. I obediently ate one helping, then a second, then a third. Every time he filled my bowl, I ate it all, until he looked worriedly at me and didn't give me any more.

"The daikon stuffing's good, isn't it?" said Second Aunt.

"Was it daikon?" I asked. Then I got up from where I was sitting on the doorsill, and a *jiaozi* burst out of my mouth, whole and unchewed.

"Are you sick, Spark?" Justice Xia asked.

"No."

"You are!" he exclaimed, and he took me to the Great Qing Hall. He walked in front, and I followed behind, picking my feet up high. On the way, I met Culture. He smiled, put his arms round me from behind, turned me right around, and pointed me back the way I'd come. It was a while before Justice Xia realized he couldn't hear my steps anymore, and when he looked around, I was on my way home. He swore at Culture and marched me in the right direction again. When we got there, Justice Xia asked Big-Noise Zhao to give me a proper consultation. Big-Noise Zhao took my pulse and gave me three medicated patches.

"Why do you use patches all the time?" Justice Xia asked.

"There's a proper treatment for his sickness, but I can't prescribe it," said Big-Noise Zhao.

"What is it?"

Big-Noise Zhao did not answer but just wrote something on a scrap of paper. Justice Xia looked at it, scowled furiously, and hauled me off back to the scorpion's tail again. What was it that Big-Noise Zhao had written? I only found out long afterward. Two words: Snow Bai.

Big-Noise Zhao was a fine doctor, good at making a diagnosis, but he couldn't cure me. No one could. When Marvel came by Justice Xia's, he looked at me and said I'd lost my soul. I didn't answer; I just sat there listening to him talking to Justice Xia.

"How do you know Spark's lost his soul?" Justice Xia said.

"Mom told me that it happened to her once when she was young," Marvel said. "It was just like this."

"It happened to her?"

"It was Master Clear-Bright at Tiger Head Cliff who called her soul back," Marvel said.

"How did he do that?" Justice Xia said.

"He tied a red thread around a hen's egg and baked it in a fire till the shell was charred. Then she ate it, and he called her name and she answered. Her soul was back."

I didn't think for a moment that Justice Xia would believe all that, but he got up, found some red thread and an egg, and put it into the flames through the stove opening.

"You should eat a charred chicken egg," Marvel told me, "and you'll get your soul back."

"My soul's gone," I said.

"What do you mean, gone?"

"Steam came out of my head, and I could see myself standing in front of me."

"And d'you see yourself right now?"

"Right now I can't see myself," I said.

"Your soul's gone, and you don't know where it is," he said.

If Marvel was right, where could it have gone? Did it go in Seven Li Gully because Snow Bai took it with her? Or did it get lost in the stove because Justice Xia had embarrassed me? Wherever it went, I didn't want Justice Xia calling it back, so I got up to go.

"You can't go!" said Marvel. "If you go, you'll be a walking corpse!"

Fine, I wouldn't go. I went back to the kitchen and sat down. Justice Xia got the cooked egg out, and it was strange: the red string was untouched, even though the eggshell was completely blackened. He gaped in astonishment. "Very strange!" he said. Then he instructed me, "Spark, go out of the gate, and when I call you, answer me, and come in here and eat the egg."

I went and stood at the entrance. There was a rooster there with three hens in tow, and it fluttered its wings and stalked up to me grandly, like it was a village cadre.

"Hey, Spark!" Justice Xia called.

"Yes!" I replied.

"Come back!"

I didn't say anything because there was Snow Bai. She had the baby in one arm, and in the other, a bundle of potato noodles. For a second, our eyes met.

Eyes can speak, and they said, "Hey!"

"Hey!"

"Hey . . ."

"Hey!"

Snow Bai squeezed sideways past me, went into the yard, and draped the noodles over the door knocker, but they fell off and landed in the dirt.

"Come back!" Justice Xia shouted again.

"Let me hang them up," I said.

"Spark!" Justice Xia was furious. "Why the fucking hell are you not answering?"

Snow Bai had already hung the noodles back up.

"Would you like a drink of water? And a seat?" I offered.

At that moment Justice Xia came out of the kitchen. He saw me offer Snow Bai a stool to sit on and rushed up and gave me a kick up the ass. "You useless little fucker," he roared. "Out!"

And then he pushed me out of the gate before I could eat the egg.

I never ate the egg, but my spirit had come back. Marvel never understood how that happened. Justice Xia knew. Three hours after he kicked me out, I sneaked back and eavesdropped on him talking to Second Aunt indoors.

"The world's a strange place," he was saying. "Wind Xia doesn't value Snow Bai, but Spark is obsessed with her."

Second Aunt said, "You should encourage Snow Bai to smile and say a few words to him sometimes. It won't do her any harm, and it might help him get better."

But Justice Xia said, "No, I can't do that."

I was so upset at his words that I decided I wouldn't go to Seven Li Gully anymore. Plus, I did something so idiotic that it made Justice Xia ill, and he had to stay in bed for three days.

Here's what happened. You might remember the township Youth League cadre, the one who invited all the village officials to his wedding so they'd bring gifts? He'd gone crazy about photography. When he heard about the giant ear of wheat we'd grown in Seven Li Gully, he came and asked me if I'd get it for him. He wanted to photograph it; he was sure the picture would win a prize in a photography content.

"I can't give it to you," I said. "Why should it matter to us if you win some stupid prize?"

"I'll give you five yuan!"

"No go."

"I just want one picture. When it's printed, it'll spread the word about all the work you've been doing in the gully."

So I took him to the shrine of the Earth God and Goddess. The wheat was hung up too high for him to get a good picture, so we got it down and laid it on the ground. When he was finished, I asked him for the money, but by then he'd changed his mind and wouldn't give it to me. What a bastard! Of course, I got into an argument with him.

Meanwhile, a hen ran in from the street and started pecking at the ear of wheat. He gave me my money, and I looked down and the wheat was gone. It was out in the street with a flock of hens playing tug-of-war with it, and it was now in three bits. I was terrified, and so was the cadre. But he was a sly one. He managed to find another wheat ear from somewhere and hung that up instead. "Justice Xia won't notice it as long as you don't say anything," he said.

I'd never deceived anyone in my life, so how could I keep this from Justice Xia? All the same, I didn't dare tell him. I gave my five yuan to Clerk's wife at the restaurant and treated Justice Xia to a bowl of *liang fen* noodles every day.

When I showed up with the first bowl, he said, "Why are you buying me *liang fen* when you're refusing to go to Seven Li Gully?"

"Who said I'm refusing? I just needed a few days' rest."

That cheered him up, and he ate all the noodles. For three days in a row, he ate my noodles and told everyone, "This fucker's really a good nephew!"

But there's no wall that doesn't let a draft through. Somehow, Tongue-Tied got to know what had happened and told Justice Xia. When I arrived with the *liang fen* on day four, Justice Xia was sitting on the bench in the courtyard with a bamboo stick beside him.

"Here come your tasty noodles, Uncle!" I greeted him.

Justice Xia lifted the stick and knocked the bowl out of my hands. Then he hit me on my legs so I fell to my knees.

"Why are you beating me?" I shouted.

And he shouted back, "What happened to the wheat? What did you do with my wheat?"

I'm done for, I thought to myself. The blows fell on my back, over and over, but I didn't move; I stayed right where I was. Eventually, when I was lying in the dust and blood was trickling out of my mouth, he did stop. He gave a couple of groans and collapsed to the ground himself.

Justice Xia stayed in bed for three days. Finally, he climbed down off the kang with great difficulty. I tried to look after him, but he ignored me. Wisdom Xia came by to see him, and so did First Aunt and Third Aunt, and everyone tried to cheer him up.

They didn't blame me, just told me to take proper care of him. All the younger Xias came, too, except for Snow Bai.

After the New Year was over, she had started to contact the others from the opera troupe. They had split into seven bands based all over the county, each band guarding their own little patch of territory, just like thieves did. No one was to encroach on anyone else's patch, and no one was to undercut ticket prices, either. Some of those who got on best with Snow Bai asked her to come and join them, but they were based near the county seat, in Guanzhen, and she didn't want to be so far from home. She contacted a troupe that was touring the villages of Freshwind, West Mountain Bend, Teahouse, and Qingyangzhai. Of course, they welcomed her with open arms and even put her on the highest pay grade. So Snow Bai left her baby in Fourth Aunt's care.

Fourth Aunt had reservations, partly because the baby was so small, partly because she thought that touring would take it out of Snow Bai, but also because people would laugh at the idea that the wife of an important provincial official like Wind Xia was tooling and warbling in a village opera troupe. But Wisdom Xia was in favor. There was nothing the least embarrassing about it. Everyone needed a singer at family celebrations. There was nothing worse for a singer than not being allowed to sing; besides, she could earn some money.

"Will it be worth it?" said Fourth Aunt. "It's not as if Wind Xia is short of money!"

Wisdom Xia got angry. "Your son's got money, sure! But did he leave a cent to Snow Bai or us before he left? He's an idiot. It wouldn't surprise me if he has another woman in town, and that's why he's trying to get Snow Bai to divorce him."

But Fourth Aunt was on her son's side. "Don't you think I'd know if my dog bites or not?" she said. "It's true they've got problems, but what couple doesn't squabble or have spats? Suppose he does have a girlfriend in town. That just means he's taking after you, doesn't it? You weren't such a good boy at that age, either! Give him a bit of time, and he'll come round. He doesn't really want a divorce."

Wisdom Xia said nothing more. Snow Bai made up her mind to join the troupe, and Fourth Aunt took over looking after the baby, so he started spending more time at home. They bought a nanny goat, and he milked it every day so the baby had warm milk to drink.

Snow Bai usually got up and left as soon as it was light, returning late in the evening. Justice Xia suggested that Rain Xia give her his motorbike, as it would make her journey to work easier, but she firmly refused. She couldn't ride a motorbike, and she had no intention of learning. So Wisdom Xia got up early every day and went out to look at the sky. If it was overcast, he put an umbrella at the gate and reminded Snow Bai to take it with her, and when they went to bed at night, they left the gate unlocked for her. As soon as they heard the gate open and shut, Fourth Aunt would get up and knock on the little bedroom window. "Is that you, Snow Bai?"

"Yes. How come you're still awake?"

"You're back late. Have you eaten?"

"Yes."

"I heated some water in the kettle. Give your feet a soak."

Snow Bai was touched at her concern. One night, she said, "Mom, I've ordered a jacket for you in the store. Remind me to pick it up in the morning."

"I'm not going to town. What do I need new clothes for? You've only just earned a bit of money, and you're splashing it around already. Send it back; I don't want it."

She got the baby out of bed and held her over the potty to pee, but the baby just cried and didn't pee.

"Let me have her in my bed," said Snow Bai.

"She's nice and warm in here," said Fourth Aunt. "If you take her in with you, she might catch cold. Go to bed. A letter came from Wind Xia today. I put it next to your bed."

Snow Bai washed her feet and went to her room. The letter lay untouched in its envelope. She eyed it as she pulled off her pants, crawled under the quilt, and warmed up a bit, then finally opened it. Inside, there was no letter, only a divorce certificate. She didn't get angry, nor did she get upset. She lay on her back staring up at the ceiling, then snuggled down under the quilt and let the envelope and its contents drop to the floor.

Snow Bai was exhausted and slept like a log all night, her arms and legs splayed out motionless. It was still cold at night, and there was a heavy dew. One last leaf hung from the tickle tree, but now it dropped, curving through the air before landing silently on the ground. There were calls from three crickets that lived in the tree roots, from an earthworm rubbing along in the earth, and from a line of ants marching up the trunk. Then Lucky barked, the cocks crowed, Clerk's pig oinked, and the dyehouse donkey brayed. Wisdom Xia woke up, but Snow Bai slept on until the baby gave a wail, and then she woke up with a start.

Fourth Aunt, in her room, was annoyed. "I got you up to pee and you wouldn't, but as soon as I put you down again, you peed me a river."

"Mom! Let me get her back to sleep," said Snow Bai.

But her mother-in-law said, "You go back to bed. I'll get her some dry bedclothes."

Fourth Aunt made kissing noises as she changed the baby, and the cries died away until she was snuffling and snorting, her face scrunched up as if she had all the cares of the world on her shoulders. But Snow couldn't sleep. She stuffed the pillow between her teeth and wept until sunrise.

That night, Compliance had asked me to go along and play mah-jongg. We played at the cultural center, with Goodness and Yang, the pig breeder from West Street. I won. I only had to think of a tile to find that I had it. I was really proud of myself. "You know what they say. Money's hard to come by like shit's hard to eat. Shit's certainly hard to eat, but the money's rolling in today."

After a while I got tired and told them I was going, but Yang wasn't having that, so I had to play on a bit longer. I could barely keep my eyes open. I thought if I lost a bit I could go, but even though I was almost playing with my eyes shut, I was still on a winning streak. "It's no good, I can't lose. Here, you have my money and let me go," I said.

I went home and fell fast asleep. I dreamed I was up in a tree, eating persimmons. There was one persimmon tree after another all along Yijia Ridge, and they were covered in ripe, orange-red fruit. I picked one that looked good, bit into it, and sucked in the soft sweet flesh. Then I blew into the empty skin, and it inflated like a balloon. I was on my third persimmon, eating the flesh and blowing into the skin, when suddenly a tooth fell out and I woke up.

They always say that when you dream of losing a tooth, it means someone in the family has problems, I thought. *But I haven't got any family left.* The only one who could possibly count as family was Snow Bai, but what could have happened to her? I began to panic. I decided that when it got light, instead of going to the stone bridge to wait for Justice Xia and Tongue-Tied, I'd go to East Street.

Wisdom Xia's gate was closed. There was no one else in the alley, so I paced back and forth a couple of times, but the gate didn't open. People were beginning to come out of their houses; I'd have to leave.

Bamboo saw me. "What are you doing here?"

"I'm waiting for your dad to go to Seven Li Gully."

"Dad and Tongue-Tied have gone to the stone bridge."

I dragged myself disconsolately to work in Seven Li Gully, where I kept looking up to see if the sky was going dark, longing for rain so I could go back to East Street. I'd decided that if I met Snow Bai, never mind whether Wisdom Xia was there or not, I'd go right ahead and ask her how she was. I was going to be like a fly buzzing around food. It didn't matter how many times you flapped it away; it always came back and settled down on the edge of the bowl again. It was disgusting, but it was brave, too! Time and again, I looked up at the sun in the sky, but it moved so slowly.

"What are you looking at?" Justice Xia asked me.

"I'm wondering why the sun has no tail," I said. "If it had one, I'd yank it out of the sky by its tail."

Snow Bai had been weeping in her room all night, but when Wisdom Xia got up, she didn't dare continue. She got up, too, and started sweeping the yard. Then she went and fetched some straw to burn in the stove and heated water to wash her face and to make some rice gruel. When Fourth Aunt got up, she said, "Mom, I have to go out."

"Which village is it today?"

"Qingyangzhai. A man's asked us to go and sing at the third anniversary of his mom's death."

"Have a good breakfast first then."

But Snow Bai wasn't hungry. She went into Fourth Aunt's room and looked down at her baby, who was still sleeping, her little mouth puckered up in a pout and one small foot sticking out from under the blanket. Snow Bai put the foot between her lips and kissed it. The tears ran down her cheeks.

When Fourth Aunt came in and told her the food was ready, she dried her tears, put her baby's foot back inside the quilt, and said, "I can't stay. I have to be there early."

"Why are your eyes so swollen?" Fourth Aunt asked as she went with her to the gate.

"I didn't sleep very well," said Snow Bai, and with a quick smile she was off.

Wisdom Xia had gone for a stroll through the village. When he got back and noticed that Snow Bai was gone, he said, "She's having a hard time, isn't she?"

"She didn't sleep well; her eyes are very puffy."

"You must tell her to look after herself. She may be young, but her health is important. I just went to visit my brother. He's always been so healthy, but look at him now! I'm worried sick about him. The pair of them, one blind, the other sick—how are they going to manage?"

"What are you worrying about him for? They've got five sons to take care of them."

"Yes, five . . . and too many cooks spoil the broth, as they say." He milked the nanny goat, then went into Snow Bai's room for the baby's bottle. He spotted the certificate lying under the bed, pulled it out and scanned it, shouted for Fourth Aunt, and then collapsed onto the floor.

That evening, I walked to East Street from Seven Li Gully with Justice Xia. I didn't see Snow Bai, but I did hear that Wisdom Xia had had another attack. Justice Xia went into their yard, but I stayed outside. I could hear Snow Bai's baby's cries getting shriller and shriller. The clouds stained the sky a rusty red, and then darkness fell all around.

Chapter 43

After his attack, Wisdom Xia spent the next two days in bed. On the third day, he started belching, the burps rumbling up from deep inside him. He'd always loved smoking, but a drag off his water pipe suddenly made his head swim, and even the smell of tobacco was enough to make him retch. At around noon that day, with the sun high overhead, he ordered his rattan chair brought out into the yard, and Rain Xia helped him settle in it. He called his wife and Snow Bai out into the yard to stand beside Rain Xia. He asked about the divorce, but Snow Bai played dumb. When Wisdom Xia told her he'd seen the certificate under her bed, Snow Bai started to wail inconsolably. Fourth Aunt and Rain Xia shuffled awkwardly, not sure what to do.

"If it's come to this," Wisdom Xia said, "there's something I need to say. I want all of you to hear this: For as long as I live, Wind Xia will never step foot in this house again. He can wait until I'm in the ground, and even then, he's not coming to my funeral! I want you to know this, too: Snow Bai married into the Xia family, and no matter what happens, she's a Xia. She's not my daughter-in-law anymore—she's my daughter!

"If Snow Bai wants to get remarried, I won't stand in her way, and I don't want anyone else to stand in her way, either. If she wants to get remarried, she'll be treated as a daughter of the Xia family, and her dowry will be looked after. If Snow Bai doesn't get remarried, I'll divide this house between her and Rain Xia. Rain Xia will get the rooms on the east side of the house and the side house on the east side of the yard. Snow Bai will get the rooms on the west side and the side house on the west side." When he was finished, he turned to his wife and said, "Is that understood?"

"It's your decision to make," Fourth Aunt said.

"Do you understand?" he asked Rain Xia.

"Yes," Rain Xia said.

"Good," Wisdom Xia said; then he leaned back in his chair and belched three times. Snow Bai fell to her knees and kowtowed to him. "What are you crying for?" he said. "No need to cry now!" Snow Bai stopped crying but knelt down to kowtow again. "If you want to kowtow, that's fine, but three times is enough. That big red sun up there is my witness, I'm taking you as my own daughter." Snow Bai knelt and bowed her head to the dust a third and final time. Wisdom Xia lifted himself out of the chair. Rain Xia went to his father's side to help him back into the house, but Wisdom Xia waved him off. As he walked into his bedroom, he shouted back into the yard, "Get the loudspeaker on! I want to hear some opera!"

"Which one?" Rain Xia asked.

"*Execution of the Son*! That's what I want to hear."

At lunch that day, the entire village shook with the sounds of *Execution of the Son* blaring over the loudspeaker. When it had played through, the tape was rewound and started again. People set down their bowls to sing along:

> Word was passed from Jiao Zan and Meng Liang,
> Mother had come to grace her master's tent.
> Not a word was spoken,
> But he still gleaned her troubled thoughts.
> Zongbao's crimes were dear and he must repent,
> Make sure the rope around his neck is taut!
> Toss him in a pot of oil!
> Young Zongbao rode to war but found a maid,
> He threw Muke into turmoil.
> Mu Guiying arrived with slashing blade!
> For Mother's sake, we'll spare the details.
> Zongbao found himself locked in marriage,
> We brought him back locked in chains.
> The law is clear.
> The sentence is death.

From that day on, Wisdom Xia's health only got worse. He felt like a lump was growing out of the incision in his stomach. It itched something fierce, and he'd always get Fourth Aunt to scratch it for him. "That doctor over at the county hospital didn't do a very good job," he said. "Why the hell is there a lump there?" The lump seemed to be growing and hardening. Despite all that, Wisdom Xia seemed to be in a better mood than before. He finally went to show his lump to Big-Noise Zhao.

"Does it hurt?" Big-Noise Zhao asked.

"Not at all."

"Then don't worry about it. I'll give you a medicated plaster."

After leaving Big-Noise Zhao's, he stopped by Concord Qin's for a visit. To his surprise, Justice Xia was there. His older brother looked even worse than before: skinnier and darker. Wisdom Xia knew he had to intervene, so when he got home, he told Rain Xia to call over Gold, Bounty, and Halfwit. He made sure to mention that Treasure and the wives shouldn't be invited. Once they'd arrived, he told them, "I called you over here to tell you something important. I was waiting for one of you to do something first, but I'm tired of waiting. I didn't want to get involved, but I'm afraid I must. You've seen what state your father is in. He's getting old. I've watched him, this past winter, this spring, getting worse and worse. Now that he's done with Seven Li Gully—"

"He's still going there," Gold said.

"I know that," Wisdom Xia said, "but he's not working there. He can't work! But your mother and father are still working Virtue's plot of land. They grow food for themselves; they cook for themselves. They're not eating right—I've seen what's on the table every night. You should be waiting on them hand and foot. I've said my piece now. What are you going to do about it?"

The four brothers agreed with their uncle that their mother and father shouldn't be forced to look after themselves. They talked for a while, hoping to come up with a plan, but quickly started arguing. Finally, a decision was reached: The five sons of Justice Xia would take turns cooking for their mother and father. No matter how poor they were or what else they had to do, each son had to make sure their parents ate well. The schedule had to be followed, and there was no option to postpone.

"All right," Wisdom Xia said and then sent the brothers off to tell their parents. That afternoon, Wisdom Xia took down a copy of his book and sat on the stairs to read it. He noticed a typo and was looking for a pen to make a correction when Gold appeared. He told Wisdom Xia that his father had refused to see Treasure and definitely wouldn't be going over to his place to eat when his week came up. "I figured that might happen," Wisdom Xia said. "Change the schedule then; leave Treasure off it. He'll do the same work as the rest, but my brother doesn't need to know about it."

"That's fine with us," Gold said, "but the wives are unhappy. They're saying, 'There are five brothers, but one of them isn't pulling his weight.' They think he's getting rewarded for being the bad son. They say that even if he doesn't cook for them, he should still contribute some food. I went to talk to Treasure about it. He says he's happy to cook for them, but he's not going to contribute food so that we can cook for them. He's worried that if word gets out that he's not involved, the neighbors are going to start talking. He doesn't want to look like the disloyal son."

Wisdom Xia grunted. "He's full of shit. He knows your father doesn't want to see him. How would giving some food be disloyal? I want you to go back and talk to the wives. Tell them that your father doesn't want to see Treasure. Go ahead with the plan as it is. Forget about him. If any of the wives have a problem with that, tell them to come and see me." He rushed Gold out the gate, cursing him under his breath.

Once Gold was gone, Wisdom Xia went back to his book, but he couldn't focus on it. He got up to play some opera, but the loudspeaker wasn't working right. He leaned back in his rattan chair, panting.

That night, the lump on his incision began to hurt. The pain continued for a few days, and Wisdom Xia finally sent Rain Xia to get some more plasters from Big-Noise Zhao.

"That lump might be a bad sign," Big-Noise Zhao said. "It could mean the cancer is back."

"What are we going to do?" Rain Xia said anxiously.

"It won't be easy. Rule of thumb with cancer is, if you make it through the first year, you're probably going to make it another couple of years after that. If you get to the third year, you buy yourself another few years. If you make it to five years, you're in the clear. If Fourth Uncle is suffering this early, maybe the surgery wasn't done properly."

"The doctor told me it was a success!"

"Then what do you think the problem is? You know, maybe it's fate. The operation might have bought him some time, but you can't cheat fate. You need to prepare yourself for the worst." Big-Noise Zhao fished around in a cabinet and took out some herbal concoctions known to fight cancer. He ripped off the labels and gave them to Rain Xia.

Rain Xia cried the whole way home. When he got to East Street, he couldn't go any farther. He sat down on a stone roller and lit a cigarette. The street was deserted. He thought to himself, *Could this actually be what kills him? Is everyone only hanging on to life by a thread? If I see a chicken on my way to the house, he'll be fine; if I don't see a chicken, then . . .* He looked up the street and said to himself, *Please. Just a chicken. I'm praying for a chicken.*

He walked slowly toward home but got all the way to the gate without seeing a chicken. He turned around and looked back, but the street was still deserted. He waited until he was calm and then went into the yard. Wisdom Xia was lying on the kang, cradling his stomach. Rain Xia gave him the medicine. "It'll make you feel better," he said.

"How come these don't have labels?" Wisdom Xia asked.

"He put the new medication in old bottles," Rain Xia said. "You have to take these three times a day, six pills each time."

"Are you sure I need that many at a time?" Wisdom Xia said. He took the bottle and put six pills in his mouth at once. He took a slug of water to wash down the pills, sipped another mouthful, then stretched out his neck and gulped.

Rain Xia couldn't take it; he went out into the yard and cried, his tears dripping off his chin and into the dust.

Rain Xia used to spend a few days away from home at a time, but after that, he started to avoid going to the House of Treasures, instead spending all his free time with his father. Rain Xia helped him mix colors for his painting and bought a box set of opera cassettes. Wisdom Xia found it odd. "Did Rain Xia break up with that girl?" he asked his wife.

"Did he say something to you?" Fourth Aunt asked.

"He was never around before. Now, he spends all his time at home. If he didn't break up with that girl, there must be something else going on."

"Maybe he's growing up," Fourth Aunt said.

"He must have broken up with her," Wisdom Xia said.

Later that day, Rain Xia came home with a soft-shelled turtle and asked his mother to make soup out of it. "Dad should drink some turtle soup," he said.

"You know your dad isn't feeling well," Fourth Aunt said. "Did you ever think about bringing that girl around to see him?"

"You said you didn't like her. She's scared to come around here."

"As long as you like her, what do you care what we think? Bring her over!"

Rain Xia did as she asked and brought over Lotus Jin's niece. The girl knew how to butter up his parents and immediately called them Mom and Dad. But Wisdom Xia only gave her a brief nod and then went to sit in his bedroom.

"They're not even married," Wisdom Xia complained to his wife, "but she's already calling us Mom and Dad. What did you think about that?"

"I thought she seemed okay," Fourth Aunt said.

"'Seemed okay'?" Wisdom Xia said. "Did you see the way she poses, always—"

Fourth Aunt shushed him.

Out in the yard, Rain Xia and the girl were getting the turtle ready. Rain Xia chopped off the turtle's head with a cleaver; the girl bent down to get the head and was about to toss it to the cats when it bit down on her middle finger. She wailed with pain.

A few weeks went by, and something really funny happened in Freshwind. It started with Clerk's second-eldest daughter getting sick. Big-Noise Zhao mixed her up seven doses of herbal medicine. After she took six of them, she was feeling better. Clerk's wife decided it was a shame to waste the final dose, so she decided to take it herself. Right after she took it, she had a tremendous pain in her gut. She had to be taken to Big-Noise Zhao, who put her on an IV. Three days later, she was back to normal.

Wisdom Xia and Fourth Aunt were over to see First Aunt when Clerk's wife showed up to borrow a scale. She started talking about the medicine. "Are you really that cheap?" Fourth Aunt asked. "How could you take somebody else's medicine?"

"I wasn't being cheap," Clerk's wife said. "I just thought it was a shame to waste it. I wasn't feeling well. I always eat the kids' leftovers, so why not take their leftover medicine? I didn't expect it to be that strong."

"I should get some, too," First Aunt said. "Maybe a dose of that stuff will be enough to kill me. I've lived long enough."

"Come on, First Aunt," Clerk's wife said. "Pavilion is a big deal now. If your son is a big deal, that means you are, too."

"So what!" First Aunt said.

As they were talking, Bounty's wife went by the gate with a sour look on her face.

"Always with the long face, that one," Fourth Aunt said. "You could hang a bucket off that chin."

Bounty's wife came into the yard. "Fourth Aunt," she said, "that Halfwit is a real bastard, isn't he?"

"What's the problem?" Fourth Aunt said.

"His parents have been over at his place for five days," Bounty's wife said. "That mother of his is blind. She knocked over a stack of bowls, broke three of them. Halfwit says all the sons have to pay for the bowls—the four of them who are helping, at least. Gold and Bamboo gave their share. They came looking for me to give my share, but I told her I wasn't paying. If Halfwit got money from the two of them, he can afford to buy new bowls. Halfwit decided to grab one of my bowls and smash it. He said we were even. What the hell is he thinking?"

"Oh, we all feel sorry for you!" Wisdom Xia yelled from inside the house. "Why don't you go out on the road and shout it for everyone to hear?"

Bounty's wife jumped with surprise. "Fourth Uncle is in there?" she said.

"Yes, he's in there," Fourth Aunt said.

Bounty's wife turned and left.

Later that afternoon, Pavilion's wife, Cutie, came back from working in the field and invited Wisdom Xia and Fourth Aunt to stay for dinner. Wisdom Xia said that they had to go. Out in the alley, he ran into his brother, who was leading his blind wife. "Who's frying onions?" Second Aunt said, wrinkling her nose.

"The only thing you've got left is that nose of yours," Justice Xia said.

663

"What do you think they're making for us today?" Second Aunt asked. "When I was taking a nap earlier, I had a dream about *jiaozi* stuffed with radish and tofu."

"Don't expect that dream to come true!"

Justice Xia saw a shadow coming toward him and looked up to see that it was Wisdom Xia. "Second Brother," Wisdom Xia said, "where are you off to?"

"We're going over to Hearth's for dinner," Justice Xia said. "Look at me, no better than a beggar!"

Wisdom Xia looked around awkwardly and then excused himself and headed home. The gate was shut. Treasure came to the gate covered in sweat. "Were you washing your hair?" Fourth Aunt asked. "What do you need to lock the gate for?"

Lotus Jin's niece came out into the yard, her hair tousled and her shirt buttons done up wrong. "Hello, Mom and Dad," she said, and went out of the gate.

Wisdom Xia seemed to figure out what was going on. "You—" he said, but he was too angry to continue. He felt the pain in his stomach grow even worse.

Wisdom Xia started to go downhill even faster after that. The pain was so bad that he couldn't eat or drink; he just lay on his kang, curled up like a cat. Big-Noise Zhao brought him some poppy-head tea, but even that stopped working after a while. Wisdom Xia started getting injections of Demerol, once every couple of days at first, then once a day, and then finally twice a day. He began to realize how serious his situation was.

When he'd first gotten out of the hospital, he'd enjoyed the attention, and talking about his illness, but now that he'd gotten worse and people were coming again, he was in no mood to talk. It seemed everyone in Freshwind was coming to visit, and they all told him, "Look after yourself. You've got an ulcer, right? Just look after yourself." All he could do in response was wave a hand or blink. He had to lean on Rain Xia every time he went to the bathroom. Rain Xia gave him a pot to piss in, which he tucked under his father's blanket, but Wisdom Xia insisted on getting out of bed. "Just stay on the kang," Rain Xia said. "Use the pot. We can change your blanket if it gets wet." Wisdom Xia lost his temper, but he was in too much pain to speak. He glared at his son, and Rain Xia finally helped him down from the kang.

Even more visitors started to arrive, but Wisdom Xia was in no mood to meet them. When he heard a knock at the gate, he'd shut his eyes and roll over. When Rain Xia asked if he should call Wind Xia, Wisdom Xia shook his head, and when Rain Xia insisted, Wisdom Xia tried to spit in his son's face. He didn't have the energy even for that, and the spittle trickled down his own chin. Rain Xia, Fourth Aunt, and Snow Bai discussed calling Wind Xia, too, but they knew that Wisdom Xia would never approve. If they did it secretly and Wind Xia showed up, Wisdom Xia's condition might get even worse. They sat in the yard together and cried.

The afternoon I went to see Wisdom Xia, the sky opened up. The rain looked muddy yellow. The wind had been blowing for two days, and the entire village was covered with dust, so when the rain came down on the third day, it seemed like the air had turned to yellow mud. Lucky was leading me, and her white coat became spotted with dirt; my white shirt turned gray. Fourth Aunt, Snow Bai, and Rain Xia seemed surprised to see me when I came into the yard, but they didn't turn me away.

"Is Fourth Uncle any better?" I asked.

"I didn't expect to see you, Spark," Fourth Aunt said.

When I went into the bedroom, Wisdom Xia had his eyes closed. He was unrecognizable. I could still see his chakra burning, but it was faint, like a guttering oil lamp. I went back into the yard and stood there awkwardly for a while, not sure what to say. I looked around and saw the tickle tree. "I know how to cure him!" I said suddenly.

"You've lost it again," Rain Xia said. "Just get out of here! Go!" Rain Xia tried to push me out of the yard, but I wasn't leaving.

"If he says he can cure him," Snow Bai said, "why not hear him out?"

"Snow Bai understands me," I said. Fourth Aunt and Rain Xia went quiet. "Fourth Uncle has a tumor," I said. "The tickle tree does, too." They looked over at the tree and saw that it did have a lump growing out of the side of it. "It wasn't there before, was it?"

"That's strange," Fourth Aunt said. "The trunk used to be smooth. I never noticed that lump. What is it, Spark?"

"If the lump grew at the same time as Fourth Uncle's tumor," I said, "there must be some connection between them." I grabbed a hatchet and went over to the tickle tree. With a few strokes, I took the lump off the trunk. "If we cut the lump off the tree, Fourth Uncle's tumor has to disappear, too."

Fourth Aunt, Snow Bai, and Rain Xia stared at me. In that moment, I felt quite proud of myself. I couldn't figure out how I had realized the connection. My own greatness moved me to tears.

From that day forward, I no longer felt sorry for myself, and I was no longer scared to go into Wisdom Xia's yard and visit the old man. Each time I went, Wisdom Xia kept his eyes shut and Snow Bai didn't say much, but nobody stopped me from visiting and nobody called me crazy. They asked me, "Is Fourth Uncle really going to get better?"

"You have to believe me," I said.

I sat down on the edge of the flower bed, and all the roses behind me burst into bloom at once.

Chapter 44

But eight days later, Wisdom Xia took his last breath.

When the time came, he could not speak. He pointed at the radio, and Fourth Aunt rushed to tune in some opera. When the music came on, I didn't know what it was at first.

Riding the beat, a voice sang, "The weather is clear and my spirit is free."

"So beautiful," I said. "I think Fourth Uncle is going to be fine."

But behind me, Snow Bai was screaming, "Dad! Dad!"

Wisdom Xia clawed at his chest and then went still. A dark shadow spread across his face as if a curtain were being pulled across it. A smile followed after it. He breathed his last breath.

When Mid-Star's dad was alive, he used to say that some people go to heaven and some people go to hell. If they're smiling when they die, you know they're going to heaven. They can see the light, they're instantly at peace, and they can't help but smile—their soul is already in flight. Wisdom Xia had been tortured for so long that his smile put our minds at ease. I'd promised I would cure him, though . . .

Fourth Aunt and Snow Bai broke into anguished sobs.

Rain Xia stared at me. "He was smiling," I said.

"He was smiling," Rain Xia repeated.

"That means he's going to heaven," I said.

"He's going to heaven," Rain Xia repeated.

"I . . ." I stopped. I saw that Rain Xia was crying.

The sound of crying floated up out of the yard, and into the neighbor's yard, and out into the alley and through East Street and through Middle Street, all the way to West Street. Everyone in the Xia family cried. They fell to the ground and wept; there seemed to be nothing else to do.

Fortunately, Goodness was ready to take charge. He sent someone to arrange the mourning pavilion, and he sent someone else to arrange the coffin, and then he called together the family and said, "It's only right to cry, but who is going to deal with the funeral?"

He gave them each a job. Bounty was told to build a stove in the yard. Rain Xia was sent to get flour, meat, cigarettes, vegetables, spirit money, incense, and candles. Hearth was put in charge of the wives in the kitchen. Snow Bai arranged a band. Gold went off to find Big-Noise Zhao and have him write a banner. Halfwit and Thunder were sent to inform all the relatives of the death. And New-Life was sent to West Mountain Bend with gifts for a fortune-teller there who would be able to tell them the perfect date for the funeral.

All the villagers of Freshwind arrived. There was no room to sit down in the house, so they stood, crowding around the bed to get a last look at Wisdom Xia. They wiped tears from their eyes and asked Gold, "What can we do?"

Gold passed out cigarettes, saying, "We have enough people, we should be fine, but come back tomorrow."

The mourners went home to prepare steamed buns, spirit money, and incense for the funeral. Justice Xia had been the first one there, and he never left. He hadn't cried. He covered his brother's face with a sheet of hempen paper. "Brother," he said, "why did you have to go and leave me alone here?" That was when his tears started to flow. Justice Xia's tears seemed to be thick. They ran sideways through the wrinkles on his cheeks and then curled under his chin and slid down his neck. He sat on the edge of the kang, ignoring everyone else, as if he were a statue.

Rain Xia and Snow Bai replaced the paintings in the main room and then took all of Wisdom Xia's painted ladles out of the cabinet to hang in the mourning pavilion.

"Goodness," Snow Bai said, "he used to say that when he died, he didn't want a pillow; he wanted to use a stack of his books instead. Can we get some of his books?"

"Of course!" Goodness said. "If you hadn't reminded me, I would have totally forgotten." He took six copies of *Shaanxi Opera Masks* and tucked them under Wisdom Xia's head. Wisdom Xia's neck had been stiff, but when Goodness lifted him to place the books under his head, he seemed to relax. When the books were back in place, Wisdom Xia seemed to stiffen again.

"Fourth Uncle," Goodness said, "is there anything else we're missing?" The sheet of hempen paper on Wisdom Xia's face slipped off. There was no wind in the room—it appeared to have moved by itself.

"New-Life's back!" someone yelled from out in the yard.

"Good, good," Goodness said. "Good to hear. I think Fourth Uncle was worried about the date, too." He turned and yelled for New-Life, who rushed into the room. "The time is set?"

"He should be buried the day after tomorrow, eleven o'clock."

"Fourth Uncle," Goodness said, "did you hear New-Life? Eleven o'clock, the day after tomorrow. You've got nothing to worry about; I'm handling things. Everything is being looked after." He put the hempen sheet back on Wisdom Xia's face, but it slipped off again.

There was complete silence in the room. Goodness went white.

Snow Bai started to cry. "He doesn't want the paper," she said; "he wants one of the opera masks." She fetched one of the masks and laid it over his face. It seemed to have been made for him.

Rain Xia had not been there to see the paper slipping off. He was out in the yard, talking to Pavilion about informing Wisdom Xia's old school, the township government, and the county government about his death. "What about my brother?" Rain Xia asked. "Should I call him?"

"You didn't tell Wind Xia yet?" Pavilion asked.

"Not yet."

"What do you need to ask me about it for? Call him right away."

Rain Xia realized that it wasn't right that everyone in the village knew, while his own brother didn't. He went to the House of Treasures and placed a call to Wind Xia. He managed to get in touch with his brother, but Wind Xia wasn't even in the city. He had gone out into the countryside, two hundred li north of Xijing, to do some research. He wouldn't be back until that afternoon. He told Rain Xia he'd be able to get to Freshwind the day after, around dusk.

As soon as he hung up the phone, Wind Xia broke down, crying bitterly. He got a ride back into Xijing and called his work unit to book a car to take him into Freshwind the next day. When the car came the next morning, he told the driver to take him to Xingshan Temple, south of the city wall. He bought sixteen candles, ten bundles of incense, and ten sheafs of spirit money.

After that, he went over to the wholesale market and picked up a carton of cigarettes and two cases of *baijiu*. It was already eleven. Wind Xia and the driver went into a small restaurant near the market and ordered a couple of bowls of hand-cut noodles. As they were eating, the waiter came back to ask if it was their car out on the sidewalk. "So what?" the driver asked.

"They're towing it."

Wind Xia ran out, still clutching his chopsticks. He yelled after the tow truck, "What are you towing it for? What are you doing?"

A traffic cop came up to them and asked, "You think you can park on the sidewalk?"

"It was an emergency!" Wind Xia said. "Can't you just give us a fine?" But the tow truck had already disappeared up the street. Wind Xia cursed a blue streak and then got on the phone to start calling around for another car. It was three hours later before he managed to get

668

a friend to pick him up. They went over to the impound lot and got the things for the funeral out of the car, and it was three in the afternoon before they left Xijing.

But that wasn't the end of Wind Xia's troubles. Around halfway to Freshwind, the car broke down, and they couldn't manage to get it started again. Wind Xia was losing his mind. He went out onto the highway to try to flag down a car, but only big trucks were passing, and none of them would stop. Finally, Wind Xia and his friend decided to spend the night in the car and try to hitch a ride in the morning.

When his brother didn't return to Freshwind that night, Rain Xia got nervous. His lips broke out in blisters.

"He has to get here by eleven o'clock tomorrow morning," Pavilion said, "or he's going to miss his chance to see Fourth Uncle one last time."

"Maybe something came up," Goodness said, "and he couldn't get away."

"Like what?" Rain Xia said. "It's going to be tough if he can't get here in time."

"We have to be prepared for that," Pavilion said. "If we wait until eleven tomorrow and he doesn't show, it's going to be too late. Wind Xia's the eldest, but you might have to take the lead, Rain Xia. Do we know who's carrying the coffin, Goodness?"

"Here's how it is—everyone who needs to be invited has been invited; everyone who should be kept away, I've seen to that, too. We're looking at about thirty-five tables for the banquet. All the food is ready. But the problem is, most of the guests are old folks, women, and children. We don't have enough able-bodied men to carry the coffin and put it in the tomb."

"You can't get some men from East Street?" Pavilion asked.

"Well," Goodness said, "let me see . . ." He counted on his fingers. "Clerk's leg is better, but he's still got a limp, so he's out. Forest Wu and Bright Chen are out of town. Back-East is working at the gold mine, and so is Water-Born. Bai Hua and Moneybags are in Xijing, working as trash collectors. Army Wu is selling herbs. Excellent is out looking for work. Good-Water fell from a scaffold while working in Zhoucheng. He's still in critical condition, and Good-Wins went to go look after him. So, there's only Marvel, Third-Kid, Shifty, and Trees left. Marvel isn't up to the job, and Shifty isn't reliable. It's down to the Xia brothers, but it's not right to have them carry the coffin."

"You're right," Pavilion said. "I didn't realize it until you added it up. This village is running out of able-bodied men! Look at the village cadres. Most of us are old, washed up, or sick! We'll have to go to West Street and Middle Street for men."

"We've never had to do that before," Gold said. "They've never come over here to ask for help with a funeral, either. It'll be humiliating for us. We can't even carry our own coffins to the tomb!"

Justice Xia, who had been sitting not far away, listening in, breathed a heavy sigh. He shot a look at Pavilion.

"What do you think we should do?" Pavilion asked.

"If Freshwind doesn't have enough men to carry a coffin, does it even count as a village?"

"We never had men going out to look for work before," Pavilion said. "Who are these village cadres even looking after now? East Street doesn't have the men to carry a coffin. Middle Street and West Street are probably the same story, West Mountain Bend and Teahouse Village, too."

"Sure, sure," Justice Xia said.

Bamboo knew from his tone that the conversation with Pavilion was about to take a very bad turn, so she rushed over to interrupt. "We had plenty of workers before," she said, "but it never did us any good. We didn't get rich, did we? And now that we're short of manpower, doesn't mean any of us are starving, does it?"

"That's exactly what it is, isn't it? If farmers aren't even working the land, can starvation be far behind?"

Pavilion ignored his uncle. "Now, as for the matter of who's going to carry the coffin, how many do we need from Middle Street and West Street?"

Goodness counted on his fingers again. "Seven," he said. Everyone agreed that Bamboo would go that night to make the request.

Pavilion stood up and brushed the dust off his rear end. "Fine then!" he said. Ignoring his uncle, he went over and sat down on a big rock in the yard and lit a cigarette.

Lucky was lying beside the rock. The day that Wisdom Xia had stopped eating and drinking, Lucky had, too. Once the mourning pavilion was set up, Lucky went in and stayed under the table. Whenever anyone came to pay their respects, Rain Xia had to kneel and kowtow to them, and Chastity thought it looked bad having a dog lying there while he did it, so she chased Lucky out. She'd been beside the rock for two days already, completely motionless.

Snow Bai was standing under the tickle tree, dressed in her white mourning clothes. Her eyes were red from crying, and the rings around her eyes were the color of a ripe peach.

"You even make those funeral clothes look good," Chastity said. Snow Bai didn't speak. "Why isn't Wind Xia back yet?" Chastity asked. "You don't think he might skip it, do you?"

"He's probably still on his way," Snow Bai said.

"He's the eldest," Pavilion said. "He has to come back."

"You're supposed to have sons to look after you when you get old," Chastity said, "but you get old just the same."

"Chastity!" Third Aunt yelled from the kitchen. "I sent you to get the wash bucket. Did you forget already?"

Pavilion reached down and patted Lucky's back. He blew a cloud of smoke, and the dog coughed. She spoke her first word in two days: "Woof!"

That night, nobody in the Xia family slept much, since everyone was preparing for the funeral. The rooster was already crowing by the time the neighbors helping in the kitchen turned in and the Xia family daughters-in-law caught a quick nap.

Instead of going back home to sleep, the helpers who had worked late into the night decided to play a few hands of mah-jongg around the dinner table. At exactly seven in the morning, Rain Xia and Gold were out at the burial spot, setting off firecrackers, burning spirit money, and opening the grave mound. The band that Snow Bai had invited began to assemble at the yard gate.

There were twelve players altogether, eight men and four women. I recognized them from Wind Xia and Snow Bai's wedding, so I went around and welcomed them back to the village. The final two to arrive were old Mrs. Wang and Master Qiu. It had only been half a year since I'd seen her last, but Mrs. Wang seemed to have aged years in a matter of months.

"So you're back, huh?" I said.

"Sure," Mrs. Wang said.

"Are you going to sing *Picking Up the Jade Bracelet?*"

"Sure," she said. I passed out cigarettes to the men in the group, and she said, "What about me?" I hurriedly shook another cigarette out of the pack for her. She took it but put it in her pocket instead of lighting it.

The summer before, the performers had been aloof, holding themselves apart from the villagers, and they had taken the stage in beautiful costumes provided by the opera company. That day, however, they looked as common as anyone else. The men were not in their fancy suits, and the women hadn't dolled themselves up like they had on their last visit. They took the invitation to sit down, ate their breakfast, then began setting up their black tent, tuning their instruments, warming up their voices, chatting quietly as they went about their work.

At around eight, a gray blanket of cloud slipped over the sun. It felt as if there wasn't enough air, and everyone seemed to strain to breathe. The yard began to fill with villagers. "Should we get started?" Master Qiu asked Goodness.

"Go ahead!" Goodness said.

"Ah! Here we go," he said, and then broke into a guttural wail, the sound of drums and cymbals rising to meet his voice.

Halfwit, who was inside the house, in Wisdom Xia's room, was just about to take out a cigarette when the drums crashed. He jumped with surprise, stuck the pack back in his pocket, and rushed outside. He watched Master Qiu, moving with the beat, approaching the mourning pavilion. Master Qiu shook the dust from his clothes, lit a stick of incense, and then got down on one knee and bowed toward Wisdom Xia. He turned and motioned for the band to approach and pay their respects.

The *erhu* player went first. He shouted, "Change clothes!" and mimed putting on a fresh pair of clothes. "Remove your hat!" he roared and mimed doffing a cap. The *erhu* player shouted, "Brush the dust!" and he beat the dust from his clothes. "Burn incense!" he said, while lighting a stick to offer. He held up a glass and called, "An offering of wine!" The *erhu* player shouted, "Kowtow!" and he went to a knee three times.

The cymbal player stepped forward and repeated the ritual. The drummer followed him. The man who sang the *xiaosheng* roles followed the drummer, then the man who sang the *jing* role, then the *suona* player . . .

While the *suona* player was beating dust from his clothes, I saw Mid-Star come into the yard.

It was the first time I'd seen him since he'd become a county head. He still had the same comb-over, a tuft of hair slicked down from his left ear to his right ear. He was carrying a bolt of black cloth, and Gold, who had been standing on the stairs into the house, rushed over to greet him and take the offering. "How did you hear?" Gold asked.

"I'm on my way back from a meeting, so I figured I should stop by. I don't want Fourth Uncle haunting me!"

Gold hung the black cloth on a rope strung from the mourning pavilion, where there were already sheets of black and white fabric hanging. Big-Noise Zhao wrote out a couplet to stick to the black cloth that Mid-Star had brought.

"I'm not ready to give him the final toast yet," Mid-Star said. "I want to take one last look at him. I never got a chance to say goodbye."

Gold led him to the bedside. "Nothing but skin and bones now," he said, looking at his uncle's body. He tried to lift the mask so Mid-Star could see Wisdom Xia's face, but it seemed to be stuck.

"I don't need to see his face," Mid-Star said. "This is fine."

The people out in the yard had been too busy watching the players paying their respects to notice Mid-Star, but when he went out of the house, a few of them came over to shake his hand. He didn't want to disrupt the musicians, so he went to stand at the side of the yard.

The *suona* player finished paying his respects, and the *banhu* player stepped forward. When the men were done, the four women in the group stepped forward. Each woman had a wooden tray with fried dough dyed in bright colors. They performed a dance with quick, intricate steps that left Mrs. Wang panting and struggling to keep up. Master Qiu glanced over at the drummers, who immediately stopped playing, and the fried dough was placed on the altar. When the players were done, Mid-Star went over to where they were resting and started shaking their hands. Mrs. Wang immediately recognized him as the former head of the county opera troupe.

"He's not the head of the troupe anymore," the *jing* singer said; "you should call him 'County Head.'"

"County Head Xia," Mrs. Wang said, "when did you get here?"

"A while ago," Mid-Star said.

"You saw us paying our respects?"

"I saw."

"What did you think?" Mrs. Wang asked.

"As the saying goes, 'With enough time, even the mighty sea might become mulberry fields.' It was very innovative."

"You sure do have a way with words, County Head Xia," Mrs. Wang said. "There's something I need to say to you, even though I know I probably shouldn't. I don't think you should have tried to force the company together. When we split in two, we could still perform. You put us all in one troupe, but as soon as you left, it fell apart, and it was even worse than before. We split into seven, eight troupes. Now, it's tough to get even this many people together."

"Who cares?" the *jing* singer said. "Whatever became of us, our company still produced a county head."

Mid-Star forced a smile, but it wasn't convincing. He reached up to slick down his comb-over again. "The opera is in decline," he said. "I don't think there's any way to change that, comrade."

Master Qiu had seen Mid-Star but hadn't gone over to greet him. "Everyone in position!" he shouted.

The players assembled again in front of the altar, and Master Qiu took a position in front of the mourning pavilion. He clasped his hands in front of his chest and began to recite a long poem.

Halfwit couldn't understand much of it, but he could tell it was a conversation between a living person and a dead person. "This is way more complicated than what Rain Xia has to do," he whispered to me. Rain Xia had a few tasks, but his main duty was greeting and bowing to those who came to pay their respects. As Wisdom Xia's son, he wasn't supposed to be the star of the show but to keep a low profile. Still, I hadn't expected the players from the troupe to put on such a performance.

"You're right," I said.

"They do this every day, going from funeral to funeral?"

He hadn't whispered that, so I gave his arm a pinch to shut him up. "Mind your own business," I said.

Master Qiu continued reciting the poem, faster and faster. The words themselves seemed not to matter as much as the rhythm. As he reached the climax, he suddenly bowed and went silent. I rushed over with a cup of water, but he twisted away from me and took a step back, into the doorway of the house, his hands held above his head. Out in the yard, the band began to play "Beating Out the Sorrow."

The next tune was "Jumping the Threshold," then "Zhang Liang Returns to the Mountain," "The Willow Tree Buds," "Longevity Convent," "South Wind Sacrifice," "The Execution of Daji," "Golden Mountain," "Deep Night," "Wang Zhaojun," and "Nailed Shut." Then the singers began to sing, the men and women trading off on "Journey to West Lake," "The Injustice to Dou E," "Blessing," "Wudianpo," "Retreat to the City of Wan," "Qin Xuemei in Mourning," and "Zhuge Liang Prays for the Eastern Wind."

Master Qiu was a tall man with an extraordinarily long neck, and as he beat his drum, his face flushed red and the comb-over that he had stuck across his bald head flopped down over his shoulder. Someone was laughing at him, and when everyone turned around to see who it was, they saw that it was White-Moth. She didn't care what anyone thought. Master Qiu glared at her, and she glared back, and he hit the drum even harder.

I'd seen enough. I went to get a cup of water to bring to the players and, as I squeezed through the crowd, I stomped on White-Moth's foot as hard as I could. The water ended up spilling all over, and she ran out of the crowd to massage her foot. Master Qiu was too absorbed in his drumming to notice anything. He sang along with the beat, directing the other players with his pursed lips and darting gaze. When another singer took up the song, he bent to his drum, and when his turn came again, he jerked his head back up. His hair managed to knock a teacup off the altar, splashing the musicians. He threw himself into the music again, drumming with even more passion than before. I saw that he was scanning the yard, and I knew he must have been looking for White-Moth. He didn't find her, but his eyes landed on Roughshod Ding. Those eyes were beady, his pupils like two droplets of black lacquer. Roughshod Ding gave a thumbs-up in response. Master Qiu turned those beady eyes on me next, and I called out, "Sounds great!" Everyone clapped for him.

"Sounds like ass!" someone behind me said. I turned and saw that it was Emerald.

"What are you doing back?" I asked her. "When did you get here?"

"So, I report to you now?"

I wasn't upset by that at all. "It's good to see you. You're good to come back. Better than your uncle Treasure, at least."

She turned and stormed off. Her face was pale, but her neck was as dark as ever. I wanted to get another look at her eyelashes—they were so long, I wondered if they were fake. Star Chen saw her, too, and gave her a wave, but she stuck her nose in the air when she saw him and went the other way.

I went over to him and said, "You're here for the funeral, aren't you? Get into the mourning pavilion; pay your respects."

"I only came to look for Emerald," he said.

"At a time like this?" I said.

As Star Chen went out the gate, Halfwit came along with a pole and bucket. He was going down to get water, but he asked me to do it. "Who were you talking to just now?" he said.

"Star Chen showed up here empty handed, not even a stick of incense with him. I told him to get lost."

"You did the right thing," Halfwit said. "If he's not going to pay his respects, just here to enjoy the show, then he shouldn't have come. You keep an eye on the gate!"

About an hour later Chastity went out to get some pepper, and when she came back, she told Goodness she'd seen Star Chen under the East Street archway playing guitar. "What is he doing, playing guitar over there while we're having a funeral here?" she asked. "A bunch of people went over there to listen."

"Is that right?" Goodness asked. He called me over and told me to go have a look. "If he's got a crowd over there, break it up."

Tongue-Tied and I went over, and just as Chastity had said, Star Chen was playing his guitar, belting out a pop song. He sang, with tears running down his cheeks, "Who can drink with me tonight? / Then grow old together."

He was in love with Emerald, and I admired him for it. I was even a little bit jealous. But it was the wrong time and the wrong place. I went up to him, told him to move on, and made sure he got the message.

When I got back, the band was still playing, and Wisdom Xia's nieces and nephews were paying their respects, but Emerald was nowhere to be found. I asked Culture where she was, and he told me I'd just missed her. She'd slipped out the gate right before I got back, but he wasn't sure where she was going. I figured she must have gone out looking for Star Chen; I wondered if he'd gone back to the archway to play his guitar again.

Right around then, Concord Qin's wife showed up, dragging her husband on her back. When he went in to see Wisdom Xia and pay his final respects, he didn't cry, but he beat his head against the kang so hard that his forehead started to bruise. Goodness had to tell Concord Qin's wife to get him out of there, but Concord Qin refused. "Spark," Goodness said, "put him on your back."

"Have you smelled him?" I asked.

"Okay," Halfwit said, "I'll carry him! But you need to go fetch some water."

I wasn't about to take orders from Halfwit, so I bent down, got Concord Qin on my back, and carried him out of the yard. When I got out to East Street, I didn't see any sign of Star Chen, but on the way back from dropping Concord Qin off, I stopped in front of the shoe shop.

I wanted to say, *You think you're a big man, huh? Why don't you sing now? I'm calling the shots here!* But the door was shut. I peered through a crack in the window and saw that Star Chen was inside, and so was Emerald. They were naked from the waist down. Emerald got down on the bed and stuck her ass up so that Star Chen could hit it from behind. While he went to work, she took a bite out of an apple.

I couldn't believe it. Her fourth uncle wasn't even in the ground yet, and she was in there, getting fucked by Star Chen! I gave the door of the shop a hard kick and then turned and left, cursing, "Wicked! Evil!" Before I'd gotten very far, I heard another sound from inside the shop; it sounded like they were fighting. I heard Emerald cussing him out, and it sounded like it was about money. The door swung open, and Emerald rushed out. I ignored her and she ignored me.

I wasn't going to tell anyone what I had seen. I shouldn't have seen it in the first place. Why was I there at the perfect time and place to witness Emerald in the act?

"Did you get Concord Qin back home?" Halfwit asked me when he saw me coming up the alley.

"Mind your own business," I said. I was worried that he'd be able to tell from my bloodshot eyes what I had just witnessed.

The afternoon before Wisdom Xia died, I'd run into him after weeding my sweet potatoes. I was leaning against the embankment between the fields, soaking up the sun, trying to forget how hungry and tired I was. I ended up drifting off to sleep, but I was woken up by the sound of footsteps. I saw that it was Wisdom Xia, coming down the path. I knew I couldn't hide from him, so I grabbed a leaf from one of the sweet potato plants and put it over my eyes. *If I can't see him,* I thought, *he can't see me, either.*

"Spark," he said, "give me a hand over in my field. Once we clear the weeds, I'll give you a few baskets of sweet potatoes."

"No."

"You're lazy!"

"I'd love to get some potatoes," I said, "but I'm not going to get up from here." Wisdom Xia frowned and kept walking. "Fourth Uncle," I called after him, "I was just joking. I'll help you weed." He ignored me and kept walking. "Fourth Uncle! Where are you going?"

"I'm leaving!" Wisdom Xia said. He pointed down the path, and I looked up to see that Rites Xia and Mid-Star's dad were waiting for him. Both of them were dead! What were they doing, walking around again? The path ran from Freshwind at one end to Bowed Ox Ridge at the other end. I couldn't figure out which way he was going.

And then I woke up. The sun was already setting over Yijia Ridge, red as a blister. It seemed to drop with a thud; then it disappeared behind the hills. My heart ached. I felt like a pincushion stuck full of pins. I couldn't shake the feeling that Wisdom Xia was going to die. *Don't think that way,* I told myself. *Just don't think that way.*

The more I told myself that, the more I couldn't stop thinking that Wisdom Xia was going to die. I got up and went back to the village and straight to Wisdom Xia's home. Wisdom Xia was still asleep on the kang, and Snow Bai was out in the yard, sticking a potato with a needle. Since Wisdom Xia needed his injections of Demerol so frequently, and Big-Noise Zhao couldn't be there every time, she knew she had to practice giving the shots. She was teaching Rain Xia how to give the shots, too. I stayed at Wisdom Xia's house from that moment on, up until he took his final breath. When he passed, I went to get Justice Xia, Gold, Pavilion, and Goodness, then I went back and spent the next two nights and three days there.

When Goodness was handing out jobs, he'd skipped me, but the Xia brothers had kept me busy with little tasks. I glanced over at Master Qiu—he and his troupe had been invited to play for the funeral, but Master Qiu was clearly playing for himself. It started to annoy me, the way he played to the crowd, trying to squeeze applause out of them. Gold seemed to be annoyed by it, too. He told Halfwit to go get more water, and Halfwit tried to get me to go with him, but I didn't feel like it. But I also didn't want to see Master Qiu, so I went and stood out by the gate, studying the couplet pasted above it.

I saw Dog-Scraps's young son out in the alley. He'd shown up earlier and eaten a few steamed buns and a bowl of tofu; then he ran outside with an extra steamed bun. He was playing a game of tossing the bun into the air, clapping his hands, then catching it again, chanting the whole time, "Buns, buns buns!" When he saw Forest Wu coming up the alley, he asked him, "Uncle Forest Wu, did you come for the steamed buns, too?"

Forest Wu wiped sweat from his forehead. "I was out o-on, uh, b-b-business. Is Fourth Uncle d-d-dead?"

"Yep," Dog-Scraps's son said. "And there's steamed buns in the kitchen."

"St-stick, uh, st-stick a bun up your m-m-mother's cunt! You filthy animal, shameless, heartless—you c-c-came here just for some steamed buns?" Forest Wu began to sob and went into the yard.

Forest Wu's wails silenced even Master Qiu. Everyone in the yard turned to watch him go into the house. He threw himself down beside Wisdom Xia's body and bellowed like an old ox stuck in the mud. Nobody expected that kind of reaction from Forest Wu.

"He must have really loved the old man," someone said.

Fourth Aunt and then a few other family members tried to pull him away, but he couldn't be moved. The band stopped playing and went to take a break, and the sound of crying filled the yard.

"Keep playing," Goodness said after a while. "Just sing something, anything!"

But the players were momentarily unsure of what tune to play. Snow Bai came out of the mourning pavilion, wiping away tears. "He loved opera," she said. "He always wanted me to sing for him, and I never did. But it's not too late." She began to sing "The Hidden Boat."

Snow Bai wept while she sang. She steadied herself against the tickle tree, which shook against her weight. I was sitting under the tree, on the clothes-beating stone, and when I saw her crying, I began to cry, too.

Her tears ran down her cheeks and into her mouth. My tears ran down my cheeks and into my mouth. The tears that ran down my cheek and into my mouth were salty. I took out my handkerchief and was about to dry my tears, but instead, without thinking, I passed it to Snow Bai. She took the handkerchief but didn't wipe her tears. She paused and stopped singing. The clouds above the village seemed to drop away like flakes of skin. The sky above Wisdom Xia's yard cleared, and the sun shone down. It was completely quiet. Everyone was looking at me. Bamboo came and stood between me and Snow Bai and nudged me with her foot. I awoke from my reverie and stood up and went to the doorway of the kitchen. My face was flushed red. Snow Bai had taken my handkerchief! I was happy about that. But I knew I would never get it back. It had been Snow Bai's handkerchief in the first place, and it had finally returned to her.

That was my fate, I suppose. Even that slight connection had meant something to me.

Goodness looked down at his wristwatch. "It's almost ten o'clock," he said to Rain Xia. "Twenty more minutes and we'll need to put him in the coffin. Why isn't your brother here yet?"

"He must be running late," Rain Xia said.

"He's got twenty more minutes. We can't wait any longer than that."

"Well, if we can't, then so be it."

Twenty minutes later, Goodness went out into the yard, where Snow Bai was still singing. "Snow Bai," he said, "that's enough. It's time to get him ready for the coffin."

"At least let him listen to some opera," Snow Bai said. "Put it on the loudspeaker." She went into the house.

With a mournful tune echoing through the village, Wisdom Xia was put into his coffin, the lid was nailed shut, ropes were fixed around the middle of it, and eight carrying poles were stuck through the ropes. The crowd cried, "Lift!" Eight men lifted the coffin, and eight more men put their shoulders to the carrying poles. The carriers struggled out of the house, weaving under the weight, and then steadied themselves as they went through the gate, out into the alley, and then onto the street. They walked through Middle Street, then back through West Street, then out onto the 312, and off toward the cemetery at Bowed Ox Ridge.

I hadn't been chosen to carry the coffin, so as they took it around Middle Street, I took a shortcut over to the grave. Lucky was running along behind me. She hadn't moved from her spot in the yard and looked like she was never going to get up again, but as soon as I went out the gate, she chased after me. I picked out a willow branch that someone had marked the grave with. There was a paper pennant on one end of it. I swept it over the ground, knocking down wheat seedlings and grass, then waved it at the sky. A cloud about the size of a stone roller seemed to fall from the sky, toward the cemetery. It settled above the road and hung there. The sound of opera grew louder. I couldn't figure out if it was coming from the loudspeaker or from up in the cloud.

Lucky suddenly reared back and stood on her hind legs. She stretched her neck out and howled along with the opera. Lucky loved the opera—she'd been a singer in a previous life—but what had there been between her and Wisdom Xia? She hadn't eaten for days, just lying in the yard, and now suddenly she was howling at his grave. I couldn't figure it out.

The funeral procession came down from Highway 312 and turned toward Bowed Ox Ridge. They went along a path that ran up on the embankment between the fields. The path narrowed until the carriers could no longer walk alongside the coffin.

"Come on!" Goodness shouted. "Let's go!"

The carriers in the front struggled to keep their footing on the path, and the carriers in the back shouted for them to keep going forward: "Get going, you slackers!"

"Keep pushing back there! Let's go!"

The two carriers at the very front finally broke down. They took a knee, panting. "That's enough," they said. "We can't go on!"

"Change carriers! Change carriers!" Goodness shouted. But there was nobody left to take the poles. Goodness motioned for Roughshod Ding, and the two of them went to lift the front of the coffin. Goodness was much taller than Roughshod Ding, and as they lifted, the pole finally came all the way off Roughshod Ding's shoulder. Goodness grunted with exertion.

Rain Xia got down on his knees and kowtowed to the carriers. "I'm begging you," he said. "Give it all you've got!"

"Bounty, Pavilion, Halfwit," Gold roared, "get in there!" They rushed over to take positions under the carrying poles.

There were twenty men straining under the load. They called out, "One, two, lift!"

The coffin finally rose again, and the men stumbled all the way down the embankment path to the gravesite. The coffin was set down, and the men staggered away, their faces flushed red, their clothes soaked with sweat.

"Fourth Uncle is fucking heavy," one of the carriers said.

Goodness went around, passing out cigarettes. A bottle of *shaojiu* went around, too, each man taking a swig. "He's not heavy," Goodness said; "we're just a bunch of weaklings!"

Wisdom Xia's nephews knelt down in their mourning clothes in front of the grave and burned spirit money, offering sticks of incense and cups of liquor. The band started to play. Rain Xia and Snow Bai knelt together beside the coffin. "My brother isn't going to be back in time," he said to her in a low voice.

"Your father said he didn't want him here," Snow Bai said. "I suppose he got his wish."

The coffin was set in the grave, and stones and bricks were piled on top of it. The coffin carriers gathered around with shovels, sealing the entrance with dirt. Finally, a tall mound of dirt and stone was built over the coffin. The band stopped playing, and the sound of opera could be heard again over the loudspeaker. "Offering Sand" was playing.

Everyone stood and listened. "This must be a long tape," Rain Xia said.

"Did someone rewind it?" Snow Bai asked.

"There's nobody over there now." He was puzzled. He looked up and noticed a car parked beside the 312. Wind Xia was coming toward the cemetery, sobbing.

Chapter 45

I should tell you more about Freshwind Village, but what is there to tell? There were the major events, life events—births, deaths and departures, the joys and sorrows of everyday life—but so what? Why bother to talk about them? People are born and die just like the sun rises and sets, the days go by one after another, and their lives are full of humdrum happenings.

Anyway, Wind Xia went back to Xijing after the "first seven"—a week after Wisdom Xia's funeral, that is. Star Chen left a day earlier, his guitar slung over his shoulder. Star Chen going like that seemed odd. Right after the New Year, he asked the county farm machinery station people to come and prune the fruit trees; then, the day before he left, he went and gave a whole song recital in the theater, strumming his guitar and singing song after song. And the morning after, he went, and he never showed his face in Freshwind again.

Then gradually, the weather warmed up, the cicadas emerged from their chrysalises, the cats yowled for a mate, the frogs spawned, and Justice Xia still spent his days in Seven Li Gully. Every evening on his way back, he passed his brother's grave and muttered about how they should get a gravestone made. "Why hasn't Rain Xia done it?" he grumbled. But Rain Xia said he'd already talked to Wind Xia about it, and Wind Xia said to wait until he was back and they'd erect a fine gravestone; he'd already gotten the stonemason onto it. Rain Xia had a question of his own for Justice Xia: Was it true that the county officials were going to come and redivide the land plots again? Justice Xia stared at him. "Who told you that?" he asked.

"Goodness. Didn't you know?"

"Fuck!"

"What are they coming to investigate? Does it matter whether we agree to land distribution or not?"

"It's like bringing the brazier when you've already drunk the wine cold," Justice Xia muttered. Rain Xia didn't answer. "Well, let them come, if they want to. At least it shows my letter had some effect!"

"Did you put in another complaint, Uncle?" Rain Xia asked.

Justice Xia said nothing; he just slapped the dust off his hands and went home. He stuck his neck out in front of him as he walked, and you could see a line of greasy sweat on the back of his neck, even though he didn't have the rolls of flesh anymore.

But just as the wheat ears were plumping up and the county officials were making their way to West Mountain Bend and then Freshwind Village, a rainstorm hit our village. To start with, it was black rain: in fact, it turned the sky so dark it was like nighttime at midday. Then it was clear rain. It lasted a whole night, and all the paper window screens turned clear, too. It rained so hard that no one put their heads out of doors, and if you held out a basin under the eaves to get water for cooking, you couldn't fill it more than halfway full.

Snow Bai stood on the steps with the child in her arms. Beyond the wall of the yard, she could see all the way to South Mound, which was smothered in dark clouds, so it looked as if a black widow spider were sitting on top. She looked away. A bit of the gate arch had fallen off, and the wooden pole poking out had grown moss. The water was so high in the courtyard that it covered the clothes-beating stone, and the drainage hole at the foot of the wall was blocked up with trash. Rain Xia prodded a stick down it to get rid of the blockage, but even then, the water wouldn't drain. He went out into the alley and shouted for the folks next door. Eventually, after he'd called them every name under the sun, someone answered.

"Are your ears stuffed with donkey hair?" he exclaimed. "Your cesspit is overflowing, and there's piss and shit all over the alley."

"It's filled up with rainwater, that's why! What the fuck can I do about it?"

"Why didn't you shore it up with earth?" said Rain Xia. And he went to clear the alley. Fourth Aunt was in her kitchen, lighting the brazier so that Snow Bai could hang the baby's diapers up to dry, when they heard a loud crash.

"Mom, someone's yard wall has come down!" said Snow Bai.

"Let it go," said Fourth Aunt. "Another day of rain and ours will be down, too."

Snow Bai didn't hang the diapers. She went and sat on the doorstep. It was so dark and gloomy in the house that it was giving her the shivers.

Another day's rain and still the Xias' wall held firm. Only a piece of plaster the size of a mat fell off the wall. But down East Street, other people's walls did come down, twelve of them. And Forest Wu's side house collapsed, a sinkhole appeared at the farmers market, and one of Shifty's brick ovens fell in. On Middle Street, thirteen houses and thirty yard walls collapsed, crushing a sow and five hens. The water transformed the streets into rivers, washing away the theater steps and making one of the pillars of the Earth Shrine tilt to one side. Ten rows of roof tiles went, too, leaving the god and goddess standing in a sea of mud. All the water drained into a stream beyond East Street, which then overflowed onto Gold's newly dug land, knocking through the stone walls that reinforced both banks. A single willow tree leaned over the new watercourse.

The Zhou River had stout stone dikes and held firm, but the water rose to within a foot of the top of the embankment, and all the villagers—men, women, old and young—were summoned with the beating of gongs to shore up the defenses. Pavilion didn't come home for several nights in a row. It was much worse on Bowed Ox Ridge: a landslide smothered the young trees in the forestry plantation in stones and mud, so that the Reforestation Center resembled a giant scalp covered in red welts and yellow pus, bereft of a single hair. The Freshwind villagers were desperately worried. "First we had drought for five years, and now we've had five years' worth of rain all at once. Heaven's trying to destroy us!" they told each other.

To be honest, I was happy when it started to rain. I can't stand quiet, calm weather, just like I can't stand people living a comfortable life—or living an uncomfortable one, come to that. The storm threw Freshwind into confusion, and while I didn't say anything when I saw all the problems everyone was having, I was happy. Maybe I'm a bad person, but I thought it was fun!

I ran around barefoot and without a straw rain hat. I went to East Street to report on which West Street houses were letting in water, and I rushed off to West Street to tell them whose roof on East Street had fallen in. When I saw Justice Xia, I told him, "Uncle, there's been a landslide at the orchard, and New-Life's lost thirty apple trees and Bright Chen's hut has gone. This is a terrible storm, isn't it? The water's gone crashing through a hundred yards of orchard!"

Justice Xia had been lying on his kang. He pulled himself upright. "Come here, Spark."

I went closer, and he gave me a couple of smacks around the face. "What are you so happy about?"

The smacks didn't hurt, but I felt deflated and sat quiet.

"Why are you hitting Spark?" Second Aunt asked.

"'Cause if I don't, he'll go loopy!" said Justice Xia. And he reached behind him and dug a tiny bit of mud out of the wall above the kang with his fingernail and popped it into his mouth.

With the rain, Justice Xia got such bad pains in his joints that he couldn't get off the kang. Once, he dozed off and dreamed that a crack had opened in the heavens and was going to swallow him up. When he woke up and opened his eyes, there *was* a vertical crack in the bedroom wall. He went and peered at it, realized it was the electric light cord, then lay down and went back to sleep again. But his head ached and his belly was empty, so he dug a tiny bit of mud out of the wall above the kang with his fingernail and popped it into his mouth.

That was weird. I mean, he wasn't a worm, was he? But Justice Xia enjoyed his bit of earth; it was delicious, and he began to make a habit of eating it from then on. At the start, Second Aunt heard him chomping in the dark and thought he was grinding his teeth in his sleep.

She gave him a kick and he grunted. "Are you awake? What are you eating?" she asked.

"Something good," he said.

"So nice you're not sharing any of it with me?" And she crawled over, grabbed a bit off him, and shoved it in her own mouth, only to find he'd been eating dirt. She pushed her fingers down Justice Xia's throat, but the old man kept saying how nice it tasted and carried on eating it. After a few days, he'd made a hole in the wall that looked like a hollow scraped out by a wolf.

By this time, it was Hearth's family's turn to prepare the food, and Hearth and Bamboo came over with umbrellas to piggyback them to their house. There Justice Xia sat down on the doorstep, absentmindedly picking at the dirt and popping bits in his mouth. Bamboo was worried enough to call Big-Noise Zhao.

Big-Noise Zhao's only comment was that when small children ate dirt, it was a sign they had worms, but he'd never in his life seen an adult eat earth. "Why are you doing that, Uncle?" he asked.

"I don't know. It just tastes good," was the reply.

"Does it make you feel sick afterward?"

"No."

So Big-Noise Zhao told Bamboo, "Don't worry about it. Birds eat stones. If he wants to eat dirt, let him."

Finally, at noon one day, the rain stopped, and Tongue-Tied came back from the dike, his legs running with blood. He'd been banging in stakes and injured himself. As soon as he came in, he fell fast asleep on the kang, dead to the world. Justice Xia tried to wake him, but no matter how much he shouted, Tongue-Tied didn't stir.

"The kid's exhausted. What d'you want now?" Second Aunt berated him.

"It's cleared up; we have to go to Seven Li Gully," Justice Xia said.

"Is this really the time to be worrying about Seven Li Gully?"

"Yes!" And Justice Xia carried on shaking Tongue-Tied. Then he started rifling through the trunk in search of the new blue-lined jacket Bamboo had just made him, and the belt, too.

"What do you want to dress up for when you're going to Seven Li Gully?"

"I've got new clothes; why can't I wear them?" said Justice Xia. "If I don't wear them now, then when?"

"You planning to die?" said Second Aunt, and she hurriedly spat in case the words brought bad luck.

Justice Xia, meantime, put on his new jacket, belted it, and picked up the shovel. Tongue-Tied offered to carry him piggyback, but Justice Xia refused. They were just passing Rain Xia's gate when they saw Snow Bai and Rain Xia. She had a pair of straw shoes on, but Rain Xia's feet were covered in yellow clay. He had a spade in his hand, and Justice Xia asked, "Have you been to the dike? Has the water dropped?"

"Yes," said Rain Xia. "And I just went to take a look at Dad's tomb."

"It hasn't been washed away, has it?"

"No, only the new saplings."

"Were you there, too, Snow Bai?" Justice Xia asked.

"No," said Snow Bai. "But I got a message from Teahouse Village. Someone died when a house collapsed, and they want me to go and sing."

"How fragile humans are!" exclaimed Justice Xia. "Let's go together. I'm on my way to Seven Li Gully."

"To Seven Li Gully? Shouldn't you wait until the weather settles and the ground's dried up?"

"You're going even though it's still wet," Justice Xia pointed out.

"That jacket fits really well," said Snow Bai as she followed him out of the alley.

On the main street a tractor was parked. I was in the driver's seat. I'm not afraid of the cold, and I sat there in a sleeveless vest, hollering out an opera aria:

> May your virtuous name be inscribed above the door
> And immortalized all down the generations.

"Spark, how did you know that I'm going to Seven Li Gully?" said Justice Xia.

"I even knew Snow Bai was going out, too!" I said. I told them to get on the tractor, but Snow Bai refused. "Sit!" Justice Xia encouraged her. "Does Spark look like a crazy?" So she sat on the tailgate of the trailer.

Now that I had Snow Bai as a passenger, I drove very slowly. The road was full of potholes from the rain, but the grass along the edges was a brilliant green and covered in flowers. The flowers were delighted to see me, and the bees followed in our wake. One bee settled on my ear and buzzed its song. Tongue-Tied went to swipe it away, but before he could hit it, the bee fell off, dead.

"Uncle Justice," I said, "the bee's died of joy!"

"What nonsense! A bee can't be so happy that it dies."

"I think it saw my bare arms and was so happy that it could sting me there that it died."

Justice Xia and Tongue-Tied laughed, and so did Snow Bai. Even the tractor gave a few laughs as it went over the bumps—it sounded like popcorn going off.

Just before Seven Li Gully, Snow Bai jumped off. The path to Teahouse Village went east past the gully fork, then around a bend. The village was two *li* farther on.

I jumped down, too, and asked, "When are you coming back?"

"Before dark."

"Then I'll wait for you!"

I stood watching her until she disappeared into the distance. Tongue-Tied banged on the side of the trailer to get me moving again. Justice Xia said nothing; he just smoked his rollie.

In Seven Li Gully, we were not surprised to find that the water had broken through the stone embankment and was pouring out the other end of the gully. Justice Xia got me and Tongue-Tied to build a new earth wall, to divert the water along the foot of the cliff. While we were working, he sat at the door of his shed, which had survived unscathed. After a while, he dug a bit of dirt out of the doorway, put it in his mouth and chewed on it, then sat staring at the place he had designated for his grave nearby. The sapling that had grown from the stick we planted was still there, and so was the bird's nest. It hadn't filled with water, but the parent birds were still anxious and chattered and chirped continuously.

"What are you chirping about?" I asked. "Did you miss us, is that it?"

The birds carried on chirping and flying around our heads, and three feathers dropped on us. I ignored them and said to Tongue-Tied, "Hey! Your granddad's looking at his grave." Tongue-Tied didn't react. "Tongue-Tied, what's he thinking about?" Still no reaction.

So I stopped talking to him. Then I heard Justice Xia speak. His words were silent; he was just thinking them.

It won't be long before I move here. Will there be anyone to carry my coffin? The harvest will be even smaller this year because of the rain, so more people will go off looking for jobs outside. Freshwind will have fewer and fewer people, and more and more grass and trees. And maybe there'll be wolves and foxes, too . . . I wonder what will grow on my grave when I'm dead and buried. A tree or a bramble bush? Or maybe a patch of wheat. Will its ears be as big as our King of Wheat?

And when will the gully ever get filled? Life's too short. I haven't managed to get Seven Li Gully done. And now everyone's leaving Freshwind. Maybe one fine day, someone will come and finish the job. Then when they sit down on my grave, what will they say? Something like, "Once there was a man called Justice Xia, but he was a failure, and Seven Li Gully was his mark of shame." But then again, in a few years' time, this grave will probably be leveled, or completely covered in soil, and the grandchildren won't even know who Justice Xia was. Nowadays, nine out of ten kids can't tell you their granddad's name if you ask them. And I'm not Chairman Mao, so for sure they won't remember me.

He got to his feet and shouted, "Spark! Spark!"

"What?"

"I'll make sure they remember me!"

"Who's 'they'?"

He didn't answer, just stomped over to where the wall had collapsed. But the ground was claggy, and so much mud stuck to his shoes that he eventually came to a halt; when he put his foot down, it sank into the mud, and he couldn't pull it out.

The family in Teahouse Village had done a very simple funeral; the mud made it difficult to organize anything. The troupe played and sang three pieces, and the coffin was lowered into the grave. The musicians and the singers didn't stop for a meal, just took their pay, and the relatives gave them a bottle of liquor each. Then Snow Bai hurried on her way home. When she got to Seven Li Gully, the sun suddenly burst through a crack in the clouds, and its rays poured down on us. Just then, I heard an odd sound.

"What d'you think that is, Uncle Justice?" I asked.

"What d'you mean?" he asked. At that moment, the parent birds flew up into the air and then dive-bombed his head. He didn't move, just repeated, "What noise? Damned birds!"

Then I looked up and caught sight of Snow Bai at the entrance to the gully. The sun was behind her, bathing her in a halo of light, like a bodhisattva on a mural. It was the first time I'd seen the Buddha aura on her, and I threw down my spade and ran toward her. Tongue-Tied roared in disapproval, but I ignored him. What was wrong with me going to the bodhisattva?

A slurry of mud splashed up behind me as I ran, and I imagined Snow Bai seeing me coming to her on water, or with sparks at my heels. Snow Bai was standing still and smiling a bodhisattva smile. Suddenly there was a thunderous roar, and the ground beneath my feet quivered like a suspension bridge, and before I knew what was happening, I was flung to the ground and sliding ten yards downhill. What had pushed me? I saw Snow Bai stumble and fall, too. There was no one with her, so who'd pushed her? It was air. Normally, you couldn't see or touch it, but just now it had hit me in the back, smashing into me like a wooden post, throwing me to the ground.

"Snow Bai!" I shouted. "What's going on?"

It felt like I had no arms or legs, or nose or eyes; I was just a mindless lump of clay.

This was the disaster of March 24. It's a date I'll always remember, and so will everyone else in Freshwind. This was the day when a landslide brought down the east cliff of Seven Li Gully. It came without the slightest warning; perhaps the rain had made the hillside crack open, but we had no inkling. Then the gully top came loose and began to slip downward, shaking the sky and the earth, burying the shed, burying Wisdom Xia's grave, burying Justice Xia while he was still cursing the parent birds. There were enough rocks and earth to fill half the gully. People came from the village to help, but the strong and able-bodied ones had all gone, leaving only old folks, kids, and women. All through the night, we cleared rocks and soil, but we managed to move less than a twentieth of what had been brought down. Goodness and Pavilion called a meeting of the Xia clan, and after much discussion it was agreed that there was no hope of finding Justice Xia alive. As it would take at least two or three days to dig him out, and another three or four days to excavate the tomb, it was better to let him lie where he was and let the gully become a giant grave for him.

The family was distraught, but there was no real alternative. Still, with Justice Xia lying under the rockfall, which would eventually become a permanent part of the mountain, he had to have a grave marker. As soon as that decision was made, his five sons and their wives all began to argue over who should pay for it. Goodness suggested that they share the cost of erecting the stone, but Treasure, Bounty, and Halfwit were firmly opposed to that idea, on the grounds that they had already agreed that Gold would be responsible for their father's funeral. Gold had already saved quite a bit of money when Justice Xia died in the landslide, so why should the rest of them fork out for the grave marker? Chastity said Gold had less to organize, true, but there was still the mourning pavilion to set up and the mourners to feed and entertain. If the rest of them wouldn't agree to share the costs, there would be no memorial stone! No one could agree, and Goodness was so upset that he was about to walk out when Rain Xia offered to donate the stone he'd prepared for his own father to Uncle Justice.

The day the stone was brought from West Mountain Bend happened to coincide with the arrival in Freshwind of the county survey team. The first person they asked to meet was Justice Xia, and when they heard that he had died, they exclaimed, "What a time for him to die!" Still, no one in the village really understood what it was that the group was surveying, and they all kept very quiet.

Gold asked Big-Noise Zhao to write a few words for the memorial stone, but Big-Noise Zhao excused himself. "We can't just write, 'Here lies Justice Xia.' It's much too basic. Before he left, Wind Xia said he'd compose something appropriate for the memorial he's putting up for his own dad. Second Uncle was a fine man, too, and he deserves nothing less, but I'm not the right person to compose the words. Why don't we set up a blank stone and wait until Wind Xia comes home again? He can write something."

Big-Noise Zhao's words made sense, so we erected a blank memorial stone on the rockfall in Seven Li Gully.

After that, I couldn't wait for Wind Xia to come back.

Afterword

BY JIA PINGWA

If you follow the Dan River down toward the southeast corner of Shaanxi, to the border of Danfeng County and Shang County (the county name no longer officially exists, and the area has been renamed Shangzhou District, with Shangluo City as its own administrative region), you will come to a village called Dihua. That is my home village. The Dan River begins way up in the Qinling Mountains as a tributary of the Han River. As the Dan River flows south, it meanders through six or seven river basins. Dihua sits in one of the smallest of those basins, surrounded by four mountains. That means that the land is fertile, it's easy to grow cereals and grain, and there are wetlands with reeds and lotus. The mountain that dominates the village is shaped like an ornamental brush rest. There is a street of wooden homes, a tall flight of steps, a large square with a pagoda, an opera theater, a bell tower, and a God of Literature Pavilion. The main road has always been called the Public Road. It was once part of the most important route from Chang'an to the Southeast, traversed over the centuries by countless merchants, soldiers, bureaucrats, and poets. The ruins of the mule and horse drivers' guild hall are still visible. Here, the songs of Qin were preserved alongside the martial arts of the "Dashing King," Li Zicheng. If you go a bit farther south down the river and look at the cliffs along the bank, you can see grottoes carved into the rock during troubled times. Some say that there are still mummies lying in those grottoes. When night comes, the bats come down from their roosts in the caves and flutter through the dark streets of Dihua. The villagers like to brag about the famous men who have come through Dihua; they say Li Bai, Du Fu, Wang Wei, and Han Yu all spent time in Dihua.

Before I was nineteen, I never went much farther than thirty *li* outside the village. I used to put on my straw sandals and my hat and walk out to the mountain villages north and south of Dihua to trade rice for potatoes and corn. When they asked me where I was from and I said Dihua, they knew not to play any games with the scale. Back then, the natural scenery and cultural reputation of the village were famous throughout Shangluo Prefecture. City folks in leather shoes came down Highway 312 to visit and photograph the old streets. But a reputation can be misleading: Dihua suffered from extreme poverty and a lack of arable land. Each spring, when the willow and locust trees budded, they were immediately stripped bare. If you went down to the village pond, you would see baskets of boiled leaf buds being soaked to take out the astringency. My younger brother and I used to help my mother grind fried sweet potato vine stems. One time I was too hungry to wait and ate a bunch of them raw; that night, I ended up with a wicked case of diarrhea. A man named Li lived next door to us. He used to weave straw sandals and sold each pair for three *fen*. On his deathbed, his only request was a bowl of cornmeal porridge. He never got it. Before the production team leader set the lid on his coffin, he put a roasted sweet potato in his arms and said, "Please, just don't become a hungry ghost."

Nobody in Dihua was fat—it was a village of skinny necks. When we had meetings in the square, everyone was dressed in the same dusty peasant clothes. Some of the villagers had surprising talents, like Kuanren, who could carve wood, and Benwang, who made clay sculptures. On East Street, the brothers of the Li family could play the *huqin*. Every night, they were out under the trees beside the village gate, playing their instruments. Dongsheng from Middle Street loved to sing Shaanxi opera. They never had enough food to eat, and his wife had to go out and beg for food. But he was always singing, anyway. He sang the *dan* roles, the female roles.

Uncle Wulin used to get us kids over on rainy days to help him take the kernels off cobs of corn; then he would gather us around and recite a story from *Investiture of the Gods*. When someone finally pulled the book out to see how his version compared, they realized he had recited it perfectly, word for word. Shengping somehow managed to get a copy of *The Book of Changes* and eventually became a yin-yang master. Baiqing learned to paint and used to scrape the soot from the bottoms of pots to use as ink. He painted pictures from *The Twenty-Four Filial Exemplars* on walls all over the village. Liu Xinchun could write drum scores. Liu Gaofu had talent as a builder—he could design buildings from the ground up—and he and his eight brothers were responsible for most of the important buildings in the county.

The two most prominent families in Dihua were the Han family of West Street and the Jia family of East Street. Han Shuji and Jia Maoshun were the most talented calligraphers in the village. They both had great skill, and their writing graced the archways of gates around the village. Every year, from the thirtieth of the final lunar month to the fifteenth of the first lunar month, there were parades and opera performances in Dihua. The performers were paid in sweet potatoes, three *jin* from each villager. When the performers went to the county seat to perform, they always came back with first prize.

When cadres went to work in Dihua, they were warned not to put on airs since the villagers would see right through them. After I made a name as a writer and went to live in Xi'an, nobody in the village thought much of my accomplishments. When my name came up in Dihua, some people even said, "Just as well he went to Xi'an—he'd never be able to cut it here!"

I lived there until the age of nineteen. I learned to read in the ancestral hall that had been converted into a classroom. I was a sickly child, but I never saw the inside of a hospital. If whatever was ailing me couldn't be cured with ginger tea, cupping jars, or raking a porcelain chip between the eyebrows to draw out the blood, then it was ruled to be a case of "running into a bad spirit," and the necessary rituals were performed.

I learned how to work the land, how to sing the local opera, and how to write couplets and banners. I am a peasant. I am good at heart, but I am selfish. I can work hard, and I keep most of my pain to myself. I owe a debt of gratitude to the soil that I was raised on; it made me what I am. I am like a firefly in the reeds, carrying my own little lamp. I am like the flowers of the cherry bush, spreading their own magnificent color across the hillside. But I hate my native place, too. Like a plant in bad soil, I never managed to grow as I should. A diet of sweet potato ruined my stomach.

When the chance came to leave Dihua, I went, and my life was changed forever. I remember sitting on a bus headed to the provincial capital, carrying my bedroll. I said, "I am finally going to shake off this peasant skin!" But when I went to make a living in the city, I realized it was not so easy to shake off. Like those dark-skinned chickens whose color penetrates to their very bones, I was a peasant through and through.

When I go back to the village to celebrate holidays and festivals, or to celebrate the birthdays of my elderly relatives, or for funerals or weddings, nobody cares that I am a writer. They say, "Jia Number Four's son is back!" I greet them and pass out cigarettes.

My room in the city has become a Xi'an destination for people visiting from back home. I have a stack of rough porcelain bowls and a couple of beds in there, and when I have visitors, we eat *laomian* with oil and peppers and big chunks of garlic. We usually crack a bottle, maybe play some drinking games, too. I get glares from the people who live down the same hallway. So if something happens in Dihua, I hear about it. If someone has a grandson, I hear whether it was a smooth birth or a breech birth. If someone's funeral banquet skimped on the meat, I hear about it. If a wife leaves her husband or if brothers feud, I hear about it.

During the ten years between 1979 and 1989, the news was always good. The contract responsibility system was introduced to agriculture, the weather cooperated with the harvest, and there was plenty of food to go around. Visitors from the village would always bring me freshly husked and polished rice, beans, or maybe even a side of pork. They came into the city and walked through the park, noting that the flowers there were even prettier than the ones in their yard. They wanted to visit the theater, and they wanted me to write couplets for them to hang in their main rooms. I used to laugh to myself and say, *These villagers are still noble, no matter what!* Those were Dihua's happiest years. The farmers threw themselves into wringing crops out of the newly divided farmland, and you could still find them working in their fields under the big winter moon, sucking on pipes, radios set on the embankment between fields, blaring Shaanxi opera. When I went back, there was only good news: this family was building a house, that family was planning a son's wedding . . . The old people were airing out the clothes that they would be buried in. For farmers, the three most significant events in life are marrying off a child, burying their parents, and building a new house. In those days, those events were carried out with dignity and ease. Villagers put Deng Xiaoping's portrait up on their walls, kowtowing to him and making offerings of incense.

I got together with my childhood friends whenever I went back to the village. We used to work in the fields, chop firewood, and steal sweet potato leaves together, but as older men we smoked cigarettes, drank liquor, and sang Shaanxi opera until we got light-headed. We call each other *gege*, big brother, but the Dihua accent makes it sound like *guoguo*. Our gang of older men looked like a nest full of birds chirping and flapping.

People who grow up in the village have an intrinsic understanding of the importance of the land. This is an agricultural country; we were fostered by the land. By nature, the farmer is decent and hardworking. But for many years the countryside has been the most back-ward place in the nation, and rural people the most impoverished. When the state began to implement reforms, the transformation of society started from the countryside; the greatest achievement of the reforms was ensuring that rural people would no longer go hungry. There is no historical precedent for the changes in Chinese society, and there is no choice but to charge forward, no matter what happens. There will be anger and confusion, but we must keep pushing.

But a problem has arisen: once hunger in rural China was solved, the focus of the state shifted from the countryside to the city. What is the solution to the ongoing problems in rural China? For the people who live there, there are concerns beyond simply filling their bellies. If you push a gourd underwater, it keeps floating up again. My father died just as we entered this new age. His death marked the beginning of the Jia family's decline, but the brief prosperity of the village seems to have come to an end, too.

Dihua has no mineral resources and no industry; the land itself has been exploited almost to its limit; and the price of fertilizer, pesticides, and seeds is rising, while crop yields are falling. The countryside has become a runoff pond for all social pressures, and the system has allowed administration of the countryside to become lax. The old way of life has disappeared completely, but nothing has taken root in its place.

The old way of life was solid, while the new way of life has proven ephemeral. The wind blows from the east for a while, then comes in from the north, and nobody has time to catch it before it changes again. The people of the countryside are like a flock of chickens, ruffling their feathers and pecking around but not moving toward any particular goal. Each step seems to take them away from the land, but their fate is tied to the land, and if they are uprooted and transplanted, they will struggle to survive.

When I return to Dihua, I notice that the highway has been renovated and now runs up along the plateau behind the village. There is talk of a railway line cutting through the hills that are now home to terraced fields, and rumor has it that an expressway might be run through the fields along the river dike. The river basin that Dihua sits in is not very large, and transportation infrastructure quickly cuts into the amount of arable land. Most people have relocated from the old streets of the village to lots along the highway. Of course, they are not building traditional homes but two-storied buildings of concrete and prefabricated panels. Those sorts of buildings are cold in winter and hot in summer. There are still flakes of yellow earth on the concrete. The rooms are large. They still use the same wooden cabinets and chests and three or four clay jars that they've always had. I don't recognize any of the women standing out in the alleys holding children. All I can do is study their faces and try to connect them to the faces of their fathers—I can usually guess correctly who their parents are. When they find out who I am, they call me "Grandpa Eight" (in my generation, I was the eighth-oldest male).

When I go down to the old village street, a few of the old buildings are still standing, but others have been left to decay. Across the rotten eaves of one of them, I come across a glistening spiderweb, home to a long-legged spider with patterns over its abdomen. It's hideous. I can't help but think it must be the avatar of some horrible demon. There is grass growing out of the road. There are no mice left, but clouds of mosquitoes rise with every footstep. There used to be shops all along this road. On some stone steps, a sloughed-off snakeskin is stuck in the cracks. One of the sons of the Zhang family comes down the road toward me—he was once a "model worker" and a village cadre. He used to strut down this road with his jacket draped over a shoulder, but he had a stroke a few years back, so when he comes up to me, drooling, smiling, trying to mumble something, I can't understand a word he's saying. One of my cousins told me about a woman in the village who held her baby out to shit, then smeared it on the top of the yard wall. Guanyin could never keep his appetite in check—after his nephew became a cadre, someone poisoned the family's rice. He was at dinner that day, gobbled up three bowls, and ended up dying on the kitchen floor.

I once overheard an argument between two men that included one of them howling, "What the hell is wrong with you—you bit my dick!" What had happened before that, I don't know, but one of the men had pounced on the other and bit his dick clean off.

Out of the dozens of villagers who have left Dihua to work, half the men went to work in the coal pit in Tongchuan or down the gold mine in Tongguan, and the other half are in the provincial capital, hauling coal or picking trash. Nobody really knows what the women do when they go to work outside the village. They don't talk about it. They come back dressed in sharp new outfits.

There have been at least ten deaths or serious injuries among the migrant workers. They get sent back in a white pine box with a white rooster feather stuck on top. And the family usually gets paid around ten thousand yuan in compensation, but it's been as low as two thousand yuan, and getting anything usually requires that they kick up a fuss. They get paid off, but the disputes are never truly resolved.

Three men from the village were sentenced to prison on robbery charges, and eighteen were sentenced to long-term detention for gambling. On one occasion, family feuds rekindled by the election of village cadres led to an armed street fight. The Public Security Bureau has had to respond to tax protests.

It is hard to find an able-bodied adult left in the village. The original reason for this was a lack of land driving people out; the soil could not sustain them. There is nobody left to carry coffins to the grave. I stood in the village one day, beside an old stone roller, and thought to myself, *Will there come a day when none of my relatives or friends remain in Dihua? Will this old village street disappear completely? Will the land itself disappear? If the process of urbanization continues, could all this disappear? And if it doesn't, what future does it have?*

Once my father died, his generation seemed to drop off, one by one. Now, it's my own generation who are the old folks. They have lived hard lives; they stayed in the village while I went to the city, and they look at least a decade older than me. And now they, too, are starting to die off.

Since I brought my mother to live with me in the city, I've been returning to Dihua less and less. My parents had been a link between myself and the village, but now that they have both left Dihua, the village has become less a real place and more of a concept. When I walk by the labor market in Xi'an, past all the country folk with their battered clothes and rough hands, there are always faces that I think I recognize. It feels like I'm seeing the reincarnations of people I knew from my younger years. I've often asked myself, *Once my mother has passed away, will I have any reason to go back to the village?*

Maybe I'll never go back. Maybe I'll go back even more often. My native place gave me life, and I am forever indebted. Back in the city, thinking back to that rotten old lane—to the old lady out in her yard, lighting up wet leaves to smoke the mosquitoes out, struggling to get them lit, only managing a few wisps of bitter smoke—I have the urge to write about it. I've written about my native place before, but that writing was always about Shangzhou in general, with only a few bits and pieces specifically about Dihua. I understand that the village is changing, becoming something else entirely, and will one day be even more unfamiliar to me than it is now. Maybe the village is like a rotten apple, still pristine on the surface but ready to spew its foul juices if pricked. Or maybe the village is like a lotus flower, growing in the mud, becoming ever more beautiful with each day that passes. But I don't belong there anymore, and that is fine with me. I continue to write about it because an emotional connection remains, and I feel as if I have some responsibility to the place. When half the True Relic Pagoda at Famen Temple collapsed, I wrote an essay dedicated to it. It was the only remembrance of the half tower that was written. I wrote this book for the same reasons. The book is a remembrance of forgetting.

I want this book to stand as a monument to my native place.

Before I finally picked up my pen and went to work on this book in the spring of 2003, I made a ceremonial toast to the villagers who had died in the years since I had left, and another to those who remained. I lit a stick of incense in the Han dynasty pot in my office and kept it burning while I wrote. The smoke curled up to the ceiling like a thick rope.

When I began to write, I found great pain and difficulty; I did not know whether to write a paean to life in the village or to curse it; I did not know whether I should write an ode for the people of Dihua or a eulogy. The list of those who had passed away included my father, my father's older brother (who had been a village cadre for all his adult life), and my three aunts. In the village, I still had my cousin, who had himself become a village cadre, and a nephew, who was an officer at the local police station. Those characters seemed to force themselves into the spotlight. Ghosts, both living and dead, flew at me, wanting to tell their story, arguing among themselves. I found myself putting down my pen to stare into the smoke rising from the pot and saw the neat column disturbed by my ragged breath. I felt as if the room was full of the spirits of Dihua.

The manuscript for this book took a year and nine months to finish. I abandoned all other tasks. I was criticized for missing meetings and cursed by my friends for turning down invitations. I wanted to write without interference. I got up every morning and went out to my office, carrying my lunch of noodles or vegetable *jiaozi*. I always made sure the window was shut tight and the door was locked. I switched on the light and took the phone off the hook.

When lunchtime came, I heated up my noodles or *jiaozi* on the gas stove, ate, then returned to my writing. I worked until dusk, and only then did I allow myself to go out for dinner or take a meeting. I kept at it, the same way, day in and day out. The loneliness was torture.

When I needed to take a break from writing the novel, I took out a brush and wrote some calligraphy or painted—I was fond of painting the monk Xuanzang. The image of the monk, who worked for years at the Giant Wild Goose Pagoda translating sutras, encouraged me. I made a painting of a dog lying on its back, looking up at the sky, howling pitifully, with a cat gingerly walking over to look at him. I made a painting called *The Qin Player* and inscribed it with this line: "When you are lonely, play the *qin*." I wrote a line above that: "In the end, even the brush disappears, and the blue sea covers everything." I put the paintings up in my office. I had two characters hung above my desk: 守侯, a request for the guardians of the soul to watch over me.

The ancients said that a piece of writing must inspire fear in the writer. I asked myself, was I afraid while writing this book? I wasn't satisfied with the first draft, so I started over again, but I still wasn't satisfied with the result. When I had completed the third draft, I wasn't satisfied, either. I started a complete revision. I have never found myself going through drafts like that. Perhaps it's because I'm getting old; perhaps I don't have the energy anymore; perhaps my talents have been used up. No matter what I did to the third draft, I could not make it work.

When my family saw me suffering through these revisions, they told me, "Stop editing it, or you'll end up driving yourself crazy!" Perhaps I did drive myself crazy. Like a man made of mud who becomes dirtier and dirtier the more he tries to wipe himself clean, maybe the more I revised the manuscript, the worse I was making it.

Throughout the entire process, I had a friend who would take each completed manuscript and copy it. He went to a tiny print shop to have them copied. Altogether, he copied four manuscripts, each about eight hundred pages. The owner of the shop managed to turn a tidy profit off my friend. That friend was one of the first to read the book. He was from the countryside, not from any sort of literary background, but he read the early manuscripts with enthusiasm. When I said my idea was for the book to stand as a monument to my native place, he said: "It's going to be one hell of a monument!" His reaction gave me more confidence, but finally, as I sat in my smoky office, the final draft complete, I started to suspect that there were still lingering problems.

Dihua is my native place, but the book is about Freshwind. Dihua is the moon; Freshwind is the moon reflected on the surface of a pond. Dihua is the flower; Freshwind is the flower seen in the mirror. But the moon on the water and the flower in the mirror are still reflections of a real thing, just as Freshwind is the reflection of a living place. Can country people, or people living in the country, immerse themselves in this kind of dense, arrhythmic narrative? What about city people? What about people from other places in the province, or from outside Shaanxi?

It's not that I don't understand conventional plotting or have no experience writing a book with a conventional plot. It's not that I'm unfamiliar with the idea of "meaningful form," or that I reject the idea. But the book had to be written this way, in this fragmentary style. A horse's legs are strong only because it must sometimes flee for its life. A bird's song is beautiful only because it must call for a mate. The only places that reveal the author are those places where I have been clumsy in, for example, my command of a character or the rhythm of the narrative. In a time when the fashion is for conceptual writing and for family epics, if I dump thick tea in a Yixing terra-cotta bowl, will anyone mistake it for spring water? If I wear a hand-spun jacket to a banquet, will I be mistaken for a poor man?

If you read closely, perhaps you will understand my confusion and bitterness. But for the many people who are used to quickly flipping through a book, will they call it "boring" and toss it aside? I expect the reaction will be even more severe from those with a prejudice against my writing. When they hear I've written a new book, they don't even bother reading it. A sow can't give birth to a lion, they might say, and don't expect a dog to spit pearls.

Many years ago, I ran into a woman who had once been in a dispute with my family over a field boundary. There was nothing the Jia family could do that would make her happy. She had cursed my mother and gone after me, too. She'd curse our chickens and our dogs, if she saw them out in the street. When I was hesitating over whether to turn the manuscript in to the publisher, the friend who had helped me copy the manuscripts said, "Don't be stupid! You're like the guy in the market selling grain, worried that some other guy who only eats seafood, or someone else who's eating only fruit to try to lose weight, isn't stopping to buy. You have your customers!"

But now I am more worried about how people in my hometown will take the book. I want this book to stand as a monument to my native place, but will the people who still live there accept it as such? All the characters and events in Freshwind have their roots in people and events in Dihua, and while it is easy to draw a ghost, drawing a person is a lot harder. I have a modicum of talent, but I fear that I have attempted to write a tiger and ended up with a hound. Also, I fear I may have violated some political taboos because I do not understand politics. When I wrote *First Records of Shangzhou* nearly twenty years ago, I was fiercely attacked. People said: "The tone is too dark. You exposed all the dirt of the countryside. This isn't writing for the people; it's not socialist writing of any kind." I acknowledge that where I come from, many people say one thing and do another, or vice versa. But I am a writer, and a writer has to be prepared to suffer hardship and abuse for telling the truth. It is in the nature of the job that a writer may have to tell uncomfortable truths about social realities, but this is never done with the intention of causing offence.

I have heard, even seen with my own eyes, how a township-level cadre reporting to county-level leadership, or a county-level cadre reporting to province-level leadership, will report their successes with boundless enthusiasm. (The way they tell it, even the lice in their villages have double-folded eyelids.) However, when the time comes to request money, they'll start shaking like a leaf and predicting disaster. I have said that I want this book to stand as a monument to my native place, but a monument is not the same as an ancestral shrine—it is far less deferential. China today longs for greatness as never before, but at the same time, its people need learning and refinement in their lives more than they ever have before.

The story of Freshwind will be the monument for a Dihua that has nearly disappeared. From this point on, my memories of my home village will begin to fade.

As a final note, while writing this book, I have drawn on relevant facts and figures from *The Series on Contemporary China's Rural Governance and Election Observations*. I would like to take this opportunity to express my gratitude to the authors of this work.

TRANSLATOR'S AFTERWORD

By Nicky Harman

Translating *The Shaanxi Opera* was an immersive experience. I think it is safe to say that we translators felt bereft as we came to the end and put the completed translation into the hands of Amazon Crossing's editors. This brief afterword gives me a chance to reflect on how we translated it and to make a stab at answering some of the questions that may have occurred to you as you read it.

I am often asked how two translators work together on a text. In our case, it was simple: We translated alternate chapters, then swapped and checked and commented on each other's translation. At the same time, we kept a running terminology list, so that, for instance, Bowed Ox Ridge was Bowed Ox Ridge throughout, not Kneeling Ox Ridge or some other variant. The emails winged back and forth between the UK, where I live, and Japan, where Dylan lives, as we delved into the minutiae of village architecture. Are the house porches small archways, or covered corridors? The latter, it turned out. What is a side house? (They are the smaller buildings on two sides of a courtyard house flanking the main rooms that face the gate.) We also had lively exchanges about the gully-filling project that causes so much heartache in the story—it is, we discovered, a technique for creating land out of deep, barren gullies by laboriously infilling them.

Not all our discussions were as high flown. We argued about whether to use *piss, pee,* or *urine* (*piss* won out), *shit* or *defecate* (*shit,* as you will have gathered), and *bathroom* or *shithouse.* You get the picture: country life in poor villages is life in the raw. Finally, Dylan curbed my tendency to drift off into British English slang, because we were, after all, translating for an American publisher.

So far, so straightforward. A bigger challenge came with the names of the protagonists, nearly one hundred and forty of them. Between Chinese and English, translators have two basic choices: transliterate or translate. So is our hero to be Yinsheng, or Spark? You will have noticed by now that, with the exception of a few of the opera roles, all the characters in this novel have translated names. Neither of us have done this before, but in this novel we found compelling reasons. First, it is hard for readers to distinguish one Xia brother from another, for example, when their names are transliterated. Xia Tianzhi and Xia Tianyi look very similar on the page. More importantly, Jia Pingwa himself has made it clear that the names of his characters are an essential part of the imagery of the story and, outlandish though they sometimes sound, are actually the kind of nicknames that Shaanxi villagers choose. We had a chance to ask Mr. Jia why he had chosen certain names, for instance, Yinsheng/Spark and Sanxue/ Shifty, and his answers gave us some reassurance that we were heading in the right direction.

Finally, you will have noticed that snatches of the local opera arias pop up on almost every page. A couple of lines here and there were comparatively simple to translate. Sometimes we managed to reproduce a rhyme; sometimes we didn't. But there are also two long poems in the novel: one is an aria from the opera *Visiting the Judge Carrying a Child*, at the end of chapter 20; the other is a serenade to the beautiful Snow Bai by a fan of her singing, in chapter 21. Serendipitously, we got one each. I know how long it took me to put the extremely bad poetry of the serenade into English, so I can only salute Dylan for his efforts with the opera aria. It is filthy and funny, rollicking but also erudite where it needs to be, and dammit, it rhymes like a dream! I'll close by quoting the first few lines:

> They're calling out, calling out, calling out for you!
> Little baby girls and grandpas, too!
> Headed to the cornfield with a yoke and a plough,
> Bumping into stalks while looking for the cow.
> Switch the bomb with the carrot-top sprout,
> Blow you right across the sky like a waterspout.
> Dung beetle fell in the ol' pisspot,
> Eat it like a pickled plum, it's all you got.
> Dung beetle fell on the butcher's block,
> Take in the scene like a soaring hawk.
> Dung beetle crawled up the bamboo stick,
> Danced all day like a lunatic.

ABOUT THE AUTHOR

Photo © Wang Lizhi

Jia Pingwa is the author of the novels *The Shaanxi Opera*, winner of the Mao Dun Literature Prize, *Happy Dreams*, *Turbulence*, *Ruined City*, *White Nights*, *The Earthen Gate*, *The Lantern Bearer*, *The Mountain Whisperer*, and *Broken Wings*. He is also the author of several short fiction and essay collections. Born in Dihua Village, Danfeng County, Shaanxi Province, Jia graduated from Xi'an's Northwest University in 1975. He is a member of the China Writers Association Presidium, deputy chair of the Writers Association Shaanxi branch, and chair of Xi'an Federation of Literary and Art Circles.

ABOUT THE TRANSLATORS

Photo © 2020 Alex Hofford

Nicky Harman is based in the UK and translates fiction, and occasionally nonfiction and poetry, from Chinese. She has won several awards, including the 2020 Special Book Award of China, the Mao Tai Cup People's Literature Chinese-English translation prize 2015, and the 2013 China International Translation Contest. When not translating, she works for the registered nonprofit Paper Republic, which promotes Chinese literature in translation. She also runs literary events, writes blogs, and gives talks.

Photo © 2018 Asumi Koyama

Dylan Levi King is a writer and translator based in Tokyo. His most recent translations include Jia Pingwa's *The Shaanxi Opera*, with Nicky Harman, and Cai Chongda's *Vessel*. King's writing on contemporary literature, politics, fashion, and crime has appeared in *Palladium*, the *Spectator*, SupChina, and *Chinese Literature Today*. For more information, visit www.dylanleviking.com.